ASSAIL

A NOVEL OF THE MALAZAN EMPIRE

Ian C. Esslemont

BANTAM PRESS

LONDON · TORONTO · SYDNEY · AUCKLAND · JOHANNESBURG

TRANSWORLD PUBLISHERS
61–63 Uxbridge Road, London W5 5SA
A Random House Group Company
www.transworldbooks.co.uk

Published in Great Britain
in 2014 by Bantam Press
an imprint of Transworld Publishers

A CIP catalogue record for this book
is available from the British Library.

ISBNs 9780593064481 (cased)
9780593064498 (tpb)

Addresses for Random House Group Ltd companies outside the UK
can be found at: www.randomhouse.co.uk
The Random House Group Ltd Reg. No. 954009

The Random House Group Limited supports the Forest Stewardship
Council® (FSC®), the leading international forest-certification organisation.
Our books carrying the FSC label are printed on FSC®-certified paper.
FSC is the only forest-certification scheme supported by the leading
environmental organisations, including Greenpeace. Our paper procurement
policy can be found at www.randomhouse.co.uk/environment

Typeset in 10½/12½pt Sabon by
Kestrel Data, Exeter, Devon.
Printed and bound in Great Britain by
CPI Group (UK) Ltd, Croydon, CR0 4YY.

2 4 6 8 10 9 7 5 3 1

This one is for the old gaming gang at the University of Manitoba: Doug and Doug, Jeff, Oliver, Grant, Ron, Martin, Henry, Craig, Laurence, Neil, Shurjeel and Arne.

ACKNOWLEDGEMENTS

I wish to offer my gratitude to my advance readers for their observations and comments, Sharon Sasaki and A. P. Canavan. You helped more than you think.

I give my love to my wife, Gerri Brightwell, without whose support and understanding this novel, and those preceding it, would never have been possible.

And to you Malaz readers. It has been a privilege to unveil these stories. I hope you have enjoyed them as much as I.

ASSAIL & environs

As compiled from diverse sources
by Reuth, son of Tulan

N

Wrack Coast

Barren Coast

PLAIN of GHOSTS

PLAIN of VISIONS

PLAIN of SIGHS

Fallen

THE BLOOD RANGE

E. SALT MTNS

Mantle

DREAMING RANGE

PLAIN of LONGING

W. SALT MTNS

Reach

First Landing

City of Many Saints

SEA of GOLD

VANISHING WASTES

Destruction

Mist

BONE PENINSULA

Holly

Press

PLAIN of CHANCE

SEA of HATE

REACHER'S OCEAN

Nomads

RANGE of the Saints

BONE RANGE

Rough Landing

BAY of TIMBER

The Fear Narrows

DREAD SEA

Anguish Coast

North

Bones

Deep Well

Wrecker's Coast

Pillar

Widden

Burnt

Run

Deep Root

TALON FOREST

Second Landing

Old Ruse

Exile Keep

Coast of Dust

Listell

Lake Fort

SHIFTING WASTES

GREYSTONE

Green River

LAKE BLESSING

BLACK FINGERS FOREST

Nomads

Yag' Quarall
(The Silent Tribes)

Shore of Sand

BLACK SEA

Ruins

Towerpoint

Shore of Stone

BLACK STONE MTNS

Black River

Spur

Thin River

Kurzan

White Cliffs

Nomads

The Yaguran
(Sons of Wind)

Nabraji

WEEPING PLAINS

The Anari Narrows

BAEL ENVIRONS

THE BLOOD RANGE

DRAMATIS PERSONAE

The *Lady's Luck*

Kyle	Given name, Kylarral-ten, of Bael lands, south of Assail
Tulan Orbed	Master of the *Lady's Luck*
Reuth	Ship's navigator, and Tulan's nephew
Storval	First Mate
Gren	Steersman

In the North

Orman	Son of Orman Bregin
Old Bear	A legendary man of the mountains
Keth and Kasson	The Reddin brothers
Gerrun	Also known as Shortshanks
King Ronal	Also known as 'King Ronal the Bastard'
Lotji Bain	Nephew of Jorgan Bain

Of the Iceblood Holdings

The Sayers

Buri	Legendary elder of the clan
Jaochim	Master of the clan
Yrain	Mistress of the clan
Vala	Sister to Yrain
Jass	Son of Vala
Bernal Heavyhand	A clan retainer, or hearthguard

The Heels

Cull Heel	Also known as Cull the Kind
Yullveig	Wife of Cull, also known as Yullveig the Fierce

| Erta | Daughter of Cull and Yullveig |
| Baran | Son of Cull and Yullveig |

The Overland Raiders

Marshal Teal	A Letherii aristocrat
Enguf the Broad	A Genabackan pirate
Malle of Gris	A Malazan aristocrat
Holden of Cawn	A mage of Serc
Alca of Cat	A mage of Telas

The Sea Raiders

The *Sea Strike*

Burl Tardin	Captain
Whellen	First Mate
Gaff	Second Mate

The *Silver Dawn*

Jute Hernan	Captain
Ieleen	Navigator, wife of Jute
Lurjen	Steersman
Buen	First Mate
Letita	Master of weapons
Dulat	A sailor

The *Resolute*

| Tyvar Gendarian | Commander of the Blue Shields and Mortal Sword of Togg |
| Haagen Vantall | Steward of the Blue Shields |

The *Ragstopper*

| Cartheron Crust | Captain |
| Orothos | First Mate |

The *Supplicant*

| Timmel Orosenn | Also known as the Primogenitrix, ruler of the island of Umryg |
| Velmar | Priest and servant to Lady Orosenn |

The T'lan Imass

The Kerluhm

| Ut'el Anag | Bonecaster |
| Lanas Tog | |

The Ifayle

Tolb Bell'al   Bonecaster

The Kron

Pran Chole   Bonecaster

The Crimson Guard

K'azz D'Avore	Commander
Shimmer	Second-in-command
Blues	New captain of the Second Company
Tarkhan	Captain of the Third Company
Bars	Also known as 'Iron Bars', formerly of the Fourth Company
Cowl	High Mage and Master Assassin
Gwynn	A mage
Petal	A mage
Black the Elder	
Black the Lesser	
Sept	
Cole	
Amatt	
Lean	
Keel	
Turgal	

The Crimson Guard Fourth Company

Cal-Brinn	Captain and mage
Jup Alat	Lieutenant
Laurel	
Leena	

Of *Mael's Greetings*

Ghelath Keer	Master
Havvin	Ship's pilot
Levin	Apprentice pilot

Others

Silverfox	The 'Summoner' created to end the T'lan Imass war
Luthal Canar	Representative of the Canar trading house, of Lether

Lyan	A female warrior from north Genabackis, a Shieldmaiden
Dorrin	King in exile of Anklos, Lyan's ward
Fisher Kel Tath	A well-travelled bard
Jethiss	A Tiste Andii castaway
Kilava	Ancient living Bonecaster of the Imass
Mist	A sorceress
Anger and Wrath	Mist's sons
The Sharrs	A mage family
The Sheers	A mage family
Giana Jalaz	A former lieutenant in the Malazan army

PROLOGUE

North territory of a new land
Of the Jaghut wars:
Seventh century of the 12th Lamatath campaign
33,421 years before Burn's Sleep

THE WOMAN RAN AT A STEADY UNHURRIED PACE. HER BREATH came as long level inhalations through the mouth and out through her wide nostrils. Sweat darkened the front and back of her buckskin shirt. Her moccasins padded silently over stones and pockets of exposed sandy soil. That she was running up a wide rocky mountain slope, and had been for most of the day, attested to iron strength and endurance. She dodged round slim poles of young pine, white spruce and birch. She jumped rocks and slid and scrambled up steep gravel talus fans. She knew she could outpace her pursuers, but that she would never shake them from her trail. Yet still she ran on.

She knew that once they tired of the chase, they would take her. She judged it ironic that the same desperate urge to continued existence that drove her also lay behind their relentless pursuit – though they had relinquished their claim to it long ago.

Still she scrambled on up the slope, for one hope remained. One slim unlikely chance. Not for her survival; she had given that up the moment she glimpsed the hoary eldritch silhouettes of her pursuers. The one slim chance lay for vengeance.

Knife-edged broken rock cut her fingers as she scrabbled for handholds. It flayed her moccasins. The surrounding steep slopes of tumbled stone and talus heaps were just now emerging from winter; ice clung to shadowed hollows and behind the taller boulders. Snow still lay in curved dirty heaps, almost indistinguishable from the surrounding gravel. She took vigour from the chill bite of the high mountain air, knowing it perfectly natural rather than any invoked glacial freeze. Taking cover in a stand of pine, she paused to risk a glance behind: no movement stirred upon the slope below, other than a smallish herd of elk just now clattering their way down-valley. No doubt disturbed by her passage.

Yet she knew she was not alone. She also knew her pursuers needed not to show themselves to run her down. She'd hoped, though, they would at least grant her this one small gesture.

A lone figure did then step out from the cover of tumbled glacial moraine. It was as if she'd willed its appearance. The tattered remains of leathers flapped about its impossibly lean frame. A dark ravaged visage scanned the slope, rising to her. The white bear hide that rode atop the head and shoulders hung as aged and wind-dried as its wearer. She and he locked gazes across the league that separated them – and across a far larger unbridgeable gulf as well.

So far behind? she wondered. Then she understood and in that instant threw herself flat.

Something shattered against the rocks next to her. Flint shards thinner than any blade sliced her buckskins and flensed the skin beneath.

She jumped to her feet and returned to scrambling up the slope. She reached a ridge that was a mere shoulder of the far taller slope: a jagged peak that reared far above. Here she paused a second time, exhausted, her lungs working, drawing in the icy air.

Then she screamed as a spear lanced through her thigh, pinning her to the bare stony surface. She fell back against a rock and took hold of the polished dark haft to draw it. A skeletal hand knocked hers aside.

The same fleshless visage that had caught her gaze below now peered down at her. Empty dark sockets regarded her beneath the rotting brow of a white tundra bear. Necklaces of yellowed claws hung about the figure's neck – presumably the claws of the very beast it wore – while the scraped hide of the beast's forelimbs rode its arms down to the paws tied with leather bindings to its own hands. Ribs darkened with age peeked through the mummified flesh of its torso. Rags of leather buckskin lay beneath the hide, all belted and tied off by numerous leather thongs. A long blade of knapped flint, creamy brown, its tang wrapped in leather, stood thrust through a belt. 'Why flee you here, Jaghut?' the Imass demanded.

'I flee destruction,' she answered, her voice tight with suppressed pain.

Others of the Imass warband now walked the ridge. The bones of their feet clattered on the rocks like so many stones. 'Caves above, Ut'el,' one of their number announced, pointing a flint blade higher up.

The Imass, Ut'el, returned its attention to her. 'You would seek to lure us to ambush,' it announced.

'If you say so.'

'I am disappointed. You have brought death to your kin as well.' It faced one of the band. 'Take scouts. They are occupied?'

This Imass dipped its hoary skull where the flesh and hair had fallen away in patches. 'Yes, Bonecaster.'

Bonecaster! the woman marvelled. A mage, shaman, of the breed! If she should bring this one to destruction then all would have been worth the struggle.

The Bonecaster returned its attention to her. She sensed its mood of disappointment. 'I had thought you a more worthy prize,' it murmured, displeased.

'As we had hoped for more worthy successors.'

'Victory is the only measure of that, Jaghut.'

'So the victors would soothe themselves.'

The undying creature raised its bony shoulders in an eloquent shrug. 'It is simply existence. Ours or yours.'

She allowed herself to slump back as if in utter defeat. 'You mean the elimination of all other than you. That is the flaw of your kind. You can only countenance your family or tribe to live.'

'So it is with all others.'

'No, it is not. You are merely unable to see this.'

'Look about, Jaghut. Raw nature teaches us . . .' Ut'el's whisper-faint voice dwindled away as he slowly raised his bone and dried-tendon features to the higher slope.

'How fare your scouts, Bonecaster?' she asked, unable to keep a savage grin from her face.

'They are gone,' he announced. His gaze fell to her. '*Others* are there.' He now shook his nearly fleshless head in admiration, and, it seemed to her, even horror. 'My apologies, Jaghut. I would never have believed any entity would dare . . .' He drew his flint blade. 'You are a desperate fool. You have doomed us all – and more.'

'I am merely returning the favour.'

All about, the remaining Imass warriors flinched as if stung, drawing their blades of razor-thin flint. 'Purchase us what moments you can,' he told them flatly. His tannin-brown visage remained fixed upon her.

The warriors dipped their heads. 'Farewell,' one answered, and they disappeared into snatches of dust.

Above, figures now came pouring from the cave mouths: stone-grey shapes that ran on oddly jointed legs, or all four limbs at a time.

'I am tempted to leave you to them,' Ut'el said. 'But we Imass are not a cruel people.'

'So you would absolve yourselves over the centuries, yes?' She took hold of the spear haft. 'That is fortunate. Because we Jaghut are not a judgemental people.' And she heaved herself backwards in one motion, yanking the spearhead from the ground to tumble off the ledge, spear in hand.

He swung, but the blade cut just short of her as she slipped from the narrow ridge. Her buckskins snapped in the wind. 'I leave you to . . .' she yelled as she plummeted from sight down the sheer thousand-foot drop.

. . . *your doom*, Ut'el Anag, Bonecaster to the Kerluhm T'lan Imass, finished for her. He turned to face the high slope. The grey tide of creatures had finished his band and now closed upon him.

In what he considered his last moments, he raised his flint blade to his face. He watched how the knapped facets reflected the clouds overhead, how the reflections rippled like waves on clear lake water.

No. This is not yet done. I so swear.

He stepped into the realm of Tellann as the first of the clawed hands snapped closed upon the space he once occupied.

*   *   *

Hel'eth Jal Im (Pogrom of the White Stag)
51st Jaghut War
6,031 years before Burn's Sleep

Here evergreen forest descended mountain slopes to a rocky shore. Shorebirds hunted for crabs and beetles among tide-pools and stretches of black sand beaches. From their perches on tree limbs and among the taller rocks larger birds of prey watched the shorebirds and the glimmer of fingerlings in the shallows.

A morning mist hung over the bay. The air was still enough for sounds to cross from one curve of the shore to the other. The figure that arose from the seaweed-skirted boulders was not out of keeping with the scene. The tattered remains of leathers hung from its withered, mummified shoulders and hips. A nut-brown flint blade hung thrust through a crude twisted-hair belt tied about its fleshless waist. Over its head of patches of stringy hair and exposed browned skull it wore a cap cut from the cured grey hide of a beast more at home on sundrenched savanna than temperate boreal forest.

Similar figures arose, one by one, here and there about the shore. They gathered around the first arrival, and though gender was almost impossible to tell among their fleshless desiccated bodies, skin little more than paper-thin flesh over bone, this one was female and her name was Shalt Li'gar, and she was of the Ifayle T'lan Imass.

'What land is this?' one of the band, J'arl, asked. In answer, she raised her head as if taking the earth's scent through the exposed twin gaps of her nostrils. 'I know it not,' she judged. 'No account of it has been shared with me, nor with those with whom I have shared.'

'Others of us must have found it before, certainly,' another, Guth, commented.

'And what became of them . . . ?' Shalt answered, thoughtfully, peering into the mist to the far shore of the sheltered bay.

The other ravaged faces turned as well and all were silent and still for a time. So quiet and motionless were they that an eagle flew overhead to stoop the waters, its talons slicing the surface. It rose with a fish struggling in its claws, and perched in a nearby half-dead fir to tear at its meal.

The faces of all the Imass had turned silently to follow the course of its flight.

'Favourable, or unfavourable?' J'arl asked into the continued silence.

'Are we the eagle?' answered another. 'Or the fish?'

Shalt extended a withered arm to the bay. 'Others are fishing as well,' she pronounced.

They started picking their way round the curve of the shore.

First to emerge from the mist were the prows of hide boats pulled up on the strand of black gravel that climbed steeply to the forested rocky slope. Smoke trailed through the trees. Shalt glimpsed a stout log structure high on the slope. Figures now came running down a trail. They carried spears armed with stone heads, maces of stones tied to wood handles. They wore stained and beaded leathers and animal hide capes.

'Humans,' Guth observed, unimpressed. 'We should search inland.'

'Pity they choose not to talk,' Shalt judged, almost with a sigh. 'We will scout inland.'

21

J'arl thrust up a withered hand, all sinew and bone. 'I ask for a pause. There is something . . .'

Shalt regarded him. She tilted her age-gnawed head. 'A presence?'

'Something,' he repeated, wary, as if unwilling to say more.

The local people had formed a line inland. They yelled and shook their weapons. Shalt studied them: much taller than she and her stock. Prominent jaws, large teeth. Similar in features – probably the descendants of a small breeding population. Such was not so unusual among her own kind, long ago.

Her band was disappearing one by one, moving on, when one of the locals shouted something Shalt understood: 'Be gone, demons from the outside!'

The words used made all her remaining band reflexively draw their blades. For they were in the Jaghut tongue. Shalt stepped forward. 'Whence came you by this language?' she asked in the same tongue.

'It is known to us of old, demon,' an elder answered, sneering.

Known? she repeated, wonderingly. *How can this be?*

'And we have been warned of your kind,' he continued. 'Be gone! You are not welcome here.'

Shalt raised her chin, the flesh worn away from one side of her mandible, and scented again, deeply. What came on the air staggered her, and were she not of the Imass she would perhaps have fainted into unconsciousness from the challenge it presented to her very core.

'Abomination . . .' J'arl breathed in an exhalation of cold air. He raised his blade.

No! Shalt cried to herself. *They are human! We mustn't slide down this path . . . it will lead us to annihilation.*

J'arl started forward and Shalt acted without thought. Her blade sliced through vertebrae at the juncture of neck and shoulder. J'arl slumped, though she knew he was not finished utterly.

Up and down the shore her band exploded into a whirling mêlée of Imass striking Imass. Flint blades clashed and grated in a burst of clamour that sent all the nearby birds skyward in alarm. A group coalesced round Shalt, who directed them into a line defending the milling locals.

'Flee the coast!' she shouted to the people as she blocked a strike from Guth. 'Flee!'

'They will be found,' Guth promised her as he strained. 'If not us, then others.'

22

Shalt cut him down as well and wept as she fought, for he had been a companion of uncountable years.

She spared the mêlée a glance and despaired. The aggressors far outnumbered the defenders. Yet she was First of the Band for a reason and she fought even as all her allies fell about her. She was last, giving ground, suffering strikes that shaved dried flesh from her limbs and cut rotted hide from her shoulders. Now her skills overcame the constraints of the attackers, who fell one by one before the two-handed blade, so thin as to be translucent, that she flicked and turned as lightly as a green branch.

A blow took her skull. It severed bone down past her right occipital ridge. Yet even as her skull shattered she dropped this last aggressor and wailed at the necessity, for it was Bruj'el, a bull of a warrior, and cousin to her mate gone these many centuries.

She turned to the people. She could sense her animating spirit fleeing its flawed vessel. Her Tellann-provided vision was darkening, withdrawing. She fell to her bony knees. She dropped her blade to brace herself with one hand and breathed out one last fading sigh to the staring, awed figures.

'Hide yourselves . . .'

CHAPTER I

KYLE SAT IN HIS ACCUSTOMED SEAT IN A SAILORS' DIVE IN KEVIL,
Mare, of south Fist, and considered his dwindling stash of
coins, and thus options, for escaping these damnably insular
Korel lands. It was a region so notoriously hostile to foreigners
that should any here find him, an obvious stranger, wounded in
the street, many would go out of their way to kick and spit upon
him.

Especially as he wore the gear of the hated Malazans.

He'd ordered a stein of beer, which finally arrived at his table only
because he'd proved himself a paying customer; something which
might end soon enough. He supposed he could afford the short jaunt
across Black Strait to Stygg on the mainland, and from there it was
but a hop and a skip overland south across the Great Ice Wastes to
Stratem, wasn't it, my lad? He had the money for that at least. Or he
could always join the Mare navy. They at least were recruiting. Not
that they'd take a foreigner, and certainly not a blasted ex-Malazan
who'd been at the naval engagement where the much vaunted Mare
galleys had been razed to the waterline by said invaders and their
allies.

He sipped the beer and damned that Katakan captain he'd hired.
Once Fist slipped below the horizon the man turned round! He
should've put his sword to his throat and forced him to sail on east.
'Course, there was no way he could've kept the whole crew at knife
point for two weeks – but at least he'd have gotten off the wretched
island.

Patience, he told himself, Kylarral-ten, son of Tulo, of the People
of the Wind. There will be other chances.

Abyss, maybe a foreign trader would put in and he'd be able to
hire on as crew. He was wondering how long it would be before that

...d whether he had enough coin, when someone eased ...n into the chair opposite.

...e looking for a ship,' the fellow said, and crossed his arms. ...wearing a canvas shirt, ragged and much patched, and ...users were similar. His face and neck were sun- and wind-d...ened to the Mare sailor's usual deep polished brown. An antler-handled dirk stood up from the strip of hair rope he wore tied as a belt. His dark eyes held the common disapproval and scarcely hidden hostility Kyle usually found directed at him as the cut of his leathers, his belt, sheath and boots, labelled him as being of those recent invaders.

Kyle allowed a guarded nod. 'Unsuccessfully,' he said.

'I speak for Tulan Orbed, Master of the *Lady's Luck*. He is interested in your talk of lands east of here across the Bloodmare Ocean.' The man's face and tone, however, made it plain that he was not.

'Those lands are so close the Bloodmare Ocean should be named a strait.'

The sailor leaned forward to push his stubbled chin out over their tiny round table. 'Listen, Malazan. We Marese are the greatest sailors of the age. If there was any such land so close then it would be our colony by now.'

Not if those lands are the ones I seek, my friend, Kyle silently rejoined. He also thought it politic not to mention that the combined Malazan and Moranth Blue navies, having defeated the Mare navy, might have a word to say about who were the greatest sailors of the age. In any case, he allowed himself a small shrug. 'What does Master Tulan Orbed say?'

The sailor fell back, scowling. Knife scars on his cheeks and chin twisted and paled a ghostly white as they stretched. 'He would meet you to discuss the matter. He would have you come on board.'

'When?'

'Tonight. Tomorrow. Whenever,' and he echoed Kyle's indifferent shrug.

'Then I will come this night.'

'We would require payment before we push out,' he warned, and he thrust his chin forward once again.

Kyle stood, tossed a coin to the table. 'That is for your master and me to discuss, I should think.'

He left the tavern not even glancing back. The fellow had made his disapproval obvious. There was nothing more to discuss. He headed to the wharf, or rather series of wharves. For Kevil, as he had discovered, like all Mare cities, was really nothing more than a land-based depot and servicing centre for their extraordinary, apparently unsinkable, galleys.

At least, he reflected, they may not sink but the Moranth certainly proved that they do burn.

He walked the uneven cobbles of the wharf's main way. It bore ruts from centuries of foot and cart traffic. The cortex of many stones had eroded through to the creamy brown flint beneath. Through the evening gloom of clouds, smoke and mist he could just make out the looming shapes of the nearest moored vessels. All thrusting so tall and proud their sculpted galley bow-figures of waves, dolphins, and, of course, the obligatory women.

Well . . . maybe not quite so proud these days.

The famed galleys of Mare, when not drawn up for repairs, were each housed in their own slip flanked by piers allowing easy access to the long slim vessels. The effect of the league-long line of such berths was of a great set of teeth deployed ready to bite the waters of the bay.

Dragging steps behind announced the resentful sailor following. Kyle searched for and found a lad lounging among the piled cargo of boxes and bales. He approached; the lad made a show of ignoring him. He cleared his throat. 'I'm looking for the *Lady's Luck.*'

A lazy sullen gaze scoured Kyle up and down. The gaze slid away. 'Her mate's a knife thrust behind you.'

'Where's his ship?'

The lad just smiled his contempt and crossed his arms, leaning farther back.

Calm, Kyle, he reminded himself. Calm. It's worth it to get out from among these ignorant inward-looking people.

He headed on. Movement on his left and the mate appeared. He decided to give the man another chance. 'This direction, I assume.'

The mate said nothing.

So, am I right or wrong? If they reached the end of the wharf, he decided he'd throw the man off.

After a long silent walk, interminably long it seemed to him, the mate edged his head over and muttered a grudging, 'The *Lady's Luck.*'

A tiny orange glow at the raised stern deck marked a lit brazier. Kyle stepped down into the longship, edged along the narrow seating of the oarsmen up on to the central raised walkway, and climbed the seven slim steps that led to the open stern deck. The mate followed all the way.

Here Kyle found two men, one old and one young, each wrapped in furs against the chill of the passing winter, roasting titbits of meat on skewers over the brazier.

The older one, a great boar of a man with a thick black head of curly hair and beard to match, eyed him while he licked his fingers clean, one at a time. His dark face carried the scars of decades of fighting and exposure to sun and wind. The younger's face was smooth and pale; Kyle hazarded a guess that he had been to sea rarely if at all. The lad glanced from his elder, his father perhaps, to the mate, then to Kyle, and back round again.

'You are this foreigner speaking of lands to the east?' the elder rumbled.

'I am.'

'I am Tulan Orbed, Master of the *Lady's Luck*.' He waved a great paw to the lad. 'This here is my nephew, Reuth.'

'Kyle.'

'The black storm cloud behind you is Storval, First Mate.'

'We've met.'

'Ha! I intuit from your tone that you certainly have. So gloomy is he we name him Black Storval.' He urged Kyle to him. 'Come, come. Set yourself at ease. We see so few foreigners here. Tell us of the world beyond Fist. You have seen these distant shores to the east?'

Kyle was rather taken aback to meet such a cosmopolitan attitude. He sat easily enough, but to one side, so as not to put his back to the ill-tempered mate. Tulan chuckled at this, and winked. Then, peering up sharply, he said, 'Another horn and more ale, Storval.'

The man scowled even more but ground out a nod. 'Aye, captain.' He thumped down the stairs.

Tulan extended a wood skewer to Kyle, who took it and jabbed a scrap of meat that he then held over the glowing brazier coals. 'I have seen them.'

The captain's gaze flicked to his nephew. 'Indeed. And does this land have a name?'

'It does. The southern lands are known to some as Bael. The northern some name . . .' and here he paused, wondering whether to mention the damned ill-omened name at all. But he ploughed on, thinking, wind toss it, no one from Korel would know it anyway: '. . . Assail.' The captain eyed his nephew once more. But the lad was watching Kyle. A faintly amused smile pulled at his mouth. They know this already, he realized. They just wanted to see if I'd lie about that name. 'Anything else?'

28

'Where were you there? A port? Did you land?'

Kyle nodded while he ate his sizzling cut of meat. Storval returned, set down a third drinking horn and a fat skin. Kyle used the skewer to pick his teeth. 'A city on the east coast. Kurzan.'

Again, Tulan eyed his nephew, who nodded.

Kyle turned to the unprepossessing pale blotchy-faced lad and looked him up and down. 'You've been there?'

He blushed furiously, his face almost glowing, and shook his head.

'Reuth's a scholar,' Tulan explained. 'But a particular kind of scholar. I paid a fortune to send him to poke through dusty records in Jasston and Jourilan. Isn't that so, Reuth?'

The lad nodded vigorously.

Tulan picked up the skin and squeezed a stream of ale into the horn. He offered it to Kyle. 'His passion is cartography. Know you this line of knowledge?'

Kyle accepted the horn, nodding. 'Charts and maps.'

'Indeed. He is only happy when bent over dusty sheets.' The captain glanced to his nephew. 'Quite the secret hoard of charts they have in Jourilan, confiscated from every vessel that ever landed or wrecked itself upon the coast. Isn't that so, Reuth?'

The lad leaned forward, all eagerness. 'Yes. And you, sir, your accent is not Malazan, sir. Where are you from? Is it Seven Cities?'

The captain raised a paw as if to backhand the lad. 'Not now, dammit to the Lady's grave!' Reuth flinched away. 'Apologies,' Tulan growled. 'The lad has spent too much time among scrolls and records and not enough time crewing among men – some of whom may not look kindly upon questions regarding their past.'

Kyle gave the young man a reassuring smile. 'I welcome curiosity. I find it . . . refreshing.'

Tulan grunted a laugh. 'No doubt you do here along these shores!' He wiped his greasy hands on his furs. 'Now to business. How many days to cross – by your estimate?'

'Due east of here? A fortnight at the least, I should think. With favourable winds.'

Again the captain eyed his nephew, who answered with a curt nod of approval. 'Good, good. Such a crossing is as nothing for us of Mare.'

Yet none of you have ventured it, Kyle reflected. On the other hand, perhaps some have . . . they've simply never returned. He sipped the ale and found it even worse than he'd anticipated; he grimaced. 'And is your goal – pure exploration?'

Tulan guffawed anew. His toothy grin was conspiratorial and he hunched forward, lowering his voice. 'Come now, friend. That you seek these eastern lands proves you've heard the rumours.'

'Rumours?'

The big man sat back and frowned behind his greasy beard. 'No need to play things so close. We of Mare are traders, sea-scavengers. Aye, I'll even admit it openly here upon the deck of my own good ship . . . marauders and raiders. No need to pretend with me.'

Kyle had no idea what the man was getting at. He swirled the dregs of the ale in its horn, considered dumping it over the side. Rumours? There were plenty of rumours surrounding Assail. Yet these were all of a kind that would send you fleeing it. Not seeking passage *to* it. He slowly shook his head, all the while keeping his gaze steady on the man. 'I'm sorry, Tulan, captain. But I have heard no recent rumours.'

Tulan once more waved a hairy hand at his nephew. 'Foreign gods, man. Even Reuth here has heard, in Kor! The ports are seething with the news.'

Kyle continued to shake his head.

Reuth cleared his throat. 'A word, Uncle, if I may?'

'What?' Tulan grunted, now all ill-humour.

'Our friend is a foreigner in these lands, yes? No one here would speak to him regarding anything. Let alone pass on choice bits of news, or even gossip to while away the time.'

The captain's dark masses of brows rose as he considered his nephew's words. He slammed his horn to the keg he used as a table. 'Of course! No one would pass such news along to some damned foreigner – ah, no insult intended.' By way of apology, he held out the ale-skin and Kyle could only answer by extending his horn for refilling. 'An offering to our journey!' Tulan laughed as he over-topped the horn, spilling ale to the deck. 'And a propitiation to the new gods to come. Though,' and he lost his smile, 'after the Lady, we've quite had our fill of gods in this region, I should think.'

'The news then?'

Tulan raised his horn to the toast. Reuth joined, and Kyle also, though inwardly dreading more of the brackish drink. 'To a profitable, ah . . . *venture*, friend. For it is all the news that gold has been discovered in the northern mountains of the lands across the Bloodmare Sea. Great wide fields of gold. Enough wealth to make kings of us all.'

So astounded by this claim was Kyle that he mechanically threw back his drink and had to force the vile liquid down. Ye gods! Gold in northern Assail? This news would draw thousands from all across the lands. Especially if word of it had reached even isolated and inward Korel. 'When was the strike made?' he asked, clearing his throat and coughing.

Tulan waved the horn airily. 'Well, admittedly, it has taken some time for the news to come to us. Apparently, word first came from a shipwreck on the Jourilan coast. Some people heralding from some backward land named Lether. The crew had heard of it first hand from a stricken vessel they'd come across and . . . ah . . . rescued.'

Kyle shook his head, unconvinced. 'Tall tales to save their skins.'

Tulan winked. 'So too would I have thought. But then similar news came by way of a vessel that put in for repairs on the north Fist coast. This ship hailed from Falar, north of Malaz. Know you it?'

'I know it. Excellent mariners, the Falari.'

'Yes. They claimed to have landed on an island within spitting distance of the Assail mainland only to find the place nearly deserted. Entire villages empty. They questioned some oldsters who gave them the news . . . gold had been discovered in Assail. Everyone picked up and went after it.'

Kyle raised his hands wide. 'Then we are too late. These strikes are usually cleaned out in months. All the rich ground worth sifting gets claimed.'

The captain winked again – it was an engaging gesture that seemed to say: 'Yes, this may be so, but we are both men of the world and we know better . . .' Kyle found himself warming to the old pirate – for pirate he had as good as confessed to being. 'But this is Assail,' Tulan said, pushing more meat on to his blackened skewer. 'We know the tales of that land.' Don't we now, Kyle silently answered, and he shook his head at the dreadfulness of them. 'Just so. Few will live to reach the fields, yes? And as to claims or owner-ship . . . well.' The big man gave an eloquent shrug.

Kyle knew this to be true. If the stories were to believed, no state existed up there to grant any rights of ownership, or to recognize any claims or stakes. It would be utter chaos. Armed bands would provide the only authority, and they answerable only to themselves. And as to those who already lived up there – petty warlords, pocket tyrants continuously at war with their neighbours – they could find themselves utterly overrun. Surely not even they could kill quickly enough to stem the tide soon to be breaking on their shores.

He almost tossed back the last of his drink but stopped himself in time. He eyed the grinning pirate captain. 'You plan to take a rich claim, empty it, and cut your way back to the *Lady's Luck*?'

Tulan blew on the cooked meat then pulled it off the skewer with his teeth. 'Nothing as crude as that,' he answered, chewing. 'Godsblood, man, you almost make it sound like hard work.' He offered his nephew a wink and topped up his horn. 'Nothing like that. Think it through, man. We don't do any of that hardscrabble digging! We let other poor unfortunates do all the hard work sifting and washing and transporting and such. We'll just lie in wait along the coast, won't we? After all, they'll want to get it out of such a godsforsaken pesthole.' He opened his hands wide at the obviousness of it. 'That's when we liberate it.'

'Ah, I see. An elegant plan.'

Tulan grinned his agreement. 'Thank you, my friend.'

'So you have a crew.'

'Oh yes, the prettiest gang of murderers and hireswords. Why, we even have a squad of ten Stormguard who are – how shall I put it – *dissatisfied* with the new regime.'

That alarmed Kyle, and he must have not made a good enough job of disguising his reaction as the captain held up a hand. 'You are Malazan. I understand your concern. But do not worry. All that is the past, no? We are now brothers together in this venture for gainful capital, yes?'

Kyle allowed a wary smile. 'Of course.' Struck by a new thought, he studied Reuth. 'So you know the coast . . .'

The lad blushed and lowered his gaze. Tulan stroked his beard and grinned like a proud uncle, saying, 'We have the best maps outside Assail itself, I am sure.'

Reuth dared a glance. 'The names,' he whispered, as if frightened. 'I don't understand the names. Have you heard those names?'

Kyle nodded his agreement. Yes. Those names haunted the stories of his youth. All of them ghost stories. 'Wrath . . .' he murmured. 'Wrack . . . Dread . . . Black Pit . . . the Anguish Coast.'

Tulan grunted, but not unkindly. 'You're young, Reuth.' He held another titbit of meat over the brazier. 'We may be ignorant provincials here in these lands, friend Kyle, but I know a tale or two. I've heard tell of lands where people name their children "Fool", "Louse", or even "Splitnose". Know you why they would do such cruel things to their own children?'

Kyle smiled his understanding. 'To turn away the attention of the gods – or demons.'

32

'Exactly. So, tell me, friend Kyle, if you wanted to ruin a place what would you name it?'

His smile twisted to its side. 'I suppose I'd tout it as Paradise. Or Bounty.'

'Exactly. And if you wanted to keep people away?' Tulan turned his questioning gaze on Reuth.

The lad nodded. 'I see.'

'Or perhaps they are just awful places,' Kyle suggested.

Tulan burst out in a great bout of laughter. 'Perhaps indeed they are, friend Kyle.' He rubbed his hands again on his already greasy furs and leathers. 'So. You will bunk here on the *Lady's Luck*, yes?'

Kyle motioned that he had no objection.

'You have gear? I could send Storval.'

'No – no thank you.'

The captain waved to Kyle's side. 'Need you another blade? We have plenty.'

He could not stop his hand from going to his belt where he carried his sword wrapped in leather. 'No. It is quite all right. I will repair it.'

The big man shrugged. 'Suit yourself. Storval will see you bunked. We'll push out with tomorrow's evening tide, yes?'

Kyle rose. 'Very good. Thank you.' He bowed to the captain and noted how Reuth now could not keep his gaze from the wrapped blade at his side. He descended to the rowing deck. Tulan bellowed: 'Storval! Rouse your worthless hide! See to this man's berth!'

While the first mate rubbed his eyes and stretched, Kyle stood with his hand still resting on his covered sword. He wondered whether these two had heard certain tales of the war against the Lady. Stories making the rounds of the invasion and rebellion. Of the Malazan commander Greymane, named Stonewielder here, and his foreign companion, and of two swords – one grey and one pale. The grey one was gone. The stuff of mere legend now. But the rumours also told of an ivory sword carried by a foreign warrior. A blade that could cut through anything. A sword he'd heard the stories here named Whiteblade. A weapon, they said, fit for a god.

These stories were closer to the truth than even their tellers knew. For the blade came to his hand from the hand of the Sky-King Osserc himself, and Kyle was beginning to suspect just what it might be. The possibilities terrified him. And so he dared not leave it out of his sight, yet he dared not show it either. The burden of it was a curse. A damned curse. So had Greymane named the stone sword he had wielded. And now Kyle understood the man completely.

33

He clenched the weapon in its leather wrap more tightly to his side. Storval motioned curtly to the steps down into the low-roofed storage cabin beneath the stern deck. 'You may sleep here tonight,' he growled, then smiled wolfishly and added, 'But after tomorrow it's the rowing benches for you – what say you to that, foreigner?'

Kyle shrugged indifferently. 'Beats the ground.'

The first mate sneered his disbelief and waved him down.

✳   ✳   ✳

Shimmer did not want to do it, but two months after returning from Jacuruku and the harrowing though successful expedition to that cursed land, she requested that a select few officers of the Crimson Guard meet her in the forest just north of Fortress Haven, Stratem.

She realized that this decision had been some time in coming. These last months of indecision and inactivity on the part of K'azz had merely provoked it. Cal-Brinn and the Fourth remained trapped in Assail and still no steps were being taken to organize their rescue. K'azz had even been told that answers to what awaited the Guard in the future lay in those lands. Yet he did nothing. No vessels had been hired nor were efforts being made to begin construction. K'azz had simply disappeared once more into the wild tracts of Stratem's interior.

It was infuriating. And it was saddening. He was allowing her no choice. She had to act. It was in the best interest of the Guard.

Yet she was also self-aware enough to reflect: *or so I tell myself.*

Even so, it cost her a full month of sleepless nights. The doubts and self-recriminations would not go away. Was she no better than Skinner? He too had expressed his dissatisfaction with K'azz's leadership – though in a far more direct and decisive fashion.

He'd buried his old commander alive to keep him out of the way. Yet she wondered whether what she intended was any gentler. *Usurpation is still usurpation,* she told herself. She'd finally decided: *look on the bright side . . . they might run me through the minute they realize what I am proposing.*

When she entered the glade Blues was already present, standing among the tall weeds. It was a clear night. The sky was dark once more. The Gods' Road arched across its spine as it always had before the invasion of the Visitor with its long arching tail of jade flame. A weak wind stirred the tall dry grass and sent a whispering and brushing among the leaves.

Not only worry pinched Blues' namesake Napan features. The man had lost weight. The mission to Korelri had been a particularly trying one. Though it too had met with success: Bars had been found and returned to the fold.

And the man brought further news of Assail. Cal-Brinn and the Fourth had been fleeing north when they parted ways. *Fleeing*. Cal-Brinn, one of the strongest mages of the Guard. An adept of Rashan and a fearsome swordsman, together with some thirty Avowed. *Fleeing* for their lives.

Blues said nothing, though he did nod a welcome. He suspects, she saw. Will he challenge? A caustic smile twisted her lips as she realized that they'd both come armed. He with the multitude of weapons he habitually carried: sticks, knives, twinned longswords, and who knew what else hidden away. Gods, he was the Guard's weaponmaster. A fish would be deadly in this man's hands.

She, of course, wore her whipsword sheathed at her back, its two-handed grip extending up over her left shoulder. The one weapon she might be the last living master of, she reflected.

Petal entered next and his appearance did nothing for Blues' sour expression.

She knew Blues saw Petal only as a mage loyal to Skinner. Blues had been on his own mission. Hadn't walked the jungled paths of Jacuruku with them. He had not shared all that Petal and she had shared. The brothers and sisters who walked into exile under Skinner would listen to Petal. She must bridge this gulf of suspicion between him and Blues.

Tarkhan arrived next and it was Shimmer's turn to clench her lips.

Always a creature of Cowl. She'd never liked this one. And now Cowl had returned . . . if in body only. For Hood's sake, the man had been captive of an Azath House! Who knew what was going on in his crazed mind? Yet Tarkhan carried the loyalty of the First company. She must win him.

The squat Wickan paused at the edge of the glade. His broad dark face was unreadable in the dimness. His eyes glittered as they shifted from her to Blues and Petal. He too had come armed: the traditional Wickan curved knives rested on his hips.

Steeling herself, Shimmer advanced into the glade. Fieldmice scurried from her boots as she pushed through the thick grasses and thorn bushes. Among the trees an owl gave an excited hoot at this rousting of prey.

When the four met at the centre of the meadow, none spoke.

35

There was no need. Shimmer read in their expressions that all had deduced why she had called them here this night. She was pained to see disappointment in Blues' frown, while Tarkhan carried a sort of smirk that seemed to say . . . and you were doubting of *my* loyalty? Petal held his hands clasped before his wide stomach and his eyes were downcast; it seemed he could not meet her eyes.

Damn. Had she lost them already? Would none support her? What then was left? Exile?

She almost wavered then. The option remained to travel half the path. Voice mere concerns. Play the worried subordinate.

Yet they would see through that and know her failure of nerve here, now, on the cliff's edge. She would lose any remaining shreds of their respect: not only disloyal, but a coward as well. Imagining such a loss stung her to draw breath, but she caught sight of a fifth, uninvited, figure entering the clearing and clamped her lips shut.

It was Cowl in his tattered finery. He came swaggering up with his maddening knowing grin. The scars across his throat – put there by Dancer himself – seemed to glow in the darkness. His unkempt black hair fell across his face like deeper shadows of night. He offered his manic grin to each.

'You have no part in this conclave,' Shimmer ground out. 'Be gone.'

The High Mage and master assassin of the Guard appeared not to hear. He continued to cast his gaze about the meadow as if he were out for a mid-night stroll.

'There is poetry here,' he suddenly announced, seemingly apropos of nothing.

The sensation of *things* crawling upon her skin that always accompanied this man's presence returned to Shimmer. 'What do you want?' she growled. She was emboldened – and encouraged – to see even Tarkhan shift uneasily and rub his arms in discomfort in the presence of his old master.

'It was not so far from here that other masks were removed,' the man said airily, as if this fully answered her demand.

'What do you mean?'

'I mean, dearest Shimmer, that this is not far from the spot where Skinner and I abandoned the pretence of searching for K'azz and he stepped forward to claim command of the Guard.'

Shimmer's throat clenched far too tight for words. Bastard! What was he trying to do? Might as well stick the knife in and be done with it!

'I don't believe Shimmer here means to try anything that radical,' Blues ground out, an unspoken warning in his voice. He turned his narrowed gaze upon her. ''Least not the Shimmer I knew.'

'No,' she agreed. 'But I cannot stand silently by either. Duty and loyalty drive me to call attention to K'azz's neglect of his responsibilities.'

Cowl brayed a mocking laugh and Shimmer fought down an urge to yank her whipsword free and add to the scars across the man's neck.

'Quiet,' Blues growled. To Shimmer: 'I share your concern. What of you, Tarkhan?'

The Wickan inclined his head in agreement. 'I, too, am concerned. We are mercenaries yet we pursue no contracts. We are idle. What, then, are we?'

'And you, Petal?' Shimmer asked.

The giant was pulling thoughtfully on his fat lower lip. He blushed beneath their attention and dipped his head, murmuring, 'I am come merely as an observer – I have no standing to vote on any of this.'

'We ain't voting on anything,' Blues was quick to answer. ''Least not yet, anyways.' His gaze fixed upon Shimmer. 'What do you propose?'

The weaponmaster's gaze flayed her to the bone and she drew a steadying breath. It was as if the man were waiting poised for one misstep from her, one wrong word, and she would feel his blade in her heart before she sensed his move. She found her throat had gone quite dry, and licked her lips to wet them. Even though she felt as if she were declaring her own death sentence, she began: 'I must formally question K'azz's fitness to command.'

Blues' hands did not rise from where they rested close to the grips of his long-knives. Tarkhan's dark eyes, like glistening obsidian, shifted from her to Blues while he brushed his fingertips across his belt. Petal had stopped pulling at his lip and now stood motionless with it pinched between his fingers.

A long slow mocking laugh echoed through the clearing and Shimmer, as did the rest, shifted her gaze to Cowl, High Mage of the Guard.

'Quiet from you,' Blues warned again.

The man bowed. 'My apologies. Please, do continue, dear Shimmer. Do go on. You now propose yourself as acting commander given K'azz's, ah, *desertion* of his duties. Yes?'

'I propose no such thing.'

The man's acid smile slipped away and he tilted his head in puzzlement. 'Oh? You do not?'

'No. I propose Blues as acting commander.'

The Napan swordsman's brows shot up. 'Now wait a Trake-damned minute.'

'I have no objection,' Tarkhan put in quickly, and he smiled evilly as if taking enormous pleasure in Blues' discomfort.

'Well *I* do,' Blues growled. 'I decline. And anyway, it makes no difference either way.'

Shimmer frowned, not certain what he meant, but sensing the truth of the man's words. They carried an echo of something out of Jacuruku. 'What do you mean?' she said slowly, almost in dread.

He waved to Cowl. 'What this jackal's laughin' about. You're not a mage, Shimmer. You don't understand. Makes no difference who we put forward to take over. Can't be done.'

'As I now have come to see,' Cowl whispered, and his toothy white smile broadened once again. 'The Vow is binding.'

What of the Vow? she wondered. Whatever did the man— Damn! We swore to K'azz! He commands . . . until we are all gone? No escape? We are . . . helpless? A strange dizziness assaulted her and her vision darkened. A hand steadied her – Blues' – and she nodded her thanks. 'Then there is nothing we can do,' she barely said aloud. The words sounded desolate to her ears. There was no hope for them.

'Make the arrangements, Shimmer,' Blues said gently. 'Just go ahead. We will go to Assail.'

'Who should come?'

'I must,' Cowl said, and his manic smile returned.

'Then I will,' Blues answered, glaring at the mage.

'And myself,' Shimmer answered. She cast an invitation to Petal.

He raised his brows, quite surprised. 'I would – if I may. And I suggest Gwynn.'

'Bars must come, of course,' Blues added. 'What of you, Tarkhan?'

The plainsman shifted his broad stance, uncomfortable. 'If you lot are going then I am certain K'azz will once more leave command of Stratem to me.' He smoothed his moustache and scowled his disgust. 'There you are. Neither Shimmer nor you get command. It comes to me, unwanted and unasked for.'

'I am sorry, Tarkhan,' Shimmer offered. 'But I am also relieved.'

The man snorted.

'We must go in force,' Blues continued. 'At least ten more swords.'

Shimmer nodded her assent. 'Two Blades, then. You take one, I the other.'

'Very good.'

'And K'azz?' Petal asked, his hand at his chin.

Blues waved the question aside. 'He can come or not. His choice. We aren't leaving Cal to rot.'

*　　*　　*

The south coastal people called her the Ghost Woman, the Stranger, or She-Who-Speaks-to-the-Wind. All anyone knew was that she appeared just a few seasons ago here on this stretch of their coast and that that day there had been a terrible battle in which the dead rose to fight all the day and all the night. Since that time this length of seashore was avoided by all and was cursed with the name, the Dead Coast.

And over the seasons the clash and clamour of battle had returned to rage from that coastline. At those times, day or night, the locals would huddle in their huts, throw themselves down before their altars, and beg that the gods and demons pass them by.

Sumaran, son of Jirel, was one of these inhabitants. A fisherman by trade. Once, when the winds pushed his outrigger too far up the coast, he spotted the woman herself. She was out walking the dunes all alone, just as others had reported seeing her – reports he'd doubted himself. Yet that day there she appeared, a lonely figure, her long hair blowing in the shoreward winds, her ragged clothes snapping and flicking as well. Then she had stilled, and it seemed to him that her face turned to him, and he thought he saw her mouth moving as if she were speaking though no one was there. Or she was casting a spell upon him. He had made the sign against evil at his heart and paddled on as fast as he could.

Now, this morning, the winds had taken hold of his outrigger once more and were determined to toss him upon the Dead Coast. He'd lowered his mast and paddled furiously but still the rising winds pushed him in towards the submerged rocks that guarded this stretch of beach. It was, he decided, as if some malevolent god or demon was working to make this day his last. He wondered what he had done to earn such wrath and realized that it could have been anything. He was no stranger to the capriciousness of the gods, and the demons and spirits of the coast were even worse. It occurred to him then, briefly, that perhaps this was the curse of the Ghost Woman herself for that single forbidden glimpse.

Then the outrigger ground up against the rocks and he was heaved over the side. Waves tossed him rolling until he knew not which way was up. Rocks gouged his shoulder; his chest flamed. The clear bright sky suddenly glared upon him and he gasped one breath before the waves pushed him under once more. His arm struck the sandy bottom and he stood, coughing, squeezing his shoulder.

He staggered to shore even though he knew he was no better off. This was the Dead Coast where the dead ruled. He had to flee. He ran, panting, the wet sands pulling on his feet, his shoulder blazing its pain and his hand slick with blood.

He ran mouthing prayers and entreaties to all the gods and spirits of the coast: please allow him to escape! Please look away! He would sacrifice half his catch from this day forth should he live to see tomorrow's dawn!

Pleading gave way to tears and curses as his feet became heavy and he tripped, falling again and again. His breath burned in his throat and his vision blurred. He rose one more time to stumble on. A dark figure suddenly appeared before him as if swirling out of the night itself and he threw himself aside shrieking his terror. There, peering down at him, was the ravaged face of death itself, and Sumaran knew nothing more.

He awoke to the cawing of seabirds. The sun was just rising. He lay upon the open sands, the remains of a fire before him. Something held him tight and he felt at his chest. Some sort of cloth was tied tightly over his shoulder. He peered about, terrified. Where was death? He thought he'd come for him. Perhaps it had been nothing more than a nightmare.

A figure approached from over the dunes. Sumaran tensed to run but his legs would not move: he was frozen in dread. It was the Ghost Woman. The wind tossed her long tangled hair. She wore a hide shirt and trousers and over this a tattered fur cloak that flapped and snapped. She was old, he saw, as wrinkled as any elder. Strings of polished green and blue stones hung about her neck. She stood peering down at him and it seemed that there was no sympathy in her hard black eyes.

'You are well?' she asked in an odd accent, using very archaic phrasing.

Remembering whom he dealt with he quickly lowered his gaze. 'What do you wish of me?' he stammered.

'I wish nothing of you. You need not fear me. I will not harm you.'

He knew not what to say. What could one say? 'I – I am grateful for my life,' he murmured, his eyes still downcast.

'It was nothing. If your strength has returned you may go. You are from the villages to the east, I believe?'

He swallowed to wet his throat. 'Yes.'

'And what is it they name me there?'

He dared not reveal that. He searched for some possible answer until the Ghost Woman chuckled and murmured, 'That bad, is it?' He ducked his head, even more petrified. 'Never mind,' she continued, 'I understand. It is not important. You should go now before—' and a catch came to her voice, almost as if she was pained.

Suraman dared a glance. The Ghost Woman was studying the horizon and for a moment it seemed as if she was far more terrified than he. He almost spoke then, to ask what it was she saw, but he feared her anger far too much to dare such a thing.

He used his good arm to raise himself up, all the while keeping his gaze downcast. 'I – I will go, then. My thanks again.'

'Certainly.'

He dared another glance: the witch was still peering aside, squinting, something like unease tightening her mouth. For a moment the strange impression struck Suraman that instead of haunting the coast, this entity was in fact guarding it. He headed off, limping slightly. Yet that startling image drove him to turn back. Glancing up, he asked: 'How, then, are you known – I may ask?'

The woman was still staring off towards the sea. Her old patched furs lashed and snapped about her. She answered, 'You may call me Silverfox.'

When he was far enough away he risked one final glance back. The woman was still where he'd last seen her. All alone, staring off towards the surging ocean waves, hands clasped behind her back. She appeared even more alone and sad to him then. Something about her pulled at his heart. He was about to turn away when suddenly she was no longer alone there among the dunes. Other figures stood with her. Dark they were, ragged and worn in outline. Bulky furs draped their odd figures, and long tatters of hides blew about them. The head of one carried gnarled antlers.

This sight drove icy atavistic shivers down his spine and he backed away, horrified once again. The dead. She is the sad Queen of the Dead. To think if he had drowned in the surf he, too, could now be standing among them!

He spun and ran. He must warn everyone! No one need doubt any longer. This was the Dead Coast in truth!

*   *   *

41

Of the countless freebooters, hijackers, and outright pirates of the south Genabackan coast and the archipelago of the Free Confederacy, Burl Tardin knew he wasn't the first to hear word of a rich gold strike in the legendary north Assail lands. He knew also that he was not the first to set out south to dare the stormy Galatan Sweep and from there pass onward, entering the semi-mythical Sea of Hate as it was known in the old lays. And he knew that though he was not even the first to succeed in said crossings, at great risk and cost, it was an achievement worthy of song all the same.

This he became certain of as he passed the shattered hulls of Genabackan vessels lying strewn along what those self-same old songs and stories named the 'Wreckers' Coast'.

He did, however, suspect that he was among the first to reach the gauntlet of rocks known as the Guardians. These rocks, and the twisted course between, choked Fear Narrows, the entrance to the inland Dread Sea – which some also called the Sea of Dread. He did believe he was the first of his compatriots to manage this particular miracle of seamanship.

And now he, his vessel – the *Sea Strike* – and his crew lay becalmed somewhere on the pale milky waters of the Dread Sea. His crew manned the oars, of course, though progress was hard to determine among the near constant mists and fogs that shrouded the stars at night and obscured the unfamiliar coast by day. Many were for putting in until the damned fogs abated, but he suspected that such conditions were unavoidable here in these strange lands and waters. Besides, each time they'd put in for water, or to hunt, hostile locals had met them and they'd put spears through four of his crew.

Banks of the thick mists drifted by like smoke to enmesh them in their clinging arms. Dark shapes seemed to loom through the fogs. Other ships, perhaps, just as lost. His lookouts shouted but only their own calls echoed back across the waters. Or so Burl assumed, as the returning shouts sounded eerily like voices in other languages calling their warning. Perhaps even crying their panic.

'Sea-monster!' a lookout warned one morning and Burl almost ordered the poor fellow to come down as his eyes were playing tricks upon him. But others called now, pointing to port, where a dark shape closed upon them. Long and tall it was in the fog. By the great sea-god himself, Burl swore, amazed: a sea-dragon.

The fog parted in swirling wafts and the lookout voiced a panicked: ''Ware! Ice!'

'Stave it off!' Burl bellowed.

The crew on the starboard side jumped to unship their oars while those on the port raised theirs and braced themselves. The huge shard of emerald ice came brushing up against the slim wooden poles. Wood shattered and crewmen grunted and shouted their pain as the oars lashed among them. Hernen went down with a shattered skull as one slammed him on the side of the head in a sickening wet crack.

The *Sea Strike* lurched under a side-swiping blow. Its planks groaned, and all aboard were thrown from their feet. Ice clattered in a gleaming shower to the decking, where the shards lay steaming.

'Check the hull!' Burl ordered and clambered to his feet. 'Clear that ice.'

'Aye,' First Mate Whellen answered.

The great ice behemoth coursed on, not even scarred by its encounter. Burl watched it go, eerily silent, once more merging into the bank of hanging fog. 'Hull's still sound,' his master carpenter reported and Burl nodded his relief.

A scream of pain snapped their attention to amidships. Whellen stood staring at his hands. Burl ran to him. 'Gods, what is it?'

The mate stood gazing at his hands, wordless. Burl yanked on his shoulder. 'Speak, man!'

The mate raised his eyes and Burl flinched away: they seemed utterly empty of awareness. 'It burns,' the mate whispered, awed. 'The ice burns.' Then he collapsed to the wet planking.

Burl ordered the man be wrapped in blankets and thought nothing more of it – he had a ship to check for soundness and an entire crew to handle. He had spare oars drawn and those that could be repaired kept. Yet they were now short of a full complement and when the crew returned to rowing they made even less progress than before.

The next day they sighted a vessel. It was a vague motionless silhouette in the mists at first. Oaring closer they hailed it, but no answer came. Burl ordered a cautious approach. The half of the crew not rowing hurried to ready weapons. As they closed the gap, the lines of the vessel revealed themselves in a form never before seen by him or his crew.

Long and narrow it was, a galley just like the *Strike*, but larger, and closed, not open-hulled. It lay becalmed, the sails of its one mast limp. To Burl it looked abandoned, like some sort of ghost ship. 'Hello, vessel!' he shouted again.

When no one answered he ordered the *Strike* closer and a small boarding party readied, led by the second mate, Gaff. Whellen still lay abed, stricken with whatever ailment it was that had hold of him.

The *Strike* bumped up amidships and the party clambered aboard. Burl and the crew waited and watched, weapons in hand. They did not have long to wait. Immediately, it seemed to him, the boarding party returned. They swung legs out over the taller side and jumped or eased themselves down. Burl searched among them for Gaff. Quiet they were, pale even. He found the man and looked him up and down. 'Well?'

His second mate just shook his head, unable to speak. Un-nervingly, Burl was reminded of Whellen's reaction to holding the ice. The man shakily drew a sleeve across his sweaty glistening brow and swallowed as if pushing back bile. 'Gone,' he managed. 'All gone.'

Burl scanned the rocking vessel. Its waterline foamed heavy with weeds and barnacles, as if it had lain becalmed in the water for years. 'Dead? How?'

'No, not dead, sir. Gone. She's empty of all crew. Not one soul, living or dead. A ghost ship.'

'Cut loose? An accident?'

The second mate rubbed his arms as if chilled, his gaze lingering on the silent vessel. 'No sir. 'Tis as if the crew up and walked off during a voyage. Ropes lay half coiled. Meals still on the table. Still fresh.'

'Fresh? How could that be? Any ship's rutter?'

Gaff shook his head. 'Didn't look, sir.'

'Didn't look? Gods and demons, man! Get back on board and find the pilot's rutter.'

Gaff jerked a negative. 'Nay, sir. The vessel's cursed. We must push off.'

Burl had been about to send the men back aboard to gather supplies and any potable water, but he noted the fierce nods that the second mate's words collected. He saw the signs raised against evil and a kind of atavistic fear in the gazes of all. And as a sailor himself he knew how deep-rooted such superstitions could lie. He also knew he led by support of these men and so he merely gestured his contempt, muttering, 'Very well. If you must.'

Gaff's nod of acknowledgement was firm. He turned to the board-ing party. 'You brought nothing, yes? Good. Can't risk the curse.' Then he shouted to the rest of the crew: 'Now cast off! Back oars!'

'And just what curse is this, Gaff?' Burl enquired, as the foreign vessel slid phantom-like into the fogs.

44

'Sea of Dread, sir. Drives men insane, they say.'

Burl had heard such stories and songs. Tales of ships mysteriously abandoned. Floating hulks empty of all crew. He'd only half believed them before now. Why would a crew abandon a perfectly seaworthy vessel? It must have come from some nearby port. Slipped free of its mooring lines, surely. The crew wouldn't just up and jump into the water!

Burl now became aware of his men murmuring among themselves. Even as they pulled strongly on the oars they spoke to one another under their breath. He heard much re-telling and re-sorting of all the hoary old tales of such ghost ships and curses. And repeated among the men he heard the name whispered like a curse itself: *Dread Sea. Sea of Dread. The Dreadful Sea.*

And now like the thick choking fog itself he felt that selfsame dread coiling about the entire ship. And he thought, perhaps it was too late. Perhaps all it took was some chance encounter with strangeness to taint the mind and the imagination – and this was the curse itself.

*   *   *

Orman Bregin's son considered himself lucky to be alive. He'd grown up outside Curl beneath the cold shadow of the Iceblood Holdings. Hardscrabble farming on rocky land was the sum of what he knew. He and all his relatives and neighbours, all the Curl townsfolk. Lowlanders, he knew he and his neighbours were called among the tall Greathalls of the high slopes, as they in turn scornfully named the coastal kingdoms. Those high forests and mountain valleys leading up to the Salt range were forbidden; the Iceblood clans guarded their holdings jealously and warred constantly among themselves over their boundaries. All trespassers, lowlanders such as he, were simply killed out of hand.

Of course, for generations he and his had been at war as well, trying to oust the damned Icebloods and wipe them from the face of the land.

And he and his were winning. Leastways, that was what he heard from the benches of the White Hart. The townships were all steadily growing, and their local baron, P'tar Longarm, Baron Longarm, sat strong in his long hall.

At least, that was so before the last raid. Orman had almost joined that one. Most of his friends had. Longarm himself had led it. Nearly fifty armed men and women had set out to track down the Icebloods and burn their Greathalls to the ground.

Only twelve returned. Longarm was among them, though sorely wounded. None of Orman's friends returned. There was much muted talk then round the White Hart of Iceblood magic. How they moved like ghosts through the woods and fought like cowards, attacking out of the night only to flee and disappear like will-o'-the-wisps.

The baron kept to his hall now and people named him Shortarm. Orman figured there'd be a new ruler soon enough. So it always was. Once the local king, or queen, or baron, weakened and could no longer hold what he had taken, others arose to take it from him.

Maybe King Ronal the Bastard out of Mantle town. Orman had heard Ronal crossed Hangman creek and cut a new settlement out of the tall pines of the Bain Holding. He also heard that Ronal kept the head of the Iceblood Shia Bain pickled in a jar at his table.

Once more, Orman congratulated himself on still being alive. Then over these last few seasons word had come spreading from town to town of rich gold strikes high up the river valleys of the Salt range – far into the Iceblood Holdings.

At first everyone he knew had been dismissive of it all. The lake to the south was called the Gold Sea and no doubt that was the cause of all the stir. The oldsters claimed it had happened before: some idiotic foreigner caught sight of that name on an old dusty map somewhere and before you knew it damned fools arrived thinking they just had to reach out to gather up great handfuls of the stuff.

But then came tales of foreigners arriving in the south. Just a trickle at first. A few tow-headed ignoramuses easily done away with. Then bands of them. Some even pushing upland, ignoring all the warnings. A few of them reappeared only as heads tossed across streams or left on stakes next to forest trails.

Now word was of shiploads arriving in the lowlander kingdoms. Two new towns had sprung up overnight along the shores of the Sea of Gold. He heard rumours of real warfare where the Bone Peninsula had been closed to these invaders.

Then late one night Gerrun Shortshanks came and sat down next to him among the benches of the Hart and started talking of this news of gold. Orman let him blather on for a time – too fond of his ale was Gerrun Shortshanks, with his gold earrings and felt shirts bought from traders up from the coastal kingdoms. So dismissive of the man was he that it took a while for the full significance of what he was whispering to sink in. He and the Reddin brothers heading out with Old Bear. And would he throw his lot in with them?

Any other night he would have brushed the fool's talk aside. But the name of Old Bear gave him pause. One of the last of the high valley hunters. Seemed to come and go as he pleased from Blood Holdings. Rumours were that he'd served as a hired spear for the Heel clan years ago – back when he had both eyes. And the Reddin brothers, Keth and Kasson. They'd been among the eleven who'd returned with Longarm. Serious and quiet both of them. So quiet few knew which brother was which.

'Why me?' was Orman's short answer, his forearms on the table, one to either side of his leather tankard.

Gerrun jerked his head, agreeing with the question. He took a quick sip, wiped his mouth. 'Old Bear says he knew your father. That's why. Says he even met you.'

Orman nodded. It was years ago. His father had been a sworn man to Longarm's predecessor, Eusta. Eusta the Ill, she'd been known, as she'd always been sick with this or that. His father had been a borderman, had even slipped into the Blood Holdings now and then – and had taken Orman along a few times.

And had told him about the ghosts. The Iceblood Holdings were haunted, his father had explained the first night as they pressed close to their small fire. Haunted, he said, by the spirits of all the dead ancestors of the various clans: the Heel, the Bain, the Sayer, and all the others. And sometimes, his father whispered, leaning close, his great spear Boarstooth across his lap, if you listened very carefully you could hear them too.

And later he did hear them – or thought he did. Voices calling. It seemed as if the very land itself, the Iceblood Holding, was speaking to him. Now, thinking back some five years, he wondered whether he'd imagined it all. That perhaps he'd only heard things because his father had suggested it.

A joke played on an impressionable boy.

He did remember meeting Old Bear on one of those trips. The fellow had his name from the great brown shaggy hide he wore wrapped about himself, its head thrown up over his own like a hood. The rotting pelt had stunk even then – imagine how it must reek now. Unless the old fool had gotten himself a new one.

He thought he understood Bear's real message now. He knew that his father had shown him around the lower vales of the Holdings. And he'd delivered the message all without leaving his mouthpiece, Gerrun, any the wiser.

He bought himself more time to think by taking a long slow pull at his tankard. He peered about the dark timbered hall of the White

47

Hart. It was late; the fire was low in the stone hearth. Only the regulars remained: those few who paid for the privilege of passing the night on the floor among the straw and scavenging dogs. None was paying him and Gerrun any particular attention, so far as he could tell.

So. The Old Bear was pulling together a party to make a strike for the gold fields. Why a party, though? The veteran mountain man could pick it up by himself, surely. Maybe he already had collected some few nuggets here and there over the years . . . He must've found a rich bed – one worth digging up.

Then it came to him: Old Bear was expecting competition. He was betting that soon, perhaps by the end of this coming season, what with spring arriving, these hillsides would be crawling with lowlander and outlander fortune-hunters, raiders and outright thieves. All fighting over the claims or the sifted nuggets and dust itself.

Best to get in early before the rush arrived, then. And he and the Reddin brothers and Old Bear had all walked the Iceblood Holdings before – no coincidence, that. All of them but for Shortshanks here. Or was that so? He studied the man covertly while eyeing the mostly empty benches of the White Hart. Never short of coin for ale was Gerrun Shortshanks, though he worked no plot of land nor laboured for others. And what of his gold earrings? The thick band of twisted gold at his wrist? Thinking of it now, how came he to such wealth? Perhaps this man Gerrun was no stranger to certain high streams in the vales where it was said a few days' panning could set a man up for years.

He cleared his throat into his fist and murmured, low, 'All right. Where's the meet?'

Gerrun smiled and took a deep drink. He wiped the foam from his moustache. 'Know you the camp up towards Antler Rock? Over Pine Bridge?'

'Yes.'

'Tomorrow, then.'

He nodded and finished off his ale. As he rose, Gerrun signed to Ost, the innkeep, for another.

It was a long chilly walk through the night back to his uncle's holding, where he and his mother lived now after being taken in on the death of his father. A light icy rain fell. The snow was hard beneath his boots, the slush frozen with the night's cold. Above, the Great Ice Bridge once more spanned the night sky, glittering and forbidding. It had been obscured of late, what with the passing of the Foreigner, or Trespasser, as some named it. People had sworn it foretold the end of the Icebloods. But no such blessing followed. As he walked the path of frozen mud he wondered whether in time it would come to be seen as a portent of this gold fever and the crushing of the Icebloods beneath the boots of a horde of outlanders ... if enough really did reach this far north. In that sense perhaps it truly was an omen – of whatever came to pass.

He pushed open the door to the draughty outbuilding his uncle had grudgingly given over to them and crossed to the chest against the rear wall. He cleared away the piled litter of day-to-day life: the wood shavings, the old bits of burlap, wool, jute and linen his mother sewed and darned to make clothes; a wooden bowl he'd carved, now clattering with buttons, hooks, awls and needles, all carved by him from bone and antler. He opened the chest and pulled out his father's leathers, rolled up and bound together with belts.

The strong scent of his father wafted over him then as animal fat and smoke together with pine sap and earth. The smell of the high forest.

'You are leaving,' came the voice of his mother behind him. He turned. She lay beneath piled blankets. Her long grey hair caught the moonlight that brightened their one window of stretched sheep-skin.

'Yes.'

'When?'

'Tomorrow.'

'I see. Where will you go?'

He squeezed the heavy leather shirt and trousers in his hands, cleared his throat. 'Down to the coastal kingdoms. Perhaps I'll join with Ronal the Bastard.'

After a long silence she said, 'Take Boarstooth.'

He straightened, surprised. Boarstooth was his father's spear. It hung now over the stone hearth of his uncle's hall. 'Jal has claimed it.'

'I did not agree to that. But I said nothing at the time. You were too young.' Her eyes, glittering in the faint light, shifted in the direction of the hall. 'Go now. They will all be abed.'

He rose, slipped an arm through a belt and adjusted the roll on his back. Inside, he knew, would be the tall moccasins that his father always wore bound with leather strips up to his knees. His mother rose as well. In her long white shift she glowed like a ghost and Orman felt a shiver of premonition of her death. She met him at the door, said, 'Go quietly.'

49

'Like Father,' he answered and she smiled, though it was tinged with sadness. A cold chill of wetness brushed his cheek as she kissed him. 'Goodbye.'

None of his uncle's household, his cousins or their hired men-at-arms, challenged him as he climbed the hill to the longhouse and entered. The hounds greeted him eagerly, nosing his hands for treats. He stroked them all and shushed them as he crossed to the wide stone fireplace with its mantel of chiselled river stones. Reaching up, he lifted the spear from its wooden rests. The thick ash haft and the broad leaf-shaped head, unique in being struck from some unfamiliar stone, felt lighter than the last time he'd held it: at his father's funeral pyre.

He was halfway across the hall when a woman's voice commanded: 'Orman! That is not yours to take.' He turned. Raina, Jal's wife, stood wrapped in a blanket at the door to their sleeping chamber.

'It comes to me from my father.'

'That is for Jal to decide.'

'I claim it as my father's bequest.'

Raina turned to the sleeping chamber. 'Jal! Rouse yourself, you great oaf! Your nephew is an ungrateful thief!'

He did not wait for the household to bestir itself. Raina's screeching shouts followed him down the hillside. 'Orman! We name you thief! None will harbour you! Outlaw! You will be hunted down like the dog you are!'

He broke into a run then, making for the woods. His breath plumed and Boarstooth felt as light as a willow branch in his hand. The blade of creamy brown stone seemed to sing as it sliced the cold night air.

Ahead rose forested hillside heaped above hillside up on to slope and ridge, climbing to the broad shoulders of the Salt Mountains. Their snowcapped heights glowed dark silver in the moonlight, home to the leagues upon leagues of the Iceblood Holdings. This wild country beckoned to him now – a near infinity of possibilities, it seemed, his for the taking. A promise made by his father years ago.

CHAPTER II

HER LIFE, SHE DECIDED, HAD BEEN NOTHING MORE THAN A STRING of failures. Wretched failures. One piled on to the other. And all after so many had sacrificed so much to bring her into her birthright; her mother, the Rhivi tribes, Malazan marines, citizens of Darujhistan – honourable and not so honourable – had striven heroically to help her become what she was fated to become: Silverfox, Summoner to the ancient undying self-accursed T'lan Imass.

Her mother had given up her own life to nourish her. The Rhivi had endured privation and the loss of many in their migrations; one of the most beloved Malazan officers had given his life championing her; and now, after she had been named the T'lan Imass Summoner come again, it was the Imass themselves who threatened to destroy her.

She had been born to unite the many T'lan Imass clans in one gathering dedicated to the dismissal of the Tellann ritual that bound them through life and death to their relentless pursuit of the Jaghut. A war that had dissolved into irrelevance countless millennia ago as that alien race faded away into isolated individuals who retained no interest in anyone's affairs. Even those of their own kind.

Yet not all the T'lan considered the war over. Here in Assail there remained one last vestige of that conflict. A soul-wrenching legacy that threatened even her sympathies for these ancient people.

Now she spent her days and nights keeping watch on the coast where the Warren, or Realm, of Tellann tended to draw those Imass guided by this lingering presence. Here they found her, and something else. Something none of them had ever anticipated, nor even imagined.

~

When she was at her very lowest Pran Chole would come to spend time with her – or perhaps to watch over her should she consider some sort of sudden drastic action to end her misery. She had yet to decide whether his silent company was a consolation or an aggravation. In the past, he'd once offered himself up as the defenceless target and recipient of her anger, her fury, and her outrage at the injustice of her fate. And she had beaten upon him the way a smith punishes his anvil. Yet she'd seen since how he had done it as a gift to her, out of love. That she should turn her fury upon him rather than herself.

Now she was not certain what her feelings were for the ancient Bonecaster – the closest thing to a father she could claim to have had. When she was at her lowest he could somehow sense it. He would come to her tent among the dunes, entering just as any living being would through the loose front flap, ducking his head bearing its broken-antlered headdress, to stand silent and watchful. Offering the last thing that remained to him to try to ease her mind: his company.

Sometimes, on nights like these, when the wind howled off the coast and the waves pummelled the beach as if meaning to wash it from existence utterly, she would sit cross-legged next to her small fire while her hide tent shuddered and jerked about her, and he would come to stand just inside the opening as if uncertain of his welcome. She was not uncomfortable in his presence; and indeed, his attention wasn't upon her at all. The dark empty pits of his sockets gazed steadily aside, towards the coast, ever sensing for newcomers.

Of course he need not have bothered with this awkward gesture of companionship. She of all people, Silverfox, was never alone. It was what she was. How she had been created. And she considered it her curse. Three entities resided within her. Pran Chole himself, among others, had pulled the three together to create what he hoped would become the first living T'lan Imass Bonecaster and Summoner in many millennia. And he had succeeded. Mighty beings, dead and dying, had been lashed to her soul as if by bloody sinew and dried roots: Tattersail, powerful Malazan cadre mage, indeed potent enough to be considered a High Mage; Bellurdan, a Thelomen giant in life and huge in soul in death; and most closed to her of all, Nightchill, a sorceress of the Malazan Empire. In life, for a time, they had served Kellanved, the first emperor. But in death they agreed to serve the child Silverfox – destined to release the T'lan Imass from their self-inflicted bondage.

And when she was at her very nadir, as on this night, she could not help but note her hands as she prodded the dying embers of the fire; their wasted bird-like lines, all sinew and bone, the skin blotched by age-spots. Not the hands of the youth she was – at least in years. By the number of seasons she had seen she should be an adolescent. Yet her purpose, what she was formed to do, had arrived early. And so was she quickened to meet it. The cost had been terrible, and not just to her. The need had consumed her mother first. It had taken the many potential decades of her life. And now it was overwhelming hers.

She flexed her hands to warm them then returned to stirring the embers with a stick of broken brittle driftwood. All this Pran Chole witnessed. The low fire cast a bronze glow across his dry withered face, though the empty sockets of his eyes remained hidden in darkness beneath his headdress of weathered, broken antlers. How many such scenes had this Imass seen? The fire's flush suited him, she decided.

Her thoughts turned then to another Imass, one who had shared many similar nights across the sea in Genabackis, and had become what Silverfox considered the closest thing to a friend among them: Lanas Tog of the Kerluhm T'lan Imass. The warrior who came bearing the message of war in Assail.

She sighed then, examining her limp useless hands, and Pran Chole, who knew her so well, broke his silence. His voice was the brushing of sand across the dunes: 'She did what she thought she had to do, child.'

That she should be so transparent irked her and she growled, 'She should not have lied.'

'She did not lie. You could say she told a half-truth. What she imagined would bring us to this land.'

'She must've known we would not join her.'

The ancient undying warrior offered the answer of his accumulated millennia of wisdom: he lifted his bony shoulders in a small shrug. 'She guessed some would.'

Silverfox felt a fury mounting at that betrayal. Within her, the mountain-shaking ire of Bellurdan bellowed anew at those who had defied her command, while an icy vow from Nightchill whispered: never forget nor forgive. Yet she and Tattersail still could not believe that there would be those who would put their ancient enmity first – even after the lessons of Genabackis and the benediction of the Redeemer who had granted the T'lan Imass the possibility of hope once more. This clinging to the past troubled her young soul the most. 'It is so utterly needless,' she murmured, watching the embers burn themselves out.

Pran Chole did not answer. After a moment she glanced up to see that she was alone.

Certainty chilled her spine then. Gods, no. Not again. I can't go. Can't bear to witness it all again. It tore her apart to see it. But she should; if her words could sway just one . . .

She threw open the loose hide flap and ran for the breakers crashing beyond the intervening high dunes.

She found Pran Chole standing knee high in the foaming surf, facing the empty ocean. 'Who comes!' she shouted over the wind and the surge of waves.

'I know not,' he answered, as phlegmatic as ever.

She scanned the water, dark and webbed beneath the chill stars and passing courses of clouds. Her hides, sodden to her thighs, pulled upon her, heavy and clinging. Then darker shapes came emerging from the trough and rise of the waves: ravaged skulls, broken caps of bone and cured leather; the jagged stone tips of spears; the humped shoulders of animal hides. T'lan Imass strode forward from the surf, some dozen or more.

'They are of the Kerluhm,' Pran Chole murmured tonelessly. He pushed into the waves.

Though she was dreading it, the news still made her clench her fists and press one to her breast. Gods, no! More of them. Will they not stop coming? Why not others?

Pran Chole raised a hand of bone and cured leathery skin. 'Greetings, Kerluhm,' he called. 'I am Pran Chole of the Kron. We honour you.'

'I am Othut K'ho,' one answered. 'We honour the Kron.' A ragged cape of sewn animal skins hung from this one's bare bone shoulders. He turned to Silverfox and lowered himself to one knee in the surf. The others of his band joined him. 'Summoner,' he murmured as softly as Pran. 'We honour you as well.'

She raised a hand for pause. Now, she knew, she had to command when her every instinct urged her to plead. 'My thanks, Othut. If you honour me I must ask you to agree to forestall any action until I have explained fully.'

His battered mien wrinkled up even more as his mostly fleshless brow crinkled. 'Explain?' he breathed. His empty sockets edged to the north and he murmured, 'We are newly reawakened to the world, true. We were caught crossing the Agadal and the ice took us. It seems we slept for ages. And while we slumbered, interned, that river of ice carried us far afield indeed. I awoke on the shore of an unknown sea and freed what companions I could find. Then we heard the Call . . .'

'Listen to me, Othut,' she interjected, speaking with all her power over the roar of the surf. 'If you honour me you must follow my command. And I command an end to the war, Othut. It is over. No more hostilities. We gather here and I will release you all. Is this understood, Othut? Are you listening?'

The Kerluhm's rotted head, its tannin-stained skull peeking from behind the mummified flesh, had edged aside to Pran, and it raised a bone-thin arm to point to the north. 'Is what I sense true?' it asked, and Silverfox heard the familiar stunned amazement in his words.

Pran answered in a slow firm nod. 'It is so. And we of the Kron name them beyond the boundary of the Ritual.'

Silverfox stood frozen, fists clenched at her sides, fairly quivering in dread. Now would come the answer, she knew. The T'lan did not dissemble. Nor hide their intent. It would happen now.

'We Kerluhm,' Othut answered, his voice even more raw and jagged, 'do not.'

'*No!*' she cried once more – as she always did – but to no effect. The waves boiled about her as Kron warriors surged through the surface and they and the Kerluhm locked blades that clashed and grated. Pran shifted to stand protectively before her, though never in all the battles played out here on these beaches did one Imass ever move to threaten her.

She fell to her knees, the water at her breast, her face in her hands. Failure! Utter wretched failure once more! The cold waves splashed over her. The surge of bodies fighting around her died away.

'It is over,' Pran Chole said unnecessarily. 'They have fled. My warriors pursue.'

She raised her face. Her tears felt hot on her chilled wet cheeks. 'Your numbers are diminishing, Pran. Some time soon too many will arrive and you will be overrun. What then?' she yelled. 'What then!'

'You will not be harmed.'

She lunged to her feet. Her wet hides slapped about her, almost pulling her over. She threw up a hand as if to strike his stone-hard face. 'I do not speak of myself!' She jabbed a finger to the north. 'I speak of them! *Them!* What will happen to all those thousands . . . so many. A crime beyond imagining, Pran! And you Imass the perpetrators. Mass murderers . . .' The enormity of it made her dizzy and she could not continue.

'Omtose Phellack remains active in the north. It protects them yet.'

'For how long!' she threw back at him. 'It is weakening. You know this! In the little time we've been here I have felt it weakening.'

To this Pran could only offer the wordless gesture of those who live long enough in the indifferent world: the subtle lift of the shoulders that says, *who is to know?*

*   *   *

Fisher Kel Tath found the Bone Peninsula much the same as when he'd left it so very long ago. Which is to say: insular, murderous, and savage. The pocket city-states still jostled and warred amongst themselves seeking supremacy. And each, in its turn, succeeded in grasping a taste of said supremacy only to be dragged down eventually by some new alliance of its neighbours, said alliance then flying apart in the inevitable betrayals and killings. And so it went. On and on. Endlessly repeating itself and none apparently learning a thing from it. Fisher was even more disheartened and disgusted than when he'd fled it all originally.

Yet he'd returned. Drawn not by the steep inlets and forested mountain slopes that so figured in his youth, but by hints from readings in the divinatory Dragons deck, by whispered rumours, and by plain gut instincts that told him that things were about to change here in the lands of Assail, so very ancient and clinging to the old ways of family, clan and blood-feud.

He lingered in Holly, at the top of the mountainous peninsula. It was one of the more northerly of the coastal kingdoms. They were named kingdoms here along the coast, though in any other region they would rate as little more than baronies, or minor city-states. He lingered because when he arrived he found himself anticipated by a horde of foreigners all come ashore from the outland vessels now crowding the tiny fishing harbour of this modest fortress and town.

It seemed that for all his seeking out of subtle readers of the deck, paying of noted prophets, and even time spent insinuating himself into the good graces of a certain priestess of the Queen of Dreams for hints of future events, he had failed to discover the news that was clearly common knowledge: that streams bedded in gold had been discovered in northern Assail lands.

He did not know whether to consider it a personal failing, or a sad comment on the skills of said clairvoyants. In any case, he now had a seat in a tavern quite taken over by foreigners – and he was thought by everyone to be among them – while strategy was being hammered out around the captain's table.

It was a raucous affair of banged fists, yelled insults, and daggers half drawn while their owners, hired swords, and plain men-at-arms watched one another suspiciously.

'We must all march together overland.' This was Marshal Teal of Lether, tall, pole-slim and sour-faced, who possessed the largest force: a pocket army of forty armed fortune-hunters, all probable ex-soldiers. He called himself 'Marshal', though Fisher couldn't recall such a rank associated with the Letherii military.

'Overland is too slow!' This from Enguf, called the Broad, a man who couldn't be more opposite to the pale-lipped Letherii commander: a squat, flame-haired south Genabackan pirate who'd landed with a crew of twenty armed, lean and hungry swordsmen. 'Those who continue on to the inland sea will take everything!'

'We have no time for such games,' cut in the third commander at the table, a Malazan aristocrat, Malle of Gris. She was an older woman, wiry, in thick layered finery of the sort that was fashionable in Unta two decades ago. Thick silver wristlets gleamed at her wrists like manacles, and kohl lined her eyes giving her something of the look of an owl. 'That you landed here betrays your intent clearly.'

'And that is?' Enguf answered, not the least intimidated by the woman's haughty manner.

She dismissed him with a wave of a skinny hand. 'We three must have seen maps or heard accounts that hint of the dangers all along the inland sea. The Sea of Dread, many style it. The Anguish Coast. Are we three not betting that few of these vessels will reach the inland Sea of Gold? Better to cut across the top of the peninsula, neh? Though the mountain passes of the Bone range no doubt hold their own dangers.'

'Quite so, Malle,' put in Marshal Teal. 'We will march for the top of the Demon Narrows. To a settlement named Destruction Bay.'

'Hardly encouraging, that,' muttered Enguf.

'Not to worry,' said Malle. Her lips thinned into a humourless predatory smile. 'I believe that to be a description of what awaits those foolish enough to attempt the narrows.'

'We are resolved then?' enquired Teal. He signed to his second, who drew a sheet of parchment from a pouch. 'We the undersigned,' he began, dictating, 'agree to equal shares of all profits accruing, after shared expenses, from our venture in gathering mineral resources from the Salt range.' When his aide had finished, he signed the document then slid it and the quill across to Malle, who also signed. She offered it to Enguf, who scowled at the sheet and the other two commanders.

'Must I?' he growled distastefully.

'Mercantile contracts must be signed and witnessed,' insisted Teal.

Enguf snatched up a candle and tilted it over the document. 'All this paper waving and scratching is nothing more than hollow mummery. What matters is a man or a woman's word.'

'Nevertheless . . .' Malle murmured.

Wax dripped to the page and Enguf pressed a ring into the cooling droplet. He pushed the sheet to Teal. 'Done. Meaningless charade though it is.'

'In a barbaric country perhaps,' allowed Teal. His second rolled up the document and slipped it away. 'But in Lether the rule of law is respected.'

Enguf stroked his thick russet beard. 'Oh yes. I forgot that being civilized means constructing laws that favour yourself while at the same time disadvantaging everyone else.'

Teal offered a bloodless smile. 'My friend, if in some manner you find yourself disadvantaged by the law then by definition you must be a criminal.'

'You take my point exactly.'

Malle threw up a hand for silence. 'We are outside our purview. I suggest we ready for the morrow.'

Teal nodded his assent. 'Of course. My thanks, Malle of Gris.'

'What?' Enguf objected, quite disbelieving. 'Not one drink to our partnership? Come now, we must drink. All mercantile agreements must be sealed by a toast.'

Teal's mouth tightened even more as his jaws clenched.

'If we must,' said Malle. 'Myself, I favour liqueurs. Wormwood, or dhenrabi blood, preferably.'

Enguf raised his brows, impressed. 'Well – I doubt we'll find such rare delicacies here. But we can only try.' He clapped his hands. 'Innkeep? Hello? Demons and gods, has the man fled?' He gestured to his crew and two men got to their feet and ambled to the rear, where, Fisher imagined, the man was probably cowering, overcome by this crowd of foreigners who had taken over his business.

Fisher noted a lad lingering about the back door. He was biting his lip and shifting his weight from foot to foot, obviously anxious. He crossed to him. 'Is something wrong, lad?'

The boy jumped, rather surprised. 'You don't talk funny.'

Fisher cursed his mistake, muttered, 'I've travelled a lot. So, what's troubling you?'

'Father sent me to give a message – but I don't know who to talk to.'

'Can you tell it to me? I'll pass it along.'

The boy brightened; clearly this was what he'd hoped to hear. He gestured to the north. 'We found another of you foreigners washed up on the shore. We brought him here but don't know what to do with him. The Countess's men won't take him.'

Iren, Countess of Holly. And north of here was a good part of the Wreckers' Coast. The gods alone knew how many of the ships making for this region had their bottoms ripped out along that length of treacherous rocks and shoals. To its inhabitants anyone not local was free game to rob and murder. It was, in point of fact, the only industry they had. 'Why bring him here?' Fisher asked, now wondering why the lad's father hadn't robbed this fellow and pushed him under as he had probably done to countless others before.

The boy now got an odd look in his eyes, wary, and touched with fear. 'He's a strange one, sir.'

A strange one? 'Well, let's take a look.'

The lad bobbed his head, grateful and relieved. He motioned to the rear. 'We'd best go this way.'

'The back? Why?'

The boy now squinted to the front. 'Ah . . . reasons, sir.'

One of Enguf's men appeared from the kitchens. 'Can't find the innkeep anywhere,' he bellowed.

Fisher eyed the sturdy hewn planks of the front door. Come to think of it, no one had come or gone for some time. He motioned the lad onward. 'After you.'

The boy took him out of the canted ill-fitting rear door, then immediately ducked behind a tall stack of firewood and crouched. Fisher joined him. 'Company?' he whispered.

'The Countess's men have closed the roads round the inn.'

'Didn't consider sharing that information?'

The lad studied him as if he was a fool. 'Not my errand.' He dashed for a rear outbuilding. Keeping low, Fisher followed. Entering a field of tall stubble the lad suddenly halted and Fisher saw that he faced one of the Countess's men-at-arms. This fellow wore a loose oversized leather jack covered in iron studs that winked as they caught the moonlight. He had a crossbow levelled upon them.

'Back inside,' he growled through a ragged beard.

Fisher motioned to the lad. 'He's not with us.'

'Doan' care. Back inside. We're arrestin' you lot.'

'What for?' Fisher asked, almost smiling at the conceit.

But the question didn't buy any time at all as the man spat to one side and smiled behind his beard. 'For bein' a damned foreigner.'

Fisher slowly raised his hands, and as he did so a coin appeared in each. Large ones that gleamed something other than silver in the moonlight. The man-at-arms' tongue emerged to wet his lips and he peered about. He took his hand from the crossbow's trigger bar and motioned for the coins to be tossed. Fisher threw them one after the other, then urged the lad onward with a hand pressed at his back. The man-at-arms ignored them as he held the coins up to the moon, squinting at them first through one eye then through the other.

The lad stumbled onward and kept slowing to peek back. 'Keep going,' Fisher whispered. Once the man was left behind, the lad scowled and hunched his shoulders.

'I didn't ask you to spend no coin,' he finally complained.

Fisher understood the lad was worried he would press the debt upon his family. 'Don't worry about it,' he answered, quite untroubled. 'The coins are from Lether and worthless. The gold plating their brass is thinner than Letherii generosity – which is non-existent.'

The lad frowned, still uncertain. 'Well . . .' he finally judged. 'All right.'

Fisher peered ahead into the night where the land fell to the coast. 'You're taking me to the harbour.'

'Aye. We have him in our boat.'

'I see.'

He was led, not to one of the fishing docks, but onward, past the built-up shore to where the waves surged among black rocks and the footing became sodden and treacherous. Here, almost invisible from shore, a tiny boat, a skiff, bobbed with the sullen gleaming waters. As they closed, a pale face rose over the worn and gouged gunwale. It was a lad even younger than the first one, fear quite plain in his wide eyes.

'Just the two of you?' Fisher grunted, surprised.

'Aye.'

He was amazed they'd brought the man all this way and didn't simply toss him overboard and call the errand finished. Something of his thoughts must have shown on his face for the lad bristled and thrust out his chin. 'We was told to bring him!' Then he shrugged, his outrage melting. 'Besides, Father said he doan't want his ghost hauntin' us in the night.'

His ghost? Intrigued, Fisher edged down the slippery rocks to where the younger brother kept a handhold. The moon and clear night's starlight revealed a tall form wrapped in burlap and rags in the skiff's bottom.

'He's a tall one,' Fisher observed.

'That's not all,' said the lad, and he nodded to his brother, who knelt down and pulled the covering from the figure's head.

Fisher almost plunged into the cold waves as the night revealed the black elongated features of a Tiste Andii.

How long Fisher squatted awkwardly on the rocks staring at that face he knew not. All he knew was that he lost the feeling in his feet and had to gingerly adjust his seating to work the blood back into them. Jesting gods! An Andii here on these shores! What could be this one's purpose for being here? Not the hunt for gold, that was certain.

Then he saw how mist wafted from the figure, and how hoar frost limned the burlap. He pointed, hardly able to speak.

'That?' said the older lad. 'That's nothing. Covered in ice he was when we dropped him in. And the water in the scupper froze solid beneath him.'

Fisher could hardly credit it. 'Ice, you say? And what of the ship – the wreck?'

The boys exchanged wondering glances and the elder stroked his chin in a gesture out of place in one so young. 'Was none that night. Now as you say it. Maybe he fell overboard.'

Fisher did not think so. The lads, he noted, had been studying him for some time now, sullen and still fearful, though covering this with a brittle truculence. 'Well?' the older one demanded.

'Well what?'

'Will you take him from us?'

Fisher almost gaped. 'Oh – aye. That is, yes. Certainly.'

The lads let out long pent-up breaths and even shared quick smiles of success. Clearly they were in dread of the curse of this black-skinned demon out of foreign lands. Fisher motioned that he would take him from the skiff. Together, the lads awkwardly eased the bundled body up to Fisher, who set it over his shoulder. At that instant he almost tumbled all of them into the waves as from within the rag cowl at the Andii's head a great mass of billowing hair tumbled free to lash in the contrary winds: a long mane of straight black hair shot through by streaks of white.

Andii – with streaks of silver! Fisher almost staggered. Jesting gods indeed! Could this be . . . *him*? Surely not. It must be another. He was not alone in his silvering hair, was he?

The lads pushed him on his way, grateful now to be free of any death-curse from this eerie demon thrust upon them by the water and the night. Though Fisher was an unusually strong man he staggered beneath his burden back to town; this Andii was an unusually solid fellow. He selected a modest outbuilding, a small barn, and kicked open the door to lay his burden within. Then he went to find means to start a fire to warm him.

As he returned carrying a brazier he'd taken from the front of another house, the noise of fighting erupted into the night. Angry shouts and the reports of crossbows reached him together with the clash of iron and yells of pain. A large fire arose to brighten the darkness towards the middle of town. Smoke billowed black into the night sky, obscuring the stars. Blasts of magery sounded, punching the air and flashing like munitions. Fisher recognized the Warrens of Serc and Telas, and wondered which of the three parties had brought such powerful attendants.

He sat on a stool in the doorway while his charge warmed under blankets next to the brazier. Soon Letherii soldiery emerged from the night, retreating, casting fierce glances back, stopping and turning to fire their crossbows, then running on. Marshal Teal's men.

After them a troop of Enguf's raiders appeared. They came jogging up the street, axes and swords loose, hugging the buildings, keeping a watchful eye behind. Spotting Fisher, a small band broke off to run his way. A voice burst out, bellowing and dismissive: 'He's with us, damn you all! Halt here!'

The raiders jogged past. Many bore minor wounds. Fisher took out his pipe to examine it and Enguf, sweating and puffing, came running up. 'Bard,' he greeted Fisher. 'Wondered what happened to you. Thought maybe you ate a sword during the dust-up.'

'What happened at the meet?'

The pirate angrily sheathed his sword. 'Monumental stupidity is what happened. This Countess's damned fool men tried to arrest us!' The idea seemed to fill him with outrage. 'I'm a lettered privateer. Have certificates from Elingarth! All quite legal, I assure you.'

'I'm sure,' Fisher supplied. Enguf ran his fingers through his beard and squinted off into the night. 'And now you are fleeing.'

'Fleeing!' the man echoed, offended. He pulled at his beard, considering. 'Ach – they got the drop on us, didn't they? We didn't come to sack them.' He called to his crew members: 'Go on! Head out!'

'No looting?' a woman answered scornfully.

The big man offered Fisher an apologetic shrug and said, his voice low: 'We were leaving anyway . . .'

'The arrest . . . ?' Fisher prompted.

The man regained his indignation. 'Hood's dead hand, yes! That dried up Malazan crone – she came with two mages! They're damned pricey.'

Fisher pointed his pipe to where Enguf's crew now kicked down doors and were in the process of throwing burning brands and lanterns into shops and houses. 'And the fires?'

Enguf pulled at his beard again, even more offended. 'Well . . . they started it, didn't they? Set our ships on fire.'

'I see.'

The Genabackan waved a paw. 'It'll slow them down. Now, we should go.' He peered in past Fisher then leered, elbowing him. 'Caught a pretty gal already, have you?'

'No. A shipwreck survivor.'

Enguf grunted his disappointment. 'Blasted wreckers. Like to hang the lot of them.'

'It's an Andii.'

The pirate's bushy russet brows rose. 'Really? That's damned unusual. Still, good in a fight – when they fight.'

The flickering glow of flames leapt up over them and Enguf spun, cursing. He charged off, bellowing: 'Not yet! What about the Malazans! They're still— Oh, Mael's damned balls!'

Fisher put away his pipe and rose. Time to find some kind of transportation – one that hadn't yet been taken, that was. He wasn't surprised that these Lether soldiers and Genabackans had found the locals tougher to handle than they'd anticipated. Such was the story of Assail. And it would only get worse inland.

Later, Fisher followed Teal, Malle and Enguf along a trail that wound up into woods and the rising slopes of the coastal Bone range. His donkey drew a travois on which the still unconscious Andii lay securely bound. Behind, smoke and the lurid glow of flames pockmarked Holly. The Countess's men-at-arms now had greater worries than a small army of foreigners invading their town. Fisher was encouraged to see few soldiers and raiders carrying wounds. Clearly, these commanders knew not to fight when it wasn't necessary. They might have been routed out of Holly, but they didn't hang about plotting vengeance.

Ahead, the only mounted figure awaited him: Malle of Gris. She sat sidesaddle astride a donkey that could have been the sister of the one he'd found. A bodyguard of hardened old Malazan veterans in leather and mail surrounded her. They parted for him and he could well imagine every one of them once having carried a sergeant's armband.

'So this is our mystery Andii,' Malle said as she fell in behind the travois. 'Has he woken at all?'

'Not yet.'

'Ah. Well, on the morrow perhaps.'

'Yes. And you, m'lady? May I impose upon you to speak?'

The woman wore a dress that consisted of many layers of severe black. Her greying hair was high on the top of her head and tumbled down her back, rather like spun iron. He imagined she must have been very handsome years ago. Black sheepskin riding gloves completed her costume. She smiled, amused, and gave Fisher a wave as if to dismiss his question. 'Speak? Whatever of?'

'Your reasons for embarking upon this perilous quest.'

Her hand went to her mouth to cover a quiet laugh. '"Perilous quest"? Now I am certain you are a bard. There is nothing perilous about this. Nor is this a quest. A mere business trip . . . the acquisition of operating capital, only. Nothing more. Rather boring, really.'

'Capital for what operation – if I may ask?'

Again a courtly wave. 'Nothing worth telling, I assure you. However, since you ask.' She adjusted the sleeves over her slim wiry arms. As hard as pulled iron this one, Fisher reflected. The sort of widow who could outlive any number of men. 'I come from an ancient and proud family,' she began as they started up a rise of rock and packed mud that would take them up into the first of the coastal slopes. 'However, our fortunes have not prospered under the Empire. What we require are funds for a new beginning. I do not know if you understand politics, bard, but it all comes down to money. Coin to purchase loyalty, to influence votes, to put seats on councils and bodies into local senates. That is why I am here. I would see my family name returned to the prestige and power it once held.'

As the trail steepened and the forest pressed in on both sides, Fisher took a moment to check on the balance of the travois and its passenger. Malle rode behind with ease, sidesaddle on the donkey, her short black boots peeping out from beneath the layered edges of her skirts. 'And what name is that, good lady?' he asked.

Her plucked brows rose in shock and surprise. 'You do not know?' Then she tilted her head, considering. 'No – how could you? Singer, I am not Malle *of* Gris. I *am* Gris.'

Fisher bowed his head. 'Ah. An honour.'

Again, a modest wave set aside such considerations. 'Gris lost its self-rule long ago.' She sighed, crossing her gloved hands on the slack leather leads of the donkey. 'Now we are merely citizens of the Empire – free to strive to improve our station.'

'Of course.'

The old woman's sharp gaze now studied him. 'And what of you? Why be here?'

He shrugged at what should be the obviousness of it. 'I would witness how all this unfolds.' He offered his half-roguish smile. 'And I will be paid in gold.'

Malle did not appear impressed. Her steady gaze did not lighten. When it shifted away to examine the front of the column, he felt quite relieved: he'd faced a great number of cunning and powerful men and women but this one struck him as particularly shrewd. He wondered now at her reasons for being here; there was gold to be had, yes, and coin could be leveraged into status and influence. Yet this was also Assail, and many stories told of what else lurked in these mist-shrouded mountain forests. Stories that he knew contained a terrifying truth at their root: raw power itself.

And perhaps this was what the representative of an ancient proud family pursued in order to regain the status of ruler.

Malle now inclined her head to him in farewell and urged her donkey onward. Her guard of some ten men and women moved on with her. There came abreast of him a man in old patched clothes much travel-stained, limping and walking with the aid of a staff. His face was a patchwork of scars, the nose a mere knob of tissue and his lips twisted. Fisher realized he knew him: Holden of Cawn, mage of Serc, and a man he knew to also be an imperial Claw – a spy and operative for the throne.

Holden grinned his mutual recognition. 'Fisher. Come for the show, hey? Count on you to be where the action is.'

Fisher shot his glance forward to Malle's back. 'Count on the Empire to keep an eye on its prominent citizens.'

'Bah.' The man spat, then grimaced as he struggled to keep up with the column. 'Retired now. Forcefully. "Served honourably", they said. "More than earned your time of ease".' He thrust a finger to his ruined face. 'Too shop-worn and mangled to be of any more use, I say.'

Fisher smiled indulgently. 'Yet here you are.'

'Job's a job. An' this one might provide damnably well, hey?' Fisher said nothing more. The man wasn't about to admit to anything – if there was anything to admit. Holden gestured to the travois. 'What's this one's story?'

'Don't know yet.' Just on the off chance, he motioned the mage over. 'Recognize him?'

Holden limped closer to bend down. 'No. Got some silver in his hair. Not too many of 'em have that, I believe. Though – what do we really know 'bout the Andii anyways, hey?'

True enough. Their society and ways were alien to humans. And he, Fisher, knew all about alienness. He steadied the travois as it jerked and clattered over the stones. 'We'd better stop soon – unless our self-appointed leader plans to march us into the ground?'

'Naw. Just a half-hike to put some room 'tween us and Holly. We'll set up camp soon enough, I imagine.' He rubbed his leg, wincing. 'Better be, anyways. M'pin's killing me an' us hardly started.'

The travois almost tipped as one branch climbed a large rock. Fisher saw that he'd have to spend much more attention on it. He nodded his farewell to Holden. 'I hope to sit down for a long talk.'

The mage nodded. 'Till then.'

Walking alongside the travois, Fisher studied his unconscious charge while the Andii rocked and jerked in the bindings that held him wrapped in place. And what of you, friend? What if you never regain consciousness? He'd heard of such cases – men and women half drowned who never awoke. Theirs was a slow death of starvation. How many days should he wait before granting the mercy of a hand pressed over the nose and mouth?

Do not make me wait so long that I grow tired of all my poetic speculation, friend.

*   *   *

In the end it was all so very much easier than Shimmer had imagined. She simply gave commands and they were carried out. At first she was loath to give any orders at all; her tone and wording were far from commanding. She almost winced as she spoke, as if expecting at any moment to be challenged, or defied.

Yet none of these imaginings arose. Guardsmen and women saluted and things got done. No one asked where K'azz was, or why he was not here to voice the commands himself. Still, whenever a

Guard answered 'Yes, Commander', she could not help but almost glance behind, as if expecting to find him there.

Blues crossed the Sea of Chimes to the other main Guard fortress, Recluse, to ready his command for transport. Shimmer organized things here in Haven. Of the Guard, she had her usual command, the Second Company. However, she remained sensitive to the First Company, Skinner's old unit, once disavowed by K'azz but now returned to the Guard. To show she bore no grudges she selected Black the Lesser to accompany her. And so was he reunited with his brother, Black the Elder. And Bars, of course, of Cal-Brinn's command, would guide them. Jacinth, once Skinner's lieutenant, was now in command of the First and would remain behind to work with Tarkhan.

Of the remaining Guard mages, she would take Petal and Gwynn. Blues himself was of course a skilled mage of D'riss, the Warren of stone and earth. And there was always Cowl, once High Mage of the Guard, though she knew she could not count upon the man. Mara, Lor-sinn, Red, Shell and Sour would remain, leaving her confident that Stratem would be well defended. She also understood that Blues planned to leave Recluse under Fingers' command. The decision left her uneasy; she'd always considered Fingers a touch unreliable. And his sojourn in Korel seemed to have only worsened his . . . eccentricities. But it was Blues' call and so she did not object.

She sent messenger after messenger into the vast interior of Stratem, searching for K'azz to inform him of the impending journey, and still no answer came. She sent another message via the fallen brothers and sisters of the Guard, the Brethren. Her unease mounted with each day that passed without word. How could they journey without him? Moreover, the best vessel to be had was hardly adequate: a fat merchantman more suited to hauling cargoes of lumber or pots of wine. Yet it was all that was available – she ordered it loaded and victualled.

The day before they were to depart K'azz had still not appeared. All the messengers had returned; none had found him. That night Shimmer laid out her replacement coat of mail on a table and oiled it thoroughly, as she did her whipsword, in preparation for the ocean crossing. Once they landed it would be back to simple rubbing with sand to remove any rust.

She worked well into the night, the wide front of the fortress smithy open to the cool night. The candles of tallow burned down around her, providing no more light than the dim fading coals of the forge. She was rolling up the coat in its covering of oiled leather when a voice spoke from the darkness: 'You should get some sleep.'

She spun. The name on her tongue faded away when she saw Petal come shuffling forward out of the night. His heavy lips were pursed and his gaze was directed down at his hands clasped across his wide girth.

'Not whom you were expecting,' he murmured, embarrassed.

She smiled despite her disappointment and anger at herself for her reaction. 'No – but always welcome, Petal. What brings you round?'

The big man sighed. 'It is my fate to always be the man women aren't expecting.'

She had heard that he and the fiery-tempered Mara, recently united, were now not getting along. She turned to her gear to hide her smile, and said, 'Women are allowed to be just as great fools as men.'

'You are too kind, Shimmer.'

Straightening her expression, she turned back to him. 'So – cannot sleep?'

'No. Sleep, and dreaming, is always problematic for us practitioners of Mockra.'

Mockra was the Warren of manipulating thoughts and the mind. 'I understand.'

'So – you may sleep. I will keep watch. And if . . . anything should happen I will send for you, of course.'

She tipped her head in acceptance. 'How can I refuse such a kind offer? My thanks, Petal.'

He leaned back against a post then jumped when the horseshoes and chains hung there jangled and rang. 'Certainly,' he managed, and smoothed the front of his dark robes.

Shimmer felt the urge to give the sweet fellow a peck on the cheek. 'Good night.'

'Ah, yes. Good night.'

The next morning she found her best shirts, gambeson, and long tabard laid out by her servants. This would be the last day of such pampering, as they would be leaving all the servants, grooms and maids behind in the fortress. She splashed her face, saw to her toilet, then dressed. Gwynn, who had somehow fallen into the role of her unofficial second-in-command, awaited her in the Greathall.

The dour white-haired mage had returned to his typical dress of hues of charcoal: a long coal-black shirt over midnight trousers. And his expression was in keeping with a priest of Hood, though he was not.

'How are we doing?' she asked, and took a bite from a scrap of yesterday's bread.

'We are behind, of course.'

Taking up a glass of watered wine, she invited him to follow her out. 'Oh? What is it now?'

'The water casks. We are still short. More were promised by the cooper but they haven't arrived.'

'We'll just have to make do.'

'We are too low on salted meat as well.'

'Why am I not surprised?'

'And dyed red cloth.'

'Red cloth?'

'For the tabards,' he explained.

'Well, some will have to go without.'

They descended the stone and dirt way that led from the fortress to Haven Town. Shimmer nodded to tradesmen, labourers and farmers as they passed. Guardsmen and women saluted her. She cast a glance sidelong to the elder mage. Did the man enjoy being the bearer of ill tidings? Did he relish failure and gloom? Or was he perhaps merely excruciatingly careful? In all the time spent with him in Jacuruku and since, she had yet to decide.

'We'll take whatever we can get,' she told him.

'Which, I must point out again, is not enough.'

'Are there enough casks and nails in all of Haven Town?'

The mage contented himself with rubbing his jowls and grumbling into his hand. Shimmer smiled tightly; that should hold him for a time.

She found a crowd of the Avowed of the Crimson Guard awaiting her at the waterfront. The sight sent a flush of gratitude and affection through her. At first she'd feared she'd been too selfish in her choice of those who would accompany the expedition: personnel from her old command predominated. No doubt, however, the other Avowed understood her preference for the men and women she had commanded for decades and knew so well. And here they all were, assembled to see them off.

She embraced many as she passed and saluted old soldiers of the Second Investiture like Ambrose and Trench. She shook hands with a glum Tarkhan, formally handing over command of Fortress Haven.

'Good hunting,' he told her. 'Come back with Cal.'

'I shall.' Leaning close, she murmured, 'Any sign?'

He gave a minute jerk of his head. 'None.'

69

Damn the man! He ought to be here. This was inexcusable, and, if anything, it strengthened her faith in the difficult decision she had made. Negligence. Pure negligence.

She caught Gwynn's eye as she shook hands and answered salutes of farewell. 'We are all aboard?'

'Aye.'

'Very good.' She motioned him up the gangway of their hired merchantman, *Mael's Greetings*, then faced the crowded dock and gave one last long salute. 'Farewell, brothers and sisters. We will return with the Fourth – then we will all be reunited once again. And at full strength!'

A raucous cheer answered her. She raised her hand in salute once more, and climbed the gangway.

The ship's master met her on deck. 'Cast off, Master Ghelath.'

The pot-bellied Falari bowed. 'Aye, aye.' He stomped off, pointing and shouting. The crew, mostly Falari and Seven Cities outcasts, all sprang into motion. Bare feet slapped the decking.

Bars stood nearby, leaning against the side, and she reached out to grip his wrist. 'About time, yes, Bars?'

The big man returned the clasp. He was smiling, but his mouth remained grim and hard. 'Yes, Shimmer. About time.'

Others of her new command lingered at the side as well: Cole, Amatt, Lean, Sept, Keel, Reed, Turgal. She answered their greetings then climbed up to the raised stern deck to watch the receding forested shore. She wondered whether he'd just now arrived – moments too late. Would she see his tall lean form on the dock?

'We are headed east round the Cape of the Stone Army?' someone asked behind her and she turned to the pilot, an old man hunched over the arm of the side-mounted tiller.

The eastern cape of the Sea of Chimes took its name from the curious formations of octagonal stone pillars that crowded the coast and extended out to sea. The forest of towers marching up out of the waves resembled to some an immense army cursed into eternal petrification. 'Yes, eastward.'

'Then on. To Assail lands, hey?'

'Yes.'

A strange conspiratorial look came to the old man's lined and wind-darkened face. 'Havvin's the name,' he offered, and he gave her a knowing wink.

Shimmer was taken aback, but before she could frame an answer another voice spoke, its familiar tone grating like a jagged blade down her neck: 'How nice to be off on another mission.' She turned to face Cowl.

'I thought you were travelling with Blues.'

'Hardly. The man won't even speak to me.'

Shimmer leaned against the side, returned to studying the passing shore. She felt, rather than saw, him join her there. 'He's not coming,' he murmured, bringing his head close.

'So you claim.'

'He's hiding.'

She glanced at him, saw the ravaged, lined skin of his face, so pale and yet so hardened, resembling dried parchment; his hanging moustache, thin and tatty; the pearly scars glistening at his neck. His pale hazel eyes glared as if heated by the blazing fevers that seemed about to consume him. 'Hiding from what?'

'The truth.'

'And what truth is that?'

'That we are cursed and he is responsible.'

'Cursed? You mean the Vow.' She thought of the inhuman Rutana in Jacuruku and what that one had said regarding their Vow. 'Yes, I've heard that as well. Cursed in what way?'

The man smiled, or attempted to: he pulled his lips back from his tiny teeth and raised a hand to shake a finger in negation. But like his efforts at a leer, or a knowing grin, the gesture was ruined by his tattered gloves and blackened, broken fingernails. Nails, Shimmer knew, that had clawed their way out of a mound on the grounds of an Azath House. The thought shook her and confirmed her impression of the man: insane. Driven beyond common reason.

'I will not do his job for him,' he said. 'If he chooses to keep you in the dark then take your complaints to him.'

'Then that is between us.' She waved him off.

His inarticulate snarl told her that her dismissal infuriated him just as much as she hoped. Yet he did go, his walk stiff with outrage. She leaned once more against the side and returned to scanning the rocky forested shore as it passed. Show yourself, K'azz, she urged the coastline. Walk out and wave. You must come with us – how can we possibly leave without you? Yet we must go. Cal-Brinn has already waited far too long for rescue. And there are questions to be answered.

She watched through noon and on into the late afternoon while the shadows deepened and the sun disappeared behind her into the western horizon. Sept brought her a bowl of stew and a crust of bread, which she ate while still standing at the rail.

71

You stupid stubborn fool, she sent to the shore. You have to come. How could you not? But if you refuse – then *I* will discover what the Queen of Dreams promised awaited us in Assail. Yet . . . as the one who invoked the Vow, what if these things can only be revealed to you?

She sighed and scraped the wooden spoon round the bowl. Surely he must have considered that. Why allow them to depart on a useless errand? Then she castigated herself: rescuing Cal-Brinn and the Fourth would not be useless, girl! Finally, she pushed off from the side and went below to find an open bunk.

Damn the man for leaving it to her to decide!

Two days later they reached Fortress Recluse. They loaded more supplies and equipment, then Blues and his Blade of chosen Avowed boarded. They set sail that eve. Four days later they were nearing their rounding of the cape. Shimmer was asleep in a hammock when a call from the night watch woke her: 'Fire on the slate shore! Bonfire ashore!'

She lay half awake for a time, still groggy with sleep. Then a sudden suspicion, almost like a breath from one of the Brethren in her ear: *what if . . . ?*

She swung her legs from the hammock and ran for the companionway, barefoot, wearing only her thin cotton longshirt and trousers. She gained the deck to find it abandoned, empty but for the night watch. 'Why are we not investigating?' she demanded.

'It's only a fire,' the sailor said, and he eyed her up and down as the wind pressed the thin fabric to her form. She cursed the man inwardly and went to the pilot on duty: not Havvin now, but a younger apprentice. 'Turn for shore,' she told him.

The tall skinny fellow peered down his nose at her. 'Only the ship's master can order a change in course.'

'It just so happens I'm *his* master,' she snarled. 'Now turn for shore.'

But the young fellow only gripped the faded wood of the tiller arm all the tighter. 'No, ma'am. The slate shore is far too dangerous.'

Oh, for the love of all the dead gods! She drew a deep breath and called in her best battlefield bellow: 'Master Ghelath! You are required on deck!'

In a few minutes the man himself appeared, puffing, scratching his wide belly, his bare chest a dense thatch of russet hair. 'What is this?' he growled, bleary-eyed.

'She wants us to head for shore,' the pilot complained.

The Master squinted at the night-hidden coast as if to confirm that it was even there. Then he turned on her. 'Are you a fool? We'd be stove in. Those are the Cursed Soldiers. No ship can come within a league of them.'

'Nevertheless,' she answered through clenched teeth, 'I wish to investigate that fire.' She pointed over the stern, where the flickering orange and gold glow was already disappearing into the gloom.

Ghelath spat over the side, then waved a hairy hand to dismiss the entire matter. 'Ach! Well, it's gone now, isn't it? Too late.' He turned to go.

'Turn us round. Drop anchor. Do whatever is necessary.'

Ghelath just waved the hand over his shoulder as he descended the stairs. 'Too dangerous.'

Shimmer crossed her arms, called, 'Gwynn . . .'

The mage appeared amid-deck. He carried a tall staff of ebony wood. This he stamped to the planking and black flames burst to life, rippling all up and down the stave. The sailors on night watch scrambled away.

Master Ghelath slowly remounted the short set of stairs that led to the stern deck, while pulling at his long grizzled beard. He cleared his throat and addressed the apprentice pilot in a weak voice, 'See if you can't get us a little closer, Levin.'

The lad didn't move. He licked his lips. 'I can't – that is . . . I don't know these waters well enough . . .'

Hoarse laughter drew everyone's attention. The old master pilot, Havvin, all bones and pale skin, came edging past Gwynn. He pushed his apprentice aside, offered Shimmer a broad wink. 'Rouse the lads, boy. Prepare to bring us round.'

The apprentice rang the bell, clearly relieved that his master had taken over. In a flurry of stamping feet the rest of the crew came pouring up on to the deck. 'Man the lines!' Levin shouted.

Havvin pushed the tiller arm over. 'Have to lose headway, don't you think?' he directed his apprentice.

The lad nodded frantic assent, shouted: 'Reef the mains'l! Lower the fores'l!'

Ghelath watched silently, one fist closed on his ragged beard. After a moment he caught the old pilot's eye and pointed to the bow. Havvin nodded a brief acknowledgement.

Blues came up to the stern deck to stand next to Shimmer. He too was peering off over the side, to the glow of the distant bonfire.

'Eyes up front, don't you think, Levin?' Havvin murmured, adjusting the tiller arm slightly.

The lad swallowed, nodding. 'Aye. Four lookouts on the bows!'

Shimmer crossed to Gwynn. 'Black flames?' she murmured.

He shrugged. 'Thought it would be impressive.'

Ghelath shook his head. 'I still don't like it, Havvin. Lose all the canvas. Prepare the sweeps.'

Havvin nodded. 'Aye, aye.' He gestured to Levin.

The lad drew a great breath, shouted, 'Lower the yardarm! Unship the sweeps!'

The crew scrambled to obey. The heavy yardarm scraped down the mainmast. Long thin oars that had been stored along the hull, just above the decking, were set into holes beneath the top railing.

'Man the sweeps,' Blues called down to Bars, who gave his curt assent and gestured to the gathered Avowed. They brushed the sailors aside to take the oars.

'Dead stop,' Shimmer called.

The Avowed levered the oars straight down then swept them back, grunting and heaving. The vessel slowed so suddenly that Shimmer had to take a step for balance against the loss of motion. The Master's thick matted brows shot up in amazement and wonder. Havvin hooted his laughter.

All became quiet but for the splash of the waves, and, distantly, the roar of an unseen surf.

'Ahead slow,' the Master called, then cocked an eye to Shimmer, who motioned for him to take over.

Blues crossed to Havvin, who was pushing and heaving on the thick tiller arm. 'Need any help, old timer?'

'Nay. A gentle touch is all's needed. Like caressing a woman.'

Blues shot an amused glance to Shimmer, who suppressed a smile. 'We're in good hands then,' Blues supplied.

'Oh, I could tell stories,' Havvin answered, and he cackled his mad laughter once again.

'Point starboard!' a lookout called.

The lashing of the tiller arm creaked as Havvin edged it a touch over. The Master still held his beard in one fist, and now he reached out and clenched the stern deck railing in a grip so tight and white it looked to Shimmer as if not even the strongest impact could dislodge him.

Yells of surprise and horror suddenly went up as something immense and night-black loomed out of the murk. One of the soldiers this was, a pillar of rock all webbed in spray, seaweed and barnacles where it met the waves. Its top stood too tall to see and its girth was a third of their vessel's length.

Levin turned to cast an appalled look to his master, who merely smiled his mad grin, then shot Shimmer another wink. Calls sounded from the lookouts and she spun: the bonfire had come once more into view.

'Lower the launch!' Master Ghelath shouted.

'Get us closer,' Shimmer called.

'Close enough!' he answered, fierce. 'I'll not risk everyone for this.'

Shimmer had to acknowledge something of the soundness of that and so with her teeth clenched tight she sent a curt nod to Bars.

Bars grasped a sailor by the nape of his neck to set him on to his oar, then ran to where sailors were readying the long slender launch. He called out names to accompany him as he went.

Mael's Greetings slowly edged closer to the pillars emerging in ever denser numbers from the waves. The sight reminded Shimmer of descriptions of the dolmens of Tien, except that those had been carved and built by humans. This formation was so immense, and appeared to be rooted so far below the ocean, it could only be the work of the gods, or of nature itself.

Some of the pillars were quite blunt, hardly topping the surf, just above the larger breakers. It was on one of these short pillars that the bonfire blazed.

As *Mael's Greetings* drifted, a figure came into view standing before the licking flames of the fire. A tall thin human shape, motionless, waiting, and Shimmer felt a shiver of recognition run through her. He'd come. At the last possible place he'd found a way to meet them. K'azz. She was certain.

Rowed by six Avowed, including Bars, the launch surged through the waves and onward into the dark.

'Turn us away a touch, Master Havvin,' Ghelath murmured.

'You worry too much,' the old man grumbled, but he obeyed. The bowsprit began to edge to the north. They waited. The vessel rocked strongly in the rough seas. The surf roared loudly now, all the more terrifying as it was unseen but for the greenish phosphor glow where the waves crashed and foamed against the base of the cliffs.

'Put up some sail,' Master Ghelath ordered. 'We need headway or we'll swamp.'

'Very well,' Havvin answered, and raised his chin to Levin. The lad cupped his hands to his mouth.

'Raise the fores'l!'

The triangular foresail edged up and billowed, catching the wind, and the bows pulled over even further. Master Ghelath leaned forward over the stern deck rail. 'Row, damn you!'

75

The Avowed, who had paused to watch for the launch's return, started guiltily and heaved on the oars. Next to Shimmer, Blues chuckled. 'Can't let them forget that,' he murmured.

She squinted off over the stern. 'We're not making too much headway, are we?'

'They'll catch up,' he assured her. 'Or break their oars trying.'

After a time a long low shape detached itself from the dark blue gloom of the waves. Sailors hailed the launch and threw lines. Shimmer went to the side. A rope ladder was heaved over. Sitting amid the Avowed, dressed in old ragged travelling leathers, was K'azz. Catching her gaze, he offered a rueful half-smile, as if mocking himself, and saluted her.

She just shook her head.

When all were aboard, and the launch stored away atop the deck, Shimmer faced her commander. He looked travel-worn but hale – as hale as the man ever appeared now. His thin greying hair blew about his skull, the shape of which showed through. 'What were you thinking?' she accused him.

'You're going,' he said, and he peered about at the gathered Avowed.

'Yes,' she said. 'No matter what. We must.'

'No matter what,' he echoed, slowly nodding. 'Yes. Well. I wish you hadn't. But I should have known you'd call my bluff, Shimmer.' And he inclined his head, acknowledging his defeat, and turned to take Bars' hand before moving on to greet all.

Blues edged close to Shimmer and the two watched their commander speaking with each Avowed. 'He really didn't want us to go,' he murmured.

'Yes.'

'That makes me wonder, then,' he said, 'just what it is that awaits us.'

Shimmer had been thinking the same thing. What could be so terrifying, or dangerous? Then the name of the rocks where K'azz had been awaiting them came to her: the Cape of the Stone Army. Also known as the Cursed Soldiers.

She closed her eyes against the night and sent a prayer to Burn: dear ancient one, please let this not be an omen you send us. If these stone soldiers be cursed, then let that be the end of your anger. Send no doom upon us. In answer to your forbearance, I offer my dream. The wish I have held within my heart all these years. It I would sacrifice to you. A future for a future. This is my pledge.

So do I vow.

Kyle threw himself into the exhausting duties of day-to-day sailing. There was work enough aboard the *Lady's Luck* for everyone, though the Stormguard held themselves apart, viewing the labour as beneath them. He did not suffer from such delusions of self-importance. He avoided the ten ex-Chosen, which suited them as they had only contempt for all outlanders. Indeed, they kept themselves apart from everyone. They stood wrapped in their thick blue woollen robes, spears never far from their fists. The regular working crew of the Mare vessel were torn between admiration for them as Stormguard, and a growing resentment at their arrogant presumption of superiority.

For his part, Kyle suffered no such quandary. His answer to their scowls and slit-eyed hard stares was a quiet smile of amusement, as if they'd become a joke – something they no doubt suspected and thus dreaded to be the truth.

His companion for much of this time was Reuth, Tulan's nephew. In terms of seamanship, the lad was far behind even him. The Mare sailors were dismissive of the lad, seeing no worth in anyone so woefully ignorant. Kyle, however, remembered his own abrupt introduction to the sea: he'd grown up on the steppes, far inland, and had never even seen a ship until his fourteenth summer.

The lad tagged along with him during watches and while he crewed. He kept up a peppering of questions regarding the outside world. A week into the crossing, perhaps halfway, Kyle drew the task of inspecting the lines, their splices and ends, searching for breaks and any dangerous fraying. He sat near the bow in the half-shade of the high prow while he sorted through the coils and bundles. Reuth sat with him. This day the lad was uncharacteristically quiet and withdrawn.

Kyle glanced up from studying a line of woven linen. 'There is something troubling you?' The lad would not meet his gaze; instead, he stared off down the long gangway that ran the length of the *Lady's Luck*. 'One of the crew kicked you aside? Cussed you up and down?'

Reuth gave a shrug of his thin shoulders. 'No worse than usual. No, they're not so bad. Remember, Tulan's the ship's master.'

'Not one to coddle you too closely, though.'

Reuth laughed without humour. 'No. That's for certain.'

Kyle set the linen line aside and turned to another, which appeared to be woven of hair. He inspected it more closely and was surprised, and a touch unnerved, to see that it was not horse hair, as he had presumed, but human hair.

'Pay no attention to what these ragged sailors say, Reuth. Continue studying your maps. You could become a navigator, or a pilot. That's a rare skill. One these hands can't even imagine.' He didn't add that he himself was barely literate – it was only after joining the Guard that he'd learned to read and write, just.

'No. It's not them.'

Kyle pulled on the woven line – it was strong. Perhaps it was somehow special; that is, special beyond the sacrifice made by the women of Mare for the welfare of their husbands and sons. Perhaps it was employed in the ship's rituals surrounding the invocations of Ruse. 'Not them?' he asked absently.

'No. It's you.'

He raised his gaze to the lad to find him casting quick concerned glances his way. He lowered the line. 'Oh? Me? How so?'

The lad licked his lips then cleared his throat into a fist. 'You are an outlander. You served with the Malazans, yet you are not of them. You have the look and bearing of what we would call a barbarian, an inhabitant of the Wastes – your sun- and wind-darkened hue, your black hair and moustache.'

Kyle eased himself back, straightening slightly. 'Yes? So?'

Reuth hesitated, then pushed on: 'You carry that sword with you at all times. You never leave it aside in a bunk or a chest. You keep it hidden from sight, wrapped and covered . . .'

'Yes? So?'

'Well . . .' The lad peered warily about then lowered his voice. 'There are those on board who say you might be Whiteblade.'

Whiteblade. So there it was. No longer *the* Whiteblade, but just Whiteblade itself. A title, or epithet. How things change and transform in the retelling as each speaker slips in one or two embellishments to make tales their own – or to move them in the direction they think they ought to go.

'You're doing it again,' the lad said.

Kyle studied the lad. He appeared serious, worried even, hunched forward as he was, his eyes searching. 'Doing what?'

Reuth pointed to his neck. Kyle lowered his gaze and jerked, a touch ruefully. The lad was right – he'd gotten hold of the amber stone he kept round his neck and was rubbing it as he thought.

'What is it?'

'Just an old worn piece of amber. The gift of a friend long ago.'

'So – are you him? Whiteblade?'

He chose to give an unconcerned shrug. 'And what if I was?'

Reuth leaned even closer. His long unwashed hair fell forward and he brushed it back with an impatient gesture that was a habit of his. 'Then you must be careful. There are those here who would like to kill you, I think.'

'Thank you, Reuth. I'll have a care.'

The lad nodded earnestly. Edging forward even closer, he pressed his hands together and touched his fingers to his nose. 'Ah . . . so . . . is it true what I hear?'

Kyle simply shook his head, smiling slightly. He picked up the sailor's dirk he'd taken as his own, honed to a thin sickle-moon, and set to cutting a hemp line to trim it.

Reuth sighed his disappointment and sat back. 'Well, I had to try.'

'Thank you for the warning, Reuth. Now I think that the less time you are seen with me the better for you.'

At first the lad looked stricken – as if he'd been told to go away – but then the wider implications came to him and he nodded once more. 'Ah! I see. Well, don't you worry about me. Tulan's the Master, remember.'

Kyle waved him away with the short blade. 'Go on with you now.'

Winking, the lad clambered to his feet and ambled off.

Kyle worked on, unweaving the coarse hemp fibres for a splice. This he could manage with his hands alone and his gaze shifted sidelong down the length of the galley to the raised stern deck where Tulan stood wrapped in layered robes that hung to his ankles. Nearby lingered a knot of the ex-Stormguard in their blue cloaks. With them was Storval, who made no secret of his antagonism. He'd often seen them together and it occurred to him that the lad was right: he would have to keep a closer eye on them. Any deep water crossing is a risky undertaking at the best of times. Tulan might be the Master, but ships are dangerous places. A man can fall overboard any time. Even by accident.

CHAPTER III

ORMAN CROSSED PINE BRIDGE IN THE NIGHT. THE TRUNKS OF ITS bed creaked beneath his feet. Frost glimmered over the pale wood as it reflected the stars above. Below, the cold waters of Fool's Creek rushed past beneath a clear skein of ice. It was still too early in the season to travel up-country – it would be months before the passes cleared – but he was no stranger to the snows. He'd hunted the valleys bordering the Holds through the winter. And with his father he'd wandered the high slopes for a full year.

He knew the territory surrounding the old hunting camp. It was on level ground next to a seasonal run-off stream. High forested ridges overlooked it on two sides. There was no true camp – it was merely a convenient marshalling ground from which to set out on longer journeys. He also knew it would be an obvious place for any pursuit to come hunting for him. This did not overly worry him. He frankly doubted they'd come. After all, he had nothing to lose now that he'd been declared outlaw. And he carried Boarstooth.

He set off at a jog-trot up the trail that climbed the first of the many ridges and mountain shoulders to come. The tall old growth of conifers blocked the stars, plunging him into deep shadow that was broken only by shafts of moonlight that came lancing down like spear-thrusts. Snow and ice were brittle and crusted beneath the battered leather moccasins that climbed to his knees. His breath plumed in the chill air.

Yet he jogged tirelessly. And Boarstooth was a joy to hold: its balance was exquisite, the heft of its slim leaf-shaped stone blade a promise of power. The wood of its haft was polished dark with oils, and the point of its balance was worn even darker by the grip of its countless owners. For it was old – older than memory. Everyone knew it was a relic from the lost past. It was famous here in the north, and so his uncle Jal had claimed it for his own.

If he continued through the night he should make the hunting camp near to dawn. If he continued. He thought of what he had left behind, and what he held, and he resolved to keep going. Nothing would stop him now. He was a free man in the wilderness, an outlaw among the lowlanders, and he would keep it that way.

The leagues passed swiftly, and he began to sweat. Short of a turn in the trail that wandered on towards the camp, he paused. Who was waiting ahead? Was anyone? After all, he had only the word of Gerrun Shortshanks, a man looked upon with suspicion by many, whom some named forsworn for his mysterious coming and going, and damned as a probable thief.

A man who knew what he, Orman, would no doubt take with him should he finally strike out into the wilds on his own.

He turned off the trail and headed up the nearest ridge slope. He slowed, circled round the densest brush, stepped over fallen logs covered in humps of snow, climbed bare rock outcroppings. He found a curve of the ridge that overlooked the stream and here he crouched, his back to a moss-covered rock, Boarstooth across his lap, to wait. He blew upon his hands for a time to warm them.

The sun's rise was delayed, for it had to climb over the eastern mountain ridge. Mists filled the valley, twining through the trees like banners of ghost armies. To the north, the rising heights of the Salts humped and reared in snow-covered shoulders and peaks, all bathed in the golden-pink of dawn.

Eventually, the mists burned off as the sun's slanting rays pierced down to the valley floor. The clearing was empty. No gear lay about. No fire sent up slim wafts of white smoke.

Orman's stomach churned with acid sourness – what a fool he was! To have made any decision purely on the word of a shiftless rascal like Gerrun. Served him right. Looked as though he'd be headed south to offer his spear to Ronal the Bastard after all.

The noise of snow brushing snapped him around and he crouched, Boarstooth levelled. A short distance away stood one of the Reddin brothers – even this close Orman wasn't sure which. He wore furs over a long leather brigandine that hung to his thighs. Furs wrapped his legs down to his moccasins, tied by leather swathings. His sword hung belted and sheathed, though one gloved hand rested on its long hand-and-a-half grip. The man's other hand was raised, signing that he meant no harm. Indeed, his pale hazel eyes even held a hint of humour.

Orman nodded to him. Then his shoulders slumped as he understood the reason behind the humour. He turned slowly. There stood the other brother, directly behind, arrow nocked, its bright iron point trained directly upon him. He straightened and brought up Boarstooth to set its butt to the snow. He crossed his arms over its haft and hugged it to him, his gaze still watchful.

This Reddin brother – damn, but he'd have to figure out which was which – relaxed his pull, then slipped the arrow into the bag at his side. Orman nodded a cautious greeting. The fellow gestured, inviting him to the campsite. Orman started down.

Here he found gear hidden under hides, all snug beneath a layer of freshly fallen snow. He turned to the brothers, who now stood side by side, watching him.

'They'll be after me,' he told them.

The brothers nodded their acceptance of this. Both were tall – taller even than Orman, who was among the largest of his friends – and both wore their straight brown hair long and loose. Both carried only a light dusting of moustache and beard, for they were still young, hardly any older than he. Their eyes held a strange sort of shy watchfulness mixed with wariness, as if they expected terrible things at any moment.

These two had survived Longarm's raid into the Holdings, Orman reminded himself. He thought he saw in their bruised gazes the possibility that they too had glimpsed the ghosts of the Icebloods beckoning from the shadows of the deep woods.

One glanced to the other and jogged off southward, obviously to keep watch. The remaining brother approached. His gloved hand still rested on the grip of his longsword. Orman knew these two fought back to back, sometimes two-handed, sometimes one-handed with a dirk or a shield in the off hand. The brother looked Boarstooth up and down then nodded as if to say: *impressive.*

'Old Bear?' Orman asked.

The brother shook a negative.

'When?'

'Soon,' the brother allowed, his voice almost womanishly soft.

'Could use a fire.'

The brother nodded, then headed off north. He crossed the ice-edged stream stepping from rock to rock. Turning, he gestured for Orman to follow.

The brother – which one, damn the man! – led him up the wooded ridge slope. 'Keth?' he called, trying a throw. The young man paused, straightening. He glanced over his shoulder, his mouth

82

drawn tight with suppressed humour, then turned away without offering any clue.

Ha! Very funny. Have your little joke. I'll find out eventually.

They came to a cave comprising leaning slabs of stone. The unmistakable musk of bear assaulted Orman, but for now the cave appeared unoccupied. The stamped-out remains of a fire lay before it. Here, the brother sat on a log and tucked his hands up into his armpits for warmth. Orman studied the fire pit. It was sunk and shielded by rocks so that its glow was hidden from below. He then glanced up at the dense branches of the spruce and fir woods. They should disperse the smoke quite well. He leaned Boarstooth up against a rock and set off to gather firewood.

When the sun reached overhead the other Reddin brother appeared. He tossed the body of a freshly killed rabbit to his brother, who pulled out his fighting dirk and set to skinning. Orman spent his time trying to decide which was which. It really didn't matter, of course – but in a fight it certainly would. The dressed rabbit went on to a stick over the fire.

While the rabbit cooked the brothers sat quietly peering down at the clearing below. Their furs differed, Orman saw: one wore sheepskin wrapped around his tall moccasins while the other wore layered leather swathings over cloth wraps.

'Is Gerrun joining us?' he ventured.

The brothers exchanged a wordless glance. Then one gave a small shrug and a purse of the lips that said *perhaps*.

He gave up trying to get a response from them then. After a meal of the rabbit, goat's cheese cut from a hard lump, and hardbread, the second brother headed off to keep watch. Orman put his back to a trunk, stretched out his legs, and allowed himself a nap.

He woke to a tap against his side. He opened his eyes a slit to see one of the brothers standing over him, bow in hand. This one inclined his head downslope and Orman instinctively understood his message: *company*.

It was late in the day. He rose and adjusted his leathers, returned his sword to his side, then picked up Boarstooth. The brother had jogged off, disappearing into the woods. A troop of men was filing on to the clearing. A hunting party – and he the quarry. It seemed he had underestimated his uncle's greed and temper. He slowly descended the ridge.

Presently one of the largest men of the party, one he recognized, raised his bearded face to the ridge, set his hands to his mouth, and bellowed: 'Orman Bregin's son!' It was Jal, his uncle. 'We know you are there! We tracked you! Come down, lad, and hand over that which you stole!'

Among the men, Orman now recognized two of his cousins. Of the rest, eight in all, seven were of his uncle's hearthguards. And to his surprise the last of the hunters was the short, richly dressed figure of Gerrun Shortshanks himself. The party spread out, hands going to their sheathed swords.

Orman descended the slope to step out from behind the trunk of a large pine. He called: 'I took only that which is mine by birthright!'

His uncle spotted him and waved him in closer. 'Come, lad. Don't be a fool! This has gone on long enough. Return it and I will let you journey south – no ill feelings. Why, I even offer a small purse to see you on to Mantle town.'

'I do not want your silver, Uncle. Just that which is mine by right.'

His uncle spread his hands in a gesture of exasperation. 'And what will you do there in the wilderness? Wander willy-nilly to no good purpose like your father? Come now, grow up.'

Orman slammed the butt of Boarstooth to the frozen ground. 'Bregin was sworn to Eusta! And I am my father's son.'

Jal shook his head. All the while, his hearthguards advanced on the woods, spreading out. A few now crossed the rushing stream, stepping from rock to rock. Their armour rustled and jangled in the cold air. 'Eusta is long gone, lad,' his uncle called. 'Your father should have bent his knee to Longarm. If he had, you could have risen in his service. But as it is . . .' and he shook his head as if at the waste of it.

A new voice bellowed then, as deep as a rumbling of rocks falling. 'Who would enter the Blood Holdings?' The challenge echoed from ridge to ridge and a crowd of rooks took flight from a slim ash bordering the clearing. They cawed and squawked as if answering the voice and swirled overhead in a dark cloud.

The hearthguards hunched, peering warily about. Weapons slid from sheaths.

Orman scanned the woods. As if by magery a hugely tall and broad figure emerged from the trees close by the stream. A shaggy bear's hide was bunched wide at the shoulders and hung in ragged lengths to brush the snowy ground. The great beast's head rode the man's like a hood, its upper jaw intact, yellowed teeth curving downward. Within that grisly headdress glared the grey-bearded, lined and one-eyed face of Old Bear.

Jal stared in amazement and wonder – he even retreated a number

84

of steps to strike his back against the trunk of a spruce. Then he nodded to himself and fury darkened his face. 'So. It is as everyone thought.' He called to Orman: 'Your father struck a pact with the Bloods. A traitor! He served them!'

Stung, Orman came sliding sideways down the rocky treed slope. He hopped fallen trunks and melt-slick rocks, holding Boarstooth high. 'Say what you will of me,' he shouted, 'but do not insult my father's name! You who cowered in the warmth of your hearthfire while he kept watch!'

'Conspired with the mountain demons, you mean,' Jal rumbled darkly. And he waved his contempt, his fingers thick with gold rings.

'Enough!' Orman yelled, furious, and he threw Boarstooth. The moment the weapon left his hand he felt a stab of regret. He did not know what he'd intended – to frighten the old man, to wound him – but the instant he loosed he knew the ancient heirloom would fly true.

Jal watched, perhaps in disbelief, as the spear flew high across the stream, then arced downward, tracing a path straight to him. It slammed home, pinning him to the tree where he remained standing, his mouth open, eyes staring wide at the haft where it emerged from his girth.

The hearthguards watched the flight and impact in stunned silence. Then they charged.

Arrows took the nearest two, one in the side, another through the head, giving Orman time to draw his sword. He parried the third – this one cousin Belard – then pommel-smashed him in the face, knocking him flying backwards in a spray of blood.

Old Bear was down from the woods in great bounds, roaring with battle-joy. With a swipe of his spear, he knocked aside the blade of a hearthguard then slashed him across the neck. The man fell gurgling and clutching at his throat. Orman's other cousin, Tomen, back-pedalled wildly, splashing through the stream then turning to run.

Two more hearthguards closed on Orman. A thrown hatchet from Gerrun took one, but the other dodged and ducked as he came. An arrow meant for him shattered on a rock. Orman met him, parrying and closing to grapple. Moments later the man jerked as a bloody arrowhead punched through the leathers of his chest, almost reaching Orman. The lad let him fall to the mud and snow, where he curled around the point like a pinned bird.

Raising his gaze, panting, Orman saw his cousins and the remaining hearthguards in full retreat from the clearing. He relaxed, or tried to: his limbs would not stop shaking. Suddenly he felt very cold indeed. He walked across the crackling sheet ice and blood-stained snow to where his uncle still stood, fixed to the spruce by Boarstooth.

Jal still lived. His bloodied hands still gripped the slick haft and thick crimson blood smeared his beard. His wide eyes followed Orman as he came. He tried to speak but coughed instead and groaned his agony. He spat out a mouthful of blood to croak: 'Kinslayer I name you. Forsworn. Damn you to the Dark Taker's deepest pit.'

Orman took hold of Boarstooth's slick haft. Jal slid a hand free to fumble at the silver-wound grip of his sword. Orman held his uncle's eyes. Hatred and wordless fury blazed back at him. He yanked on the spear, twisting and levering, until the eyes lost their focus and the man's head slumped forward. He pulled the weapon free. His uncle fell in a heap at the base of the tree.

Orman stared at the gleaming gore-smeared blade. Steam rose from it into the chill air. I am a kinslayer, he realized. So many stories of vendetta and feud surround this weapon. Is it cursed? Am I?

'Well met, Orman Bregin's son,' a deep voice growled behind him. He turned, wonderingly, still feeling as if he were in a dream, or a nightmare. There stood Old Bear, wrapped in his bunched bearskin cloak, leaning on his tall spear. His one good eye held calm evaluation, as if still taking his measure, while the other glared frosty-white like an orb of ice. Behind, the Reddin brothers now stood with Gerrun, all three silent and watchful.

'I did not mean to . . .' he began.

'I understand, lad,' Old Bear said, his voice gentle. 'But Boarstooth, once loosed, would have its blood-price.'

'Blood-price?'

Old Bear nodded solemnly. 'Aye. Jal insulted it. Had no right to lay his hand upon it.'

'And I do?'

'Oh, aye. When your father was hardly older than you are now he wrested it from the dead hand of Jorgan Bain. It was a storied duel. They fought in Green Rock Valley on the border of Bain and Lost holdings. There they duelled through two days. Stopped only to rest at night.'

Orman blinked, hardly understanding. 'But I heard none of this . . .'

Old Bear snorted his disdain. 'These southern lowland scum aren't worthy of such tales, hey?'

Feeling oddly cold and shivery, Orman nodded. 'I see . . . I think.' Then he bent over and vomited ferociously, hands on his knees, gagging.

Old Bear rumbled a laugh and slapped him on the back. 'There, there. The first one's always the hardest!' He chuckled again, greatly amused, then roared: 'You three! Pack up! Kasson, we leave at once!'

'Aye,' Kasson answered, and it irritated Orman no end that he didn't catch which brother had spoken.

*   *   *

Three days after Burl and the crew of the *Strike* came across a ghost ship adrift on the Dread Sea, men and women of the crew began disappearing. No one saw anything. Burl questioned everyone himself, as did the second mate, Gaff. Those on watch neither saw nor heard anything. Nor were there any discernible signs of violence; no blood, no marks of forcible abduction. Over the course of the day or night people simply went missing. Sometimes it even happened during their time on duty. Burl had no explanation for it; the crew members seemed to have merely up and jumped over the side to sink without a call or a struggle.

It happened sometimes. Over the course of his decades at sea Burl had known of a few cases when seamen had taken their own lives. Their disappearances had been similar to these: no struggle, no blood, no yelling. One time, when a young mate, Burl had been watching over the deck, glanced away, and looked back to find one less crewman at work. The man had simply thrown himself quietly over the side and allowed himself to sink to Mael's own boneyard below.

Over three decades it had happened two or three times. Now more than twice that in mere days. So he was not surprised when he found a contingent of crew members confronting him one foggy morning.

Gaff, the second mate, led the knot of men as First Mate Whellen was still abed, apparently unable to awaken from whatever it was that ailed him. Burl crossed his arms and waited for Gaff to say his piece. He was not too concerned; the crew had every right to be fearful. It had hold of him as well. Perhaps more so, as he wasn't sure they understood that they were far past turning back. He no longer had any clear idea of their direction, and hadn't had for some time.

The second mate finally clawed a hand down his wiry beard and cleared his throat. 'Me 'n' the crew,' he began, his voice hoarse, 'we say you can't deny it no longer, captain. These disappearances 'n' such. They're the work of the curse.'

Burl made a show of his annoyance. 'What curse, man? What? I know of no such thing. It's just this place. The fogs and cold – it has an unhealthy effect on some.'

The man hunched and ran his hands over the thighs of his frayed canvas trousers, but his mouth was set in a stubborn line. 'There're stories. Old songs. The Dread Sea . . .'

'Tall tales. Made-up fireside imaginings. Nothing more.' Burl raised his gaze to take in everyone. 'Have any of you ever actually *seen* anything?'

None of the assembled crew would meet his eyes. None but Gaff, who scowled anew. 'It's been weeks, captain. The sea isn't this large. We should've reached the north shore long ago. The curse has us, I tell you. Soon there'll be none of us left and the *Strike* will be like that ghost ship we come across. Act now before it's too late, captain.'

'Act? How so? What is it I'm to do?'

The second mate's gaze slid past Burl to the stern, to the door to the cabin where Whellen lay abed. The realization of what his second mate intended came to Burl and he felt real anger clench his throat – that, and disgust. So, we have finally come to this. Funny how all must band together to throw just one off the ship. 'That's enough of such talk, Gaff,' he growled, fury rasping in his voice. 'Are we superstitious fools to sink so low? You think you can pin such things on any one person – all in some craven effort to save your own hide? No. We're not of Korel, where I hear they practised such things against the Stormriders – not that it did them any good. No more such talk. We'll be through this soon. Things will look up. Think of the gold ahead – we may be the only ones to actually make it, hey?'

Many of the crew, those who had been with Burl the longest, now looked shamed by his words. Gaff saw this and clenched his lips against saying more, though his hardened expression made it clear he was only temporarily silenced. Burl waved the crew back to work and pulled open the door to the cabin.

Within, he went to where Whellen lay sleeping, or under some sort of spell. The man looked deathly pale and Burl pulled another blanket over him. What ails you, man? he wondered. If they only knew. If he only had a ship's mage; but such men or women were few in the Southern Confederacy. For now he would wait. Things had to change. And Gaff – he would hear from him again. Perhaps he'd made a mistake in not running the man through the moment he understood just how far he would go in his mania. Yet if Gaff dared not move against him because he could not count on the crew's support, then so too was he constrained. If he wanted to remain captain he couldn't go round running crew members through over a few heated words.

He sat down heavily. It was cold in the cabin, and the aura of frigid air seemed to be wafting from his stricken first mate. Burl set his elbows on his captain's table and held his head in his hands. By the thousand-faced god, you'd better not be some damned curse-carrier, Whellen. Because if you are . . . Ach!

He slumped back into his chair. Never mind. The one who carries any curse is always the last to know, yes? It wouldn't be a damned curse otherwise, would it? This last thought chilled him and he pulled his gaze from Whellen.

So it could just as easily be me, couldn't it?

*   *   *

Two days into the climb into the Bone range, Fisher's guest awoke. Officially within the party, Fisher was appended to Malle's Malazans. The expedition's overall leader, Marshal Teal of Lether, had been against taking him on, as, in his words, he 'saw no profit in hiring a mere wandering player'.

Fisher had then rather reluctantly revealed that he had travelled through this region before. After demonstrating local knowledge to the satisfaction of Malle's own expert on Assail, the mage Holden, the Gris noblewoman offered to take him on, she said, to play and sing tales for her edification.

Therefore, it was in a Malazan-style field tent that Fisher sat idly strumming his current instrument, a stringed idum, consisting of a long narrow arm on a round gourd-like body. It was a traditional instrument of the Seven Cities region.

He was strumming and plucking, exploring possible composition elements for his current travels, when a voice spoke from within the tent. 'You play well.'

He lowered the instrument's arm from where he'd held it close to his ear and turned on his stool next to the open flap. Outside, the fires of the expedition crackled and cast a flickering light within the tent. His guest still lay under his blankets on the travois, but now his eyes glittered as dark as if the night itself was watching.

'You are with us!' Fisher came to his side. 'I am Fisher. Fisher Kel Tath. And you are?'

'I . . .' The Andii frowned. 'I am . . .' He rubbed his brow and the frown rose into growing alarm. Fisher glanced away from the open panic that surfaced in the man's night-black eyes. 'I – cannot remember,' he confessed, almost awed. 'I cannot remember anything.'

Fisher pulled his stool next to the travois. 'It is all right. I understand you nearly drowned. No doubt your memories will return in time. Do you remember anything of the sea, or drowning?'

'No. That is . . .' The man rubbed his brow with both hands as if struggling to pull memories from his mind. 'Perhaps. I think I remember . . . fighting for breath.'

Fisher studied the man. Could he in truth be amnesiac? He'd heard that sometimes a near death by drowning could do that to a person. Of course, a sceptic would note how that was all too convenient. 'So. You do not remember your name. What of your past? Any images, or places?'

The Andii gave an angry shake of his head – angry only with his own failure. 'No. Nothing.'

'Yet you are of the opinion that I play well.'

The man offered a half-smile. 'Perhaps I should say that your playing was pleasing to my ear.'

'Ah. Well, I thank you. Now, what of a name? I cannot just say hey you.'

'No. That would certainly not do.' He sat up in the travois then rubbed his brow anew, as if dizzy. He looked to Fisher and the bard thought the man's glance uncharacteristically open and unguarded for an Andii. Or for any adult, for that matter. It was too much of the honest artlessness of youth. 'Can you give me one?'

Half wincing, Fisher lowered his gaze. Ye gods, what a responsibility! Naming an Andii was not something anyone should casually take on. Yet he knew many old Tiste Andii lays, and they were jammed full of names and ancestries. 'I . . . could,' he allowed.

'Very good.' And the man sat waiting as if Fisher was about to bestow it right away.

Fisher gave a rather nervous laugh. 'Let me consider the matter. Such things require . . . care.'

'Ah. I see.' And the man nodded his acceptance.

Fisher cleared his throat into the silence. 'In the meantime, let me see to kitting you out properly. We are headed into mountains.

Your thin cloth trousers and shirt, though they are of an expensive weave, will not do. And you need footgear of a sort – that will be a challenge. And some sort of weapon. Do you use a sword?'

With the mention of the word 'sword' the man's head snapped to him and for an instant the black eyes held an expression that was far from innocent openness. Then the mood cleared and the Andii smiled as if having discovered something. 'Yes. I remember . . . a sword. Something about a sword.'

Fisher slapped his thighs and rose. 'There you are. Progress already. Soon it will all come back. Now wait here – I'll see what I can pull together.'

He made the rounds of the three camps. Marshal Teal offered to sell him equipment at an insultingly inflated price. Enguf's raiders had no extra gear, and were in fact short of everything themselves. He returned to the Malazan camp and headed for Malle's tent.

Three guards sat on stools before the closed flap. A small fire burned low in front of them while behind a thin slit of lamplight cut through the tent opening. They were three of a kind: gnarled veterans in battered light armour, the heaviest item of which was a shirt of mail. Like three boulders, Fisher thought, that had rolled and bashed their way across countless fields and continents until every edge carried a bruise or a scar.

'Lookee here,' one commented, nudging his fellow. 'It's that foreign screecher. Where's that cat you keep stretched on a stick and torture every night?'

'Evening, lads,' Fisher said placidly. 'Here to see the mistress. And it's an idum. An instrument out of Seven Cities.'

'Oh, I know that,' the first said. 'Heard them played. Broke every one of them I saw after that.'

'You wasn't in Seven Cities,' the one on the right objected.

'Was so.'

'Yes, he was,' said the one in the middle. 'I remember it distinctly – he was advertised as the famous Malazan dancing boy.'

The one on the right now nodded his agreement. 'Oh, I remember now. His bum was everywhere.'

The first joined in the nodding. 'I distracted them and you stuck your knives in – or something like that.'

Fisher struggled to keep his face straight. 'Gentlemen . . . your mistress?'

'Now I know *she* wasn't in Seven Cities,' the middle one said.

The one on the right rubbed his jaw with a gnarled paw. 'She mighta bin.'

'Would you announce me?' Fisher asked.

'As what?' the first asked, looking him up and down. Fisher raised his eyes to the night sky. The guard nudged the one in the middle. 'Your turn.'

This one kicked the one on his right. 'Your turn.'

The last dropped his hand from his jaw and sighed his annoyance. 'I can't believe I have to be the one to go to all the trouble.' He lifted his head and shouted: 'Hey, Malle! It's that foreign bandolier here to see you!'

'That's balladeer, Riley dear,' Malle called from within. 'Now send him in.'

'What's the difference?' Riley asked out of the side of his mouth.

'He wouldn't fit so well across your chest,' the one in the middle answered.

'Oh, I dunno about that,' Riley answered, eyeing Fisher up and down. 'He just might.'

Fisher sketched a salute and edged between them.

Inside, a number of lamps cast a warm yellow glow. Tables and stools cluttered the front half of the tent. Hangings concealed a private rear sleeping chamber. With Malle were her two hired mages, one of whom he knew: the old and battered Holden of Cawn, mage of Serc. The other was new to him: a young plain lass, obviously the mage of Telas he'd sensed earlier. A low table between them lay cluttered with scraps of food, glasses, and rolled sheets of parchment he recognized as charts and maps.

Malle waved to a stool. 'Fisher Kel Tath,' she invited. 'Please be seated.'

'I thank you, m'lady.'

She waved a black-gloved hand to Holden. 'Holden of Cawn.'

'The songster and I know each other of old, ma'am,' Holden explained.

'Oh. How convenient.' She indicated the girl. 'This is Alca of Cat, new to my service.'

Fisher bowed to the girl, whose pale lipless mouth drew down as if anticipating some sort of insult from him. He merely inclined his head in greeting once more, and indicated the rolled parchments. 'You come well prepared.'

'These?' Malle snorted her scorn and tossed back a tiny glass of some thick blood-red liqueur. 'Mere traveller's tales. Might as well draw monsters on their borders.' She eyed him speculatively. 'You, however, have travelled through here before.'

'Along the coast only, ma'am. Never inland.'

'And why not?'

'Very dangerous.'

She eyed her mages. 'How very encouraging. Dangerous in what manner?'

He shrugged, extended his legs. 'I do not know exactly. All I can say is that those who attempt to cross the spine of the Bone range are never seen again. There are stories, of course. Many rumours.'

Malle refilled her tumbler from a tall thin crystal decanter. 'And have these stories a common theme?'

'A monster. A threat. A price to be paid.'

The woman held the tiny glass between the fingertips of both hands and studied him over the rim. Under her steady gaze he was thankful that he had told her the truth.

'Interesting . . .' she said at last.

Fisher frowned at that. 'How so?'

'Holden?'

The old mage cleared his throat and spat into a bronze pot next to his feet. 'The oldest accounts have a road that tracks the top of the Bone Peninsula. Know you of that?'

Now Fisher regarded Malle steadily. 'I have heard stories of such an ancient traveller's account. It is said that the imperial archive in Unta possesses it.'

Behind the glass a small tight-lipped smile came and went from the old woman's mouth. 'Archivists can get into debt as easily as anyone.' She waved to invite him to speak. 'What have you heard?'

Fisher wasn't certain that he believed the woman's explanation, but outwardly he gave the appearance of not particularly caring either way. 'I am a singer, a collector of songs and tales. And there are very old ones from this region that speak variously of the Bone Road, the Bridge of Bone, or the Way of Bone.'

'Colourful,' the old woman commented dryly. 'Any other hazards we should be mindful of?'

Fisher opened his arms. 'Well, there are always bandits, thieves, and mountain tribes.'

'I doubt that any ragged bandits would attack a party of some hundred armed men and women,' the girl sneered. 'Hard knocks for poor rewards.'

Fisher shifted his gaze to her. 'Some might fight to defend their territory.' The girl just snorted, looking sour.

'Anything else?' Malle enquired.

Fisher nodded. 'Then there are the supernatural dangers.'

Holden chuckled and winked. 'Ah yes. The legendary ghoulies, ghosties and giants of Assail.'

Fisher did not share the man's amusement. 'The ghosts are real, my friend. The further north you go the worse they get. That and the cold.'

Alca leaned forward. She slid her forearms along her thighs to her knees. 'These stories of cold and ice interest me. Since we landed I have sensed it. It is Elder. Omtose Phellack. This land was once held by the Jaghut – is that not so?'

Fisher studied the girl more closely; not so young as he had thought. And a scholar. Perhaps a researcher into the Warrens. He crossed one leg over the other and clasped his hands over his knee. 'Some say all lands were once held by the Jaghut. But yes. It is thought that their mark lingers.'

'And beyond the Jaghut there lies the threat of the namesake of this region,' said Malle.

Fisher simply blinked at her. 'Those are just stories, m'lady.'

'Indeed? Let us hope so.'

Her tone told Fisher that his audience was at an end. He bowed his head and rose.

'You had wished to speak of some matter?' she enquired.

Fisher's brows shot up – ah yes. He'd quite forgotten. 'Our guest is awake and I wish to request equipment for him. Warm sturdy clothes and a weapon.'

'And does our guest possess a name?'

Fisher shook his head. 'Unfortunately, he remembers nothing. The shock of nearly drowning, perhaps.'

The old woman's smile of sympathy was cold. 'Perhaps.' She gestured curtly to Holden. 'See to it.'

'Aye, ma'am.'

Bowing to all, Fisher ducked from the tent. As he crossed the camp it occurred to him that he'd entered to make a request only to find himself the object of an intense cross-examination regarding the peninsula and the lands beyond. Understandable, he supposed, given that they intended to penetrate within. Yet among the rolled charts and pressed fibre sheets he'd glimpsed a flat wooden box, closed and clasped. And he knew such boxes. They held draughting instruments: compasses, tools for measuring angles and scales. These people were not only consulting maps – they were assembling their own.

The party might in truth be after gold, but he considered it a good bet that these Malazans were after something else as well.

Once Jute Hernan, late of Delanss, was certain the *Silver Dawn* had passed beyond of the maze of rocks that choked the entrance to the aptly named Fear Narrows, he loosed the terror that squeezed his own chest like bound cordage and inhaled fully. He allowed his gaze to rise inland, up the calm channel of the long twisting narrows itself.

What he saw waiting ahead did not give him much cheer. Tall sheer cliffs on both sides offered little or no anchorage. And the *Dawn* was in desperate need of refit and repairs after threading through the Guardian Rocks; she was leaking at the seams, stores were water-spoiled, and she was desperately short of sweet water. Once more, he did his best to dredge up the tales of this region that he'd soaked up with his warm milk and bread when a boy. They told of how those vessels with enough luck, or piloted with enough skill, to navigate the Guardian Rocks could look forward to shelter within a protected port called Old Ruse, itself one of the many wonders of the region.

Scanning the rearing cliff walls, he saw no hint of any such tranquil or welcoming harbourage. Perhaps it was all sailors' fancies and flights of tale-telling round the alehouses. Yet so far the stories had proved accurate to some degree. Yes, the lands could be found more or less south of Genabackis; yes, the north-east coast was warded and ringed by hidden rocks and shoals; and, yes, an even worse hazard along this stretch of shore was its inhabitants, who, having no interest in trade or relations with the outside world, treated any vessels within their reach as sheep to be slaughtered. Thus supporting the mariners' universal wariness of the Wreckers' Coast. And if one did pass beyond all this, one came to a narrow inlet warded by series after series of jagged rocks. A formation any vessel would only dare attempt during the hours of highest tides. The Guardian Rocks.

Now, according to all the tales, what lay before his crew of the pick of all the mariners and pirates of Falar was Fear Narrows: a hostile inhospitable chute which allowed access to the broad calm Sea of Dread. Deceptively calm. Or so the stories always went.

Jute headed for the *Dawn*'s quarterdeck, nodding encouragement to the men and women of the crew as he went. Not that he felt it – it was simply his role as he saw it: reassuring these volunteers, each of them daring and intrepid enough to answer his call to join a voyage like none before. A voyage to the ends of the world in search of riches, though for most, including himself, such a voyage was a reward in itself.

He thought of what might lie in wait for them beyond the Sea of Dread: fortresses constructed from the bones of earlier travellers foolish enough to trespass there; strangling mists; limitless fields of ice taller than any city tower; forests guarded by giants of ice and rime. And beyond all these, mountains harbouring a race said to be willing to offer any gift a traveller daring and tenacious enough to reach them might think to request, yet no gift worth the harrowing price demanded by these legendary Assail.

Jute mentally cast all such unknowns overboard. One threat at a time! Right now his job was to see to finding safe anchorage for the *Dawn*, and such harbourage looked to be scarce indeed.

At the stern stood their master steersman, Lurjen, a short and broad stump of a fellow, gripping the side-mounted steering arm. His leathers were darkened with sweat and more ran in rivulets down his bald, sun-burnished pate. His massive arms still appeared to quiver from the exertion of heaving the ponderous oar to the directions of their navigator, who sat on a short stool behind him, leaning forward, chin almost resting on her walking stick. Ieleen of Walk, Jute's navigator and his wife. A legend she was among the mariners of Falar, and some whispered witch or sorceress of Ruse, for her seeming miraculous intimacy with wave and channel. All the more fantastic as she was completely blind.

'Sorceress you are, my dear!' Jute called. 'Your reputation is un-shakable now.' Sorceress indeed, dearest, he added silently. How else did you steal my heart away?

'I just listen to the waves, luv,' she answered, and she winked one staring wintery-white eye. 'Our friends are still with us,' she added, motioning to the rear with a tilt of her head.

Jute cast a glance behind where the last of the rocks now disappeared from sight. Indeed, some three or four vessels were still treading their wake. When they'd arrived out beyond the mouth of the narrows they'd found a great mass of foreign vessels at anchor awaiting the right tide. Or just waiting and watching to see who would be the next fools to dare attempt the jumbled currents and hidden tearing teeth of the Guardian Rocks.

For a time they too had waited and watched as well. They witnessed six vessels make the attempt; each went down in a mass of shattered timber. Jute thought he could almost hear the screams of the crews as they were sucked down into the curling, tumbling currents and dashed against the rocks. And after each attempt a wash of corpses and litter of rope and broken wood rode the waves out on to the equally aptly named Sea of Hate.

Then, one day just before dawn, Ieleen gave him the nod and he ordered all the crew to the oars – no sails for this narrow passage – and they'd set out, following her directions. Their navigation through the shoals down the Wreckers' Coast must have impressed the masters of other ships, for five other vessels quickly followed their route.

Of his part in that turning twisting run Jute was not proud. Ieleen barked her commands while Lurjen grunted and huffed, heaving the steering arm back and forth. The *Dawn* yawed and pitched so steeply that half the time one or the other side's oars waved uselessly to the sky. Yet his love seemed to have taken all this into her calculations as she sat staring sightlessly, her head tilted ever so slightly, as if listening to someone whispering in her ear. All he could do was hang on tight to the mainmast, shouting to keep order among the crew as oars struck rocks to throw men bodily from the benches, or knock them senseless. Timber groaned as hidden rocks scoured the sides and keel. Many times the crew were not so much rowing as using the oars as poles to fend off looming black pillars that jutted from the foaming waters like saw-teeth.

Then, of a sudden, like the passing of a thunderstorm, it was over. The waters streamed beneath the bow as smooth as glass. The crew slumped where they sat, breathless, utterly spent, though with enough energy to weakly laugh and cuff one another. And he'd planted a kiss on Ieleen's cheek and called her a wonder.

Now, glancing back, he saw only three of the five vessels that had set out following their lead. They also coursed along, oars idle for the nonce. Obviously just as relieved, or disbelieving, as they. 'Yes,' he told Ieleen. 'They're still with us. Two are of a strange cut to me, though one's a Malazan galley or I'm a Kartoolian eunuch.'

'You're no eunuch, luv. I'll attest to that.'

Pained, he lowered his voice. 'Not in front of the crew, dearest.'

She waved a hand. 'Oh, they're happy when we're happy. They just don't like it when we fight.'

Jute cleared his throat. 'Well. Where we go from here is a mystery to me.'

'Something's ahead,' she answered and lifted her chin. 'The wind sounds different.'

He grunted his acknowledgement. 'A touch of sail, Buen,' he called to his first mate.

'Aye, aye.'

'Dulat, get up top and get an eye out.'

The youngest and slightest of the crew jumped up from a bench and exclaimed, 'Thank the gods for that!'

'No use anyway,' Sarsen, a giant of a fellow out of Gano, grumbled. 'It was like having a flea on my elbow.'

'Someone has to show the ox where to go,' Dulat retorted.

Sarsen peered up at him, squinting. 'Better run up to your perch, little flea.'

Dulat set his feet on the mast and started up. 'Now I have to show *everyone* where to go!'

Jute grinned; the crew were in good spirits. And they should be, given what they'd just accomplished. He waited until Dulat had had a good look then called, 'Anything?'

'Might be a cove or a channel ahead on the starboard cliffs.'

'Very good.' He turned to Ieleen. 'Anything more?'

She sniffed the air. 'There's a settlement close.'

'Old Ruse, then.'

'Perhaps.'

He returned to Dulat. 'Direct us over!'

'Aye.'

'We're seeping, Buen. What's the rate?'

'Too fast for comfort. We have to make repairs.'

After a time Dulat shouted down: 'Our shadows are following.'

Jute mentally shrugged. Nothing they could do about it. Moreover, since this journey promised to be a long one, they'd no doubt be seeing a lot more of each other in any case. And there's strength in numbers, a more cautious voice whispered in his mind.

The crew rowed at a slow easy pace; in the slim cut of the narrows the sail did little to help. Jute kept his eyes trained on the gap in the cliff wall ahead. Steadily it became clear to any who cared to look that it held some sort of channel. When they came abreast of the opening, everyone saw at once that it opened on to a broad cove that was a natural harbour. Wharves, slips and docks lined its shore, while above rose the stone buildings of a town. Old Ruse, apparently.

'Make for port!' Jute bellowed, relieved. Thank hoary old Mael himself! He'd feared savages populated the entire land and they'd not be able to put in anywhere.

Lurjen grunted and grumbled anew as he swung the steering arm over. Ieleen sat still, hands atop her walking stick, humming a tuneless song to herself. As usual she was content to let him handle the mundane tasks. He knew she'd step in should she sense anything awry.

The channel was a narrow one. There was hardly room for the oars. Before entering the wide cove they passed tall towers to either side at the end of the channel – some sort of defensive installation against raiders or pirates, no doubt.

Within, the crew eased up on the oars to peer about in wonder. It was a town hacked from the very stone of the narrows' cliffs. Great clouds of sea-birds crowded the ridges of the surrounding cliffs. Their screeching and cawing drowned out all other sounds.

'Make for the nearest berth,' Jute told Lurjen. The *Dawn* curved across the smooth waters on its own for a time. Lurjen directed it to the north side of the broad arc of the harbour.

'Our friends are with us,' Dulat called down.

Jute glanced to the stern: so they were. Their entourage nosed into the cove one after the other. Closer now, Jute recognized the lines of the first vessel: Genabackan. No doubt some damned pirate out to make a quick fortune. The middle vessel, a tall three-tiered ship, remained a mystery. He'd frankly never seen anything like it on any sea, from Quon to Seven Cities. The Malazan galley brought up the rear. Quite dilapidated Jute thought it. A veteran, that one. Or just damned sloppy.

'Movement all about,' Dulat called, sounding bemused.

Jute turned to the wide arc of wharves and slips. Indeed, crews were swarming out on to the ships and boats, which, it now occurred to him, were a mishmash of various styles and origins. Oars slapped the water up and down the harbour.

Behind him Ieleen had stopped humming. 'Luv . . .' she began tentatively.

A small voice whispered in Jute's thoughts: oh, dammit to Mael.

'Swing us round!' he bellowed to Lurjen though the man stood right next to him. The squat fellow savagely heaved the thick wooden steering arm over. 'Port side back oars!'

The port side oarsmen raised their arms high to bite deep then pushed with all their might, gasping and grunting. The *Dawn* lurched into a tight circle. Glancing back, Jute saw their companions reach the same conclusion as all three vessels now struggled to bring themselves about. The Malazan galley was the quickest to respond, obviously crewed by old hands. The Genabackan vessel followed. The foreign ship, however, responded slowly and awkwardly; she was clearly a top-heavy ungainly design. How she could possibly have made it through the rocks was a mystery to him.

'Archers!' Dulat warned from atop the mainmast.

Jute cast a quick glance over the arc of ships approaching under oar. Arrows flew here and there, but not a steady volley. Not yet. Just testing the range. No, too distant yet. It appeared to his eye that these Old Ruse pirates had sprung their trap too soon. They might all make the channel before being intercepted and engaged. All except the tall three-tiered vessel that, now that she was circling near, had the look of a strange class of oared galleon about her.

'The entrance!' Dulat yelled, and real alarm choked his voice. 'The towers!'

Something was happening at the channel entrance. The water across the way was foaming and tumbling. Squinting, Jute made out chains rising from the course. They climbed each tower wall, crossing the narrow channel from side to side.

A gods-damned harbour chain. No wonder they jumped to the attack. We're trapped within. It occurred to Jute that in a way they were still on the Wreckers' Coast, after all. And, he supposed, this town must be its damned capital city. They'd avoided every hazard, side-stepped every pit so far, only to walk right into the mouth of the very last trap. He almost hung his head at the injustice of it.

'I know your moods, luv,' murmured Ieleen. 'Don't you despair.' She shifted her blind gaze to starboard. 'That foreign vessel near?'

'Yes,' he answered, his voice heavy. 'We're passing her.' Not that any of it mattered any more.

'Well. You call me a sorceress . . .' and she offered another wink.

Jute frowned his confusion. Sorceress? Even if she was, they were still trapped.

'The Genabackan trader's circling behind!' Dulat called.

Jute looked. The Genabackan vessel was now heading to brush past them as if meaning to intercept the entire fleet. As she stormed abreast, oars flashing, a man hailed them from her side. 'Wait by the channel!' Then they were gone.

That was strange enough, but what was really odd was that the man was armoured like a heavy infantryman. He wore a white tabard over a banded hauberk of iron with iron greaves and vambraces, was bearded with a great mane of black hair. In one hand he held a full helm, while the other rested on the tall grip of what must be a bastardsword.

But what was strangest of all was that the entire deck was jammed from one side to the other with soldiers all armoured alike. All wearing white tabards. And on the chest of each tabard a triangular shield shape of a pale sky blue.

'There must be over two hundred soldiers on that ship!' Dulat cried out, and he threw his hands in the air in amazement.

'We're not out yet,' Jute growled under his breath. Blue – that struck a chord in his memory somehow. 'Who in Togg's name was that?' he murmured to himself, and he crossed his arms to tap a thumb to his lips.

'The voice of command, dear,' Ieleen answered. 'Now do head for the channel.'

His response was a snort, but he nodded to Lurjen.

'And I may be blind but shouldn't we ready our own archers?' she added sweetly.

Jute let a hard breath escape between his teeth. Not that it would matter. He searched amidships, found their master-at-arms. 'Letita! Ready archers!'

'Aye!' she answered, ever eager.

Half the crew at the oars stood for the detail. Jute knew he was lucky; some of the greatest sea-fighters in Falar had volunteered for this voyage, archers and swordsmen and women. If this were an even fight he'd place his bet on them any day – but they faced over a hundred damned ships.

'The Malazan's drawn near one o' the towers,' Dulat shouted. He was shading his gaze. 'They're readying springals and arbalests at stern and bows.'

Jute squinted at the far galley. Siege weapons? Did they mean to try to take the tower?

'Engagement with them Genabackans!' Dulat called.

Jute almost shook his head; the lad was actually excited by all this. Couldn't he see how it would play out? It would soon be his own guts spread upon the waters.

The Genabackan pirate ship with its crew of soldiers had pretty much ploughed into the front rank of wrecker vessels. It was now surrounded by the rag-tag flotilla of ships and boats. Grapnels flew. They were being boarded from all sides.

'That foreign ship!' Dulat shouted.

The tall vessel had fallen behind as well. It too was being sur-rounded as it and the Genabackan now held the rear, engaging the wreckers, while the *Dawn* closed on the Malazan vessel.

Jute watched the fighting, fascinated despite his dismay. Hordes clambered up the side of the Genabackan ship. From across the smooth waters of the cove came the clash of iron and screams of the wounded. Shapes came tumbling over the sides. Most fell limp to splash into the water or crash on to decks.

'They're slaughtering them,' Dulat breathed, awed.

Aye, for the nonce, Jute added darkly. But eventually they'll be overrun. Numbers will tell. He shifted his gaze to the foreign ship. The wreckers appeared to be having trouble climbing the sides of the supernaturally tall vessel. Some few made it, clambering hand over hand on ropes, up and over the side. But what became of them he couldn't see. Nor in all this time had he seen any crew on board either, for that matter.

No shouts or noise of fighting crossed the water from that vessel.

Then he physically jumped as explosions thumped the air behind him. They slapped him in the back to concuss the air from his lungs and the *Dawn* shuddered from stem to stern. Some of the oarsmen lost their grips, so shocked were they. He turned, gaping. 'What in the name of the dead god of death was *that*?'

Blossoming clouds of smoke enmeshed the top of the north tower. Even as Jute watched, disbelieving, amazed, stone shards came flying through the swelling black clouds to arc over the waters before they struck, punching great tall towers of spray.

Dulat, atop the very highest spar, threw his arms in the air, howling in triumph: 'Munitions! The damned Malazans are demolishing the tower!'

Jute felt an immense weight lift from his shoulders. By the Queen's soothing embrace . . . there's hope yet. He swung his gaze to the Genabackan; but have we the time? The vessel was completely surrounded, its sides aswarm with boarders – yet from the furious action on the deck, the soldiers fought still. The foreign vessel was equally engulfed and overrun, but oddly, disturbingly, quiet.

'Send us a touch southerly there on the channel,' he told Lurjen, who nodded profoundly, his eyes huge.

'Yessir.'

'They're reloading their arbalests!' Dulat called.

Jute ignored that to study the wreckers closing upon them in what he now understood to be a fleet of captured launches, traders' coasters and unsuspecting travellers' galleys. 'Take the range,' he called to Letita. She nodded, now fully armoured, her iron helm with its long camail of chain link hanging past her neck, bronze cheek-guards closed. She raised her bow.

The shot fell just short of the prow of the closest vessel.

'Target that nearest one,' Jute ordered.

'Ready archers!' Letita shouted. 'Fire!'

All forty archers loosed. Most of the flight struck true over the open galley, raising chaos among the oarsmen. 'Fire at will,' Jute called. 'Pound them!'

Buen appeared on the quarterdeck and handed Jute his blade, wrapped in its belt, which he tied on. The first mate then thumped into the wood of the deck next to Lurjen the wicked cross-hilted parrying daggers the man favoured for close-in fighting. The steersman grinned and winked his thanks.

Jute turned to Ieleen. 'Sorry, lass,' he said. 'It's time you went below.'

His wife shook her head. 'I can't hear so good down below.'

'Ieleen . . .'

'Never mind 'bout me.'

Jute sighed his exasperation. 'Lass . . .'

She just smiled. 'Every time we have this argument. And every time you lose. Now, forget about me and mind our speed.'

Jute spun to the bow and choked. They were so close to the channel opening he could make out the individual weed-draped links of the chain swinging and dripping ahead. 'Ease off, y'damned blind fools!' he bellowed. 'Back oars!'

Movement above caught his eye: Dulat hunching, one arm covering his head and the other hugging the very tip of the mainmast where he sat atop the yardarm. Oh, for the love of D'rek . . . *'Back oars!'*

Multiple punches assaulted his ears and chest. Clouds of pulverized stone and black smoke blossomed above. A rain of stone shards came arcing for the *Dawn*. 'Take cover!' he yelled and bent over Ieleen, hugging her to his chest.

The striking rock sounded like cloth ripping as it punished the decking and splashed all about. It reminded Jute of the impact of shot from arbalests during his naval engagements. Men and women of the crew grunted their pain or slumped, unconscious or dead, from dull thumping impacts. The huge links of the sea-chain rattled and bumped as they swung. Jute grunted himself as small stones and gravel pelted his back and shoulders. He cast an eye to the barrier and the length appeared to slump lower in the water.

Beneath him, Ieleen squeezed his arm in empathy. He straightened to see that Letita had not allowed her archers to let up. The foremost boat that had been heading for them now wallowed, having lost all headway, and she'd turned her attention to the next – but some six more now came closing in upon them.

'I think this is it, dearest,' he murmured to Ieleen.

'You're always saying that.' Then her head snapped up as something captured her attention. Her brows rose and she breathed an awed, 'Oh my.'

He followed her blind gaze; it was fixed upon the tall foreign vessel. Something strange sounded then. Or failed to sound. It was like the tolling of a massive bronze bell as tall as a house, but silent. Something came rolling from that ship. It struck sharp expanding waves in the water. It swept over all the wreckers' vessels. Wood of oar and hull snapped and splintered as the invisible wave engulfed them.

'Here it comes!' Jute shouted, but heard nothing of his own voice. Indeed, at that moment it was as if he was deaf to every sound.

The *Dawn* rocked as if punched, pitching from side to side. Yet the concussion merely passed over them while at the same time utterly crushing the nearest wreckers' boats as if clenching them in a giant's fist. Ieleen, wrapped in his arms, let out a gasped breath, and he heard, faintly, 'Now *there's* a sorceress!'

Atop the mainmast Dulat threw his arms into the air. 'Yeaw!' he howled, or Jute thought he did, for he barely heard the man. 'We won! We won!'

Won? Jute snorted. The spell, or ward, or whatever it was, had only bought them time. Behind this first wave of attackers far more were oaring down upon them. Even their Genabackan defenders, he noted, were assembling oars to withdraw from the wreckage of broken timbers and canted half-sunk hulls surrounding them. And something told him they shouldn't count on their foreign ally to rescue them a second time.

He turned his attention then to the Malazans. Squinting, he could make out figures still working frantically to wind their springals and arbalests. Amazingly, the crew had kept to their duties through the sorcerous blast and the fusillades of rock and the threat of impending boarding. But then, he reflected, they must have seen much worse – should all the stories be believed.

The arbalests swung into position at stern and bow even as he watched. At some unheard command they fired in unison. He caught a momentary glimpse of the fat munitions flying up like dark eggs to disappear into the billowing smoke obscuring the tower's heights. Fresh eruptions punished his ears and punched his chest. Cussors, he judged. They must be throwing waves of cussors at the installation. Those boys are damned serious about getting out of this trap.

A new sound grated its jagged course along Jute's skull and

spine. Through the swelling clouds of dust and smoke he thought he glimpsed the very stone of the tower, itself chiselled from the rock of the cliff-side, split in two there at the top. A teeth-shaking thunder announced the length of bronze links, each perhaps as great around as his own waist, slithering and thumping its way down the stone side of the tower to crash into the channel. The top of the tower followed. It burst into shards as it fell then punched the water, sending up great spouts of foam and spray that reached even to the *Dawn*, spattering its decks.

A great roar went up from the crew and Jute slapped Lurjen's meaty shoulder. 'Ahead easy, master Buen!' he called.

'Aye!'

'I want pole-men at the bows!'

'Aye.'

Buen called commands, setting the rowers' pace. Jute bent down to plant a kiss on Ieleen's head. 'I'm for the bows, love.'

'Wouldn't do to get stuck and block the channel, yes?'

'I do believe our Malazan friends would blow us to Hood's own cellar if we managed that.'

She laughed and waved him off. 'I do believe they would.'

At the bows, Jute picked up a pole and leaned over the side. He felt a twinge of guilt at striking for the channel first, after the Malazan did all the work. But of the two vessels, they were unquestionably in the better position to make for the opening. Even as he watched, the Malazans were turning to follow. Further back, the foreign vessel's bow was sweeping their way in an ungainly broad arc; to the rear, the Genabackan soldiers had turned their vessel broadside to the incoming second wave of ships and boats and were exchanging racking arrow-fire with some ten of them even as their oarsmen worked to keep them mobile.

Jute had time to wonder, amazed, how they'd fitted so many men on that ship when the grey shapes of jagged rock blossomed in the water beneath him and he readied his pole.

'Two rods!' one of the pole-men, Anli, announced.

'Steady on!' Jute shouted.

'One rod!' Sill called from the starboard side.

'A touch to port!' Jute yelled to Lurjen.

Oars scraped the sheer cliffs to either side. It was suddenly very dark and chill in the shadow of the narrow slit. The pole-men kept jabbing. 'A half-rod!' Anli shouted, alarmed.

Damn the Twins! Nothing for it. Jute turned to Buen. 'Keep going. Don't stop for anything!'

Rock from on high pattered down upon the deck. Wood groaned and creaked as the hull grated over stone. Jute hoped to Mael that it was just piled wreckage and not some great obstinate boulder. The terrifying scraping and creaking passed, then the debris field fell away to reveal deep black waters.

Jute straightened in relief. He considered asking for more speed but decided against it. There was no need to risk banging against the cliff sides. When they broached the entrance the crew cheered again but Jute was quiet – for now there was but one thing to order. He caught Buen's eye and called, 'A westerly course up the narrows, First Mate.'

'Aye,' the man answered. His sun-burnished long face dropped its unaccustomed smile.

'Slow,' Jute added, then he turned to watch the entrance as it dropped behind them.

The Malazan was the first to exit, as Jute expected. It was a very long time before the next vessel emerged; by then a curve in the narrows was taking them out of sight. The tall foreign ship it was and Jute shook his head in amazement. Ye gods! The Genabackans covered the retreat of that great lumbering beast?

Then they were too far up the main channel and Jute turned his attention to finding some beach or cove to put in. He returned to the quarterdeck. Along the way he stopped at the mainmast to shout up, 'Find us a landing, Dulat. Or you're not coming down!'

'Oh, no worries there, cap'n. We'll sink long before that!'

Or be wallowing so bad we'll have no control. In either case, time was limited. At the stern he called to Ieleen: 'How's the wind, lass?'

She tilted her head, her brow wrinkling in thought, and was quiet for a time. He and Lurjen kept quiet as well, awaiting her judgement. 'It's freshening ahead,' she finally allowed. 'Though how far I cannot say.'

Jute turned away, frowning. One good thing about sailing west: it was damned clear how much daylight they had remaining. That would put an end to things. There was no way he could sail into unfamiliar waters after dark. Have to drop anchor next to the base of one of these cliffs and risk being driven up against it.

He glanced behind, searching the narrows. There was the Malazan. Its master had it tagging along in the far distance, just keeping line of sight. Jute was puzzled. They could easily catch them if they wished; Jute had the *Dawn* keeping a slow pace.

Then he realized that the Malazan was holding back for the foreign vessel. Probably doing its best to keep a line of sight on her. But why bother? They were in a channel; there was no chance anyone could get lost. But what if he, Jute, found a slim hidden cove or inlet and put in? What if the way opened into a maze of islands or sand bars? That captain was playing a careful game.

It occurred to him then that if he wished, he could lose them now. Order chase speed and dash ahead to find this freshening wind then free all *Dawn*'s sail. This was a race after all. A selfish lunge to grasp what riches one could find and damn the slow ones to failure or death. Wasn't that the point of chasing after gold or coin or any other fortune to be snatched from others or seized at sword-point? He'd leave them all completely lost, or he was an Untan dancing girl.

Yet they'd saved his life. Or, more important, saved the *Dawn* and all who served on her. Including his love. And so he could not in good conscience abandon them. Besides, travelling with Malazans armed stem to stern with munitions, a powerful sorceress, and a pocket army – if they survived taking on the entire wrecker fleet – could have its advantages.

'The cliffs are slipping away!' Dulat called from his perch. Jute was startled; he'd quite forgotten about the lad.

Indeed, the cliffs appeared to be smoothing out, sloping down as they advanced through the narrows. Perhaps the end of this interminable chute was near.

'Strand on the south shore!' Dulat called again, pointing.

Jute squinted; he couldn't make it out. The light was gold and near straight on as the sun was falling to the horizon. 'Take us in!' he shouted up.

'Three points to starboard,' came the answer.

Jute turned to scan to the rear. No other vessel was in sight. The Malazan vessel may have sunk. They'd looked uncommonly low in the water. He turned to find Buen on the mid-deck walk. 'Light a smudge,' he called.

The man gaped at him. 'A smudge? Here? On an unknown shore?'

'Do it!' Jute snapped, suddenly annoyed at having his word challenged.

Buen seemed to remember himself and he ducked his head, touching his chest. 'Aye, cap'n.'

'Everyone's on edge, luv,' Ieleen murmured from his side.

'I'll give him the edge of my hand.'

'It's a steep gravel strand,' Dulat shouted. 'Wide, though.'

'Have to do,' he answered.

'Steady on,' the lad shouted to Lurjen.

Black smoke now wafted in a choking thick cloud from the pot Buen had set. Sailors moved the iron brazier to keep as much of the ship upwind as possible. The smoke plumed low and heavy over the waves, as if the *Dawn* were unravelling a scarf.

The shore now hove into view. In the deep gold of the setting sun Jute made out a steep rise of black stone gravel leading to the last remnants of the narrows' cliffs: an inland rise of perhaps no more than a chain, topped by long wind-whipped grasses. And spread across the wave-washed gravel lay a litter of broken timbers, barrels, torn sailcloth, tangled rigging, and the blackened skeletal hulls of two ships.

Jute tried to remember the stories he'd heard of the region and came up with a name. The south shore of the Dread Sea – the Anguish Coast. Wasn't that the best of Oponn's jests! They were like sailors on leave staggering blind drunk from one rats' nest to the next. And he'd thought things couldn't get any worse. 'Any sign of survivors?' he called up.

After a time the lad answered: 'None as I can see.'

Jute wiped a hand across his brow and found it cold and sweaty.

'Another ship!' Dulat shouted then, making Jute flinch.

'Whereaway?' he snapped, alarmed.

'Following. That Malazan galley p'rhaps.'

Jute let out a long breath. A hand brushed his and he snapped his head down: Ieleen reaching out. He took her hand and she gave a squeeze. Jute's chest suddenly hurt with a great swelling pressure and he answered the squeeze. 'Very good, Dulat,' he said. 'Take us in, slow and steady.'

'Aye.'

The lad directed them to a relatively clear swathe of strand and Buen drove them in at a strong speed. The bow ground and grated its way up the gravel and crewmen and women jumped over the sides, pushing and tugging on the hull. Buen then tossed out two stout hemp lines that most of the crew grasped to heave the *Dawn* as far up the slope as possible. The lines were staked into the gravel.

Jute climbed down over the side. Ieleen, he knew, would remain on board. She hadn't set foot on land for some years now and he'd chided her on it, but she remained adamant and so he'd relented. It was a silly superstition to his mind, but it was important to her and he really couldn't care either way.

The black gravel crunched under his boots. Letita stood awaiting him, still armoured, helmet under an arm. 'I want a perimeter, a picket, and a watch. And send out some scouts. What's past that short rise?'

She saluted. 'Aye, captain.'

He next tracked down Buen. 'Gather some of this wrack for fires. Both for cooking and for signals.' The man nodded his assent but appeared unhappy with the idea of casting signals far and abroad. Jute then ran into a grinning Dulat, who was inspecting the unpacked casks and kegs of their remaining foodstuffs. Jute made a show of studying him long and hard as if puzzled.

The lad's smile faltered and he asked, uneasy, 'Yes, captain?'

'Why aren't you at your post, sailor?'

'My post? Ah, well – we've hauled up, haven't we?'

'What has that to do with anything?'

'And it's getting dark.'

'You coming down makes it lighter, does it?'

The lad had to think about that, his head cocked. 'No . . .'

'Then get back up there and keep an eye out for those ships or any others!'

Dulat cast one last glance at the stores, sighed his longing, then saluted and jogged off for the ship. Jute clasped his hands behind his back and paced off to a vantage from which to scan this most southerly bay of the Dread Sea. The Malazan ship was a black dot making its way to their location; of the other two vessels he could see no sign. As he watched it occurred to him that the Malazan silhouette was canted rather alarmingly to starboard. There's seamanship, he told himself. Keeping afloat despite every reason to be underwater.

The dark silhouette limped nearer. Its oars, a single bank on each side, flashed in the weakening sunset. The fires piled on the beach sent out clouds of grey smoke that sometimes blew over Jute as the contrary winds gusted and shifted. He spotted one of Letita's marines, Gramine, and waved the man over.

'Any word from the scouts?'

'No sir. Not yet.'

'Send Letita over when there's news.'

'She'll come, sir.'

Jute gave a light snort. Nerves. Damned nerves. 'Yes,' he allowed. He returned to examining the Malazan galley. 'I suppose she will.'

The vessel drew nearer, silent but for the faint splash of oars. 'I see the other ship!' Dulat shouted then from his post atop the mainmast. 'She has signal beacons burning at the bow!'

'Very good, Dulat.' He returned to watching the Malazan's

crippled approach. After a time, boots crunching through the gravel announced Letita. Jute turned and she saluted. 'Grasslands inland,' she reported. 'Empty.'

'These wrecks?'

'Looted then burned here, on site.'

Jute eyed the charred skeletal ribs. He wondered aloud, 'Burned on shore?'

'Aye.'

'Then someone's here.'

Her gaze slid to the north where it rested, naturally narrowed and wary. 'They're gone now.' Attractive eyes, he reflected as he had a number of times. Warm brown with a touch of sea-green, if he had it right. The wind cast her ragged-cut black hair about.

'You do not mix much with the crew,' he observed.

Her gaze snapped to him. It remained narrowed, challenging now. 'Nor do you.'

'There is someone awaiting your return home to . . .'

'Strike, sir. Yes.'

Strike still? He'd known she was a graduate of the famed military academy on that island, but was surprised to hear that she still considered it home. 'Well . . . we'll make it back. That's the point of any journey, yes?' and he gave a small laugh. She watched him in silence. He cleared his throat. 'Well, that's all for now.'

She saluted, 'Very good, captain,' spun on a heel and marched off.

So serious, he reflected. Well, she was early yet in her career. He returned to watching their companion's progress. Closer now, the ship appeared even worse for wear. Battered and scarred. Its planking faded with age. He couldn't make out the name scrawled below the bowsprit. It ground up on to the beach, but far lower than the *Dawn*. Some of his crew helped secure lines that they hammered into the gravel. Two figures clambered down its side. Jute went to meet them.

The foremost of the two was a squat wiry fellow, quite old. His leather armour was much-worn, and scoured where Malazan sigils of rank would once have ridden. His unkempt grey hair blew about in the winds and a grey-shot beard matched. His wrinkled features bore the faded slate hue of a native Napan. The second was equally wiry, spidery even, in common sailor's jerkin and trousers, barefoot, with a mane of thin white hair and a pinched, worried face.

Jute extended an arm to the first fellow and they clasped wrists, sailor-style. 'Jute Hernan, Master of the *Silver Dawn*. At your service, sir. You have my eternal gratitude for getting us out of that trap.'

This fellow waved his other hand, dismissing the topic. 'Ach – it was my own arse I was worried about. Cartheron, of the *Ragstopper*. Our thanks for leading us through the rocks. We'd never have made it otherwise.'

Jute stared, quite taken aback. Cartheron? *The* Cartheron? One of the legendary captains of the Old Empire? Unlikely . . . yet how many Cartherons could there be? He released the man's hand and nodded at the compliment. 'Well, as you say. We were worried about our arses as well. How fare our companions?'

The Malazan captain glanced away, squinting to the east. Jute noted that squinting suited the man's face, either through a lifetime's habit, or perhaps naturally. 'The galleon was limping along. Umryg is no sea-faring state.'

'Umryg? I know nothing of such a land.'

'As I said.'

Jute blinked, rather at a loss. 'Well. Can you effect repairs here?'

The Napan's squint soured into a scowl – the expression also no foreigner to his features. 'Not my first choice, that's for damned certain. Rather have her up and dry.' Then he laughed. 'But she'd probably fall to pieces so p'raps it's for the best.'

His companion pressed forward, outraged. 'We can't manage any of the necessary repairs here in this forsaken land. Gods, the keel needs inspection!'

Cartheron turned on the man, his first mate, perhaps. 'The keel needs no inspection,' he snarled. 'It's rotten through and through and that's that!'

The first mate spluttered, searching for words. He pulled at his hair in his passion. He finally yelled back: 'And so what do you suggest, O great Captain Cartheron?'

'Stuff more rags into her.'

'More – *more* rags? She's more rags than wood!'

'And yet she floats. There's philosophy for you, Orothos.'

Hands grasping fists of hair, the first mate glared back, dumbfounded. '*What?*'

'Beacon fires on the water!' Dulat yelled from the gathering twilight.

Vastly relieved by the interruption, Jute stepped away from the two Malazans, who continued their furious argument until a threatened cuff from Cartheron sent the first mate ducking. 'How far?' he called.

111

'Hard to say. Coming this way, though.'

'Good.' Jute studied the beacon fires on the shore for a time, then, satisfied with their strength, scanned the water for some sign of the approaching vessel. Cartheron came ambling over in a side-to-side wide-legged walk that only those who have spent most of their life at sea can manage. At first Jute was tongue-tied as he considered just who he might be standing next to all alone in the dark. What stories might he hear? What sudden, unlooked for intimacies or unburdenings of secrets? Was this the Cartheron Crust, one-time companion to the old ogre emperor and his killer and usurper, Laseen? Victor, with Nok, of the battle of Fenn Bay, where the combined Falaran navy was scattered in a rout? His grandfather had fought at that battle and told stories of the sorcery unleashed.

Finally, he was unable to contain his curiosity any longer, and, gaze still shaded on the waters, he cleared his throat. 'So, sir. Are you *the* Cartheron?'

'How many damned Cartherons do you know?' the man growled.

'Well . . . just you.'

'Good. For a moment there you had me worried.'

Jute cleared his throat once more. 'Well, I was wondering because—'

'There she hails,' the Malazan said, pointing.

Jute squinted. He could just make out the flickering glow of the fire, and his eyes were far younger than this man's. 'Who is she?' he asked.

'A sorceress. Damned powerful one. That's all I know. We met while we were all anchored there waiting for someone to dare the rocks.' Jute glanced to the man and saw him grinning. 'You. As soon as I saw your light galley dart for the rocks just at the peak of high tide I knew you had a good chance. Trust a Falaran at sea, I always say. When there's no Napan to be found, mind you.'

'What of your pilot, then?'

The Napan lost his grin. 'My pilot's a souse. Nerves.' Jute frowned at that. Nerves? 'Here we are,' Cartheron announced. He raised his chin to the surf.

The huge silhouette of the sorceress's galleon detached itself from the surrounding gloom. A fire burned in a brazier atop the raised castle at its bow. Jute estimated that height at a good six fathoms above the waterline. A launch was being lowered over the side. He and Cartheron waited.

The launch reached the surf far from them. The eight oarsmen remained seated within while two figures climbed out. The first was an aged fellow, all in dark clothes, his hair long and brightly glowing in the murk. He held out a hand to his fellow passenger. As soon as the woman stood – for it was clearly a woman, though wrapped in loose windswept robes – it was also clear to Jute that she hardly needed the old man's help. Unusually tall one might've described her – alarmingly tall, even. Strapping and sturdy would perhaps be kind. She was fully taller than he or any man of his crew and her presence was accented even more by her long flowing headscarf, a face veil that revealed only her eyes, and her equally disguising layered robes.

He and Cartheron bowed to the woman and he introduced himself.

The old man, his face sun-burnished and wrinkled and dominated by a long nose, carried a tall staff – thought not so tall as the woman. He stamped this to the gravel and announced: 'Timmel Orosenn, the Primogenitrix of Umryg.'

The woman waved a hand as if to brush this pompous announcement aside. Jute noted the hand was large enough to encircle his head like a fruit. 'Lady Orosenn will do,' she said in a rich honey tenor. 'Falaran,' she added, addressing Jute. 'We are in your debt. Your navigator is a sorceress indeed . . .' and she gave a small laugh as if sharing some unspoken secret.

Jute laughed as well; he'd always thought so. 'That she is, my lady. But it is we who owe the debt. Your actions in the harbour saved us all.'

'I merely did what I could to buy us time.'

'Speaking of the harbour, what of Tyvar?' Cartheron asked.

'They exited the channel,' Lady Orosenn answered. 'What has become of them since I cannot say.'

'Tyvar?' Jute asked.

'The Genabackans,' Cartheron explained. 'He sent a launch among us while we anchored earlier. We'll let him introduce himself – if he hasn't sunk.'

'Then we wait,' Lady Orosenn said, agreeing.

The old man frowned at the news. He peered about glowering into the dark and muttering to himself. Finally, he raised his voice. 'M'lady,' he urged, 'it is not safe for you to linger here on shore. Best you remain on board your vessel, yes?'

The Lady's eyes, so very enticing behind the veil, shifted to the south. Jute followed her gaze but saw nothing. She nodded then, reluctantly. 'Very well. If I must. Give my thanks should Tyvar arrive.'

'There is a danger?' Jute asked.

'Only to me. There are . . . old enemies that I must be wary of.' The old man urged her back to the launch and her crew pushed off.

'So we wait,' Cartheron reaffirmed, and he wiped his mouth then eyed Jute. 'Care for a drink? I have damn fine Untan distilled grain spirit on board. I could send for a bottle.'

Jute immediately felt his mouth water. 'That would be wonderful. My thanks.'

Cartheron's first mate had glared at the proposal and now he hissed aside to his captain: 'You're drinking the manifest!'

'Manifestly. Now be a good man and have a bottle sent over.'

The first mate glared anew but threw his hands in the air and stalked off, grumbling and gesticulating. '. . . not a rat's arse left . . . empty hold . . . utter loss . . . chicken farm . . .'

Some time after that a sailor in a tattered shirt and torn canvas trousers arrived carrying a bottle in one hand and two small glasses in the other. These he handed to Cartheron then walked away, all without a word or salute. Jute had the impression that standards had rather fallen on board the *Ragstopper*.

Cartheron inspected the glasses, blew in them, and wiped them on his very dirty shirt. He used his teeth to pull the cork free then splashed out a liberal measure of the spirit and handed Jute a glass. Jute's enthusiasm had fallen off with the polishing, but he set aside his reluctance and raised the glass. 'To a successful venture,' he offered.

'To ample wine and rich women,' Cartheron answered. 'Or is it the other way round?'

They drank. The liquor was indeed very fine, and very strong – including the undercurrent of sweaty shirt. Jute coughed into a fist. 'This Tyvar – you believe he'll make it?'

'Oh yes. Very impressive fellow. Reminds me of the old days. But I'll let him introduce himself. We should see him soon.'

They had another glass and Jute stood in the flickering firelight longing to question the man regarding those 'old days' he had so casually mentioned. But tact kept him quiet. If the man wanted to talk, he would. Besides, he understood that these veterans were often unwilling to discuss the past – it was usually painful. He was old enough himself to understand that.

'Hear that?' Cartheron asked after a long near-silence of crackling fires, the slow crash of the waves, hissing grasses, and the calls of night-hunting animals out on the plain beyond.

Jute started – he'd been fading. Exhaustion and alcohol. 'I'm sorry? What?'

'Listen.'

Jute struggled to focus. Then he finally heard it: the strike and ripple of oars out upon the water.

'He's here,' Cartheron announced. 'Good.' He raised his drink to Jute and downed it, sucking his lips. 'Our chances have just improved materially.'

A launch emerged into the firelight's reach. Several of the oarsmen and women jumped overboard to drag it in through the surf. Jute noted that all wore belted layered gambesons or leathers that were the underpadding of heavy armour. All the crew fought, it seemed. Two men thudded down on to the gravel shore, both still in their armour. One was the bearded fellow who had called to Jute from the vessel earlier. The other was his virtual twin, similarly armoured, only older, his beard shot with grey.

The pair doffed their helmets and tucked them under their arms, then strode up the shore to Jute and Cartheron.

'Captain Cartheron,' the bearded fellow greeted him. 'I am glad to see you still with us.'

Cartheron gestured to Jute. 'May I introduce Captain Jute Hernan, of the *Silver Dawn*.'

The man bowed from the waist. 'Captain. May I compliment you on your pilot? He is worth his weight in gold. I would follow him on any sea in any storm. But I am remiss.' He indicated the man at his side. 'Allow me to introduce my companion. This is Haagen Vantall, Steward of the Blue Shields.'

The man bowed, as did Jute, who strove to keep his amazement from his face. The Blue Shields! Of course. One of the fighting religious cults out of Elingarth. A brother order to the Grey Swords who had fought the Pannion threat years ago.

Haagen motioned back to his companion. 'And this is Tyvar Gendarian, Commander of the Blue Shields. Mortal Sword of Togg.'

Tyvar shook his head. 'Mortal Sword in title only. Togg has withdrawn, as so many of the gods have now, yes? We are all left with only our own prayers to comfort us these days.'

Jute took a steadying breath. He felt as if his head was swimming. 'Well. My thanks for interceding in the harbour. You saved all of us.'

Tyvar waved it aside. 'It was nothing. I would have remained and slain them all as a service to our fellow mariners, but time is pressing and we are yet at the very beginning of our journey, are we not?' He looked to Jute expectantly.

Jute suddenly felt his mouth grow dry. He swallowed, or struggled to do so, nodding. 'Yes. Yes, quite so. These southern reaches are said to be the easiest portion of the passage. They say it gets progressively more deadly the further one travels north. We have only just entered the southernmost bay of the Dread Sea.'

Tyvar shared a glance with his companion. 'And does your pilot know these waters?'

Despite feeling strangely shamed to fail this man, Jute had to shake his head. 'No. But I would dare the Stormriders with her and will sail on.'

Tyvar burst out a laugh and slapped his thigh with his bunched gauntlets. 'Excellent. May we accompany you then and sail north under your guidance?'

Jute stared, utterly amazed. 'I'm sorry?' he finally stammered in disbelief.

'Perhaps our good captain is concerned regarding the apportioning of shares . . .' Haagen murmured to Tyvar.

The Mortal Sword's brows rose and he nodded, 'Ah! I see. Do not concern yourself, captain. We of the Blue Shields are not interested in what gold or plunder may be amassed—'

'Hear, hear,' Cartheron muttered into his glass.

'We wish only to reach the north. Aid us in this and we offer our swords. What say you?'

Jute gaped, staring from one to the next before settling upon the wrinkled grey-hued features of Cartheron Crust. The old sailor cocked a brow and held out the bottle. Jute offered his glass, which Cartheron filled. 'Then I say we travel north.' And he raised the glass to toss its contents to the back of his throat, gasping and coughing.

The commander of the Blue Shields let out a great shout and slapped Cartheron on the back. 'Excellent! Two days for repairs, yes? Then we sail.'

Two days was far less than Jute would have wanted, but the deadline reminded him that they were not alone in this rush to the north. Others were on their way, or already ahead; who knew how many. And so he nodded his agreement. 'Very well. Two days.' And he added, gesturing to Tyvar, 'If I may ask, sir, why do you wish to journey to the north? If not for the gold or the plunder, then what?'

The tall man nodded again, sombre. 'A very good question, captain. Before Togg withdrew, he set upon us one last task, one last mission. That when certain portents were fulfilled, we of the Blue

Shields would venture to the north of this region and there fight to right an ancient wrong. And to prevent a great tragedy.'

Jute frowned, uncertain. 'A great tragedy, sir? What would that be?'

Tyvar waved as if the answer was obvious. 'Why, the death of innocents, of course.' He bowed his farewell, then turned to Cartheron. 'My regards to our Lady,' he offered. 'Come, Haagen,' and the two men returned to their launch.

Jute and Cartheron watched them go. It was now the middle of the night, and darkness quickly swallowed the small boat. The bonfires snapped and popped on the beach, sending sparks high amid the stars of the night sky. Most of Jute's crew lay asleep around them. He sighed and rubbed his aching, foggy brow.

Cartheron slapped the cork back into the bottle and regarded him, scratching meditatively at the bristles on his cheeks. 'Take my advice, lad,' he said. 'Don't get caught up in all this talk of missions and god-given purposes. I've seen it before and it only leads to misery and pain.' He offered the bottle, which Jute took. Then he inclined his head good night and walked into the dark, crunching his way across the gravel strand to his launch.

Jute stood alone for a time. He studied the night sky as if he could somehow discern there a portent of what might lie ahead, but he was no seer or mage. He turned to the ridge with its tall tossing grasses – who knew what enemies or dangers lay hidden within? Finally, he drew a deep breath and headed to a fire to find a place to lie down.

*   *   *

Silverfox walked the dunes of the coast. Her hair, long uncut and uncombed, whipped about her head. She hugged herself as she went; the wind was cold this day. Sea-birds hovered overhead, their wings backswept like strung bows. It was odd, she considered as she went, how she was alone yet felt as if she had to be on her own. Because of course she was never truly alone. Within her Bellurdan, the giant Thelomen, raged for action, while Nightchill, the ancient Sister of Cold Nights, and the true wellspring of her power, counselled patience. Closest to her in her humanity was Tattersail, the mage, once of the Malazan imperial cadre. She too urged patience.

And yet what of Silverfox? What of her? What did she wish? The sad fact was that she had no idea. Hers was the frail soul of a girl, full of doubts and fears. How could she set herself against such potent beings? How could she even be certain which thoughts were her own?

She raised her hands to study them, turned them over. Skin sun-darkened, stretched thin and dry, age-spotted, joints knotted and swollen – not the hands of the young girl she held in her mind's eye. Her creation, birth, and maturation had consumed the life of her mother. As now it was consuming hers. Yet she was content; it was just. She only hoped there would be enough time. The Imass had waited untold thousands of years for her arrival, a living Bonecaster who could release them from their ritual, and now that life was slipping away. Should she fail, how much longer would they have to wait again?

If there ever could be a second chance for redemption.

The wind gusted, sands hissing about her, lashing her, and she turned her face away. The stiff brown grasses clinging to the dunes shushed and grated. She saw Pran Chole standing alone on the shore, facing out to sea, and her chest tightened in bands of dread. No – not again.

Though it was the last thing she wanted to face, she clambered down the sand slopes to the strand. He did not turn when she joined him. 'What is it?' she asked.

Pran was slow to answer. 'I am not certain. I sense something . . . different.'

'Different? How?'

Dry tendons creaked as he turned his ravaged face to hers. 'Powerful.'

She suddenly found it difficult to breathe. Nightchill wavered close to her consciousness as if to reassure her with the message: *do not fear, I am here.*

I am no child to need such soothing, she cast against the presence in her thoughts.

Regardless, I am here should there be need.

'It comes,' Pran breathed, and he extended a skeletal arm, all bone and desiccated flesh, pointing.

Silverfox sought out her own powers as a Bonecaster, a shaman in her own right.

A head broke through the waves, its owner obviously walking the rising shore, approaching. Patches of long hair clung here and there over the bare dome of a tannin-stained skull. Dark empty sockets beneath thick brow-ridges, full wide cheekbones over lipless jaws that still carried strips of muscle and tendon. Next came chest and shoulders of bone beneath a ragged hide shirt, coarsely sewn, with sleeves all torn and stained.

At her side Pran Chole made one faltering step forward, as if half moving to greet the newcomer. A dry breath, like a sigh, escaped his throat.

'What is it?' Silverfox asked.

The newcomer approached, bowed on one knee to her. 'Greetings, Summoner,' he murmured in the T'lan voice that was the mere brush of falling leaves. 'It is an honour.'

Pran Chole took another hesitant step closer. 'I am Pran Chole. We of the Kron salute you.'

'I am Tolb Bell'al,' the newcomer answered, 'Bonecaster to the Ifayle T'lan Imass. And long have I been absent.'

And to Silverfox's utter astonishment, the two Imass embraced. For a time they held one another at arm's length, seeming to study each other. *Ifayle*, she marvelled, amazed. According to the Kron they'd been lost long ago. Some even claimed they were lost here, on Assail.

'Long has it been since the steppes of the Has'erin, Pran,' said Tolb.

'Indeed. That was a parting of many tears.'

'Yet we meet again.'

Silverfox stepped up. 'Pardon, Tolb of the Ifayle, but I must know . . . have you been here before?'

The two relinquished their grips. The newcomer turned to face her. She felt the full power of his regard, and it was potent indeed. This one may be the last and only shaman of the Ifayle, she thought. He carries their fate upon his ravaged shoulders. 'No, Summoner,' he answered. 'But the Ifayle are here and I have searched everywhere to know the answer to their fate. I found it nowhere, and despaired. Until your arrival. I see now that we merely had to wait for you to come to us.'

Merely! Silverfox felt her knees weaken at the ages of weight that one small word carried.

'So . . . you know.'

'Yes. I alone escaped and have spent all this time in search of an answer. And now here you are.'

'I?'

'Yes.' He bowed once more. 'Summoner, we must travel north. The answers are there. In the far north.'

Pran Chole also faced her. 'Summoner? What say you?'

The moment Tolb spoke she'd felt the right of it. In truth, she'd known it since they arrived on this shore. Yet she had avoided it. Dreaded the final irrevocable hard choices. She rubbed her hands up her arms and held herself. 'I must face Omtose Phellack unveiled. Something the world has not seen in tens of thousands of years.'

'Not you,' said Pran.

She blinked at him, a touch irritated. 'Not I?'

'No. Tolb and I and the remaining Bonecasters shall. As during the ancient unveilings when the Odhan was scoured clean by rivers of ice leagues thick. Or the war over the rich fields of the Gareth'eshal, which yet lay lost to us beneath the sea.'

'Then what of me?'

'Summoner,' Tolb spoke gently, 'you must bring the Kerluhm to heel. You must stand before them and deny them their war.'

'*Your* war,' she corrected. 'You also swore the ritual.'

The Ifayle Bonecaster nodded deeply then, his neck creaking, and it seemed to Silverfox that a great exhalation of repentance shuddered from the ancient. 'A question of interpretation. They choose to fight it. We choose to end it.'

This near confession touched her deeply and she felt an urge to console the man though he was a walking corpse to her vision. Yet, she wondered, what differences truly lie between us? Only the accidental timing of birth. I could easily have been hearthmate to him, or he born of the Rhivi. She swept an arm to Pran. 'Gather everyone.'

'Summoner,' Pran said, a warning in his voice. 'It will be a long journey.'

'How so?'

'We cannot move through Tellann – Omtose inhibits this. We must travel across the land. So did the Jaghut deny us tracts of land and slow our progress in the elder ages.'

Silverfox stared, speechless. Walk . . . on foot all the way north across this enormous continent? It would take months! Still, was she not of the Rhivi? Why let yet another migration deter her? She smoothed her layered hides down her hips. 'Then let us go at once.' And she headed for her tent to pack.

Behind her, Tolb Bell'al and Pran Chole shared a glance that could almost be said to contain humour. 'You chose well, Pran,' Tolb murmured, his breathless voice nearly lost in the wind.

'It was she who chose to come to us,' he answered.

*   *   *

When the lookouts of the *Lady's Luck* sighted land in the east, Kyle counselled that they turn south to travel round the horn of the continent. Tulan Orbed, however, ordered Reuth to find their position first to see how far north the winds had taken them. That night Reuth studied the stars, their setting and rising, and determined that they had indeed been driven quite far to the north. Kyle's advice against travelling round the northern coast was rejected.

Two nights later Reuth came to where Kyle slept wrapped in blankets in the bows. The lad reached out to wake him but his approach had already roused him; he now slept as wary as when on campaign.

'Kyle . . .' Reuth urged over the shush of the bow wave.

'Yes?'

Tears gleamed on the lad's face. 'I'm so sorry,' he whispered, choking, his voice thick.

Kyle understood immediately, and reached up to squeeze the lad's shoulder. From the stern came a knot of men – the majority of the crew all told – headed by the ex-Stormguard and Storval. Kyle pushed Reuth away. 'Hide yourself now, lad.'

After one last anguished look – which Kyle answered reassuringly – the youth slid down amid the rowers' berths and disappeared. Kyle stood. The crew confronted him, spread out, the ex-Stormguard at the fore.

'The lad warned you, did he?' Storval growled.

Kyle ignored the glowering mate. He spoke to Tulan: 'You should be proud that your nephew finds murder distasteful.'

The master of the *Lady's Luck* at least had the grace to appear embarrassed. He pulled on his thick black beard, his gaze downcast. 'My apologies, outlander. But we must know . . .'

'Show us the blade,' Storval demanded.

Kyle glanced to the east where the coast lay as a dark line that brought the horizon close. With his foot, he drew the pack he used to rest his head on towards him. 'You want to see the sword, do you?' And he reached behind his back.

Storval yanked his shortsword from his belt. The ex-Stormguard levelled their spears. The front line of the crew reached for their knives. The rest raised cocked crossbows.

Kyle slowly drew the weapon and shook off the leather wrap. A glow immediately suffused the bows, cast by the curved, translucent, cream-hued blade.

'Whiteblade,' one of the crew breathed, awed.

121

Storval's gaze remained fixed on the sword. He took a steadying breath. 'Hand it over.'

'Before I was in Korel lands,' Kyle said conversationally, hefting the blade, 'I was with a mercenary company. The Crimson Guard. And with them I acquired a rare and mysterious skill. I will demonstrate it now.'

Storval frowned at him, puzzled. 'What?'

Kyle kicked the pack up to his free hand and turned to the side. He planted one foot on the gunwale and leapt over. Roars of outrage followed him until his head plunged beneath the frigid water.

He emerged into darkness. The sword in his grip was a murky glow in the water as he struggled to open the pack. The ship was a diminishing dark blotch in the night. A great cheering whoop reached him from it – Reuth's shout of triumph – followed by Tulan's barked: 'Shut up, lad! Come about!'

They might bring the *Lady's Luck* about, but Kyle was confident they'd never spot him here in the dark of night amid the waves. Holding the sword beneath the pack, he drew out the water-bladders he'd half inflated, and began blowing into one. It would be a long swim to shore and he'd have to keep topping up the bladders, but he should make it – provided he didn't freeze to death first.

*

Dawn saw a man drag himself by his elbows up through the surf, his hands mere pale blue clubs. He lay on the beach of coarse gravel, half in the waves, exhausted and immobile, warming himself in the gathering light.

Later in the morning, Kyle pushed himself up and blew on his hands. He pulled at his wet clothes then faced inland. Eroded cliffs topped by scrub and brush hid what lay beyond, but he knew what awaited him: a broad flat steppe-land of grasses and copses of trees, arid, a near desert in regions, that swept all the way east to the foothills of the near-mythical Salt range.

He drew the sword from his shirt, wrapped it in the empty sack, and tucked it through his belt. Then he pushed back his sodden hair, tied it with a leather strip, and set off.

CHAPTER IV

A STORM CAUGHT THEM WHILE STILL WEST OF THE SOUTHERN Bael coast. Master Ghelath saw them through, bellowing commands, solid on the deck though chilled blue from the spray. The towering cliff-high waves would have overpowered Havvin at the tiller arm had not Bars and Amatt taken hold to follow the canny old pilot's orders.

Storms were one of the main reasons Shimmer hated these deep ocean crossings. It seemed to her that no frail construct such as a ship should dare challenge the might of such vast depths and lengths of open water. The pitching and yawing below decks made her sick; that and the clattering of loose equipment and the ominous groaning of the mere finger-widths of timber that separated her from the cold dark depths. The noise and stink of vomit drove her to seek the fresh air above decks – even when 'fresh' meant gale-force winds and driving sleet.

She found Lean and Sept taking their turn at the tiller arm, following Havvin's commands yelled above the crashing of waves. K'azz was also above decks, an arm round the mainmast, staring forward into the roiling cloud cover. She climbed the stern to the pilot's side, noting the length of line that secured him to the tiller arm. The old man, his long white hair a plastered layer upon his knobbly skull, sent her another of his intimate winks.

She planted her legs wide, lowered her head against the blowing spray, and offered him an uncertain frown.

The old man laughed his amusement. 'Know you why Master Ghelath named her *Mael's Greetings*?' he called.

'No,' she shouted back.

'Because Mael, having sent his greetings, need not send them again!' and he cackled anew.

Sailors, she thought. The oddest sense of humour.

The pilot sliced an arm forward, yelling, 'That one! Straight on!' Lean heaved her considerable bulk against the arm while Sept pulled. 'Further!' Havvin urged. 'Hard o' port!'

'I don't remember volunteering for this,' Lean gasped as she strained.

'Beats marching,' Sept grinned.

Lean, her jaws set, shook her head. 'Never the right weather, is it? Always too hot or too cold. Too wet or too dry.'

Shimmer saluted them and headed back below. If they could still joke, then things were in hand. She descended the steep ladder to find Bars and Blues awaiting her at the bottom. Water poured down over her shoulders in one last chilling wash. 'I'm beginning to hate these journeys,' she told Bars.

'I'm with you, Shimmer. Only way to get anywhere, though.'

They braced themselves on nearby timbers in the darkness of the low deck. Water sloshed about their boots. 'And you, Bars,' she asked. 'Where were you in Assail lands?'

The man grimaced at the memory. 'Exile Keep. On the shores of the Dread Sea. Turned out to be two inbred families of mages battling each other for control of the coast.' He paused and ran a thumb along a scar on his chin. Blues' eyes glittered in the dark as he waited and watched, just as Shimmer did. 'Somehow they got it into their crazy paranoid heads that we were plotting to take the keep, or some damned fool thing like that. Both the families turned on us. Every last one of them. Anyway . . .' Bars cleared his throat. 'Cal an' the rest withdrew. Pulled 'em all off so me and my Blade could escape in a local's fishing skiff. That was the last I saw of them. Headed north along the Anguish Coast.' He lowered his head to study the knuckles of one hand.

'That was Cal's plan, wasn't it?' Blues said gently. Bars nodded. 'So stop beating yourself up about it. The plan worked. Now we're back because of it.'

Bars curled the hand into a tight fist, lowered it. 'Right.'

Ah, Bars, Shimmer thought. Always feeling everything so keenly. Like a raw exposed nerve. The man's emotions were like a storm; it would be attractive if it were not so exhausting.

'Where's K'azz?' Blues asked.

'Up top. Watching the storm.' Shimmer shook her head, mystified. 'It's like he's not afraid one whit. Just curious. As if he wants to experience it.'

Blues snorted. 'Well I'm damned afraid, if he's not. Don't like being out of sight of shore. Too far to swim.'

Of course, Shimmer reflected, being a mage of D'riss Blues wouldn't like being out of sight of land. 'We're none of us happy sailors,' she said.

The two chuckled their appreciation. 'That's for damned certain,' Blues agreed, and he peered up nervously through the open hatch to the black churning mass of clouds above.

The next day the churning clouds passed to the north and *Mael's Greetings*, sails tattered and seams leaking, limped under oar to the south-east. Havvin was aiming for an island he had sketched into his personal rutter from descriptions and stories he'd heard over the years in sailors' taverns in Delanss, Strike, and the Isle of Malaz.

Ghelath and K'azz ordered head-counts and were relieved to find that no one had been lost during the four days and nights of the storm. All the Avowed and ship's crew not rowing were then pressed into labouring at the pumps and buckets in a continuous struggle to keep Mael from delivering his final greetings to his namesake. Shimmer was too busy to return to questioning K'azz regarding their destination. Indeed, she welcomed the distraction of exhausting physical work and threw herself to the task; she found ocean crossings, when not terrifying, damnably boring.

Three days later the call went out from the crow's nest: land to the south-east. At first no one else could see it as what had been glimpsed were the merest tops of what proved to be tall mountains that seemed to rise straight out of the sea.

Havvin nodded as if expecting this and explained that such were the accounts he'd heard: an island of mountains nearly free of any land a person could stand upon. It was therefore often referred to as the Pillars. He skirted the island's coast, circling to the north-east. Soon a narrow ribbon of beach, or strand, came into view and he threw over the tiller. Approaching, they saw numerous plumes of smoke, and presently spotted the long dark shapes of four ocean-going vessels anchored close to the shore. Their cut was unfamiliar to Shimmer. They appeared to be broad-beamed merchant ships adapted into war-vessels, with archers' platforms added fore and aft.

'Do you know those ships?' she asked Ghelath, who shook his nearly bald head.

'K'azz?' she asked her commander, who was standing with Ghelath. He also shook a negative.

Bars came climbing the short stairs to the quarterdeck and joined them; he looked unaccountably grim. 'I know them,' he said. 'And I wish I didn't. They're Letherii.'

Shimmer was impressed. Letherii? She'd heard much of them but had never met any. 'Accomplished merchants and businessmen and women, I hear.'

Bars gave her a strange look, then muttered beneath his breath, 'That's one thing you can say about them.'

'Four vessels armed for war . . .' Ghelath pointed out.

'We have no choice,' K'azz said flatly. 'Put in and we'll go ashore to see about repairs.' Another might have taken offence at K'azz's now belatedly stepping in to give commands, but all Shimmer could think was: *about damned time.*

Ghelath shook his head, dubious, but signalled Havvin.

The pilot took them to the stretch of the narrow shore farthest away from the Letherii vessels and ordered the anchor dropped. An informal landing party of Ghelath, K'azz, Shimmer and Gwynn drew together. Others could have joined, but with K'azz and Shimmer departing Blues elected to remain, and no other Avowed expressed an interest in negotiating with the Letherii. At the last moment, however, Bars slid down the rope ladder to join them in the launch. He looked ill-tempered already, and Shimmer wondered just what the man was expecting. They would merely be foraging for supplies and water, or, if necessary, purchasing them from the Letherii.

They drew the launch up the strand and headed towards a file of tents. The narrow strip of flat land proved to be something of an armed camp. Troops were in the process of erecting a palisade of timbers that had possibly been salvaged from a fifth, wrecked, ship. The palisade, Shimmer noted, faced inland, where precipitous cliffs of a chalky white stone rose like walls themselves.

A party came down to greet them; one far larger than theirs, she noted.

'Welcome.' The party's spokesman hailed them. He was bearded and wore banded iron armour that was polished to a bright gleam. Closer now, Shimmer saw that his armour was engraved with intaglio swirls and that the trimmings of his mantle and collar were of silk and white fur. 'I am Luthal Canar, of the Canar trading house, of Lether.'

'Greetings,' Ghelath answered. 'Ghelath Keer, Master of *Mael's Greetings.*'

'K'azz, of the Crimson Guard.'

Luthal nodded cheerily to them, while his party of some forty soldiers spread out around them. All were armed with crossbows. 'Yes. Welcome to my island.'

'*Your* island?' Bars spoke up sharply, and he sent Shimmer a significant glance.

The man opened his hands in a sort of shrug of apology. 'Well. The private property of the trading house of which I am the appointed representative.'

'I see,' K'azz murmured.

Luthal's answering smile was wide, but hard, rather like the blade of a knife. 'So I am sorry to say you are trespassing on a private commercial establishment. Luckily, we of Lether are not barbarians. We have not attacked you. We are enlightened. Our laws contain provisions for the peaceable restitution of crimes against property.'

'Here we go,' Bars grumbled to Shimmer beneath his breath.

Ghelath had been blinking rather confusedly for a few minutes and now he gazed about, his face reddening. '*Establishment?*' he burst out. 'What by Mael's breath do you mean, an *establishment*? This is an island!'

Luthal nodded his pleasant agreement. His men, now ordered in double ranks, raised their crossbows. The front rank sank to one knee. 'I agree that on the surface this piece of property might resemble an island. But it is in fact a mine.'

'A mine,' Ghelath mimicked mockingly. 'A bloody mine?'

'Indeed.'

'And what by Hood's dead grasping hand could you possibly mine here?'

'Shit.'

Ghelath blinked anew, startled. Shimmer frowned at Bars. K'azz, for his part, was eyeing the distant cliffs as if studying them for climbing.

'What was that?' Ghelath asked, obviously completely lost.

Luthal had not lost his convivial façade, which Shimmer now recognized as the Lether way of conducting business. It was the bland merchant's mask that covered chicanery, deceit, chiselling, theft, slavery and murder. The man gestured to the ground. 'Bird shit, to be exact,' he explained. 'You are standing on it. This entire shore is made up of layer upon layer of bird shit. And it is really quite valuable.'

Ghelath waved that aside. 'Well, we have no interest in your damned shit. We just want to purchase supplies for repairs.'

It seemed to Shimmer that Luthal's smile became even more

smooth. 'Purchase, you say? That is not necessary. Because, you see, the penalty for trespassing is confiscation of your vessel.'

'Confisca— *What?*' Ghelath grunted, appalled. He lunged for the man but K'azz caught him by the back of his shirt. The forty crossbowmen tensed, adjusting their aim.

K'azz slowly raised his open hands. 'I understand. We broke your laws – and this is your price.'

'We didn't know you'd claimed the entire damned island,' Bars ground out.

'Ignorance is no defence before the law,' Luthal observed. 'Surely you are not such a complete barbarian that you are unaware of this concept?'

To the Letherii, K'azz may have appeared unmoved. But Shimmer read his anger in his fixed expression and the deep lines bracketing his mouth. 'We are not unaware,' he answered. 'Seeing then that we require a ship . . . may we purchase one of yours?'

It was Luthal's turn to appear confused. The man lowered his chin to study K'azz from beneath his brows. 'I believe in truth you do not understand. The confiscation of your ship includes all cargo, chattels and equipment on board. Considering this, I do not see what you could possibly possess as collateral to guarantee such a purchase.'

'None the less, I wish to enter into a contract with you for the purchase of one of these vessels.'

'And do you accept the price for default upon such a debt?'

'I do.'

Shimmer grasped his shoulder, hissing, 'What are you doing?'

'I know what I am doing, Shimmer,' he answered firmly.

Luthal crossed an arm over his chest and propped his other elbow upon it to tap a finger to his chin. 'I set that price at one hundred peaks.'

'One hundred!' Bars burst out. 'That's absurd! That must be half the coin in all of Lether!'

'One tenth, I estimate,' Luthal answered, his gaze fixed upon K'azz, one eyebrow arched.

'I accept your price.'

'Very well.' Luthal held out his hands as if such a mass of coin could fit within them. 'Produce it.'

K'azz dug in a pouch at his side then dropped a single coin into the merchant's hand. Luthal examined it, nonplussed. 'A Quon quarter-moon? What jest is this?'

'A tip above the asking price. I believe you set the price at the

128

sum this entire beach would fetch at current rates on the market in Lether. I assure you that I could take this beach from you should I wish. However, I have restrained myself, thereby giving it back to you. Price paid by anyone's measure.'

Luthal lost his smile. He glanced to his crossbowmen then returned his narrowed gaze to K'azz. 'I do not accept your assurances. I consider you forfeit of the amount and you and your crew indebted to me.' He raised a hand to his archers.

'What of a trial of payment?' K'azz asked sharply.

The merchant paused, then lowered his hand. He studied K'azz. 'A trial?'

'Is that not in keeping with the laws of Lether?'

'Well, yes . . .'

'And the debt is considered discharged should I succeed?'

Luthal chuckled, but his eyes remained flat and hard. '*If* you should succeed . . . yes.'

'Very well. I accept payment by trial.'

Luthal waved his guards forward and they took hold of K'azz. Shimmer felt just as confused as Ghelath. 'K'azz, what is this?' she demanded.

He glanced down at her. 'Do not interfere.' Then his face softened and he added: 'Promise?'

She grated her teeth as she watched the guards yank him away. 'If I must,' she murmured savagely. Infuriating! She had thought that after Jacuruku all his secrecy would be done with. But it seemed that after all nothing had been resolved. What had he gained from Ardata in any case? A name. A location. Nothing more. Assail. A place he was then seemingly completely unwilling to travel to. And now that he was so close – despite his every effort! – he would rather indulge this pompous Letherii merchant.

Someone was laughing and she spun to see the scarecrow figure of Cowl approaching along the beach. He was clapping silently and chuckling his eerie unnerving laugh. It was all Shimmer could do to restrain herself from slapping the man. She looked to Bars, who was frowning as he watched K'azz being marched off. 'You know what's going on,' she accused him.

Grimacing, he lowered his gaze and nodded. 'Yeah.'

'Well?'

He glanced up. His lips were pressed tight but he eased them, sucking in a breath. 'Seen one of these trials while I was in Lether.'

'Yes?'

He cleared his throat and dragged a hand across his chin and his growing russet and grey beard; he appeared to be searching for the best way to present what he'd seen. 'They load the debtor up with chains and weights and drop him into one of their canals. If he'r she can walk the canal, then they've discharged their debt.'

Shimmer felt her brows rising in growing disbelief and horror. 'And has anyone ever managed this feat?'

'Ah – only one, as I heard tell.'

'This is absurd.' Shimmer dismissed him to chase after K'azz.

'You swore to obey,' Cowl called in warning.

Shimmer felt again the grating jagged blade the man's voice drew down her spine. She slowly turned to face him. 'You would have him killed?'

Something strange crossed the man's features, almost a secretive knowing amusement, and he chuckled anew. 'I would have his orders followed,' he said, still laughing.

She looked to the knot of Lether soldiers escorting K'azz, and Luthal following after, his hands clasped behind his back. 'Well,' she murmured. 'There're no canals here.'

Bars cleared his throat. Having her attention, he motioned to the waters of the lagoon beyond where the Lether ships rested at anchor.

'Oh, dammit, no . . .'

Indeed, the soldiers were taking K'azz to the launches drawn up on the beach. 'What do we do?' she asked.

The big man hunched his rounded shoulders, considering. 'Well,' he ventured at length, 'I believe you can request to witness the trial.'

It turned out that Letherii law allowed two individuals, relations or acquaintances of the accused, to witness their trial. Shimmer and Blues attended. Avowed brought Blues to the island and rowed them across to the flagship of Luthal's merchant flotilla. To Shimmer's eyes the proceedings in no way resembled a trial as she knew it. K'azz stood bound while stone weights were hung upon him by way of stout rope. No questions were posed. No charges were read. No opportunity was given for a response from the accused. She supposed that being away from civilized lands, Luthal had dispensed with such finer points of the law.

All the while she held K'azz's gaze. She knew her expression conveyed her questions, doubts and fears. He answered with calm forbearance. He even raised a bound hand, as far as he could, to further reassure her.

Meanwhile, Blues at her side was seething. 'What is this Togg-forsaken nonsense?' he muttered. 'We should step in . . .'

'He doesn't want any bloodshed.' And she noted the many Letherii soldiers about the deck, all with crossbows cocked and readied.

'No bloodshed in drowning, that's certain,' he growled.

'Those are his orders.'

'Seems he really does want you in command, Shimmer.'

She glanced to him, the grey-blue hue of his face even darker in his anger, and had opened her mouth to dismiss such a thing when Luthal spoke.

The guards had turned K'azz to face the ship's side, out over the water of the lagoon, towards the shore. 'The indebted has chosen a trial,' Luthal began. 'In order to win free of his obligation he merely has to carry his burden underwater to the shore. It is his free choice. No one forced the accused to take on these debts and burdens. The lenders and creditors are the innocent aggrieved parties in this exchange.'

Luthal coughed into his fist and nodded to the guards. Seeing his expression of untroubled solemnity, it occurred to Shimmer that the man actually believed the nonsense he was spouting. As if watching one's children starve, or struggling to salvage a lifetime of work, wouldn't force anyone to do anything. No, there was no coercion at all in the battle to keep a roof over one's head and survive in this world. Such a belief – and the circumstances that allowed it – must be a convenient and soothing balm indeed.

'Let the trial begin,' Luthal announced, and the guards pushed K'azz over the side.

Shimmer and Blues lurched forward, but K'azz shot them a glare over his shoulder as he slipped from sight and shouted, 'No!'

The pair halted, exchanging looks of disbelief and horror. It was as if both had fully expected that somehow K'azz would escape, reverse the proceedings, or otherwise win through as he always had in the past.

Flanked by his guards, Luthal approached them. His expression was sad, but behind it Shimmer read satisfaction and an untouchable smugness that almost tipped her into a blind fury. 'I am sorry,' he said, obviously not sorry at all. 'However, justice had to be done. The debt is now abrogated and discharged. You and your crew are free to land on the beach – though fees must be levied for such occupation, of course.'

Shimmer stared at the man, stunned by his false assurances of sympathy, his lofty, breathtaking arrogance. Free to land on the beach! Oh yes, quite free. Or equally free to stay on their slowly sinking vessel and drown. Obviously, they were free to choose! No possible coercion here at all.

She longed to stab the man through his uncomprehending skull, but then they'd be forced to kill the rest of them as well – which was clearly what K'azz had wished to avoid. She'd even moved her hand to the worn grip of the dirk at her belt when shouts of disbelief and alarm sounded from the ship's side.

Luthal's sailors and soldiers crowded the rail. Shimmer was hardly paying them any attention. She'd already decided to return to *Mael's Greetings* and from there launch an attack upon one of the Lether vessels, sinking all the rest as well if it should prove necessary.

Which was what they should have done in the first place! She glanced to Blues and the man edged his head up and down in the slightest of nods. So it was decided, without any words, as only two who had campaigned side by side for years could decide.

As for K'azz and this absurd manner of throwing away his life . . . what could he have been thinking? Had he hoped for a different sort of trial? That Luthal was bluffing? She had no idea – she only felt tired by it all. Now she wished he hadn't come with them after all. If the man had wanted to kill himself, he should have simply gone ahead and thrown himself into Lake Jorrick.

Luthal suddenly pushed himself back from the side and hurried to her. Anger darkened his features and he jabbed a finger out over the waters. 'What trickery is this?' he demanded.

She blinked at him, her brow crimping. 'What do you mean?'

'Do not play coy – you outlanders with your magery and magics. This is simply unacceptable.'

She and Blues brushed past the man. The crossbowmen tracked them with the iron tips of their quarrels as they crossed to the side. Rather reluctantly, she glanced down; she had not wanted her last vision of the man to be of him drowned under fathoms of water.

The lagoon, or stretch of shallowing water, was a clear pale turquoise over the rising slope of the beach, probably because of the sand floor. Shimmer imagined that slope to be quite steep beneath the vessel as it dropped off precipitously into deep midnight blue. Far below there appeared to be a dark figure struggling, moving side to side with a kind of exaggerated gait. For lack of anything else it resembled some sort of monster of the deep making its ungainly way to the land. Yet she wasn't absolutely certain as the motion of the waves partially obscured it, as did the sunlight glinting and glimmering from the surface.

'I dismiss this trial as a corrupted test,' Luthal announced.

Shimmer continued to watch the dark wavering figure as it made its slow laborious way up the white sand slope. To one side lay the half-buried rotting hull of a wreck. Peering down, she noted a number of other such skeletal remains littering the deep lagoon bottom. 'You mentioned no such provision in the trial,' she answered, rather distractedly. She fought to keep a smile from pulling at her lips: why hadn't he told her? Obviously he'd worked out some sort of solution with Gwynn, or Petal, or perhaps all the company mages combined.

'It is understood,' Luthal huffed. 'Everyone knows this.'

'Sadly, we outlanders are ignorant of such niceties. Everyone knows this.'

Luthal peered over the side and his eyes fairly goggled at the progress the figure below was making. 'You cannot mean to hold to such an absurd demonstration!'

'I agree that your practices are absurd. But you insisted.' The merchant adventurer appeared ready to order his crossbowmen to fire upon her. 'Perhaps we should take the boat to shore,' she suggested. 'To see how the trial ends.' Luthal snarled under his breath, but he snapped an order to the sailors and they set to lowering rope ladders to waiting launches.

Shimmer found it uncannily odd to find herself floating over her commander's head while he struggled below to heave his load of stones up the submerged slope. Who was aiding him? she wondered. Could it be Petal on *Mael's Greetings*? Or Gwynn? Yet neither of these had ever confessed to any knowledge of Ruse magics. It certainly was not Blues here beside her, frowning down at the water, apparently as completely perplexed as she. However, it occurred to her that the Warren of High Denul, the healing and manipulation of the flesh, could also serve to sustain K'azz. And every Crimson Guard mage, out of necessity, possessed some familiarity with the healing magics of Denul. Perhaps Petal was even now completely engrossed in maintaining K'azz's breath. This must have been what K'azz had had in mind from the beginning; why the man had pressed so hard for a trial. He'd worked it out with the company mages but had not included her. She had to admit to feeling a touch put out.

Didn't he trust her?

The boat ground ashore and Luthal and his escort of six guards clambered out. She and Blues followed. The guard kept a steady bead on them with their crossbows as if they would throw themselves upon Luthal. She ignored them. Together they all awaited K'azz's arrival. Other than they, the beach was deserted. When she and

Blues had headed out, Ghelath and the rest of the Avowed had returned to the *Greetings*, there to await the outcome of the trial – and to avoid any further fees the Letherii might invent to level upon them.

Out of curiosity, Shimmer peered about at the so-called 'establishment'. What immediately came to mind was an impression of general shabbiness. That, and the temporary, transient character of everything. No buildings of any sort had been erected. Canvas tents, pole-framed, stood here and there. Fire pits were in evidence everywhere. The Letherii soldiers – private hired guards, she corrected herself – lounged about in the shade of the tents, all but those manning the palisade that ran across the inland edge of the beach. The entire band appeared scruffy, ill-fed, and lacking in any discipline.

They would prove no challenge should Shimmer choose to act.

K'azz, however, held his company to a higher standard. No mere brigands were they to simply take what lay within their power to take. And Shimmer found that she agreed, though it galled her to have to endure the smug self-righteousness of Luthal.

The palisade troubled her. Clearly they were not alone on the island. Who were the locals? Hostile in any case, she assumed. And the palisade itself was not built simply of logs. It was an uneven mishmash of adzed timbers and sections of what appeared to be decking and hulls of ships. The entire construction was made up of bits and pieces of salvage from many wrecks.

She studied the rising pillar-like slopes above and noted that while grasses and low brush covered the rock, anything larger was entirely absent. Not one tree grew here – or they'd all been harvested for cooking or building. Had K'azz seen this earlier when he'd been studying the island?

A grunt of outrage from Luthal drew her attention to the lagoon. A dot had emerged from the waves: K'azz broaching the surface. Hunched forward, the man doggedly carried on, step after laborious step. And the shifting sands couldn't be helping.

His shoulders emerged, each looped by the numerous ropes supporting his load of stones.

'Impossible . . .' Luthal murmured at Shimmer's side. His voice, she noted, held a touch of awe. He turned to her, now scowling. 'This is your foreign Warren-magic.' He swept a hand down in dismissal. 'This is illegal. You are forfeit.'

'Forfeit?' Blues snarled. 'You set a trial. We pass it. Now you back out?'

The crossbowmen, Shimmer saw from the corners of her eyes, were spreading out in a semicircle facing them. K'azz was now only knee-deep in the surf. With each step the stone weights hung upon him clattered and knocked as he heaved himself up the steep grade of the beach. Shimmer tried to catch his eye but his head was lowered in his struggle to stay erect.

'Mistrial!' Luthal shouted. 'I call mistrial! Outside influence!'

Shimmer had had enough. 'Oh, shut the Abyss up.' She ran down into the waves to help K'azz. Together, she and Blues half dragged their commander the rest of the way until he sank to his knees. The stones rattled and Shimmer noted the deep gouges the ropes had pressed into his shoulders. Blues had already begun cutting.

'This proves nothing,' Luthal continued, his voice rising.

K'azz heaved himself to his feet. Shimmer was amazed to see that he was not even out of breath. He pushed back his sodden hair and studied Luthal. Shimmer knew him well enough to read the fury in his narrowed impassive gaze.

'You will not honour even your own laws?' he ground out. His voice was level but Shimmer heard the disappointment, and disgust.

The Letherii showed only defiance, arms crossed, his expression one of arrogant superiority. 'You did not follow the spirit of the law,' he objected.

Shimmer found the man's blindness to his own hypocrisy breathtaking. Moreover, he was obviously incapable of even understanding the possibility of it.

K'azz appeared to have reached the same conclusion as he blew out his breath and wiped the remaining water from his face. 'Very well. Since there is no way we can ever satisfy you . . . we shall go.'

'Go? You cannot go – there remains the matter of the debt!'

For the first time a hard edge crept into K'azz's voice: 'I fulfilled your trial yet I choose to forgo the hundred Peaks. Consider yourself lucky not to be the one indebted.'

Luthal's mouth twisted as he tasted the sourness of his position. Curtly, he waved them off. 'Go then. Renegers. Men and women of bad faith. I cannot do business with those who refuse to honour even the most basic laws of commerce.'

Blues drew breath to answer but K'azz wearily raised a hand for silence. Together they walked to the small skiff that Ghelath had left pulled up on the shore.

'They gonna shoot us from behind?' Blues murmured to K'azz, without looking back.

'I suspect not,' K'azz answered. 'That would precipitate a pocket war between our forces. Bad for business.'

'You've shown some restraint yourself,' Shimmer observed.

K'azz nodded his tired agreement. 'I gave the man every chance, Shimmer,' he said. 'Witness that. Every chance.'

Back on board *Mael's Greetings*, Shimmer immediately sought out Gwynn and Petal. She found them already together at the ship's side. 'How did you do it?' she asked. They exchanged surprised, and rather alarmed, glances.

'We thought . . .' Petal began, 'that is . . . we were just discussing how Blues could have managed . . .'

'But he didn't do it.'

'As I said,' Gwynn cut in, looking satisfied, 'I detected no active Warren-manipulation at all.'

'Yet there must have been *something*,' Petal murmured. The possibility that there hadn't been seemed to terrify him.

They looked past her, nodding their greeting, and she turned to see the man himself flanked by Blues and a second figure, the scarecrow-tattered High Mage Cowl, wearing his usual mocking smile.

Of course. Cowl.

The one mage she'd forgotten. And why? Because she so very much wanted to forget the bastard. Ghelath edged his way forward through the gathered Avowed as they congratulated K'azz. 'We can't sail,' he complained. 'The moment we leave the bay we'll wallow and capsize!'

'Yes, Master Ghelath. Unship the oars. Make for the nearest Letherii vessel. It's time to collect a down payment on my debt. Bars – organize a boarding party. Minimum bloodshed. Just throw them overboard.'

Bars gave a savage grin and saluted. ''Bout goddamned time.'

K'azz caught Shimmer's eye. 'Every chance, Shimmer,' he said, as if by way of apology.

'I understand.'

'I'm doing them a favour, actually,' he added, and he motioned to the island. 'You saw the palisade? The guards?'

She frowned, puzzled. 'Yes.'

'I could order their other ships sunk, yes? But I won't. That would condemn them all to death. Seems the locals don't want them here – and there's no food or water on that narrow strand of shit.'

He gave her a small smile then and turned away, heading for his cabin. Cowl remained behind and she caught his eye, beckoning him aside. When they had a modicum of privacy, she asked, her voice low, 'How did you do it?'

The man's maddening, mocking grin deepened. 'Do what?'

She bit down on her irritation. 'Sustain him.'

The mage appeared to be enjoying the discussion so much he had to wrap his arms around himself. 'I did no such thing, Shimmer.'

'No?' She did not bother to hide her confusion. 'You didn't? Then who . . . ?'

'No one did. That is, other than K'azz.'

'K'azz? But he is no mage – is he?'

'He is not.'

'Then . . . how?'

The man just smiled all the more. And he slowly turned away, grinning and chuckling. Shimmer wanted to strangle him. But that had been tried before. Cowl had had his throat cut and been strangled by Dancer himself. Yet he'd lived. Somehow he'd lived. Was that the secret these two shared? If so, she felt a new sensation stealing over her. She realized she no longer simply feared *for* her commander. She faced the closed cabin door. Now, she knew a strange new sensation: a feeling of rising dread *of* her commander.

K'azz – what are you becoming?

*   *   *

Burl slept poorly after his confrontation with Gaff and the crew. Over the following nights he jerked awake at every slight creak of hull timber or tick of wood from the cabin panelling. Whellen still slept soundly, as if under some sort of spell. The crew worked quietly, subdued and watchful. It did not help that there was so little to do; the *Strike* hardly moved at all. Only the weakest of icy winds urged it on.

As the days passed, Burl quit his cabin less and less. Why bother? There was nothing to see or do. And he did not like the way the crew watched him; as if these troubles were all his fault. He suspected that they were planning to throw not only Whellen overboard, but him as well for protecting the man. As the days passed, he became certain of it. He took to sitting facing the door to his cabin, sword across his lap. He even slept in the chair, jerking awake and snatching up the weapon whenever he nearly slid from his seat.

Hunger finally drove him out. He gave the form of his still immobile First Mate one last glance, then eased open the door. Sword readied, he edged out on to the mid-deck. The soft diffused light of the day made him think it was late afternoon, though he couldn't remember the last time he'd heard the ship's bell.

To his surprise and horror he discovered the deck empty of any crew. Not one soul was in sight. He drew breath to bellow his outrage but something choked his throat, some nameless dread and suspicion: if everyone was gone then couldn't who or whatever did it – couldn't *it* – still be about?

He hunched into a fighting crouch, sword raised, and padded onward as quietly as he could. When he edged past the mainmast some instinct, or faint rustle, made him glance upwards and he thought he caught a glimpse of movement there at the lip of the crow's nest high atop the mast. A pulled-away dark lump against the ice-blue sky that might have been the silhouette of a head.

He tried one leaf of the cargo hold doors but found them secured somehow from within. Strange, that. He searched the bows and found that indeed the ship was empty of all crew. He came across no sign of violence or struggle; no blood, scattered gear, or damage. Everything was secured, tied down and squared away. It was as if the crew, after taking care to ready for ship's inspection, then piled into launches and abandoned the vessel. But that was not quite so: the two small-boats remained in their moorings.

Gaff's description of the ghost ship returned to him then and he shivered as something clutched his throat, almost cutting off his breath. They'd found it looking clean and in order – simply empty of all souls. Gaff had even mentioned unfinished meals on the common table in the galley.

As if everyone had merely walked away . . . or been taken.

He shook his head to clear it of such fancies. This was no ghost ship. He and Whellen were here. He returned to the stern and the narrow companionway. Here he found the door to the stores closed and barred. He banged upon it.

'Open up, damn you! This is Burl! The captain! I order you to open up!'

He waited, but no one answered. He raised his fist once more but froze as he sensed someone there, listening, perhaps pressed up against their side of the door. 'Who's there?' he murmured, lowering his voice. 'Who is it? Gaff? Are you there?'

Something shifted behind the door, cloth brushing against wood. 'Gaff is gone,' came a strangled whisper.

'Gone? Gone where?'

After a long silence he thought he heard a gasped, 'Taken.'

'Taken? By who, man? Who? Answer me!' He waited, listening.

Only his harsh breathing sounded in the companionway, that and the weak creaking of the timbers as the vessel coasted onward over the still waters. 'Who?'

A voice, speaking perhaps through choking misery, sobbed, 'Maybe you!' The sobbing climbed into abject weeping and someone slid down the boards of the door.

Burl flinched away as if the man's fit were somehow contagious.

He climbed to the deck, perhaps hoping for open clean air, but he was not refreshed. The atmosphere was chill and dead. His breath plumed about him in a cloud. On a hunch, he started up the rigging for the crow's nest. When he was halfway up the head reappeared above and a voice called, high and strangled: 'I'll jump! I swear! Come no closer!'

Burl was angry at himself for not being able to identify the crewman, so choked with terror was the voice. Was it Juth? Or maybe Bolen? 'That you, Bolen?' he called.

'Stop or I'll jump!' the voice shrieked.

Burl halted. He raised a hand. 'All right! I'm stopping. What is it? What's stalking the crew?'

The man was weeping. 'I don't know! Could be anyone!' The head ducked from sight. 'So keep away!'

Burl cursed under his breath. Anyone? And why? What's to gain? A lone person can't possibly sail a damned ship. It didn't make any sense.

He started back down the rigging. On the deck, a suspicion took him and he ducked into the cabin. Whellen lay within. He went to the galley and collected a handful of dried biscuits then returned to the cabin, shut the door, adjusted the chair once more to face the entrance and sat, sword across his lap.

He chewed on a biscuit and waited for whatever was stalking the crew to come for him.

Some time later, he jerked awake at a noise – or at least he thought he heard a noise. He thought it sounded like a splash. He straightened on numb stiff legs and reached for the latch. Then he remembered something and stopped to look: Whellen still lay beneath his blanket. Hoar frost gleamed on the coarse wool weave. Burl clenched and unclenched his hands to warm them, then pulled open the door. The iron latch was so cold it burned his fingers.

Again he found the deck empty. The waters of the Sea of Dread remained calm – unnaturally so. Any body of water of its size ought to have considerable waves. The sky above was darkening into twilight. Stars shone through and Burl blinked and rubbed his eyes as he gazed at them: he recognized none of the constellations. Where was the Rudder? The Cart? The Great Cowl? It was as if he were staring up at another sky.

He spun, raising his sword: for a moment he'd been certain someone was behind him. Indeed, he still had that prickling feeling that someone was watching him. Glancing about to be sure he was alone, he sheathed the sword, then started up the rigging. This time no one challenged him. He reached the crow's nest and peeked within – empty. Perhaps what he'd heard had been a splash. He climbed back down.

Everywhere he checked it was the same: doors that were formerly locked and barred now hung open. None showed any sign of having been hacked or forced. The stores and armoury were empty, as was the hold. As far as he could determine Whellen and he were now the only two souls on board the *Strike*.

He returned to the mid-deck.

This time he was not alone. Another stood at the side, facing away out over the limpid waves. A familiar blanket lay draped about his shoulders: Whellen.

So. Now it was his turn. Someone had slain all the rest of the souls on board and now only the two of them were left alive. And Burl knew it wasn't him. He raised his weapon and advanced upon the man. 'You'll not find me so terrified,' he called.

Whellen turned and Burl was surprised by his expression. He'd expected a snarl or gloating, but the man just looked sad and worn. He wasn't even armed.

'I've been dreaming,' he said, and his gaze slid away to the sea.

This drew Burl up short. The blade quivered as he shook. 'Dreaming? Dreaming of what?'

'Of dread.'

Now he was certain the man was mad. He'd harboured an insane murderer. Against all the crew's exhortations, he'd sheltered the man. What a fool he'd been. He probably deserved to die far more than they. He clenched the shortsword in both hands but still it shuddered. 'Why?' he managed, his throat almost choked off, so dry was it.

'Why?' Whellen echoed, thoughtful, his gaze still narrowed upon the iron-grey waters. Then that gaze shifted to Burl and in it he read only the grief that bowed the man's shoulders. He appeared sorrowful beyond tears. 'You think I did all this,' he murmured, and gestured to indicate the ship.

'Who else?'

'Not you then?' he asked, and a sort of weak smile plucked at his lips, as if acknowledging a poor joke.

Burl swallowed his terror and redoubled his sweaty grip upon the blade. 'What kind of lunacy is that? Listen to yourself.'

'I mean, are you certain the crew is gone? Perhaps it is just you who is gone.'

'What?' Burl didn't want to listen to any of this craziness, but he could not bring himself to run the man through in cold blood. Perhaps it hadn't been him after all. 'What do you mean, man? Speak sense, damn you to the Enchantress! I mean it . . . or I'll kill you!'

'I mean that there have been no murders here. No one has killed anyone.'

'Bullshit! What happened to everyone, then?'

The first mate raised his open hands and examined them. 'It's this place, Burl. It's where we are.' He gestured to the waters, the sky. 'We don't belong here. It's not for us. That's what everyone's been feeling. As if an enemy has been stalking every one of us. But that enemy is just our own fears.'

Burl almost thrust his blade through him for concocting such a preposterous story, no doubt to squirm out of his guilt. Yet somehow he wasn't entirely convinced that this man was the murderer. Hadn't he lain ill or in a faint all this time? Or had he been duped somehow? Perhaps he had an accomplice . . . and Burl snatched a quick glance behind. Seeing nothing, he wet his lips and muttered a weak, 'I don't believe you.'

Whellen nodded his understanding, or acceptance. 'There is no way I can convince you, is there?' he murmured softly, as if he were speaking to himself. He shrugged to drop the blanket from his shoulders. 'Except perhaps this way.'

'What?' Burl answered. But the man wasn't listening. He merely gave Burl one more nod, as if in farewell, and leaned backwards. Burl lunged, snatching at him. 'No!' But all he touched were the man's sandals as he slipped over the side to fall to the water below.

Burl leaned down, reaching, his hands empty.

The Sea of Dread was a particularly clear sea, and Whellen remained visible for some time as he sank, staring upwards, his face a pale oval, in no way panicked or desperate, only so very sad. Or regretful. As if all this were nothing more than an unfortunate accident of fate. Burl watched until the man's outline disappeared into the murk of the depths. Then he threw himself away from the side as if it burned to the touch. He snatched up the sword and continued backing away until he reached the door to his cabin, then he quickly jumped within and slammed the door.

'Now we'll know for certain,' he whispered, fierce, as he readied the chair and sat once more, sword across his lap.

'Now we'll know!' he shouted at the door and whatever *things* were gathering beyond. 'If no one comes – we'll know!'

He wet his lips, clenched and unclenched his hot grip on the weapon. 'Come on!' he screamed at the door. 'Come on!'

He listened, but all he heard was his own hoarse breathing. He took one clumsy hacking swing at the door, croaked, 'Come on!' He listened again while he held his breath. Something was there. He was certain of it. Why wouldn't it come? Why this agony of waiting? Won't it just end it?

After a time he could no longer hold his chest tight and his shoulders sank. His face was chilled by tears. 'Come on,' he moaned, utterly exhausted by the waiting.

Gods, man – won't you just end it?

*　　*　　*

They crossed the West Whitewater on the second day of climbing. It ran steep and swift out of the high valley. Orman's breath caught as he stepped ever deeper into its icy course. He carefully picked his way between submerged boulders while the torrent surged as high as his waist. The charging water pulled at his legs and he relied upon Boarstooth to keep his footing.

Ahead, Old Bear seemed to have merely leaned into the course and bulled his way across. His ragged bear cloak had danced and whipped atop the waves as the stream appeared to be attempting to yank it from him. He climbed the opposite bank, guffawing, slapping at his sodden leathers, and Orman could actually hear his great booming laughter over the roar of the mountain stream. The Reddin brothers followed, while Gerrun brought up the rear.

They climbed steadily, half the time descending steep rocky ridges as the Old Bear's path took them from one high valley to a higher, until it seemed to Orman as if the snow-draped slopes of the Salt range loomed directly over his head. Legendary birthplace of the Icebloods themselves. What the old legends named Joggenhome. They were now long past the point where the ghosts first came to him as a boy, and this time he saw them too: grey translucent figures in the distance, watching from among the trees and rocks. Many held spears, some shields. Some wore helmets and mail coats, others only leathers and ragged cloaks. He would have remarked upon them but for seeing the others ignore them – and so he chose to as well.

On the third evening they ate a stew of rabbit and roots and berries that the Reddin brothers had collected. One of the brothers cooked it in a smallish iron pot over a fire, and they served it out in wooden bowls. Orman's bowl warmed his hands in a very welcome manner. The other brother tossed over flatbreads, like cakes, that they'd baked overnight in the ashes of yesterday's fire.

Old Bear sat in the glow of the fire, hugging his spear. His ruddy lined face seemed to glow like heated metal in the dancing light.

From what Orman could remember of his father's tales, they were currently in lands claimed by either the Sayer clan or the Bain clan. 'Which Hold is this?' he asked Old Bear.

The man's single dark eye shifted to him. He nodded at the appropriateness of the question. 'We are in Sayer Hold.' He gestured north-east with his crust of bread. 'Next valley over lies within Bain Holdings. Further east climbs the Lost Hold, though I've never met a Lost. They say they've hired many mercenaries to fight for them these last years. Must have a lot of gold, those Losts . . .' Orman knew most of this already from his father, but he was quiet, taking it all in once more from the mouth of Old Bear himself – a figure out of legend he'd never imagined he'd meet again.

The old man shifted to point west. 'The Heels. I have treated with the Heels and visited Heel Greathall. Beyond them lie the Myrni.' He shook his hoary head. 'Never met any of them.'

'Will they challenge us?' Orman couldn't suppress a slight tremor of dread at the thought. He'd never been this high in the Holdings before. Retreat was no longer an option for any of them.

Old Bear circled a crust of bread in his bowl, stuffed it into his mouth, chewed thoughtfully. At last he opined, 'I have lent my spear to the Sayers now and then. We should be allowed passage.'

'And the stream. Is it the Upper Clearwater?'

Old Bear's gaze shifted to Gerrun across the fire, where the little man sat with his booted feet stretched out close to the embers. 'It is. The seam is high in the headwaters. Gold lies strewn down the water's course where it falls from rapid to rapid. Is this not so, Shortshanks?'

The little man smiled thinly. 'It is.'

'Will we reach it soon?'

'We are moving quickly. Another two days, I should think.' The old man tilted his head to examine him with his one good eye. 'You are keen to collect your gold, are you?'

Orman looked to the fire. 'I will need money to travel. I cannot stay in the north.'

The old man nodded his assent. 'That is true. You are now out-lawed. Kinslayer. You have claimed Boarstooth. Your name will now be added to your father's, and Jorgan Bain's before him.'

Orman was not pleased by the man's light tone. 'You would mock me?'

Old Bear held up a hand. 'Not at all, lad. I am merely repeating the tale that is no doubt making the rounds of the taverns even as we speak. Boarstooth has returned to the Holdings – a tale worth the telling.'

Orman could not be certain the man was entirely in earnest. He didn't think any of this was worth telling at all. He picked up a branch and poked at the fire. 'That was not what I wanted to happen.'

Old Bear produced an apple from within his cloak. He bit down loudly and chewed while he regarded the fire. 'I know, lad,' he said. 'These things rarely go the way we want them to.'

The next day they traced a course up the valley. The way was stony, steep, and rough. A stream had once run here, but it had long since dried up or shifted course. They came to a pond no bigger than a stone's throw across where pines grew thick and the air was heavy with their scent. Standing in the water, as if awaiting them, was a ghost.

Old Bear raised a hand, signalling a halt.

The Reddin brothers moved to either side of Orman so that the three of them formed a triangle, back to back. Of Gerrun, Orman saw no sign. Run off, the faithless bastard. Best that they found out this early, he supposed.

Old Bear approached the ghost alone. It was a woman. Tall and slim, her opaque form wavered slightly as if caught in an other-worldly wind. Orman wondered why she'd chosen to stand in the pond. She wore a thick cloak of some sort of animal hide clasped by a large round brooch, like a shield. Her hair was full and long and bunched like a mane itself. For some reason he imagined it must have been black.

The two spoke; or at least she spoke to him. She raised an arm to point to the east. Old Bear nodded and backed away. The woman's form wavered and disappeared.

'There is a trespasser,' the old man announced, returning to them. 'From the east.'

'A trespasser?' Orman repeated. 'What is that to us?'

Old Bear studied him. 'The Sayers will allow us to cross here, but not for free. This is their price. We must . . . look into things for them. Do you refuse? Would you turn back?'

Orman looked to the Reddin brothers; they studied him, but not narrowly, not frowning. Merely coolly evaluative. He shrugged his indifference. 'No.'

'Very well. Let us go greet our visitor.' Old Bear gestured with his spear that they should spread out and head east across the valley towards the ridge.

'What of Gerrun?' Orman asked the nearer of the Reddin brothers – he still didn't know which was which. This one waved vaguely southwards before continuing on, unconcerned.

Orman hefted Boarstooth. Fine. I can play that game as well. Though he had many more questions, such as what were they to do with the trespasser should they find him or her? He pushed his way through the tall grasses and brush in silence.

Ahead, the woods thickened in a mixed forest of pine, aspen and cedar that climbed the valley's slope. A voice called from the trees. 'Greetings! I have come to talk! Is that a senile old bear I see with you?' Orman halted, crouching for cover.

Old Bear stepped out from dense brush and cocked his head to examine the woods. He shouted back: 'Is that a young cub come to receive yet another lesson?'

A figure emerged, tall and lanky, and loped down from among the trunks. Orman had the impression of the relaxed bounding of a wolf. The fellow closed on them, his grin exposing prominent teeth in a long jaw. Kinked brown hair blew about his head. He wore leathers that had seen hard use, and tall moccasins climbed to his knees. A longsword and two fighting dirks hung at his waist.

He and Old Bear embraced. 'What about that lesson then?' Old Bear rumbled.

'Your heart would burst, I fear.'

'What brings you to Sayer lands?'

The fellow glanced to Orman, or, more precisely, to the weapon in his grip. 'News.'

Old Bear followed the man's glance, then gestured to where one of the Reddin brothers was closing. 'Kasson,' he said, then of the other, 'Keth.' So, it's Keth in the sheepskin leggings, Orman told himself. Old Bear gestured to him: 'Orman Bregin's son. And the last one is named Gerrun.'

'He must be the one trying to get behind me,' the young man said, grinning all the more.

Old Bear let out a long-suffering sigh, waved to the trees. 'Get in here, Gerrun!'

The newcomer glanced again to Boarstooth. 'So it is true.'

'Yes.' Old Bear cleared his throat. 'Fellows, this is Lotji Bain. He is nephew to Jorgan Bain.'

Orman started, and tensed his grip upon Boarstooth's haft.

'I knew your father,' Lotji told him.

'You did?'

'Yes. He visited Bain Hold.' He pointed to the spear. 'I see that the whispers are true. Boarstooth – as you call it – has returned to the Holdings.'

'You cannot challenge upon Sayer lands,' Old Bear rumbled in warning.

Lotji gave an easy laugh. 'No.' He waved Orman to him. 'However, if you wish to step on to Bain lands I would gladly meet you.'

'That is not our mission,' Old Bear quickly cut in.

Orman was relieved. For his part, he had no intention of accepting a challenge from anyone. Not to mention that he'd had no time to practise with the weapon.

Lotji laughed again. It was an easy laugh, but Orman detected a strong grating of iron beneath. 'As you wish.' He backed away. 'We will see one another again, I am sure, Orman Bregin's son.' He raised a hand in farewell. 'Until then.'

They watched him go. As he entered the denser growth another figure stood from cover to one side. Gerrun. Old Bear turned to Orman. He was pulling thoughtfully on his thick tangled beard. 'Well, Orman,' he said, low and rumbling. 'What do you think of that?'

'I think I need to practise.'

The old man threw his head back and roared with laughter. The echoes boomed out across the valley. He slapped Orman on the back and started off once more. 'I think we can help you with that, my lad. I truly do.'

Two days later they came to the high valley of the Upper Clearwater. The mountain stream ran milky with run-off from the ice-fields and snowpack above. It rushed and surged into the valley from the rock cliffs above. The valley itself was long and comparatively flat. The pale-green stream meandered among silt channels and sand bars, chaining and twisting, until it reached the bottom, where the valley dropped off through a gap in another ridge line. From there the river continued on its course until eventually, far below, it emptied into the Sea of Gold.

It was cold here and spray seemed suspended in the air, chilling them. Snow lay in the shadows behind rocks and trees. Their feet crunched through thin layers of ice over the soil and compressed snowmelt.

They startled an elk cow and the brothers took off in pursuit, but Gerrun called out that he would stalk it and the brothers returned. Old Bear led them to a long bare gravel bar – a stranded shoreline where the river once ran, bordered by tangled brush. The old man used his spear to push through. They walked the gravel in a crunching of stones. Old Bear paced with hands clasped on his spear behind his back. He was peering down at the rocks as if searching for a particularly pretty one. The brothers and Orman couldn't help but glance down also.

'This is it,' Old Bear announced, gesturing to encompass the stream bed. 'This valley. This is the richest deposit in the Sayer Holdings. A season's gathering and sifting here will leave any man rich beyond measure – rich in coin, at any rate.' He beckoned to Keth and pointed to the rocks with his spear. 'Here. What do you see?'

Keth knelt, then grunted. He rose examining something in his fingers, and indicated that Orman should hold out his hand. Grinning, he dropped something into the palm.

It was a gold nugget, still wet and half covered in silt. It felt unnaturally heavy for its size. Like a lead sling bullet. Orman was astounded. Without effort Keth had found the largest nugget he'd ever heard of. What more riches might lie hidden here?

He blinked to see Old Bear watching him through his slit eye. The fellow cleared his throat. 'As you've no doubt gathered by now, we serve the Sayers, Gerrun and I. We brought you here to offer you lads a choice.'

He peered off across the valley, squinting. Took a great breath, planted the butt of his spear in the gravel and set both hands upon it. 'Two paths stand before you. Here, you can collect as much gold as you wish. You can return with it to the townships and be rich men – for a time. Or you can come with me and swear your spear to the Sayers and live defending the Holding – for a time. The choice is yours.'

The Old Bear scanned the valley and what he saw seemed to disgust him. 'But tell me . . . do you wish to be a slave to gold? Do you wish to live on your knees scrabbling in the dirt like a dog? For do not fool yourselves – that is what those who are enslaved to gold must do. If not here, then elsewhere. Always chasing after it. Never possessing enough. Grasping, hoarding and fearful for what you do have. Lusting, envious and covetous of what you do not.

'Or . . . do you wish to live as a man? Never needing more than the good sword or spear in your hand? Slave to no one or no thing? For all the Sayer require of you is your word and that you swear to live and die by it. Nothing more. For nothing more than that need be asked of a man or woman with honour.'

Still looking away, he asked, 'What say you?'

Orman glanced to the brothers, who exchanged flat looks. Keth rested his hand on the worn leather-wrapped grip of his sword; Kasson let out a long breath and shifted to a more relaxed stance. Orman realized he was beginning to read the brothers. They would prefer to stay.

He studied the broad valley. How much gold might be hidden here? Shiploads? It was enough to leave him dizzy. Yet somehow it left him unmoved as well. He examined the dull nugget. So much struggle, blood, and scheming spent by those in the towns below just to grasp the barest fistful. A lifetime's worth of toil and sweat. Yet here it lay scattered about like so much chaff. He could only shake his head at the absurdity of it. So what if he were to descend into Mantle, or the cities beyond such as Holly or Lillin, with a great fat sack at his side? Once word got out he carried such a fortune he'd be dead within the hour. Useless. Utterly useless to him.

The decision, he realized, had been made for him long ago. For he now understood it to be the same one his father had made.

He tossed the nugget back to the gravel bar. 'I would swear my spear to the Sayers – if they will have it.'

The brothers nodded their agreement.

A broad smile split Old Bear's craggy features. He slapped Orman on the back with a resounding smack. 'Good, good! I am glad. Very glad.' He waved them onward. 'Come, then. Let us travel higher, to the Hall of the Sayer. You will swear your fealty and we will feast and drink until we pass out.'

They climbed for three more days through dense forest of spruce, pine and birch, ever upwards. The lingering snow cover thickened. Orman's breath plumed in the air. He tore a ragged piece of cloth he carried and wrapped his hands. Distant figures shadowed their advance. They were too far off and too hazy for him to be certain whether they were real or ghosts. He wondered if perhaps half the 'ghosts' sighted by travellers were in fact Icebloods – or the other way round.

They ate well. Gerrun carried a haunch of venison wrapped in burlap and leather. The cold allowed it to keep for longer than usual. Old Bear pointed out plants and roots that could be boiled or cooked in the fire. They slept huddled up next to the embers and took turns keeping watch.

Orman came to look forward to his time standing through half the night. The sky was so very clear from this extraordinary height. So high were they, and the Salt range was so very steep, that he thought he could even make out the glimmering reflection of the Sea of Gold, far to the south. He felt that he could reach up and touch the stars. It was cold, yes, but it was bracing and enlivening. He did not know how to say it exactly, but he felt strong. His senses – his hearing, his sight, even his sense of smell – all seemed keener than before.

On the fourth night a ghost came to him. It emerged from the trees and walked straight up to him. As it came closer he felt a shiver of preternatural fear as he realized that it was certainly not human. Very tall and broad it was, even more so than the Icebloods. It wore clothes of an ancient pattern: trousers of hide, a shirt that was little more than a poncho thrown over its head and tied off with a coarse rope. Hides were similarly tied around its feet. It carried an immensely tall spear, which Orman realized was the bole of a young tree topped by a knapped dark stone that bore an eerie resemblance to the spearhead of Boarstooth.

The figure stopped in front of him. Its hair was a great unkempt mane twisted in leather. Beads and pieces of bone hung within it. The face was long and broad, the jaw heavy. The teeth were large, the canines especially pronounced. For some time it stood regarding him in silence. Orman wondered if it could see him at all. He saw now that the figure was female, thought its hips were not broad and its chest not especially prominent.

'I am come to give warning,' she suddenly announced, startling him.

'Warning?' he managed through a dry and tight throat.

'A time of change is coming,' she continued as if he had not spoken at all. 'Old grudges and old ways must be set aside, else none shall survive. Pass this warning on to your people.'

My people? 'Why me? I am not – why speak to me?'

'You carry *Svalthbrul*.'

Svalthbrul? Ah. He looked to Boarstooth and she nodded. 'I am sorry,' he began, 'I do not know how old you are, but much has changed—'

She looked away, to their surroundings, scanned the night sky. She shook her head. 'The stars remain. The mountain remains. Little has changed.'

'But . . .' He stopped himself as she turned away and started walking.

'They will come before summer,' were her last words over her shoulder.

The next morning Old Bear announced that if they pushed hard, they should reach Sayer Hall that day. Orman walked in silence for much of the time. The way was steep for most of the morning; he used Boarstooth as a walking stick to aid in his climbing. Then the slope smoothed out and the forest returned.

He gnawed on the question of whether to broach the subject of the ghostly visit with Old Bear. It seemed fantastic. Why should some ghost come to him when he was not even of the Icebloods? Surely it must have been a dream – or a delusion. Perhaps just holding such an ancient weapon brought the fancy upon him. He decided to keep quiet about it and not risk the old man's scepticism, or mockery.

Old Bear led them onward to a trodden path through the woods. After a time the wilderness gave way to cleared fields bearing the stubble of last year's crops. Cows grazed here. The straight lines of what looked to be an orchard of apple trees lay on the left. Woodsmoke hung in the air. A distant figure was minding the herd – a youth, perhaps.

Ahead, up the gentle grassy slope, rose a tall building constructed of immense tree trunks. A Greathall. Its roof was covered in faded wooden planks and a great thatch of grasses grew upon it as if it were a field itself. A crowd of ravens walked and hopped about the roof like a troop of guards. A wide dark opening dominated the front. The sun's last amber light struck the building almost from below, so low in the west was it compared to their present height. For a dizzying moment Orman had the impression that they were somehow separate from the world far below.

He was also struck by how familiar the farmstead seemed. Just like home. Old Bear led them on towards it, chickens scrambling outraged from his path. A woman emerged from the doorway. Her

150

hair hung in a long black braid over one shoulder, and she wore tanned leathers. A long-knife stood tall from her belt.

Old Bear raised an arm in greeting. She lifted her chin in response. Orman wondered where everyone was. Back home a hall like this would have been busy with the comings and goings of family, servants and hearthguards. So far, all he'd seen had been the cowherd and this woman. Old Bear led them up the wooden stairs to the threshold.

The woman was tall, like all Icebloods. Orman thought that some would consider her plain and mannish with her thick bones and wide shoulders, but he saw a haunting beauty in dark eyes that seemed full of secret knowledge as she, in turn, studied him.

Old Bear bowed. 'Vala,' he greeted her, 'these are the Reddin brothers, Keth and Kasson. And this is Orman Bregin's son.'

The woman's eyes closed for a moment and she nodded as if she'd already known. Her dark gaze shifted to Boarstooth. 'You carry Svalthbrul,' she murmured, her voice deep and rich. 'As the Eithjar – our elder guardians – whispered.'

Orman simply nodded. 'It comes to me from my father.'

She closed her eyes again. 'I know.' She raised an arm to the broad open doorway. 'Enter, please. You are most welcome. Warm yourselves at our poor hearth. Food and ale will be brought.'

Before they could enter, a great pack of shaggy tall hounds came bounding out to Old Bear. Standing on their hind legs they were nearly fully as tall as he. They barked happily and licked his face while he swatted them aside. They sniffed at Orman and the Reddin brothers and nuzzled their hands as if searching for treats.

Old Bear pushed on in. The interior proved to be one great long hall. The ceiling of log rafters stood some five man-heights above Orman's head. Halfway up the hall's length lay a broad circle of stones enclosing an immense hearth where a banked fire glowed. Smoke rose lazily to a hole in the roof far above. Beyond the hearth stood a long table flanked by wooden benches. Past the table, at the far end of the hall, rose a sort of platform, or dais, supporting three oversized chairs carved of wood: crude thrones of a sort, if that was the right word. Furs and hides lay draped everywhere, even underfoot. Tapestries featuring scenes of nature, trees, streams, the mountains themselves, hung on the walls. Most were dark with soot and half-rotten. What looked like bedding, rolled blankets and more furs, lay bunched up next to the walls.

Old Bear eased himself down at the long table and began searching through the clutter of half-stripped bones and old bread, wooden bowls and drinking horns. He picked up a stoneware jug, peered inside, and grunted happily. He selected a drinking horn, dashed its contents to the floor, and filled it anew.

Orman and the rest watched from next to the hearth. Catching sight of them there, Old Bear impatiently waved them forward. 'Come. Sit. Eat.' He pointed to Gerrun and waved him from the hall. 'Go see what needs doing, hey?'

Grinning, Shortshanks gave an elaborate courtly bow and wandered off. Old Bear chortled at the bow. Orman leaned Boarstooth against a bench and sat. The Reddin brothers sat on opposite sides of the table, facing one another. 'Where is everyone?' Orman asked.

Old Bear was gnawing on a chicken leg. 'Hm? Everyone? Well, now. That's a good question. Never were too many Sayers to begin with. Down to five now. You've seen two of them. Vala, and maybe you spotted her son, Jass. Buri is eldest, but we see him rarely. Always out patrolling the Holding, he is. That leaves Jaochim and Yrain. Master and mistress of the Hold.' He swivelled his one eye about the hall. 'Not in at present.'

'That is all?'

'Mostly. A couple of servants, Leal and Ham. And one other spear, Bernal Heavyhand – heard of him?'

Orman felt his brows rise in surprise. 'Yes. Father spoke of him. I thought he was dead.'

'Not yet. Works as our smith. Game in the leg from the battle of Imre's Ford.'

Orman glanced away. That battle had seen the shattering of Queen Eusta's supporters – his father included. He helped himself to a drinking horn and a share of the warm ale. He sipped the rich malty beer while studying the faded tapestries, the smoke-darkened rafters, the floor of packed dirt covered in straw, and the hounds growling and gnawing on bones under the table. He decided that he'd probably just made a very great mistake. He didn't know what he'd been expecting. But this certainly wasn't it.

Should've taken the gold and his chances down south.

He glanced to the Reddin brothers, but their faces were always so closed it was impossible to see whether they shared his dismay. They sat quietly, peering about the hall, neither eating nor drinking.

Old Bear finished the dregs in his drinking horn and wiped the back of his hand across his beard. 'Well,' he announced. 'It has been a long day's journey.' He gestured to the rolls of furs and blankets against the wall. 'I plan to sleep soundly this night.' He stood, stretching and groaning, and crossed to a pile of bedding which he dragged next to the hearth. He wrapped his old bear cloak about himself and lay down. Two of the huge shaggy hounds padded over and curled up next to him. Orman could only tell which was which from the colours of the ragged pelts: the hounds were an iron-grey, while Old Bear was a ruddy brown.

The brothers shared a glance then followed suit. They unrolled blankets on opposite sides of the broad hearth, set their spears down next to the bedding and began unbuckling their leather hauberks.

Orman, however, did not feel the call of sleep. Restless, he walked down the hall to the doors and stepped out into the gathering dusk. The air was already quite chill. The cold of night came quickly in the heights. Below, the sweep of dark forest descended on and on to end at an arc of glimmering black – the Sea of Gold. Beyond, he thought he could make out the jagged silhouette of the Bone range.

Above, the sky was clear but for a few passing scraps of cloud. The stars seemed so bright and crisp he again had the impression that they were gems he could reach out and pluck. He stood still, enjoying the cold breeze upon his face. While the hall was enormous, far larger than his uncle's, which was the largest outside Mantle town, he'd felt enclosed and uncomfortable within. He much preferred to be outside.

Noise of a footfall brought his attention to a figure climbing the stairs. It was the youth he'd glimpsed minding the cattle. The lad might be younger than he, but stood fully as tall, though lean and gangly. Orman thought him perhaps thirteen. He carried a spear much too large for him.

The youth gave him a solemn nod. 'Welcome to Sayer Hall. I am Jass.'

Orman inclined his head. 'Orman.'

The youth faced the south, gestured down the valley slope. 'You are just come from the southern lands, yes?'

'Yes.'

'You have been to Reach?'

'Yes.'

'You have been to Mantle town?'

'Twice. When I was young.'

'They say there is a keep in Mantle. A Greathall, but built of stone. Is this so?'

Orman glanced to Jass and caught him studying him; the lad quickly looked away. 'Yes. Taller even than your hall.'

The youth pulled at his lip. 'I thought it a story. You have been to Many Saints?'

'No.'

The lad frowned, disappointed. 'But you have seen the shores of the Sea of Gold?'

'Yes, of course.'

'Is it true that they are lined in gold?'

Orman smiled to himself. 'There is some gold in the sands of its beaches. But it is mostly gone now, sifted out over the years. You would like to see the southern lands? Broken Sword? Lillin?'

The youth looked affronted and clasped the spear in both hands. 'Not at all. I'm just curious, that's all.'

Orman worked to keep his face expressionless. How things were the same everywhere! How like himself and his own friends, yearning to see distant lands. Yet this one was an Iceblood – one of the legendary fiends of his own upbringing. Forest demons and child stealers. Dwellers in the misty forests of Joggenhome. He remembered how the mothers of his homestead invoked the name to quiet their children. 'Behave! Or the Icebloods will take you!' Now, standing next to one of their kind, all he could think of was how very similar this lad seemed to him.

He inclined his head in farewell. 'Good night, then.'

Jass answered the gesture with a formal short bow. 'Good night. You may sleep well. I will guard.'

Orman turned away to hide his smile. 'My thanks.'

*

He awoke to licks in the face and dog breath. Groggy, he pushed the hound away and sat up, wiped his mouth. An old woman, heavy at her middle, was setting out bread and jugs on the long table. Leal, he assumed. She gave him a nod in greeting. Apart from the two of them, the hall was empty.

Great bellows and roaring sounded from without. Leal chuckled and shook her head. At his puzzled look, she pointed to the rear. He headed that way. To either side of the slight dais slim passages led to the very rear of the building. Here doors opened on to private chambers. Beyond these, he came to a kitchen area and further narrow doors that opened out to the rear. The bellows and laughter were coming from there.

He stepped out to find a yard of piled firewood, outdoor ovens and fire pits, a chicken coop, outhouses, and a large garden plot. The roars were coming from Old Bear, naked-chested, squatting in a wooden tub while an old man poured jugs of water over him. So hairy was the man over his chest, back and arms, it was as if he still wore his bear cloak. Watching were the Reddin brothers, Gerrun, and a great bald bull of a fellow, with arms as thick as Orman's thighs, a reddish-blond beard, and gold rings in his ears. He wore a thick leather vest that could pass as armour, and buff leather pants. Seeing Orman, he limped over and extended a hand as large as a mattock.

'Greetings, lad. Bernal—'

'Heavyhand. Yes. Old Bear told me you were here.'

'Ah.' He eyed Orman up and down, nodded to himself. Orman raised a questioning brow. 'I see him in you,' the man said. 'Your father.'

'My thanks.'

The huge fellow nodded thoughtfully. 'He was a good friend.'

Old Bear spluttered and gasped anew. 'That is quite enough, Ham,' he gasped. 'You enjoy your chores too much, I think.'

'One must take pleasure from one's work, sor.'

'You look like a sad bear that has fallen into a river,' Bernal called out.

Old Bear pointed to him. 'You are next.'

Bernal laughed and waved him off. 'I think not. I have work to do – can't swan the day away with baths and shaves,' and he limped off around the side of the hall.

Old Bear peered about, looking very alarmed. 'Shaves? Who mentioned shaves? There will be no shaving this bear.'

Keth and Kasson, side by side on a bench, their arms crossed, sat grinning at him. Gerrun called out: 'If we shaved you the only thing left would be a heap of hair.'

Ham threw Old Bear a blanket. 'If you insist, sor. No blade is up to the task in any case, I fear.'

Leal stepped into the yard and half bowed. 'The morning meal.'

Old Bear straightened from the tub and threw his arms out to her. 'Come to me, my dove of love!'

The old woman let out a squeak of terror and ducked back inside.

Orman saw that, impossible as it might seem, the man was twice as hairy from the waist down.

They ate a morning meal of barley porridge and apples. Then Old Bear announced he'd trounce them with any weapon they cared to name. They sparred with spear and staves, then moved on to wooden practice swords. Orman found that while Old Bear could, literally, overbear any of them, his technique with the spear was poor. With the sword he was useless. He wielded it like an axe. After a few bouts Orman began to wonder how on earth the man had lived so long through a lifetime of battle.

With the Reddin brothers it was the other way round. In just a few moves they always had the better of him. Just when he thought it could not be any more embarrassing Kasson reached behind his back to draw twinned long-handled hatchets that he then employed to systematically destroy Orman's defence with spear and sword. Orman was amazed by the weapons. The brothers could weave the spiked and bearded axe-heads to catch swords and yank them aside or deliver a killing thrust that could penetrate mail armour.

As if this humiliation was not enough, it was then Gerrun's turn to beat him armed only with a knife. 'You let me in,' the little fellow warned him. 'Never let a knife-fighter get inside your reach.'

Orman waved him away. 'This is stupid. No one is going to come at me with a knife when I hold a sword.'

Old Bear growled from where he sat on a bench, quite winded. 'If all they have is a cooking pot then that's what they'll come at you with!' He gestured Gerrun forward. 'Again.'

They practised through the full day, taking breaks in which they discussed various techniques and moves. It was during one of these rests that a thought occurred to Orman while he sipped water from a ladle. He looked to the Reddin brothers. 'You two marched north with Longarm's Fifty,' he said. 'When you were here, in the Blood range, did you . . . you know . . .' He motioned to Sayer Hall.

The brothers shook their heads. Keth studied the edge of one of his hatchets, sheathed it at his back. 'The Bains,' he answered, low.

'The Bains,' Orman repeated. 'Did you face, you know, that one – Lotji?'

'We didn't,' Kasson said. 'But we saw him fight.'

'And?'

The brothers exchanged a look, said nothing.

Old Bear loudly cleared his throat. 'Lad,' he said. 'It's one thing to learn how to fight. Any fool can do that. But it's a damned ugly business, risking death and hurting people. Few really enjoy it. But that one does. To him, it's a game. As in the old days, when the fighting was constant between the clans. Now there's too few of them.' The old fellow pulled his fingers through his scraggly beard. 'He misses those days, I suppose,' he mused. Rousing himself, he slapped his hands to his thighs and stood. 'Now, more spear work, I think. Try to keep us at a distance, hey?'

Orman groaned inwardly, but he understood what they were doing. He was carrying Boarstooth: he would be the mark of anyone
they met.

In the evening they ate a meal of freshly baked bread, a steaming
soup of boiled vegetables and barley, baked pheasant, apples, and
weak beer. Old Bear was in a great humour. He entertained them
all with the story of Ruckar Myrni and the slaying of the ice-drake
in the heights of the Salt range, and all the frozen maidens he found
greatly in need of warming. 'You can be sure,' he finished, 'that
Ruckar thawed the heart of each of them!'

Noise at the entrance brought their attention round. Vala was
there with Jass. She pushed him in and followed behind. The lad's
light brown hair was slicked back, and he wore a belted shirt of mail
that was far too long for him and a large knife at his hip, its ivory
handle wound with silver wire. They climbed the platform at the
end of the hall, where Vala sat in the centre chair while he stepped
forward to stand before her.

He shot one uncertain glance back to her, and she nodded for
him to continue. He faced them once more. 'Greetings,' he began,
and cleared his throat. His voice was still a touch high. 'I am Jass
Sayer. In the name of our clan I welcome you to our hearth and hall.
I understand that there are those among you who would pledge your
spear and arm to guard our Holding. Would these men stand forth?'

Orman recognized the formula – though it was an oddly archaic
form. The swearing of the hearthguards. Keth and Kasson also no
doubt knew it. He looked to them. They shared a glance, then Keth
stood and approached the raised dais. It came up to his knees.

Jass clasped his hands behind his back. With the aid of the dais
he stood eye to eye with the rather tall Keth. The lad glanced back
to Vala. She mouthed something. He turned back. He cleared his
throat once more, obviously quite nervous. 'Say your name so that
all within may know it,' he said.

'Keth, Reddin's son.'

'Keth, Reddin's son, we Sayer swear that these lands, this hall,
our Holdings, shall be your home so long as you shall defend it. Do
you pledge your spear, your arm, and your heart to its defence?'

'I do so swear.'

A cold breeze tickled Orman's neck and he turned, sure that
someone had passed behind him. But no one was there. He had the
sudden feeling that far more Sayers than Vala and Jass were now
present in the hall as witnesses to this swearing.

'Very good. We accept your pledge and give our own.'

He turned back to Vala and she handed him a basket. From this he took a small round bread and gave it to Keth. Then a small cake of salt. And finally a tiny round object that flashed gold – a ring. These Keth gathered up.

'Welcome, Keth, Reddin's son. Guard to our hearth, hall, and Hold.'

Keth sketched a slight dip of his head and backed away.

Kasson followed and exchanged the same pledge. Then Orman approached the dais. Jass gave him a shy smile. 'Say your name so that all within may know it,' he repeated.

'Orman, Bregin's son.'

The smile was whipped away. Jass gaped, then spun to Vala. She gave a straight-lipped nod to indicate that he should continue. He slowly turned back and Orman saw wonder in the lad's eyes. He wasn't certain what he'd said or done wrong – was Bregin un-welcome here?

The lad appeared quite shaken. He had to clear his throat before he could go on, and when he did speak again it was distractedly, his voice faint and weak. Orman received his bread and salt and gold ring from the lad's hands, then gave a small bow and returned to his seat.

Jass sat down in the chair on Vala's left. He still could not take his eyes from Orman. Vala leaned forward, calling, 'Leal! Ale for our hearthguards! Let them never know need or want here within our walls.'

'Yes, m'lady.' The servant woman disappeared into the kitchens, while Old Bear swatted the Reddin brothers and Orman about the back and shoulders.

'Well done! Well done. Now you need not kill yourselves sweating for starvation wages among the lowlander filth. Serve well and you will be rewarded!'

Leal returned carrying a large tray bearing flagons. Gerrun jumped up to ease the heavy burden from the elderly woman's hands then shooed her back for another. He thumped it down on the table and Old Bear rescued a jug that was about to fall.

Keth took up a round loaf of bread, tore off a piece and thrust the rest at Orman, who was slow to take it as he was watching Vala and Jass. The two had their heads together, Jass imploring, animated, she soothing and calm, a hand at his shoulder. They must have reached some sort of agreement as he pulled away from her hand to jump from the dais. He came to Orman's side. 'May we speak?' he asked, his voice stiff and very formal.

Orman nodded, still rather bemused. 'Of course.'

Jass motioned to the front. Orman followed him outside.

They stood side by side again, both peering out over the sweeping descent of this shoulder of the Salt range. Evening was gathering once more, and the wind was cool and damp. Orman reflected that spring was coming to the heights. Soon all the passes would be open.

In time, Jass took a breath and raised a hand to point downslope. 'Jaochim says there are many more fires below and lights upon the Gold Sea. Is this what you saw in the south?'

Orman thought of his ghostly visitor and her words: a time of change was coming. He nodded. 'Yes. Many foreigners are coming. They want the gold on your lands.'

'We will defend our Holding,' the youth said, utterly assured. 'It is us and we are it.'

'Of course.'

The young man answered Orman's nod. He swallowed, his jaws clenching, and Orman could see he was steeling himself to raise something. 'Here we are once more,' the youth observed. 'Studying the night.' Jass turned to him, his eyes almost level. 'Orman,' he said, 'I am the son of Vala Sayer. But I am only half Sayer, as I am also my father's son. I am Jass, Bregin's son.' He held out his hand.

Orman could not breathe. The outstretched hand. So small, he thought. So vulnerable. Then for some reason his vision swam and his chest burned like a forge. Finally, with difficulty, he managed to swallow the lump that was throttling him and he took the hand in his and squeezed.

'Greetings and well met, elder brother,' Jass said.

'Well met, little brother,' he choked out.

CHAPTER V

AFTER CONSIDERING FOR TWO NIGHTS AND A DAY WHAT TO CALL their Andii guest, Fisher offered the name Jethiss. The man accepted it graciously as Fisher knew he would, for whatever else the Tiste Andii might have lost he had not forgotten his manners. As was the custom among the older races, gifts were not to be disputed or examined, but received with gratitude and an understanding of the obligation that binds giver and receiver.

The name was the best Fisher could parse out of the ancient lays and hero-songs that had come down to him from Tiste-influenced sources. It translated, roughly, as one-who-comes-from-the-sea. He thought it appropriate, descriptive, and poetic. The man simply took it on without question and was, from then onward, Jethiss.

He was kitted out from among the Malazan party, and so he wore thick sailor-style trousers tucked into tall leather moccasins that were bound by wrapped cloth and leather. He was given a faded gambeson of quilted linen and hide and a leather hauberk sewn with iron rings and lozenges to pull over it. A scuffed belt and worn gloves completed his accoutring. He was offered a battered iron pot-helmet, but turned it down, preferring instead to go bareheaded, his long hair loose.

The only thing missing was a weapon. After much cadging and harassing, Fisher was able to wheedle a set of Wickan long-knives out of a sympathetic veteran. The man had them at the bottom of his kit as souvenirs of an old campaign. The curved knives were wrapped in oiled cloth but were badly corroded none the less. Jethiss selected a flat rock and scraped the blades as he walked along through the days.

The party ascended winding mountain trails. The way was rocky, the slopes bare, and Fisher wondered if perhaps it was this feature of the landscape that lay behind the name the Bone Peninsula. He wondered, but was not convinced. Marshal Teal and his Letherii soldiers led the column. Malle and her Malazan guard followed. Enguf and his Genabackan pirates came bringing up the rear, puffing and sweating, unaccustomed as they were to any long overland march.

Fisher and Jethiss walked with Malle's guard of twenty Malazan veterans. The Gris matriarch still rode her donkey, as sure-footed as any of its kind. Its hooves clicked and clattered over the stones as they climbed. At times the Cawn mage Holden walked with Fisher, but most of the time the mage walked alone, taking notes and making sketches – all for his hobby of natural philosophy, or so he claimed. Fisher wished he would simply drop the pretence, as he believed he knew what the man was doing. Especially as he once came quietly upon the fellow and heard him counting his steps as he paced along.

It was no surprise to him that the Malazans would be taking an interest in the interior of Assail, although if he'd been consulted he would have advised them not to get involved; in his opinion it was a pit that would swallow any entity foolish enough to jump in.

However, if the Malazans were casting an appraising eye over these lands, it was not his concern. Politics was not his province. It was history that interested him, both ancient and current. The mystery of their guest, for example. Who was he? What was his past? There were fewer and fewer Andii to be found these days. The fall of Moon's Spawn had marked the end of an age for their kind. He'd heard that they had departed Coral. There were rumours that they'd withdrawn to the island of Avalli; one of the many rumours constantly swirling about the Andii and their supposedly devious plans and intentions.

He did not know any of the Andii personally. Few outside their society did. And they were a race well known for their similarity in face and kind. To put it bluntly: to outsiders they all looked alike. This one had the build and grace of a swordsman. His mind might be smothered by the trauma of his near-drowning, or perhaps as the result of a sorcerous attack, yet his hands knew what to do when they took up the long-knives. No clumsiness or hesitation there.

When they first walked together Fisher felt a strong temptation to quiz the man – to aid in the recovery of his memories, of course. Not to mention for the satisfaction of his own curiosity. Yet he held back, for he did not wish his company to become trying and thereby drive the fellow from him. And so as they walked he avoided all direct interrogation, preferring instead to amplify upon any questions the man posed, hoping that such information might elicit a memory or two.

Music seemed to please the Andii. And so Fisher had his idum out as they went, freely strumming, composing lines and melodies. The Malazan veterans in line about them were just as free with their comments. Most involved uses for which the instrument was not intended. However, none, he noted, ever actually told him to put it away.

He had an ulterior motive for strumming fragments of songs, of course. He knew that music could pluck the deepest memories from the recesses of human minds. He'd seen it often enough wherever he played, were it in the field around a fire, in the most isolated back-woods tavern, or in the richest court. A scrap of melody, or a turn of phrase, could summon images just as powerfully as any magic – and so indeed were bards considered to possess their own sort of sorcery.

He'd seen tears brought to the eyes of oldsters as they relived a childhood memory long thought buried. He'd heard people confess that they could almost hear the sea or smell the forest where they last heard this or that song. Or feel again the touch of a departed lover. It was not precisely why he pursued the craft and art of his calling. But it was close.

And so he strummed phrases from old lays and ballads as they climbed the paths through thick forest and over steep bare slopes of broken tilted stone. And occasionally their guest's pace faltered. He would pause as if distracted, cock his head as if searching for some flitting scrap of something. Sometimes he would frown and his hands clench as if he were reliving some powerful emotion. Yet the man seemed unaware of all this himself. He would walk on without comment. Perhaps shake his head once or twice as if freeing it from some clinging fugue or daydream.

Fisher was not surprised. He knew that music spoke to the emotions, not the intellect. The heart was where people truly lived, and died. He also knew that this magic that music and poetry were said to possess was the power to touch that heart. So he pursued his phrasings from melodies and strumming from ancient hero cycles and lays. Perhaps at some point Jethiss might stop and turn to him and say with wonder: *that reminds me . . .*

The inland valleys and forests they crossed were not entirely empty. Tiny villages huddled here and there. Their inhabitants were a trickle of homesteaders slowly journeying inland and north from the lower, more settled, part of the peninsula. To a man and woman they looked with stunned incomprehension upon the arrival of this pocket army of outlanders.

To Fisher's relief, Teal was strict in keeping his guard in hand. If they came across a clutch of chickens, not all were taken. Maize cribs were not entirely emptied. Larders were thinned, but not cleaned out. It seemed the Letherii officer was more than familiar with the art of taxing to the very bone – but not beyond. The Malazans under Malle were particularly watchful of the women and girls. It seemed they did not want to leave behind a name synonymous with wholesale rape and murder, and this also Fisher could not fail to note.

Enguf's Genabackan pirates, however, clung hard to their traditional right to rape, murder, loot and burn. It took the threat of turning upon them from both Teal's guard and Malle's veterans to bring it to a stop. Even then, the Letherii and Malazans had to divide their time between scavenging for provisions and guarding the cottages and farms. Enguf's crew were mutinous, but their captain kept reminding them of the real reward ahead – all the gold they could carry. As it was, Fisher believed a number of the crew members had dropped away as they'd journeyed inland. Deserted with an eye on plain old-fashioned brigandage, probably.

On the seventh day he found the Cawn mage Holden waiting for him as he slogged past along a forest trail. He stepped out of the column and raised his brows in a question. The mage waved him over, then led him up a thin path through the woods. A cottage built of wattle and daub stood ahead, roofed in straw. The young and rather sour-faced mage of Cat, Alca, was standing with what Fisher presumed was the settler himself, a youngish fellow in tattered shirt and trousers with a defiant look on his lined face.

'What is it?' Fisher asked Holden.

'Intelligence – if you can call it that.'

Fisher nodded a greeting to the farmer, who returned the gesture.

'Would you care to repeat what you've said?' Alca asked him.

The man nodded, his jaws set. 'Aye. I'm not afeared.'

Fisher wanted to ask what the man was not afraid of, but decided not to interrupt.

'You are travelling the Wight Road,' the farmer said, addressing himself to Fisher. The way was actually more of a path, an old trail that linked passes through the high ridges, but Fisher did not correct him.

163

'Yes.'

'You should turn back.'

Fisher glanced to the mages. Holden's face held scepticism, even tolerant amusement; Alca was grim, as if she was conducting an interrogation. 'Oh? Why is that?'

'Because o' the Bonewight.'

Fisher nodded. This was the 'monster' he'd warned Malle about. It was the 'lurking threat' mentioned in the old lays. 'I know the old stories. All that was long ago.'

The man shook his head. Fisher now saw that he was even younger than he'd thought. The hardscrabble life here in the wilderness had aged him brutally. ''Twas and 'twasn't. It was and it still is. It will come. It wards the way north.'

Now Fisher frowned, struck by something. '"Wards"?' he asked.

'How do you know this?' Alca demanded. 'No one else has said anything.'

The settler shifted his attention to her. He held his chin high, defiant still. 'They are all afeared o' the Jotunfiend.'

Holden scowled his impatience. 'Jotunfiend? You mean a ghoul? A ghostie?'

'It's as real as you strange foreigners.'

'And where is this monster?' Alca demanded.

'It waits under its bridge.'

Holden let out a snort and pressed a hand to his forehead. 'Ogres under bridges . . .' He shook his head, looked to Fisher. 'Never mind. Seems our friend here has heard the same old ghost stories you have.' He waved Alca off. 'Let's go.'

The two mages left to return to the column. Fisher studied the slate-hued overcast sky where it showed between the trees. It looked like rain. He returned his gaze to the settler, who glared back, his jaws set once more. 'Thank you for the warning,' he said.

'It is real,' the man growled resentfully.

'Thank you.' Fisher turned to go.

As he was walking up the trail, the man shouted after him: 'It took my brother!'

Fisher glanced back but the man had turned away to return to his work, cutting wood. The bard stood for a time, watching, but the man said no more. Fisher returned to the column.

When he fell in with the Malazans once more, Jethiss gave him a questioning look. Fisher gestured ahead, where the ground climbed to another ridge and another high pass. 'Some sort of possible threat ahead. Something haunting the highlands.'

164

Jethiss nodded. 'Ah. I saw your mage friends. They did not appear convinced.'

Fisher chuckled. 'No. But then, they have not seen what I have seen.'

'And neither have I, it would seem.'

Fisher studied him, his lined face, his blowing white-streaked hair. 'I believe you have. You just do not remember it.'

The man gave an easy shrug. 'Perhaps. Immaterial now. What is gone is gone. How could I miss that which I do not even recall?'

Sidelong, Fisher studied the man. Could he cultivate such an untroubled equanimity if he'd lost all that he'd ever been? He doubted it. It would take a strong and centred spirit to awake into a strange new existence and still keep one's sanity. Let alone one's sense of humour, or irony.

He shivered in the cold wind blowing down out of the heights and shaking the trees. Dampness chilled it. A late snowstorm? Would the pass be open? He pulled his travelling cloak tighter about himself. 'The old songs and stories are consistent on it. There must be *something* there.'

'Perhaps they merely reference one another, perpetuating the myth.'

He walked for a time in silence. Ahead, Malle, the old Gris matriarch on her donkey, raised a parasol and opened it. Fisher held out a hand; a few drops struck. A cold rain. And perhaps snow in the upper passes. This late in the season, too. He drew his idum from his back to check its oiled leather wrap. 'Perhaps,' he allowed. 'We shall see.'

That night it snowed. Fisher watched it from the open front of his tent. The fat flakes hissed and melted as they slapped the ground.

He played late into the evening. At times Jethiss stirred, thrashing on his bedding. It was not until Fisher put away the instrument and lay down upon his own Malazan-issued blankets that he realized he'd unconsciously been playing themes from *Anomandaris*, his epic lay concerning Anomander Rake.

Yelling from somewhere in the camp shocked him awake in the dead of night. He bolted up, pulled on his boots, and ran out of the tent in his leather shirt and trousers. Almost everyone was up and milling about, most running to the perimeter. He spotted Marshal Teal with a bodyguard of four men, jogging for Enguf's camp, and followed. The pirate commander was shouting and waving to disperse his crew back to their campfires and tents.

Marshal Teal closed upon the captain. 'What was it?' he demanded. 'What happened?'

Enguf was bleeding at the mouth. He wiped away the blood with the back of his hand. 'Just a difference of opinion regarding this expedition of yours.'

Teal's brows arched. 'A difference of opinion? Really.'

'We were debating its merits.'

'A debate? Is that what this was? Sounded more like a damned tavern brawl.'

The captain rubbed his jaw. 'For the Southern Confederacy, this was a debate.'

'I see. Well, perhaps next time you could conduct your debating in such a manner that you do not alarm the entire camp.'

'Well, perhaps I'll just raise that at the next meeting!'

'Gentlemen,' Fisher interrupted. 'It's over now, whatever it was. I suggest we continue this discussion in the morning.'

Marshal Teal eyed him up and down, his mouth a sour line. 'Very well. However,' and he waved at him, 'next time you respond to an alarm . . . I suggest you bring a weapon.' And he stormed off.

Fisher watched him go, then looked down. It was true; he hadn't brought a weapon. Not even his belt.

Enguf muttered under his breath, 'The lads and lasses don't like it. All this marching, with no loot in sight. Plenty of targets left behind along the coast . . .' He shook his shaggy head and peered closely at Fisher. 'How far now, would you say?'

Fisher let out a breath. His shoulders were damp and chilled with melted snow. 'We're close to the highest passes. Downhill from then on to the Sea of Gold.'

'The Sea of Gold so close, you say?' He nodded, impressed. 'They'll like that. Maybe that'll keep 'em quiet.' He frowned then, looking Fisher up and down as well. 'And don't come running without a weapon, y'damned fool.' He lumbered off.

Fisher turned away to go back to his tent and flinched, almost jumping. Jethiss was there. The man seemed to have appeared from nowhere, emerging from the dark like magic. He held something out to him: his sheathed sword wrapped in its belt. Fisher ruefully shook his head and took it from him.

*

Two days later they tramped through the slush and muck of lingering snow cover. They were high here, but nowhere near the treeline. The spine of the Bone Peninsula did not rise anywhere as high as the

Salt range. They marched through coniferous forest; the tall pine and spruce growing far apart, with moss and bare rock and patches of snow between. Ahead lay a pass, the ridgeline not far away.

Fisher was just thinking how quiet everything had been so far when he spotted Teal's forward scouts come running pell-mell back to the column. He jogged up to the front along with some of Malle's people.

The scouts were panting and short of breath. 'What is it?' Teal snapped.

'Some kind of bridge,' one of them managed, gulping and pointing ahead. 'Spans a defile. Looks like the only way across.'

Fisher caught Holden's eye; the mage rolled his gaze skyward. Teal grunted. 'Imagine that. Let's take a look.' He turned to his men, called, 'Spread out,' and signed the order. The Letherii troops quickly shuffled to right and left, forming a skirmish line. The Malazans and Genabackans followed suit. Malle remained behind with a guard of five veterans. Fisher and Jethiss joined the line.

Hunched, dodging from tree to tree, Fisher edged up next to Holden. 'A bridge . . .' he murmured.

'Just because there's some old relic bridge doesn't mean . . .'

The scouts signalled from the forward right, and the skirmish line shifted that way. They came to the broken rock of the ridge. Mixed snow and rain swirled down. Fisher's hands were becoming chill in the cloth he'd wrapped around them. He edged forward to peer over the lip. A steep slope of bare rock overlooked a dark defile. Blowing snow obscured the further distances.

Holden murmured from next to him, 'Where in Togg's name is the way down?'

Fisher peered around as well – where was it?

Down the ridge behind him, Jethiss pointed off to the south. Fisher nodded and touched Holden's shoulder, and they pushed themselves back from the lip. Off to the south of their position Teal was conferring with his scouts and a few of Malle's veterans. The pair jogged over to join them.

'One at a time, I reckon,' one scout was saying.

'A night-time descent?' Teal asked.

The scouts shook their heads. 'Too dangerous.' Teal looked even more sour.

'So where's this bridge?' Holden asked.

'Switchback trail leads down to it,' a scout said.

'See us coming five league away,' one of the veterans grumbled.

'No signa any guards so far,' another scout pointed out.

'Not yet,' Teal breathed absently, peering away into the gusting snow. Then he scowled, muttering, 'Darkness take them . . .'

Fisher glanced over. Enguf and a handful of his crew were sauntering up.

'What's all this?' the Genabackan called out.

The scouts all winced. The veterans hung their heads.

'Quiet,' Teal hissed.

'What's that?' the man shouted back. 'What?'

Fisher could swear veins were writhing in the Letherii commander's temples. Through clenched teeth he grated, '*Quiet*.'

Enguf was now close enough to hear and he nodded. 'Ah! Quiet. Very well. May I ask why?'

Teal was pressing his fingertips to his brow, his head lowered.

'The scouts think they saw a bridge down the trail here,' one of Malle's old veterans said. 'But the clouds closed in on us so we can't be sure. Why don't you take your boys down and have a look?'

Fisher glared at the man, but the rest of the veterans were grinning. One had a strip of dried meat held in his teeth. Sucking on it to soften it, Fisher knew.

'No thank you,' Enguf answered. 'We're happy where we are.'

It was good to know that the Genabackan wasn't a complete fool.

'You Malazans go down under cover of these clouds,' Teal said, raising his head. 'Reconnoitre.'

The four veterans exchanged slow looks. 'Don't think so,' answered the one who'd spoken earlier.

Teal studied the man for a moment. 'You don't . . .' He drew a breath. 'Go down and reconnoitre . . . soldier.'

The Malazan's stare was steady. Then he gave a small shrug of his rounded shoulders. 'I don't take orders from you.'

Teal appeared ready to bring the rocks down around them excoriating the man, so Fisher jumped in, saying, 'What's your name, soldier?'

The man's gaze swung to him. It was half-lidded, distant, the eyes a pale hazel. Fisher recognized the loose watchfulness of someone poised to kill at any moment. Not your usual veteran. A trained bodyguard, perhaps? But field experienced, obviously.

'Stub,' the man said. 'Sergeant Stub.'

Teal nodded brusquely. 'Thank you, Fisher.' To the sergeant, he said: 'I will have a word with your employer regarding your insubordination, soldier. You can be sure of that.'

The man actually gave Teal a wink, saying, 'You do that.'

But irony appeared lost on Teal, who merely nodded, indicating that he most certainly would.

There seemed to be an impasse, as none of the three parties was willing to risk men on the steep twisting trail down to the hidden defile below. Fisher blew on his hands to warm them; his homeland's chill cut deeper than any he'd encountered elsewhere. It struck him that one man might sneak down whereas a full party would make too much noise.

'I will go,' he said.

Teal's quick nod of acceptance seemed to say it was about time he did something useful. The veteran, Stub, frowned, either displeased or uneasy, Fisher wasn't certain which. He started down the trailhead. It was extraordinarily steep; to keep from falling he had to lean into the slope, running his hands along the rock as he descended. Gusting curtains of snow obscured the bottom. The sky was iron-grey, the rock slate-hued, or black with melt and ice, while the snow seemed to swallow everything down its swirling leaden throat.

After many switchbacks, he stepped out on to a relatively flat ledge. It was wide and deep. He thought he could make out a structure of sorts at its far end and was about to step towards it when movement in the corner of his eye snapped him round, sword out.

It was Jethiss. Fisher let out a breath, sheathed his sword. 'You needn't have come,' he whispered.

'I could not let you go alone.'

'You are very quiet.'

'Thank you.'

Fisher gestured ahead. 'What do you sense?'

The Andii's long-jawed face hardened in distaste. The contrary gusting winds whipped his white-streaked hair. 'Something terrible. A crime.'

Fisher nodded his agreement. They spread apart and advanced. The structure emerged from the flurries: tall and thin, the landing or buttress of a bridge that went on to span the defile ahead. The bridge, however, was not a suspended arc of rope and wood, as Fisher expected. It was the trellis sort, one that descended in segments all the way down into the darkness where, presumably, it rested upon the uneven ground below.

He heard a grunt from Jethiss at his side, a gut-punched exhalation of shock, or revulsion, and the man stopped advancing. A few steps later the bridge resolved clearly in his vision and he halted, stunned. The whole thing, the tower buttress, the bed, the trellis supporting structure, was built entirely of bones.

Not an exaggeration then, he mused. Nor poetic metaphor. The majority of the upper segments appeared to be built of thinner, less robust bones, while the lower he cast his eye down the immense edifice the thicker and heavier became the bones. Some seemed even gigantic, though the scale was difficult to make out. He was curious as to how they were all attached, or woven together, as it were, but he did not wish to approach any closer.

They backed away. At the base of the trail they found the four veterans, including Sergeant Stub. Fisher sent him an arched brow. The man raised his eyes to the sky. 'Couldn't let you do m'damned work.' He gestured ahead. 'So? What is it?'

'It is a bridge,' Fisher allowed. 'Made of bones.'

'Hunh,' the man grunted. 'That's not you bein' all bardish, is it?'

'No. Sadly not.'

'Well. Ain't that a curiosity, then.'

'It is a perversion,' Jethiss supplied, his voice hard.

Fisher was surprised by the man's vehemence. He might be without conscious memories, but this artefact seemed to have touched him. It outraged something deep within him. Through slit eyes the sergeant studied the Andii for a time. He rubbed his thumb over his scarred chin. Then he motioned his companions forward. 'Take a look-see.' Before they could obey, tumbling gravel and rocks announced the arrival of Teal and the van of his force.

'Afraid we found a copper sliver and he won't get his share,' Stub murmured to Fisher, who answered with a quick grin.

'What is it?' Teal demanded.

'It really is a bridge of bone,' Fisher said.

'Sounds unsteady,' the marshal remarked, as if its engineering was the only question of relevance. Holden and Alca arrived, slipping and sliding down the sheer trail.

'This stinks of Elder magic,' the ex-cadre mage warned, short of breath.

'I will examine it,' Alca said.

Holden thrust an arm out before her. 'Don't be a fool!'

'We should go around,' Fisher said.

'And how many weeks would that cost us?' Teal answered impatiently.

'Thought you'd be all cat-curious,' Stub said to Fisher, grinning.

Jethiss suddenly spoke over everyone: 'You are all in great danger here. You should all leave.'

Stub and Teal examined the man as if questioning his sanity. Teal arched a brow. 'Thank you for the valuable insight.' He gestured, inviting Stub forward. 'Shall we look?'

The sergeant shrugged once more. 'I'll take a peek.'

The party edged forward together, the Letherii and Malazans drawing swords or readying crossbows and bows. Fisher heard Malle descending the trail on her donkey, along with Enguf and his party. He advanced with the soldiers through the gusting snow until the edifice resolved into view once more. The soldiers grunted or swore as they made out the grisly details of its construction. It seemed to Fisher that the snowstorm was thinning. He could see further down into the defile, which was far indeed.

The mages snarled warnings then, leaping back. Jethiss pulled Fisher by the arm. The soldiers shuffled backwards. The very ground they stood upon was heaving. Bones of every sort and description were pushing their way up through the dirt and gravel: animal scapulae, pelvises and femurs, all sturdy and large; dirty human bones still holding tatters of ligaments, these mostly the long limb bones of femur, humerus, and tibia. Mixed in among them all came enormous bones to which Fisher could not put a name: the remains of giants, he wondered, or perhaps dragons. Bones as tall as he and as thick around as his torso.

The macabre collection slid and grated together into a heap before the entrance to the bridge. As the parties continued to retreat, the bones assembled themselves before their eyes into a gruesome skeleton of gigantic size that reared fully some four man-heights above them.

Its legs were built of the most massive of the remains, the dragon or elephant bones. Its pelvis was constructed of many such pelvises, lashed and articulated by slithering ligament and tendon. Its ribs might have been those of the fearsome sea-behemoths, so massive was their arch. Its spine was a pile of segments, any one of which was probably as large as Fisher's own pelvis. The flat blades of its scapulae were constructed of many taken from elk or similar giant ungulates. The longest of the bones banged and scraped together to build its arms, the reach of which made Fisher despair. It had them all easily within its sweep.

Yet Fisher saw no skull of any kind. Was it headless? Or the skull yet to be assembled? The hands, constructed of the lesser human bones, now clutched and flexed. They swung down, digging into the ground, working and probing. When they emerged, throwing up a great swathe of dirt and gravel that everyone raised their arms against as it came pattering and clattering down, they held an immense object that rained more dirt and mud. The creature set it upon its own shoulders. As the dirt fell away, Fisher made out the elongated muzzle and fleshless grin of a dragon skull.

Cold intelligence regarded them through the empty dark sockets. No one, Fisher noted, had run; all had understood that the creature had them within its reach. All gripped weapons, were hunched for battle. The Malazan veterans had even readied their broad heavy-infantry shields.

All except Jethiss, who stood with arms crossed, an expression upon his face that Fisher could only interpret as disgust.

'Pay the price,' the creature boomed in a voice that brought rocks tumbling down the trail, 'and you may pass.'

The Cawn mage Holden stepped forward. Fisher had to give the ex-cadre mage his due: the man was damned brave. 'What is your price?'

'One in three must give his bones.'

Malle, just behind Fisher, let her breath out in a furious hiss. 'This is not to be borne,' she murmured.

'And if we merely turn round?' Holden asked.

'Fight or flee, the bones of all will stay behind.'

'A steep price then,' Teal whispered to Malle. 'But better than . . .' He tailed off, because Jethiss had stepped forward.

'What is your name?' the Andii demanded.

Teal glared at Fisher. 'Shut that damned fool up before he gets us all killed!'

The giant's dragon skull turned to examine Jethiss. 'You ask my name,' it boomed. 'You who do not even know your own.'

Fisher could have sworn that Jethiss literally jumped into the air at that. His arms fell to his sides, his hands clutched. He edged even closer to the creature. 'Give me my name.'

The dark empty sockets regarded him steadily. Fisher thought he glimpsed dark blue-black flames flickering within. 'I will strike a bargain with thee, child of the Andii.' Its voice growled and rolled, and struck echoes from deep within the defile below. 'Give me your bones and all others may keep theirs.'

'And my name?'

'That you shall have – for a time.'

Fisher lunged forward. 'No!'

'Done,' Jethiss called out, sweeping a hand to seal the bargain.

Fisher gripped his arm. 'Are you a fool? What have you done?'

The man offered a crooked smile. 'I have bought my name – at a fair price.'

'At the price of your life!'

'At the price of saving near twenty.'

Fisher released him, let out a ragged breath. 'Well, yes. But still . . .'

'All must pass now!' the creature boomed. 'Go!'

Marshal Teal approached, inclined his head to Jethiss. He regarded him for a time as if searching for the right words, then said, 'You may not believe me when I say this . . . but I understand what you are doing. We in Lether believe that everything has a price, but we are not fools. We understand that the most important things are paid for with blood. And so I salute you. You have found something more precious than life . . . I can only hope to find a thing so precious myself one day.' And he bowed again, then waved his guard forward.

Malle came next – on foot. One of her guards led her mount. She studied Jethiss closely, peering sharply at him. 'This is distasteful to me,' she said. 'Especially when,' and she leaned forward, lowering her voice, 'as you fighting men say, I believe we could have taken him.'

Jethiss smiled again. 'At the price of many more than twenty, I should think.'

Her mouth remained a tight slash. 'Still, I do not like it.' She shook her head, cast a quick glance to the creature, which had raised its notched skull and now stared into the distance, seemingly paying no attention, and whispered, 'Remember your ancestry.' She bowed, and moved away. Her Malazan guard of veterans followed. Every one of them saluted.

Enguf came last. He was rubbing the back of his neck and looking quite sheepish. 'A third of my lads and lasses thank you heartily. I tell you, they were all for running off. But now . . . well. We can hardly do that, hey?' The man obviously wanted to say more but couldn't find the words. Finally, tears in his eyes, he lunged forward and enveloped the much taller Andii in a great hug, thumping him on the back. Releasing him, he growled, 'I hope you find what you're looking for, man. I truly do.' He waved his Genabackan crew onward. Some of these, when they passed, just stared at Jethiss as if they thought him touched.

Then Fisher was alone with him. Jethiss gently urged him onward. 'Go on. Go with my blessings. You saved me. Brought me to my name. You have my thanks.'

Fisher found himself shaking his head. 'I'm not going.'

The Andii frowned. A touch of anger hardened his face. 'Now who is playing the fool . . .'

Above them, the giant was stirring. Its titanic skull was lowering to regard them. Fisher leaned close to Jethiss. 'You see . . . I too would like to know your name.'

Then the gigantic bone hands swept in and closed upon them, sweeping them off their feet and swinging them into the air, and Fisher screamed his surprise and terror as the creature took one great leap into the defile.

It thrust them into a cave that opened directly on to the sheer cliff. Fisher could see no way down as he was pushed within. The hands released them to fall to a rocky floor.

'My name!' Jethiss yelled into the absolute night surrounding them.

The rumbling voice echoed back, mocking. 'I did not say when you would have it.' Then Fisher sensed they were alone in the inky black.

'I am sorry,' Jethiss said from off to one side.

'It's all right. We still have our bones.'

'For a time,' Jethiss agreed.

Fisher felt at his back then, alarmed. He whipped the idum from where he'd slung it and gingerly felt along its wrapped length to find that the neck was broken. 'Damn.'

'What is it?'

'Broke my neck.'

'Your neck!'

Fisher snorted a laugh. 'Sorry – the neck of my instrument.'

'Oh.'

A hand clasped Fisher's arm and helped him upright. 'You can see?' Fisher marvelled.

'I see fine. Why?'

'I cannot. Although . . .' He squinted in one direction. 'I believe I see some sort of a glow off that way. A fire?'

After a moment Jethiss answered, 'I see it as well.' The hand pulled lightly. 'I will guide you.'

Fisher shifted the hand to his elbow. 'There.'

'Ah. I see.'

It couldn't have been that far, but the walk seemed excruciatingly long to Fisher. He lost count of the number of times he barked his shins on rocks, or twisted his ankles on the uneven cave floor. At times Jethiss had him duck under low-hanging formations or ledges. Eventually, as they neared the fire, he could see better and better, and finally he eased free of the Andii's hand.

They came to a very modest little fire that gave hardly any light or heat. It appeared to be built of old dry roots and other such burnable trash. In the utter black of the cave, however, it felt wonderful to Fisher. He knelt to warm his hands at it.

Jethiss breathed a low warning: 'We are not alone.'

Fisher straightened.

Two figures came emerging from the murk. Twins they appeared, so alike were they, both in rough torn leathers, both squat with extraordinarily burly muscular builds, like wrestlers, and both as hairy as bears. One was mostly bald, with gold earrings; the other sported a great massed curly nest about his head. Twigs rode in their thick black and russet beards. Long-knives and hatchets were tucked into their leather belts.

For a time they stared at each other, wordless. Then the massively haired one struck the bald one in the chest, saying, 'It's that songster, Fisher. Hey, Fish. Remember us?'

Fisher squinted. He knew the accent. It was a northerner's . . . 'I'm sorry . . . I don't . . .'

The hairy one thumped his companion in his massive chest again, once more raising a cloud of dust. 'It's us! Badlands and Coots! Remember us? We're of the Losts!'

And Fisher remembered, and he pressed a hand to his forehead. 'Oh, no . . .'

*   *   *

A warband ambushed Kyle when he was a few days inland. He was not surprised. He knew that though these lands might appear a wasteland to some, to those who lived here it was their territory, their home, to be guarded against trespassers who would strain its already slim resources.

They were on foot, and arose all at once from the stiff grasses and brush of the rolling hills. He halted and raised his hands to demonstrate his peaceful intent. They wore headscarves and treated hides laced together as leathers, and carried spears, with bone-handled knives at their waists. What Kyle noticed right away was the striking similarity they bore to himself: short and broad, skin a dark olive hue, and thin facial hair of moustache and mere tufts of beard.

'I would speak with your hetman,' he called out.

'You walk alone across our land and then you make demands upon us?' one answered. 'You are either an arrogant fool or a warrior worthy of our attention.'

'I intend no challenge . . .' Kyle began.

'Your presence here is a challenge,' the spokesman answered, his face hard, and he nodded. Kyle spun in time to knock away a thrown spear. He turned back to find the spokesman almost upon him in a silent rush, knife out. He dodged two quick thrusts, retreating. 'Do not—' He got no further as the man bellowed a war-cry and attacked again.

Though he hated to do it, Kyle drew and brought his blade up to cut through the man's forearm. The hand flew free, still gripping the knife. The surrounding party of men and women all flinched back a step. The man clamped his remaining hand around the stump and stared in stunned wonder. Kyle picked up the thrown spear and cut through the haft in one easy slice. He raised the shortened weapon high, circling. 'Let me pass,' he told them. 'I mean no challenge to you. I merely wish to pass through.'

'What blade is that you carry?' the man breathed in utter awe.

Kyle glanced down. The curved blade glowed its pale honey-yellow in the afternoon light. He wiped it on his trouser leg and tucked it into his shirt. 'It is mine. Given to me and for none other.' He swept an arm to the south. 'Go now, report to your elders what you have found. I suggest none of you return.'

The warband leader straightened. His face was ashen with pain, his hand tight around the bleeding stump of his wrist. Yet he scowled, unbowed. 'We will go to tell of this. But we shall return. You will not find us craven.' He flicked his head and the rest of the warband turned as one and jogged off.

Kyle wanted to howl: I care not if you are craven or brave! Just leave me alone! But he remained silent. He knew what the clan would do was not up to him – he could only hope to minimize any damage he might have to do.

The leader shuffled to where his severed hand lay, and bent to retrieve the knife.

'Leave it!' Kyle barked. 'It is now mine. Is this not so?'

The man straightened. His face had darkened with the effort – and with rage. 'It is so,' he ground out through clenched teeth.

Kyle motioned him away. 'Then go.'

For an instant Kyle thought the fellow might launch himself upon him, attacking with his teeth alone. But he let out an inarticulate snarl of frustration, his eyes blazing his fury, and backed away. Kyle waited until he had shambled from sight before bending down and collecting the knife.

Now he had two weapons. He set out jogging east.

~

The second night after that encounter he jumped awake to darkness and crouched, knife and blade out, circling. His feet raised dust as he shifted. The moon was out, a thin sickle. The Visitor was a fading green smear just above the western horizon.

'Come out,' he called. 'Let us speak.'

A shape straightened from the brush, advanced. It was an older warrior. Grey streaked his hair. He carried a hatchet in each hand.

'The blade glows,' the man remarked. Kyle glanced down. The strange material of the sword seemed to collect the moonlight and shone now with a silver lustre. 'What is your name,' the man continued, 'that I might recite it before the Circle?'

Kyle thought about that, then said, 'Kylarral-ten is the given name of my youth.'

The man cocked his head, surprised. 'In truth? Of what clan?'

'The Sons and Daughters of the Wind, to the south.'

The man nodded. 'We know them. We are the Silent People. What brings you to our land?'

Kyle did not take his eyes from the man as he slowly circled, his arms out, hatchets readied. He inclined his head a touch to the east. 'I journey east and north. To the mountains.'

The man's eyes shifted momentarily to the north. They glittered in the moonlight. He nodded. 'Ah. I understand. A hero quest. You go to stand before the ancient ones. The ancestors. To prove your worth.'

'Ancestors?' Kyle said, surprised.

The man snorted his disgust. 'Have you Children of the Wind forgotten everything?'

Kyle vaguely remembered stories. But his father had not been much of a one for stories. And he died when Kyle was young and then his mother's brother had sold him into slavery. There had been little time to sit and listen to the old tales around the fire.

None of this did he say.

'Our forefathers,' the man continued. 'You must recite your lineage to be allowed into the Greathall. There you shall fight and feast for ever, shoulder to shoulder with all the heroes of the past. And should you defeat me – here is my name. Swear you will not forget to commend me to our ancestors . . . Ruthel'en.'

Kyle nodded, quite serious. 'I'll not forget.'

'Very good.' Ruthel'en started circling once more.

'We needn't . . .' Kyle began.

'We must.' And the man charged. But the charge was a feint. He

177

halted abruptly to heave one of the hatchets. Kyle barely had time to raise his blade. Somehow it caught the thrown weapon, but not in time to prevent it from striking him a blow on the top of his forehead. Stunned, he just managed to deflect a disembowelling sweep across his midsection that raked through his jerkin, leaving a flaming eruption of pain behind.

Ruthen'el staggered back. His right arm hung useless, severed to the bone across the inside of the bicep. Panting, he reached across to take the hatchet into his left hand. Kyle stood weaving, blinking to clear his vision. Warm wetness covered the right side of his face, blinded that eye. He hugged his left arm across his stomach, terrified at what might happen should he let go.

Ruthen'el straightened, leaned forward to close once more. Kyle circled in a drunken stagger. He held the point of his blade straight out at the man. Ruthen'el batted the blade aside and closed. Kyle brought the sword around underneath, managing to catch the man's side and slicing through. The shock of that blow caused Ruthen'el's hatchet to strike flat and weak against Kyle's shoulder, numbing the arm rather than taking his head off. Ruthen'el slipped backwards off Kyle's blade, half eviscerated. He fell in the mess of his own blood and fluids and lay staring skyward, still conscious.

Weaving, Kyle sheathed his blade. He kept his arm pressed across his stomach and half knelt, half fell to the man's side. Ruthen'el's gaze found his face. 'Remember me to the ancestors,' he whispered wetly.

Kyle swallowed to gather spit to speak. 'I will remember. You are the best I have ever faced. Tell me, this place of the ancestors . . . what do you call it?'

'Joggenhome.'

Kyle straightened, wincing and gasping. Ruthen'el stared up at him. 'You will not finish me?'

'You are done.' Kyle motioned to the east. 'Perhaps you will last until the dawn and you will feel the warmth of the sun upon your face before you go.'

The man smiled dreamily. 'A nice thought. But I think not.'

Kyle staggered to the dropped hatchet. He leaned down awkwardly to pick it up, then tucked it into his belt. Now he had three weapons. He shuffled off into the night.

The next day he washed his head wound at a waterhole. He inspected his torso and was relieved to see that it was merely a flesh wound: a slice across his upper stomach that had failed to sever any muscles. He washed it as well. He killed a lizard and cleaned it and ate the meat raw on the run.

The day after that the next warrior found him, a youth. This one he finished without taking another wound. Though strong and quick, he was far less experienced than Ruthen'el. He did not even give his name. He did shock Kyle, however, and nearly gained an advantage, by calling him 'Whiteblade'.

He jogged now, through the rest of that day and the night, straining to put as much land as possible between himself and the Silent People. The next morning he was limping across the grassland, hardly awake, staggering and stumbling, when someone leapt up directly before him, yelled a war-cry, and bashed him to the ground.

He lay dazed, staring up at a young woman in a full coat of battered mail. She held a longsword to his throat. 'Why are you following us?' she demanded.

He blinked to clear his vision. 'What? Following? I'm not . . .' He swatted the blade aside, struggled to rise. The woman watched him closely, the sword still extended. He eyed her, thinking that he must be seeing a mirage. 'What are you doing here?' he said, amazed.

'Never mind that. What of you? What are you doing here?'

He glanced to the west, covered his gaze to scan the gently rolling steppelands. 'I . . . I was travelling east when the locals set upon me.'

She grunted her understanding, sheathed the longsword. 'They're a murderous lot. We wrecked on the coast. Been travelling ever since. I understand there're towns on the east coast. Civilization.'

'We?'

'Myself, my brother, and others. Now there's only me and my brother.' She whistled loudly and a head popped up from the tall grasses. She waved him in. The lad, about eight, came to stand shyly behind her. He wore a tattered shirt and trousers that might once have been very rich indeed, sewn of crushed velvet and fine leather.

He examined the tall woman more closely: thick auburn hair, pale, high cheekbones, slim but athletic build, an old scar across her right cheek from a blade. Her accent hinted of north Genabackis. 'Who are you?' he again asked in wonder.

She surprised him by studying him narrowly, as if wondering why he would ask such a question. Then she shrugged. 'No one. Just stranded travellers.'

'You do have a name?'

For a moment he thought she wouldn't answer, but she gestured to the lad. 'Dorrin. I am Lyan.'

'Kyle. You are of north Genabackis, yes?'

The young woman visibly flinched. She turned away, waved Dorrin off. 'Get the gear.'

Once the boy had gone, she allowed, reluctantly, 'Yes.'

He opened his arms to encompass the surrounding leagues of steppe. 'May I ask what in the name of the jesting Twins are you doing *here*?'

She gave a snort of disgust. 'Money, of course. Word came of gold in northern Assail. Rivers of it. We came to win our fortune. But,' and she waved a hand, 'fate had other plans for us. Damned ship's master didn't know the coast nearly as well as he claimed.'

'No one does,' Kyle remarked.

She nodded her agreement. 'Forty of us made it to shore. Been fighting our way north ever since.' Dorrin reappeared, dragging two packs. He dropped one before Lyan and shouldered the other.

'Well, I'm headed east.'

She searched his face. 'You would abandon us? Just like that? A woman and a child?'

He didn't bother pointing out that she could probably cut him in half with her longsword. He glanced back to scan the western hills. 'It's best that I travel alone.'

'Oh, I see. On the run and we would only slow you down. Is that it?'

'No, it's not . . . I'm being hunted.'

She eyed him up and down. 'I can see that – you're a right mess. But we're being stalked as well.'

'Trust me. It's not *quite* the same.'

'All trespassers are hunted down and killed here. There is only security in numbers. But go on . . .' She waved him off. 'I do not want any company I cannot rely upon.' She started walking. Dorrin followed. The lad cast him a last wistful glance.

'Well . . . where are you headed?' he called.

She pointed a mailed arm to the north where foothills rose all alone like boulders from the surrounding steppes. 'There may be water, and shelter.'

'And then?'

She glanced over her shoulder, offered a mocking smile. 'Then east . . . to this Sea of Gold.'

He pressed a hand to his forehead then hissed, yanking it from the swollen cut. Damn it to Hood's own pit. Damned difficult woman! Could have just said . . . He cast one last glance to the west, then followed.

*

180

That evening they found a stream coming down out of the hills, and shelter in a cave. He watched the approach while she bedded the lad down. When she emerged, she wore only a long quilted gambeson, stained with sweat, and cut through in places from old sword-strokes. She glanced about in the twilight and frowned.

'No fire?'

'No.'

She grunted her understanding and returned to the cave to come out carrying her sword. She sat on a rock, unsheathed the weapon, and began working its edges.

'A handsome weapon.'

'Thank you. It was my father's. I wish it had never come to me.'

'You did not want it?'

She scowled as if this was an idiotic question. 'My grandfather carried this weapon against the Malazans. As did my father.' She took a heavy breath. 'No. I prayed to the gods every day that it would never need to come to me.'

'I'm sorry.'

'As am I.'

'Your family fought the Malazans in the north. Where? In the west? The east?'

It was obvious to Kyle from her hesitation that she was reluctant to discuss it. Yet she drew a breath and said, 'The east coast. Taph.'

Kyle dredged through what he'd heard of the northern Genabackan campaigns. Taph, he believed, had been among the very last cities to fall to the Malazans. 'Those eastern Free Cities hired the Crimson Guard. Did you see them?'

She blew out a long breath. 'Togg's teeth, man. I was just a child. I met one. Blues was his name. He seemed kind. Why?'

He considered telling her that he'd been of the Crimson Guard but decided it best not to say anything. Given his present unimpressive condition she'd probably think him the worst liar she'd ever met. He shrugged. 'Just curious. I've heard much of them.'

'They're fools.'

He raised his brows. 'Oh?'

'You can't defeat an empire. It's just too damned huge.'

'Then what have your family been doing all these years?'

She ran her sharpening stone down the blade's length. 'Only thing you can do when facing such a giant beast. Make your own little patch of ground too much trouble to bother with and it'll just lumber on and swallow someone else.'

He thought about that. Sound, he supposed. Provided everything you cared for hadn't been swallowed yet. He realized, with a small start, that once more he'd taken hold of the amber stone hanging about his neck and was rubbing it between finger and thumb as he considered his options. He let his hand fall.

A call sounded then from the dark and he stilled, listening. Lyan also froze, her hand poised above her weapon. It called again. Neither beast nor bird. It was a girl's voice in a rising and falling song, taunting from the night: 'White . . . blade . . .' it beckoned, 'white . . . blade . . .'

His gaze went to Lyan. She closed her hand on the grip of her weapon. He signed a negative, shot his gaze to the cave. She nodded and began backing away to the cave mouth. He went out to meet the challenger.

She stood plainly lit in the open among the monochrome grasses under the moon's watery silver light. He pushed his way to her through the knee-high stiff blades, thinking Ruthen'el must have lasted far longer than he'd imagined. Long enough to talk to whoever it was who had found him.

When he was close enough, he shouted: 'Listen, whatever your name is – just turn around and head home. I'm tired of this. I don't want to kill—'

Something crashed into his head from the side and the next thing he knew he was staring up, blinking, at two faces peering down at him. What was strange was that the faces were practically identical. He wondered whether he was seeing double.

'We could've killed you,' one girl said.

'But we want you alive,' said the other.

'For the moment,' finished the first.

Kyle felt his head; his fingers came away dark and wet. A birding arrow, or a sling stone. He felt for his weapons, but they were all gone. One of the girls, he saw, carried the sheathed sword.

'We want you to take our names with you,' the second said, 'so that you can tell our forefathers and foremothers who killed you.' She pointed to herself: 'I am Neese.'

'And I am Niala,' said the one holding his blade. 'You killed our cousin and our uncle.'

'Ruthen'el will be ashamed to hear you avenged him with an ambush,' Kyle croaked.

'You killed all the ones with honour,' Neese said. 'We decided to win instead. Isn't that so, Niala?'

'It is so, Neese.'

Niala hefted the blade. 'So this is it . . . We have heard the stories. I will use this to cut you to pieces. Then it will rest among our clan heirlooms as proof of our power.' She took hold of the sheath to draw it.

'Careful with that,' Kyle warned. 'You have to know how . . .'

Sneering, Niala yanked – and the blade slid through the leather and wood of the sheath taking her fingers with it. She stared at the streaming bloody stumps of her four fingers then screamed, dropping the blade to clench her hand.

Kyle lashed out with his foot, catching Neese in the knee as she leaned to take the weapon. She fell. He threw himself on her and they wrestled for the blade. Something crashed against Kyle's head. Once more stars burst in his vision: it was Niala, standing over him, her crippled hand gripped in the other.

'Bastard,' she hissed, and drew back her foot for another kick.

A war-cry froze her for an instant. Something silver blurred the air over her shoulders and her head toppled from her neck. Blood jetted. Neese screamed. Lyan lunged, turning the blade, and impaled the other sister to the ground through her chest. Kyle climbed awkwardly to his feet.

'Couldn't take two damned girls?' Lyan said.

'I was on top of things.'

'They were all over you.'

'I didn't want to kill them.'

'Bullshit.'

A wet cough brought their attention to Neese. She'd turned her head to where the blade lay in the grasses. It glowed with a gold-tinged light, like coming dawn when the moon is still high. 'We thought . . .' she breathed, 'just stories . . .'

Kyle limped to the blade, took it up. He raised his gaze to meet Lyan's staring, wide eyes. Grimacing, he picked up the sheath and hid the blade within, holding it edge down. He wrapped it in a leather belt. 'Can't leave them here,' he said.

'There's a pit over there.'

He nodded. 'I will head east tomorrow.'

Lyan hesitated, cleaned her blade on Neese's leathers, then bent her head in assent. 'We will go east tomorrow.'

'You're better off—'

'We're better off together,' she cut in, firm.

Kyle chose not to argue the point. There was no way he could stop them from following him if they would. And he was grateful, though twice as worried now. There was no way he would see them killed because of him. He studied the bodies. 'We should take their gear.'

They journeyed east for three days without catching sight of another human being. On the third day Kyle found his attention wandering to his travelling companions. Dorrin kept up as they jogged through the days until losing their breath, walked for a time to recover, then set off once more. Kyle had shouldered the other pack and so the lad ran unencumbered. Kyle hoped this was the main reason Dorrin could keep up. Not that he was getting old.

The boy also did exactly as Lyan told him. All without complaint, or face-making, or rebellion, and this struck Kyle as unlike any brother–sister relationship he'd ever heard of. He wondered whether they were in fact mother and son. But nothing in their manner reflected that. He saw no gestures of affection from either, no hugs or touches. Their behaviour to one another was in fact very formal, almost businesslike.

This drove him to say to her, as they walked along, with Dorrin distant for the moment: 'You are not brother and sister, are you?'

Lyan bristled at first, taking breath to mount a strong objection. But she seemed to reconsider and subsided, shaking her head. 'No. We are not related.'

'Yet you are more than just chance survivors. You have been together for some time.'

'Yes.'

He simply waited, walking in silence until she sighed and waved as if capitulating. 'I am his guard. The last of his bodyguard.'

Kyle peered over at the blond-haired lad where he walked, his shirt dark with sweat, swishing a stick through the tall grasses as he went. 'He is of noble blood?'

'Yes.'

'From north Genabackis?'

Again the woman paused, reluctant to continue. Kyle just shrugged. 'I am from the south of these lands. Bael, it is sometimes called. I haven't even been to Genabackis.'

Lyan sighed again, accepting this. 'Well – you have heard that the fighting in the north-east of the continent was far more savage than the west?' Kyle nodded; he had heard. 'There were . . . powers there,' she continued, 'that the Malazans only overcame with great difficulty.'

'Caladan Brood commanded the Free City armies of the north.'

'That was later,' she said. 'There was no alliance of "Free

Cities" before the Malazans arrived. Only competing city-states and personalities. One of the most powerful cities was Anklos. Its ruling family – the Batarius family – was the one that originally hired Caladan. They were the ancestral rulers of Anklos until the Malazans forced them out and they fled into exile.'

Kyle felt his brows rising higher and higher. 'Are you saying that Dorrin . . .'

Lyan jerked her head in assent. 'With the death of his father he is now king in exile, rightful ruler of Anklos.'

'Then . . . may I ask – why here? Why in the name of the Sky-King are you here?'

Lyan gave a long troubled breath. 'I advised against it. But his father insisted. You see, word had come of gold in Assail. Rivers of gold.' She eyed him sidelong. 'Do you have any idea how much gold it takes to mount a rebellion? To build an army? A very great amount indeed.'

Now Kyle was even more troubled. He walked in silence for a time, frowning. 'And why are you telling me all this?'

'Because,' and her gaze was constant upon him now, 'I have also heard songs of the Malazan campaign in Fist. Of its leader, Greymane, Stonewielder . . . and of his companion, now known as Whiteblade. Who, I have also heard, abandoned the Malazans with the death of Greymane, his friend. Such a champion would have no use for the empire that used his friend so cruelly, I imagine.'

He lowered his gaze. 'I walked away from all that. I have no intention of returning.'

'You will do what you must. In the meantime one can at least keep watch while the other sleeps.'

He gave a stiff nod of acceptance. 'At the very least.'

Towards the end of the afternoon, as the light darkened to a deep amber, he raised a hand in a halt. Lyan, who had been walking with Dorrin, jogged to him.

'What is it?'

'I smell smoke – and worse.'

Her gaze went to Dorrin, who crouched now in cover, as he'd been instructed. 'I see.'

'Should I scout ahead?'

She shook a negative. 'Let us keep together.'

'Very well.'

They advanced warily. Lyan hovered close to Dorrin, sword out. Kyle scanned the hillsides. In time, he spotted the source: a long patch of flattened and disturbed grass stretching between hills. They passed outliers of the attack – a burst wooden chest, spilled trampled clothes. A child's rag doll. The smouldering remains of a two-wheeled ox cart. Staked out amid the wreckage lay bodies, and seeing this Lyan steered Dorrin aside. Kyle approached.

They had been left alive but had had their skin flayed from their bodies. Eyes gouged out, hands hacked off. Incredibly, two still breathed. Kyle crouched next to one, a thing that might have once been an old man. 'Can you hear me, oldster?'

The head moved as if its owner were searching for the source of the voice. Kyle allowed a few drops of water to fall on to the man's split and mangled lips. 'Who are you?' he asked. 'What are you doing here?'

'Alana?' the oldster whispered hoarsely. 'Little Gerrol? Reena?'

Kyle had seen no remains of women or children. He did not wonder as to their fate. The clans here were similar enough to his own. Children adopted into the clan, and women of childbearing years taken to replenish their numbers.

'Taken,' he said.

The man's head fell back. He moaned long and low – a sort of keening.

'Old man . . .' The fellow did not answer. He now seemed oblivious, lost in his pain. Kyle glanced to the surrounding hillsides. Had the clans left scouts? Had they eyes on the remains?

'Old man!' The head shifted once more, blindly searching. 'Why are you here? Why are you trespassing?'

'For the gold. We came north. Trains of travellers. Heading north . . . for the gold . . .'

Kyle straightened. The fools. As if the various clans of the Silent People would allow them to cross their lands. He jogged to where Lyan waited, her hands on Dorrin's shoulders.

'Trains of wagons travelling north,' he explained. 'It's a rush to collect this gold of yours.'

She squinted to the south, appalled. 'The clans are slaughtering them all.'

'Yes.' He examined Dorrin, who peered up at him, quite direct in his gaze. 'You have a weapon?'

'Yes.'

'You know how to use it?'

'The Shieldmaiden is training me.'

He raised his gaze. Well, it seemed he was not the only one with secrets. One of the legendary Shieldmaidens of north Genabackis.

Her lips remained tight and her eyes wary as her thick auburn hair blew about her. 'Well, lad, here's another one.' He handed over one of his extra hatchets. To Lyan he said: 'We'd best get going.'

She gave a curt nod of agreement.

Two days later the wind again brought hints of smoke. Lyan had the lad kneel in the grass and keep watch as she and Kyle advanced up a hillside. From this rise they could see another hilltop, this one fortified and occupied. Kyle counted more than thirty swords.

'We should go round,' he said.

'Yes, we should. But . . . who are they?'

'I should warn them.'

'Warn them? Warn them about *what*?'

He handed her his weapons, water, and gear. 'Take these. Hunker down. If I'm taken, just go on without me.'

Lyan stared, uncomprehending. 'What are you doing?'

'I'm going to talk to them.' Hunched, he edged down the hillside.

'Don't be some kind of fool hero!' she hissed after him.

This gave him pause. It reminded him of Ruthen'el's words. But he wasn't trying to be a hero; he was just trying to do these people a favour.

When he got close enough, he shouted, 'You there! On the hilltop! Let me speak to your commander.'

The men and women guarding the perimeter of heaped wrecked carts and baggage all sprang to their feet. They scanned the hillsides, readied crossbows.

After a moment a gruff voice called out: 'Yes? What is it? Show yourself.'

'You can't stay here,' Kyle shouted. 'You have to keep moving.'

'Show yourself! Are you one of them?'

Damned fools. Couldn't they tell he couldn't possibly . . . oh, fine! He stood. The guards pointed. A man climbed the barricade. A fat fellow, in leather armour.

'I see you there. So, a traveller like ourselves.' He waved Kyle up. 'Very well, come. Join us.'

'No. You're in a death trap. Your only hope is to keep moving.'

The commander appeared taken aback for an instant, then he gave a great belly laugh. 'We're holding them off!' He glanced about to his people. 'Isn't that so?'

Kyle resisted raising his hand to press it to his forehead. Blind idiot. 'Listen – they're coming in twos and threes, yes?'

The man frowned, losing patience. 'Yes? What of it?'

187

'They're just using you. They're sending their least experienced warriors to blood them. You don't understand. It's like a game to them. They've got you right where they want you.'

The fellow was scowling now, rubbing his bearded jaw. 'Wait a moment . . . it's *you*, isn't it? *You're* the one they're after. You caused all this!'

Kyle raised a hand for a pause. 'Now wait! I didn't cause any of this . . .'

'Kill him!' the commander ordered. 'Fire!'

Bows and crossbows thrummed. Kyle dived for cover. Bolts and arrows hissed through the grasses about him. 'Get out there,' the fellow bellowed. 'Get his sword! It's worth a fortune!'

Kyle ran hunched almost double, straight south. Bolts and arrows continued to punish the grass about him, but luckily none struck. One did slash his arm. He ran on until he judged it long enough, then cut due east. He kept glancing back to look for any pursuit but saw none. It appeared these men and women were unwilling to travel too far from the security of their redoubt.

Their voluntary burial ground, as far as he was concerned.

He jogged east until twilight came. Only then did he start to worry; he hadn't really organized a firm rendezvous with Lyan. What if he'd lost her too? He assumed she'd been watching. Wouldn't she have started east, knowing that this was his chosen direction?

He walked now in the open, scanned the gently rolling steppe lands as he went. It was getting cold as night gathered. Then a light flashed on a distant hillside. He raised a hand to shield his vision. It came again from north of him, flashing and flickering on and off. A signal? He set out jogging in that direction.

He came to a long winding hillock, not too tall, but broad with steep sides. A figure rose from the deep shadows there and descended towards him. He went to meet it.

It was Lyan. She held out his weapons and gear. He took it all and re-girt himself. Dorrin rose from cover nearby and came dragging the two heavy packs.

'So,' Lyan said. 'That went well.'

Kyle just made a face.

'Your diplomacy skills at work again, I see.'

He merely gestured, inviting her eastwards.

'Making friends all over the region.'

He let out a long breath. 'Try to help someone and what do you get?'

'No good deed goes unpunished.'

'No indeed.'

'Now what?' she asked. 'Just going to leave them to be ground down?'

'They deserve it. I recognized them. Slavers out of the south. A city named Kurzan. I have a particular dislike of slavers.'

'Slavers! In truth? Then they do deserve it.'

He took a pack from Dorrin. 'Thanks, lad. You're doing just fine, you know?'

'Thank you, sir.'

Kyle laughed. 'Sir? You don't have to call me sir.'

'Oh, but I should,' the lad returned quite seriously. 'All champions should be called sir. As a sign of respect.'

Kyle's gaze snapped to Lyan, who looked away as if disinterested, but he thought her face a touch flushed.

'Who says I am a champion?' he said, still gazing over the lad to Lyan.

'Oh, I've heard the stories too,' Dorrin continued, unaware. 'From my tutors. They said that Whiteblade cut through a ship's chain as thick about as a man's thigh.'

'A wrist, perhaps,' Kyle conceded.

'That the sword Whiteblade cut a goddess that none other could touch.'

'That is true.'

Lyan seemed to flinch at that, reddening even more.

'They said Stonewielder broke the Shieldwall – though many in Fist claim it was just an earthquake.'

'It was he,' Kyle said, his voice hoarse and faint, and he looked away to scan the hillsides.

Lyan cleared her throat. 'That's enough, Dorrin.' Then, to Kyle: 'This sea to the east . . . it is the Sea of Gold, yes?'

He shook his head. 'No. It is another. It has many names. My people called it the Sea of Terrors. Everyone knows it is cursed. We will not go near it.'

'Then . . . what is our route?'

'North, skirting its shore.'

'Then . . . we remain within the Silent People's territory?'

'No. I understand their territory ends just to the north.'

'And who is next? What murderous clans?'

Kyle did not answer immediately; he shaded his gaze to the west, squinted into the sunset, glanced away. 'We'll need to find a camp soon.'

'What tribes?' Lyan continued stubbornly.

His gaze lowered, he drew his hatchets, tested their edges with his thumbs, hooked them back into his belt. 'There are stories,' he began slowly. 'Only stories. The further north we go the less I know of things.' He took a steadying breath. 'The Silent People's territory ends north of here because they are afraid of those lands. As were my people.'

'Who lives there?'

He cast her a quick bleak smile. 'No one knows. We call it the Vanishing Lands. That is because those who venture there are never seen again. None have ever returned.'

Lyan halted. 'And we are walking into it? You would . . . I would take Dorrin to such a terrible place? I would rather take my chances with this sea.'

Kyle halted as well. 'Believe me, you would not. I know more of this sea than the north – that is why I would avoid it.'

'There will be ships! Surely one will be headed south, away from these dreadful lands.'

'There is only death on that sea. All agree it is cursed with madness.'

'A few days on a ship will see us free of here!'

Kyle raised his eyes to the darkening cloudless dome of the sky. 'There will be no ships coming south out of the Sea of Terrors.'

Lyan dropped her pack and waved a dismissal. 'How do you know? Have you *seen* this? Countless ships are entering it now. Heading north even as we speak! Yes? Do you deny that?'

'No, I do not deny that.'

'Then why are you even arguing? They will come south again.'

Dorrin came and stood between them; he looked from Lyan to Kyle.

Kyle shook his head. 'None of them will ever return.'

She laughed. 'Oh, come now. Listen to yourself: "None will ever return." *Some* will.'

He drew a sharp breath.

Dorrin announced loudly, 'We need to camp. It's late.'

Kyle clamped his jaws shut. Lyan glanced away. She clenched and unclenched her gauntleted hands.

Dorrin headed for the nearest hilltop. Kyle watched him go. After a time, he murmured ruefully, 'Wise beyond his years.'

Lyan hitched up her pack and followed. 'I'm glad one of us is.'

There was little talking the next morning. Kyle walked ahead and apart. He thought through yesterday's conversation. How close could they get to the sea? And what of water? They were in desperate need. Yet the narrows could sometimes reverse their flow and seawater would wash into the basin. It was unhealthy to drink much of it, although some claimed it was the water itself – run-off from the great ice-fields and snows of the north – that carried the curse.

They passed the scene of an old attack. Grass grew through the spokes of burnt cartwheels. Tiny scavengers had gnawed the leather of scattered rusted equipment. A skull half bare of flesh grinned from the dusty dry earth. Its hair was long and black. Kyle scuffed dirt over it before Dorrin arrived.

Later, he and Lyan walked together. He cleared his throat. 'We do need water . . .' he began.

'But as you say – if it is too dangerous . . .' she answered. 'And you should know. You're the local. I should defer. I'm sorry . . . command is a hard habit to break.'

He laughed. 'Yes it is. And I am sorry. I swear that if I see any ship headed south I will personally swim out and shake the captain's hand.'

Lyan was quiet for a time, then she peered sideways at him, her brows raised. 'You can swim?'

They walked east for four more days. The grasses grew taller here, and greener. Copses of brush and short trees occupied the depressions. Kyle sought out each hoping to find a pool or a soak. So far he had found none.

He did his best to maintain a watch for possible challengers but it was harder and harder to maintain the necessary heightened awareness and readiness. He felt that they were being watched; yet now these Silent warriors were keeping their distance. It was exhausting, and he was feeling the weakness and drain of lack of water. Dorrin hadn't realized it yet, but he was now the only one drinking.

Kyle could sometimes feel moisture on his face in the breeze out of the east. White birds flew in the eastern sky. He stopped walking and gestured to the rolling horizon. 'The sea is close. Just beyond those rises, perhaps. Some call this the Shore of Fear, or Anguish Coast.'

'Pleasant names you lot have here.'

He grinned. 'They are meant to keep people away.'

'They don't seem to be working.'

He nodded. 'Unfortunately, they just seem to have piqued everyone's interest.'

'We turn north?'

He nodded again, wearily, already tired. 'Yes. I wonder if we should start moving at night now.'

'Dangerous. I've seen predators watching our camp at night. Jackals and spotted cats.'

'Yes.' He drew a sleeve across his brow, let the arm fall. 'Perhaps I should head to the top of those hills. Have a look.'

'We'll all go.'

He eyed her; she still wore her heavy mail coat. Sweat ran in rivulets down her temples and her hair lay pressed and matted to her skull. Her eyes were sunken and dark. He nodded heavily. 'Very well.'

The slope was gentle; in fact, it was hard to tell that they had reached a hilltop so lightly did the land rise and fall. He stopped, shaded his gaze in the harsh noon light. Between hills he could just make out the iron-grey shimmer of the sea. He raised his chin to Lyan. 'There it is.'

She lifted her hand to her brow. 'Looks harmless. We could reach it by the end of the day.'

'Yes.'

'But we won't. So . . . what?'

He gestured north. 'There are a few streams that run to the sea. We should come across one eventually.'

'If we have the strength,' she murmured as Dorrin was close now. 'And what of our friends?'

He scanned the surrounding horizons. 'I have the feeling that they're letting us weaken.'

'Not very fair of them.'

He drew a fortifying breath. 'Well, it's our own damned fault, isn't it?'

Dorrin arrived to peer east. 'So that is your Sea of Dread. I don't like the look of it.'

'Neither do I,' Kyle agreed. He held out a hand, inviting Lyan northward, and they started off.

The next day Kyle sucked on stones. He pinched the skin of his hand and it did not fall back at all. The moisture coming off the sea was a torment, but no matter how much he feared the Silent warriors shadowing them his instincts told him that the true threat lay to the east.

Even so, if the Silent People's strategy was to wait until they were falling down weak, then it was working. The next day he stopped

Lyan from donning her mail coat. He'd found the poles of two dead saplings that he used to build a travois. He motioned to the packs. 'Keep only what you need.'

Lyan did not even bother answering, merely set to tossing things away. With the travois finished, the poles and cross-sticks lashed with leather straps, they loaded it with what remained of their gear: armour, wrapped dried meat, a sack of meal stuffed into a cooking pot, and the empty waterskins. Lyan hung a leather pouch around her neck and tucked it under her tunic. What remained of the lad's royal inheritance, Kyle assumed. They set off, Kyle dragging the travois by the length of two leather belts. At noon they switched over.

In the late afternoon they came to the dried bed of a stream. Kyle clambered down among the exposed rocks and gravel and started digging with a hatchet. Lyan joined him. About an arm's length down, the mixed mud and sand became damp. Kyle pressed the cold wet sand to his face and sighed in delight.

A gasp from Dorrin brought them jumping to their feet, weapons drawn.

Across the dried stream bed five people faced them: two clan elders, male and female, and three of what must be their most senior warriors, two men and one woman. The warriors wore white face paint while their mostly naked bodies were smeared in ochre mud. The elders were draped in leather skins and furs.

'Let me drink first,' Kyle called.

The female elder smiled, revealing blunt nubs of teeth. 'No pleading, Whiteblade? Good. That is as it should be.'

The old man jerked his head back towards the north. 'You are truly headed north?'

'I am.'

The two elders exchanged a glance that greatly troubled Kyle, for it was an uneasy one. Then the old woman stamped her staff to the ground and announced, 'It is the Quest, then. Child of the Wind, you go to the great mountains, Joggenhome, to stand before our ancestors and prove our worth as our champion.'

'It is not agreed,' one of the male warriors, the most scarred one, snarled.

'Quiet, Willow,' the old man warned. 'The clans have lost enough blades. He has proved his worth. And we are shamed by Neese and Niala. They were not chosen.'

'It is only the blade he carries,' Willow answered scornfully. 'Let us see him fight with no advantage.'

Kyle raised his chin to the elders. 'I am half dead of thirst, but if the elders wish it I will face this one without the white blade.'

'The Quest is a not a trifling matter,' the old man muttered.

'We must be certain,' the woman agreed.

The old man gave a curt nod. 'Very well. You have two nights and two days. Rest, drink, eat. We will meet again at the dusk.' He gestured to the female warrior and she tossed something to Kyle. He caught it: a skin of water. The five climbed the slope up out of the stream bed and melted away.

'You should not have agreed,' Lyan said.

'I had no choice. It was a test. It was all a test. If I had failed they would have killed all of us.'

'What do you mean?'

'A test of honour. A test of bravery. A test of my resolve – they had been waiting to see whether I truly would turn north.'

'And this last stupid duel?'

'It is their . . . well, our, way. Formalized war. Some might call it a kind of game. Only we two need be wounded or killed. More humane, really.'

She was shaking her head. 'Stupid. Damned stupid.'

'Thank you for your faith in my abilities.'

She just waved an arm, dismissing him, and climbed the stream bed.

For two days they rested. They drank the water and boiled the last of their grain meal. As the afternoon of the second day slid into evening, Kyle began stretching. He decided to use his two hatchets and keep two knives tucked into his belt at the rear. Dorrin stood cradling the white blade in its sheath and leather wrap.

The Silent People appeared soon after. They approached in the open, out of the west.

'Remember,' Kyle again told Lyan, 'follow the coast. It should curve to the east and you should come to some sort of estuary, an outlet to the Sea of Gold. There should be people there. A fortress named Mist.'

She had objections, plenty, he could tell. But she swallowed them. Instead, she slipped her hand behind his neck and pulled his lips to hers to kiss him.

He stood blinking, quite stunned.

'There's some motivation for you,' she said, looking fierce. 'Now slit him open and let's get going.'

'Yes, ma'am. You really are a Shieldmaiden. Where is your shield anyway?'

'Lost it in the shipwreck.'

'Have to get you another.' And he walked away, swinging his arms to loosen them and kicking at the dry dusty earth.

The Silent People's warrior, Willow, stepped forward. He drew two fighting knives. Kyle was surprised to see that both blades were of chipped black stone, obsidian. The warrior saw him eyeing the blades and held them up. 'You have set aside your white blade, and so will I face you in the old way, with the traditional weapons.'

So the man hadn't been seeking his own advantage when he demanded that Kyle set aside his sword. He'd given up quite a lot in choosing those brittle blades. A solid blow from his hatchet should shatter one. But then, even a fragment from such a weapon would be deadly sharp.

The warrior twisted the blades before him as he circled. Sometimes he reversed them, spinning and jumping. Kyle saw that the grips were wound in leather. As they circled, he glimpsed Lyan standing aside, Dorrin before her, her hands on his shoulders. She wore her sword.

'Do you know why I challenged you, Son of the Wind?' Willow called.

'No.'

'Because when I defeat you I will take your place in the Quest. *I* will stand before our ancestors and it will be *my* name they will know.'

'Then you are a fool,' Kyle answered simply. He put all the tired contempt he could muster into the observation.

The man jerked, stunned, then snarled and charged in. The charge was a feint as the man slid aside at the last moment, slashing, but Kyle was prepared, as he had learned the hard way from Ruthen'el – these people were deadly knife-fighters. The deadliest he'd ever faced. But he had been taught by the best as well, by veterans of the Crimson Guard, and by Greymane himself. Grey had been a legendary brawler. 'Just win,' his friend had always berated him. 'Never mind the fancy shit – just win.'

Kyle parried and countered lazily, disguising his own speed. Willow returned to circling.

And so the duel slid into a pattern. The two circling, darting in to test one another, sometimes counter-attacking, sometimes feinting a move, always watching their opponent's reactions, searching for openings.

Twilight thickened. Their shuffling feet raised clouds of dust that wafted heavily off to the east. The man was quick, Kyle realized.

Probably faster than him. Yet he seemed to be losing patience. Most of his duels must have been long over before this. Even weakened, Kyle believed he could probably outlast him. And so he pulled back, circling more, parrying, holding himself loose and relaxed, conserving his energy. *Just win*, Greymane's words returned. *The only ugly fight is the one you lose.*

Willow streamed with sweat now, his arms quivering with suspended energy. He glared, enraged. 'You are frightened, yes?' he taunted. 'You would run away if you could.'

Kyle decided that silence would frustrate the man further and so he didn't answer.

Willow darted in with breathtaking speed, weapons reversed, slashing low. Kyle slid backwards, parrying. He managed to kick one knee, bringing Willow to the ground, and came down hard with one hatchet, but the man rolled aside. A flame of pain erupted across Kyle's shoulder.

Sharp! A voice screamed in Kyle's mind. So sharp! Already a warm wetness was spreading down his back. From behind he heard a suppressed gasp from Dorrin.

Not even thinking consciously through the mist of pain, he allowed the left arm to hang loose. He circled, even warier.

Willow was panting, sheathed in sweat, but grinning now. He nodded to himself. Kyle kept his right side to him, hatchet extended. The warrior darted in, batted the hatchet aside; Kyle shifted backwards without bringing his left arm up. Willow slashed with both weapons but chose not to press the attack, easing back instead, watching. It looked to Kyle as though the man was ready to let him bleed out.

He loosened his left hand and let the hatchet fall free to thump into the dust.

Willow suddenly changed direction, hunched, weaving the obsidian blades before him. Kyle followed, shuffling slowly. He still had his reserves and he meant to expend them all in one burst.

The warrior's feet shifted, his weight easing forward. He held one blade high, the other low. Kyle knew the danger lay with the raised blade. He faked his own falling back, as he had done so often already. Willow lunged in, the high blade ready to dart for neck or chest.

Kyle reached behind to his belt with his left hand to pull free a knife and snap throw from his waist all in one motion. The Silent warrior was so fast he managed to shift so that the blade only grazed his side. But in that moment of distraction Kyle swung his hatchet up and the raised obsidian blade exploded in a burst of fragments. The low blade thrust for him but Kyle deflected it with his left forearm.

Willow stabbed Kyle's side with the remains of the shattered blade still gripped in his hand even as Kyle brought his hatchet up between them to thrust the killing spike up behind the man's jaws, piercing his palate and entering his brain.

They stood locked together. Held in each other's arms. A moment that seemed frozen to Kyle. Long enough to watch the man's gaze fade from bewilderment to unfocused emptiness. Still, they held one another's arms. Then Willow slid down to slump to the ground. Kyle stood panting, his blood roaring so loud in his ears as to drown out all other sounds, his vision blurry with lancing agony. Hands took him, arms, and he relaxed into them.

He awoke to glaring sunlight and he winced, hissing in pain. 'It's all right,' Lyan said from nearby. A shadow occluded the glaring light; a hand pressed his chest. 'We're safe. We have food and water. Thirsty?'

He nodded. Turning his head he could just make out that his torso was wrapped, as was his shoulder. Lyan held the spout of a waterskin to his lips, gently squeezed the skin. He drank.

'What happened?'

'You won. Barely. It was stupid, but impressive. He was fast, that one. Damned fast. You have all the time you need to recover. We're guests of the Silent People now.'

'I see. Well, if you don't mind I'll pass out again.'

'Go ahead.'

It was night when he opened his eyes once more. He tried to rise and failed when agony shot up his side. He relaxed back on to the blankets. In the morning Lyan spooned him a mush of boiled vegetables and grains. 'I need to get up,' he told her.

'Why?'

'I need to . . . you know.'

Her brows rose. 'Ah. You shouldn't, really. But . . . all right.' She took hold of him under the arms and gently lifted him so that he could draw his legs beneath himself. He snarled and hissed in suppressed pain but managed to stand. 'Help me walk a bit.'

She rolled her eyes. 'I've nursed a lot of men – no need for shyness.'

'Humour me.'

Tsking, she took his weight so that he could limp off a few steps.

'Good,' he said, his voice taut. 'Thank you.'

'Fine. Call if you fall down.' She walked away.

'I most certainly will.' He unlaced the front of his pants and eased his bladder. How embarrassing that when you were wounded you couldn't even get up to see to the most basic of things. He resolved not to be wounded again.

Slowly, very slowly, he tottered back to camp. Lyan came and took his arm. 'I should lie down,' he gasped. He'd broken into a cold sweat. She eased him back down.

'I will call for their healers,' he heard her say as through a roaring waterfall.

When he next awoke he felt much better. The stabbing pain was gone from his side. It was late afternoon. Dorrin dozed in the shade nearby. 'Hey, lad. How are you?'

Dorrin jerked awake, sat up. 'I'll get Lyan.' And he ran off.

After a moment Lyan jogged up, wearing only a sweat-soaked shift and trousers, her sheathed sword in one hand. 'You are awake.'

'Yes. What happened?'

Her face grew serious. 'A needle of obsidian was left behind in your side. It was digging in, slicing you up. They found it and drew it out. The old lady used her teeth for that, by the way.'

'I'll have to thank her.'

'Better?'

'Yes.'

'Good.' She cleared her throat, then motioned to his throat. 'That necklace you wear. A remembrance, perhaps? From a girl?'

He raised a hand to touch the smooth amber stone at his neck. 'From a friend. He was of the Thel Akai. An ancient race. Giants, some name them. You have heard of them?'

'You mean a Toblakai? We know them in the north.'

'Related.'

'Ah.'

'What were you doing?'

Lyan peered down at herself, jerked. 'Oh, yes. Practising.'

He nodded. 'Good.' He thought the view from down here looking up at her was wonderful and she seemed to see something of this in his expression.

She gave him a sour face. 'Rest. I'm not done.' She walked off.

He eased back, then frowned; he smelled something disagreeable. He realized it was him. He smelled to the heights of stale sweat and urine – and worse. He must have had a touch of fever. Of course –

Lyan's taking care of me and I stink like a pig.

Yet he was too weak to get up to wash himself. For now. He shut his eyes. Great Wind he was hungry.

At dawn the next morning he decided to try to get up. With Lyan's help, he managed. She'd fashioned a kind of crutch from one of the poles of the travois and with this he hobbled off into the tallest grasses to squat for his toilet. This took a great deal of time, and by the time he'd managed to straighten he was sheathed in sweat from the effort of bending down. But he was standing. He hobbled back to camp.

That day he limped about, regathering his strength. In the afternoon Dorrin came running up, pointing to the south. 'Look! Look what's coming!'

Kyle squinted, shading his gaze. Up a slight valley between two gentle rises came one of the Silent People leading three horses. Kyle stared, amazed. Gods. Horses! Rare as pearls on this continent. Where'd they come from? What were the Silent People doing with them?

The one leading the horses was the old man from the challenge. He nodded to Kyle. 'You are recovered.'

'Getting better.'

'Good.' He gestured proudly back to the horses. 'You can ride, can you?'

'Yes.' He looked to Dorrin. The lad nodded vigorous assent. 'Yes we can.'

'Good. We Silent People do not. These are yours, then.'

'Ah, may I ask . . . how did they come into your possession?'

The old man was untroubled by the question. 'Foreigners bring them from their houses that float. They land them and try to ride through our lands – but they still do not escape our blades.'

Kyle blew out a breath. 'I see. Well . . . we thank you for the gifts. They will aid us greatly.'

'Very good. Farewell, then. Remember us to the ancients. Prove your worth and bring honour to us all.'

Kyle inclined his head. 'I will try. Farewell.'

The old man walked away. Lyan already had a hand on the neck of the biggest of the three, a broad roan. 'That one's mine,' Kyle called.

'No she ain't. I'm heavier than you in my armour, so she's mine.'

Kyle just shook his head. He wasn't about to argue with her over that subject.

Aiken was out hunting birds when he saw the smoky ochre cloud to the south. A storm, but one unlike any he'd seen before. He shouldered his bow and ran for the village.

When he arrived many of the elders were already out peering to the south. They were quiet, and to Aiken they appeared strangely troubled by a mere storm. He found his mother standing before their hide and pole hut. 'A storm!' he announced, excited. He'd always enjoyed storms: the lightning and thunder of gods battling overhead.

'I see, little grub,' she answered distractedly, her gaze still to the south. 'Get inside.'

'But Mama!' She clenched his arm and thrust him within. 'Mama!'

A warband ran past the hut, led by Hroth Far-seer. They ran with their knives in their hands.

'Who is it?' he asked, now wondering if perhaps he should be afraid.

'Stay within,' his mother barked. She pulled her blades from her belt, and ran.

A rumbling and crackling reached him, as of thunder, and a dark wall burst over the hut obscuring almost all the light. Dust washed within, choking him. Of course! A dust-storm! He'd seen one of these before. But what was there to fear? Save the animals wandering lost?

Footfalls sounded all about, sifting and thumping. He heard the crack and grating of weapons clashing, gasped breaths, hisses of pain, and the grunt of mortal blows taken. He stared out of the opening, now an ochre curtain of shifting and gusting dust. Blurred shapes ran past, wrestled, duelled.

He recognized the outline of his own, and was chilled by the hoary shapes they battled: cloaked in wind-blown rags, skeleton thin, some bearing armour of animal bones.

The demons of his people's legends. The demons of dust. Come for them at last, as their oldest myths warned.

Then he screamed as a shape darkened the doorway. His mother burst within. Her head was bloodied, her hide trousers slit at the leg, streaming blood. She scanned the hut, her eyes wild, found him, took his arm and thrust him amid piled hides and blankets.

Tears streamed down her face. 'Quiet, love,' she croaked, hoarse.

'Mama – what . . . ?'

'Quiet now as a woodlouse, yes?'

She pressed her hand over his face, left behind a smear of warm blood, pulled the hides over his head.

Through a gap in the layered hides he watched her feet as she crossed to the doorway. From her stance he could see she was crouched, blades ready. The feet shifted, scuffing. He heard blades clash and scrape, heard his mother growl and gasp. The feet shifted anew, weakly. Blood came running down one leg. Something hissed through the air and his mother's feet tilted and she fell.

New feet entered the hut. Inhuman. Earth-brown bone and sinew in tatters of thick leather hide. The skins were yanked aside and he stared up at a demon face of bone, dark empty sockets, and naked amber teeth. Riding atop the head of patchy hair was another skull of some sort of gigantic horned beast.

'This one?' the demon asked someone outside.

'Nay – the scent is too thin. Come, they are fleeing.'

This demon thrust him back into the hides, stalked from the hut, was swallowed by the swirling dust. Aiken crawled to his mother. She lay staring sightlessly skyward, thrust through the chest. He rested his head upon her breast and, weeping, gently closed her staring eyes.

Three days later a lone rider came galloping up from the south. Aiken happened to be with the mourners that day. He'd brought flowers to his mother where she lay on her tall raised bier, exposed to the sun's kiss and the wind's embrace. Others were out as well, his neighbours, cousins, and aunts. Those who'd survived the demons' attack.

Everyone snatched up their weapons, of course. Even Aiken, as warriors were few now.

But it was an old woman. She threw herself from her lathered mount and ran to them. Her hunting leathers were dust-caked. Bead necklaces rattled about her neck. Her hair was a thick tangled nest.

'How many?' she gasped; she clutched a thin weathered hand to her throat. Aiken thought her a maddened survivor from another village.

'A full third of our people,' answered Jalia, Aiken's great-aunt. Then she hissed, flinching from the newcomer. She pointed to her waist. Aiken glanced there and saw that the knives thrust through the old woman's leather belt were of nut-brown stone, knapped, the grip leather-wrapped.

'Demon weapons . . .' Jalia snarled, and she went for her own daggers.

The ground erupted around them. Bone arms yanked clear of the dirt. Skulls denuded of flesh burst free. Aiken backed away, terrified yet fascinated. Jalia thrust for the woman but a demon stepped up between them, taking her arm and tossing her aside.

'Do not harm them!' the old woman bellowed. Then her wild gaze found Aiken and she yelled to him: 'Go! Run!'

Aiken turned and fled.

*

Silverfox, alone but for the dead, stood quivering. She wiped her hands down her thighs. She felt intensely cold, on the verge of collapse. She studied the funeral biers all about. The custom of these lands. And how many new? Some forty? From this village alone? She closed her eyes and staggered, righted herself, headed back to her mount.

Pran Chole came to her side. 'You must rest.'

'They are close, Pran.'

'True. A few days ahead. They flee you, Silverfox.'

'Then I must continue to press. Push them along. They won't have time . . . time to kill everyone, will they?' Gaining her mount, she took hold of the saddle to steady herself. 'Who were these people, Pran?'

'These clans name themselves the People of the Yellow Grass.'

She pressed her forehead to the saddle. The leather was warm and damp with sweat. 'It is all my fault . . . all this. My fault.'

'By no measure.'

'If I had pressed harder for the release . . .'

'We refused you, Summoner.'

She nodded wearily, her eyes closed. She tried to raise her leg to mount, failed. 'Who . . . who is north of us?'

Pran turned his dark empty sockets to the north. 'A far larger confederation of clans.'

She nodded once more, exhausted. 'A third here, Pran. A full third! Next it will be half. Then two-thirds. Then, to the very north. None there shall be spared. Who are these next clans?'

'They name themselves the People of the Wind.'

With a grunt of effort, Silverfox managed to mount. She twined her fists in the reins. 'I must warn them. And Pran,' she added, 'find me another horse.' She kneed her mount and it kicked away, obeying her though exhausted itself.

Pran Chole stood for a time watching the Summoner ride off. Tolb Bell'al joined him. Tatters of the Ifayle's hide shirt flapped in the wind revealing curves of age-stained ribs. Patches of long hair blew and whipped. 'She will not rest,' Pran breathed.

'Just as we,' Tolb answered.

'What should be done?'

'We will continue to sustain the horse.'

'We are cruel.'

'The need is cruel.' Tolb's voice was no louder than the murmuring wind. 'Lanas Tog must not reach the mountains.' He turned to face Pran directly. 'At any cost. In this we are in complete agreement, yes?'

Pran's ravaged visage of dried and withered flesh, bared nostrils and yellowed teeth turned slightly to follow Silverfox's retreat. 'Agreed,' he breathed. Tolb knew the ancient man Pran had once been well enough to feel the clenching dread of that admission. He knew the Summoner was as precious to his friend as his own child. Indeed, were they not all their own children?

And what would a parent not do to secure the future of their own?

Indeed, what not?

CHAPTER VI

REUTH KEPT A WARY EYE OUT WHEN TULAN ORDERED THE *LADY'S Luck* in to land a party to search for water and provisions. This northern coast had proved singularly unpromising; long stretches of black gravel beaches, hillsides of low brush, and bare smooth stone highlands. But provisions and water were low, and so Tulan dropped anchor in a bay and lowered a launch carrying a landing party under Storval.

That was four days ago. Four days since the party was last seen walking inland to be lost behind the lazy curve of a coastal rise. Short trees – large bushes, really – provided the main greenery of this coast. That and lichens and moss. Far inland, on the clearest of days, a distant range of gleaming mountain tops could just be seen. From his research Reuth alone knew their names: the Salt range, east and west. Or, on some charts: the Blood Mountains. Their destination.

Why then did he dread the sight of them?

On the morning of the fifth day – the last day Tulan said he would wait for them – the crewman atop the mast called out a sighting. Reuth ran to the side. Two figures came shambling into sight. Limping, running, helping each other along. They heaved the launch out and struggled over its side as it rose and fell in the surge.

'Only two,' Reuth breathed and Tulan shot him an angry glare. Reuth realized, belatedly, that everyone had seen this but that only he had been foolish enough to say it aloud. It was as Tulan said. Too long in the dusty halls bent over manuscripts and not enough time spent among sailors. Well, after this voyage, he would have spent more than enough time at sea.

That is, should they ever get home.

The two managed to ready the oars and steady the nose of the

204

launch to point it out to the bay. Reuth glanced away to scan the beaches of rolled gravel for signs of pursuit, but saw none. Where were the attackers? Surely these two couldn't have outrun them. Yet no followers betrayed themselves amid the ash-hued naked rock.

Then movement on the nearest hilltop caught his attention. Figures came walking out into the open to stand atop the domed rock. Tall and slim, wearing tanned hide jerkins and trousers. They carried long spears, or javelins. Long brownish hair blew unbound in the winds.

Crewmen spotted them and shouted, pointing.

Tulan just grunted and muttered something about 'damned natives'.

The launch reached them. Lines were thrown, attached to it. The two climbed up a rope ladder. It was Storval and Galip. Both carried flesh wounds, cuts and slashes.

'The others?' Tulan demanded.

Storval just shook his head, still winded, breathing heavily. He dropped two fat skins of water to the deck.

'This wouldn't have happened if you'd had Kyle with you,' Reuth told Storval.

The first mate turned on him, his face flushed, enraged, his hand going to the dirk at his side. Tulan slapped the man's hand aside, grasped Reuth's arm and dragged him off. 'You're supposed to be a smart lad,' he hissed. 'So think before you open your damned hole.'

Reuth peered past his uncle to the first mate. 'Well . . . it's true.' And he walked away.

He leaned on his elbows over the side while Tulan bellowed to get the crew moving for departure. Sailors readied the running rigging. Arms crossed on the railing, Reuth eyed the figures on the shore, who still had not moved. *Seeing us off.* The Barren Shore, he knew, was one name for this stretch of the northern coast. *Fitting.* Another name was the Plain of Ghosts.

He decided he did not want to discover whether or not that appellation was accurate.

Some charts he'd studied had included an inlet in the northern coast that led to rivers and a settlement. A fortress named Taken. But on this coast, on these lands of Assail, Reuth decided not to lead the ship to a fortress with the name of Taken. No, not in these lands. He hoped instead that they would find water before then – some unnamed stream or trickle – anything.

Again, while he daydreamed, his thoughts went to Kyle, as they often did. He must have made it to shore. He'd seemed completely confident that he could. And ashore, he must have headed north. If anyone could make it, he could. Perhaps of all of them he would be the only one to succeed.

Wouldn't that be an irony? And the probable truth, too, given how the gods seemed to relish irony, reversals, and fitting unanticipated rewards for deeds both good and evil. And on that account, Reuth believed they had earned what they had so far received – the very real possibility of an ugly anonymous death on some desolate shore like this.

It had been wrong of them to turn on Whiteblade like that. His uncle should have thought further ahead. Given the dangers, they would have been so much more secure with him among their crew. Reuth did not think much of their chances now. And that was fitting. For he too had known it was wrong, yet he'd shrunk from drawing a blade and standing with his friend.

He was a coward, and he deserved whatever shameful death the gods had set astride the path of his life.

He heard Tulan come stomping up behind him. 'Are there no rivers marked on this shore?' he demanded.

Reuth turned round and peered calmly up at his uncle. 'We're bound to come across a stream eventually,' he assured him.

Tulan cocked an eye beneath his tangled bushy brows, as if troubled by the answer in some vague manner that he could not pin down. Then he snorted and lumbered off, muttering darkly beneath his breath.

Reuth returned to contemplating the iron-grey waters. Yes, eventually they would find water. Or they would not. It did not matter. Eventually, just as certainly, they would meet their end.

And there was nothing any of them could do about it.

*　　*　　*

Shortly after the *Silver Dawn* set sail, leading the convoy of four ships into the Sea of Dread, Ieleen became ill. She refused to go below and would not budge from her seat behind the tiller. She sat all day leaning forward, knuckles white on her walking stick, her head bowed, pressing against her hands.

The times Jute had come to urge her to go below and lie down she'd snarled tersely and he'd backed away. They'd been under sail for six days now, although for the majority of the last day the description 'under sail' had no longer been accurate. The canvas

206

hung limp. Only the barest of chill breaths brushed Jute's neck. He ordered the crew to the rowing benches and they carried on.

But he was worried. He'd never seen Ieleen like this. It was as though she was being crushed beneath a terrible weight. Towards evening he went to her once more. He bent over her, but dared not touch her – she didn't like to be touched when she was casting ahead. 'Lass . . .' he whispered. 'Where away?' She seemed to flinch. Her body beneath its layers of shawls shuddered as if in the grip of an ague. 'What is it, lass?'

'I can't . . .' she whispered. Her voice was thick with sorrow. Leaning closer, he saw that the planking of the deck beneath her head was wet. A teardrop fell even as he watched.

'Rest, dearest,' he urged. 'Gather your strength.'

'I haven't the strength,' she answered all in a gasp. 'I can't see us through!'

'It's all right, lass. Tomorrow. Tomorrow you'll feel better.'

'No!' She drew a great shuddering breath. 'Makes no difference. It's too late. I can't see ahead. And . . . I'm afraid . . . I can't . . .' She choked then on her words, collected herself, and continued, huskily, 'I can't see behind.'

Jute straightened. He studied the southern horizon out past the following three vessels. Then he glanced to the north. The flat horizons appeared identical. A thickening sea mist obscured both. The waters were uniformly calm. Not even the winds gave any hint of which direction was which. If they were to be turned round in the night, how was anyone to know? Other than studying the night sky, of course. But should this fog close in about them . . .

He knelt to her once more. 'What am I to do, love?'

'Just keep going,' she answered curtly. 'Try to chart us a course tonight.'

'Aye. Tonight. You just hold on then, dearest. Hold on till then.'

He paced to the bows. He might have reassured Ieleen but he held little hope. How could they escape if they had no heading? They'd oar in circles until they ran out of water and provisions and that would be the end of them.

Later that afternoon a launch came aside the *Dawn* and Cartheron himself climbed aboard. The old man peered about the deck and nodded to himself, evidently approving of what he saw. Jute greeted him. 'To what do we owe the pleasure?'

'A word, captain, if I may,' and he lifted his chin to indicate the cabin.

Jute swept an arm to invite him onward. 'This way.'

Inside, the Malazan captain glanced about the cabin as if searching for something. 'You wouldn't still have that bottle I handed over, or such like, would you?'

'In fact I do.' Jute produced the bottle and two tiny glasses.

Cartheron frowned at the small glass but shrugged and held it out.

'And what can I do for you, captain?'

Cartheron tossed back the liquor and held out the glass again. 'I was just hoping that you knew where you were headed. Because we sure as Mael's own bowels don't.'

Jute studied the clear fluid in his glass. 'I won't dissemble. My . . . pilot . . . has been having trouble in that regard. But tonight we hope to get a heading from the stars.'

Cartheron threw back his drink, sucked his teeth. 'Hunh. The stars.' He squinted at Jute. 'Have you been studying them these last few nights? No? Well, I tell you – they've not been of much help. But . . .' he drew a steadying breath and set down the glass, 'I leave it to you.' He slapped Jute on the shoulder and opened the cabin door. 'Because, other than you, we've no damn hope of ever finding our way out of here.'

Jute laughed, a touch uneasily. He walked Cartheron back to the side and saw him off.

Tonight then. They had to make some progress through the night. Some measurable progress.

He waved Buen over. 'Have the crew take a rest. We'll resume at the evening watch.'

The first mate frowned, not liking loss of motion, but nodded and went to give the orders. Jute turned to Ieleen, meaning to give her the news, but one glance at her rigid back, her hands bloodless upon the walking stick as if it were a lifeline, and he decided not to disturb her.

If they made any headway this night, then she could rest. He'd see to it.

He ordered a general rest. The crew took turns napping. He would've himself, but Ieleen wasn't getting any sleep so he couldn't bear to lie down. He knew it would be useless.

Behind, the following three vessels slowed as well. Jute ordered the smallest launch lowered, a tiny skiff used for repairs, to be taken across to the others to let them know to be ready this night. Then he sat to await the dusk.

When twilight thickened, Buen came to him. 'Permission to resume rowing?'

'No. Wait for a bearing. No sense running off chasing our own shadow.'

The first mate appeared dubious, his brows rising. 'As you say, captain. But I really think . . .'

Jute gave him a sharp look. 'You think what?'

The man ducked his head. 'Nothing, captain.' He marched off.

Jute watched him go. That had been a strange outburst. Becalmings could be hard on the nerves – was the man feeling it already? Damned soon for that.

He stared out across the rippling waters. Calm. Too calm for a body like this. The winds should kick up larger waves over all these leagues of water. Strange. He was not a man given to brooding, but something about this sea troubled him. He drew a hand down his face, rubbed his gritty eyes, perhaps he was just reacting to Ieleen's troubles.

Gradually, the stars emerged. Jute's mood darkened with the night as he realized that he couldn't recognize any of the constellations. It was as if he was staring up at someone else's night sky. Yet how could that be? Must be a trick of the night and the mists here on the sea. Even so, none of that would matter if he could just identify a pole star: a star that did not move.

Yet which was it? Amid all this panoply of glimmering infinity . . . which?

He hunched, defeated. The only explanation that he could think of was sorcery. They'd been ensorcelled. In which case, as well as Ieleen, they now had a further authority to turn to.

He called to Buen. 'Ready the launch!'

Four oarsmen took him across to the side of Lady Orosenn's intimidatingly tall galleon. No watch or officer hailed him from the darkened vessel. As they'd approached he'd seen a single brazier burning towards the bow. Now, from so low next to the side, it was only visible as a faint glow above.

'Ahoy! Lady Orosenn! It is Captain Jute, come to talk. May I come aboard?'

They waited in silence for a long time. Jute was finally driven to bash an oar against the thick planks of the side. A bump appeared above: a head peering down.

'Who is that?' Jute recognized the voice of the old man who'd accompanied the sorceress. He'd quite forgotten his name, if it had been given at all.

'It's Captain Jute, come to speak to Lady Orosenn.'

'A moment,' the man called. Shortly afterwards a rope and wood ladder came clattering down. Jute stared up. 'Wait here,' he told his oarsmen, who all nodded, quite happy to remain.

He found the deck empty but for the old man. Jute peered about, a touch confused. Normally such a huge vessel would require an equally large crew. Yet the vessel was unnaturally quiet but for the normal creaking and stretching of cordage and planks. Indeed, the old man appeared quite put out by his presence. It occurred to him that very possibly the only reason he now stood upon the deck was the fact that he had been raising a ruckus below.

'What do you want?' the scrawny old fellow growled, his voice low.

'To speak to Lady Orosenn,' he replied loudly.

The old man winced. 'Keep your voice down,' he hissed.

'Why?'

'You may disturb the Primogenitrix!' the man shouted, angered, then ducked, glaring his rage.

'I see. Well, won't you go and see if she may be disturbed?'

The old fellow chewed on that for a time, his expression sour. Then he gave a curt jerk of his head and scuttled off. Jute waited. Alone now, in the quiet, he cast about for some hint of the crew's presence, but all he noticed was the smell. The ship fairly reeked of foreign spices, and unpalatably so, too. He held a hand to his nose. Beneath the cloying scents he believed he also detected a faint whiff of rot. Perhaps even of decomposition.

The old man returned. He waved Jute off. 'She won't see you. Now go away.'

'Go away?' He peered past the scarecrow fellow to the stern cabin. 'She seemed very approachable before . . .'

'Well, she's busy now.'

'Doing what?'

The fellow frowned even more darkly, knotting his brows. 'Sorcerous things. Now go – you are in great danger.'

'Danger of what?'

The fellow drew breath to shout or argue, but caught himself and clamped his mouth shut. He leaned close, conspiratorially, and lowered his voice: 'Perhaps you would care for a tour of this curious vessel, yes? I think you would find the lower decks of particular interest . . .'

'Velmar,' came the rich tenor of Lady Orosenn, 'who is that you are speaking to?'

The old man jerked upright, still glaring his rage. 'Captain Jute, m'lady.'

'Is that so?' The woman emerged from the murk. She loomed just as impressively tall as before, still wrapped in her loose robes, her head hidden in a headscarf, her veil in place.

Jute bowed. 'I'm sorry to disturb you, madam.'

'Not at all. You are concerned, no doubt, about the choking wardings that have settled upon us.'

Wardings? Jute wondered. 'Yes,' he replied. 'We seem to have lost our way.'

'Such is one of their purposes.'

'My, ah, pilot is attempting to find the way. But I fear the task is beyond her.'

The woman tilted her head, regarded him with her large, almost luminescent, golden-hazel eyes. 'And you are concerned for her.'

'Indeed.'

The woman nodded her great head, and Jute thought he heard a sigh. She turned away to the ship's side, resting a hand atop the railing. 'Your feelings do you credit, Jute of Delanss. I must admit I have been selfish. I had hoped to remain anonymous. To not have to . . . *exert* myself . . . as yet. But I see now that in doing so I have allowed a terrible burden to fall to another. A burden that should rightfully be mine.'

Velmar raised a hand. 'My lady! This is none of your affair.'

She regarded her attendant then offered Jute what he thought a dry chuckle. 'We work at cross purposes, my priestly guardian and I. You must forgive him. His only concern is my safety. Whereas the safety of others concerns me.'

She turned back to the railing, gazing off towards the *Silver Dawn*. 'I sense your pilot's struggle, Jute. She is drowning. The Sea of Dread will swallow her . . . as it would you all. Unless I finally choose to announce myself.' She raised a hand, gesturing. 'So be it. It is done.'

'My lady!' Velmar hissed, uneasy. 'We are not yet far enough north.'

She looked back at him. 'We are now, Velmar. The Dread Sea is far enough. Do you not feel it?' She spread her arms, expanding her robes like sails. 'Never have I sensed it so strongly.' She shifted her attention to Jute. 'I am a child of exile, Falaran. Yet I am returning home.' She extended a long-fingered hand, inviting Jute to the side. 'Return to your ship. You will find your pilot at ease. I shall take

211

the lead in the *Supplicant*. You must secure your vessels to mine. On no account must you become separated. Spread the word, Jute of Delanss.'

Jute could not help it: he bowed to the sorceress. 'I will. My thanks – *our* thanks.' He climbed down the ladder, stepped into the rocking skiff. 'Head across to the *Ragstopper*,' he told the men at the oars.

After the *Ragstopper*, they crossed to Tyvar in the *Resolute*. Chase launches were lowered, lines were unwound, and the coming dawn saw them arranged in line: the *Supplicant* leading, followed by the *Silver Dawn*, the *Ragstopper*, and the *Resolute*.

When Jute, exhausted, finally climbed aboard the *Dawn* he found the stool next to the tiller arm empty and peered about frantically. The steersman, Lurjen, pointed him to his cabin. He lurched within. Ieleen lay in bed. He sat gently and laid a hand to her cheek.

She was asleep, breathing gently. He let out a long breath of ease and rose from the bed. Good. Let her rest. She is in need of a long rest. He exited the cabin and eased the door shut. He needed a rest as well; everything was blurry. He looked to Lurjen, pressed his fingers to his sore eyes. 'I'm going to find a hammock.' He went below.

*

Three days later they encountered the first drifting vessel. It was a broad-beamed merchant caravel, dead in the water. Its sails hung limp. Jute hailed it from the *Dawn*'s side, but no one answered. A launch was sent across from the *Resolute*. It carried some ten Blue Shield mercenaries. More than enough to meet any danger. Word came back that they'd found the ship empty of all life. As if the crew had just up and abandoned it mid-voyage. Meals lay half eaten, ropes half coiled. All without signs of any violence. No corpses, no evidence of any struggle.

It made even Jute uneasy, and he was the least superstitious person he knew. The crew began muttering of curses and becalmings, haunts and murder. Everyone was on edge. Buen reported to him the bizarre rumour that accused the sorceress, Lady Orosenn, of dragging them all to their doom.

He'd laughed out loud when Buen repeated it to him, yet the strange thing was that the man had actually appeared hurt, as if he'd half believed it himself.

Ieleen had been bedridden since Lady Orosenn's intervention, and when he'd told her of the rumours she hadn't laughed. She'd looked very worried, and murmured, 'We have to get through here as quickly as we can.'

Every day they sighted more of the drifting, abandoned vessels. Seventeen so far. They stopped bothering to send out launches to investigate. That was until they came abreast of a two-masted galley that Jute recognized as a Genabackan vessel, a craft the pirates of the south preferred. And there, standing amidships, was a man.

Jute hailed him, waving. The man did not wave back. He stood immobile, as if staring in disbelief. Jute looked at his own crew and was unnerved to see that they, too, were not waving or hailing. Why in the name of Mael not?

'Buen,' he called, 'lower a launch.'

The first mate stared back up at him, rubbed a hand over his jaws. 'Why, sir?'

'Why? How can you ask that? There's a man on board that vessel, that's why.'

Buen peered about among his fellow crewmen. 'We saw no one, captain.'

'No one? You saw no one?' He snapped his gaze back to the vessel. The figure was gone. Had he been there at all? Had it been . . . a ghost?

Jute slammed a hand to the railing. No! No damned ghosts! A man. Nothing more.

'Ship's boat coming alongside!' the watch announced. Jute hurried down to the side. It was the dilapidated launch from the *Ragstopper*. Half the oarsmen rowed while the other half bailed furiously. Cartheron sat within, his legs stretched out, his leather shoes wet in the swilling water. He hailed Jute: 'Going to take a look. Interested?'

'Yes I most certainly am!' He turned to Dulat. 'Lower the ladder.'

The rope ladder was thrown over the side and he climbed down to the launch. It took a while to settle into the battered rowboat, as it was so low in the water he was afraid his added weight would swamp the thing. But it took him, although the freeboard was a bare hand's breadth. The Malazan sailors, in their tattered shirts and trousers, scarves tied over their heads, looked more piratical than any pirate crew Jute had ever seen. They pushed off and started rowing.

'Thought I saw someone,' Cartheron said from the bow.

'As did I. The crew claimed they didn't, though.'

Cartheron sagely nodded his grey-bristled chin. 'Beginning to think you see or don't see what you want on this sea.'

Jute shook his head. All part of the curse. Tricks of the mind. Delusions become real while reality itself drifts away.

They came up beside the dead vessel, which they saw was called the *Sea Strike*. No one answered their hail; Jute hadn't expected them to. Cartheron ordered one of his sailors to climb the side and the man impressed Jute mightily by clambering up the planking as agile and sure as a monkey. Shortly afterwards a rope ladder came clattering down.

The deck was empty and abandoned, just like all the others. This one was far worse for wear, however. Bird-droppings covered the deck, and the lines and sails were faded and frayed. Still, like the others, there were no obvious signs of violence.

'Hello!' Cartheron called. No one answered. The Malazan captain went to the cabin door. 'Let's have a look.'

Jute had turned away, meaning to investigate the bows, when a shriek spun him round. A shrill voice, hardly recognizable as human, had screeched: '*At last!*'

Cartheron stood impaled on a sword that a man, lunging from the cabin, had thrust straight out.

The Malazan had his hands pressed to his stomach around the blade. While everyone stared, stunned, the sword's owner shrank from them, hands raised, his face white and his eyes rolling in mad terror.

'*Ghosts!*' the man yelled, and charged the side, toppling straight over.

'No!' Jute yelled. He lunged, but there was no sign of the fellow. It was as if he'd simply allowed himself to sink.

A wet cough brought his attention back to Cartheron. The Malazan had yanked the blade free and fallen to his knees. Jute and the sailors blinked away their stunned confusion and went to him. Jute gathered up folds of the captain's shirt and pressed it to the wound. 'Make a seat,' he shouted to the gathered crewmen. 'We have to lower him.'

Cartheron actually laughed, albeit without breath. 'Ain't this just the funniest comeuppance, hey? You drop your guard for a moment and . . . there you go. Damnedest thing.'

Jute wrapped the wound as tightly as he could. 'Quiet, now. We'll take you to the sorceress. Maybe she can heal you.'

'Don't you bother, lad. Bound to happen sooner or later. Long past time, in my case.'

214

'Don't even think of it.'

They tied him into a makeshift plank and rope seat and lowered him into the launch. From the *Sea Strike* they oared straight across to the *Supplicant.*

This time the sorceress herself appeared at the side. Jute shouted up that Cartheron was wounded. She gestured for a rope to be thrown up, and after a moment the seat, with the unconscious man secured within, began rising steadily up the tall ship's side. A rope ladder came banging down. Jute climbed alongside the rope seat, attempting to steady it. On deck, he and Velmar struggled to raise Cartheron over the side until the lady herself took a hand and easily lifted him across.

'I will take him to my cabin,' she told Jute, and carried him within.

'You should all just turn round,' Velmar grumbled, and he glared as if all their troubles were Jute's fault. Jute ignored him.

They stood silently for some time. The launch from the *Ragstopper* bumped the side below. The lines creaked and stretched. Velmar glowered sullenly, as if the very heat of his disapproval could drive Jute from the deck.

The captain sat on the edge of a raised hatch leading to the cargo hold. Curious, he glanced down through the wood grating. It may have been a trick of the shifting light, but he thought he glimpsed figures below, standing crowded together, motionless. He turned to the priest to ask him about them but the wolfish mocking grin that now climbed the man's lips somehow stilled his tongue.

'You're sure you wouldn't care to have a look below?' the man asked, and the downturned smile widened.

Jute had no idea what the priest was hinting at, but didn't think it sounded healthy. 'No, thank you.'

'Aren't you curious?'

'Not at all.'

'Later perhaps,' Velmar said, thoughtfully tapping a finger to his lips.

'Certainly – later.'

The priest was nodding now. 'Yes, I think so. Definitely later.'

Jute merely bunched his brow. Such games were of no interest to him.

Movement among the shadows of the stern brought him to his feet. The sorceress emerged. She still wore her headdress and veil. All he could see were her eyes, and these appeared worried and saddened.

'I have done what I can. He will not die. But neither is he certain to recover. Many organs were damaged. And he is old, and very tired.' She glanced back to the stern. 'Then again . . . he is an extraordinary fellow. He may just recover.'

Jute bowed to her. 'Our thanks, Lady Orosenn.'

'It is nothing. I am glad to be of help.'

Jute crossed to the side. 'I'll tell the crew. He is to remain here, then?'

'Yes. He mustn't be moved any more.'

'Very well.' He took hold of the rope ladder, swung his legs out over the side and climbed down.

Velmar's shaggy head appeared above him at the side. 'Later, Captain Jute,' the man called down in his enigmatic tone. Jute just shook his head, while below the rowers from the *Ragstopper* steadied the launch.

In the days that followed they met fewer and fewer abandoned becalmed ships until the outlook was again clear of all other vessels. The sea was improbably calm, as was the wind. No breeze ruffled the air, no ripple disturbed the iron-grey surface. To Jute it was as if they sailed a sheet of misty glass.

Yet they were not entirely alone. Now and then crew members shouted their surprise and dismay, pointing down at the astonishingly clear water. Rotting vessels lay beneath them, in various stages of decomposition. And all, it seemed to Jute, from differing epochs or periods of history. Older-style galleys lay stacked upon even more archaic open-hulled longboats, which in turn appeared to rest upon even cruder hulls, some perhaps nothing more than dugouts. It was as if the Sea of Dread were one great graveyard of vessels, all heaped upon one another, each slowly settling into, and adding to, the mud and mire of the sea floor.

So too would they have ended, he imagined, were it not for the guidance, and shielding, of the sorceress with them.

For the next few days a dense mist enshrouded them. It clung to the masts in scarves and tatters. Jute found it almost hard to breathe the stuff. The noises of their passage returned to them distorted, even unrecognizable. It was almost as if the sounds were from other vessels hidden in the miasma, calling to them.

Then, slowly, the light ahead began to brighten ever so slightly. Took on a pale sapphire glint. The vapours thinned and they emerged as if through parting veils to find themselves once more behind the *Supplicant*, only now approaching a forested rocky coast bearing the last patches of winter's snow. Great jagged spires of ice floated in the waters between them and the coast.

The fog thinned even more, revealing that beyond the shore the land climbed to rocky jagged ridges. Behind these, distant and tall, reared the white gleaming peaks of mountains. Jute gazed, entranced. Could those be their destination? The near-mythical Salt range?

A breath caught behind him and he turned, surprised. There stood Ieleen, gripping the doorway, walking stick in hand. He went to her. 'Lass! You're up!'

'Aye.' She sounded deathly hoarse. He guided her to her stool and she sat heavily, sighing her gratitude. 'Aye. At last.' Her sightless clouded eyes darted about. 'I dreamed . . . troubled dreams. Someone shielded me from their worst.' Somehow, the eyes found him. 'We know who, hey?'

He nodded, then remembered. 'Ah, yes. So, what do you smell?'

'The scent that has been tormenting me for days now,' she growled, displeased. She closed both hands atop the walking stick and set her chin there. 'The stink of ancient rotting ice.'

*　　*　　*

Two days after departing the Isle of Pillars, Master Ghelath came stomping up to K'azz and Shimmer. They stood at the bow of their new vessel, the Letherii-commissioned merchantman named the *Venture*. The captain was mopping his brow and scowling.

'This vessel's a useless tub,' he announced.

'Don't pull your punches,' K'azz answered, not looking away from the waters to the north.

The Falaran sailor threw his arms wide. 'We're hardly making any headway at all!' He thrust a finger down to their feet and the raised archer's castle they stood upon. 'These platforms fore and aft make us top-heavy. We're squat, too broad at the beam, wallowing, and slower than a Cawnese river-barge!'

'Speak for yourself,' K'azz murmured.

Shimmer compressed her lips to hide a smile. 'And what do you suggest, captain?'

Ghelath waved his arms as if they could start anywhere. 'Hack off these half-arsed platforms for a start,' he finally spluttered.

K'azz frowned. 'There are easier options, master mariner.'

The captain daubed at his flushed glistening forehead. 'Such as?'

'Light a smudge.'

217

The man gaped at K'azz. 'A smudge?'

'Yes, captain.'

'That'll attract every ship within leagues!'

'Yes, captain.'

He squeezed the cloth in his hands, twisted it. 'That's yer orders, is it?'

'Yes. I agree with you, captain – we do need to make better headway. See to it.'

Ghelath wiped his face with the rag. 'Well . . . if you say so, sir.' He went off shaking his head.

Shimmer regarded K'azz. 'It could bring the Letherii.'

He turned away to lean against the railing once more. 'I do not believe they are following.'

'You underestimate the blind spitefulness of the self-righteous.'

That raised a faint smile. 'Perhaps so, Shimmer. Such emotions feel distant now.'

She considered the statement. Indeed, she couldn't remember the last time she felt an intense emotion. Such as rage. Or – and here her breath caught – even *passion*. And yet the pain I feel now burning in my chest is real. I *feel*. But I do not reach out. What is wrong with me? Am I still even capable . . .

She went to find Bars.

He was below talking with Blues, Sept, and Black the Elder. 'A word, Bars. If you would,' she said.

He nodded. She led him to the main cabin, which was quite sumptuously decorated – the Letherii merchant Luthal Canar seemed to have valued his creature comforts. The bed, she noted, was much wider and longer than the usual sailor's bunk. Good. Blasted awkward to be banging your head when you're trying to enjoy yourself.

She closed and latched the door behind them and stood before it.

He turned and peered down at her with a rather puzzled look. 'Yes, Shimmer?'

This close she found she had to tilt her head back quite far. Damn, but he's a big one. She'd quite forgotten. She drew a hard breath to steel herself, and said, 'Kiss me.'

First his brows fell, then they rose higher and higher. The colour of his face actually deepened.

Oh, come on, you great ox! You're not making this any easier. I can't do all the work here. Without looking down she started undoing her belt. 'Does a woman have to ask twice?'

Now he was shaking his head. 'No, Shimmer. Don't . . . not like this . . .'

Her weapon belt hit the floor and she started on his. 'Come on, Bars. Don't you feel anything? I want to. I want to *feel*.'

He snatched her hands in his. 'No! Shimmer. No . . .'

She gazed up at him, saw hurt in his eyes. *Hurt?* Why that? Am I so—

She yanked her hands from him, flinched away. 'I may not be some soft courtesan, Bars. My nose may be broken and I may have calluses on my hands . . . but I am a woman!' She turned to the door. 'And you are a fool.'

'You are beautiful, Shimmer,' he said, very quietly. Her hand lingered on the latch. 'I've always thought you beautiful. You do not know how long I've wanted . . . longed . . . well.' She heard him cross the cabin. Wood creaked as he sat on the framed edge of the bed. 'I don't want something so beautiful if it will just be taken away from me tomorrow. That would hurt too much, Shimmer.'

She slowly turned back to him. Oh, Bars . . . I didn't know . . . How could I have known? You said nothing. Why didn't you at least *say* something? She pulled her mail coat over her head. It dropped to the floor in a crash of jangling metal. She came to him. 'How was I to know, you great oaf? You never said a thing!'

A wistful smile crossed his scarred face. He wiped something from his cheeks.

Tears? Oh, Bars . . . you great fool!

He cleared his throat. 'There's a saying where I come from, Shimmer. If you have to chase and corner the wild animal, then it's not yours. But if you stand very still and let it come to you – then it *is* yours.'

She stood very close before him. 'So I'm a wild animal, am I?'

A smile crooked his lips as he peered up at her. 'The wildest. And the most frightening.'

'Frightening? How so?'

'Women are terrifying to men,' he whispered, 'because they can break them with the simplest word or briefest glance.'

Now she smiled. 'Not if they care for them.' She took his head in her hands and gently pressed his cheek to her stomach. Even through the layers of padding and undershirts she could feel his heat. She closed her eyes at the pleasure that warmth gave her. 'I think we have a lot of catching up to do,' she said, and her voice was very faint, and husky.

He ran his hands up under her shirts along her thighs.

Her breath escaped her in a gasp.

~

219

The light streaming in through the opaque window glazing deepened to the gold of late afternoon and still they did not leave the cabin. Even shouts and the stamping of running feet across the deck did not rouse them. Only the thrumming release of crossbows and the muted sound of Ghelath shouting orders caused Shimmer to raise her head from his shoulder.

'What is that?' she murmured.

'Blues can handle it,' he answered, and pressed his mouth to hers. She clasped his head again and straddled him.

Later, a quiet knock on the planks of the door brought her head up. Groaning, she stood and dragged off the embroidered quilt to wrap around herself as she crossed the cabin. She yanked open the door. 'What is it?'

Master Ghelath stood in the way. His grizzled brows shot up and his already ruddy cheeks darkened further. He swallowed and pressed his hands together. 'Ah . . . we've another ship, ma'am. If you're ready to move . . .'

She peered out past him. The masts of another vessel rose beyond the side of the relatively tall merchantman. A lower vessel – probably a far faster galley. She gave a curt nod. 'Very good, captain. What does K'azz say?'

She pushed back her hair and the quilt fell partially open. Ghelath quickly glanced away. He blew out a long breath. 'He awaits your pleas— Ah, that is . . . when you're ready, ma'am.'

'Very good. You may begin.'

He bobbed a bow. 'Yes, ma'am. At once.'

She slammed shut the door, threw aside the quilt. 'Get moving. K'azz has captured a better ship.'

Bars groaned and sat up. 'It's about time.' He massaged a knee. 'You're killing me, standing there. I still can't believe it's you.'

She searched for her shorts and chamois. 'I have no complaints either.'

'Is that flattery?'

She pulled on her trousers and undershirts. 'How about: now I know why they call you Iron Bars?'

'Ouch!' He drew on his trousers. 'And what about you? Will I ever see you dance?'

She planted a kiss on his shoulder, tasted salt and sweat. 'I hope we'll have the chance.'

His smile turned sad once more. 'I hope so too, Shimmer. I hope so.'

She nodded her answer and returned to the door. Outside, she watched the sailors handing stores over the side to the new vessel. In the middle of the deck, crowded together under guard, stood its former crew, a ragged band of would-be pirates hailing from the southernmost shores of this new continent, Assail. Bruises darkened the faces of many. They looked bewildered and thoroughly cowed.

'We'll be gone soon,' Blues was explaining to them. He opened his arms wide. 'Welcome to your new ship.'

She went to the side. The new ship was much smaller, two-masted, with low cabins fore and aft.

Have I just made a terrible mistake? she wondered. No. Reaching out for companionship – for a human touch – is not a mistake. Withholding such a thing is the mistake. She thought of all the years she had held herself apart and shook her head.

She had been the fool.

Blinking against the blur of tears, she glanced away. She caught Blues watching her, a teasing smile on his lips. 'What're you grinning at?'

'Nothing, Shimmer. Nothing at all.'

'Isn't there any privacy around here?' She stomped off to pull together her few possessions.

*   *   *

For nearly a week, the Reddin brothers and Old Bear beat against Orman's spearwork. Even Bernal Heavyhand took a turn; the man's blows rocked Svalthbrul and numbed Orman's hands. On the fifth day they were out in the fields practising when a distant figure came jogging up the valley to the Greathall. The shaggy hounds howled their welcome and bounded out to meet him. Old Bear gestured for Orman and the Reddin brothers to return to the house.

They found the newcomer sprawled in one of the raised wooden chairs, petting a hound. Vala was bent down at his side, speaking to him. The man rose and waved them forward. 'Welcome to Sayer Hall,' he called.

'Jaochim,' Old Bear answered, bowing. He gestured to the Reddin brothers. 'This is Keth and Kasson Reddin.' He motioned to Orman. 'Orman Bregin's son.'

'Greetings!' the man called. 'I am Jaochim. Brothers, you are welcome. Orman – I knew your father and I honour his name.' Orman could see that the man was eyeing Svalthbrul. 'My thanks for joining us. We have need for more spears.'

Old Bear cocked his brow. 'Oh?'

'The Eithjar have sent warning. A gang of some twenty raiders have entered the Holding. Take our new spears and drive them off, yes?'

Old Bear bowed again. 'With pleasure, Jaochim.' He slapped Orman on the back. 'Our first sport, lad. Let us blood your spear!'

Jaochim stepped down from the platform and examined Svalthbrul. In turn, Orman examined the head of the Sayer clan. Very tall and wiry he was, like all the Icebloods. Long-jawed, with large canines and a deep brow. His long earth-brown hair hung in a dirty mass about his shoulders. His eyes were oddly shaped; oblong, they seemed, and glowed a deep amber. 'So it is true,' he said admiringly.

'I am proud to carry it,' Orman said.

Jaochim smiled. His canines made it a wolfish grin. 'As you should be. Your father's winning of it is a grand tale. The Eithjar speak of it still.'

Feet slammed the dirt of the floor and Jass came running in. 'Jaochim!' Uncle and nephew embraced. 'I am so very glad to see you!'

'And I you.' Jaochim looked Jass up and down and nodded to himself. He gestured to Old Bear. 'Take the lad with you, Bear. It's time he blooded his spear as well.'

Orman couldn't help himself: 'No!'

Jaochim turned a frown upon him. 'No, you say?'

Orman shot a look to Vala, but she stood motionless, her arms wrapped around herself, her lips drawn tight. Obviously she was fearful but would not interfere; perhaps she saw the need, or the obligation. He swallowed his sudden dread and cursed himself. 'There are twenty . . .'

Jaochim nodded, patted Jass on the shoulder. 'All the more need for another spear.' He urged Jass out. 'You will leave at once. The Eithjar will guide you.'

Old Bear bowed. 'At once, Jaochim.' He waved Orman off. 'Get your gear.'

He waited before the Greathall. He had little gear to ready, just his father's travelling leathers, his knives, a sleeping roll and a pouch of dried meat and hard cheese. And Svalthbrul, of course. Keth and Kasson emerged side by side wearing their heaviest armour of boiled leather hauberks with mailed sleeves and vambraces. Helmets were pushed back on their heads. They carried shields on their backs, longswords at their sides, and spears in hand.

Old Bear came out escorting Jass, who now wore a leather hauberk that was a touch on the large side for his gangly frame. The sword at his side also looked rather too big for him, and he carried his spear.

Orman went to Old Bear's side. 'Is this it, then?' he whispered, low and fierce. 'Just we five?'

'Six,' Bear answered, grinning – foolishly, Orman thought. 'Gerrun is probably with them.'

'With them? What do you mean, with them?'

The big man winked, and the gesture – as if this were all in good fun – infuriated Orman. 'Don't you remember the hunting party that came chasing you? Gerrun joined it. He's with most parties that come up from the lowlands. Offers his services as a guide, he does.'

Old Bar headed off, jogging down the path that led to the trail out of the valley. Orman followed. He thought now of Gerrun, offering to guide his uncle, or perhaps merely joining the party for coin. How many times had the man gone alone among enemies? He shook his head in admiration. And he'd thought him a coward!

Later, as evening darkened beneath the trees, their pace slowed. The uneven ground was treacherous, the path nearly non-existent. Orman had the rear and Old Bear had fallen back to join him, or rather, the party now kept the old man's pace as he puffed and lumbered along. 'I understand your reluctance regarding Jass, lad,' Old Bear said as they descended a steep rocky stretch. Orman didn't answer. 'Don't you worry now. We'll all look out for him, won't we? And you can bet the Eithjar will also.'

'Can they stop a sword?' Orman growled.

The old man hawked up a mouthful of phlegm and spat. 'Well, no. But there're other things they can do here on the lands of their Holding, you can be certain of that.'

Orman grunted, unimpressed. 'Then they had better just stay out of my way.'

At an old campsite Keth called for a stop. They threw themselves down and rested until sunrise, then ate a quick cold meal and set off once more. Ghostly shapes wavered into view occasionally: the Eithjar directing them onward. Three days later a translucent womanly shape, all in ghostly furs, appeared before them and motioned to the ground. All fell to their stomachs and rolled to cover.

After a moment, Kasson edged forward on his elbows, then waved them onward. They all slid forward to what proved to be a shoulder of a wooded slope offering a view of the valley. Here a party climbed alongside a slim tumbling stream of meltwater. Orman counted fewer than twenty and decided they had scouts out.

Keth must have come to the same conclusion as he gestured them all into thicker cover. They grouped together under a rock ledge. Keth motioned to the top of the thick trees that rose about them. Orman nodded and handed Svalthbrul to Jass, then set to climbing.

He had to swing round the trunk and lean out to glimpse the party as it advanced. He spotted Gerrun with them, but this time the man probably wasn't laughing inside. He was tied up and being led along. This group, it seemed, wasn't nearly as trusting as prior parties.

Something else about them troubled Orman. Then he had it: they were all dressed alike in battered banded leather armour that looked to have once been painted or enamelled a dark green, with shortswords at their sides and shields on their backs. And they climbed as a unit, not dragging out in a long straggling line. Soldiers. Veterans, probably. Not your typical fortune-hunters, though soldiers sought gold just as anyone did. Very bad news for their small band. There was no way they could take such a large party of experienced fighters. He climbed back down.

Old Bear, however, was not impressed. 'We'll come at them in the night,' he said. 'When they're all asleep.'

'There'll be guards!' Orman answered hotly, hardly believing his ears.

'So there will be a few guards,' the old man answered, waving it aside. 'We'll rush 'em.'

'Rush them?' Orman echoed scornfully. 'They're soldiers! Trained for such a thing!'

Old Bear merely turned to Jass. 'Are we to retreat? Allow them passage?'

The lad, who had been following all this with a serious face, now shook his head. So serious was he it somehow made Orman's chest ache. Oh, lad, he thought, we're asking too much of you – we really are. 'Jaochim has laid the task on us,' Jass said, his eyes downcast, as if unwilling to look at them or let them see what was in his gaze. 'So we must see it through.'

Orman groaned inwardly. Oh, lad! What other answer could you possibly give us? You're too young to be brave enough to say no.

Old Bear grinned his approval. 'Aye, lad!' He cast a severe one-eyed glare on Orman, who nodded as well. For what else could he do? Had he not sworn his loyalty?

'I will watch them,' Keth said, and started pulling off his shield.

'No,' Old Bear interrupted. 'The Eithjar will shadow them. We can follow at a distance.'

The Reddin brothers accepted this without further words. They sat back and started working the edges of their weapons. Orman laid Svalthbrul across his lap. These Eithjar had better be a big help, because he did not like their chances against an organized party of soldiers.

With dusk one of the dead ancestors of the Sayers came to them and beckoned them onward. They crept forward in a line, the Reddin brothers leading, Orman following Jass, and Old Bear bringing up the rear.

The night was very dark. The Visitor had withdrawn to a faint sea-green dot among the stars. The moon was a silver arc, while clouds bunched up from the lowlands. Orman thought it unaccountably warm for this early in the spring. Jass knelt then, raising a hand for a pause. He tilted his head as if listening to something only he could hear, then gestured for them to spread out.

Orman edged to his left. He used Svalthbrul to part the brush and saw the glimmer of a campfire. He motioned to the Reddin brothers and signed ahead. Keth readied his bow and Kasson drew a hatchet. They all crept forward.

Against the flickering gold glare of the flames, he made out one of the guards. The man was standing with his back to the fire and Orman mentally cursed. Damned veterans! They know every trick. He almost backed out then, feeling that they were walking into a trap – yet how could that be with the Eithjar keeping watch? A bowstring thrummed and the guard pitched backwards.

Orman charged, Svalthbrul readied. At that moment the prone figures about the fire all threw off blankets and leapt to their feet – and not groggily, for they were armed and armoured, ready for the attack. There was no time to curse as one charged Orman directly. The man had his medium-sized round shield ready and he batted aside Orman's thrust, but Svalthbrul was no ordinary spear as the edge of the lanceolate blade caught the copper lip of the shield and Orman used this to yank the shield aside and curve round it inward to thrust again, taking the man through his chest armour and sinking deep. Too deep. The blade would not come free as the man fell. He held on hard, twisting, forgetting for the moment the boiling charging figures around him.

Someone shield-bashed him, knocking the breath from him and raising stars in his vision. The blow was so powerful it yanked Svalthbrul free and he turned it on the man, snapping up the haft as if it were a whip, taking him across the face so that he screamed as blood flew skyward.

Orman backed off. He searched among the dark milling shapes for Jass. He found him being pushed backwards by an opponent, his spear held sideways across his chest. The lad's footing became hung up on a corpse and he fell. The soldier reared over him, sword pulled back for a thrust. Orman screamed as he threw Svalthbrul. The spear pierced the man completely. He fell leaving the weapon standing from his back. Jass recovered his and backed away.

But the Reddin brothers were surrounded, while Gerrun had gotten free somehow and was duelling with a soldier though armed only with short knives. Three more were coming for Orman. He drew his heavy fighting knives and despaired. Too many. Just too damned many.

Then the very ground shook beneath his booted feet. A roar burst upon everyone like a blast of thunder. A massive mountain of russet shaggy fur came bowling in upon the scene, paws the size of shields swiping men left and right. Massive jaws crunched on an armoured arm and threw a soldier flying, legs and arms spinning. Another swat sent the two facing the Reddins down in a crunch of broken bones.

The remaining soldiers broke, running. The titanic humped bear roared again and gave chase.

And then it was quiet. Orman stood dragging in cold air, weaving on his feet. He retrieved Svalthbrul and staggered to Jass, who stood motionless, staring off where the great bear – Old Bear – could still be heard crashing through the underbrush.

'Just in time,' he gasped.

'So it's true,' Jass murmured in amazement.

'What's true?'

'The old tales. Shapeshifter. Old Bear. The last of them.'

Orman wiped his cold slick face. 'Or a spell, perhaps.'

Wet coughing pulled his attention round. A soldier. Orman moved off to stand over him. The man lay peering up, his chest a crushed ruin. 'They warned us,' he croaked.

Orman crouched on his haunches. 'What's that?' He could barely make out the man's foreign speech.

'Them townsfolk,' the soldier said. 'They warned us.' He tried to laugh, but had no air for it.

'Where are you from?' Orman asked.

'Don't matter.'

'Where?'

'Long ways away. Half-fort, Genabackis.'

'You soldiers?'

'Mercenaries, lad. You won this one . . . but I'd run . . . I was you.'

'Why?'

'Straw hut in a flood is you, lad. Compared to what's comin' . . . straw hut . . .' The mercenary's mouth fell slack and his gaze fixed. Orman pressed a hand down the man's face to close his eyes.

The Reddin brothers came up, Keth limping and Kasson cradling his bloodied left arm. Gerrun was hunched over the dead, rummaging through their clothes.

Orman studied the three of them: the brothers and Jass. He motioned uphill. 'Let's go.'

'What about Old Bear?' Jass asked.

'He'll find us.'

'And these bodies?'

'Leave them for the scavengers – as a warning.'

Keth nodded. He and his brother bound their wounds then waved to Gerrun. They headed back the way they'd come.

They could only limp a few leagues before bedding down for the night. They kept a watch just in case any of the soldiers came hunting them. Orman didn't think that any of them would have escaped Old Bear, but it was best to be careful.

The next day Old Bear emerged from the brush to join them. He looked himself, except perhaps the great shaggy bear hide he wore appeared a little worse for wear, hacked and slashed even more. Now, though, Orman knew he would never again look upon the man in the same way as before.

'You could have told us,' he accused him.

The old man grinned hugely. Even his frosty bad eye seemed to glint in delight. 'And ruin the surprise? Should've seen your faces! I'm sure you soiled your breeches, Orman Bregin's son.'

'Only from your smell.'

The old man guffawed his huge laugh. He slapped Jass's back. 'There you go, lad. Not so bad, hey?'

But Jass shook his head. 'We would've lost.'

At that morose evaluation a huge weight eased from Orman's mind. Good. The lad sees it. The victory – such as it was – hadn't fed any false youthful cockiness. 'I lost my duel,' the youth said, and the pain in that admission squeezed Orman's chest.

'It's all right, lad,' Old Bear said. 'Why, I'd be surprised if you won your first. That's why we're together. We cover one another. Next time maybe you'll save Kasson's life, hey?'

Jass merely shrugged. 'It wasn't . . .'

'Wasn't what?' Old Bear asked.

'. . . wasn't what I thought it'd be.'

Over Jass's head, Old Bear's single eye caught Orman's gaze and fixed there. He patted the lad's shoulder. 'It never is, lad. It never is what we think it's going to be. It's ugly, and confusing, and a blur and full of the acid of fear. Then it's over and you don't quite remember what happened but you're either alive or you're not. And there you are.'

Orman was nodding. 'Yes. That's how it was for me.'

Jass looked up at him. 'Really?'

'Yes.'

'You were scared?'

'Yes I was. Only a fool wouldn't be.'

The youth let go a long breath. 'Well . . . I was very frightened.'

Old Bear cuffed him again. ''Course you were! Only natural. First time's always the worst – hey, Orman?'

And Orman nodded, frowning with the memory of it. Yes, it had been.

The next day Gerrun announced that he ought to return to the lowlands to see what was going on. Old Bear waved him off, as did Orman and the brothers. They watched him go and Orman couldn't help reflecting that the man was now headed down to the towns loaded with the coin and goods he'd pocketed from all those dead mercenaries. It occurred to him that perhaps Gerrun was enjoying the best of both worlds – the fine clothes and wine of the lowland towns, and the comradeship and belonging of the highlands – and he felt a hot surge of resentment towards him. Then he recalled the man's role in hiring among the invading parties, even the armies, spying on them and guiding them to ambushes, and he decided that the fellow pretty much earned every lead penny of it.

They returned to the highlands. From time to time grey shapes appeared in the woods to walk alongside them. Orman found that he no longer paid their ghostly visitors any mind at all.

He passed the time speaking to Jass and was rather embarrassed when the lad truly did treat him as an elder brother, though he was no Iceblood. He found that, indeed, there were only five living Sayers. Only these few defended the entire Holding. The bonded couple Jaochim and Yrain ruled – if that was the word for such a small clan. Of Buri, Jass confessed he had seen the man only a few times. He kept to the far north and when he visited even Jaochim bowed to him, for he was the eldest living of any clan of the Icebloods.

When they climbed the highest valley and emerged into the fields the hounds came bounding out to greet Old Bear. They leapt up upon him, licking his face and barking. He swatted them aside and tousled their ragged pelts. In turn they pulled and gnawed upon his cloak.

'They smell the bear in you,' Jass teased.

'That they do,' he answered, grinning. 'Ale tonight, lads!'

Keth and Kasson shared small tight grins. Orman winked at Jass.

They found Yrain had arrived. She and Jaochim oversaw the evening meal in two of the three raised chairs. The middle one remained empty – for Buri, Orman supposed.

Old Bear entertained them all with the tale of his appearance in the battle. How Orman fainted dead away on the spot like an old widow and how he chased the foreign soldiers up trees, into streams, and even to the very walls of Mantle town.

Everyone laughed as the tale went on and on, until it transformed into another tale, the story of one of their ancestors, Vesti the Odd-handed, and his journey to the tallest of the Salt range peaks. There, so he claimed, he met the matriarch of all their kind living in a tower of ice, and had his amorous advances rebuffed.

'Was this Vesti older than Buri?' Orman asked Old Bear.

'He was not,' Yrain answered, cutting off the man's answer. Orman inclined his head, accepting this. The woman shared Jaochim's rather distant and cold manner. Her hair was long, deep flame red, and wavy. She kept it loose about her shoulders. Her build was lean and her skin had an odd hue to it, as if she possessed a touch of colour: a pale olive. She wore leathers, old and much worn, with strings of red stones, garnets, about her neck and wrists.

'Winter is the eldest of us,' Jaochim explained.

'Winter?' Orman asked.

Jaochim made a small gesture with one hand. 'We call him that. When he visits he seems to bring winter with him.' The man frowned then, eyeing Jass, who sat next to Old Bear. 'Bring me your spear, Jass,' he called.

The lad rose, puzzled. He came to the platform and handed the weapon to Jaochim, who studied the iron spearhead.

'This weapon has taken no life,' Jaochim announced. He handed it back butt-first. 'I told you to blood your spear and you return it unblooded?'

Old Bear straightened on his bench. 'The lad fought two of the soldiers. I saw with my own eyes . . .'

'Yet he slew neither.'

The old man waved a thick arm. 'Well, I'm sure that if I hadn't come charging in—'

'It is so,' Jass answered, lifting his chin. 'I took no life.'

Jaochim pointed to the front of the hall. 'Then go. And do not return until you have taken a life in defence of our holding.'

Orman almost stood from the bench to object, but for the heavy paw of Old Bear upon his arm. This was too harsh! Yet Jass bowed. He turned away. As he did so, Orman saw his gaze flash to his mother, Vala. She sat rigid, her lips clenched against all she might say. Her eyes sought Orman's and he saw there a silent plea – the beseeching of a mother for her son. Aware of Jaochim's disapproving glare, Orman allowed himself only the smallest nod. The woman eased back in her seat, her shoulders falling as she let go a pent-up breath.

Jass gathered up his pack and headed for the wide front entrance. Orman half stood to follow but Old Bear's great paw closed upon his arm again and yanked him down to his seat.

'Let me go,' Orman grated, his head lowered.

'Not now, lad. Later.'

'Why?'

'It's their way, lad.'

'Their way is damned harsh.'

'That it is. Now let it go.' He filled Orman's tankard. 'Drink up. Celebrate. Today you're alive, lad.'

'What of it?'

'What of it?' Old Bear appeared horrified. 'Why, lad. That's everything! Live every day as if honourably facing death then celebrate if you live to see its end, hey?'

Orman snorted, but he had to grant the point. Living without fear. Trusting wholly in one's skill. That was something he had yet to achieve. It was an ideal. One he fell woefully short of.

He raised the leather tankard and gulped down the ale, spilling some down his front. There! To the Abyss with everything! Damn the odds and damn these Icebloods' rigid notion of honour. He would have none of it. He threw an arm about Old Bear's shoulders. 'When can I go?' he murmured, holding his face close to the old man's.

Old Bear laughed and slapped his back. He answered beneath his breath: 'With the dawn.'

Wrapped in old furs, Orman lay awake listening to the night. Old Bear snored terribly. Distantly, somewhere in the forest, wolves howled to the night sky. He decided he couldn't wait any longer, never mind whether he was stepping upon Jaochim's edicts. He threw off the hides and dressed. Across the hall Kasson's eyes glimmered in the firelight as he lay awake, watching. Orman thrust his heavy fighting knives into his belt and snatched up Svalthbrul. Across the way, Kasson raised a hand in farewell. He gave the brother a nod and jogged from the hall.

Outside, he headed south. His breath plumed in the cold night air. He wrapped cloth rags about his hands as he ran, Svalthbrul clamped under an arm. Once he reached the forest and the steepening descent into the first of the lower valleys, he stopped and peered about the dark woods.

'Eithjar!' he called. 'I am searching for Jass! Which way?'

He waited, but no answer came. Well, I guess they don't come when called . . .

He started down the trail.

When the sun rose above the lower ridges of the Salt range he was crossing a valley. A run-off stream churned down its middle, no deeper than his shins, but frigid as it splashed and hissed among the boulders and rocks of its naked bed. Across the stream he stamped his sodden feet to bring feeling back into them. He raised a hand to his mouth and called, 'Which way?' His shout echoed among the steep valley walls.

He almost missed it then, in his impatience and disgust. A thin ash-grey shape flickering at the treeline far to the east. He frowned at the indistinct visitation, uncertain whether his eyes were playing tricks upon him. Then the shape raised an arm pointing to the east and was gone.

Orman rubbed his gritty eyes, blinked them. Gods, the east! This high that would be . . . No! The little fool! Bain Holding! What could he possibly mean to . . .

He set off at a run the way the shade had pointed. He smashed into the dense brush, limbs snapping and lashing. He vaulted from rock to rock. The way steepened as he approached the valley side. Ahead, past the trees, the ridgeline climbed bare and rocky. Snow yet lingered in the shadows and capped the highest shoulders. The air was frigid, yet it seemed to burn his lungs as he panted onward. And all the while, Svalthbrul's keen knapped edge sang as it cut the cold air.

CHAPTER VII

FISHER KEL TATH SAT IN THE GLOOM OF THE CAVE BY THE SMALL sputtering fire. With his fingertips, he massaged tiny circles over his temples. 'So let me get this straight,' he said. 'You wrecked on the coast while you were returning home?'

Coots and Badlands, both of the Lost clan, nodded vigorously. 'Aye,' Badlands answered.

'And you've been down here for how long? Months?'

The brothers shared guilty glances. Coots started counting on his fingers, frowned, shrugged, then scratched his ridged bald pate.

Fisher stared his disbelief. 'Why haven't you escaped? You could climb out, couldn't you?'

Badlands waved a hand. 'Oh, yeah. Might fall to our deaths any time, though.'

'But you don't intend to stay down here for ever, do you? Don't you want to get home?'

Another quick guilty glance shot between the brothers. Fisher looked from one to the other. 'What is it . . . what aren't you saying? That is, if it's any of my business.'

Coots laid more moss and dried bracken on the modest fire. He hung his big gnarled hands over his knees. 'Well . . .' he rumbled, 'we kinda had a fight with Stalker.'

'Stalker?' Fisher echoed. Then he remembered. 'Stalker Lost – head of the clan.'

Badlands was nodding. 'Yeah. He was all for coming back. We had us a falling out over it. Back when we was captured by that crazy mage in the Galatan Sweep.'

Coots looked offended. 'Wasn't then. Was when we tried pirating but got chased down by that Elingarth navy convoy.'

232

'Was not! Was when you shacked up with that queen o' them troglodytes!'

'They wasn't troglodytes – they just had an aversion to sunlight.'

Fisher raised a hand for a pause. 'Well, you can't mean to stay, surely? What are you eating?'

Coots looked to the low soot-blackened stone ceiling. 'Oh . . . lizards, salamanders, bats, rats, birds, eggs, mushrooms, roots, frogs, and a cliff-climbing mammal kinda like a marmot.'

'And a mountain goat,' Badlands added.

Coots snapped his fingers. 'Right. Forgot about that. There's mountain goats on these cliffs too.'

Fisher's brows rose. 'Ah. I see. So you're out hunting mountain goats?'

Badlands nodded. 'Yeah. And there's fish in the stream below.'

Fisher glanced over to Jethiss, who stood to one side, frowning his confusion. 'But this Bonewight means to take your bones, yes?'

Coots waved that aside. 'Not till after spring break-up. That's when the flood coming down the valley might damage the bridge's foundations. Least, that's what Yrkki says.'

'Yrkki?'

'Yeah. Yrkki. An' he's not a bone*wight* – he's a bone*wright*. He's real particular about that.'

'He says he knows my name,' Jethiss said from the darkness where the glow from the fire barely touched him.

Both Coots and Badlands eyed the Andii for a time. Badlands gave a musing frown. 'Well, if he says he does, then he probably does.'

'I want it from him.'

Coots blew out a breath, stretched. 'Real cagey with what he knows is Yrkki. Been hanging around here for ages. Treats us like we're equals, though. Funny that.'

An ancient verse came to Fisher and he sang, low and slow, 'Set in stone to ward the way, spirit guardians await the day.'

Coots and Badlands blinked at Fisher, then Badlands scratched his scalp beneath his bunched hair. 'I've heard that before. That one o' yours, Fish?'

'Not originally. I transcribed it from a much older poem.'

Coots cracked his knuckles one by one. 'Hunh. So you're sayin' Yrkki's a prisoner himself? Set here to guard the way. Set by who?'

'By the Jaghut,' Fisher answered. He kept the rest of his suspicions to himself.

Badlands laughed. 'Them old stories. Ghost stories. Hobgoblins and ghoulies in the night. All them hoary old ones is all long gone.'

'An' who's he supposed to be guarding against, then?' Coots asked.

'The Jaghut's enemy.'

The brothers lost their smiles. 'That's not funny, Fish,' Coots rumbled.

'I thought you said they were all gone?'

Badlands' lips drew tight over his large teeth. 'You know they ain't.'

'Exactly. Kellanved changed that. We need to warn the north.'

'I'm thinking the Eithjar know,' said Coots.

'What is this you are talking of?' Jethiss asked from the darkness.

Fisher straightened, set his hands on his knees. 'Sorry, Jethiss. Local history. Old feuds.' He motioned to Coots. 'In any case, we should bring word.'

The brothers shared a measuring glance. 'Well,' Badlands allowed, 'only if you talk to Stalker.' He cut a hand through the air. ''Cause we swore we weren't comin' back.' Coots nodded his firm agreement.

Fisher looked to the low roof and sighed. 'Fine. You don't have to come all the way.'

'So – we are going?' Jethiss asked.

'Yes.' Fisher stood, dusted his trousers. 'I'm sorry he did not give you your name.'

Jethiss nodded his sour agreement. 'Yes. Nor is he likely to, I suspect.'

Badlands pointed towards the distant cave opening. 'We was thinking we'd climb along the trelliswork. Plenty of handholds there.'

Fisher thought of going hand over hand across that grisly construction and shuddered. What horrors might he encounter among those bones? Still, it was probably the best plan. He nodded. 'Very good.'

'Let us wait until night,' Jethiss said.

Coots raised his opened hands. 'Night, day. What difference does it make?'

'It might make a difference to me.'

'Fine,' Fisher said. 'We'll wait.' He motioned to Coots. 'What do you have to eat?'

'Got some dried bat.'

'Never mind.'

~

The night sky was clear. The stars glimmered sharp and cold. The moon had yet to rise. Coots led the way out of the cave mouth. He scrabbled along a thin ledge using hand- and footholds. Fisher followed, then came Badlands, and Jethiss last. Coots edged along the rough rock of the cliff face. The ghoulish pale latticework of the bridge neared. They were perhaps a chain down from the walkway. Below, the trellising extended far deeper into the ravine, to be swallowed by the dark. Fisher heard the crash and hissing of churning water.

Here, dried ligaments and sinew secured the bones to the rocks of the cliff. Fisher felt his stomach rebelling at the thought of having to grasp such gruesome handholds. Coots, however, swung out on to the bones without any pause or outward show of scruples or disgust.

Reluctantly, Fisher followed. He found the bones dry and rough to his grip. They actually provided very secure holds. Many were not tied at all, being merely locked together as if they'd grown, or been bent, to fit one over another like hooks or woven rope. Fisher wondered anew at the creature's self-proclaimed title: *Bonewright.*

He slipped his feet into convenient pelvic curves, used ribs like ladder rungs, edged along gigantic femurs that must have come from titanic ancient ungulates such as the legendary giant elk or caribou. At times the full visceral realization came to him of what he was suspended upon and he would break into a cold sweat, shivering, as his vision darkened. But these fits would pass, or he would force them away by concentrating upon other things – the sanctuary of the far side, for example – and he would continue after a few moments.

One by one they made the opposite side of the ravine. Jethiss came last. He swung out on to the cliff face and was helped up by Badlands. The brothers then faced one another and threw up their hands, yelling at the same moment: 'Run for it!'

Fisher stared after them as they legged it across the dirt landing. It cannot possibly be this easy, he thought to himself.

And indeed, at that moment the ground rocked beneath their feet. Thought so, Fisher managed before stumbling and being pulled from the edge by Jethiss. The dirt landing erupted beneath the brothers, sending them flying skyward amid a spray of dirt and gravel.

The Bonewright, Yrkki, heaved himself up from the ground.

Coots landed heavily amid broken rocks, but as if he were made of nothing more than a twisted knot of muscle and gristle he was up in an instant, long-knives in hand, to launch himself at the creature.

Bone chips flew as he slashed at a limb. Badlands latched on to the other leg and began to pull himself up the massive bone.

Yrkki tottered and kicked. Its roars brought rocks crashing down from the surrounding cliffs. Fisher and Jethiss began working their way around it, if only to avoid being crushed beneath its enormous feet.

'Go for its spine!' Coots yelled.

'You go for the damned spine!' his brother yelled back.

Yrkki swatted at Coots. 'Do not make me break your bones,' he thundered.

Fisher and Jethiss had circled around the battle. Fisher drew his sword. 'We cannot leave this to the brothers,' he told Jethiss.

'No indeed,' the Andii answered. He startled Fisher by running out into the open. 'Yrkki!' he bellowed. 'I demand that you give me my name!'

The creature straightened and turned round. He held a struggling brother in each hand. The giant dragon skull lowered to regard Jethiss more closely. The otherworldly deep ocean-blue flames seemed to brighten in its empty sockets. 'Your name would only make you weep,' he boomed in his basso voice.

'No!' The word seemed torn from Jethiss. He thrust out his hands as if refusing to accept what he'd heard. Darkness flew at the Bone-wright. Ink-black folds seemed to coalesce from the surrounding night to enmesh it. It threw the brothers free to claw at them.

'What is this?' Yrkki bellowed. 'Galain?'

Jethiss thrust out his hands again and the monster tottered backwards, flailing. The folds and scarves of night appeared to be yanking it back into the ravine. The naked talons of its feet grated and gouged at the dirt as it slid. 'None shall remember your name!' it boomed as the black folds enmeshed its skull and it fell backwards, bone legs kicking, to disappear over the cliff's edge.

Jethiss slumped to the dirt. Fisher ran to pick him up. Badlands joined him and threw the Andii over his shoulder. 'Run!' the man yelled, spraying blood from a split lip. They ran. Coots came behind, weapons out, covering their retreat.

They climbed a switchback trail that led to a knife-sharp ridge of rotten rock. The far side sloped down into a high mountain valley. Clouds moved in but Fisher could make out a stretch of woods below. Badlands set Jethiss down in the hollow of two large leaning halves of rock, then sat rather heavily. Fisher eased himself down next to him. Badlands felt at his mouth. 'I think I lotht a damned toof!'

Coots came to stand over them. 'You're always okay 'cause you land on your head.'

'Same as you 'cept it'th your ath!'

Coots gestured to Jethiss, who lay unconscious. 'How'd your friend do that?'

'I don't think even he knows,' Fisher answered.

Coots grunted his acceptance, then rubbed the wide bulge of his stomach. 'I'm hungry,' he said, peering about. 'I'm gonna hunt something up.' He walked off into the dark.

'Better be thoft and thewy!' Badlands called after him, then groaned and cupped his mouth.

Fisher tucked a roll of bedding under Jethiss's head. 'I'll take watch, if you like,' he told Badlands.

The brother waved a negative. 'Naw. You thweep. My mouth hurths.'

Fisher nodded, edged down further into his seat against the rock, tucked his hands under his arms, and let his chin fall. After the exhausting rush of the encounter with Yrkki, sleep came quite quickly.

The delicious smell of roasting meat woke him. He sat up, blinking. Badlands and Coots were crouched at a small fire. Two skinned and gutted rabbits roasted on sticks over the flames. Jethiss sat nearby, arms draped over his crossed legs. He appeared troubled and distracted; Fisher could imagine why. What the man had accomplished was the manipulation of Elemental Night. Something open to the mages of his kind, yet he had made no mention of such a capacity. Who knew what else might lie hidden in him?

'Found the trail of your buddies,' Coots said, and licked fat from his fingers.

'Thank you.'

'Easy to follow. They only have a few days on you.'

'Thanks.' Fisher searched among his feelings. He found no desire to return to the raiding party. He'd much rather strike straight north. 'I thought we were heading to the Lost Holding.'

Badlands carried a swollen purple-bruised mouth and cheek. He slurred: 'It's othay. You doan' have to come.'

'I want to. What of you, Jethiss?'

The Andii was staring at the fire. 'It matters not to me,' he murmured.

'We'll come with you, then.'

The brothers exchanged dubious looks. 'We move pretty fast,' Coots explained.

237

'We'll keep up.'

'Suit yourself.' He gestured to the rabbits. 'Eat up and we'll go.'

Fisher discovered that the brothers were not exaggerating. After they'd eaten and drunk from waterskins and Fisher had rubbed his teeth with a green twig, the brothers kicked dirt over the fire then took off at a run. Fisher was quite startled, but followed quickly. Jethiss came after. Soon, Fisher found that he had to increase his pace considerably in order to keep the brothers in sight.

The Losts ran pell-mell down slopes, dodged trees, jumped from fallen logs and leaned into steep slides of loose talus and broken rock, guiding themselves with a hand. Fisher struggled to follow. His breath came hard and his chest burned. But as the sun climbed overhead his legs loosened up and his breathing eased. He found his pace, and glancing back saw that so too had Jethiss, as the man followed with an easy loping gait.

He came abreast of Badlands. Or rather, Badlands fell back to him; the man ran with a hand pressed to his mouth, breathing loudly, leaning over to spit blood, cursing and wincing as he went. He fell back behind Fisher, then Jethiss as well.

Coots did not stop for any sort of mid-day rest or meal and so Fisher had no choice but to follow. The man appeared to be striking a course far more east than north. They crossed steep mountain shoulders and narrow valleys, scrambled up naked rock ridges, shuffled and half tumbled down the other sides into dense forests of conifer and slashing stiff-branched brush that exploded in sharp bursts when Coots bulled through.

By late in the day Fisher was stumbling, exhausted, hardly able to lift his burning bruised feet. He pushed through a thick copse of spruce and caught the welcome sight of Coots standing motionless on a rock outcropping that jutted from the mountain shoulder they were descending. The sun cast an amber-gold light over the valley side from where it sizzled on the western horizon.

Coots stood shading his gaze to the north. Fisher joined him, panting and gulping the biting chill air. The Lost brother shot him a sidelong glance and grunted his approval.

Fisher swallowed to wet his burning throat. 'What is it?'

Coots gestured, inviting him to look. He stepped up, shaded his gaze. To the north, the mountain slopes graded down in falling arcs to reveal hazy foothills beyond. Past the hills, a body of water glimmered golden yellow in the sunset. Beyond the flat glittering field of water, mountains rose so far away as to be deep blue. These rearing heights climbed to snow-white peaks tinged with a hint of sapphire. The sunset washed the ice-capped heights in a glow of salmon-amber.

'The Salt range,' Fisher said. He did not add that the mountain range looked no different from what he remembered growing up beneath its looming bulk.

'Aye.' Coots pointed a blunt finger below. 'And the Sea of Gold.'

'Hazy,' Fisher observed.

The man's eyes, narrowed beneath his shelf-like hairless brows, appeared troubled. He rubbed one of his gold earrings between a thumb and forefinger. 'Aye,' he murmured, thinking.

Jethiss joined them. Fisher cast him a glance and was envious to see that the Andii did not even appear winded. That was just not fair.

'We'll camp here,' Coots said, and he eased himself down on the rock, grunting and grumbling. He unrolled a strip of leather to reveal what was left of the roasted rabbit, and passed it round for them to pick at.

Badlands finally came staggering in. He had a hand pressed to his mouth and was keeping up a steady stream of slurred cursing as he came. He sat heavily. Fisher offered him the rabbit but the man winced at the sight of it and waved it off.

'I'd better have a look at that,' Coots said.

Badlands flinched away. 'Theep y'ham hanths off, y'ox!'

'You might get an infection,' Fisher said.

'Thalker can thake a look.'

'Stalker does the cutting and bonesetting,' Coots explained.

'He might not make it . . .'

'I'll make it!'

Fisher shrugged. Fine. They'd see, he supposed. He turned to Jethiss. 'How are you?'

The Andii shrugged.

Fisher wished to improve the fellow's mood. 'There are powers in the north. Perhaps one of them might find your name . . .'

The man's head snapped up at that, his gaze suddenly sharp and fierce, as if Fisher's words had awakened something within him. A memory, perhaps. For some vaguely troubling reason Fisher wished he hadn't mentioned the possibility.

When night came Coots stood and peered out over the cliff's edge. Curious, Fisher joined him again. He squinted down to the black glimmering slate-like expanse that was the Sea of Gold. A blush of lurid yellow light glowed in a halo around the sea.

'A lot of fires,' Coots rumbled, explaining. 'Smoke by day, fire by night. Looks like war in the lowlands.'

'We go round, I take it?'

The big fellow nodded. He ran a hand over the ridged and scarred armour-like pate of his skull. 'Aye. We go round.'

* * *

On the eighth day riding north skirting the Sea of Dread, Kyle, Lyan and Dorrin pulled up short to stare at an amazing sight.

As far as they could see in a line running behind the low bare hills along the coast there stood a forest of bare spires: ships' masts. A long parade of them, slowly edging along. Kyle and Lyan exchanged wondering glances. Then Kyle urged his mount east in a slow walk for a closer look.

They topped a hill that allowed line of sight to the shore and stopped. It was an immense convoy. A long train of roped ships being pulled by teams of men, plus the occasional horse and mule. Kyle had seen such things before, of course, mule teams pulling barges on canals, but this was the first time he'd seen the concept applied on the shore of a sea. He counted over twenty ships in this one flotilla.

'Looks like they've found a way around your Sea of Dread,' Lyan remarked.

Kyle rested his forearms on the saddle pommel and shook his head in awe. 'Nothing like naked greed to find a way through any barrier.'

A susurration of noise reached them from the nearest teams of men and women heaving on the ropes. Individuals came running inland from the shore, knelt, and trained crossbows in their direction.

'They think us hostile locals,' Lyan said.

'Yes. We'd best be going.'

A chuff of dirt behind stiffened Kyle's back and in that instant he realized their mistake – they'd all been looking in the same direction. He turned his head, knowing what he would see. A cordon of soldiers advancing upon them from farther inland. It looked like they meant to drive them to the coast.

Lyan's blade shushed against its wooden sheath as she yanked it free. She kneed her horse to stand between Dorrin and the soldiers. Kyle did not draw his weapons. He urged his mount down the hill a short distance. The men raised their crossbows and spears. 'What do you want?' he shouted in Talian, knowing exactly what it was they wanted.

'Give up your horses and you can go,' one answered in thickly accented Talian.

'They are ours and we will keep them!' Lyan shouted.

One of the crossbowmen brought his weapon up to aim and a fellow near him knocked it down. 'Don't shoot, y'fool! Might hit a horse.'

'Here's mine!' Lyan yelled and kneed her mount into a charge down the hill. She whooped a war-cry as she went and Dorrin followed in her wake.

She thundered past Kyle, who could only urge his mount onward to join her. A spearman directly in her path jabbed but she parried with her blade and the man leapt to save his life. Dorrin followed close behind. A crossbowman drew aim on Lyan, and Kyle twisted his mount over to charge him; the man dropped the weapon and leapt aside.

Then they were through, galloping for a draw between the next two shallow hills. But when Kyle brought his horse over he saw Dorrin's mount running riderless, its saddle empty.

He yelled, turned in his saddle. The lad lay in a heap on the flat between the rises. The soldiers were closing on him. Kyle yanked his mount around, just as a scream of shock and rage announced that Lyan had discovered what was happening.

Kyle reached Dorrin first. Dismounting at a run, he yanked the boy up by one arm and flinched upon seeing a bolt impaling his leg. Some crossbowman had snapped off a lucky shot. He tossed the lad over his saddle and drew a hatchet. 'Hang on!' he ordered. Dorrin nodded, his face snowy pale and glistening with sweat, and wrapped the reins around his hand. Clenching his teeth against the necessity of it, Kyle struck the horse's flank with the impaling spike.

The horse screamed and reared, then took off in a spray of kicked-up dirt. Dorrin hunched low, hugging its neck. Kyle turned to face the closing men and women. He counted fifteen.

Damn the Twins' luck. Nothing for it. He switched the hatchet to his left hand and drew his blade.

The men and women spread out in an arc, facing him. He snapped a quick glance behind, saw Lyan leading Dorrin away on his mount, the lad's horse following.

'Togg turd!' one man shouted. 'At least we can make you pay!'

Then one of the spearmen stepped forward, pointing. 'You!' he bellowed, and charged. In the instant Kyle noticed that he wore a tattered blue cloak. *Shit.*

'Die, Whiteblade!' the ex-Stormguard yelled in rage.

In a single movement Kyle swung, hacking the head from the spear, spun, sliced through the haft and the man's leading arm at

241

the elbow, looped his arm in an arc and took off the fellow's head cleanly through the neck.

The dismembered corpse fell, spraying arterial blood from neck and arm.

In the stunned pause that followed, Kyle charged.

The first he reached actually turned to run. Kyle cut him across his back, severing his spine. He caught a sword blow from another with his hatchet, then swung, cutting through the sword arm. He severed a spear as it thrust, took off the spearman's leading leg at the knee.

A crossbow bolt hissed as it brushed past his head and he wished he had a damned helmet. The thought drove him to charge the remaining crossbows. The nearest, a woman, reflexively raised her weapon to protect herself; Kyle sliced through the stock and ironwork and took her forearms with it. The woman stared in horror at the severed stumps of her arms, her eyes rolled up white, and she toppled. Kyle meant to close on the remaining two crossbowmen but four swordsmen were dangerously close. He remembered the trick he had learned from the Silent People and threw his hatchet, taking one bowman in the stomach, and charged the other. This one backpedalled, terrified. Kyle pressed forward until the man tripped then took off one foot as it flew upwards. He spun to meet the swordsmen, blade raised in a guard, but no one was pressing the attack. The survivors were running.

He eased his stance, let out a long hard breath. The wounded crossbowman, screaming curses and clutching his ankle, he left alone. He bent down to retrieve his hatchet, and walked away. Their friends might, or might not, come back for them. The lesser wounded might make it to the coast.

He didn't care. He was just tired of the stupidity of it. The needlessness of it. He had been forced to defend himself and now he was a killer. He cleaned the blade on the blue cloak of the dead Stormguard, carefully sheathed it. This one he didn't recognize, but it made sense that many of them would now be out selling their spears. He walked on, trying to spit, but his mouth was too dry.

Atop the next rise he found Lyan tending to Dorrin. She'd torn his trouser leg and removed the bolt and was now tightly wrapping the wound. Mercifully, the lad was unconscious. Kyle was worried as the boy had lost a lot of blood.

He cleared his throat to speak, croaked, 'We have to move.'

'I know,' she answered without stopping her work. Kyle nodded, though she wasn't looking. 'Saw you fight,' she said, and glanced up. He saw something new in her eyes, something that troubled him. 'That was plain butchery.'

He went to collect the horses.

That night, across the small fire, Lyan cradled Dorrin to her chest, giving him her warmth. He'd woken only for brief moments, groaned his pain, and shut his eyes once more. Sweat now gleamed on his face and Kyle feared a fever. It occurred to him that the lad might not make it and the thought brought a terrible squeezing pain to his chest that made it hard to breathe. The boy had shown such good sense, such endurance, such patience and wisdom beyond his years. Kyle suddenly realized that if he had a son, he could only hope for one such as this. The band across his chest became a burning acid gash and he blinked away a swimming blur in his eyes.

He decided, then, what he would do.

In the morning, when Lyan mounted, Dorrin held in her arms before her, Kyle did not mount as well. Instead, he stood next to her leg looking up at them. She drew breath to tell him to hurry, then realized what was going on and swallowed.

'Take the horses,' he told her.

She shook her head.

'Take the horses and bargain for healing for the lad.'

She continued shaking her head, only now looking away, blinking.

'Go.'

She nodded then, curtly, and lowered her head. He sought her mouth and found it hot and wet with tears. 'I'm sorry,' she whispered, half choked.

'As am I,' he answered just as faintly.

She twisted away, kneed her mount gently forward. The two other horses followed. Kyle watched them go then turned to face the north. He had already looped the straps of a few waterskins over his shoulders, and now he set off at a jog.

*

After two days he imagined he had entered the region of desert plains that his people's stories named the Vanishing Lands, or the Lands of Dust. It was a broad northern desert of dwarf trees, lichens and brittle brush, with a scattering of clumped grasses and tiny wild flowers. Clouds did pass overhead, occluding the sun, but none released any of their life-sustaining rains here. The air was frigid and painfully dry. His lips chapped and split. He was ruthless with his limited supply of water; one mouthful in the morning, and one at noon. The heights of the Salt range, a deep aqua-blue in the distance, taunted him with their gleaming shoulders of snow and ice-field.

He passed the remains of people, and even of horses. Most lay half buried in clumps of meagre soil. Wild flowers surrounded them like burial wreaths. The bones were very old, or at least appeared so, wind-gnawed down to stumps where exposed to the gusting dry air.

The nights were the worst. There was no cover to be found any-where. He lay wrapped in a blanket, exposed to the buffeting winds. At times these rose to storms that lashed him with tossed sand and gravel. All the warmth would be sucked from him and only un-controllable shivering kept heat in his bones. He would wake with dunes of blown dirt gathered up his sheltered side.

One night something large banged into him, tossed by the wind. He reflexively lashed out to snatch it. It took him some time peering at the thing in the starlight to identify it, but eventually he realized that what he held was an eroded, battered, wind-tumbled human skull.

He kept it with him as he walked the next day, turning it in his hands. It wasn't old, that much he was certain of. Bones yellowed or greyed with age. This skull still held that bright whiteness of bone picked clean. Bones also roughened with age, became more porous, and lost mass. This skull still held heft, and was smooth where not abraded through rolling and bumping.

While he paced along studying the skull, something bright caught his eye on the ground and he stopped. His arms slowly fell and he let the skull thump hollowly to the bare rock beneath his feet. He had wandered into a field of bones. The remains lay as far as he could see in every direction. They gleamed whitely, humped together in small depressions where the winds had swept them up. Ribs lay snug in natural cracks of the exposed granite bedrock. Wide scapulae lay flat where the winds could not budge them. The round dome of a skull was caught up against a knot of rock.

Kyle reached for the grip of the blade snug at his side to reassure himself, and continued on. None of the bones that he passed showed any signs of violence: no shattering, no gashes or cuts. They had not even been gnawed by scavengers. Fat femurs had not been cracked open for the rich marrow.

Equipment lay scattered about, corroded armour, metal fittings, wind-smoothed coins, and naked rusted blades. But no leather, cloth, padding, or even wood. How could it have rotted away so quickly?

That night the winds returned with redoubled violence. It was as if they wished to pick him up and send him tumbling back down to the prairie of the Silent People. They seemed to punch him from all directions and sent needle-sharp lances of sand that stung and burned any patch of exposed skin. He tucked himself entirely under his blanket in a desperate effort to escape their constant lashing and hissing.

In the morning, when he shook out the blanket, he found it full of holes. Patches of it had been eaten away entirely. Something about this troubled him far back in his mind: memories from the ancient stories he'd heard in his youth. *The Land of Dust . . . the Land of Winds*. He shook his head. Surely the winds alone couldn't kill a man. But perhaps they could scour the padding from discarded armour.

He rolled up the blanket, took a sip of water, and moved on. The silver heights of the Salt range beckoned. The distant peaks shimmered suspended over a layer of haze, or clouds, like ships at sea.

Towards noon a dust storm struck. It swept down from the north. A swirling churning mass of solid yellow that engulfed the entire plain ahead. Kyle tore off a strip of cloth and tied it over his face leaving only his eyes exposed. He ducked his head, raised a hand to shelter his eyes.

The wall struck like a blow of rage. Sand and grit blasted at him. It gnawed the flesh of his hand, bit at his scalp. The noise was a howling and a grinding avalanche combined. Kyle walked blind, a hand extended into the murky haze of gusting blankets of dust. There was no cover anywhere at all. If it became unendurable, he supposed he would have no option but to lie down and curl into a self-protecting ball.

And the thought came: *As so many others had done before him . . .*

Land of Winds. Land of Dust. Put these two together and you have a desolate uninhabitable desert that scours all life from itself.

Then a shape resolved out of the sweeping scarves and twists of sand and dust. Vaguely humanoid. A shape of seething hissing winds and grit. A blunt arm pointed. A moaning wind-voice spoke, 'You I would allow to pass. But you carry a thing of chaos. This cannot be allowed to pass.'

Thing of chaos? Kyle clutched at the blade. He called uselessly into the winds: 'What do you mean? This is the sword of Osserc!' He heard no sound of his own voice yet the creature answered.

'Yes. This thing he carried for a time. Yet its origins are older than he. Know you not what it is?'

'It is a sword.'

'It is no sword. Lay it down and you may pass.'

'No! It was given to me by Osserc himself!'

'Then he did you no favour. All that will be left of you will be that artefact. And that I shall grind until its dust is spread across the continent entire.'

Artefact? 'No!' Kyle yanked the blade free, swinging across his front. The winds flinched. At least that was how it felt to him. He almost tumbled forward into a lull that lasted a fraction of a moment. The winds' howling doubled. It rasped and growled in what seemed like frustration.

'Then die!' the creature bellowed, and raised its arms of churning dust.

Kyle charged, rolled forward, and swung. The blade bit into the shape at its broad base, and, just as when he had struck the manifestation of a goddess on Fist, an enormous blast of unleashed energies threw him backwards to land on the rock, depriving him of breath and bringing stars to his vision.

When he regained his senses, he raised his head to see the dust storm dispersing. It fell in uncoiling scarves of particles that came hissing down. He stood brushing a thick layer of it from his chest and hair. He raised the blade still gripped tightly in his hand. He remembered that someone had once told him it wasn't made of metal – it certainly didn't look like metal. It was creamy amber, opaque at its thick spine verging down to translucent towards the curve of its keen edge. He ran his fingers down the side of the blade. It felt organic to him, like horn, or scale. An artefact? Artefact of what? And chaos? What had that being meant about chaos? Yet he didn't imagine he'd killed the creature. Just as at Fist, when he'd struck the Lady, she had merely dispersed for a time. So too here, probably. Shrugging, he resheathed the blade, carefully, edge up, and walked on.

The air was clearing. The wind was dying. The rock and snow peaks and slopes of the distant Salt range emerged from the haze of dust once again. He raised his last remaining waterskin, shook it to listen to its meagre sloshing, and let it fall. He angled his route a touch to the east.

*　　*　　*

This village was larger than any of the ones she'd yet found. The sight of the collection of round hide roofs had been a gut-punch to Silverfox when she topped a slight rise. She paused, nearly toppling from her quivering lathered mount. Pran appeared at her side, ready to catch or steady her.

She flinched from his presence, kicked her mount on. It started forward with heavy clumsy steps.

As before she found them strewn where they'd fallen. As before, kites and crows lifted like dark shadows from her advance to hover overhead, waiting for the momentary disruption to move on. The vultures merely spread their wide black wings and waddled to one side.

Occasionally, foxes and wild dogs scampered off into the grasses, their muzzles wet and dark with blood. There they lurked, awaiting her departure.

But this time it was quiet. So quiet she could hear the hide flaps tapping and slapping in the wind, the grasses shushing, the wind moaning through gaping open entrances. No strained voices rising in near-crazed grief shattered the silence. No screams of rage. No weeping.

This time all was silent. Silverfox slid from her mount, let the reins fall. She stepped on to soil dark and wet with blood yet hardly noticed. She found that she had to consciously urge her legs to move. Pran appeared from behind a hut ahead of her.

'Summoner,' he began, and she thought she heard pain in his voice, 'you need not—'

'Yes,' she snapped. The word felt torn from her. 'I must. I must . . . witness this.'

She brushed past him. She walked between silent huts of poles and hide, stepped over knifed women, men, and children. Many had fallen curled round their young, protecting them. Slaughtered. All. She raised her gaze, found it blurred. All? *All?*

Lanas . . . how could you? What will they say of you? Of the T'lan?

She lifted her wrinkled, age-darkened hands to her face, turned them over and over. Yet what was this but a glimpse of the old ways? Her people's hands were no more clean. No one's were. How could this have once been the norm? How could the ancestors have named this a great victory and boasted of it? The slaughter of children? Perhaps it was a good thing to be reminded of this – once in a while.

Sound reached her. So wrapped in her horror was she that it took some time for it to register for what it was: the wail of a baby. She started, jerking, and ran in the direction of the noise. Rounding a hut she came up short, her breath catching.

All were not dead. A woman stood ahead. She cradled a tiny squirming bundle awkwardly in her muscular arms. A woman not of this village, nor even of this continent. For Silverfox knew her, and as she advanced, the young woman's sharp gaze reflected their mutual recognition. Dark earth-brown she was. Sun-darkened even more over her wide arms. Sturdy-boned, heavy-browed, with smooth silken black hair, in old buckskins.

Kilava. Last living Bonecaster of the Imass.

Silverfox inclined her head in greeting. The baby writhed in its wrap of a coarse blanket. It squalled anew. Silverfox found she had to swallow hard to wet her throat to speak. 'Just . . .'

'. . . her,' Kilava finished. 'Yes.'

Silverfox peered anew round the silent village. 'Who were they?'

'They called themselves the Children of the Wind.'

Silverfox regarded the babe. 'It is hungry.'

'I have no milk to give,' Kilava said. She arched a brow to Silverfox. 'We neither have any milk left, do we?'

Silverfox shared the knowing look. 'We are neither the nurturing sort.'

Kilava gestured to her hair. 'You have come into your name.'

Reflexively, Silverfox lifted and examined a twist of her long ash-grey streaked hair. 'So I have.'

They regarded one another for a time in heavy silence; the ancient Bonecaster's gaze shifted to peer behind Silverfox. She turned to see both Pran and Tolb standing at a respectful distance. 'They would remain out of my reach,' Kilava muttered to Silverfox.

'They have tasted your temper.'

'I have not changed my mind!' Kilava shouted.

'I would not have thought so,' Pran answered.

The Bonecaster snorted at that. She lowered her attention to the babe. 'I will take this one south. Find willing arms for her. Then I will return to warning the tribes.'

Silverfox's breath caught. 'Then some have escaped . . .'

'Those who have heeded my warnings. I've been sending them to the west. The Kerluhm are headed to the mountains – I do not believe they will divert for refugees.'

'Thank you, Kilava.'

'I did not do it for your benefit, Silverfox. Your task remains and I wish you'd taken hold of it.'

Silverfox felt her cheeks heating. She snapped, 'We've been through this already.'

Kilava did not answer. She adjusted the babe in her arms then brushed past to walk on to the south. Once she was gone, Pran and Tolb came to Silverfox's side.

'A powerful ally,' Pran observed.

'We cannot count on her aid,' she warned them.

Behind her, Pran and Tolb shared a silent glance. Silverfox examined them. 'Where's my horse?'

'We have found another,' Tolb said.

She turned to peer among the silent empty huts, rubbed her eyes. 'I can't stay here. I'll keep going – have it brought to me.'

The two Bonecasters bowed. Silverfox walked on. The two stood motionless for a time, then Tolb spoke, 'Should we reach the very north it will be good to have her with us.'

Pran's dry sinews creaked as he nodded his agreement. 'Even she would not stand aside . . . then.'

*

Atop the heights of a rocky cordillera, a file of skeletal figures came to the lip of a tall hillock of mixed gravel and sands. Here, ages ago, a continent-spanning mountain of ice ground to a halt, piling up this near mountain of debris. Wordlessly, they spread out to line the edge. The bones of their feet clattered and grated across the stones. The rag-ends of hides and furs snapped and lashed in the cold dry wind. Here they stood still as statues of bone and ligament. The wind whistled through dry chest cavities and gaping fleshless jaws. Several times the sun rose, traced its path across the sky, and set. They waited, as patient as the stones themselves.

Beneath the cold light of the moon, the shifting and grinding of stones announced movement within the slope. Rocks came sliding down, banging and clattering. The talus heap shifted, slipping. A fist punched free of the gravel and a forearm of bare aged bone emerged. A skeletal shape straightened. Dust and sand plumed in the wind from a long tattered bearhide cloak that glowed dirty white beneath the moon. It lifted a ravaged head half scoured of flesh.

Another figure, nearly identical but for the cloak, advanced to greet this newcomer. They clasped hands to bony forearms. 'Ut'el Anag,' the cloakless one said. 'Long have we been parted.'

The newcomer nodded its battered skull. 'Lanas. It warms my spirit to see you once again.'

Further Imass now came dragging themselves free of the heaped moraine. Ut'el raised his head as if to sample the chill night air through his naked nostril slits. 'Omtose retreats before us.'

'As it ever has.'

The Kerluhm Bonecaster turned his head to the east. Lanas shared his gaze. Across a shimmering plateau rose slopes limned in silver, deepest blue and iron-grey. 'The stain has spread,' Ut'el observed, 'and the source remains.'

'We arrive to wash it away – as ever. Though we are opposed.'

The head snapped round. 'Who?'

'Remnants of the Ifayle . . . and now the Kron.'

Ut'el nodded. 'They will come round and will thank us before the end.'

'As it always has been.'

Without further word Ut'el stalked off to the east. Lanas remained. 'There are survivors here,' she called.

Ut'el turned. 'Forget these lesser ones. The source lies to the east.'

'The source?'

'The Matriarch. The mother of their kind.' He raised an arm of ligament and bone sheathed in tattered leathers, pointed to the distant peaks. 'She awaits us, Lanas. She's known we would come. Like the thawing of the spring, we come. Eventually.'

'It will be a long walk,' Lanas answered.

'As it has ever been, Lanas.'

She inclined her head in assent and came abreast of Ut'el. Together, the two struck a path to the north-east over the rocky slope. The rest of the Imass followed in a rattling and clack of bone over stones. Behind, more of their brethren dragged themselves free of the eroding moraine, sloughing off a rain of dirt and mud.

*   *   *

Orman jogged downhill from one high mountain valley to the next, ever angling to the east. For two days ghosts, Sayer ancestors, pointed the way. On the third day he came to a ridge separating the Sayer Holding from the Bain. Here, an immense half-dead white pine stood taller than all its kind. Pinned to the trunk by a hunting knife hung Jass's cloak.

He understood the message, for he recognized the knife. He'd last seen it pushed through the belt of Lotji Bain. He ran on, leaving the challenge hanging for others to find. Should any others be following.

He descended the ridge, crossed a forest towards a stream rushing over a wide bed of naked broken rock. Here, a shout sounded over the pounding waters.

Lotji stepped forth from the cover of the wide bole of a pine. He held Jass before him, a knife to his throat, the lad's hands tied. He bellowed up: 'I'm glad you came, hiresword! You've saved me a lot of time. You know what I want. You and me! Now!'

Orman squeezed the haft of Svalthbrul so tight it seemed to squirm in his hands. He picked his way across the tumbled rocks. He so wanted to meet this man – to cut him to pieces with Svalthbrul – but what if he lost? What of Jass then? Jass, as he'd known all along, was far more important to him than any weapon. No matter how storied. He raised the spear. 'I have something you want, Lotji . . . and you have something I want. Let's exchange.'

The offer brought the man up short. His face wrinkled in distaste. 'An exchange?' he shouted, almost in disbelief. 'An exchange? You would part with Svalthbrul for this useless pup?'

'I would.'

'Why?'

Something in Orman resisted revealing his true reason and it took him a moment to identify it – the man was not worthy of such an intimacy. It was a family matter, not for outsiders. 'Honour!' he shouted over the pounding stream. 'I swore to serve the Sayers!'

Lotji shook his head, his gaze scornful. 'Hearthguard,' he snorted. 'Hearthguard you are and hearthguard you will ever remain – nothing more!'

They closed further and Jass choked out, 'Leave me to die! I deserve no better.'

Lotji shook him by the neck like a disobedient dog. 'Quiet!' He motioned to the rocks between him and Orman. 'Far enough. Set the spear there and back away.'

'Release the lad!'

'Back away first!'

Orman jammed the butt of the spear amid the rocks so that it stood tall and straight. He backed away one step. 'Release him!'

Lotji waved him off. 'Further!' He pressed a knife blade to Jass's throat.

Orman snarled a curse but backed away more steps until clear of the spear. Lotji edged up almost within arm's reach of it.

'Now the boy!'

Lotji just shook his head. 'You stupid fool!' He snatched up the spear. 'Now I have both and you have nothing!'

251

Orman felt his shoulders fall. *Damn. Should've fought him.*

Lotji examined Svalthbrul's knapped stone spearhead, then cast an arched glance to him. 'You do have one thing left, though. And now I'll take that . . .'

Orman moved to draw his hatchets.

Lotji lunged, Svalthbrul lashed out and crashed against Orman's skull. He was unconscious before he hit the ground.

*

He snapped to wakefulness in a panic, fighting for breath. Something was choking him; he strained to raise his hands to pull at whatever it was, but his arms were secured behind his back. He saw that he hung from a branch. Lotji was tying off the rope round the trunk even as he watched. Jass lay to one side, weeping, his hands tied behind his back.

Lotji appeared before him, peering up. 'I was looking forward to killing you in a duel, hearthguard. But you stole the pleasure from me. Therefore, I demand a blood-price.' He extended the nut-brown faceted stone head of Svalthbrul to Orman's face. He tried to squirm aside but the spear licked forward. Fire engulfed his head. He screamed, or tried to, lurching and spinning as he struggled. The rope squeezed tighter about his throat.

'Farewell, fool,' Lotji called, now yanking Jass to his feet. 'Perhaps this will teach you wisdom.'

Orman fought to scream, to curse, to beg, but nothing could escape the twisting noose strangling his throat. His vision, oddly restricted now, darkened. He felt nothing, sensed nothing – only a swelling balm that seemed to soothe all pain and tension from his body.

He felt as if he were floating.

Pain roused him; some sort of sharp blow. Cold air scraped his throat and he gagged, coughing. He lay for a time possessing only the strength required to draw a breath into his straining body. After this, he managed to open his eyes – or one eye, at least. The other remained stubbornly closed.

Someone was leaning over him. A dark man, skin almost black, his face deeply weathered and lined. He wore a plain leather hood. Orman tried to speak but no words would come.

'Quiet now,' the man urged, his accent strange. 'No talking yet. Hard to access anything here but I think I can stop the bleeding.'

He was bleeding? He pursed his lips, managed to croak in an exhalation: 'Who . . .'

A smile touched the man's lips. 'Same as you. A hiresword working for these Icebloods. The Losts. We have to stick together, hey? You're with the Sayers, yes?'

Orman nodded his head weakly.

The man grunted. 'Good. I fix you up and you go back to the Sayers and let them know the Bains are broken. They've retreated halfway up their Holding. Soon us and you Sayers will be flanked. Understand?' Orman nodded. 'Good. Now, let's see what I can do.'

The man bent over him. He slithered his warm hands up under Orman's shirt to press against his chest. Something happened and Orman felt strength flow into him. His breathing eased. The man then pressed a hand to his face and the searing yammering pain there dulled to an aching throb.

'There,' the fellow said. 'Best I can do. I'm no expert at Denul.'

'Thank you,' Orman managed in a hoarse whisper.

'No trouble. I've seen worse.' He helped Orman stand. He tottered on his feet, but remained upright. He touched a hand to his neck and hissed, snatching it away. 'Nasty that,' the man said. 'But it will heal. Sorry about the eye, though.' Orman blinked at him. His eye? He raised a hand to investigate but the man caught it. 'Don't touch. Not yet. Let it get a scab.'

Lotji had taken his eye. He might as well have killed him. How could he fight now?'

'Name?' he croaked.

The man just shrugged. 'Call me Cal. Listen, sorry I can't take you with me, but any lowlander army comes advancing up here maybe we can pinch it between us, hey? Put it to the Sayers. We'll keep watch.' And the fellow saluted him: a hand to the brow swept down and out.

Orman just nodded, still a touch confused and bewildered. The fellow jogged off to the east. As he watched him go Orman realized that everything he wore, his hooded cloak, his leather armour, was stained a deep dark blood red. He found that he could not move. Perhaps he should simply remain here upon these rocks until his very flesh rotted away and his bones fell between the cracks and gaps of the stones.

For a brief time he thought he'd found something. Something worth fighting for. Now he'd thrown it away. Lotji had taken his eye, but he hadn't taken his honour . . . that he'd thrown away himself. He should've died this day. Should've died fighting the man. Only that could have redeemed him.

Now it was too late. The valley blurred as tears burned and smarted. He felt as if he could no longer breathe – something new was binding his chest from expanding.

Why hadn't he? Why?

Then he remembered something more important. Something vastly more important than his selfish worries over his honour or his name. The reason why he hadn't thrown his life away beside this pounding stream of frigid meltwater.

It seemed that he had learned wisdom after all.

Released from paralysis, he turned and limped back the way he'd come.

Once he topped the ridge, he started down the other side, sliding and gouging a trail through the loose rotten rock, stumbling and half falling down to where the slope shallowed to allow brush and trees to take hold. Here he stopped and brought his hands to his mouth. 'Sayers!' he called, hoarsely. 'Come to me! I have news!'

He tottered on then, knowing that any of the ancestors, the Eithjar, could appear before him should they choose to. He walked due north now. He meant to keep going until he could go no further.

Eventually, as the day waned, he pushed through spruce woods to find a shape awaiting him, translucent, wavering, a tall man in leathers, smoky knives at his hips. Orman stopped before him. 'I have news,' he gasped. The figure nodded. 'Lotji Bain has taken Jass, the youngest of your line. He has taken Svalthbrul as well, though to you that should matter far less than what else I have to say. The Bains are broken, retreating. Soon a lowlander army will advance up their Holding. The Losts propose to attack it in concert from both sides. Take this news to Jaochim.'

'You should speak to Jaochim or Yrain,' the ancestor spirit answered, its voice hardly more than the brushing of the wind through the trees.

'No. I go north.'

The figure's gaze shifted away and rose to the heights. 'North? To what end?'

'I go to seek the one who should care the most regarding your line.'

The Eithjar shook its head. 'He will not listen to you. You will perish in cold and hunger on the great ice.'

'So be it.'

The ghost nodded grim acceptance. 'Indeed. Farewell.'

Orman answered the curt nod. He walked on.

He knew it was as the Eithjar said. He would win through or die in the attempt and he was satisfied with either end. Both were better than meekly offering his head to Jaochim in payment for the failure to observe his duty. He would run on, heading north, until those legendary serpents of ice consumed him.

It would be a fitting end. He remembered all the many nights he'd spent watching the sapphire crags. How they glimmered like jewels strung about the neck of the Salt range peaks. Now he would finally have his chance to see them before he died.

*   *   *

They followed the coast of the Sea of Dread eastward, where legends and sailors' stories told of a settlement and a fortress: a great stone keep named for its ruler, Mist. Jute thought the coast unpromising, the soil too rocky and thin for decent farming. Pine forest dominated. It swept up broad slopes of foothills that disappeared into fog-shrouded distances. At least the wildlife was rich. Fish were plentiful, eagles soared overhead, and one or two large tawny bears were spotted ambling through the brush.

Word came via the many fishing launches and ship's boats oaring between the four vessels that Captain Cartheron was recovering and that he'd chosen to remain on board the *Supplicant* for the while. Ieleen had chuckled throatily at that news and when Jute made a questioning sound she explained, 'Gettin' together, those two. Much to talk about, no doubt.'

Jute had frowned at the news, baffled. What could such a potent sorceress see in that battered old veteran? Certainly, he'd had his heyday as a top lieutenant and confidant of the hoary old emperor, but all that had been long ago.

The further east they ventured the thicker and more persistent the ground fog and banks of mist became. Jute could even watch it pouring down the forest slopes and out over the calm waters like some sort of liquid itself. At first he was alarmed, as it reminded him of the enchanted fogs of the Sea of Dread. But Ieleen did not seem concerned, and so he decided it must be a purely natural phenomenon.

Also growing in number were those chunks of floating ice. Some as large as the vessels themselves. Jute kept a number of the crew permanently armed with poles to fend the hazards off. They also occasionally encountered great sheets of ice loose upon the surface. These passed lazily, drifting south. Some appeared no thicker than a skin, others a good arm's depth of rock-hard ice.

It occurred to Jute that they were witnessing a spring break-up, and that somewhere to the east there must lie a great congestion of ice.

Farmsteads of modest log and sod huts amid clearings hacked from the forest emerged from the mists. Rounding a bay, they came to a broad low headland, cloaked in fog. Here, a single tall keep of stone reared close to a rising cliff behind. A clutch of huts and cleared fields surrounded it and the shore was crowded by vessels heaved up upon the flats. Jute counted some fifty of them.

East of this lay an inlet choked in ice. Jute could hear the grinding and groaning of the massive sheet. Behind the inlet, further inland, rose what appeared to be a mountain of ice – a great sky-blue dome that gleamed like a sapphire jewel.

'If only you could see this, dearest,' he told Ieleen, awed.

'I see *something*,' she murmured, and she did not sound pleased by it.

The *Supplicant* anchored clear of the shore, while Jute had the crew drive the *Dawn* up on to the flats. The *Ragstopper* anchored next to the sorceress's vessel. The *Resolute* drew up next to the *Dawn*. Jute was troubled to see all the nearby ships were empty of any crew. No guards or watches, and no teams working on repairs even though most were quite badly in need of it.

He ordered a watch, armed himself, and kissed Ieleen on the cheek.

'Have a care, luv,' she told him. 'I've a sense our friend isn't the only power here.'

The mud was thick and chill. It clung to his boots like weights as he made his way up the shore. Tyvar emerged, fully armed and armoured, helm tucked under one arm. His long cape dragged in the mud as he came.

'Greetings!' the mercenary called out, grinning behind his beard, as friendly as ever. 'How fares our pilot?'

'She is recovered, thank you.'

'Excellent! And our Malazan friend is also in good care, so I hear.'

'Yes.'

Tyvar gestured a gauntleted hand to the keep. 'And what do you make of the settlement?'

Jute peered round. Distant figures worked the many fields where scarves of fog drifted. 'Quiet.'

Tyvar's smile hardened and he nodded. 'Ah! Here comes our, ah, ally.' He motioned to the flats. A launch had pulled up, oared by crew that Jute couldn't identify over the distance. The tall un-mistakable figure of Lady Orosenn straightened then, and stepped out into the mud. She made for shore. As she neared, Jute saw with some surprise that she had changed her outfit. She now wore tall leather moccasins laced to the knees over buckskin trousers, belted, with a shirt and a long thick felt jacket hanging open at the front. Her hair blew long and midnight-black about her shoulders. Her face, now uncovered, revealed a broad tall brow, deep ridges shelter-ing the eyes, and a long heavy jaw.

He and Tyvar bowed. 'Greetings, Lady Orosenn,' the mercenary rumbled. 'You are dressed for the weather, I see.'

She laughed, waved a hand deprecatingly, took a deep breath of the chill air. 'I am dressed for home, friend mercenary.'

'Home?' Jute blurted, then regretted opening his mouth. 'You are from here?' he finished weakly.

The lady laughed again. 'No, friend captain. I am not. Yet this is home all the same.' She waved them onwards. 'Captain Cartheron sends his regrets – he yet remains too weak to walk. Come. Let us greet our hostess, the Lady Mist. Though, I am certain she will not be so pleased to see us.' She swept on, and Jute and the mercenary captain hurried to follow.

As they neared the keep they passed more of the locals, though, in point of fact, Jute noted that none were local. Most were men and all were quite obviously from elsewhere. Jute recognized Genabackans and Malazans and glimpsed many other types unfamiliar to him despite his extensive travels. Most wore the ragged remains of sailors' sturdy canvas trousers or leathers; most carried hoes and other farmers' implements. None would meet their gaze as they passed. Some even turned away, or shook their heads.

Jute glanced to Tyvar. 'Solemn lot.'

'I see fear,' the mercenary rumbled.

'They are trapped,' Lady Orosenn commented.

Tyvar's gaze narrowed. 'As we shall be?'

'I will do my best to extricate us.'

The mercenary captain grunted in answer, but his hand now rested on the grip of his bastardsword.

The iron-bound door to the keep stood open. No guard challenged them as they entered. The way led to a long main hall. All was dim as the only light shone in through high slit windows. No torches or braziers burned. Against the far wall a woman in glowing white robes waited. She was seated upon a tall-backed chair, or throne, of rough-carved wood.

As they neared, Jute realized that the long snowy robes spread out around her in ragged tag-ends actually reached all the way to the sides of the long hall. Disturbingly, as he watched, these banners seemed to twist and writhe as if possessing a life of their own. He hastily pulled his gaze away.

The woman smiled and motioned them onward. Her hair was ash-grey and hung about her in long swathes that also spread out across the stone flags.

Tyvar approached and knelt upon one knee. Lady Orosenn bowed deeply. Jute hastened to follow suit.

'Lady Mist,' Tyvar began, 'we thank you for this audience. I am Commander Gendarian, Tyvar Gendarian, of the Blue Shields. With me are Captain Jute and Lady Orosenn. May we take this opportunity to beg for supplies and timber to repair our vessels, as the passage here has been a most trying one.'

'Greetings, travellers,' the sorceress answered. 'I extend to you the protection and security of residency here in the settlement of Mist.'

Residency? Jute cast an uneasy glance to Lady Orosenn. The tall woman was shaking her head, her expression one of sad displeasure. Even Tyvar glanced back to share a rather stunned look. 'I'm sorry, m'lady, but I'm not certain I understand . . .'

Lady Mist opened her arms. 'I should have thought my meaning was plain. You are now my subjects. You will surrender your weapons and armour and join the rest of the men and women here tilling the soil and building a settlement. You have until tomorrow to comply.'

Tyvar cocked his head, as if confronted by something bizarre. 'And if we do not?'

The sorceress did not answer. She merely returned her arms to the throne's thick armrests. The silence dragged on and Jute almost turned to whisper to Lady Orosenn, but something caught his eye down upon the stone flags and he flinched instead. Scarves of mist now coiled about Tyvar's feet and even as Jute watched they began writhing up his legs like winding sheets.

Tyvar hissed, sensing something, and glanced down to bat at his legs. The ropes cinched tight and he fell to the floor in a clatter of armour. His helm skittered off into the dark.

'Sorceress!' Lady Orosenn suddenly called out, commandingly.

The ropes of mist fell away and dispersed like smoke. Tyvar was on his feet in one quick leap. A gauntleted hand went to the long grip of his bastardsword. Lady Orosenn reached out to gently touch the man's shoulder and he immediately released the weapon.

The sorceress was nodding through all this. 'A very wise decision. For you see . . . I am not entirely unprotected.' And she gestured, waving her hand forward.

Heavy thumping steps sounded from the dark corners behind the throne. Out stepped two giants, or so they appeared to Jute. Hoary shapes out of legend. Jaghut? Trell? Fabled Toblakai? Who was to know? Fully two fathoms tall they must have been. One wore a long heavy coat of bronze scales that hung to the floor in ragged lengths. He was bearded, his hair a thick nest, his jaw massive with pronounced tusk-like upward-jutting canines. He carried an immensely wide two-headed axe. This he thumped to the flags before his sandalled feet in a blow that shook the floor. The other stood nearly identical but girt in armour of overlapping iron scales. Thrust through his belt was a greatsword fully as tall as any man, from its tip to its plain hexagonal pommel of bevelled iron.

Both favoured the party with hungry eager grins.

'Allow me to introduce my sons,' Mist continued. She extended a hand to the left. 'Anger.' She gestured to her right. 'Wrath.'

Lady Orosenn lurched one step forward as if she would charge Mist. 'You have not been kind to your sons,' she grated.

Mist thrust a finger at her. '*You* I will allow to continue on to the north. All who come to pay tribute to our great ancestors are welcome.'

'They are not my ancestors,' Lady Orosenn growled, low and controlled, and Jute was shaken by the uncharacteristic ferocity in her voice. 'They are more my great-nephews and nieces.'

Mist's hands convulsed to claws on the armrests and she gaped. Then, recovering, she gave a girlish laugh and waved the words aside. 'An outrageous claim. In any case, you have no stake in this. Stand aside.' Her eyes moved to Tyvar, and she pointed to the entrance. 'Go now, and convince your crews to cooperate. Any resistance or rebellion will be utterly crushed.'

Tyvar recovered his helm and marched from the hall. Jute glanced from the mercenary's retreating back to Lady Orosenn, who had not moved, and chose to follow Tyvar. Leaving, he heard Lady Orosenn say, in a voice now touched with sadness, 'It seems that we never learn, Mist.' Then he heard her steps following in his wake.

The village, if it could be called that, was deserted. So too the slope down to the ships. Everyone knew to keep indoors. Jute noted with alarm the creeping banners of fog. They were coursing in towards them from all sides, as if they were streams of water sinking into a basin. Tyvar muttered to Lady Orosenn, 'We cannot counter this sorcery. Togg is no longer with us.'

'I will do my best. Push off immediately.'

'I am not used to this crouching behind the cover of another.'

'Think of me as your priestess, then.'

The big man barked a laugh. 'Would that were so, m'lady.'

She urged him onwards. 'Quickly, set the crew to work. No time for talking.'

'Yes, ma'am.' Jute ran for the *Silver Dawn*. Drawing near, he waved, shouting: 'Push off! All crew! Now!'

First Mate Buen appeared at the side. He shouted back, 'What's that?'

Jute came stumbling and slogging through the mud. 'I said get the crew out, damn you!'

Buen gestured to the bay, now shrouded in dense mists. 'It's too foggy to set out. Can't see a thing.'

Jute nearly screamed his frustration. He drew the shortsword at his side – the first time he could recall ever doing so – and pointed it at his mate. 'Get everyone over the side now! We're leaving or we're dead!'

Buen raised his hands. 'All right, all right. What's the big rush?'

'*Just do it!*'

The mate turned away. 'You heard the cap'n. Over the side.'

'But it's muddy out there,' someone complained. Dulat, perhaps.

Jute leaned an arm against the slick planks and rested his head there in disbelief. He glanced across the flats: Lady Orosenn stood in the muck next to her launch, facing inland. Her oarsmen, stiff figures in rags, hardly stirred a muscle. Something about them made him jerk his gaze away to examine the *Resolute*. Tyvar was of course making far greater headway than he. His crew had jumped down and even now were crowding around the bows to push.

We're going to die, he told himself.

Movement up the slope caught his eye. A lone figure, running, arms waving. It was a sailor by the rags he wore. 'Take me!' the man bellowed, his voice cracking. 'By the merciful gods – take me with you!'

Buen appeared in the muck at Jute's side. He pointed. 'Who in the green Abyss is that?'

Jute glared, then shoved him to the planks. 'Push, damn you!' More of his crew came jumping reluctantly into the clinging mud. 'Push, all of you! Push!'

'Please take me wi—' Something choked off the man's call and Jute turned to look.

Coils of mist enmeshed the sailor. As Jute watched, those ropes and scarves lifted the man up into the air where he struggled in eerie silence. Then the ribbons of shifting gossamer fog about his middle yanked tight. The man vomited – but not the normal stomach contents. The very organs themselves came bursting from his mouth in a rain of escaping fluids to slap to the ground as a mess of pulped viscera. Jute fought his own gorge. The corpse, nearly cut in half now, blood-red organs dangling from its mouth, jerked as the banners of mist yanked each limb clean off, one after the other, the arms first and then the legs.

One of Jute's crew gagged and vomited.

The tendrils then lashed like whips and Jute ducked as the dismembered parts of the corpse came flying at the *Dawn* to bang against the hull. The torso thumped wetly to the deck.

'*Fucking Abyss!*' Buen yelled, ducking.

'I told you to push,' Jute observed. He was surprised by how calm he sounded.

The crew dashed themselves against the hull. Feet dug and slid frantically in the muck. Someone was whimpering and Jute couldn't blame him.

A strange sort of pressure brushed against him then and he turned. Lady Orosenn had her arms out, as if pushing. Jute glanced about – the mist was rolling backwards as though in a stiff wind. Though no true wind ruffled any of them. It lashed and whipped on all sides yet was driven back, if only a short distance.

Two great bellows of rage sounded from the obscuring banks of fog. Jute's head sank once again. Do these foreign gods never tire of their jokes? Two enormous shadowed silhouettes came lumbering down the slope.

As if this new threat were the key, the bows of the *Dawn* lurched backwards. The sailors followed, heaving. Water kicked up about them as they pushed into the weak surf. The hull lifted free of the flats. Jute could've kissed every one of the damned crew as those few left on board now reached down to help lift them up and in. He clung to the top rail, his feet dangling in the surf, and peered back. Lady Orosenn still had her arms outstretched yet even from this distance Jute could see them shuddering with effort. All about, in a clear semicircle around the ships, whips and tatters of fog lashed and writhed.

We are clear – but what of her? Jute wondered, horrified. How will she . . .

As he watched, the sorceress took one shaky step backwards into the launch then tumbled the rest of the way as if thrown. The stiff upright oarsmen started rowing and the launch surged out into the surf. The scarves of mist came unravelling down the slope just as the brothers, Anger and Wrath, emerged like two fiends out of myth. The brothers stopped on the shore and shook their fists, bellowing their rage. The mist, however, did not halt. It came on, brushing sinuously over the waves like a horde of sea-snakes, straight for him – or so it seemed.

'Pull me up, damn you all!' he roared.

Hands yanked at him, heaved him up. On deck he straightened to peer at everyone gaping at the shore, then turned as something crashed into the waves just short of the bow. It sent up a towering burst of spray that splashed everyone.

On shore, Anger stooped for another boulder.

Jute turned to his astonished crew. 'Don't just stand there!' he roared. 'Man the sweeps!'

The spell of fascination was broken; the crew scrambled for the oars.

Jute returned to studying the shore. Anger had a boulder raised over his head that wouldn't shame any siege onager. This he heaved at the *Dawn* in a mighty throw. The rock came whistling down to splash to the port side. Spray from the impact doused the oarsmen.

A distant crash of timber snatched Jute's attention to the *Resolute*. A boulder thrown by Wrath had struck the tall bow-stem, snapping it off. Their oarsmen kept heaving and the vessel kept its headway so Jute surmised the keel remained true.

As for Lady Orosenn, her silent crew pulled her out to the waiting *Supplicant* with breathtaking speed. They climbed rope ladders up the side.

All along the receding shore, the bank of fog thickened to a near opaque wall. It was as if Mist were sealing off her realm in an impenetrable barrier of cloud. Only the giant brothers remained. They stood as blurred twin shadows, roaring their namesake ire and heaving rocks that now fell short in tall towers of spray and haze.

Jute went to the stern. 'Swing us round,' he ordered Lurjen.

'Heading?' the man enquired, his gaze fixed on the rippling fist-waving shadows.

'East. There's a channel there or I'm a Letherii philanthropist.'

'Hit it off with the locals?' Ieleen enquired dryly, her hands resting on her walking stick and her chin atop them.

'The usual miscommunication, dearest.'

'The channel may be impassable,' she pointed out.

262

'We'll take our time.'

'We're too low on supplies.'

'Then we'll send out launches to fish or hunt – there may be seals.'

'You're determined, then,' she sighed.

Jute turned to her. 'Why, of course. After all this?'

She pensively tapped her stick to the decking. 'I was just thinking that perhaps we've gone about as far as we should. All things considered . . .'

He squatted next to her. Sensing his nearness, she gave him a smile, but it was a wistful one. 'I'm worried, luv,' she whispered. 'We've about pushed our luck as far as we ought.'

'We're about,' Lurjen murmured.

'Ahead slow,' he answered without turning from his wife. 'Find open water.'

'Aye, aye. Ahead slow, Buen,' Lurjen called.

'Aye,' the first mate answered. 'Get a man up that mast! Two at the bows! With poles!'

'We've a sorceress with us, lass,' Jute said. 'And a mercenary army.'

She shook her head. 'Leave it to them. Who are we? Just common people. We don't belong in this land of ogres and powers. It'll be the end of us. I feel it.' He pressed a hand to her shoulder and she took it, squeezing tightly. 'Not much farther, yes?'

'All right, lass. I swear. If it looks too rough. Not much farther.'

'Too rough!' She laughed. 'Luv – what is it now, pray tell?'

'We escaped.'

'You may not the next time.'

'I'll be careful, love.'

'See that you are,' she snapped, then sighed and gave his hand a squeeze.

'Ice ahead, captain,' Buen called from amidships.

Jute straightened. 'Very well.' He faced the bows and squinted to where the light held a bluish glow from the thickening flow of great ice slabs. 'More men on poles. And let's have a touch more sail.'

'Aye, aye.'

*　　*　　*

Neither Storval nor any of the hired swordsmen would admit it, but Reuth's navigation saw the *Lady's Luck* south through the Wreckers' Coast. Only his uncle offered any acknowledgement of the feat, and this with mere cuffs across Reuth's shoulder. Meagre fare, but more affection than the coarse, bluff fellow generally granted.

Reuth kept apart from the band of fighters Storval had gathered about himself: the sneering Stormguard and other disaffected swordsmen from Fist. The Mare sailors generally avoided the fighting men as well, siding now with his uncle in any discussion regarding strategy or ship's business.

It was, he knew, a very dangerous situation for the future of their venture – and for the future of his uncle, for that matter. Not to mention himself, he slowly began to understand. Navigator or no, the swordsmen in no way hid their contempt and dislike of him.

Again he wished Whiteblade were still with them. *He* would've sided with his uncle, he was certain. But then, who knew? Had the champion revealed himself these Stormguard might have attacked him immediately, as they had every reason to loathe him for the loss of their Lady.

In any case, there was no way to know now.

Under Reuth's guidance, the *Lady's Luck* successfully rounded the tip of the Bone Peninsula and reached the mouth of the narrows. Here they found a great flotilla of vessels from seafaring cities and states from all four corners of the world, all at anchor while their pilots and steersmen studied the maze of jagged spars and stone teeth that were the Guardian Rocks.

Tulan ordered them to drop anchor here as well, and the *Lady's Luck* joined the informal queue of vessels all awaiting some change in the currents, or a fellow navigator's brash attempt to dare the rocks. Reuth had no doubt that everyone carefully watched how well these ventures fared: what course to follow, what turns to avoid.

For the rest of that day and the next they watched as well. They witnessed two attempts to thread the maze, both at high tide. One in the evening and one at the next dawn. Four ships set out in the evening. None survived the twisting, foaming course, though one nimble galley nearly made it through.

The wreckage of broken timbers and tangled rigging came washing out to pass between the anchored vessels. Few of the sailors waving their arms and begging amid the flotsam were picked up; it was harsh, but few ships could take on more mouths to feed. Most of the survivors coursed onward past the flotilla to bob out into the grey waters of the Sea of Hate, where, Reuth was certain, all would eventually drown or be consumed by sharks.

At one point in the day Storval came ambling up to where Tulan and Reuth stood close to the bow. 'Well, *captain*?' the mate asked. These days the man said 'captain' in a strange tone, as if he were winking, or worse. It came to Reuth that now they'd arrived, the mate and his gang must think themselves close to free of them. *He* knew that they had a long way to travel as yet, but he also knew there was no way Storval would listen to him.

'We'll see,' his uncle answered.

The first mate just nodded, rather insolently, and ambled off.

'Can you get us through there, lad?' Tulan whispered to Reuth as they faced out over the waters, away from the crew.

'I think so,' he said, with far more certainty than he felt.

'Well,' his uncle answered in an almost apologetic sigh, 'seems we've no choice in the matter now. Damned if we do, damned if we don't.'

'So we might as well.'

His uncle didn't speak for a time and Reuth glanced over; he found the older man eyeing him with something like surprise. Tulan grinned then, and cuffed him, far harder than usual. 'There you are, lad!' he exclaimed. 'This voyage will make a man out of you yet.'

Reuth rubbed his shoulder. 'If I live long enough . . .' he muttered.

Tulan jerked a thumb out towards the narrows. 'What do you think?'

Reuth just shrugged. 'Doesn't matter. The crew won't follow my commands.'

'They'll bloody well follow mine. Least till they throw me overboard.' He leaned down to rest his thick forearms on the railing. 'These fools are such asses that all you have to do is give me the commands and I'll shout 'em out.'

'Would that really work?'

'Sadly so, lad. Sadly so.'

Reuth shook his head in disbelief. Seemed he truly was learning a lot on this trip regarding the nature of men. He returned to studying the mouth of the narrows.

An angry hiss from his uncle brought his attention round to the stern. Three vessels were coming up from the south, all alike in cut and banners. Three fat merchant ships specially altered for fighting, with archers' castles fore and aft.

'Where do they come from?' his uncle asked.

Reuth frowned as he ransacked his memory of the sheets of ships' sigils and heraldry he'd scanned. Plain dark blue field, a black chair or throne, with horizontal bars of gold beneath. Then he had it. 'Lether.'

His uncle grunted. 'Hunh. No competition at sea from them then.'

Reuth agreed with his uncle's assessment. Not known for their seamanship, these Letherii merchants.

The gathered Stormguard suddenly raised a great ruckus, cursing and raising their spears at a ship now hugging the side of the *Lady*. It dropped anchor not very far from them.

Reuth saw immediately why as it was an obvious pirate vessel, a long low galley.

'Bastard chisellers!' Storval yelled. 'Ready to ride our wake in, the scum. I'd like to swing over and clear their boards.'

Reuth studied the large contingent of warriors crowding the deck. Most in metal armour, banded or mail, with shields. All in similar dark tabards. Quite grim-looking, too. Serious and watchful. Reuth wasn't sure that the Korelri swordsmen would have an easy time of it.

He returned to watching the eddies and churning currents. If these pirates – if that was what they were – wanted to try to follow them in then they were welcome to do so. Personally, he didn't think they'd have any chance.

Finally, he decided on his course. He told Tulan to ready for a dawn run.

His uncle pulled on his greying beard and nodded sagely. 'We'll show these outlanders just what a Mare galley can do, hey? Join me at the stern.'

'The stern? Must I?'

'Aye, next to Gren.' Gren was their best tillerman. Reuth nodded, though unhappily. He hated being at the stern, where Storval and the Stormguard held court. Yet it made sense.

Tulan reached out but this time gently squeezed Reuth's shoulder in his big paw. 'High tide, then.' Reuth nodded. 'Good. Get some sleep till then, won't you? Rest, hey?' Reuth nodded again, and slid down the side to sit with his back to the timbers.

He wrapped himself in a blanket and tucked his hands under his armpits. His uncle might be eager to show off to everyone the superiority of a Mare galley, but what he wanted to do was wipe the superior sneers off the faces of these Korelri soldiers with a clear demonstration of his skill and worth.

He just hoped to all those false foreign gods that he didn't mess it up.

His uncle's barked orders woke him before dawn. He had the crew readying for the run in a rush of stowing gear, preparing the sails for quick deploying, and drawing out every pole and oar on board. Reuth made his way to the stern deck. Gren was already at the tiller, his broad arms hanging over the wooden arm. The veteran Mare sailor gave Reuth a wary nod. Other than Gren, Reuth and Tulan, the stern was empty. Tulan had everyone, the Stormguard included, manning the oars, or ready to step in. Storval paced the main walkway, overseeing the oarsmen. He would pass along Tulan's orders.

Reuth already had a shaded eye on the waterline of the foremost rocks where the honey glow of the false dawn shone across the narrows. He was alarmed as the waters were rising faster than he'd anticipated. He caught his uncle's gaze. Tulan raised a brow in an unspoken question. Reuth nodded. Tulan leaned against the stern railing, shouted, 'Lower oars! Full speed.'

Storval echoed the orders.

The oars slapped the waves to either side of the narrow galley and they shot ahead with such power that Reuth had to take a backward step. Gren shot him a grin, but not a superior one; the man was actually grinning a kind of savage anticipation. Reuth was fascinated to see him wrapping one of his arms in a rope attached to the tiller.

'Better tie yourself off there, lad,' the veteran warned.

Reuth started, surprised, then peered around. He found a line and wrapped it about his waist, then secured himself to the side.

'Going to see us through, hey, lad?' Gren observed.

Reuth felt his cheeks heat.

Gren drew a bone-handled knife from his side and slammed it into the tiller close to the rope.

'No – Tulan's in charge. What's the knife for?'

'In case we capsize, lad, an' I have to cut m'self free. Now, none of this talk of your uncle. We're Mare sailors, you 'n' I. These Korelri Chosen, what do they know of Ruse? Nothing. In pointa fact, they hate the sea. But between you 'n' me – you have the Ruse-sense, lad. I seen it.'

Reuth blinked at the burly fellow. 'You've seen it?'

Gren winked. 'Oh, aye. When they look out over the water they scowl and glance away. They're frightened. But when you watch the sea, you smile. That's why they don't like you, lad . . . you're not scared of the sea.'

Reuth stared, speechless. Such an idea had never occurred to him.

'Full speed I said, damn you!' Tulan shouted again. He glanced back to Reuth then glared past him, his face darkening. 'Damned shadows sneaking in after us!'

Reuth glanced back to see that numerous ships were under way, all sweeping into line along their wake. The first was the local pirate vessel. He thought them foolish to come chasing in – their galley had far too little freeboard for the manoeuvring that would be needed here.

'Over ten ships, lad!' Gren laughed. 'There's a compliment. They know we're Mare sailors, and this is a Mare vessel. If any sailor can thread this needle, it's us!'

Tulan shot Reuth a questioning glance, which he answered with a nod. He turned to Gren. 'Hug the starboard shore as we come in the mouth. Be ready to swing full to port.'

'Aye.'

Tulan nodded at this, reassured, and returned to facing the bows.

The roar of churning waters swelled. In the unruly yawing and bucking of the galley, Reuth felt the currents beneath them swirling and hammering as the incoming high tide wrestled with the narrows' outflow. The first of the rocks passed as dark blotches in the channel – submerged now, but still lurking tall enough to snatch a keel. Already Reuth's face was chill and wet from the spray suspended in the gusting winds that howled down the constricting cliffs of the narrows.

Gren stood hunched over the tiller arm, his bare feet splayed wide. 'You do what you have to do, lad,' he urged, winking.

Reuth swallowed hard and drew a hand down his face to wipe away the spray. 'Chase speed,' he shouted.

'Chase speed!' Tulan immediately bellowed, hands to mouth.

'Chase speed!' Reuth barely heard Storval echoing. He did notice that the first mate no longer paced the walk. Now he stood with an arm round the mast, probably gripping a line.

Gren had lost something of his grin now as he studied the oars. Reuth spared a glance and saw right away that they were far from the ideal unison in their slashing dip and rise. He recognized the interference of the inexperienced swordsmen – regrettable, but necessary for power. He'd have to take it into account in his estimates. 'Ramming speed,' he called.

'Ramming speed!' Tulan bellowed.

The *Lady's Luck* surged ahead, rocking Reuth on his feet. They shot between the first of the black jagged teeth of the Guardian Rocks. The foaming slew of waves danced about them. One fat swell of webbed olive-green water rose taller than their side. Reuth now kept his vision far ahead of their position. 'Ready on the turn,' he warned.

'Aye.'

Reuth delayed until he dared not wait a heartbeat longer and yelled, *'Full port!'*

Gren drove the tiller arm aside, grunting, legs straining. He even set his shoulder against it. The *Lady's Luck* groaned around them as she slewed over. Tulan steadied himself against the stern railing. Reuth grabbed hold of the line holding him upright as the galley rolled frighteningly. They started across the narrows and Reuth saw immediately that their line wasn't what he was shooting for.

'Port oars ease off!' he called, panic now in his voice.

'Port oars ease off!' Tulan roared.

Reuth assumed Storval was relaying the commands but he heard none of it over the grinding thunder of the waters about them. The port oars rose to stand straight out from the side. The *Lady's* bow nosed over as the opposite row of oars powered on. 'Resume oars!' Reuth yelled.

Tulan relayed the command. The line of port oars dipped. Reuth breathed a sigh of immense relief. Their line looked good to him, but they'd lost speed. He leaned, pointing, to shout to Gren: 'I want a line between that short rock and the cliff for another sweep to the middle.'

The steersman's thick brows rose, but he nodded. 'Aye.'

The *Lady's Luck* jumped then, flinching as if stabbed, and slewed aside. The grinding of wood over rock momentarily silenced the water's roar. Reuth leaned over the side in time to see a black shadow sweep past beneath the surface. They'd struck a submerged rock a glancing blow.

Gren strained to bring the bow back into line. 'Chase speed!' Reuth yelled.

Tulan repeated the command with a good deal of cursing and fuming.

Reuth felt the surge of renewed speed as the oarsmen leaned into their work. The swordsmen were useless on their timing, but they had real power. And the *Lady* was responding as before: she didn't feel sluggish at all. The planking held, thank their Mare carpenters and Ruse enchantments of seam and timber.

They were coming abreast of the short black tooth of rock that Reuth had named the pony in his mental map of the route ahead, and he called, 'Ready for the return!'

'Aye!'

'Now! Sweep to the middle!'

Gren cursed and heaved, bringing the heavy timber arm back the opposite way. The *Lady*'s bows now swung over, but heavily, as they fought the swifter current in this narrow pinch close to the port cliff.

'Ramming speed!' Reuth called out.

'Ramming speed, you dogs, or we'll drink with Mael this night!' Tulan roared.

The oars dug in, pulling. The *Lady* shuddered. So close did they draw to the cliff that one rear oar on the port side clattered from the face. They gained speed as real panic seemed to take hold and the *Lady* shot out towards the middle of the channel.

Reuth was pleased. They'd avoided the worst of this lowest section of the Rocks. Stretches where the waters swelled and boiled signalling many hidden teeth below. The line ahead promised smooth glassy portions. Briefly, he wondered how the trailing vessels fared, but he dared not glance to the rear to search for them.

He pointed to the coming maze of rocks. 'Take that first one on the port side, Gren.'

'Aye.'

After that first turn of the crowded middle section, Reuth couldn't be certain of the route. He had only split seconds to send the bow one way or the other and the answers came to him more or less on instinct: the fat curl of one swell; the deeper blue of one particular channel; the foam gathered in one side pool that promised a slower current. The teeth brushed past so close Tulan stepped in to order oars raised, or poles deployed to fend the *Lady* off a rock the current was pressing her against. Wood scraped in tortured groans. Oars cracked on stone, or were bashed aside in a rattling head-smashing sweep of the benches.

At one point a sideswipe knocked the entire starboard side into disorder in a running clatter of breaking oars. Tulan leapt the stern railing to help clear the chaos. Here the discipline of the Stormguard paid off as they immediately followed every command. Reuth glimpsed one of them pulling blind, his face a solid sheet of blood pouring from a gash in his scalp. Another yanked one-handed while his other hung useless, the bone of his forearm shattered.

These men know how to fight the sea, he realized. This was their life, their sworn calling. He had one moment to realize that this was why they'd left Korel – they could no longer find a battle there – then the next instant he had to select an escape route even as the *Lady*, losing headway, began a spin driven by the current.

'Back round!' he yelled to Gren. 'Circle the rock for another try!'

The steersman shot him a mad grin and laughed. He pushed the arm fully over.

This particular rock was a huge one, which was why Reuth could try the move. He only hoped that Tulan and Storval could knock the starboard banks into order before they came round once more. As the *Lady* made its dancing turn round the great tooth, Reuth was treated to a view back up Fear Narrows. He glimpsed many ships yet in play, all galleys, the pirate vessel closest behind. Its sweeps flashed in poor timing but with massive deep bites that seemed to lift the entire ship.

Spelling, he said to himself. They must be spelling the oarsmen – no one could sustain such an effort for longer than one quick rush.

The bow continued its arc and then came the time for them to catch the current once more. Reuth looked to the banks: the port oars were raised waiting to start, but disorder still reigned among the starboard sweeps.

'Trapped,' Reuth breathed aloud. 'We're caught!'

'What for it then, lad?' Gren answered.

'Port side drag oars!' he yelled. Gren took up the call as well, yet Reuth could well imagine that their voices hardly carried over the thunder of the churning waves pounding on all sides.

Then Tulan's great bull-roar sounded out: 'Drop them port sweeps! Back oars! Push, you dogs! Break your backs!'

The drag pulled on the bow and in the widening gap a portion of the starboard sweeps bit into the swell.

'Take us into the open,' Reuth told Gren. He nearly dropped then, quivering, his legs almost without strength.

The steersman nodded. 'The line?'

Reuth gestured up the middle. 'It looks to be opening up.'

The *Lady* limped along now, but the narrows broadened here, the current slower. The vertical cliffs still allowed no respite for any crippled vessel, but they made headway. Reuth allowed himself a glance to the rear. Incredibly, many vessels still followed.

He returned to scanning for the best route ahead. Don't fail now, he told himself. Not when we must be nearly through. He examined the waters emerging from round each looming rock ahead; some frothed far more than others, suggesting a rougher path. He decided to keep to weaving through the middle to avoid getting pinched against a cliff.

This long drawn-out section of the way wore hardest upon him. He was already exhausted, unable to focus as well as he had. He dragged a hand down his face and rubbed his stinging eyes. Then he thought of the oarsmen still pulling below him and shook off the mood. None of them had been spelled through any of this. The *Lady* simply didn't have a large enough complement.

'We might be through,' he told Gren.

The steersman rolled his massive shoulders to loosen them. 'We might.' Then he frowned. 'I smell smoke.'

Reuth squinted ahead. Smoke? How could there be . . . He caught coils of black smoke now curling round the rocks ahead. What in the Lady's name . . . ?

The stern of a tall three-tiered vessel came edging out from behind the looming centre tooth – an enormous galley entirely engulfed in flames.

Shouts of alarm sounded from the crew below.

'Lad . . .' Gren murmured.

Reuth simply stared. A sea battle ahead? A sea battle in the middle of the narrows? But the *Lady*'s entire crew was given over to the benches. How could they possibly hope to—

'Lad, choose . . .' Gren prompted, louder. 'Now.'

Reuth shook himself. Choose? Now? He studied the vessel's aimless spin as it came heading broadside down towards them like a wall of fire. Black smoke billowed, cloaking a portion of the channel.

'Hard port!' he shouted.

Gren thrust the tiller arm over. The *Lady*'s bow swung towards the port shore of the narrows while the burning vessel, helpless in the current, coasted directly across their line. Smoke blew across the deck in thick sooty billows that blinded Reuth.

'Pull!' Tulan urged, coughing. 'Keep pulling!'

The hungry roar of flames now overtook the rush and hissing of the waters about them. Gouts of flame penetrated the wall of smoke like bursts of those damned Moranth munitions. A firestorm much taller than the *Lady* came crackling and thundering, as searingly hot as an enormous kiln, directly past their starboard side. Reuth covered his face. He coughed and gagged in the thick oily smoke. Something hot kissed his hand and he yelped, jumping and waving the hand.

'Put those fires out!' he heard Tulan barking. 'Douse those embers!'

The pall of smoke began to clear. 'Sail's caught!' Storval shouted.

'Drop it!' Tulan ordered.

'Cut the ropes!' Reuth heard Storval call.

Blinking, Reuth felt more than saw the bundled sail come crashing down, crossbar and all, while flames licked about it. 'Overboard!' Tulan bellowed. 'Now!'

Men grunted and heaved. Wood grated, then a heavy splash announced that the burning bundle had struck the waves.

Reuth started then, remembering his duty, and called out: 'Back over, Gren.'

The steersman grunted his surprise and slammed the arm across. 'Sorry,' he murmured.

Reuth wiped his face and his hands came away black with soot. 'Is it a sea battle, Gren?'

'Don't know, lad.'

'Because we can't—'

'Never mind. You just get us through.'

Reuth gave a quick shamed nod. 'Yes. Sorry.'

He studied the possible paths ahead. The way appeared to be broadening. He did his best to choose the turns that would send them into a line that would allow the most options. His main concern now was their waning speed. The men were spent, of course, and their headway was flagging. Yet the current was also weakening. Even portions of this section ran smooth.

After a few more slow turns they emerged into a full wide channel marred only by a few isolated rearing teeth. It appeared they'd run the Guardian Rocks.

Gren shot Reuth his mad grin.

Tulan came stomping up to the stern. Soot blackened his sodden furs and his beard seemed to have caught fire along one side. He was drawing in great breaths as he laid a hand on Reuth's shoulder and squeezed. 'Well done, lad,' he croaked, his voice almost gone. 'Well done.' He turned to peer ahead, drew in a great lungful of air. 'Now what?'

'There are a few mentions of a settlement here. Ruse, some write it.'

Tulan grunted. 'Fair enough. We'll make for it. We need safe moorage for a refit.'

Gren began untying himself from the tiller arm. 'You've your sea legs now, I think, hey?'

'I've had enough of the sea.'

Gren laughed. 'There you go. You've the way of it now.'

A sailor Tulan had sent up the mast now called, 'Our shadows are with us. One close, others distant.'

Reuth glanced behind. Indeed, more vessels were limping out from among the rearing teeth. They were far behind, but it appeared that the lead one was their pirate friend.

The crew continued to row, but at a leisurely pace. The narrows broadened. There was almost enough of a breeze to warrant lowering a sail, if they still had one.

'Something ahead,' the lookout shouted.

Reuth shaded his eyes but couldn't make anything out. Tulan called up, 'What is it, man?'

'Hard to tell . . . ships! Looks like a mass of ships!'

Reuth thought of his worries about a sea battle. Tulan's brows crimped and a hand went to check for the sword at his hip. 'See that everyone's armed,' he ordered Storval.

'Aye.'

They closed at a slowing pace. What awaited ahead was a mass of ships, but no fighting. The forest of mismatched galleys, launches, fishing boats and cargo vessels were congregated around a slim side channel. As they neared, it became clear that most had seen heavy fighting. Reuth made out archers crowding almost every deck. 'Don't like the look of this,' he murmured to Gren.

'We'll surprise 'em,' Tulan answered. He leaned over the stern railing. 'Full speed! Looks like a reception committee.'

'You heard the man,' Storval announced. 'No more easing off! You and you – back to your positions.'

Ahead, a single arrow took flight above the ragtag navy and with that signal the vessels dispersed like a swarm of bees. It looked to Reuth as though they meant to cordon off the entire narrows.

'Chase speed!' Tulan bellowed out.

The *Lady's Luck* surged ahead, though with not nearly the power and crispness of earlier in the day. It was now a race. Reuth motioned to the opposite cliff face and Gren nodded. He slowly angled the bow aside.

'Ramming speed!' Tulan ordered. In answer, the *Lady's Luck* hardly accelerated. 'Row, you wretches!' the huge man raged. 'Put some effort into it for a change!'

The fastest of the navy vessels was leading the dash to the opposite cliffs, but it looked to Reuth as if they might just slip past first. He congratulated himself on being of Mare – the greatest seafarers and shipbuilders on the earth.

He turned to Gren with a smile on his lips. 'We might just—'

'Get down!' the steersman cried, and yanked him by an arm.

A rain of arrows came slamming into the *Lady's Luck*. Men yelled all up and down the benches. The sweeps clattered and slapped into chaos. Some caught the water to drag. The *Lady* lost headway as if sliding up a sand bar. Tulan was now bellowing among the oarsmen. A second volley of arrows swept the deck and Gren held Reuth in the cover of the ship's side.

Something rammed them in a snapping of sweeps and grinding of timbers. Reuth's head struck the side, leaving his vision blurry. He peered up to see that a smaller galley had struck them a glancing blow. Grapnels flew from the enemy vessel while a crowd of archers continued to rake the *Lady*.

'Cut those ropes!' Tulan roared.

A second blow shuddered through the *Lady's Luck* as another vessel scoured alongside.

'Repel boarders!' Storval called.

'Doesn't look good,' Gren hissed, looking down. Reuth followed his gaze to see an arrow standing from the man's thigh.

'Gren! What should I do?'

'Be a good lad and tear a piece of cloth for me.'

Reuth tore at his own shirt. The steersman snapped off the standing length of shaft then reached under his leg, clenched his teeth, and yanked on something. He grunted his agony, then lifted a hand holding a bloodied arrowhead and shaft. He tossed it aside then sat heavily, nearly passing out. Reuth tied off his leg.

Another impact threw him from his feet to roll across the stern deck. He clambered up and peeked over the side. They'd been rammed from behind to be knocked clear of the ships that had surrounded them and now they drifted with this new galley – the pirate vessel that had followed them in.

Armoured men and women, all in deep blood-red tabards, leapt from its bows to the *Lady*'s stern. One of them, a shorter fellow with a strange grey-blue pallor to his skin, peered down at him. Surprisingly, the fellow carried no weapons, only two short sticks. 'Where is your captain?' he demanded.

'I command here!' Storval answered, climbing the stern deck, sword out.

The newcomer raised his hands, fingers spread. 'Man your sweeps. We'll cover your retreat.'

'And who in the Lady's name are you?' Storval sneered.

'Doesn't matter. Get your banks in order. They're closing again.'

Storval peered past the man to the rear, grunted his assent. He sheathed the sword and thumped down to the main walkway. 'Man the sweeps!' he called. 'Everyone! Now!'

Reuth leapt the stern railing. *Storval?* Why Storval? Where's . . . He searched among the benches then found him lying sprawled among the bodies. His uncle, fallen, motionless. Dead.

The newcomer now stood at his side. 'Lad? What is it? Are you all right?'

Reuth raised his gaze to the man. Behind, across a gap of water, three of the leading chase vessels suddenly burst into flames for no reason that Reuth could see. Figures dived overboard. But it was all muted and distant. As if everything was a long way away. He heard himself say woodenly: 'My uncle is dead.'

'I'm sorry, lad,' the fellow murmured. 'You are the pilot? We saw you here, at the stern.'

Reuth nodded. The fellow was looking at him strangely, and nodding to himself. 'We are in your debt,' he said. 'And the Crimson Guard pays its debts.'

CHAPTER VIII

ORMAN JOGGED NORTH WITHOUT PAUSE, EVER UPWARDS. HE collapsed only when it became too dark to see. The next dawn he drove himself onward again. He stumbled and tripped the entire way. He found himself missing handholds, or falling over rocks as he misjudged them. He cursed the throbbing blindness of his left eye then. He also knew he was climbing faster than he should for his own safety. The change in altitude was making him light-headed. His nose bled. He was so short of breath he sometimes gasped, bent over, almost blacking out. His legs burned as if he was dragging them through coals, and the vision of his one eye swam.

Yet he pushed on. Soon the bare rocky rises and ridges gave way to snow cover. It was dense and heavy and wet. A white fox yipped at him as he waded through the knee-deep crests. After half a day's journey across these broad fields of whiteness, he came to a halt at the barrier of a cerulean face of sheer ice pockmarked by streams of run-off. The roaring of the combined waterfalls seemed to shake the heaped gravel he stood upon. His breath plumed while he searched the sculpted gleaming ice face for the best route up. Satisfied, he tore strips from his trousers, wrapped them about his hands, and started up.

His fingers immediately became numb. His route sometimes took him past cave openings that gushed icy waters. The spray sent him into uncontrollable shivers. A few times he nearly lost his grip upon the knobs and undulations he clung to and so he drew his hatchets and proceeded up by hacking and hammering at the ice face.

Halfway, he paused to glance back and behind. The massive shoulders of the Salt range descended below in gigantic sweeps of ash-grey stone and misted forests. Low foothills obscured the Sea of Gold. He knew that if he could see it, it would appear no larger than a puddle. And he was only halfway up this enormous slab of ice. It must be a good four chains thick.

He climbed on and at last pulled himself up on to a vast plain of gently undulating snow and ice. He'd reached the top of one of the ice-rivers that dominated the upper crags of the Salt peaks. What some named the Frost Serpents. He stumbled on. Winds of stinging ice rime lashed him, yet he hardly felt the cold. At night he wrapped himself in his plain cloak and curled up next to ridges of naked gleaming ice that reflected the night sky like mirrors. He felt as if he were floating among the stars. He awoke with a solid layer of iced hoar frost over his thickening beard.

On the third day of climbing, the crackling of ice halted him. He paused to listen. All this time he'd heard the distant booming and grinding of this massive ice tongue. Only now did the cracking and snapping sound near. He edged one foot forward, hunched, knees bent, meaning to test the ice. Then the ground fell from beneath him. He tumbled, clawing at a passing sheer face. The ice slashed and tore the flesh of his palms and fingers. He struck something that punched his legs into his chest and knew nothing more.

Some time later he awoke to the wet kisses of heavy fat snowflakes. He blinked to clear his eye and saw stars glimmering down upon him through ragged gaps in thin cloud cover. He watched them for a time. Their graceful deliberate progress was so stately and beautiful it made his heart ache. They appeared within a slim opening between ice cliffs. A narrow slash some three man-heights above the perch he lay upon.

He would have yelled for help but he knew there was no one to hear. He relaxed then, and tucked his hands – numb clubs of blood – under his arms, and watched the show.

The Realm-Lights shimmered into view next, the wavering sky banners that some said marked a gate to other realms. Perhaps the land of the giants, the Thel-kind. Or the Tiste, the Children of Night. Or the Joggen race, as some named the hoary old Jaghut, in northern Joggenhome. The storied creators of winter itself in the times of heroes. He found these curtains and graceful banners breathtakingly beautiful. He'd always admired the lights. Especially those few winters when he'd trapped and hunted the borders of the Holdings with his father. It was consoling to see them now, somehow. As if he'd come home. Home to where he belonged.

He felt himself drifting off to sleep and a small voice railed against this, screaming somewhere far off. But he was tired, so very tired.

Something hit him in the chest. He looked down: a coil of knotted fibre rope. He peered up, narrowing his one eye. A shape obscured the gap above. Mechanically, dully, he began wrapping an arm in the coils. He could not use his hands – they were beyond feeling, beyond use. After numerous turns of his arm through the rope, it began to rise. It stretched, tautened. He was pulled upright. He knew that if he hadn't been so very far gone in numbness, he'd be in agony. His arm was probably being twisted from its socket.

Hanging limp, he was drawn up the ice face, unable to help in any manner. At the top, he was heaved over the lip of the crevasse and allowed to flop into the snow, where he lay staring up at an extraordinary figure – a giant, so tall was he. Yet painfully slim, and so pale he seemed to glow. His wild mane of hair was snow-white, as was his long ragged beard, and despite the frigid cold he wore nothing more than a loincloth. He peered down at Orman with something akin to startled bemusement, like a fisherman who'd landed a particularly puzzling catch.

'What are you doing here, child of the lowlands?' he asked in a quiet and gentle voice.

Child of the lowlands? 'Are you Buri?' Orman gasped, his mouth numb, the words slurred. 'The eldest who brings winter?'

The giant's silver brows rose. 'Is that what they say in the lowlands?' He shook his head. 'I am Buri, but I am not the eldest. Come, I will take you to shelter.' And the ancient being bent down, lifted him and set off with him in his arms like a child. Above his mane of white hair, the dancing curves of the Realm-Lights circled his head like a crown.

When Orman next awoke he lay in a cave, a glittering cave of ice. A fire burned over exposed naked granite. He was alone. He allowed his eye to fall shut once more and slept again.

The mouth-watering scent of roasting meat roused him. He opened his eye to see a large bird carcass roasting over the fire. Buri sat opposite, watching him, his long thin naked arms and legs akimbo.

'What is a child of the lowlands doing here amid the ice-fields?' the ancient one repeated.

And Orman told him everything. Slowly, piece by piece, while he picked at the roasted bird. Including his shameful behaviour at the stream. The loss of his half-brother. All this Buri took in without making a sound. He started only once, when Orman described how he jammed Svalthbrul into the stones and Lotji took it.

When he finished, both were silent for a time. The fire snapped and crackled between them. Dawn's light brightened the ice cave opening with a pink glow. Finally, Orman could stand the silence no longer and cleared his throat. 'Will you not come, then? Lend your help? Your clan is sorely outnumbered. The invaders must number in the thousands.'

Buri raised his gaze from the fire. In the light of the flames, his great mane of hair and beard, so pale as to be colourless, now glowed orange and red. His eyes, however, held a deep amber radiance, like embers themselves. 'No, little brother. I am gathering my strength.'

'Gathering your— The enemy is upon us! Now is the time to act. Surely . . .'

But the ancient shook his head. He crossed his legs, rested his elbows on his knees. 'These invaders, these pathetic seekers after gold and riches . . . they are not the true enemy. It is for others that I am preparing.'

'Who—'

Buri silenced him with a raised hand. 'What must be done is clear.'

And Orman believed he knew exactly what the ancient meant. He hung his head. 'Yes.'

'You know what you must do.'

'Yes.'

'You must return and challenge Lotji for possession of Svalthbrul.'

Orman, his head lowered, nodded. 'Yes.'

'Very good.' Buri rose smoothly, towered over Orman. 'I will show you the swiftest descent.'

At the base of a looming cliff of ice, Orman waved to Buri, a nearly indistinguishable shape amid the cornices and curves of snow above. Then the ancient was gone. Nearby, a waterfall pounded the bare rocks and gravel. The stream wound into a forest of spruce and pine. Orman followed it.

Jogging downslope, only now did he wonder about Buri's use of 'little brother'. He decided the giant must have meant it affectionately. Perhaps for his dedication to young Jass.

And he felt it again. That strange tightness across his chest. That feeling of belonging that he knew when Jass had held out his hand. He realized then that it was for the sake of this feeling alone that he now scrambled down through the evergreen forest for Lotji.

*   *   *

The Lost brothers led Fisher and Jethiss north-east, round the forested north shores of the Sea of Gold. Having grown up in this region, Fisher was much surprised when their path brought them pushing through virgin forest to suddenly enter overgrown fields, or discover the rotting log remnants of abandoned homesteads. Some obviously dated from years long gone; others appeared to have been hacked from the woods only a few seasons ago. When he'd left to travel the world, this shore had been uninhabited. But then, that had been a long time ago.

On the third day, they emerged from a copse of mature ghost-white birch to see cleared fields, trampled and ragged, and a log homestead, sod-roofed. Coots reached the homestead first, and, receiving no reply to his call, pushed open the wooden door and went in. Almost immediately he came outside again and stood against the wall, his arms crossed as if hugging himself.

'What is it?' Fisher asked.

'Lowlander family,' Coots answered, his voice faint. He dropped his gaze, let go a long breath. Fisher passed him. 'You needn't go in . . .' the Iceblood called. Fisher ignored him.

Within, he found the corpses of two boys, both hacked to death by axes. On a simple bed nearby lay a woman he presumed was their mother, naked, beaten to death. She had been badly abused before finally being strangled. The dark of that tiny cabin closed in upon Fisher then and he backed away as if being physically pushed. Outside, in the cool air, he found that he could breathe once more. He raised his gaze to the sky for a time, blinking. *She had been repeatedly raped while her own sons lay dying next to her* . . . He shook his head as if to force the image from his mind.

'Who was it?' he finally asked, and it hurt to speak.

Coots shrugged. 'Raiders.' He motioned to the rearing peaks of the Salt range. 'They'll push north . . .'

Fisher felt his blood run cold. 'We can't let that happen.' He moved to pass Coots, but the man caught his sleeve.

'Those're just stories, Fish. Tales we bloods tell when the fires die down and the Greathall darkens. There ain't none of them Forkrul left – if there ever was.'

Fisher yanked his arm free. 'No.' He glanced away to the plume of clouds; the highest peaks flew like banners. 'I have been there, Coots. I've seen the caves. We can't risk it.' An old line came to him and he recited:

> 'Abiding they wait in caverns of stone
> Ruthless in innocence,
> Children of Earth,
> Bearers of justice
> Sharper than swords.'

Coots shot a glance to his brother, who stood cradling his jaw. He pinched his gold earring, rubbed it thoughtfully. 'Well,' he grudgingly allowed, 'they won't get through our cousins, will they?'

'There's a damned lot of them.' Fisher waved Coots onward.

That dusk they were ready to stop for the night when the glow of flames shone through the forest far higher up the slope, while white smoke climbed into the purpling sky.

Fisher looked to Badlands. 'Same ones, you think?'

'Or others. Makes no difference.'

'We should take a look.'

Badlands shrugged. 'They're lowlanders.'

'We'll go,' Coots said from where he'd been working on starting a fire. He straightened, brushed his hands, and headed off.

Jethiss came to stand close to Fisher. He murmured, low, 'What if . . .'

Fisher nodded curtly. 'Yes, I know. I know . . . But we must see.'

They followed the brothers into the deep shadows of the forest. Coots and Badlands were, of course, master woodsmen and moved in utter silence from cover to cover. Fisher had once possessed the talent, but too long from the wilds had dulled his skills. Jethiss, however, was in no way hampered by the dark and he showed Fisher the way.

They came to the scene of a siege. Flames pillared into the dark behind a tall palisade of logs topped by a barrier of hung antlers. Archers lined the walls. They fired down upon a gang of raiders who jeered and answered the fire from the dark.

The sight of the antlers jogged a memory within Fisher and he recalled the name of a small settlement far to the east: the Keep of the Antlers.

From within the palisade came the scream of a woman – a terrified hopeless shriek of someone burning alive. Fisher bolted upright. *Gods, women and children burning?*

Yells of surprise tore from the night, followed by the ringing of iron. A man howled, wounded. Cursing, Fisher lunged forward, Jethiss with him. He drew as he ran. Jethiss, far surer of his way, outstripped him, and he followed. A bolt or arrow cut the air near him; he could not tell from which direction it came.

Four shapes charged Jethiss from the dark. The Andii met them at a full run. He ducked, spun, kicked one man down, took the top of the last's head off in a wide swing. Fisher arrived to find all four dead or crippled. He eyed the Andii, amazed. 'That was—'

But the Andii was off again. A bellow from the dark announced Coots. More iron rang and clashed. Curses and orders sounded out from a knot of men Jethiss was now closing upon. A line of raiders set shields as he came. The Andii jumped at the last instant, planted his feet square upon one shield, and knocked its owner backwards. He fell within the knot and the line broke apart as the men turned for him. Fisher arrived and hacked down one fellow in an inelegant two-handed blow. Then all was the chaos of churning groups of men and women in the dark, some running, some closing upon him.

He fought using strong hacking blows that knocked aside shields and parrying swords – this was not a battle for the finer points of swordmanship. An axeman charged him, his two-handed double-edged weapon held high to split him in half. Arrows flashed between them, shot from both sides. Fisher sidestepped the blow then swung in to take the man at the back of his neck, severing his spine.

He spun then, turning to all sides. He recognized Genabackans together with a mishmash of others. Some looked like nothing more than casual bandits, while others were armed and armoured as mercenaries.

One of these, in thick layered leathers and iron helmet, charged him now, shield-bashing him. He took the blow but tripped, falling on to his back. The man raised his shortsword then coughed, hunching. Staring up at what he thought was his death, Fisher saw a dark wet arrowhead standing from the man's chest. The fellow toppled on to him.

Fisher heaved the man off. Close now, face to face, he realized that the raider was of Lether. Stunned, he forgot the roaring and stamping feet surrounding him. *Great Burn, no.* Was this Teal's work? Was the marshal somewhere among this force? Was . . . Malle? But no – they'd gone to such pains to remain friendly. Other adventurers from Lether must have arrived, surely.

Feet scuffed the dirt nearby and he started, twisting around. Jethiss stood over him scanning the dark. 'You are hurt?'

Fisher climbed to his feet. 'No.' He peered around: the raiders were decamping, leaving dead and wounded to lie where they fell. Badlands came racing into sight as he chased after them into the woods. Fisher nodded to Jethiss. 'You are good with those blades.'

The Andii was in no way flattered. He glanced away, troubled. 'Not that I wish to be.'

Coots approached the main gate where the archers crowded, backlit by the burning keep. 'Hello there!' he shouted. 'We've run them off! You can—'

'*Bastard Iceblood!*' someone shouted.

Bowfire sounded. Coots grunted and stepped backwards as if absorbing several blows.

Fisher charged for him, yelling, '*No!*'

'Hey now,' Coots slurred, almost chidingly, 'that's no way—' More blows rocked the man. He half spun, fell to one knee. 'That's . . .' The archers fired almost continuously now. Arrow after arrow punched into Coots. 'Hey . . . now . . .' he said, sounding very disappointed. He tumbled backwards.

A scream sounded from the woods. A harrowing call that raised Fisher's hair in its elemental rage and hurt. Arrows whisked past Fisher as he was almost upon Coots. 'Take his head!' someone shouted from the palisade. 'Take that Iceblood's head!'

Then something knocked Fisher over and absolute black night fell upon him. 'Iceblood magic!' someone yelled, real terror choking his voice. Fisher climbed to his feet completely blind. He extended his arms to feel into the blackness. He could see nothing, though he could feel the heat and hear the roar and crackle of the huge fire just a stone's throw from him. A hand took his arm from the dark and he jerked away despite knowing who it must be.

'This way,' Jethiss said from the wall of ink.

'You have him?'

'Yes.'

'And Badlands?'

'He ran into the woods howling like a madman.'

Arrows thudded around them as the archers fired blind. They cursed and yelled from atop the palisade. 'Let's go from here,' Fisher said.

'Yes.' Something brushed Fisher's arm. He felt at it and found a pair of moccasined feet. Coots'. He took hold of one. Jethiss led him on through the blackness.

They walked for some time. Jethiss coached Fisher through brush and over rocks. The slope climbed. The roar of the burning fort diminished to a distant murmur. It occurred to Fisher that to sustain such a large aura of elemental dark, Kurald Galain, must cost its summoner great effort, yet Jethiss betrayed no strain in his voice or breathing. Perhaps such raisings were natural for the Andii. He wondered, though.

Eventually, their pace slowed. Fisher bumped Jethiss, who had stopped. 'I can go no further,' the Andii murmured, his voice husky.

'You have done a miracle, Jethiss. Saved us for certain. They would have pursued. Tried to take our heads.'

'There is a tree here,' he said. 'There is a view over the lowlands.'

Like a passing deep shadow, the absolute black faded away. The sunshine glare of mid-day stabbed at Fisher's eyes. He winced and shaded his gaze, peered around.

They had climbed far into the forested slopes above the Sea of Gold. Below, it glimmered now in the sunlight with an amber-like shine – hence its name, perhaps. Jethiss sat heavily, arms draped over his knees, his head sunk, utterly spent. He'd set Coots in the nook of thick roots at the base of an old knotted spruce. The body faced downslope; Fisher thought it appropriate. 'Have you belts or rope?' he asked.

'I have my weapon belt.'

'Keep that.'

'No. Take it. I have no more use for it.'

Fisher shook his head. 'You'll still need to defend yourself.'

The Andii lifted and dropped his broad shoulders. 'I broke the knives.'

'You broke them?' Fisher marvelled. Wickan knives were a finger thick at the hilts. Thinking of weapons, he realized he'd lost his own as well. He pulled off his belt. Jethiss offered his own. Using both, he secured Coots' body to the tree, tying him under his arms and across his chest. Something told him to leave the multitude of arrows still residing there and so he did so, careful not to snap one shaft.

Jethiss watched. Fisher took Coots' long-knives and pressed them into his stiffening fingers, then laid his hands in his lap. He stood back to examine the corpse – still so broad and huge, seemingly full of life, as if asleep.

He cleared his throat, raised his head and began to chant: 'I name these twinned long-knives the Wolf Fangs. Let it be known they did not betray their bearer. I name any hand that takes them without due respect or honour cursed to see all hands raised against them. Cursed to lose all honour and respect. Cursed to fall as crow carrion.'

'This do I so too vow,' Jethiss added, his voice cracking.

'*Coots of the Lost clan*,' Fisher sang now:

> '*Loyal brother, mighty in wrath.*
> *Mighty in wrestling, mighty in laughter.*
> *Far-reiver, beloved companion.*
> *You are lost to us, and Lost you shall remain for ever.*
> *None shall undo this till these mountains are ground to*
>   *the sea.*'

He lowered his head. 'So ends my honour song of Coots of the Lost clan.'

After a long silence, Jethiss motioned down the rocky slope. 'Look there.'

Fisher turned. A figure had emerged from the treeline. Staggering, falling, it made its agonizing way up the rocks, mostly on all fours, crawling over the stones, pulling itself up.

It was Badlands. His leathers were torn. His limbs bled from countless cuts. His face was a glistening mask of mud and blood and tears. He crawled on, weeping, sobbing, right past Fisher's and Jethiss's boots till he came upon one of Coots' moccasined feet and this he grasped as if drowning. He pressed his face to it and gave a heartbreaking groan that drove Fisher to look away. This was not for him to see. This was the private grieving of family.

He touched Jethiss's arm and together they walked off down the gently falling rock slope. The light gathered its amber colour. The shadows of the trees lengthened. Fisher turned to Jethiss. 'You broke those Wickan knives . . .' Jethiss nodded. Fisher eyed him speculatively. 'Mane of Chaos – does this name mean anything to you?'

The Andii tilted his head, considering. He shook it. 'No. Should it?'

'It is another name for Anomander Rake. Is that name familiar?'

The man turned his face to regard him directly. There was a wariness in his dark eyes now. 'There's something . . .' The eyes became alarmed. 'Are you saying . . . that I might be . . .'

Fisher shook his head. 'I don't know. His hair was white, though. But . . .' He took a heavy breath as if steeling himself. 'They say he gave himself to Mother Dark. To elemental night. And if he did . . . is it not possible that perhaps it, or she, gave him back . . .'

'Yet he had white hair.'

'True. A mark of the Eleint, the ancient songs say. The chaotic touch of T'iam. Those Elder songs also say that Mother Dark never accepted the gift of Chaos. She would not take it in, and so he would return without it . . .'

Jethiss lowered his gaze. 'I cannot say. I do remember something . . .' He shook his head.

'Yes? What?'

'Something about a gate. I remember a gate. An opening on to . . . something. And battle and pain. Then suffocating as if drowning. And last of all, I remember something about a sword . . .' He shook his head again. 'I'm sorry.'

'It's all right. I should not pry.' Fisher set his hands to his thighs. 'Should we see?'

Jethiss nodded. They walked up the rock slope. Badlands stood now, facing his brother, his hands clasped before him. They came and stood just behind. 'I'm sorry,' Fisher said.

Badlands turned to them, but he kept his gaze downcast and for that Fisher was grateful, for he didn't think he could bear what might lie in the man's gaze. His face still glistened with tears, though the blood of countless gouges and scratches had dried and cracked. He moved to step past them, as if to descend the slope. Alarmed, Fisher asked, 'Where are you going?'

Still refusing to raise his eyes, he croaked, 'To kill them all.'

'No you're not.'

Badlands halted. 'Don't stand in my way, Fish.'

'I am only reminding you of your duty.'

'Oh? An' what is that?'

'Your duty to your family. Stalker needs you now. Your other sisters and brothers and cousins will need you even more.'

Badlands barked a harsh laugh, startling Fisher. He raised his gaze, and though Fisher had readied himself, the fires of desolation burning there made him flinch.

Jethiss had stepped aside as if to make room. Now he slowly moved to Badlands' rear.

'You don't know nothing,' Badlands growled and Fisher heard the abandonment of utter feyness in the words.

'What do I not know?'

'Outta my way, Fish.'

'Go to your family, Badlands.'

'Don't make me—'

Jethiss grasped the man round the middle and lifted him from the ground. Fisher lunged in and snatched a knife from Badlands' belt, reversed it and smacked it across the man's temple. Badlands fell limp in Jethiss's arms. The Andii gently lowered him to the ground.

Fisher stood hands on hips, staring down at the big fellow. Of course, if the brother had truly wanted to be rid of them he could have easily won through. He could have drawn upon them. Neither of them was armed, after all. He sighed and looked to Jethiss. 'My turn.'

* * *

The north coast of the Sea of Gold was a graveyard of broken ships. Some lay half sunk just offshore, a mere few leagues beyond the mouth of the channel up from the Dread Sea, their crews only able to coax a last few leagues of distance out of their tortured vessels. Others lay on their sides on the mud flats between ice floes. Stranded crews and passengers waved and called to them amid great piles of cargo.

At the *Dawn*'s side, Jute heard some astounding offers shouted in accents out of Quon Tali, Malyntaeas, Falar, and even Seven Cities. Half the cargo in return for transport, one fellow bellowed. A tempting offer; but the large armed crew of hireswords surrounding the heaped crates put Jute off.

Buen suggested, 'Perhaps we should pick 'em up. Easy money.'

Jute shook his head. 'They'd swamp us. Probably try to take the *Dawn*.'

The first mate sighed wistfully. 'Too bad. All that cargo brought all this way just to rot. Might be kegs of wine from Darujhistan out there . . .'

'Drop it.'

Buen pushed himself away from the side. 'Thought we came to make some money,' he grumbled as he went. Jute ignored the muttering. Always griping; it was the man's way. He walked back to the stern and Ieleen next to Lurjen at the tiller. He studied the vessels following. The Malazan *Ragstopper* had swung in behind, the *Resolute* next, while the *Supplicant* followed far offshore. Seemed Lady Orosenn wished to keep some distance between herself and everyone else.

'What do you see?' Ieleen asked.

Jute scanned the shore once again. He saw . . . futility. And greed. 'Blind stupid avarice,' he said.

'We're here.'

He snorted. True enough. And what had they brought in their hold to the largest gold strike in living memory? Food. Not weapons or timber or tools or cloth. Food. Flour and molasses, crates of dried fruit, stoneware jugs of cheap spirits. Goods for sale. And once the hold was empty, why, what to fill it with but sacks of gold, of course!

Jute shook his head at the stunning naïvety of it. It had all seemed so easy back in Falar.

Now . . . well, now he believed they would be lucky just to get out of this alive.

The coast passed in a series of flats and lingering sheets of ice. They passed vessels drawn up on the shore and raised on crude log dry docks, while crews worked alongside sawing logs into planks and burned fires to reduce resin to recaulk seams.

Then the stranded vessels and would-be fortune-hunters thinned. Those ships that couldn't limp along any further had all pulled in or sunk by this point. Those that could continue did so, leaving their fellows behind. The old unspoken law of reaching out to take what one could and damning the rest to Hood's cold embrace.

The raw ugly ruthlessness of it sickened Jute. What a waste! What a stupid urge to enslave one's fortune to – the empty promise of unguarded riches to be picked up by anyone. Where was the merit in any such gathered power or riches? Merely because you were first to snatch it up? Could not the second person there simply kill you and take it for himself?

Best not to invest in such easily transferable value, Jute determined. His gaze fell to the blind face of his love and he rested a hand upon hers.

'I feel your eyes on me,' she murmured. 'What's on your mind, luv?'

'I just realized that I've risked everything to reach a destination I don't even want to be at.'

A secretive smile broadened Ieleen's lips. 'Glad to hear that, luv.'

Jute frowned. 'But you didn't object . . .'

'That's what journeys are for, my love. You have to *take* the path to learn where you want to be.'

'The philosopher wife speaks.'

She gave an exaggerated sigh. 'We mates sit and wait. And, if we're lucky, our partners finally catch up to where we've been all the while.'

Jute crossed his arms. 'Oh? Been a long wait, has it?'

'Damnably long. But now that you're here, maybe we can go home.'

'Certainly, light of my life. We'll just sell our goods at outrageously inflated prices, load up with successful fortune-hunters groaning beneath the weight of all their gold, and head home.'

'We should just cut out the middle and turn round now.'

Jute laughed. 'And what would the crew think of that?'

Her frosty orbs shifted as if to look ahead, and though he knew her to be blind, Jute couldn't shake the feeling that her sight was penetrating all the distance to their goal. She sighed. 'We're sailing into a nest of pirates, thieves and murderers.'

Jute tried to shake his premonition of trouble. 'Then it's a good thing we have a mercenary army with us, isn't it?'

She shook her head. 'A *last* mission, Tyvar said. Have you not thought about that?'

Indeed, it hadn't occurred to him. He waved it off, then remembered, and made a non-committal noise. 'Don't you worry. We'll raise anchor and ship out if we must, don't doubt that.'

They sailed through the day and night. The *Ragstopper* and the *Resolute* kept pace, while the *Supplicant* held out in deeper water, far offshore. Jute wondered at Lady Orosenn's strategy, but it was the listing *Ragstopper* that held his attention; the vessel was so low in the water, so sluggish and lumbering, it was a wonder that it still held its bows above the surface. The collection of rotted timbers that it had crumbled into seemed little more than a glorified raft.

Late on the second day, smoke hazed the air further up the coast ahead. A stink reached them, the commingled reek of human settlement: smoke, excrement, rot, and cooking. Jute had been long from it and it churned his stomach. They rounded a low headland still gripped in ice and there ahead lay a broad bay fronted by wide mud flats. An immense tent city swept in an arc all along the shore. Smoke rose from countless fires. What must be a hundred vessels lay pulled up on the flats, or anchored in deeper water out in the bay. The coast swept up from here in broad forested valleys and ridges that climbed to foothills obscured by hanging banners of fog. Above this vista reared the snow-draped shoulders of a range of mountains. The Salt range, according to sources he'd heard recounted.

Jute was astounded by the number of ships that had succeeded in the journey – yet this must be the barest fraction of the entire fleets of vessels that had originally set out. All testament to the driving power of greed and the lure of easy riches. He felt saddened by the spectacle though he himself was a merchant, a businessman; it struck him as a damning condemnation of humankind.

'Which way?' Lurjen asked from the tiller.

Jute shook himself from his reverie. He gestured ahead. 'Make for one of the docks there near the centre.'

'Aye, aye.'

Lurjen chose one of a number of log docks that stood tall above the flats and extended out over the water. The *Silver Dawn* came alongside, ropes were thrown and secured to log bollards. His crew wrestled with a gangplank. Jute studied the jumbled mass of countless tents, the men and women coming and going, the crews cutting wood to repair vessels, build more docks, and raise buildings. He estimated the numbers here in the several thousands. A city. An instant city utterly without planning or organization, as far as he could see. Tents lay like fields of mushrooms, all without logic or order. No straight thoroughfares existed, no streets or lanes; all was a chaotic mess. He was dismayed to see men and women squatting over latrine pits right next to open-air kitchens where the steam from boiling pots melded with the steam rising from the pits to waft over the entire mass of humanity.

A far worse reek rose from the flats where cadavers lay rotting, most having sloughed their flesh. An open-air graveyard where the dead were obviously simply thrown from the docks and shore. Hordes of ghost-crabs wandered from corpse to corpse like clouds of locusts, gorging themselves.

The ragged fortune-hunters who crowded the dock waving and shouting were no more reassuring. Ragged and starving they were, in tattered shirts and canvas trousers, with mud-caked bare feet. They shouted their services as stevedores. Jute wouldn't trust a pot of shit to any one of them.

Lurjen gestured further along the dock and Jute was relieved to see the *Ragstopper* coming alongside. Thank the gods for that. He peered around for the *Resolute* and was troubled to see she had dropped anchor in mid-bay, not far from the *Supplicant*.

The crowd actually had the temerity to try climbing the gangway. Buen was pushing them back. He cast a questioning glance to Jute, who shook a negative. 'No work,' Buen yelled. 'Not today. G'wan with you!'

'Bastards!' one shouted back.

'You'll get yours! You'll see!'

Buen pulled his truncheon and waved them off. Someone new pushed through the crowd: short, grey-haired, in rags just as dilapidated and dirty. Cartheron Crust. Jute hurried down the gangway to meet him.

'How are you?'

'Better. Been better.'

'Recovered?'

The old captain pulled a hand down his patchy beard. 'Somewhat. Hard bein' reminded of one's mortality like that. Feelin' old now, have to say.'

Jute gestured to the shore. 'What do you think?'

'Fuckin' mess.'

'Quite.'

Cartheron waved him on. 'C'mon, let's go see who's in charge of this dump.'

Jute held back. 'Just the two of us?'

Cartheron didn't stop. 'Yeah. Trust me. It'll be just fine.'

Jute shouted back to Buen on the gangway: 'Making arrangements!' and hurried after him.

A knot of eight armed men and women blocked the base of the dock. They wore styles of leather armour from all over: the detailed engraved and enamelled leathers of Seven Cities; the plain layered leathers common to south Genabackis; even an expensive set of leaf-shaped scaled leathers clearly crafted in Darujhistan. The probable leader stepped up. He was a big black-bearded fellow in a long coat of mail. A longsword hung shoved through his wide leather belt.

'Welcome to Wrongway,' this fellow announced as they neared.

'Wrongway,' Cartheron echoed. 'Funny.'

The bearded fellow grinned. 'Yeah. Lying Gell thought so.'

'Lying Gell . . . ?'

The man hitched his belt up his broad fat belly. 'Lying Gell, Baron of Wrongway.'

Cartheron turned to Jute. 'There you go – that didn't take so long, did it?' He addressed the spokesman: 'And you are . . . ?'

The man's grin widened over broken browned teeth. 'They call me Black Bull.'

'Black Bull? Why's that?'

The grin sank into a scowl. 'That you don't want to find out.'

Cartheron waved the man off. 'If you say so. Thanks for the welcome.' He moved to pass.

Others of the eight shifted to block the way. Black Bull chuckled. 'You don't get it. Docking fees.'

'Docking fees?'

'Aye. Docking fees.'

Cartheron shrugged his bony shoulders. 'How much?'

The spokesman cast a lazy glance over to a scarred woman with long hair the colour of straw. She wore the expensive Darujhistani leather armour. She supplied, 'Two vessels – forty hundredths-weights.'

'There you go. Forty hundredths-weights.'

Jute asked: 'Forty hundredths-weights of what?'

Black's grin became crafty. 'Why, of gold dust, a'course.'

'But we just got here. We don't have any gold dust.'

Black shrugged his humped shoulders. 'Well . . . that's just too bad. Have to escort you to our exchange tent.'

Cartheron raised a hand for a pause. 'Listen, if it's all the same to you, I'd rather not exchange money in a tent owned by a guy named Lying Gell.'

Black pursed his lips. 'Fine. You can just turn round and go home then.'

'How about coins in equivalency? Silver?'

Black shot a glance to the woman, rubbed his chin. 'Well now, that's highly irregular. Have to be a surcharge on that. An extra fee of . . .'

'Fifty per cent,' the woman said. To Jute, her grin was far hungrier and scarier than Black Bull's.

'Fine,' Cartheron sighed. He gestured to Jute. 'Pay the man.'

Jute blinked. 'Pardon? Me? Pay?'

Cartheron waved him forward. ''Course!'

The hireswords parted to reveal a table. The woman in the expensive armour leaned against it and urged Jute onward. Jute pulled out his purse and started setting coin on the scarred wood planks. The woman crossed her arms, counting. Upon closer inspection, the scars appeared to be knife slashes. As if someone had deliberately savaged her face. She caught Jute eyeing her and pointed a finger down. He quickly lowered his gaze. In the end, it took every silver coin he possessed to satisfy her. Sighing her irritation, she finally waved him off and brushed all the coin into an ironbound wooden box.

Black Bull held out an arm, inviting them onward. 'There you go. That wasn't so hard, was it? Wrongway welcomes you.'

Cartheron pushed forward and Jute followed. The old Napan captain picked what seemed a random narrow mud trail that led up the gently rising slope of the shore. Before they'd made five turns Jute had had to step over three bodies. One he was certain was dead, what with his throat slit and the stream of blood that stained the already ochre-red mud a far deeper crimson. The other two, a woman and a man, he suspected to have merely passed out dead drunk in the muck.

Cartheron appeared to be making for the noisiest – and largest
– tent nearby. Within, under the raised eaves, was the equivalent of
a tavern. A band, of sorts, played stringed and wind instruments.
The crowd roared their encouragement from tables assembled from
wave-wrack and ship's timbers. Fights broke out and spilled into the
mud surrounding the great tent. A long bar separated the patrons
from the kegs of spirits. On the counter stood several fine weight
scales of the sort one might find in a goldsmith's.

The skinny old captain mortified Jute by stepping right up on to
the nearest table. The men and women drinking there yanked their
leather and earthenware tankards from beneath his muddy boots.
'What in the name of the Matron you doin'?' one huge bear of a
fellow bellowed and Jute flinched – an ex-Urdomen from the old
Pannion Annexation, for certain.

Cartheron ignored him. He set two fingers to his mouth and
emitted the most piercing whistle that had ever punished Jute's ears.
The entire tavern became instantly silent. Every face turned to him.
Even the musicians froze. Cartheron raised a hand, signed something, circled the arm overhead, then stepped down from the table
and exited the tent. Jute, still somewhat stunned, hurried to follow.

Outside, he caught up. 'What was that? What's going on?'

'Now we wait.'

The music started up once more. The crowd laughed and jeered,
perhaps at Cartheron's expense. After a few minutes two men
came out, followed by a third. The first two were thick-shouldered
and heavy, obvious ex-soldiers. Both possessed bushy flame-hued
beards.

'Names?' Cartheron demanded.

'Red,' said one.

'Rusty.'

'How's the gold-huntin' business treating you?'

'Piss-poor,' said Rusty.

'You in?' Both nodded. 'Okay, spread the word – Cartheron's in
town.'

Red's arm rose to salute but he stopped his fist before it struck his
chest and lowered it. 'Sorry.' They ambled off.

The third man approached. He looked like nothing more than
a starving itinerant, thin unto emaciation. His mussed pale brown
hair was going to premature grey. His face was pinched and his
small close-set eyes were yellow with what Jute recognized as a
heavy addiction to the khall leaf. Indeed, one cheek was fat with
a ball of it.

'You look like you are in need of some gold dust,' the fellow called out, quite loudly.

'No we're not,' Jute answered. 'Get out of here, y'damned khall-head.'

Cartheron raised a hand to quiet Jute. He was studying the man closely, frowning in something like wary recognition. 'Sure,' he said, 'we're lookin' for gold dust.'

'I know who has it – and who doesn't.'

'Good. Show us round and we'll send some your way.'

The man smiled dreamily. Something in his lazy distracted manner made Jute's skin crawl. It was as if he was moving under-water. And he was constantly brushing at his tattered shirt, tapping his fingertips together, and shifting his weight from side to side in a kind of weaving dance. 'Need to get some to have some,' he murmured.

Jute thought he saw Cartheron sign something to the man before the fellow waved an arm, inviting them on. 'This way,' he said vaguely.

He started off ahead of them and Cartheron pulled Jute back, whispering, 'You keep out of this one's way, yes?'

Jute was utterly confused, but nodded. 'Certainly. If you say so.'

The khall-head glanced back at them, a languorous smile on his lips, and urged them on. 'Come, come. This way.'

He led them to a tent containing another of the informal bars and here Cartheron repeated his performance. Afterwards, he led them on a lazy walk round an intervening set of tents before squatting on his skinny haunches in the mud.

Three men and one woman came ambling in from different directions to join them. Jute was startled to see by the cut of their hair and facial scars the mark of north Genabackan tribals – Barghast half-breeds perhaps. But veterans, cashiered Malazan veterans. They stood stiffly before Cartheron but couldn't stop shooting each other excited grins.

Cartheron looked them up and down then nodded to himself. 'Make the rounds. Tap any old hands you can find. Spread the word. We'll rendezvous at . . .' He turned to their guide. 'I'm looking for a place with a nice view.'

The man tilted his head to stare off into the distance. He smiled, but emptily. 'Anna's Alehouse,' he said.

Cartheron waved the four away. 'There you go.' They nodded and their grins turned savage with glee. They wandered off in different directions.

Jute watched all this feeling his brows crimping harder and harder, and finally he had to ask: 'What's going on? What are you doing?'

'Crewing up.' Cartheron urged their guide onward. 'Let's go.'

The khall-head led them to three more tent-bars and three more times Cartheron repeated his performance. By this time, Jute noticed among the crowds of men and women coming and going about them a number of the ex-soldiers here and there, surrounding them, keeping pace. Like some sort of guard. At last, Cartheron turned to their guide. 'Anna's Alehouse now, I think.'

It was long past twilight when they ducked under the raised sides of the large canvas tent that was Anna's Alehouse. Their guide had waved them on, absently and vaguely, as if he could hardly make the effort, then wandered off.

The alehouse was jammed with fortune-hunters. Jute recognized many of the ex-Malazan soldiery. Cartheron headed to a table towards the centre that, as he approached, somehow became empty in a scuffle of spilled drinks and upset chairs. When Cartheron sat he pulled Jute with him and suddenly the table was crowded with the most hardened, scarred and battered veterans Jute had ever sat down with. It was like the old days, before Ieleen, before he swore off pirating for her.

She'd be so mad if she saw him here in this company.

A man in an apron approached and Cartheron ordered ale all round. The man held out a hand and Cartheron set a coin in his palm: a Malazan gold crown. Jute saw it and sent a bloody glare to the old captain. He raised a hand, murmured, 'Just getting some attention.'

A moment later the crowd parted for a woman – a very large woman. Her hair was a fright and her very ample bosom spilled out of a barely laced top. She planted both meaty hands on the table before Cartheron and leaned forward, purring, 'What can Anna do for you, sailor?'

The old captain twisted his bearded lips into something resembling a smile. He pulled a leather pouch from under his shirt and felt about within it then drew out two fingers pinched together and held them out. Anna pursed her fat painted lips in a silent ohhhhh and raised a hand.

Cartheron dropped something into her palm. It was tiny, frosted, and faceted.

Jute leaned forward to study it: a raw diamond. Or a wondrous fake.

Anna snapped her hand closed. She leaned even further forward. 'Anything catch your fancy, sailor?'

He offered her a wink. 'Like to have a private party, Anna. If I may. Invitation only.'

'Certainly.' She gave a husky laugh and wiggled. Though, to Jute, it was more like a wobble. 'I *love* private parties.' She straightened, opened her arms. 'The place is yours.'

'Clear the house,' Cartheron said.

Men and women all about jumped to their feet. They took others by their shirts and necks, marched them to the sides of the tent, and threw them out into the mud. Anna watched with growing horror. One thick hand gathered together her shirt while the other went to her neck.

'Lower the sides,' Cartheron ordered.

The hanging leather strips were pulled and the sailcloth sides of the tent fell. In the muted light of the front flap, open still, Anna turned on Cartheron. 'Those were paying customers!'

'I've paid for the premises,' he growled. 'I suggest you take the night off.'

The big woman peered about at the gathered men and women, rough-looking ex-soldiers all, and a growing unease replaced her outrage. Her chin wobbled as she slowly nodded her head. 'Lentz! Kora!' she called, 'Take the night off! These gentlemen have private business to attend to. Business,' she added, 'that we know nothing about.'

Cartheron glanced to the front and the woman took the hint; she marched stiffly out. His men now held the doorway. Some patrons they turned away, others they allowed in. Lamps of cheap fat were lit. Cartheron scanned the gathered crowd while nodding to himself.

'How many men does this Lying Gell have?'

''Bout three hundred,' someone supplied.

'Quality?'

'Thugs, strongarms, bandits. Nothin' more.'

Jute was listening and nodding his head and now he exclaimed, 'I see it now! You're taking over!'

Cartheron eyed him frostily. 'No, I'm not doin' that. This place is an indefensible swamp.' He peered round once more. 'There was supposed to be a regular town up here.'

'There was,' someone said. 'All these waves of invaders ran 'em off. Took some fighting, I tell you.'

'Where'd they go?'

'Mantle.'

'That's some kinda fortress, right? What's the situation there?'

'Some Lether captain and a few other principals have the place surrounded. But they don't know siegework worth crap.'

'Does this keep, or whatever it is, have a harbour?'

'Yeah. That's blockaded right now.'

'We'll see about that,' Cartheron muttered.

'You're going to take the fortress?' Jute asked.

The old captain ignored him. 'Okay,' he barked. 'Here's the drill. I want a head-count. I want you lot to shake out into squads. Then I want sergeants and up to come present themselves. Is that clear? Okay, let's go. Don't have all night.'

It seemed to Jute that everyone started talking at once. Cartheron turned to him. 'I'm gonna send you off with an escort back to the ships. Have them ready to cast off at a moment's notice, right?'

Jute waved to indicate everything around him. 'What's going on? What is all this? You've just collected your own army.'

Cartheron pulled a hand through his patchy salt and pepper beard, sighed. 'Sorry, captain. Haven't been entirely honest with you. I *was* on my way here when I was contacted by . . . by some old acquaintances. I was asked . . . well, a proposition was made that I help out up here.'

'So you're working for the Empire.'

The old man scowled, offended. 'Done with that. Free agent now. Just contracted to lend aid to certain parties. That's all.' He raised his attention to the crowd surrounding them. 'I want one squad to shadow my friend here down to the docks and help guard his ship. Are we good with that?'

A woman raised her hand. 'We'll take it.'

'Okay.' He motioned Jute to the front. 'See you later. Be ready to cast off fast.'

Jute reluctantly pushed himself away from the table. 'But what are you up to here? What are you going to do?'

Cartheron waved him on. 'Don't you worry 'bout that. Go on with you.'

The woman waved him out and accompanied him through the maze of tents. Torches burned at various main intersections of foot-paths. Gangs hung about seemingly ready to waylay anyone who appeared relatively defenceless. Passing one such group, the woman pulled her muddy cloak away from her side to reveal her longsword and the men stepped back from blocking their way. Jute also noticed members of the 'squad' down side alleys, shadowing their progress.

He studied the woman: stocky fighter's build, a pretty face, after

298

a fashion. Thick dark brown hair that fell in waves to her shoulders. Fair-skinned. Armoured in a battered hauberk of banded iron over leathers. 'You're of north Genabackis.'

'Yeah.'

'You are a Malazan veteran?'

'Yeah. Cashiered.'

'You know Cartheron?'

The woman snorted. 'Abyss, no. How old do you think I am?'

'I'm sorry. I just thought . . . since you showed up . . .'

She shrugged. 'Coupla lads from my old command swung by, said he was looking to hire.'

'So you know *of* him . . .'

The woman snorted again. 'Abyss, yes. Who doesn't?'

'Then you came here on your own?'

'Yeah. Overland from the west.' She shook her head. 'Only a handful of us made it. And for what? There's no gold left. Only people rakin' it in are those selling booze or shovels. Or stealing it from those that got it. Ended up trapped here. Can't afford to stay. Can't afford a ticket out.'

'I'm sorry.'

She shrugged again. 'How it goes. Had a family farm outside Mott. Sold it to raise the money for this trip. All gone now. Fortunes of life. Gotta take risks to achieve anything.' She eyed him up and down. 'Same as you, hey? You just arrived with a ship, hey?'

'Yes. A full cargo to sell.'

'Whatcha bring? Timber? Anvils? Chandeliers? Ice for drinks?'

'Oh no, nothing fancy like that. Just basic staples. Barrels of flour, molasses, rice, salted pork, jugs of spirits.'

The woman looked him up and down again. '*God-damn*,' she breathed, in something like awe.

Jute and the woman – a retired officer? – made it down to the dock without incident. Perhaps it was the eight or so burly ex-soldiers surrounding them. In any case, they followed him up on to the *Dawn* and he checked in with Ieleen. He found her where she always was, sitting at the stern next to the tiller. 'Back, love,' he announced.

'And who's the woman?' she asked.

Jute blinked. 'Ah . . . she works for Cartheron. Here to help guard the ship. How did you know?'

'I can smell her. She's pretty?'

'Ah . . . well, I suppose so. Yes.'

'Aren't you going to introduce us?'

'Ah . . . of course.' He waved the woman to the stern. 'This is Ieleen, my wife and ship's pilot. And this is . . . ah . . .'

The woman bowed. 'Lieutenant Jalaz. Giana Jalaz, of Mott. At your service, ma'am. Here to help out defending the ship.'

Ieleen inclined her head. 'You are most welcome. Our ship's master of weapons has had her hands full beating away thieves trying to sneak on board.'

'We will give her a hand, then,' Lieutenant Jalaz said, and went on her way.

'She seems nice,' Ieleen said. Jute blew out a long breath. Then he jerked, remembering Cartheron's words.

'Oh! I have to go to the *Ragstopper*. They have to ready to cast off – as do we.'

Ieleen urged him away. 'Well, then. Off with you.'

He headed to the gangway but froze as Giana barked: 'Stop him!'

The men guarding the gangway shifted to block his way. Suddenly, a sinking realization came to him: By the gods . . . I've just handed my ship over to a pack of Malazans! What a purblind fool! I deserve whatever it is they have in store for me. An unexplained disappearance, probably.

He slowly turned to face the lieutenant. She came to stand quite close before him. 'Where do you think you're going?'

In his peripheral vision, Jute caught his master of weapons, Letita, edging in close, her hand at the grip of her longsword.

He swallowed hard and gestured up the dock. 'Cartheron's ship, the *Ragstopper*.'

'Why?'

'Cartheron wants both ships ready to cast off.'

'Oh.' She pointed to two men. 'You two, go with him. Cartheron wants you guarded.'

Jute felt his legs weaken. Gods! Was that good or bad? Am I under unofficial arrest? Maybe I'm not being fair to the commander. But he's of the old guard – infamous for their treachery.

He raised a hand to wave off Letita. Either Giana missed the gesture, or, more likely, she chose not to notice it, and did not react. One of the Malazans headed down the gangway first, and Jute followed. The second trailed him.

Scruffy would-be stevedores and touts came shuffling up. They made offers for work, or offered women, d'bayan dust, rustleaf, durhang, khall fixings. The guards brushed them aside. Jute did not think himself in any danger; the poor wretches obviously hadn't had a decent meal in some time. They did, however, seem to have access to a lot of drugs.

Reaching the side of the vessel, he shouted: 'Ho! *Ragstopper*! Permission to come on board?' He waited, but no one answered. 'Ahoy! *Ragstopper*?'

He eyed the peeling and barked-up timbers of the galley's side. A single rope hung over the rail – the only means in and out? 'Stay here,' he told his guards, and took hold of the rope to haul himself up. It was a trick he imagined only a fellow sailor could manage.

He pulled himself over the side. The open galley benches were mostly empty. A few ragged sailors lay sound asleep. Jute carefully picked his way between them and up on to the centre walk. A familiar figure lay slumped and snoring amid jumbled rope here – Cartheron's putative first mate with his thin mane of frizzy white hair. The sight of the fellow asleep – probably on watch – inflamed the lifelong sailor in Jute. He picked up a coil of rope nearby and heaved it on to the man, shouting, 'Wake up, you useless whore's son!'

The man sprang to his feet with a yell. He peered wildly about while squeezing some small object in both hands. '*We'll die to-gether!*' he howled.

Jute flinched away. The man's wild rolling eyes latched on to him and he blinked. 'Oh, it's you.' He wiped his gleaming brow. 'By all that's holy – don't you ever do that again.'

'What's that you've got there, then?'

The man whipped the round fruit-sized object behind his back. 'Nothing. Nothing 'tall.'

Jute had a hard time believing the man would've been crazy enough to fall asleep while holding a munition. Still, the *Ragstopper* seemed a floating asylum.

Now the first mate was frowning suspiciously. 'What're you doing here, anyway?' he growled.

'Orders from Cartheron – he wants you ready to cast off some time this night.'

The first mate gaped, then his lower lip began to tremble. 'But he just got here . . .' He gazed about in a panic. 'We can't . . . Do you have any idea . . .'

'I'm sorry. I'm just relaying—'

The man threw himself at Jute and hung on to his shirt. 'But we have to sell our cargo!' he blubbered. Alarmed, Jute saw that indeed the man held a munition in one hand; he gently eased it from his grip. The fellow was weeping uncontrollably now. 'You have no idea what we've been through! No harbour allowed us to drop anchor! We've been turned away from every city. Every port. We've been at sea for years. It's like a curse!' He tried to shake Jute by his shirt but was too weak. 'You have to talk some sense into him! Please . . . for the love of all the gods. Have mercy on us!'

Jute took hold of the man's hands and gently eased his grip free. 'Yes,' he soothed, 'I'll talk to him. I promise. We aren't going far – just the next town. I promise.'

The first mate was nodding with him, his eyes swimming. 'You promise . . .'

'Yes. Absolutely. On my word.'

The fellow slumped back down into his nest of rope, hunched, head hanging. 'Doomed . . .' he was murmuring. 'Retirement, the man said . . . golden years . . .' He covered his face. Jute gently set the munition down nearby and slowly backed away.

Back on the dock, he blew out a long breath and shook his head. Poor fellow! Clearly addled. Strain of the passage, no doubt. He returned to the *Dawn* flanked by his two new guards. On board, he went to the bow to watch the darkened slope of the tent city. Torches burned here and there, as did fire pits. A few of the tents were lit from within, though most were dark. The noise of the countless tent-bars, taverns and inns came and went with the wind – as did the stink – though already he was getting used to it. He waited. For what, he had no idea. Considering Cartheron's reputation, however, he suspected it would be dramatic. Whatever it might be.

He glanced over and flinched, surprised. Next to him stood the skinny pinch-faced khall-head guide, also leaning against the side. 'How did you—' he began angrily, then, remembering Cartheron's warning, cleared his throat and repeated neutrally, 'How did you get on board?'

The man merely gave his dreamy smile, more vague than secretive. 'Same as you,' he said.

Jute rolled his eyes. 'What do you want? A stake?'

The man's smile widened as if the thought amused him. He swung his head in a tilted negative. 'Oh, no. Just here to keep an eye on things.'

He frowned at the man. For the life of him, he couldn't see what Cartheron saw in the fellow. However, having just witnessed conditions onboard the *Ragstopper*, it occurred to him that the fellow would fit right in.

Fire suddenly blossomed in a quarter of the tent city. Its billowing eruption lit the tent tops. The noise of the blast washed over the

Dawn. 'What the . . .' he stammered. A second blast, this one in a different quarter, now lit the high slopes. The guide smiled again and nodded to himself. 'What's this?' Jute demanded.

The man gave an easy shrug of his bony shoulders. 'Oh, Lying Gell had a number of caches of food and equipment stashed away. Looks like they've been doused in alcohol and set alight.'

Jute gaped at him. 'But that means . . . they'll all be after . . .'

The fellow nodded again. 'Oh, yes. My guess is the boys are runnin' for the dock right now with the entire encampment hot on their tails.'

Jute wasted an instant trying to utter his disbelief, outrage and horror, only to throw his hands in the air and lurch from the side. '*Man the sweeps!*' he bellowed. 'Ready poles! Raise anchor! Cut all but one rope there!'

Lieutenant Jalaz and her cohort ran pounding down the gangway then dashed for the base of the dock. Would-be stevedores and touts went flying from the wood slats to land in the mud. A gang of hire-swords had been lounging at the base of the dock amid crates and bales. Now they jumped to their feet and peered upslope to the fires. From the bows of the *Dawn*, Jute watched as the Malazans crashed into them. In a moment, it was over. All of the toughs were down, either knocked unconscious or heaved over the side where they struggled knee-deep in the mud.

Lieutenant Jalaz now held the dock.

'Captain?' Jute turned. Letita stood armed and ready, helmet cheek-guards lowered. He shook his head. 'Stay on board, master-at-arms.' The woman's mouth hardened but she did not object. Jute pointed out over the bows. 'However, we do have a good view of the dock from here . . .'

Her lips climbed in a savage grin. She turned to the mid-deck. 'Archers! Form up!'

The shouts and iron-clash of fighting now washed down to the *Dawn.* A gang of Gell's thugs rushed Jalaz's squad. This time blood flowed as swords were drawn.

More tents burst into flame. The yells and cries swelled to a steady roar. Jute could now make out a running mêlée making its way down through the tent city. Everything in its way was trampled and destroyed as it came. Men were running both away and towards it.

A solid crowd now pressed against Jalaz's position. Jute nodded to Letita. 'Archers,' the weapons master called, 'thin them out – try to avoid our crew.'

Her team of forty archers opened fire on the crowd.

303

A strange clacking noise pulled Jute's attention to the rear. He glanced back and blanched: *Benevolent gods forgive us.* The *Ragstopper*'s springals were being brought round to bear on the shore.

He'd seen what they'd done to the fortifications at Old Ruse, and now . . . civilians? Yet could any soul here truly be counted as an innocent civilian? Very few, no doubt. And those should be fleeing the scene rather than closing on it.

The springals released with twin bangs and fat bolts shot overhead in trajectories lower than the *Dawn*'s tops'l. Twin explosions lit the darkness and sent geysers of wet earth to the night sky – along with cartwheeling doll-like figures. Mud and debris came pattering across the dock and smacked into the flats like wet fists.

Into the profound silence following the eruptions, Lieutenant Jalaz's voice came bellowing out of the darkness: 'Watch where yer shooting, y'damned apes!'

The pause was only momentary as the fighting renewed itself. The running scrum broke into the open close to the waterfront. Jute could make out individual figures within the press, such as the two Falarans who'd given their names as Red and Rusty – which was a joke, of course: all Falarans tell outsiders their name is Red. And in the middle of the pack, a scrawny grey-haired figure pointing and shouting commands – Cartheron. The roiling knot now made for the dock. Sword blades flashed in the light of waving torches. Men and women cursed and grunted at blows given and taken.

The huge figure of Black Bull reared into view before Lieutenant Jalaz. He leaned in swinging two-handed. She met him with twinned shortswords. The weapons slid and grated across one another in blows and parries until one of Jalaz's swords flicked up across the man's beard and he reared back in a spray of blood. He clasped his throat, his eyes rolling white in the darkness. She raised a boot to his chest and kicked him down.

Jute couldn't fathom the numbers of these would-be miners and fortune-hunters all piling in, all struggling to tear the Malazans apart. He'd been there when they'd been told Lying Gell's thugs numbered some three hundred. Yet far more than that – a horde of over a thousand – now clamoured to pull them down. And more were arriving every minute.

Something, it seemed, had turned the entire tent city of Wrongway against Cartheron and his crew. Lying Gell couldn't command that sort of loyalty, could he? But then, maybe it had something to do with them having just blown up or burned all the supplies in the town.

The crew, or gang, pushed through to the dock and linked with Jalaz and her squad. The entire troop now retreated up the dock. Letita kept up her punishing volleys of arrow fire. Then the springals released once more and Jute couldn't help but duck.

The end of the dock disappeared in twin concussions that shot bodies and timber high into the air to come raining down as debris that knocked more people from the dock. When the smoke cleared, Jute glimpsed the Malazans backing away, headed for the *Ragstopper*. In their midst, lumbering like two laden oxen, struggled two of the Barghast veterans. They carried between them a huge iron trunk.

Jute almost laid his head on the ship's railing. Oh, no . . . Cartheron . . . y'damned pirate. Don't tell me you . . .

Lieutenant Jalaz came bounding up the gangway. 'Push off!' she yelled.

Jute blinked and shook his head; at her cry it was as if his daze from the explosion had snapped away. 'Cut that rope!' he bellowed. 'Push off! Lower sweeps!'

Arrows and crossbow bolts thudded into the *Dawn*'s side and Jute ducked. It looked as if the entire population of Wrongway now lined the shore. Many were striding out into the deep mud, waving swords and torches. The roar of the mingled yells and curses drowned out everything.

They pulled away. The gangplank tumbled into the water.

Something flaming arced from the shore to burst on the deck spreading fire. Everyone not manning the sweeps dashed to help smother the flames. More flaming pots came flying their way. All but one fell short and that one smacked the sternplate. The crew dashed water over the flames as the dock receded into the darkness behind.

'Well,' Ieleen said into the relative silence. 'What got them all in a tizzy?'

Jute held his head. 'You don't want to know.'

Lieutenant Jalaz joined them, her helmet pushed back far on her head. 'They'll give chase,' she said, and she brushed her sweaty matted hair from her face, breathing heavily.

Jute turned on her, furious. 'Oh, you think so, do you? Think they'll give chase – *seeing as you just stole all their damned gold!*'

But the lieutenant merely shook the blood from a deep cut across her hand. 'Well, what in the name of the forest gods did you think we'd do?'

Jute kept his hands on his head, if only to stop himself from grabbing hold of the woman. Gods' blood! Fifty ships pushing out to chase them! Nowhere to run! But . . . there was *one* place. He raised his head. 'We've been had, dearest,' he said.

'How so, luv?' Ieleen answered.

'Cartheron . . . This is what he intended from the start – or was hired for!' He thrust a finger at Jalaz. 'Were you sent ahead?'

The woman's face wrinkled up in a scowl. 'What in the name of the Sky King are you talking about?' And she cursed, studying the blood dripping to the decking from her hand. Letita had joined them and now she pulled a strip of cloth from her belt and began tying up the wound.

'Calm yourself, luv,' Ieleen said. 'Lieutenant – why don't you tell us what Cartheron told you?'

Lurjen, at the tiller, cleared his throat. 'Shall I follow the *Ragstopper*, cap'n?'

'Aye!' Jute snapped. 'We can't let him out of our sight now, can we?'

The lieutenant shrugged. 'He just asked whether we wanted a share o' all that gold those lying bastards had been cheating from everyone. And we were all in, of course.'

'Nothing else?'

'No, why?'

Jute gestured to the dark waters of the bay. 'Because anchored out there are a sorceress and a pocket army of mercenaries who could sweep this entire northern region if they wanted to, that's why. And if they're not interested in this sorry-ass tent city then the question is . . . why are they here?'

Jalaz glanced ahead to the starlit bay. The dark silhouette of one ship was just visible. It appeared that the *Ragstopper* was making for them. 'I see only one vessel.'

'Trust me. Those are the Blue Shields out there.'

'Bullshit.'

Jute blinked at the woman, surprised by the strength of her reaction. 'What do you mean?'

'Listen, Malazan, I may be from the north, but even I have heard of the Blue Shields and the Grey Swords. The Blue are not really mercenaries – they fight only for Togg. You can't *hire* them. They're a religious order. Fanatics.'

Jute gestured ahead again, invitingly. 'Well, they're here. Along with their Mortal Sword of Togg, Tyvar Gendarian.'

Giana glanced away once more, scanned the waters. She drew a hand down her face, rubbing away the sweat. 'Great gods,' she murmured. 'He's actually left Elingarth?'

'*Ragstopper* veering east,' Dulat, the lookout, shouted down. '*Resolute* and *Supplicant* drawing anchor, raising sail.'

'What's east of here?' Jute asked the retired officer, though he suspected he knew.

She looked back, blew out a long hard breath. 'Some sort of fortress at Mantle. Ruled by a fellow who calls himself King Ronal the Bastard.'

CHAPTER IX

THE LAND ROSE THE FARTHER NORTH KYLE TRAVELLED. HE HAD yet to find any open water. The grasses grew far taller and thicker here, attesting to rainfall, but the high spring clouds passed on south without pausing to disgorge any of their moisture. He pushed through lush green growing shoots that brushed his thighs. Today, he knew, he had to find some source of water or tomorrow he might not have the strength to rise. As it was, he barely made any progress at all. His vision was blurry; he often had to pause to gather his wits to remain certain of his direction; and he had to stop himself from wandering here or there in a futile search for a pond or a stream.

Straight. Straight east of north was the way to go. Upland. Wandering in circles would be the death of him. Yet he was so thirsty – he might have passed right by a creek off to one side! He was just thinking that perhaps he really ought to search about for water before it was too late when he fell forward.

He lay thinking that he'd misstepped. But no, the ground fell away here into a depression, and, strangely, his hands felt cold where they pressed against the earth.

Cold . . . and damp. He dug at the thick mat of grass roots that covered the earth here. It was wet and frigid. He couldn't tear through – he was too weak. On his knees now, he drew his blade and pushed it into the ground. Two-handed, he cut a triangle, then wearily, as carefully as he could manage, he resheathed the weapon. He gathered up a handful of the grass and heaved. He had to put all his weight into it, leaning back. It came in a ripping and tearing of roots and he fell on to his back.

It took a while for the dizziness to pass.

He crawled forward and sank his arms up to the elbows to dig at the cold earth beneath. He came up with a fist of hard dirt, frosty-white, and speckled with earth. It took him a while to understand what he was looking at: the very ground frozen solid. A knot of ice that must have resided here for years, perhaps for untold centuries. He thrust the entire ball into his mouth and held it there.

The pain was exquisite. His head numbed and ached. It felt as if that knot of frost had expanded to engulf his entire body. Something told him that if anyone from another region, another land, had tried what he had just so impetuously done they would have died. Something, some power, residing in this ancient ice would have overcome them.

Yet he felt somehow . . . rejuvenated. He stood, steady now on his feet, and lurched onward.

He entered a wide forest of tall, ancient conifers. Game was plentiful, yet he chose not to take the time to hunt. He contented himself with fish taken from a stream. The ground rose more steeply now.

He had just crossed another shallow stream of frigid glacial run-off when a crossbow bolt slammed into a tree on the shore next to him. He froze and turned.

Two men and one woman came pushing into the water from upstream. Two covered him while the third reloaded.

'This is our claim!' one fellow shouted.

The accent was unfamiliar to Kyle. He kept his arms wide. 'It is none of my business,' he said, 'but I do not think this land belongs to you.'

'You're right,' the woman answered as she drew near. 'It is none of your business.'

The three were armoured alike in plain soft leathers sewn with bronze rings. The swords and crossbows they carried appeared rather shabby and mass-produced.

'What are you doing here?' the first fellow asked.

Kyle motioned up to the distant ridgeline. 'Just passing through.'

The three eyed one another, uneasy. The woman looked him up and down in obvious disapproval. 'You don't look like you're too well equipped to take on the ice giants, stranger.'

'Ice giants?'

The three laughed. 'Just arrived, hey?' the woman said. 'Yeah. The locals call them the Icebloods.'

'Ah. I see.'

'You see what?' the woman snapped, annoyed. 'Anyway, you're right about that moving on.'

The other two laughed again.

Hands up, Kyle dared a small gesture to the woman. 'If you'll forgive me . . . you don't look much like prospectors yourselves.'

She glanced to her two partners – no more than hangers-on, Kyle thought them. 'That's right. We're no dirt-grubbers or sifters. The plan is to guard this stretch of creek. Then, when everything else has been tapped out . . .' she shrugged, 'we offer this virgin patch on auction to the highest bidder.' The two men nodded, grinning. 'We should make a peak each, hey boys?'

'That's right, Gleeda,' one answered.

'And what will you do with it?' Kyle asked.

The woman screwed up her face. 'Do with what?'

'This . . . peak. All the money.'

'Who the fuck cares? I'll buy a house so big there'll be rooms I never use. I'll eat quails' eggs and fucking bird liver all day.'

'A life of luxury. Doing nothing.'

'That's right.'

'So your goal is to do nothing with your life,' Kyle affirmed. 'I don't know. Sounds . . . pathetic to me.'

The woman's mouth turned down and she raised her crossbow. 'For someone on the sharp end of three bolts, you've got a big mouth on you, fellow. Now, you can throw *your* life away, but it would be a shame to waste a fine-looking ivory-handled sword like you got there.'

Kyle glanced to the weapon at his side. 'I wouldn't touch this, if I were you.'

'Shut up. Cover him, boys.' Gleeda carefully reached in to pull the weapon from its sheath. 'Damn, that looks sharp,' she said, and, cradling her crossbow in her arm, she moved to touch her thumb to it.

Kyle tensed, readying himself.

The woman goggled at the naked slit where her thumb had been. She screamed.

Kyle rolled forward through the shallow wash to kick one fellow down. A crossbow thumped, releasing. No lancing pain stabbed him so he charged onward, pulling the second fellow's crossbow down and smashing a fist across his jaw. He turned to Gleeda. She was fumbling to bring up her own weapon. A single leap and he snatched it away and turned it on her.

Gleeda glared her bloody rage. Then her gaze went to the blade lying on the naked gravel bed of the wash. It gleamed there like glowing ivory. 'You're . . . him,' she half mouthed. 'That fella.' She backed away while squeezing her mangled hand. 'Whiteblade . . .'

Kyle gestured them off with the crossbow. The three stumbled back across the creek. He picked up the blade and carefully resheathed it then edged away, weapon raised until he entered the woods. He jogged on for a time. Once he'd gone far enough he shot off the bolt and slammed the weapon against a tree to break it and threw it away.

Three days later, in a valley far higher above the dry prairie plateau, he knelt at a pond of run-off next to humps of shadowed snow. Beneath the snow rested a layer of deep sapphire ice thicker than his arm. It crackled and almost seemed to steam in the heat of the gathering spring.

He was kneeling to scoop up the frigid ice-water when a voice spoke, close and gruff: 'You are bold.'

He held out his arms, turned, and was quite startled to find a near-giant standing directly behind him. The man must have possessed a good full third again in height over Kyle, though he knew he wasn't all that tall to begin with. The fellow wore thick leathers and possessed a wild mane of mussed brown hair tied up with leather strips, and an equally wide and bushy beard that touched his chest. A sword hung on one hip, a long-hafted axe at the other. The fellow regarded him from within his nest of hair with something like an eager grin, as if hoping Kyle would go for his sword. He kept his arms wide. 'I'm just passing through.'

The grin broadened on the man's ruddy features and he scratched his scalp beneath his bunched and matted hair. 'You pass through to what? To peak? You'll not like it there, I think.'

'I'm looking for someone.'

The expressive brows rose. 'Oh-ho! Looking for someone! You have friends here, yes?'

'Yes, in fact I might.'

The giant slapped Kyle's side, nearly sending him tumbling into the pond. 'Ho! You are funny little man! I give you chance. You go south now. Don't come back.'

Kyle rubbed his ribs. 'Do you know a man named Stalker? Badlands? Coots?'

The fellow dropped his grin. He edged backwards from Kyle. A hand went to the bearded axe at his side. 'The Losts? Yes, I know.'

Losts? Kyle wondered. Well, that made sense. They called themselves the Lost Army. 'Well . . . they named me Lost as well.'

'Did they?' the man rumbled. He threw his arms wide. 'Cousin!'

He wrapped Kyle in a crushing hug and lifted him from the ground. Only when he set him down again could Kyle breathe once more. He leaned over, hands on knees, sucking in air.

'I am Cull Heel!' the fellow announced, his voice booming over the valley. 'Come! You go with me to Greathall!'

Hardly able to talk, Kyle nodded. 'Thank you, yes,' he gasped. 'Thank you.'

Cull set off upland. Kyle hurried after; the fellow set a fast pace with his great strides. 'I know lowland ways,' he was saying. 'I travel. Sail as pirate. Work as mercenary. Much fighting, little coin. Wife not happy.'

'I see.'

'You?'

'Oh – I was a mercenary as well. For a time.'

'Same as Losts. They go too, I hear. They come back.'

It took some time for Kyle to realize that he'd been asked a question. 'So they said.'

Cull grunted his understanding. 'We go but we come back. Always. Cannot escape.'

'Escape?'

By way of answer, the big fellow opened wide his arms as if to embrace the entire valley. 'The land. The Holdings. We are one.'

'Ah. I see.'

They climbed steeply for the rest of the day. Towards evening, Kyle was surprised by a shadowy figure awaiting them in the woods. Cull walked on, giving no clue that he'd seen the stranger. When they were quite close, Kyle cleared his throat and gestured ahead. 'Someone's there.'

Cull bunched his thick brows as if vexed. 'Yes?'

'Oh – so, a friend?'

'No. No friend,' the man answered darkly.

Closer, Kyle paused as he saw how the black trunks of the trees shone through the outline. Some sort of shade, or revenant. Cull walked on. He passed quite near to the tall wavering shape with its frayed tattered leathers and long face, yet made no effort to acknowledge its presence.

'There are trespassers on the Holding,' the shape called after them.

Cull waved the back of his hand at the outline. 'Yes, yes.'

'You must deal with them!'

'Certainly.'

As they walked on, Kyle following Cull who did not slow, the last thing the shade said was a murmured, 'We are ashamed.'

312

Kyle decided not to ask what all that had been about.

They only stopped when Cull led him to what was an obvious campsite, complete with a lean-to of cut boughs and a ring of stones. The big fellow set to cutting wood with his bearded axe. Kyle followed his lead by gathering more wood. It was dark when Cull got the fire going by taking out a tinderbox and striking flint to iron over a bed of dried moss.

Once the fire was sure, the big fellow sat back. Overhead, the aurora was out in wide draping bands of green and yellow frilled in pink.

'That was ancestor,' Cull said, throwing another stick on to the fire and raising a great gust of sparks that flew up into the night. Kyle watched them rise on and on, as if they would join the aurora itself. He decided that Cull was talking about the shade. 'Tell me to kill all trespassers.' He poked a thin stick into the fire then pointed it at him. 'Like you.'

'Thank you for not killing me.'

The giant frowned at the glowing tip of the stick. 'I have enough killing. Besides,' he shrugged, 'too many come.' He eased himself back against a log. 'Too many to kill.'

'They are coming for the gold.'

The fellow swished the glowing tip through the air, making circles and snake-like lines. He seemed delighted by the designs. 'Yes, the gold.'

'Why don't you just let them take it?'

'Gold in the land. They take the land.'

He felt like a fool. 'Yes. Sorry.'

'I'm sorry for them.'

Kyle shook his head in amazement. 'They are running you from your land and you are sorry for them?'

Cull continued swishing the stick. 'Gold least important thing in land.'

'Really? Then what is the most important?'

The fellow thought about this for a time. Frowning, he peered about at their forested surroundings, his brows crimping. Finally, a big infectious grin split his lips, and he offered, 'Life.'

Kyle thought that a strange answer but decided he wouldn't argue with his host. They slept then. For a time the blazing banners of the aurora kept him awake. It reminded him of Korel and the lights that glowed above the Strait of Storms. But they had been far fainter, more diffuse. Here they appeared so bright and low he thought he could pinch them between his fingers.

Over the next three days of climbing snow-patched slopes, Kyle decided that his host was very strange indeed. The man didn't seem to think the way he did. At times he seemed a child in a giant's body; at other times he was just plain odd. When Kyle remarked on the great rush of run-off streaming down the rock faces and the gathering summer, the man answered: 'Sun not the enemy. Time the enemy.'

Another day Kyle found him standing very still and solemn as he appeared to be doing nothing more than studying the mossy forest floor. He stood with him for a time, but soon became bored and moved off to sit and rest for the unannounced, extended stop. Cull woke him with a gentle touch. Kyle started up, peered back to where the man had stood for so long. 'What is it?' he asked.

'Powerful ancestor fall there long ago,' Cull answered, and started off.

Curious, Kyle crossed to the spot, which appeared no different from any other patch of needle-strewn ground. Then he noticed how the dirt was darker here, far wetter than the surrounding earth. He knelt and brushed aside the leaf bracken and litter. Something gleamed amid the dirt. He dug deeper into the dark wet humus. A layer of it came away in a swathe. Below gleamed a black smooth face of buried ice. Kyle flinched backward in shock and surprise. His hand throbbed, numb yet tingling. How like the Stormriders – but different. Theirs had been an alien cold, seemingly anathema to flesh and blood as he knew it. This was not so alien. Frigid, yes, but somehow far more comprehensible. Like . . . well, like a snow-capped mountain peak: formidable and inhospitable, but also majestic and awe-inspiring at the same time.

'Little brother,' Cull called, sounding far away.

Kyle shook his head and blinked to clear his vision, as if emerging from a dream. 'Yes, sorry. Coming.'

Towards late afternoon, they exited the forest to push through the tall weeds and saplings of what had once been cleared land. Fields, Kyle decided, now abandoned – or neglected – to fall back to the forest from where they'd been taken. The fields climbed a rising slope that allowed a magnificent view of the haze-shrouded lowlands.

Cull led him to the burnt ruin of what once must have been a very long hall. Only the butt-ends of its huge logs had escaped the fire, many as broad in girth as a large shield. Its fieldstone foundation lay as a mute line of rock among the weeds. The Iceblood waved to the fallen shell. 'Behold, Greathall.'

Kyle did not reply at once. He took a wondering breath. 'Very . . . impressive . . .'

Studying the wreckage, Cull nodded his solemn agreement. 'Yes. Very impressive.' He motioned Kyle onward. 'Come. We find wife.' He led the way round the ruins to the rear. Here was the much more modest structure of a cabin of smaller logs, chinked, with a sod roof. Smoke curled from a roof-hole.

'Ho! Wife!' Cull boomed out.

A crash such as a dropped plate or bowl sounded from within. The door of adzed planks was thrust open. A woman of a scale to match Cull emerged, towering and broad, bearing an even greater tangle of wild unkempt auburn hair. She wore a tanned leather jerkin, trousers and moccasins, and a knife the size of a shortsword was sheathed at her side.

'You!' she called, glaring.

Cull raised his hands defensively. 'Now, now . . .'

She started for him, a hand raised as if to clout him on the head. Cull backed away. Spying Kyle, the woman halted, surprised. 'Who is this?'

'He—'

'A lowlander? You bring a lowlander here!'

'I—'

'Are you an even greater fool than everyone knows?'

'We—'

She turned on Kyle. 'What is your name?'

'Ah, Kyle, ma'am. I don't have to stay. I could just—'

'Shut up.' She thrust a finger at Cull. 'Find the cows. They've wandered off again.'

Cull bowed low. 'Yes, my chick.' He headed off.

'Why did you bring him?' she called after him.

'Because he is Lost!' Cull shouted back, and laughed. He continued on, chortling to himself as he went.

The Iceblood woman now cast her sceptical eye to Kyle. 'What did my fool of a husband mean, lost?'

Kyle cleared his throat. 'Stalker and his brothers, ma'am. We were in the same mercenary outfit years ago. He made me a Lost.'

The woman grunted at this, eyed him up and down. 'Hmph. I see it now. So, Stalker made you a Lost, did he?'

'Yes, ma'am.'

'Well, then. Better make yourself useful.' She pointed to the trees behind the cabin. 'There's a cache back there. We might have a smoked haunch or two left. Bring one in.'

315

Kyle inclined his head. 'Yes, ma'am.'

'Name's Yullveig.'

He nodded again, 'Yullveig.'

It took him some time to find the cache. It was a hut very high up in a tree. All the lower branches had been cut away. The ladder that led up to it consisted of staves of wood lashed to the trunk. They were fixed very far apart. After thrusting the haunch of venison into a burlap sack the only way he could manage the descent was to tie the sack to his belt.

He returned to the cabin and knocked on the timber jamb. Yullveig invited him in. The little furniture within – a table, chairs of lashed wood, and a bed – were all on a scale that made him feel an infant. It didn't help that when she urged him to sit his feet barely touched the dirt floor.

'I must apologize for Cull,' she said as she minded the pot simmering over the stone hearth. The steam wafting from it smelled of parsnips.

'Apologize? For what?'

The answer brought a small smile to her otherwise severe lips. 'He fell climbing a cliff when he was a child.' She tapped her head. 'Never been the same since.'

'Ah. I see.'

'But he has a good heart,' she said, adding, 'Too good, his brothers said.'

Kyle peered about the rather cramped cabin. 'There are just the two of you?'

'A son and a daughter. Baran and Erta.' She started slicing the haunch. 'Cull left with two sons and returned with one. Not that I am complaining. He left at my urging.' She pointed the knife at the remains of the Greathall. 'In his absence the hall was burned and everyone killed by lowland raiders. Just the four of us now.'

'Yet Cull won't kill the trespassers.'

'No. He says death does not erase death.' She cast him a significant glance. 'A view not popular here among the Holdings, you can imagine. Our son did not understand. Damned him as touched. He's off fighting now and Erta with him. Defending the Holding.'

'I'm sorry.'

Her gaze snapped to him. 'Sorry? Why?'

'That he did not understand your husband's choice. I do.'

She nodded as she trimmed. 'Yes. I see it in you. The blood-price.'

'Blood-price? I owe no blood-price.'

The woman snorted, almost derisive. 'You lowlanders and your fixation upon vengeance, vendetta, honour and debts owed.' She waved the carving knife. 'That is the cheapest and simplest of blood-prices. It is self-aggrandizing. Self-righteous. And self-defeating. No, I speak of the only real cost of blood that matters – the price it exacts from the one who spills it. I see that within you and I respect it.'

'Yet there are those who think nothing of spilling blood.'

She nodded. 'There will always be such. They are the enemies of order among people. They must prove their worthiness to enter into any accord. And if they fail . . .' she shrugged, 'someone must take it upon themselves to drive the dogs off.'

'I think there are many dogs braying at the borders of your Holding, Yullveig.'

She laughed aloud at that. 'I think you are right.' She set a wooden bowl before him. It contained a splash of the boiled parsnips, slices of venison, and a portion of heavy dark bread.

'Should we not wait for Cull?'

'No. There is no telling when he might return – if at all. He comes and goes of his own pleasing. I am used to it. Indeed, it would gall me to have him here underfoot at all times.'

Kyle could not restrain himself any longer. He was famished, and tucked into the offering as if he were one of those exiled dogs himself. She watched him for a time, clearly taking pleasure from his appetite.

'You wish to try to find Stalker Lost, yes?'

Kyle nodded, his mouth full.

Yullveig thought about this while she cleared up. 'It will be difficult,' she began, after a long silence. 'The Losts are far to the east. You must cross all the surviving Holdings to reach them. You will probably be killed out of hand.' She crossed her arms and stared down at him. 'I suggest you return to the lowlands and journey east from there.'

Kyle could not keep from shaking his head. After coming all this way? 'That will not be so easy either.'

'Less dangerous than the Holdings, I think.'

'Perhaps.'

Yullveig did not argue the point further. 'Sleep here tonight. Rest. Tomorrow I will escort you to the edge of the Holdings. You can make your way from there.'

'Well . . . thank you, Yullveig. I am grateful for your kindness.' A thought occurred and he ventured a question. 'Did you say *surviving* Holdings?'

'Yes. Far more existed once. Larger Holdings covered the south. They extended down all the way to what you call the Bone Peninsula and the Dread Sea. I and my daughter Erta are from one such. The Fanyar, we were named. Gone now with the retreat of the cold and ice. Cull took us in when others would not.'

'I am sorry, Yullveig. I did not know.'

She shrugged again. 'Few do in this day and age.'

Kyle did not know what to say after that. Yullveig went to the rear of the cabin. 'We have a few hides and blankets. You can sleep by the hearth.'

'My thanks.'

'Save your thanks till the morning – the nights are very cold up here.'

Kyle did not doubt her. And true enough, no matter how closely he crowded the stones of the hearth, no warmth seemed to reach him through the frigid bite of the night air.

In the morning, Yullveig had no hot tea or drink to offer. She handed over slices of the smoked venison wrapped in burlap, then collected an immense spear from next to the door and headed out. Kyle followed. They spoke little the entire time; Yullveig proved a far more sombre guide than her voluble husband. She struck a south-east route and four days' hard journeying brought them to a stretch of forest that betrayed patches of recent clearing.

'Homesteaders,' she explained.

Kyle listened but heard no reports of further chopping, nor voices calling out. He wondered if Baran and Erta had been through recently.

'You are on your own from here, cousin. Give our regards to the Losts.'

'I shall. Give my thanks to Cull, won't you?'

'Yes. Fare you well. Oh,' she gestured to his side, 'I'd cover a weapon such as that if I were you.'

'Ah – yes. I usually do. Goodbye.'

Yullveig turned and jogged off. She disappeared in what seemed an instant among the dark trunks of the spruce and pine. He thought there must be some sort of magic in how these Icebloods came and went so quietly and suddenly here within their Holdings.

He did indeed wrap the sword in leather before heading into the clearing. But he kept it at his side in case he had call to use it. He travelled easily down among the foothills; parties crossed his path now and then, but none challenged or harassed him. He supposed he looked too much like what he was: just another ragged fortune-hunter.

He met more and more gold-chasers the further he went. They were a friendly lot away from the actual bearing fields and stream beds. Some invited him to join them at their fires. They told tall tales of the difficulties of their passages north, and of the hard knocks and precious few rewards since. Every day Kyle listened for the mention of a fierce warrior-woman, a Shieldmaiden – for most of the men and women he met hailed from nearby Genabackis, and would know her as such.

The trails that had been newly tramped out of the wilderness led him down to the shores of the Sea of Gold, and a rambling tent city its fortune-hunter founders named, ironically perhaps, Wrongway.

At a tent-tavern, he heard that a band of Malazan marauders had attacked and half burned the place to the ground. After this, the thug who ran the town, one Lying Gell, died of a mysterious knife-thrust and most of the gold-hunters decamped to join the crowd pressing the siege of the last independent local settlement, Mantle. The prospect of loot on hand, it seemed, was preferable to trying to track it down and dig it up. Kyle reflected that an invasion of fortune-hunters had now made the transition into a plain invasion. Inevitable, he supposed, when these rootless blades appeared to out-number the locals by far.

'Who are the leaders?' he asked the crowded table.

It turned out the captains were from all over, though none were Malazan, given the recent attack – which everyone seemed to regard as some sort of betrayal. A betrayal of what, Kyle couldn't quite understand. There was a Lether captain who called himself Marshal Teal; a number of ex-ship's captains who'd kept their crews together, and a Genabackan troop pulled together by a woman who'd actually served in the north, under the Warlord Caladan Brood.

'This woman,' Kyle asked, 'what's her name?'

The fortune-hunters glanced to one another, uncertain. One fellow spoke up. 'Don't know her name,' he offered. 'Only know what they call her.'

'What's that?'

'They call her the Shieldmaiden.'

And Kyle sat back, sipping his drink of watered ale. Lyan. Served under Brood? Neglected to mention that . . . But then, she knew he'd served with the Malazans, didn't she?

He stood from the table.

'Headed out?' someone asked.

Kyle finished his drink and saluted the table. 'Yes. Going to join up.'

*   *   *

The seventh day after they entered the Sea of Dread, a long low vessel came storming out of the west to intercept them. The Crimson Guard led the convoy of twelve in their captured local raider ship, which Captain Ghelath insisted on rechristening *Mael's Forbearance*.

The strange vessel was long and sleek, and moved with extraordinary speed – all the more astonishingly as she showed no sail nor sweeps. Like a shot arrow, it darted straight for the *Forbearance* and pulled up alongside, slowing to match the ponderous pace of the sweeps that pulled the *Forbearance* along, as there was no wind to speak of.

A lone figure straightened from the deck. It was a thin old man, mostly bald, wrapped in a ragged cloak. 'Permission to come aboard,' he called up in a reedy voice.

Gwynn, next to Shimmer, muttered: 'That vessel is soaked in magery.'

'Raise your Warren,' she answered, and signed likewise to Petal and Blues.

A rope ladder was lowered. The foreign vessel manoeuvred alongside. The old man climbed aboard – quite vigorously for such an ancient. K'azz came forward to meet him. The fellow scanned the deck with eyes tiny and dark, like deep wells.

'What can we do for you?' K'azz asked.

'You can surrender this vessel and all those behind to us.'

'I'm sorry . . .' K'azz began.

The old man snapped up a wizened hand. 'Do not argue. And do not resist. We will destroy—' The fellow stopped himself, his gaze narrowing. He murmured, 'Wait a moment . . .'

Someone very big and sturdy brushed past Shimmer: Bars pushing his way forward. 'Just a minute,' he called.

The two met at mid-deck. The old man's gaze widened and he gaped; Bars rocked back, pointing. 'You!' the old man growled.

'It's them!' Bars called. 'The Sharrs of Exile Keep!'

Snarling, the old man spun, sending his cloak flying across to enmesh Bars, who went down in its smothering folds. Beneath, bands and belts wrapped the old fellow from head to foot, all holding short blades that shone like polished silver. He threw his arms out and every one of the blades, an entire forest of them, flew from their many sheaths.

The blades scattered over the deck. Shimmer staggered at a blow to her chest, then threw herself flat as several glinting shards flew for her face. She heard the slivers punch into someone near, and his answering grunt as he fell. Sept, thrust through the throat. Multiple impacts now sounded as Black the Elder closed on the man behind his shield – the blades thudding home. But the slivers of metal flew like birds, and many swung round to strike Black from the rear, hammering into him so hard they disappeared fully into his back. He fell as well.

She glimpsed Gwynn lying against the side, a hand pressed to one eye, blood coursing between the fingers.

A thrown rope took the mage round his neck and yanked him viciously from his feet, but the spinning blades flew and severed the rope. The new figure of a young man wielding lengths of slim chain in each hand appeared at the bow. These he lashed about, clearing the space round him. The tearing of cloth revealed Bars freeing himself. K'azz and others were closing on the old man, all crawling forward.

With another snarl, the Sharr mage jumped over the side. Shimmer leapt to the rail where she saw him straightening on his own vessel. A panicked yell snapped her attention to the bow. Blues was closing upon the youth, the chains now wrapped about his twinned fighting sticks. Bars lunged in, blade overhead, for a ferocious swipe that hacked through the lad's shoulder, collarbone and ribs and stuck in the spine. A kick sent the body over the side. As one, like a flock, all the flying shards converged upon Bars. Rather coolly, he simply rolled over the rail to follow the lad into the sea below.

At that instant Reed, Cole and Amatt all bounded past Shimmer to throw themselves after the mage. K'azz and she yelled simultaneously, 'No!' But all three thumped to the strange vessel's deck, rolling, and came up, blades readied.

K'azz joined Shimmer at the rail. 'Get off there!' he yelled.

Chains, Shimmer noted, lay all about the decking. The old man laughed and gestured, and the chains snaked to life. They lashed their fat links about the three Avowed, then tumbled over the side in huge splashes. She caught one last glimpse of Cole before he disappeared, and she wasn't certain, but she thought the man flashed her one last typical roguish smile, as if to say: *well . . . had to happen sometime.* She had one boot up on the rail when a firm hand on her shoulder urged her back down – K'azz.

A sudden blur of motion next to the Exile mage, and the fellow fell stiffly to the deck. Or rather, most of him did: Cowl stood holding his severed head. The last links of chain slithered off the deck to sink into the water, and all was quiet.

Shimmer stood staring at the waves where moments before three good friends had disappeared. She shook her head in horror and disbelief.

'By the gods . . .' someone murmured, in awe.

She rubbed her chest where one of the flying slivers had rebounded from her mail armour. K'azz was staring at her, a strange expression on his face. She frowned at him, distracted.

A call sounded from the water below: 'Hello? Some help here?'

Everyone dashed to the side. Bars was splashing about. Ropes were thrown and soon the man was up over the side, dripping water to the deck. Shimmer embraced him, but he did not share her pleasure. 'How many?' he asked K'azz.

Their commander opened his mouth to answer, but stopped himself. He looked to Shimmer. 'How many?'

She scanned the deck. Gwynn, she saw, now stood, a cloth tied over one eye. 'Five, I believe,' she answered, hardly able to speak, 'Black the Elder, Sept, Cole, Amatt, and Reed.'

K'azz, she noted, had not taken his eyes from her the entire time. The man was obviously in anguish. The flesh of his face was drawn so tight as to seem parchment. 'Yes . . . five,' he managed, his voice breaking. 'I'm sorry . . . Shimmer.'

She nodded, whispering, 'As am I.' She gestured to the Exile vessel drifting alongside. 'Take that ship under tow.'

'No!'

She turned. Gwynn approached. He had a hand pressed to his ravaged socket. 'It's cursed. Burn it.'

'If you insist.' Her gaze fell to the still figures of Sept and Black the Elder prone upon the blood-soaked deck.

'And them?' Gwynn asked.

She sighed, rubbing her chest. 'Burial at sea, Gwynn.'

He inclined his head in agreement. 'Very well.'

She turned away, only to nearly run into Cowl standing behind her. 'What?' she snarled, in no mood for the man's games.

Fresh slashes and gouges marked where many of the shards had struck the High Mage. His crooked smile appeared even more manic than usual. 'Nothing.' He turned away, brows raised. 'Nothing at all.'

She frowned her irritation. *Lunatic.*

Bars came to her side. Water still dripped from him. 'I'm sorry,' he murmured, his gaze lowered. 'I tried to warn you.'

She wanted to embrace him – *I could have lost you!* – but held his shoulder instead. 'It's all right. Now we know why Cal-Brinn chose to break off.'

He took her hand. His was so icy cold she almost yanked hers free. 'If only . . .' he began.

'If only we were somewhere else,' she finished. 'Some*one* else.'

His answering smile was a half grimace. 'Yes . . . if only.'

They held a short ceremony for Sept and Black, then slid the weighted bodies over the side. May Mael embrace them, Shimmer prayed. The short invocation reminded her of her earlier prayer to Burn, the ancient goddess, to guide them through these dangers. It seemed her prayer was going unanswered.

After this, she found she was spending almost all her time on deck, staring at the unnaturally smooth surface of the Dread Sea. It was all too familiar: the sliding water, the seeming spell of timelessness. Far too familiar.

The fourth night after the attack, she decided she'd seen enough. It was too much like a land half the world away. A land named Jacuruku. 'Gwynn,' she murmured into the dark, though it was after the mid-night bell and the deck was deserted.

A moment later he appeared. He wore a strip of cloth across his face now as he'd lost his right eye.

'Yes?'

That was all. No *What?* or sleepy resentment at being disturbed. No, he knew she wouldn't call unless there was a reason. She extended a hand to the water. 'Look familiar?'

The mage's remaining eye narrowed on the barely undulating milky surface. He let go a tired sigh. 'I see your point.' He'd been a long time in Jacuruku.

'Get on it.'

He bowed, and returned below. Shimmer returned to studying the waves where they glimmered, reflecting the stars above.

Three days later, three mages came to see her. She was again at the rail of the 'liberated' pirate vessel. Something told her she was not alone; that, in fact, she was the object of a great deal of regard, and she turned. The Guard's mages faced her: Gwynn, as sour as ever; Petal, looking uncharacteristically concerned; and even Blues, ostensibly second-in-command, but a company mage as well.

Now that they had her attention, Blues waved a hand to indicate those self-same waves. 'Casts quite the spell, don't it?'

Shimmer flicked her gaze to Petal, who nodded, his thick neck bulging.

'Can you do anything about it?' she asked.

Blues tapped one of his fighting sticks to his chin – Shimmer hadn't noticed them slipping into his hands. 'Petal here is of the opinion that maybe we can. But it'll take all three of us working together.'

Shimmer was surprised. What could possibly be so potent? 'Why all of you?'

Blues looked to Petal. The big mage actually blushed. He lowered his gaze to study his hands, where they clasped his stomach. 'It's not just another Warren, Shimmer. This is a Realm. Jaghut magics. Omtose Phellack. And we're not welcome.'

'If you need power then bring in our vaunted High Mage.'

Petal shrugged his humped shoulders. 'He said his participation would only make things more difficult.'

Difficult bastard. Typical. 'So? What's stopping you?'

The three exchanged uncomfortable glances. Blues finally supplied, 'Could be fatal.'

Fatal? To *all*? 'I see. So . . . should we risk all our mages . . .'

Blues gave a curt nod. 'Right. So I'll do it.'

Gwynn snorted. 'Idiotic.'

'It would make most sense,' Petal stammered, 'if it was me . . . don't you think?'

Shimmer had had enough of this. She brushed past all three. 'Won't be any of *you*.' Difficult, my arse! Trying to duck a dangerous job!

She stamped her way across the mid-deck, scanned the stern, saw no hint of the fellow. 'Cowl! Come out from under your rock! We need to have a chat!'

'Yes?' The answer was gentle, unforced, and directly to her rear. She turned round slowly. The man stood uncomfortably close. In kissing range, in fact. His eager, avid gaze seemed to be daring her to act: either embrace him, or knife him.

She forced herself not to flinch, began calmly, 'I understand that attempting to ease us through Omtose Phellack could kill the mage who tried.'

'True.'

'Then shouldn't you be the one to make the attempt – High Mage?'

His habitual mad mocking smile climbed even higher, as it always seemed to whenever they spoke. He shook his head in a negative. 'Oh, it would be worse if I tried. Much worse.'

'Why?'

The man fairly hugged himself in his glee. 'You'll see . . .'

She raised a hand to cuff the man across his face, thought better of it, and stormed off. *Fool!* Where's – ah, there he is. She marched up to K'azz at the bow.

'K'azz! Your pet is becoming more and more obnoxious.'

'Shared a frank exchange of views, did you?'

'I'd like to share my sword.'

'He is still High Mage, Shimmer.'

'Meaning?'

'Take his word for it.'

She almost flinched. There it was – the lingering ghost of the old chain of command. Was she able to give orders or not? Damn the way the past just wouldn't go away! She turned on her heel and left the man standing alone.

She returned to the gathered company mages. Her gaze found Petal and rested there. 'You said it should be you – why?'

The huge man seemed to shrink under her stony regard. 'Well,' he began, stammering, 'Blues' D'riss is not appropriate to this. Nor is Serc. Nor Shadow.' He pressed his hands together and touched them to his chin. 'I believe my insights into the Mockra Warren – the magics of the mind and perception – should guide us best.'

Shimmer nodded. 'Very well. You have the task.' The fellow blinked, quite surprised by his success. 'Blues, Gwynn, give him any aid necessary.'

The mages murmured their assent and the three went off, already arguing and sharing opinions on the coming job.

Shimmer crossed her arms and returned to staring out over the water. Familiar. Hood-blasted familiar. Like Ardata. But not as heavy-handed or powerful. More subtle. More . . . insinuating.

Days passed. Eleven vessels followed their lead, including the Lether ships of that ruthless merchant general, Luthal Canar. Eleven now, as one morning the sun rose to reveal that one of their number had simply gone missing overnight. No further losses appeared after that. The ship immediately following theirs, the Mare galley the *Lady's Luck*, kept close, and the others followed them.

One day Blues joined her at the rail, where she was studying the unchanging heavy cover of fog. 'How is Petal doing?' she asked.

'Holding up.' He glanced back to where the mage sat cross-legged on the deck, wrapped in blankets. He let out a hard breath. 'I gather from his muttering that what he's facing – Omtose Phellack unveiled – is fading even as he wrestles with it. Unravelling like rotten cloth. Probably be impossible to push through, otherwise.'

'Good. Maybe we'll make it through this without any further losses.'

They stood together in silence after that. The sun sank to a dim reddish smear close to the horizon. She remarked, 'The Brethren have been silent of late.'

'Petal says the Jaghut magic is holding them off.'

Shimmer grunted her acceptance. The night darkened. The unvarying haze of the Sea of Dread thickened to an impenetrable blanket that blinded her.

With the sounding of the mid-night bell, Blues remarked, 'There were ex-Stormguard on that Mare vessel. The men who used to fight the Riders of the Strait of Storms. They'll be useful in a dust-up.'

She nodded at this information. Yet she wished to say so much more: to thank the man for his support, for his extraordinary lack of jealousy that would have driven others to undermine her position; for frankly just being him all these years. But something stopped her, something intervened and closed her mouth like a clenching fist, and she wondered – was this the clichéd isolation of command? The weight she'd heard described so often? Ridiculous. Yet there it was. Something had driven itself between her and all the others of the Guard. Something she hadn't felt before.

But she said nothing of this. She remained silent. She was no longer the one to give explanations. She gave orders now. And a voice within her remarked, scornfully: *how like K'azz!*

Days later – Shimmer had no idea how many, and felt no impulse to ask – the banks of fog that choked the Sea of Dread parted before their bow, revealing a rugged rocky coast, forested hills beyond, and distant jagged snow-peaked mountains.

Shimmer went to find K'azz. He was at the stern, hands clasped behind his back. 'We're through,' she reported.

For some time he did not answer, then his eyes fluttered, blinking, and his head turned to her. It was as if he was surfacing from some deep dive, such as his undersea walk at the Isle of Pillars. He nodded. 'Good.' He gestured to the line of vessels emerging from the fog-banks behind them. 'Nine now. Lost two more.'

'When?'

326

He shrugged. 'Some time ago.'

'An attack?'

He shook his head. His dirty-grey hair, she noted, was thinning even more. 'No. No attacks. I understand that here, on the Dread Sea, crews just give up. Or disappear. Vessels lose headway, then coast, and finally lie adrift, empty. Abandoned. A sea of ghost ships.'

'We made it through.'

He nodded again, the muscles of his jaws bunched in stark contrast beneath his parchment-like skin. 'How is he?'

She jumped, flinching. Petal! She ran to where the man sat close to the side rudder and knelt before him. His head hung so low she couldn't see his face. 'Petal? Hello? Are you with us?'

The blankets heaped about the man stirred. The head shook, as if its owner were waking, then rose. Sweat sheathed the pale rounded cheeks, dripped from the chin. He peered about, puzzled, as if he'd forgotten everything, then his gaze found her face and fixed there and he smiled, rather self-consciously. 'Thirsty,' he croaked.

She straightened. 'Water here! A drink!'

One of Ghelath's crewmen ran up with a skin of water. Petal just blinked at the thing. Shimmer snatched it away, unstoppered it, and held the spout to his lips, squeezing gently. Water poured down his chin but he managed to swallow some few gulps. He nodded his thanks.

Only now did Shimmer realize how neglectful they had been. Who had taken care of him? Gods, how could they have been so . . . forgetful? But no, Blues, surely . . . With Petal awake, Blues was here with her now, along with Gwynn.

'Did you check on him?' she demanded.

Blues blinked his surprise. 'Well . . . no. I thought . . .' and he gestured vaguely, as if to indicate the ship's company in general.

Shimmer gazed down at the mage as he stirred. He wanted to stand, and so they helped him to his feet. The blankets fell from him and steam rose into the air from his sweat-soaked robes, as if he smouldered with heat. How many days, weeks, had it been, she wondered. Or had it only been a few? In any case, how could he have survived? It was inhuman.

She studied the fellow as he weaved on his feet. He looked to have lost a full two stone.

They passed a number of bare rocky headlands, a few yet sheathed in scabrous ice, then came to where the coast flattened and here they found the shore littered with the broken husks of ships.

Blues pointed a stick ahead, where cliffs rose; there stood a keep, a heap of rock exactly the same slate-grey hue as the surrounding cliffs. The land before it lay checkered in fields in various degrees of care and cultivation. A bedraggled clutch of wooden huts hugged the shore.

A rain that had fallen on and off through the day started in earnest. It pushed down the smoke climbing from holes in the shack roofs. Though Shimmer had longed for land, it was a dour and depressing sight.

'We should go ashore first,' said K'azz from beside her and she started, surprised; she hadn't sensed his presence.

'Of course.'

The landing party consisted of her, K'azz, Blues, Gwynn, and Keel. She was startled to see K'azz actually carrying a sword – a hand and a half. He caught her gaze and said, explaining, 'Cole's.'

The losses still burned in her chest, and she nodded. 'I'm sorry, K'azz.'

'As am I, Shimmer. As am I.'

A launch took them to shore. They tramped up the wet sand then climbed a ratty set of stairs built of timbers taken from stricken vessels. The huts were likewise constructed from ships' timbers. But so much wood was in evidence, Shimmer began to suspect deliberate wrecking. The shacks were roofed with sod, bundled grasses, or wooden shakes. What few men and women they met turned away, or stopped in stony silence to watch them pass. One woman, her rags gathered about her, murmured, 'Run while you can,' and hurried off herself.

Shimmer looked to K'azz, quite uneasy. He motioned her on to the stone fortress. Blues, she noted, had drawn his sticks. These he tossed and spun as they went, and she knew this was his habit when nervous. Keel walked with his enormous rectangular shield readied on his arm.

They found the wide wooden door open upon its heavy iron hinges. The hall within was flagged with broad cut stones, yet littered with wind-blown leaves and twigs as if from long neglect, and thick with tramped-in mud. The entrance hall led to a much larger reception hall. It was very dark after the outdoors. The only light streamed in from the open doorway behind them, or from thin slit openings high up the walls. Here a woman awaited them. She sat in a wooden chair also constructed from battered ship's planking, and wore a flowing white dress that hung down to spread in long reaching lengths all about the floor. Her hair was similarly snow-white and extraordinarily long – it appeared to even reach the stone floor around her. The proud way she sat in the chair of faded old timbers made it clear to Shimmer that she regarded it as a throne.

K'azz stepped forward and bowed in a courtly manner, as when he had dealt with the prickly Quon kings and nobles long ago. 'Greetings,' he murmured, his head lowered. 'I am K'azz, commander of the mercenary company the Crimson Guard. With me are members of my troop: Shimmer, Blues, Gwynn, and Keel.'

The woman favoured them with a hard glare; she did not respond to K'azz's greeting. 'A mercenary company,' she said, musing. 'An army – of sorts.' Her glare narrowed. 'Are you the enemy I was warned to expect?'

K'azz turned round to examine each of them. Gwynn stood leaning upon his staff. He adjusted the new leather patch he had fashioned for his eye, frowned his confusion. Shimmer was completely mystified and shook her head. K'azz turned back to the woman. 'I do not believe we are . . .'

'Mist,' the woman supplied. 'You may call me Mist. Normally, here I would also say that I am your queen as well. But there is something about you . . .' She turned her head as if to regard them first through one eye, then the other. 'Something about you I do not like. Therefore, while I would usually give you until tomorrow to lay down your weapons, *you* I will ask to depart immediately. Or you will be executed.'

K'azz pulled thoughtfully on his chin. 'Executed? Then we are your prisoners?'

Mist shook her head. 'No. Not prisoners. Trespassers. Meddlers. Troublemakers here among my peaceful farming community.'

'Perhaps we may be permitted to purchase a few small parcels of food – kegs of potable water? We must travel north, as we have business there.'

The woman's features hardened even more. 'The north does not want your business. But I see that you are not to be convinced. You are armed and experienced fighters – perhaps you think you can win your way through by strength of arms.' She snapped her fingers.

Heavy steps sounded from the darkness behind the woman's throne. Two gigantic shapes emerged. Twins they seemed, two giants. They resembled those of the Jaghut race Shimmer had seen over the years, but differed in the coarseness of their enormous jutting tusks, the thick shelves of brow ridges entirely shadowing the orbs of their eyes, and the massed ropy manes of hair that tumbled about their shoulders. One wore a long coat of scaled bronze, and carried a two-headed axe thrust through a wide belt. The weapon was fully as tall as Shimmer herself. The other wore a similar set of shell-like scaled armour, but of iron. This one carried a massive two-handed sword taller from tip to pommel than Keel's full height.

Both set their shovel-like hands to their belts and grinned to expose uneven teeth. Both obviously enjoyed the reactions their appearance evoked.

Shimmer heard Gwynn's breath leave him in one long hiss of revulsion. She cast him a questioning look. He whispered low, 'Twisted, these two – in the womb.'

She could not help her hand climbing to where the grip of her whipsword rose over one shoulder. Gwynn shook a negative, inclined his head to the gloom of the chamber. Shimmer squinted. At first she saw nothing, but slowly details emerged. She had thought the ragged scarf-ends of this sorceress's dress and hair ended in the small circle of light she could make out, but in fact they did not. They stretched on across the full breadth and length of the hall. Then she realized something even more remarkable: they were moving. The tatters and ribbons writhed and twitched – and they surrounded them.

Like cats' tails, she thought to herself. Lashing. And we are the mice.

'May I introduce my sons,' Mist said, sounding quite proud. She extended a hand to her left, 'Anger,' and she indicated to her right, 'Wrath.'

'Impressive,' K'azz allowed, and nodded his greeting to each. Their low rumbled amusement sounded like rocks shifting. 'We will leave you, then, to your peaceful farming community,' and he bowed again, motioning for Blues and Gwynn to back away.

'Go then,' Mist called as they retreated. 'You I do not like. But the others . . . the many vessels dropping anchor even as we speak . . . they may stay.'

Shimmer could not help but shoot K'azz an anxious look. He waved her on. Outside, the commander motioned for a hurried retreat to the shore. 'Why did she let us go?' she demanded.

'We are an unknown. She senses there is more to us.'

'Such as what?' she snapped.

He would not meet her gaze. 'The Vow, I imagine.'

They found that a thick ground fog had arisen while they'd been inside. Shimmer did not imagine it coincidental. The meandering streamers of fog reminded her too much of Mist's lashing white

330

dress. In fact, she began to wonder whether they were in very great trouble; certainly K'azz seemed to think so as he hurried them along.

'Get to the ships,' he told them as they jogged. 'Warn them off. None should put in.'

She gave a quick nod and ran for the nearest launch already ashore. These sailors she warned away. The next lot she found by nearly running into their boat in the dense soup-like miasma. They were clinging to the boat's side as if afraid they'd sink in the fog and she recognized them as sailors of the Mare galley, the one with the pilot K'azz said knew most about these waters.

'Put out,' she told them. 'It's a trap. A sorceress is here.'

'Mist?' A youth spoke up, standing from within the boat.

'Yes. She calls herself Mist.'

'We must leave,' the youth said to another sailor, presumably his superior. 'The Fortress Mist and its witch. It's mentioned in some few accounts. She enslaves all those who land.' The officer grimaced his scepticism.

'We need water, Storval,' another said.

'Shut up,' the officer growled. 'Let me think.' He eyed Shimmer. 'Couldn't we find a—'

A scream sounded from the distance. Its source was utterly obscured by the layers of dense fog surrounding them. It bespoke chilling terror, and was all the more horrible for being cut off in a gurgle, as if the man had fallen from a gallows.

'Push off now!' Shimmer commanded, and ran into the fog. She headed for where she thought she'd glimpsed another longboat. Her feet splashed through the waves and sand hissed beneath her boots, but for all that it was as if she waded through a sea of blanketing soup.

She doubled over as she ran into the next boat, nearly falling in. 'Push off!' she gasped.

None of the sailors within answered. Nor would they again. They lay sprawled, contorted, hands at throats, their features swollen and purple, although paling now. Scarves of thick fog drifted from their necks even as she watched. She threw herself from the boat, scanned the coursing banners of mist. Damn it to Hood! Where was their boat?

She ran on along the strand. Thicker gravel crunched beneath her boots and the normality of it comforted her; the fog was so leaden it was as if she'd wandered into another world – perhaps Hood's demesne itself, which some theorized as a land of mists.

The loud shock of a boot-step sounded nearby, one far heavier than any she or any person might make. Something hissed above her and she sidestepped – a fluid motion as swift as thought that only a trained sword-dancer could execute. Something sliced the fog beside her to slam into the gravel like a battering ram. She found herself within a hand's breadth of the beaten bronze blade of a two-headed axe, one pounded so heavily into the strand that she could step over it, though she knew it to be as tall as she.

A gnarled fist larger than her head yanked the weapon free and it disappeared once more into the swirling mists above her.

Shimmer ran.

Cries of terror continued all about, most cut off in throttled gurgles. She stumbled over boulders, flinched when her boot pressed down on a yielding body. It was galling that just nearby, out of sight, waves slapped against boats. If she could only find theirs!

A voice called then, from nearby in the mist, and she recognized it: Petal. 'Shimmer!' It was spoken, not shouted, as if from just next to her.

She shouted, 'Yes!' and was chagrined by the note of panic she heard.

'This way. Follow my voice.' She set off, feeling her way. Petal spoke every few heartbeats to reacquaint her with his location: 'Keep going,' he sometimes said, or, 'More left.'

Distantly, she heard the creak of cordage and the banging of sweeps as the ships and launches were pulling out. From across a portion of the strand she could make out the silhouette of one of the giant brothers, Anger or Wrath. The massive shape knelt at the shore then rose, roaring, and she recognized the shadowy curve of a boat's side rising with him. A mass of panicked shouts and screams was abruptly cut off as the longboat, overturned, fell upon its crew.

The giant's roar of laughter was an avalanche of falling rocks.

'Swim for it,' Petal told her.

'What of you?'

'Never mind me. Swim!'

Snarling her displeasure, she pushed her way into the surf. It was a good thing she'd chosen not to wear her armour, but then it had been weeks since she'd donned it. Her feet left the bottom and she paddled – she'd only ever had a few basic lessons from Blues. Something snagged at her and she flinched, gained a mouthful of water, and almost slipped into blind flailing terror. Blues' first lesson saved her: don't panic, he'd told her. As in a fight, panicking is the worst thing you can do.

She forced her eyes open, stilled her slapping of the water, and saw that she was engaged in a struggle with a corpse. Its limp arms kept bumping up against her. She pushed it away and carried on.

'To the right.' Petal spoke again and she realized then that he'd never been with her at all. It was a sending of some sort, or he was watching for her from his Warren. She paddled on.

'Shimmer!' a new voice shouted. She recognized Bars' bull bellow.

'Here!'

'Follow my voice! This way! I have an oar! Do you see it?'

Something splashed the water nearby through the cloaking fog. She headed that way. A tall cliff of darkness emerged from the bank – the side of a vessel. 'Here!' she called.

An oar came sluicing through the waves. She grasped for it but missed. She caught it on the second try.

'There's a rope here,' Bars said. The oar pulled her along through the water to where a rope ladder hung from the side. She took hold and started up. On deck, she was met by all the landing party.

'You're last,' Bars told her.

She scanned the shore but the coursing banners of fog still obscured everything. The rest of the Guard were manning the sweeps. She noticed that, oddly, Lean was at the rudder.

'Where's Havvin?'

Bars and K'azz exchanged glances. 'I'm sorry, Shimmer,' K'azz said. He motioned to where several shapes lay bundled in sailcloth.

Shimmer suddenly felt very cold as she stood dripping wet in the fog. She shivered. 'How many?'

'Eight,' K'azz said. His voice, and his features, did not change at all, and Shimmer realized that he was holding himself under a terrifying degree of will. 'Taken by the mist.'

She swallowed to dare her next question: 'Any of us?'

'None.'

She was vastly relieved, but then fixed her gaze upon him. She wished to take hold of his shoulders and shake him. 'Why? *Why?*'

'The . . . Vow . . . I imagine.' He lurched away and seemed to totter off.

She let him go. He knows more than that – *he must*. She met Bars' gaze, but the man just shook his head.

'I'm very sorry, Shimmer.'

'As am I, Bars,' she sighed.

The Avowed helped on the sweeps, a skeletal few, yet *Mael's Forbearance* made steady headway. They finally emerged from the fog and she found that they were a good way out in the bay. Behind, the thick bank obscured the shore for several bowshots. Utterly unnatural, that concentration of mist. She peered round, counting ships. Found nine. Every vessel, it seemed, had escaped – though most of the ship's launches and their crews probably hadn't. She turned to face ahead, and while the sky was a leaden hue, overcast, she still had to squint in the light. Three vessels were far ahead: the Letherii modified merchantmen. It seemed Luthal Canar was in no mood to offer anyone any aid. Well, that was fine: they could face whatever lay ahead first.

At that, she shifted her gaze to where a pale light seemed to glow to the north-east. 'What is that?' she asked Bars.

But Blues answered, sounding uncharacteristically grim: 'An ice-field.' She remembered that he'd crossed the immense plain of ice that separated Stratem from the lands of Korel to the north.

'Can we get through?' she asked.

Blues shrugged. 'There must be some way.'

She nodded at that. Yes. Surely some vessels must have made it through ahead of them. Her gaze fell on the wrapped bodies. 'We should give them a proper send-off.'

'Yes,' Bars agreed, and he sounded very firm on that.

It was a channel. A narrow gap of open water that ran between tall cliffs of white and a deep sea-blue of glacial ice. They reached it near to dusk, but such was the peculiar light held by the ice from the moon, and the star field where it shone through gaps in the cloud cover, that they continued on.

Luthal's command ahead did likewise. They too neither paused nor let up, and Shimmer began to wonder whether the Letherii merchant had – rather stupidly – decided that this was some sort of race. And the gold to the winner.

Behind, the rest of the ragtag convoy straggled along. Next in line was the Mare galley. Privately, Shimmer was of the opinion that if any ship survived, it would be that one. She had a great respect for the vessels and crews of that seafaring nation.

The passage narrowed alarmingly in places. The cliffs reared nearly overhead. At times great reports cracked the night air and carriage-sized shards of ice came crashing down ahead or behind to send up fountains of frigid spray. Some of that spray even reached them on board the *Forbearance*.

Something about these avalanches of shards troubled Shimmer, and not just that any one of them could crush them into splinters. As they proceeded through, the sweeps hissing through ice-mush and clattering off floating chunks of sapphire-blue ice, it came to her.

The ice was only falling near them.

She watched to the rear for a time: no ice shards burst from the cliff faces behind them – at all. She turned ahead to study the three Letherii vessels and the full length of the channel and saw no movement at all. No fracturing, cracking or rumbling.

She turned to K'azz.

Cowl suddenly appeared next to their commander. His scarred, ghostly pale face was upraised to study the overhanging cliffs. 'We must back out – now,' he said.

K'azz frowned his puzzlement. 'Back out? Why?'

The High Mage lowered his face to peer straight at K'azz. 'You know why.'

K'azz snapped his gaze to the cliffs. 'You don't think . . .'

'I do.'

K'azz spun to the mid-deck, roared, 'Back oars! Back off!' The Avowed on the oars pushed hard, heaving. *Mael's Forbearance* came to a slow sluggish halt amid the wash of growling crushed ice. 'Back oars!' K'azz yelled anew.

It appeared to Shimmer that they had just made a terrible mistake.

Reports like munition blasts erupted from the near port-side cliff. Cracks zigzagged up and down the translucent gleaming facets of the face. Chunks ranging in size from barrels to horses and wagons came crashing and tumbling. They sent up great fountains of spray that punched down to slap the decking of the *Forbearance*. One single massive crag now pulled away from the entire cliff. It extended from halfway up to the white snowy top. As slow as night falling it came, leaning farther and farther out from the body of the great ice wall above them.

Shimmer caught Blues' wide gaze. 'Do something,' she said.

He shook his head in utter helplessness. 'D'riss is of no . . .'

'Cowl!' K'azz demanded.

Shimmer snapped her gaze to the High Mage, but the man only stared, his face now uncharacteristically severe. 'There is nothing.'

Brutal explosions of tons of crushed ice thundered above. A dark shadow engulfed the *Forbearance*.

K'azz drew a savage breath and bellowed, *'Abandon ship!'*

The crew and the Avowed on the oars let them fall. Everyone dived for the sides.

The last thing Shimmer remembered was the intense cold of the water. She struck the ice mush first, and it parted for her, but not before imparting numbing blows to her protecting forearm. She churned her one good arm, fought for the surface.

She never made it. Some immense dark shape came plunging into the water and it dragged her down with it, down into the frigid night of the depths below. For a time she fought to free herself from the weight that drove her on and on deeper into the darkness. But in the murk and the utter cold, her strength gradually seeped from her, and she knew nothing more.

*   *   *

'We must go back!' Reuth thrust an arm to the stern, his gaze fierce upon Storval. 'Search for survivors!'

The first mate waved his dismissal. 'You saw. None survived. Only wreckage surfaced.' He nodded to the oarsmen, motioned for them to continue.

'But we should wait. Search the wreckage!'

'Too dangerous. The entire cliff fell on them. More might come down.'

Reuth stared, appalled beyond words. The foreign mercenaries saved them at Old Ruse and here at Mist, yet this heartless bastard was prepared to turn his back upon them. He clutched the man's leather sleeve. 'I see why you won't stop – you're a coward!'

He did not see the blow; next thing he knew he was on the deck, blinking, his head ringing. Hands clutched his shirtfront, yanked him to his feet. 'You little puke,' Storval hissed in his face. 'You're only living because I've allowed you to live. Maybe if you keep your trap shut and do your job I'll continue to let you!' The hands thrust him backwards and he stumbled into the ship's side.

Storval straightened his jerkin and paced off. Reuth caught the gazes of nearby Stormguard but he saw no sympathy there, only their maddening haughty airs. 'They saved us at Old Ruse,' he said, and rubbed his head where he'd been struck.

'We guided them here,' one of the Stormguard answered.

'We?' Reuth gaped, nearly speechless. 'I guided us here!'

The Stormguard merely shrugged, unconcerned. 'We all have our job to do.'

Reuth almost answered, but caught himself in time: and yours is a glorified spear-rack. Instead, he turned away, pointedly giving these fools his back.

His uncle wouldn't have bulled through the wreckage. He would've stopped. And Kyle would've supported him against these

Stormguard. Still, it was hard to imagine that anyone could've survived such an enormous blow. It had been as if the hand of some vengeful god had slammed down upon those mercenaries. No other vessel had even been touched! Reuth slapped the timbers of the stern cabin. All for naught now. He was a captive – Abyss, a *slave* to this cowardly wretch's commands.

He knew then what he would do at the first opportunity. The decision had been coming for some time now in his unhappiness and frustration. Come his first chance he'd jump ship, abandon these bastards to their own fate. Then they'd see how well they fared without a proper pilot.

It would be simple enough; there were no charts or rolls of maps to burn or steal away. His uncle had seen to that – forbidding him from bringing even the simplest scroll. Now he understood why. Bargaining power and value. Where there were no charts, the knowledge he held in his head made him priceless.

Reuth suddenly realized just how much he must have meant to his uncle – and what pains Tulan had taken to ensure his survival.

He wept for him then, hugging himself, kneeling hidden as deep in the stern notch as he could wiggle. All he had seen was his uncle's gruffness. His coarse ways. And how he had resented him for it. Now a hotter grief clutched his throat and he recognized the certainty of his own unworthiness. His ingratitude! His sullen pouting childishness!

Someone kicked his flank. It was Storval. 'Hey,' he urged. 'Which way? What now, damn you?'

He wiped his sleeve across his burning eyes. 'Hug the north shore,' he answered, his voice thick. 'There should be . . . settlements there.'

Storval – he still could not bring himself to think of the man as *captain* – simply grunted and turned away.

Reuth watched him go. The first settlement they reached . . . he'd be gone.

*   *   *

Stones rattled from a switchback trail down a steep ravine as a file of silent figures descended in the night. At its base they spread out upon a narrow cleft of dirt to regard the amazing sight ahead of a deep chasm spanned by a construction of bones lashed and hooked into a bridge. None spoke; they all seemed to be waiting.

The ground before the bridge shifted. Ancient stained bones emerged, shook off the dry dirt. A titanic entity of bone slowly straightened from the stony ground. Last of all came a colossal battered dragon skull that it set upon its broad neck with skeletal hands.

A faint blue flame flickered to life deep within the sockets of the skull as the entity regarded the eerily silent figures – who studied him in turn.

'I am Yrkki,' the giant boomed. 'And you, most of all, certainly may not pass.'

The foremost of the travellers strode closer. Passing clouds allowed the moonlight to shine upon this one, revealing him to be wrapped in ragged leathers, a fur cloak at one shoulder, his sockets empty and his lips curled back from grinning teeth stained the colour of wet dead leaves. 'I am Gor'eth of the Kerluhm T'lan Imass,' he announced. 'And we have no quarrel with you.'

'That is true,' the giant rumbled. 'Yet I have a claim upon you.'

'We are newly wakened after an ages-long sleep. We seek the north. Stand aside, ancient spirit, and you may continue your guardianship.'

'My guardianship – my custodianship – is of this bridge. Long have I awaited your arrival, T'lan. When I was set here ages ago to ward this passage my price was but one request.'

Gor'eth shifted, his skeletal hand slipping to the worn grip of the stone blade that hung at his pelvis. 'And that was?'

Yrkki stretched his wide arms to encompass the cleft. 'The bones of the T'lan Imass for my bridge!'

Gor'eth rolled to avoid an immense hand that flattened the ground he stood upon. His fellows surged forward. Flint and chalcedony weapons slashed the fat mammoth legs Yrkki stood upon. Bone chips flew. A swatting hand knocked Imass aside to land shattering among rocks. Gor'eth swung his two-handed blade of milky flint, severing one clutching hand of bones. Imass charged. They levered stone spearheads into the vertebrae of the giant's exposed spine.

Yrkki roared and crushed a handful with a descending blow then swept the rest aside. But more of the warriors gathered to encircle him and he could not defend himself on all sides.

More stone-headed spears thrust at the joints of the naked vertebrae, and levered. Yrkki roared his panic and spun. A rock-shattering crack sounded and the vertebrae parted. The giant gave one last desparing bellow as it tottered in two directions. The rain of enormous bones came crashing down upon the remaining T'lan Imass.

Gor'eth righted himself and approached, kicking through the wreckage. He stopped before the fallen dragon skull and regarded the faint azure flame still guttering within its sockets. 'Your masters have not been kind to you, Yrkki.'

'Omtose Phellack has withdrawn,' came a faint breath. 'That is true. But as a spirit of the earth, I sense its stirring. I tell you, the ice shall once again claim these lands.'

Gor'eth extended a finger that was no more than flanges sheathed in cured leather flesh. He traced a suture where it ran in a jagged line between the rises of the orbital ridges of the dragon skull's sockets. Then he gripped his stone weapon in both fists and brought it high up overhead to swing it crashing down upon the skull, splitting it into fragments.

He turned to his gathered brethren. 'Let us go.'

The file of silent figures climbed a trail that led to a bare rock ridge. Behind them, spanning its dark gap, the trellis-like bridge groaned and tilted ponderously from side to side. Thunderous cracking and popping split its length and sections fell, toppling, to disappear into the depths. After one immense shudder, the remaining structure collapsed in an impact that shook the ground the Imass stood upon and brought a small avalanche of loose rock and gravel tumbling down the slope.

Making the crest of the ridge, Gor'eth paused, glanced back down into the murk of the valley. A great billowing cloud of dust obscured the site where the bridge once stood. He returned his attention to the north, then studied his own skeletal hands.

Another Imass joined him. This one's skull bore a hideous crack that revealed withered fibrous remains within. 'I sense our brothers and sisters to the west.'

'Yes, Sholas. While we must yet walk.'

'Tellann lies beyond our reach – as yet.'

Gor'esh lowered his hands. 'Those broken must thus remain.'

'They will re-join us – eventually.'

The tendons of Gor'esh's neck creaked as he nodded his agreement. 'Yes, Sholas. Eventually. As before.'

They started down the slope to where the grade shallowed and a forest of thin spruce boles gripped the bare talus.

CHAPTER X

ON HIS THIRD DAY DESCENDING INTO THE VALLEYS AND RIDGES of the Bain Holding, Orman spotted something strange in a meadow of waving tall green grasses far below. It was the single figure of a large man running. But ponderously, awkwardly so. And, breaking from the cover of a nearby treeline, a pursuing party of some ten men. Orman froze in his sliding descent down a steep scree slope. He shaded his one good eye. He might be mistaken, what with his different vision now, but that shambling figure practically had the appearance of a bear running on two legs.

He charged down the slope. He skittered and slid, kicked up a great fan of tumbling gravel and rocks. These he leapt in greater and greater jumps until an ankle turned on a loose rock and he joined the minor landslide as one more object making its way in the inevitable rush, rolling and tumbling, down to the rocky base. As the hissing wash of stones slowed he jumped up and cleared the mass of boulders awaiting him, rolled, and leapt up to continue running.

He drew his hatchets as he ran. He jumped fallen logs, or attempted to, as he still was not used to his differing vision and fell a few times. Standing, damning the irreversible loss, he shouldered through dense thickets then burst forth on to the meadow. The roars of battle-joy he heard from over a nearby gentle rise confirmed his suspicions, and he charged.

From the crest he saw Old Bear himself below, surrounded by spearmen. The man held a body in front of him and this he raised in both arms over his head and threw upon a spearman, then charged. The ring flinched, men backpedalling. Old Bear batted the glinting spearheads aside.

Orman was spotted and the ring eased back into a line, facing the two of them. He charged in headlong. He took one prodding spear on the notch of his bearded hatchet and yanked the haft aside, then smashed his blade into the nook where shoulder met neck and half decapitated the man. A spear thrust at him from his blind side, appearing from nowhere, and he was rocked by the surprise. He had only an instant to realize what a disadvantage he now possessed and took to bobbing his head from side to side. He successfully knocked aside two more thrusts.

Roaring with laughter now, Old Bear picked up another corpse to hurl on to the spearmen. He took a thrust in the shoulder for his trouble.

'Stop fooling around!' Orman yelled.

Another spearman lunged forward. Old Bear snatched the weapon from his hands and cracked the butt-end across his head, felling him. 'Fooling around?' he bellowed, affronted. 'Why, you young pup!'

Three charged. Orman hurled a hatchet, taking one in the chest. The remaining two Old Bear somehow managed to force to cross hafts, and these he yanked from their hands. A blow from one of his huge fists felled one. The other fled. The remaining ones also backed off then turned to flee.

Old Bear simply waved them off as he stood puffing and drawing in great lungfuls of air. He eyed Orman and a wide grin spread across his shaggy features. Then he frowned. 'I resent your interference,' he said, practically wheezing.

'I saved your life, you old fool.'

Old Bear waved a dismissal over the fallen men. 'All you did was cheat me of a great boast – should I have succeeded.'

'Should you have succeeded,' Orman agreed.

The grin returned and the old man opened one arm – his good arm – and Orman embraced him. Old Bear pounded his back. 'Good to see you, y'damned fool!' He took hold of Orman's shoulder and pulled him away to give him a good look up and down. Orman noted the flinch as he examined his face. 'Running off north! What do you think you could accomplish?'

'I saw him.'

The old man's tangled greying brows rose. Even the one over the blind milky eye. 'Really? You met Buri? What did he say?'

What Buri said returned to Orman's thoughts, and he half turned away. He shook his head.

Old Bear pulled a hand through his thick beard. 'Ach – you tried, lad.' He winced and gripped his shoulder. 'Damned bastards tickled me.'

Orman took his arm. 'Let's find a stream. Clean that wound.'

Old Bear motioned to Orman's patch as they made their way down the slope. 'We're practically twins now!' he chortled.

Orman laughed as well. 'Yes – how will they ever tell us apart? So, what's going on? What in the name of the ancients are you doing here?'

'Your plan was accepted, Orman. We're working with the Losts.'

'My plan? It wasn't my plan. Was one of the Lost hearth-guards' . . . Cal, I think.'

The old man made a face as if insulted. 'Of course it was your plan! No dim hearthguard of the Losts could come up with a decent plan!' He grinned anew. 'Only the Sayers.'

Orman just snorted. Then he drew a hard breath, tensing himself. 'Any word . . . on Jass?'

Old Bear lost his grin. He cleared his throat as he limped along. 'No, lad. He's a hostage of the Bains. They'll keep him safe. Don't you worry. It's the old ways.'

'And Lotji?'

'He's out there somewhere. It's one big running battle. We're trying to herd them together. Us 'n' the Losts. But they just ain't organized. Just a bunch of raiding bands, all independent.' The man grumbled under his breath. 'Like herding cats.'

'Well . . . I'm for Lotji.'

The big man shook his head. 'Don't do it, lad. He'll run you through with Svalthbrul.'

'I'll just have to take my chances.'

But Old Bear would not stop shaking his shaggy head. 'No, lad. Don't you lot there in Curl tell the old tales?'

Orman snorted his scepticism. 'You mean that it never misses?'

'That's right, lad. Svalthbrul, once loosed, never misses its mark.'

He had no answer for that. Yet Buri had advised he challenge Lotji, and he must know the truth of those old tales, if anyone did. Anyway, he really had no choice in the matter. It would be confronting Lotji, or abandoning everything he believed about himself. It was no choice at all.

They found a stream and Orman cleaned and bound Bear's shoulder. Then they headed south, down the valley. The shadows lengthened; the sun sizzled atop the ridge to the west. Twilight already pooled in the depths of this particularly steep mountain vale. Orman was considering finding a place to settle in for the night when he heard the clash of fighting echoing from the very bottom of the valley. He and Bear broke into a trot, started jogging down the forested slope.

He glimpsed figures through the trees running parallel to them. Too many to be any allies of theirs. In his rush he'd left Bear behind, and now he broke through a dense thicket of tearing brush to nearly fall into a shallow stream. Halfway across the rushing water, hunched amid gleaming wet boulders, were the Reddin brothers with Vala, Jass's mother. Even as he watched, arrows glanced from the rocks; they were pinned down by a band of archers on the opposite shore.

Lowlanders came charging out past the line of bowmen, making for them. Bodies lay in the stream all about the hearthguards and Vala, like boulders themselves. The rushing waters coursed over them as over any other obstruction.

Orman charged out as well. He hoped that the archers on the far shore would merely take him for one of their own. Some eight attackers now engaged the brothers and Vala. The three formed a rough triangle amid the rocks. The archers held off, not wanting to hit their fellows. When Orman neared the fight he lashed out with his hatchets, chopping down through the shoulder of one attacker, then stabbing another through the ribs with the spike of his second. The brothers and Vala instantly shifted to the attack. Both brothers had their shields up and were using their swords one-handed. Vala fought with long-knives. She cut down two of the attacking men, and a woman, in swift blows that amazed Orman. Her power was such that she nearly severed a man's leg at the thigh.

An arrow cut angrily past his head and he threw himself low in the frigid stream, on his haunches, next to Keth – or the brother he was fairly certain was Keth.

'I did not think I would see you again,' Vala shouted from where she crouched.

'I've come for Lotji,' he called back.

She gave a fierce nod, answered, 'As have I.' Roaring gusts of laughter sounded from the forested slope above the stream and Orman shared a grin with the Reddin brothers. 'Old Bear is keeping them busy,' Vala said.

Keth – or was it Kasson? – directed Orman's gaze to the stream. He peered about for a moment, uncertain, then he saw it: where the waves slapped up over the fallen bodies the water left behind a wash of sand, and amid the sifting granules tiny flecks gleamed in the fading light. It was as if someone had tossed a handful of gold dust over the corpses.

Orman could only shake his head at the poetry of it. 'They came seeking gold . . .' he said.

'. . . and they found it,' Keth finished.

The other brother motioned to Kyle's patch. 'The Eithjar reported you had lost your eye. They say that one who loses an eye gains a second sight.'

Orman offered a weak smile; they were trying to cheer him up, but they all knew what a handicap he now carried in any battle.

Vala had been studying both valley slopes, and now she nodded to herself. 'Very good. I believe we've drawn them in. Now it's time to push them.' She faced the north, upstream, and waved a hand low over the surface of the chilling water. It looked to Orman as if she were casting something out across the stream, or perhaps summoning something.

The arrow fire intensified. It seemed more of the outlanders had arrived. He dared a glance over the top of his cover; some twenty archers were now creeping out into the stream, stepping over the wet rocks, searching for sound footing.

Damn the hoary old Taker! It would be the end if they succeeded in flushing them.

Keth tapped his shoulder, inclined his head upstream. Orman squinted into the shadows of the gathering dusk. A fog was rising. It came tumbling down the stream in thick billows and rolls. And it was no normal mist or haze as Orman could hardly see through it.

Curses sounded from the archers, along with mutterings about Iceblood magics. A new party of attackers came crashing through the thick verge along the shore. Here they halted, blinking. They took in the descending wall of fog, the archers now retreating before it, and they too ran.

The treacle billows washed over them, and the shocking chill stole Orman's breath. Stars of frost appeared on the iron of his hatchets. He felt his beard frosting over. Yet while the cold was sharp, even biting, he did not feel uncomfortable. Instead, as before, he felt refreshed, even invigorated.

They straightened. Their breath plumed in the icy fog. Vala gestured anew by thrusting her hands down the slope, then she waved for them to accompany her and started slogging through the water.

Far off, disembodied in the fog, came Old Bear's booming laughter.

'Was that them?' Orman asked.

'Who?'

'The invaders.'

Vala's laugh was just as loud and unreserved as Old Bear's. 'That was a scouting party. The main body is camped to the south. We will attack on the morrow.'

Orman almost laughed himself. 'Us? Attack? How many of them are there?'

'Some five hundred,' she answered, indifferent.

'So all ten of us have them surrounded?'

'The Losts have hired mercenary hearthguards,' Kasson explained in his soft voice, perhaps so quiet he never used it.

'Must have amassed a lot of gold . . .' Keth mused.

That was the most he'd heard from either of them; they seemed to get quite voluble during a fight.

'Find a campsite and start a fire,' Vala told them.

'A fire?' Orman wondered.

Vala smiled indulgently. 'None will see it in this fog. I have no use for it – but you might wish to dry yourself.'

Her leathers were rimed with ice, yet mist drifted from her as if the Iceblood woman were afire. Orman knew it was not heat driving those tendrils of mist; he knew that if he touched her, his hand would probably freeze. He ducked his head. 'Thank you.' Then he remembered he was walking with Jass's mother – a lover of his own father – and what had happened, and he hung his head even more. 'I'm sorry,' he murmured.

'Do not chastise yourself. The Eithjar told me of it. Your only mistake was in not understanding that Lotji is very . . . old-fashioned.'

'Old-fashioned?'

Her mane of black hair was frozen down her back and it crackled when she moved. 'For Lotji, the old bloodfeud and vendetta remain everything. That is what drives him. These invaders, these low-landers . . . he cares nothing for them.'

'I see. So he is here for you Sayers.'

'And you.'

The Reddin brothers had selected a copse of trees to camp in and had started gathering dry branches for a fire. The fog remained dense about them as if they had been transported to some other-world where shapes emerged suddenly from shifting walls of haze, and sounds returned distorted and echoing eerily.

'Me?'

Vala's smile appeared touched with melancholy. 'Haven't you seen it yet, Orman?'

He had no idea what the Iceblood woman was hinting at. 'Seen what?'

'We are the same, you and I. Your people and mine. We share the same ancestors from long ago.'

Orman stared, dumbfounded. Impossible, he thought. How could that possibly be? They are Icebloods!

Vala continued, her voice calm, almost wistful. 'Your clans separated from ours long ago to make their own way in the southlands. They mixed with humans they found there. Over the generations we drifted apart. Yet not so far apart. Orman, our numbers are few, we remaining clans. Our blood is too similar. When we wish to add to our numbers we take a mate from among you lowlanders – our distant cousins. Or, sometimes, we offer a position in our families to those few who arise every generation or so who seem to fit in among us.'

She regarded him directly now. Her strange oval eyes seemed to glow amber in the shadows. 'Such an offer was made to your father. And so . . . whatever should happen . . .' Her gaze released him and he found he could breathe once more. 'Well . . . please know that I am glad you and Jass met. Glad that you did what you could for him.'

The Iceblood woman seemed to be suggesting that nothing more could be done for her son – his half-brother. Yet Old Bear had told him not to worry. He fought to find his voice, murmured huskily, 'We'll get him back. I swear.'

Her half-smile simply eased into a purer sort of wistfulness and she walked away to disappear into the shifting banks of fog. Orman knelt on his haunches with Keth and Kasson, who were minding the fire. 'Where's Shortshanks?'

'With them,' said Keth – or was it Kasson? He was no longer certain he had them straight after all.

'Sleep,' said the other. 'We'll trade off watches.'

'What of Bear?'

They shook their heads. 'He will not come to the fire,' said one. 'He says he does not want to smell of smoke but I think he doesn't like fire when he's raising the bear.'

'Raising the bear? So it's not some sort of spell? He truly is a shapeshifter?'

'Have you not heard all the old tales? It was quite common, once. Now he is the last.'

'And the morrow? What is the plan?'

But the brothers appeared to have used up their store of words, and merely glanced to one another, shrugging.

Orman lay down on a brushed-together bed of dried leaves and needles, facing the fire, and watched the tendrils of mist rising from his drying leathers wend their way up to the surrounding billows and there mingle among them.

*

Dawn came as a diffuse pewter-grey light. The fog cover remained. If anything, it had thickened. The cold was intense. Frost glazed the blades of his hatchets and the grass blades and brush crunched underfoot. Vala motioned them on; she appeared to be able to penetrate the dense soup of haze. Orman reflected that, while she might claim they shared an ancestry, he still couldn't see a damned thing.

They descended a dividing ridge into another valley, this one not so steep. Fog still obscured all the distances where trees stood as ghosts, and boulders emerged like cave openings into darkness. Distantly, Orman could make out many voices and the jangle and ringing of equipment.

'They are searching the fog,' Vala snorted. 'Fools.' She motioned to the Reddin brothers. 'Time to push them in. Spread out. A slow sweep down the side.'

The brothers nodded and moved off. They were readying their shields when the mist swallowed them. 'What of us?' he asked.

'We will stay together. We are after the same thing.' She motioned him off a little. He refreshed his grip on his hatchets and stepped aside until Vala became a shadow amid the haze. Then he began edging his way down the valley side.

Men and women called to each other further down the slope. Their accent was strange, yet he could understand some of the basic words. Outlanders. He considered shouting confusing orders, then decided a silent approach would be best.

The clash and grating of weapons sounded from his right, followed by the yell of a wounded man, cut short. As Orman felt his way down, a figure emerged ahead from the coursing banks of fog. It was a man shielding his gaze to peer up into the haze.

'Who is that?' the fellow called. 'Name yourself!'

'Greki,' Orman answered.

'Greki? Greki who?'

Still advancing, Orman said, 'Greki . . . the False,' and lunged, swinging a hatchet upwards to catch the man under his jaw, splitting it. The fellow gurgled a howl, clutching his face, and fell. Orman finished him with a cut to the back of the neck.

'Who is that?' someone shouted from further down among the

347

brush. More than one came running. Orman crouched to ready himself. Fortunately, they came in a disorganized rush; stumbling upon him almost one by one. Every advantage was Orman's as he knew that whoever appeared would be his enemy. He did not bother with the niceties but took out knees and arms – whichever was nearest – then finished with single crippling blows and moved on.

The panicked calls and clash of blows exchanged and shrieks of wounded was constant now up and down the thinly treed valley side. The fog remained so thick Orman could make out none of the battle, and neither, he knew, could the invaders. It seemed that only the Icebloods could penetrate the haze. A powerful advantage for any engagement.

He felled three more as he edged further down the slope. The last actually still held a raised crossbow as he futilely searched the fog for a target. Orman almost felt sorry for the fool.

A shape appeared next to him so close and so silently that he flinched, almost falling to the ground as the tall figure of Jaochim reared over him. The Iceblood wore mere hunting leathers, and held two long-hafted bearded axes. 'You are falling behind,' he growled. 'The battle is on the valley floor. Speed is our ally. We must break them before they organize a defence.'

'I am sorry,' Orman stammered.

Jaochim raised one axe almost in salute. 'Never mind.' Then he paused, frowning. 'Did you really meet with Buri?'

'Yes.'

'And what did he say?'

'He said he was readying himself for the true enemy.'

The Iceblood appeared startled by that. 'The true enemy,' he murmured to himself. 'Those words?'

'Yes.'

Jaochim scanned the fog. Again he seemed to speak aloud to himself: 'Then we are wasting our time here.' He suddenly waved all such concerns away, a gesture that reminded Orman of Old Bear. 'Hunh. Well, run now. Hack and run.' Then, unaccountably, he suddenly offered a fey smile that bared his prominent canines. 'Lotji is here.' And he loped off, to disappear into the swirling mist.

Reminded of what he should be doing, Orman set off running pell-mell down the slope.

Figures appeared through the fog's chiaroscuro of shadow and light. He merely slashed at them in passing. What a fool he'd been! Wasting his time among these outlying pickets and scouts! It was

Lotji he wanted – and he'd cut his way through the middle of this army to find him.

Following the clashes and shouts, he tracked down the main engagement. Figures charged him but he did not pursue the duels: he slashed and ran on. He passed knots of mêlées, glimpsed the Reddin brothers, back to back, surrounded but calmly defending – he left them to it.

He burst into the ruins of a temporary camp of trampled tents, smouldering fires, scattered fallen spears and equipment. And bodies. Many bodies. All invaders as far as he could see.

He turned full circle to scan the banks of mists. This was useless. He could search until the dawn and not come across the man. Then it struck him: the one thing that would draw him in.

He lifted his hands to his mouth. '*Lotji!* I am come for you! Where are you? Coward!' He stumbled on. 'I challenge you!' Rounding a half-fallen tent, he practically crashed into a band of invaders.

'Get him!' one screamed.

Orman yelled a war-bellow and threw himself upon them, slashing right and left. But there were far too many. He spike-thrust one in the mouth and tried to disengage while they shifted, working round to his blind side. Then one threw his cloak on to his neighbour, knifed another, and leapt to Orman's side – Gerrun Shortshanks. 'Heard you yelling,' he grinned.

Orman nodded his gratitude then turned to the remaining troop, who were edging inward, wary but determined. Gerrun startled him by charging one side. 'Don't wait for them!' he yelled, taking a sword-swing on one dirk blade and kicking the man down.

Orman followed his example. It was a shifting, swirling mêlée from then on. He blocked blows with his hatchet, took out knees with counter-attacks, dodged, and shifted his head left and right, ever circling. One canny fellow kept him pinned on his blind side until he surprised him by tossing a hatchet to wind him and slow him down long enough to snatch up a fallen spear and run him through. He spun then, quickly, but not quickly enough as another invader slipped inside the spear from his left, blocking the haft to slash a blow that Orman only slipped by throwing himself backwards. He lost the spear in doing so.

The outlander closed, shortsword reversed. Orman rolled, and as he did the fellow grunted and clasped a hand to his chest. The grip of a knife stood there from his leathers. He fell to his knees, cursed impressively, and toppled.

Orman straightened, panting, his limbs quivering. He retrieved the spear. Gerrun appeared next to him. The short man grinned up at him and winked. 'You let him get inside,' he said.

'I'll try to watch for that,' Orman allowed. His mouth was as dry as stone.

'This way,' Shortshanks said, and headed off. Suddenly, he stopped, and tottered back into Orman's arms. His front was slashed open and blood and inner fluids now poured down his fine felt trousers all the way to his cured leather boots. Orman gently lowered him, dead already, to the trampled grasses. He straightened then, knowing what he would see: Lotji standing a short distance off amid the fog, leaning upon Svalthbrul.

'It is I who must challenge you,' the Bain said.

'Don't be a fool! There are hundreds of invaders! We must work together to turn them away!'

But the Bain only shook his head. He straightened, levelled Svalthbrul at Orman. 'A challenge, once given, must be answered.' He smiled then, and Orman was reminded of Jaochim's smile. 'And thankfully we are upon Bain lands.'

The knapped stone spearhead gleamed wet with blood. This close, it appeared enormous. Lotji's arms tensed for the thrust. Orman realized he held no weapon and snatched his fighting knives from the rear of his belt. 'Fool!' he damned the man, fully expecting this to be his last moment.

Both he and Lotji froze then, utterly shocked by a bellowed roar bursting so close that Orman swore he felt the hot breath. An enormous black shape burst through the mist. A swatting paw the size of a shield knocked Lotji tumbling away, to disappear into the swirling scarves of haze. The beast, the size of a wagon, lumbered off in pursuit and disappeared. Orman shouted uselessly, 'No! He has Svalthbrul!' Cursing the old man for a fool, he gave chase.

The crashing and roars of their battle guided him. He stumbled amid the wreckage of flattened torn tents, scattered cook-fires and abandoned equipment. Invaders ran straight past him in their panic to flee the duel. The trail of debris and deep pawprints torn in the soft ground led onward out of the camp to a copse of ghostly alder and birch. Orman found shattered trunks and trees that had been knocked askew and were now leaning drunkenly. The ground was torn by claws. Blood lay splashed across one fallen bole. He followed, knives readied.

The tumult subsided. Amid the coursing banners of fog, he glimpsed a huge dark figure lying across shattered trunks. Old Bear.

He quickly sheathed his blades and cradled the man's bloodied head.

'Speak to me, old man.'

Old Bear drew a long, shuddering breath. 'What use is a glorious duel,' he growled, 'when no one can see a blasted thing!'

Orman burst out a laugh. 'Y'damned old fool!'

'It would have been something to boast of,' Old Bear answered, his voice far softer now. 'Anyway,' he swallowed, said wearily, 'softened him up for you.'

'Should've stayed out of it. It's my fight.'

The old man attempted to rise. 'No, no. Would've been . . . would've . . .' He eased back, his limbs relaxing.

'Would've been something for the hero songs,' Orman finished.

Old Bear just nodded his shaggy head. His remaining brown eye closed and Orman felt his massive frame ease into death. He gently set the head down and stood.

It was strange, he reflected. Outland invaders were here to steal the land from his own people, yet it was one of his own who had taken everything from him. 'I know you are there!' he called to the mists. 'Let us end this now.'

As if answering a draught of fresh wind, the fog thinned. Off a short distance stood Lotji. 'I wanted you to see your end!' he shouted. He drew back his arm and launched Svalthbrul. Orman flinched. For some reason he hadn't expected the man to simply throw the spear. He thought he'd have a chance to engage. Some sort of fair chance.

A grating thud sounded then and Orman blinked, surprised. Instead of being thrust through as he'd expected, he found the spear Svalthbrul jutting from the ground not an arm's length from him. Its thick haft stood quivering.

Just as he had left it, he realized. When he had given it to Lotji.

Given it. And he remembered Old Bear's words: 'wrested it from the dead hand of Jorgan Bain . . .'

Svalthbrul, it seemed, was still his.

He snatched it up. Raised his gaze to Lotji. The Bain was staring, his eyes widening now. Unaccountably, he laughed, almost in approval or resignation, and gravely saluted Orman. Then he turned and walked away to disappear into the mists.

Orman brought the cold faceted stone head of the spear to his lips and did what he knew Lotji now understood, and accepted, as his unavoidable fate. *Find the bastard,* he whispered, and heaved the weapon as high as he possessed the strength to do. Svalthbrul flew

351

from his hand, almost leaping, and vanished. He drew his fighting knives and followed the line the weapon's passage had cleaved through the mist.

Distantly, it registered upon him that the noise and tumult of battle had faded almost completely. He stepped over the corpses of fallen outlanders. Ahead, three standing figures solidified from the haze. He heard their laboured exhausted breathing. Sensing his approach, they tensed, swords rising.

He met three soldiers, two women and one man, armoured alike in long mail coats, belted, with broad shields and helmets. Their shields featured a much battered and scraped field of dark red with some sort of wiggly line across.

'Identify yourself,' the man ordered.

'Orman, hearthguard to the Sayers.'

The three relaxed. The man sheathed his longsword. 'Jup Alat. We are with the Losts. This is Laurel and Leena. Fight's over, I think. What can we do for you?'

He motioned onward behind them. 'I'm tracking someone.'

The big fellow frowned. 'No one passed us.'

'Nevertheless. If I may?'

The three parted. 'Certainly. If you wish.'

Orman nodded and continued on. The three stood motionless, peering after him until the coursing fog closed between them once more.

He walked until he began to suspect that he'd somehow lost the trail, or had perhaps passed where the weapon had fallen. He paused then, listening. A stream of some sort rushed and hissed a good distance off. A freshening wind shushed through tree boughs. Far off, people called to one another through the fog.

An explosive wet cough sounded to one side. Orman tightened his grip on his weapons and closed. He found Lotji standing, tottering. The spear Svalthbrul had driven through him straight up and down; its end stood above his head, the haft disappearing into one shoulder. The spearhead stood forward, almost straight down, from his pelvis. At some noise from Orman the Bain turned, slowly, in lurching steps.

His grin was a smear of blood-red. The mouth worked and out came a gurgled, 'You win.'

'I care nothing for your damned feuds. Where is he?'

'Who?'

'*Jass!* Damn you!'

'Ah. Him.' The man drew a shuddering breath. His eyes closed, then fluttered, blinking. It occurred to Orman that the man could not fall even if he wanted to. The haft of Svalthbrul held him rigid, tree-straight. His knees buckled and he fell straight down. Svalthbrul's blade drove into the ground and the man moaned an agony beyond reason. His head rose, revealing that he grinned once more as if at some cosmic jest. 'I would try the Greathall,' he mouthed.

Enraged, Orman kicked him down. He fell and lay motionless.

Bending, Orman took hold of the wet, bloodied haft close behind the spearhead and yanked. He set one boot against the man's thigh and yanked again. The haft came sliding free in a slither of fluids. Mist curled from the gore-slick length.

'And what of Jass?' Vala spoke from behind and Orman spun. She stood breathing deeply, her long-knives bloodied to the grips, her forearms splashed.

'He said to try the Greathall.'

The news rocked the woman. Open dread filled her alien oval eyes. 'The Greathall is more than a day south of here,' she breathed, appalled.

Orman wasn't certain he understood. 'But then . . .'

Vala did not pause to answer. She spun and ran. He took a few faltering steps after her, calling, 'Vala! Vala . . . Dammit to the Abyss.'

Twin figures came jogging up through the thinning fog: the Reddin brothers. Both appeared hale, if sliced and cut by minor wounds. Neither carried his shield, which must have been battered to pieces in the fighting. 'Here you are,' said one, Keth perhaps.

'Where is Bain Greathall?' he demanded.

'South of here,' answered the other.

'South? Where?'

One brother extended an arm, gesturing downhill. 'South.'

Orman took off at a jog. After a short time he found the brothers flanking him. 'What is it?' one asked.

'Jass is at the Greathall.'

They entered a more mature forest of tall pine and birch and the ground opened up. They had left behind the localized banks of fog. Orman glimpsed other figures also fleeing south through the woods. He ignored them.

'If there are any Bains left they will be defending the Greathall,' one brother offered.

'Let us hope,' Orman muttered beneath his breath.

~

Through the rest of the day and into the night they alternated between walking and jogging. The sky was clear and bright. The Great Ice Bridge could clearly be seen spanning the entire inverted bowl above. It glittered from one horizon to the other. The moon, battered and blurry still from the strange fires that burst upon it years ago, was a sickle blade waxing.

They ran straight past camps of some few stragglers, or latecomers. These men and women watched them without a shouted curse, a yell, or a fired arrow. It was as if they considered them some sort of ghosts, such as the Eithjar.

Dawn's orange light brightened behind an eastern ridge. In its glow Orman spotted the faint smudge of black smoke rising from the forest canopy below. He broke into a run.

The pall was quite distant. He had to splash through two small streams and push his way through dense underbrush. He heard the brothers following. He burst through to cleared fields and saw ahead the Bain Greathall, aflame. Figures surrounded it.

Orman could not be certain, but he believed he howled something as he charged. Faces turned his way. He crashed into armed men and women, thrust right and left. He was now truly blind in a red mist of fury and a crushing dread. More lowlanders came closing in from surrounding the hall. The brothers joined him but instead of remaining within their cover he charged from one man or woman to the next. Some remaining rational part of him seemed to watch this and wonder whether Old Bear's talent of ferocious shapeshifting had passed to him.

He then became aware of himself standing motionless, spellbound, exhausted, his limbs quivering, before the dark opening of the gaping entrance. The arrow-pierced corpse of an Iceblood, an old man, lay upon the stairs. Vala held the doorway. Smoke gouted out about her in a black river. Embers glowed in her hair. Her leathers were slashed over countless wounds – but that was as nothing to the agony in her wild staring eyes. Devastation had hollowed them completely. But most of all what held him breathless and fascinated was their grim and absolute despair.

He reached out to her; she flinched away as if some wild beast, turned, and ran within to disappear among the licking flames and smoke. He lunged up the stairs but hands held him back. He believed he howled and fought then froze, transfixed.

Through the billowing smoke he'd glimpsed something.

Amid the churning coils, the collapsing roof-timbers, something hung from the immense log that was the roof crossbeam. A small figure swinging ever so slightly. His leathers were curling and smoking in the intense heat. His hands were tied behind his back and he'd been thrust through the chest.

Thrust through by Svalthbrul – the weapon he now held in his hands. A burden he now knew to be wholly and inescapably cursed.

He screamed then. Bellowed to the sky. Howled on and on until something struck him and he fell, knowing nothing more.

*

He awoke in an out-building, a small hut of chinked logs. He smelled stale smoke. Svalthbrul stood leaning next to his cot. He left it there and arose to push open the door of thin wooden slats. It was late in the day. White smoke wafted from the collapsed ruins of the burnt Greathall.

Keth Reddin stood without, arms crossed. Orman nodded him a greeting.

'The Bains are no more,' Keth said.

'Yes.'

'I am sorry for the loss of your half-brother.'

'Thank you.'

Keth nodded; he'd said what he meant to say and was finished.

Orman took a deep breath of the reviving air. 'We must return to Sayer Hall to bring word of this . . . this loss.' Keth nodded again.

The Reddin brother shifted to peer back through the open door. Orman followed his gaze. Yes. Svalthbrul. He took a hard breath to steel himself and re-entered the hut. Yes. He closed a fist upon the weapon. Though he now hated it, it was his. His burden to carry. His curse. If it could speak, he now understood it would be laughing at all the blood it had drunk, the discord and violence it had sown.

He ducked from the hut and crossed to the smouldering ruins. The brothers followed. He stood for a time facing the pile of ash and blackened logs, Svalthbrul cradled in his arms. He adjusted the patch of ragged leather he'd cut to cover his eye. He bowed to his fallen kin. There were no words to say. No tears to shed. His heart had been thrust through as irrevocably as Jass's. He was done, finished; as burnt and ashen within as the hulk of this Greathall.

He set off north.

*   *   *

It had taken only one salvo from Cartheron's springals to destroy the foremost of the vessels pursuing them. It erupted in a blast of

355

flying timbers and cartwheeling men, then sank as if pulled from beneath. The rest of the flotilla eased up oars. Their bow waves disappeared in a wash of dispersing foam, and Jute watched them diminish to the rear.

Another two days' journey brought them rounding a headland to enter a broad bay, its shore one of tall rock cliffs. Jutting from these cliffs, hard up to their very edge, stood the blunt cylinder of grey rock that was the Keep at Mantle town. As they approached, he kept an eye on the structure; something about its dimensions bothered him.

He leaned on the railing next to where the ex-Malazan officer, Giana Jalaz, stood with her bare forearms over the wood, an apple in one hand. 'I see ships,' he commented. Indeed, the masts of some handful of vessels rose from the waves at the base of the cliff beneath the tower. 'They are blockaded, you say?'

She took a bite, chewed. 'So I was told,' she answered round the mouthful. She raised the apple. 'Good thing you brought supplies.'

'That was not my intention, you can be sure . . .' he said, but she was moving now, signing something to the other soldiers who had accompanied her. They began pulling on their armour.

Giana herself simply yanked her thin blouse over her head and tossed it to Jute. Mechanically, unthinkingly, he caught and held it. It was warm from her body. Her upper torso was wide and muscular, her breasts small and high, the areolae dark. Only then did Jute realize he was staring and spun away.

'Hang on to that,' she told him. 'That's my one good shirt.'

He stammered, 'Of course.'

A low laugh from Ieleen made his ears heat. 'Getting changed, are we?' she enquired sweetly.

'Could be a fight,' Giana explained. He heard leather brush as she pulled on a gambeson, then the rattle and jangle of armour. 'Buckle me up, won't you?'

Still with his back to the disturbing north Genabackan woman, he said, 'Perhaps someone else . . .'

'Well, seeing as I'm blind,' Ieleen offered, 'she might not like the result if I took a hand. Go ahead, dear. You can tell me all about it later.' Then, even more disturbingly, the two women shared a laugh.

Jute decided that he was at a distinct disadvantage and that perhaps it would be best if he just went along with things. He turned and found the ex-Malazan officer waiting, her side to him, buckles of her hauberk presented. He set to work.

He was almost done when the woman yanked forward out of his grip. She growled, 'What in the name of the nitwit Boles is he doing?' Jute found the clasps again and finished up, squinting ahead where the *Resolute* had surged onward, its sweeps flashing.

'Charging the blockade, looks like.'

The woman turned to where the *Ragstopper* continued its steady pace. 'No flags. No signalling . . . Cartheron's letting them go?'

'They pretty much do whatever they want.'

She sent him a sceptical glance. 'You say those soldiers are Blue Shields?'

'Aye.'

'This I *have* to see. Can we close up?'

Jute considered. They could, he supposed. The Malazans would fight if it came to that – not that he was expecting any real resistance to Tyvar and his Blue Shields. He nodded, went to the stern railing, called, 'Follow the *Resolute*, Buen.'

'Aye, captain.' His first mate started chivvying the men and women at the oars.

He asked Giana, 'And once we are at Mantle? Then what?'

'That's Cartheron's call.'

'You must have some idea. What would you do?'

'Me?' She rubbed her jaw. 'I was never staff level. Strategy's not my strength. But seeing as that gang outside the walls wants our blood already . . .' She shrugged. 'Ever work as a mercenary, Captain Hernan?'

Mercenary? Him? He glanced back to Ieleen. She sat with her chin resting upon her walking stick. Her head was tilted as if she was listening to something faint and far off. Her expression was intent and focused, but not alarmed. 'I'm a businessman, not a mercenary,' he told Giana.

'Same thing,' she said. 'One just cleans up better than the other.'

As they neared the cliff's base, the blockade resolved into five man-o'-wars anchored in a wide semicircle, presumably just outside the range of what appeared to be two mangonels just visible atop the cliffs.

The *Resolute* did not pause. It pulled alongside the middle vessel, sweeps were shipped and grapnels flew to span the gap.

At his side, Giana allowed a grudging, 'Well executed, that.'

Yet the action at the vessels could not capture Jute's attention. Something about that squat so-called fortress kept nagging at him and now he recognized what it was: the damned thing was hardly larger than a guard tower.

This was it? The fabled fortress of the north? A wretched three-storey pile of rock that wouldn't count for more than a border keep back home in Falar?

Giana grunted a soft, '*Damn* . . .'

He spared the attack a glimpse. The *Resolute* had moved on to the next vessel to port, while the first, obviously captured, was now moving towards its brother in line on the starboard. He cleared his throat. 'Have you *been* to Mantle, Lieutenant Jalaz?'

Apparently unable to tear her astonished gaze from the attack, she shook her head. 'No. Never.'

'Well . . . you're looking at it.'

'A coupla fellows said there's not much to it— Gods! That's three now.'

Jute glanced to the attack. Tyvar's pocket army had now captured three vessels and these were all in motion, closing on the remaining two. As for the *Resolute*, she was hanging back, perhaps reduced to the barest skeleton crew.

The way to Mantle's harbour, such as it might be, was now completely open. Jute leaned over the stern railing. 'Take us in, Buen.'

'Aye, aye. Ahead now, lads!' the first mate roared. 'Take up all that damned cloth!'

Jute then turned to the bay. The *Ragstopper* was also closing. The *Supplicant* still held back. He wasn't troubled by that – typical of the sorceress's preference for staying low in the weeds.

Sweeps alone drew them in close to the bottom of the cliffs. Here awaited a meagre wharf of driven logs covered by planks that extended a few paces out over a shore of boulders and fallen rock. One low two-masted galley lay at berth here, and its crew members helped them tie off the *Dawn*.

The *Resolute* and her captured vessels of the shattered blockade looked to be dropping anchor further out. A longboat was on its way from one of them. Presumably it held Tyvar himself. The *Ragstopper* was limping in after the *Dawn*.

Jute turned to his wife. 'Going for another negotiation, dearest.'

'Let's hope this one goes better than the last,' she commented.

Jute simply winced. 'Buen,' he called, 'master-at-arms . . . guard the ship.'

'Aye, captain,' Letita answered in a loud shout, shooting a glance Giana's way.

A plank was being levered into place as a gangway. Here Jute motioned, inviting Giana to join him. She shook her head. 'Like I said, I'm not staff level.'

'Then you will remain?'

'Yes.'

Jute remembered his earlier alarm at the prospect of all these ex-Malazan soldiers on board his vessel – now he felt reassured. Leaning against the side next to the gangway was the khall-head Malazan Cartheron had saddled him with in Wrongway. The man was eyeing him with his typical dreamy smile, which appeared knowing but was no doubt just empty-headed. A wad of the leaf was fat in one cheek.

'Give my regards to King Ronal,' the fellow murmured as he passed. Jute ignored him and walked on to descend the gangway.

The fellow who met him on the dock was a fat rascal who had the look of a pirate about him. Certainly not a local. Jute pegged him as a Genabackan. Most of the fortune-hunters were from that nearby continent.

'Hello,' the fellow greeted him cheerily. 'Welcome to Mantle!'

'And you are?'

'Name's Enguf. Enguf the Broad they call me.'

'Are you surrendering?'

The fellow's thick tangled brows rose in surprise. 'What, me? Surrender?'

'You're an outlander.'

'Not at all! Well, yes . . . However, you are now looking at Mantle's own navy.'

'Since we saw the Blue Shields,' another of the crewmen muttered, and Enguf shot him a dark glare.

The *Ragstopper* drew abreast of the wharf and crewmen caught tossed lines. Jute inspected the cliff, searching for a way up. A set of wooden stairs switchbacked up the sheer rock face. The prospect looked more dangerous than any sea battle.

Cartheron joined him on the wharf. Jute gave him a hard stare, said, 'You just had to do it . . .'

The old Malazan officer waved his glower aside. 'I saw I had a chance so I took it – what d'y expect?'

Jute shook his head.

The longboat arrived and Tyvar, accompanied by his second, Haagen, climbed up on to the wharf. Enguf, a Genabackan, bowed to the two. 'An honour, sors,' the big pirate greeted them.

'And you are?' Tyvar enquired.

'Ah, Enguf, sir. Enguf the Broad.'

Tyvar grinned behind his thick beard and thumped a gauntleted hand to Haagen's arm. 'There's a name well known to the Southern Confederacy.'

'He claims to be what's left of the Mantle navy,' Jute explained.

Tyvar looked the man up and down and made a show of stroking his beard. 'Is that so? Working with us, are you?' He pounded Enguf on the arm as well. 'Excellent!'

The pirate bobbed his head, smiling rather stiffly, and rubbed his arm.

Cartheron was squinting up the cliff face. 'We have to climb *that*? Don't think it's worth it.'

'Perhaps . . . just to be careful,' Tyvar murmured, and unbuckled his cloak and started on his hauberk below. Enguf waved over a crewman, who took up the equipment. Divested of his armour, the mercenary remained just as impressive in the sweep of his shoulders and chest. He wore a loose tunic of quilted and padded linen that hung down to his knees, and soft leather trousers beneath. Jute felt like something of a bedraggled drowned rat next to him, while poor Cartheron resembled more the dock-sweeper. 'Rather than hold prisoners,' Tyvar told Enguf, 'my men will be dropping the captured crews on the shore a distance from here. Is that acceptable, captain?' He rebuckled his belt at his waist and hung his bastardsword.

Enguf bobbed his head again. 'Oh yes. Quite, ah, acceptable.'

'Excellent.' The Blue Shield commander gestured an invitation towards the stairs. 'Shall we?'

Jute was not one for heights. He kept his gaze raised to the top where the stairs ended at a landing of planks. Each wobble and groan of the wood made his heart hammer, and his hands were slick upon the worn timbers. Tyvar led while Cartheron came last. Jute knew the old Malazan officer was falling behind, but he couldn't force himself to turn to look back. 'Are you with us, sir?' he called.

After a long silence the man's weak answer came drifting up with the wind: 'Fucking stairs.'

Eventually, far beyond the length of time Jute thought it should take them, they reached the creaking and trembling landing atop the last switchback. Jute forced his numb wobbling legs to continue on to the exposed granite of the promontory itself.

From this vantage he had an excellent view of the site. The first thing he noted was that he'd been too harsh in his earlier impression: what the main tower lacked in height, it more than made up for in sheer bulk. And although it did possess only three storeys, these were three very tall storeys. It rose a stone's throw from him at the rear of an enclosed bailey that was a gently falling slope of trampled grass, beaten dirt, and exposed rock. A quite tall wall of what looked like piled shards of slate and other rock encircled it, forming a broad arc touching the cliff on both sides. Beyond the wall rose many plumes of white smoke – presumably the campfires of the besieging outlanders.

The bailey itself was currently jammed with humanity. They lay under awnings and tents, walked about, or just sat. He realized that here was where a good portion of the locals had fled.

Cartheron arrived, puffing and panting. He was rubbing his chest and wincing. 'I've lost my appetite for all this running around,' he grumbled to Jute.

Next to them, Tyvar drew a great breath of air, nodding to himself. 'Stone. All stone. A strong defensive position,' he said approvingly.

'Let's go meet the local tin-pot tyrant,' Cartheron said, and started forward.

The locals stopped them before they reached the tower. They weren't soldiers, but they obviously knew how to handle their spears and axes. Jute thought them rather negligent in not having a guard atop the stairs. But then he reflected on the nature of those stairs, and decided that maybe they were right in not expecting any horde to come charging up that way.

'May we have an audience with your ruler?' Tyvar boomed out. He held his hands far out from his sides. 'We have come to negotiate.'

'Your weapons,' one of the local spearmen commanded. 'You cannot speak with King Ronal while armed.'

Tyvar was all broad smiles and cheerfulness. 'Of course.' He unbuckled his belt and handed over his sword.

Jute looked to his own waist. All he carried was his eating dirk. This he offered, but a spearman just scowled at him as if he were a fool. Cartheron, it appeared, wasn't armed at all. They were escorted round the fat girth of the tower.

Jute's wonder at the construction of the edifice grew as he saw that the walls consisted of mammoth roughly dressed fieldstones that were clearly far too huge for any man, or gang of men, to raise. Who could have built using such immense rocks? Their techniques must have been far more sophisticated than this crude result.

The main entrance disturbed him further. An open portal it was, without a door. Visibly narrower towards the top than the base. And its top! Jute stared as he walked beneath: a titanic single rock lintel longer than any man.

Within, it was dark. Very dark. Its builders, it seemed, considered windows a luxury. Fires burning in braziers and torches in wall sconces provided what little light there was. The main floor was mostly all one great chamber. Spearmen and women crowded it. Straw was thick upon the stone-flagged floor. Dogs chased one another among the forest of legs. The guards parted for them while their escort urged them onward. Towards the far end of the chamber, the last file of guards grudgingly parted to reveal a long table of coarse-hewn timbers and a seated row of what Jute assumed to be the local dignitaries. The one at the centre wore a simple crown that was nothing more than a ring of bronze atop his long unkempt brown hair. This was fortunate, as otherwise Jute would have had no clue that this was the king. The man was small, and possessed the manic stare of a terrified predatory animal.

'What do you foreigners want?' this fellow demanded. 'You capture the vessels blocking the harbour and you expect a reward?' He waved them off. 'Take them and good riddance to you!'

Tyvar bowed. 'Greetings, King Ronal. My name is Tyvar Gendarian and these are my travelling companions, captains Cartheron Crust and Jute Hernan. Please be assured, we expect no reward at all. In fact, we are here to offer our swords in your service. I command two hundred mercenaries, while these captains offer their vessels.'

Jute marvelled at Tyvar's diplomacy and patience. He'd imagined that any man in his position would be unable to swallow such insults, yet the discourtesies merely brushed off the man as if he really did not give a damn about any of it. He was also rather taken aback to hear that he was offering the service of the *Silver Dawn*.

The king, and Jute wondered whether the man really was, or whether he merely chose to style himself one, snorted his disdain, or tried to, as one of his eyes kept twitching. He turned his head to peer at the men and women seated along the table. These were all quick to emulate his disapproval, with shakes of their heads and pursed lips.

'First,' he began, addressing Tyvar, 'the title is King Ronal the Bastard. And second, what do you expect for this service? Gold, no doubt. Well, you'll get none of it. If you think I will allow a crowd of armed foreigners into my fortress, you're a fool!' He waved Tyvar off. 'I'm not hiring outlanders. Take your ships and go!'

At the far end of the table a skinny old woman cleared her throat and the king shot her an annoyed glance. 'If I may, my king,' she began, and Jute recognized an unmistakable high imperial accent, 'I will countenance these mercenaries . . . if I may.'

362

King Ronal slouched back in his chair. He picked at the carcass of a bird before him. 'An outlander would vouch for fellow outlanders . . .' he mused, rather petulantly. Then, peering from Jute to Cartheron, he straightened. 'Ah, my apologies. Please know Malle of Gris, an adviser who has proved her value and trustworthiness. She is empowered to speak for the distant Malazan Empire, whose name we are not ignorant of. Her emperor offers his support. He would not see a fellow monarch driven from his lands. And understandably so.' He tore apart the remains of the bird. 'Very well. You have liberated the waterfront. It is yours to hold. Remain there. No more than ten of your number may enter Mantle at any one time.'

Tyvar bowed again, even deeper. 'My thanks, my king. We will defend the harbour to the death. You can be assured—'

King Ronal flicked his greasy fingers. 'Yes, yes. You may go now.'

Still bowed, Tyvar backed away. Jute followed his lead, backing away, facing forward, until the many spearmen closed the gap before him. He, Cartheron and Tyvar then turned and walked away.

Outside, Tyvar took a great breath of the cool mountain air and brushed his hands together as if to say: *and that is that.*

Cartheron let out a heavy sigh and rubbed the back of his neck. He muttered, perhaps to himself, 'For this I quit drinking?'

Tyvar set his wide fists to his waist, turned, and regarded them over the tangle of his russet beard. There was an almost mischievous glint in his eyes. 'Well . . . let us at least study the competition.' He started across the bailey. Jute and Cartheron hurried to keep up.

The stones of the wall enclosing the bailey proved as titanic as those of the tower. On the inside, the wall rose some two man-heights, or about half a rod in measure. Tyvar bounded up one of the earthwork ramps inside the wall. His mere presence seemed to bring into existence a path between the many spearmen and women crowding the way. Following more slowly, Jute and Cartheron had to weave through the scowling and suspicious northerners.

When Jute gained the wall he found that it was coarse indeed, archaic even; the huge flat stones merely lay atop one another without shaping or chiselling. At least a wooden catwalk ran behind – a later addition, perhaps. Outside the wall, a deep ditch doubled its height to any attacker. A cold wind buffeted him. The chilled air descended off the Salt range, visible above the rising forested foothills.

Beyond the ditch lay the sprawling encampment of the besieging outlanders – his countrymen included. The modest houses of Mantle town, mere shacks and huts, had long been occupied. Tents sprawled in an arc beyond, from cliff edge to cliff edge, in a broad semicircle. Multiple cook-fires sent up thin tendrils of smoke that were swiftly brushed to the south, out over the Sea of Gold. The besiegers sat about the fires, warming themselves, talking and joking. Snatches of laughter reached him, carried by the wind. Jute added up an estimate of just under three thousand. He turned round and studied those within – all of whom were armed – and came up with some five hundred. The usual ratio necessary to take a well-defended position is at least three to one. The attackers outnumbered such figures by far, yet so far they had failed to take the keep. That told him that these defenders were not the usual sort. The way each carried a spear or sword told him that they'd all lived their entire lives fighting already.

'Who commands this rabble?' Tyvar asked a northern woman who stood nearby, leaning on a spear.

The woman looked him up and down – Jute noted that she was almost as tall as Tyvar himself – and said, 'I know not nor do I care.' She pointedly turned away.

'Perhaps I may be of assistance . . .'

Jute turned as he again recognized the accent that belonged in the imperial capital at Unta. It was indeed the wiry old woman from the king's table. He offered her an Untan bow, which brought a smile to her thin pinched mouth, and she offered her hand, which he brushed with his lips.

'Very gracious of you, Captain Jute Hernan of Falar,' she said.

Tyvar imitated Jute's gesture, though he invested it with far more grace. 'I am honoured, Tyvar Gendarian,' the woman, Malle, said, with obvious feeling. Then she turned to Cartheron.

'Malle,' Cartheron said. 'Good to see you again. Been a while.'

She nodded. 'Crust. Glad you made it.'

'It weren't easy, I tell you.'

Jute looked between the two. Well, well. Here's a turn-up, as his wife would say.

'Thank you for your help.'

'So, can I go now?' Cartheron asked.

'Not yet.'

'I was promised I'd be cut loose after this,' the man growled in the closest note to anger Jute had heard from him.

'You will,' Malle assured him.

His answer was a dubious scowl. Malle turned to Tyvar. 'The only leader out there is a retired Letherii military officer named Teal. However, new soldiers and veterans are arriving all the time.'

'I thank you,' he replied. 'You are uncommonly well informed.'

Her smile turned thin, almost acerbic. 'That is my business. Also, I have in my hire two ex-cadre mages who are pledged to the defence.'

Jute shot Cartheron a glance, the obvious inference being Lady Orosenn. The old Malazan commander shook his head.

Tyvar no doubt caught the look, as did Malle, probably. He peered about, then lowered his head. 'We need not worry on that front,' he assured her.

Malle raised an expressive brow. She glanced back to the bay. 'The fourth ship? A mage?'

Tyvar nodded. 'She has granted me permission to speak of her. However, she prefers to remain . . . anonymous.'

'I see. Thank you, commander.' She inclined her head fractionally. 'If that is all, I can be found at the main table . . . where I busy myself listening to all of Ronal's relatives' offers to support them against him.'

Tyvar drew himself straight and bowed once more. 'Affairs of statehood. I quite understand. Until later, madam.'

Jute quickly sketched a bow.

Cartheron merely raised his chin in a lazy see-you-later farewell. After she was gone, he turned to Jute. 'About that lady there . . .'

'Don't get in her way – yes, I gathered that.'

Cartheron gave a very serious nod. 'You're a quick study.' He turned to Tyvar and crossed his arms. 'So . . . what do you think?'

'I think that if these defenders can hold on, then this rabble will just wander off.' He pulled at his beard thoughtfully. 'That is, unless someone out there can give the besiegers some sort of spine.'

'Riches – loot – are a great motivator,' Cartheron supplied.

Jute frowned his confusion at that. 'How do you know there are any riches here?'

Cartheron gave him a look that, back in the tent in Wrongway, he'd given one of his crew who'd asked a particularly stupid question. 'That doesn't matter,' he said, as if explaining something to some new recruit. 'What matters is what someone out there tells them.'

Jute felt his brows rising. 'Ah. I see.' Such a ploy as actually lying – deliberately or innocently – to one's people hadn't even occurred to him. However, if it got the job done . . . well, never mind, hey?

'And you, Tyvar?' Cartheron continued. 'Is this your fight?'

The big man frowned at the question. 'I do not know. Here is a battle. Yet . . . we've been forbidden from participating. I feel that

365

this is not it. However, best remain hopeful, eh?' And he slapped Cartheron on the back, almost toppling him from the wall.

For his part, Jute did not like being the object of so many hostile and evaluative eyes as he stood there exposed upon the defences. 'Perhaps we should retire?' he offered. Cartheron and Tyvar agreed, and they descended the beaten dirt rampart.

They crossed to the cliffs, and, in despair, Jute realized he'd have to descend the damned stairs in order to return to the *Dawn*. Only that could possibly have convinced him to set foot once more on the rickety construction. He managed it, but he had his eyes closed for most of the descent.

Back on board, he immediately went to Ieleen. 'Well,' he began, 'they're under siege. But they don't want our help.'

Her hands resting on her walking stick, she nodded her understanding. 'They're proud. This is their land. They don't want us here.'

'However,' Jute added, 'Tyvar pledged our support . . . and our vessels.'

She tilted her head in thought. 'Perhaps in case evacuation is necessary.'

Jute rubbed his chin; he hadn't thought of that. Where in the world would they take them? 'No. I don't think so. But good point.'

'So we wait.'

'Yes.' He cleared his throat. 'And, dearest . . . about this woman, Giana . . .'

'Yes?'

'Now, you know there's nothing there – really, there isn't.'

His wife gave a low throaty chuckle and shook her head. 'Oh, I know that's so.'

For some reason Jute felt rather piqued. 'Why would that be so?'

'Because she has eyes for our master-at-arms.'

Now he was confused. 'But she's . . .'

His wife was nodding. 'Yes, dearest. She most certainly is.'

*   *   *

Badlands refused to rest, and quickly shook off any help from Fisher. He led the bard and Jethiss north, and he did so in utter silence, without a glance to either of them. For his part, Fisher eased into the role of returning to the land of his youth. He'd grown up on the Myrni Holding, just to the east. They had taken in his mother, who

366

was of the ancient Fanyar Hold, long pushed out of her homeland. As such, a half-blood, he came to find that he was welcome in neither world. And so he had renounced his place among the Myrni, swearing never to return, and went to find his way in the world.

Yet return he had, from time to time. The last being some three decades ago – in the wider world he'd found that those of Iceblood descent lived a far greater allotment of years.

Each time he returned he'd encountered the same festering blood-feuds and vendettas, the same blind hatreds and stupid bigotries, and each time he'd vowed never to return again.

Yet here he was once more. For the last time, he suspected, as he had seen this same tragic story of invasion and obliteration play out before in many lands. Any subsistence society, even one that is small-scale horticultural, cannot possibly compete against the invasion of a full-scale agricultural society. The inequity in numbers is simply too great. The locals find themselves swamped every time. If not in one generation, then in two or three. Such has been the story for every region of human migration and settlement. Even regions that boast of themselves as 'pure' or 'native' stand upon the bones of forgotten predecessors.

But he was a bard – he could not forget, nor would he.

Now the same inexorable story had finally reached his homeland. Long though the region might have withstood this process, it had finally arrived on its shores. And here he would witness the playing out of its final chapter – and upon his own people, as the fates would have it.

Poetic, that. Something for him, as a bard, to relish.

Walking the pine and birch forest, he reflected that the singing of this song would wring his heart.

Badlands led them onward through rough untrammelled forest and up steep valleys to a slope so high that snow still lingered in the shadows behind boulders and fallen logs. Here they found the Lost Greathall.

It was raining that afternoon, a cold downpour from clouds so low one might as well name them fog. Dense overgrown woods surrounded the hall. Any fields that might have once been cultivated around it had long since fallen back to the woods' encroachment. One ancient white spruce, as fat about as his arm-span, grew next to its moss-covered log walls. Its roof was a tangle of live growing brush and grasses. Its front entrance gaped open. Rainwater pooled on beaten bare earth.

Badlands tramped onward up the huge length of the hall. Birds flew overhead to perch on murky rafters. A long table stood across the far rear wall. Embers glowed within a massive stone hearth and in this flickering orange light a single occupant sat at the table's centre, a conical helmet next to him, a bowl before him.

Badlands halted and ducked his head. 'Stalker,' he murmured.

Stalker Lost pushed himself back from the table, brushed his long hanging moustache, and eyed his brother with a gaze that seemed to glow brighter than the embers. 'How'd it happen?' he grated.

Badlands flinched beneath the harsh glare. 'Arrow fire.'

Stalker simply shook his head. 'Damned fool.'

Fisher stepped forward. 'He saved the people in Antler Fort.'

The Lost's narrowed hazel gaze shifted. 'This doesn't involve you, Fisher.'

'It involves all of us, I fear.'

Stalker grunted at that, picked up his wooden spoon, and ate another mouthful. 'Yeah, well. You got a point there.' He raised his voice, shouting, 'Ain't that so, Cal?'

Badlands, Fisher and Jethiss turned. Figures had entered the hall behind them. Two men and a woman. The lead figure was very dark, of Dal Hon extraction, Fisher recognized. Older, his kinked hair greying, in leather armour stained a deep blood red; the rainwater that dripped from him appeared almost as dark as blood itself. The other two wore banded armour, with shields at their backs, longswords at their sides. The tattered remains of a red cloth tabard hung from the woman and upon it Fisher could just make out an undulating line of silver.

His breath eased from him in a long exhalation of wonder and he turned to Stalker. 'These are Crimson Guard.'

Stalker nodded, eyeing his brother. 'Yeah. Funny that, hey? We was joined up for a time with the Guard. Then I come home and who do I find out in the woods? Cal's troop here. All hands raised against 'em. Fighting everyone on all sides. So I offer them a place so long as they pledge to defend the Holding. And there you are.' He raised a hand to Badlands. 'We got us hearthguards.'

Fisher turned to the one he assumed to be Cal. 'Why did you remain, then? You could've made the coast.'

The wiry old Dal Hon looked him up and down. 'That's our business.'

Stalker chuckled while he ate. 'Same old answer. Cal here claims the Guard has a stake here in this region. Though what he means by that I got no idea. Still . . .' He brushed his moustache again. 'We do

368

keep running into each other, don't we? It's like fate, maybe, hey?'
And he laughed.

He motioned for Fisher to sit. 'Welcome. And you are?'

Fisher almost jumped – so quiet had his companion been, he'd
almost forgotten his presence.

'Jethiss,' the Andii said.

Stalker nodded, his gaze lazy. 'Can't say as we've ever had an
Andii visit these parts. What brings you here?'

'As you said. Fate.'

Stalker snorted a laugh. He spooned up a last portion from the
bowl. 'Guess I asked for that. Anyway, sit, everyone. Eat. We have
boiled mountain goat. I recommend it as it's all there is.'

Badlands scooped up a bowlful and sat heavily to lean hunched
over the table. Fisher spooned out a portion and offered it to Jethiss,
who shook his head. He sat with it instead. The Crimson Guard
bowed and exited – as hearthguards they could not sit with the
Icebloods and their guests in the Greathall. They would eat later at
the hirelings' table.

Stalker watched his brother for a time, then turned to Fisher.
He cleared his throat. 'Anyway, you missed all the action. Had
us a regular old-fashioned dust-up over on Bain lands. Broke and
scattered the lowlanders' army. Jaochim Sayer thinks that's them
dealt with.'

Fisher thought over the Lost's words while he chewed on the
tough tasteless meat. He swallowed with some difficulty. 'But not
you,' he offered.

'No. I've been abroad. That was just a first incursion. They'll be
back. And in greater numbers.'

Fisher was much relieved; he'd feared the man believed himself
unassailable here in his northern Greathall. He nodded his agreement. 'You cannot hold out for ever.'

'No. We can't.'

'Then . . . you will abandon the hall? Head to the coast?'

Stalker shook his lean hound's head. 'No.'

'But you just agreed . . .'

'Yeah. That's true.'

Fisher thrust himself from the table. 'Don't be a fool, man!'

Badlands half rose from his seat, glaring. Stalker gently urged
him down, then studied Fisher with his pale hazel gaze – the yellow
of sun-dried grasses, Fisher thought.

'You're a guest in my Holding,' he said. 'That's enough for now.'
Fisher bit his tongue and jerked his head in assent. 'Anyways . . .'

and the man went to a barrel and drew a glass of what looked like red wine. 'There's news to relate.' He offered the glass to Fisher, who took it wonderingly. Stalker caught his gaze and motioned to the barrel. 'That? Ah, raiding them outlanders.' He drew another and offered it to Jethiss, who accepted it with a bow of his head. He took one for himself. He did not offer one to Badlands and neither did his brother move to collect one; the man just sat, now, elbows on the table, his head lowered.

'News is,' Stalker began again, 'that Svalthbrul has been taken up by Bregin's son, Orman.'

Fisher sat back in wonder. 'Bregin? That Sayer hearthguard lad?'

Stalker nodded, his brows raised. 'And that's not all. Orman used it to slay Lotji.'

Fisher blew out a long breath. 'So much bad blood there.'

'Aye. Blood-feud back generations. But . . .' and Stalker raised his chipped glass of wine as if in salute. 'The outlanders burned Bain Greathall to the ground and the last of the Bains are gone.'

Astonished, Fisher matched the gesture, as did Jethiss. 'Farewell, honoured foe,' he murmured, and they all drank, all but Badlands.

His head lowered, Badlands growled into his knotted fists: 'Sing us a song, bard.'

Fisher was quite taken aback; it had been a long time since he'd been in service to a patron – though his last, Lady Envy, used to test him that way, as if hoping to catch him out. He shook his head. 'I am not in the mood, truly. I would not wish to do a disservice.'

Badlands slammed a fist to the table, upsetting Stalker's glass and making the bowls jump. '*Sing!*'

Fisher, luckily, was cradling his glass on his lap, and he tossed the last of it back, sucking his teeth. Jethiss, he noted, was watching him closely now. He nodded a slow thoughtful assent and cast his gaze to the massive log rafters cloaked in the gloom above. Birds flew about them and guano streaked them white. Then he looked to the far entrance and saw how the wind drove the rain within where it pooled on the dirt floor. He noted the rotting straw kicked about the ground, the mere four of them huddled about the dying embers of the broad hearth before them, and he sang.

> '*Here, all possessions wrought by our hands are fleeting*
> *Here, we are passing. Our kind is fleeting*
> *Those who come after us shall peer at ruins*
> *And wonder what giants these were from long ago*
> *Only twisted tales shall remain.*'

Badlands lurched from the bench and staggered off into the dark. Stalker regarded the bard for some time. The man's eyes did indeed seem to glow brighter than the embers. He finished the dregs of his wine, stood. 'Don't forget to add how stubborn and foolish we were.' He followed his brother to disappear into the darkness at the rear of the hall.

'I should,' Fisher muttered to himself.

'I understand them,' Jethiss offered, surprising Fisher.

'Really?'

'Yes.' He appeared almost embarrassed. 'I don't know why. I just feel the same way.'

'Perhaps the Andii share something of their – our – way of thinking.'

'Perhaps so.' Jethiss rose, refreshed their glasses. 'So, what shall we do?'

'What of your . . . quest?'

The Andii clasped the glass in both hands. 'I believe I was sent in this direction for a reason. I do not know the reason, but you mentioned someone, or something, in the north that might provide an answer. What is it?'

Fisher shook his head. He considered taking up his glass, but reconsidered and left his hands crossed on the table. 'I will not speak of them.'

'Then they are there. Thank you.'

Fisher bit his lip. Gods! He was a bard! The stories he could tell of the Forkrul! But he took up the glass and drank instead. 'I will not encourage you in this.'

'Neither do you dissuade me.'

'That is not for me to decide. Each of us possesses a Wyrd – a fate – and nothing we do can undo it.'

Jethiss thought about this while the birds roosted overhead, cooing and fluffing their feathers, and the rain pattered, hissing. He answered, musingly, 'You think everything is foreordained?'

'No. I believe we follow our natures. That our natures determine the choices we make. In short . . . we do it to ourselves. There is no one else to blame.'

'Not even the gods?'

Fisher threw back the last of his wine, sucked his teeth. 'The gods are determined by our natures. But if you decide to quibble them down to nothing more than mere causation – then why have them at all?'

'Things happen regardless?'

'It is a logical deduction.'

The Andii nodded, sleepily. 'I suppose some other justification would have to be found, then, for their existence.'

'I suppose so.'

Jethiss pushed himself to his feet. 'Well, there you have it. The world's troubles sorted out over a cask of wine.'

Fisher smiled fondly. 'A nightly ritual.'

'I am off to find some bedding.'

'Good night.'

Fisher sat alone in the amber glow of the dying embers. He listened to the rain pattering and wished the night would whisper an answer to the quandary he faced. To survive, these Icebloods – *we Icebloods* – must retreat north, ever higher. Yet, if the legends and tales were to be believed, a peril far greater than any human invasion slumbered there. A threat to all, no matter what breed or kind.

What was he to do? He listened again, intently, but the night seemed only to sigh. He answered the whisper with a sigh of his own.

*   *   *

Wrapped in a ragged dirty cloak with its hood raised, Kyle entered the sprawling besiegers' camp. He carried a battered shortsword at his side, dirks at his belt and the white blade in leathers and firmly tucked in his shirt. No one challenged him as he came walking in from the west, no picket or posted guard, and this alone convinced him that this mob was doomed to failure.

It was a bright and lingering twilight, the sky a beautiful shade of purple. He stopped where a gang of fortune-hunters, now soldiers – of a kind – lingered beneath the awning of a tent. 'I'm looking for the Shieldmaiden,' he said.

'Who isn't?' answered one, and took hold of an imaginary set of hips before him. 'This time of night, hey?' Kyle ignored him and continued east, as the man's gaze had flicked in that direction when he'd spoken. 'Hey!' the fellow called. 'Where're you from?'

'Cordafin,' he called back.

'Where's that?'

Kyle kept walking. *How the fuck should I know? I just made it up.*

He continued round the broad arc of the camp. There were enough of them, he decided. But they had to be kicked into shape. Was Lyan the one to do it? He found one larger tent, a possible command tent. It at least was guarded, and almost entirely by Genabackans. This convinced him. As he'd thought; they'd recognized her. He approached the guards before the closed flap.

'I'd like to speak to the Shieldmaiden.'

The guards, two burly veterans, exchanged annoyed looks. 'You can't just saunter up and meet a commander,' one said. 'You look like a veteran, you should know that. Chain of command. Who's your sergeant?'

Inwardly, Kyle cursed. 'I just arrived.'

'Thought she'd welcome you personally?' another commented with a sneer.

'You know her or something?' the first demanded.

'We've . . . met.'

'When?'

Kyle licked his lips. This was rapidly degenerating and now he couldn't just walk away. 'On the . . . the passage in.'

The first grunted. 'Congratulations. That's nice.' He straightened, pointed off. 'You just arrived? See that big house, the one with two storeys?'

'Yes.'

'You want to join, you go sign up there.'

'Right. Thanks.'

'You Malazan?' the second asked.

Kyle managed a scowl. 'What d'you mean, Malazan? I'm from Jasston.'

'Jasston? Where the Abyss is that?'

'Korel.'

This second guard grunted, only slightly mollified. 'There's a guy here from Theft. You know Theft?'

Kyle struggled to appear indifferent, shrugged. 'Yeah. Why?'

''Cause you don't look nothing like him.'

Kyle gave a negligent wave then ended the gesture by tucking his hand into his shirt where he took hold of the grip of the white blade. 'That's because Theftians look like rats.'

The guard blinked, then they all broke into huge guffaws. Kyle allowed himself a tight grin. After the guards stopped chortling the first looked to him and frowned. 'Well? Why're you still here? Go sign your papers.'

Kyle gave a curt nod, then forced himself to amble off. As he walked away, he heard one say, 'That Theftian did kinda look like a rat . . .'

He took care to walk in the direction of the two-storey frame and plaster daub house for a time, then, when he was certain he must be out of sight, he cut to the south and lost himself amid a maze of pitched tents. He had no intention of signing anything. So far no one had pointed him out directly as having quite a resemblance to the southern tribes of this region, but he wasn't about to push his luck.

He'd almost given up hope of coming up with a plan to reach Lyan, short of storming her tent, when through the crowd of armed and armoured men and women he glimpsed the slight short figure of a youth – Dorrin. The sight filled him with pleasure, and with hope; the lad would take him to Lyan. But it also twisted his throat, as the lad was walking only with the aid of a crutch. His left leg was gone below the knee.

Kyle halted, stricken. Whatever treatment Lyan had bargained for among the convoy hadn't been good enough to save his leg.

It took a great deal of effort to shake off the shock of the sight. The lad was so young. But perhaps it was fortunate as he'd get used to it quickly. And it would win him credibility with the troops – a youth and already a veteran.

Speaking of troops, he also noted the two Genabackan guards escorting the lad. Lyan was of high enough rank to rate bodyguards for her and her 'family'. Indeed, to listen to the talk, it sounded as if she was second-in-command out here.

Still, approaching Dorrin was his only hope of reaching her. He'd have to play it carefully and hope the lad could think on his feet. He jogged off, dodging around tents to get ahead, then waited just round the corner of a shed. When Dorrin approached, with his slow limping gait, Kyle stepped out and made a show of spotting the lad. 'Dorrin!' he shouted, 'It's me – *Kyle*! You remember, *Kyle*, yes?'

Dorrin had frozen, gaping. His mouth actually opened in an O as if to begin the sound of 'Wh—'

'Kyle! Yes? You remember, don't you?'

The guards had recovered and one was striding forward to brush Kyle aside when Dorrin reached out to him, calling, 'Kyle! Yes! How wonderful to see you!' The guards looked to the youth, frowning. 'We met . . .'

'. . . on the ship,' Kyle completed.

'On the ship, yes,' Dorrin said.

Kyle pushed forward and knelt in the mud before the youth, looked him up and down. He almost said, sorry about the leg, but caught himself in time: Whiteblade had been there, after all. So he asked, 'What happened to your leg?'

Dorrin looked confused for a moment, but recovered quickly. 'Oh. I, ah, lost it. Sickness in the bone.'

'I'm sorry, lad.'

The boy shrugged. 'It's okay. I can still get around.'

'So you can. And well, too. I assume Lyan's here?'

'Oh, yes! She would so much want to see you!'

'I'm glad. Should I wait with you?'

Dorrin peered up to one guard. 'Can he stay with me, Turath?'

This fellow, an older Genabackan, probably a veteran from the look of him, possibly of the Pannion wars, scratched his greying beard while glaring his ill-disguised suspicions of Kyle. After a moment of consideration – Dorrin had just handed him a very troubling poser of a problem – he reached a decision: 'The Shieldmaiden should be informed, little sir.'

'Oh! Of course,' Dorrin answered.

Turath jerked his chin to his fellow and the guard jogged off. Then the veteran settled his scarred hand on the grip of his shortsword and planted his feet wide right next to Dorrin. 'We'll wait just here,' he said. A lazy smile of anticipation quirked his lips.

Kyle ignored him and studied the lad. He did appear to be in good health; he was smiling, his eyes were bright, and he looked well fed. 'Are there any others here your age?' he asked. 'To talk to?'

Dorrin shook his head regretfully. 'No. No one.'

'I'm sorry. It must be hard to be all alone.'

He brightened again. 'But we aren't any more! You're here!'

Kyle just chuckled and squeezed his shoulder, rising. He found himself looking into the veteran's troubled gaze. The man was frowning while he scratched his beard once more, as if chasing after a thought.

Kyle looked away. After a time of silent waiting, he saw the guard scowl his displeasure and he glanced over to find the second man jogging up. Obviously, Turath was disappointed not to see him accompanied by ten more troopers.

He nodded to Turath. 'She says he can wait in their quarters.'

Turath grunted a non-committal sound.

Dorrin raised his trimmed tree-branch crutch. 'This way, ah, Kyle.'

Lyan had one of the remaining houses – only a small one-room cabin, but a structure all the same. The front of the cabin was a general meeting room and living quarters, while hung blankets separated sleeping quarters for her and for Dorrin. The guards waited outside at the door. Dorrin clumped to a chair and sat. Kyle spotted a tall earthenware jug of water and poured himself a drink. 'Some water?' he asked Dorrin, who shook his head.

'She will be awfully pleased to see you,' the boy said.

Kyle smiled his thanks, but already he was beginning to see the foolishness of coming here. There'd been survivors from the fight on the Dread Sea shore. And at any turn in the encampment he could stumble on another Stormguard, or a Korel veteran. It was plain now that they had to get out as soon as possible, preferably this night.

'She said we were lucky,' Dorrin said.

He blinked. 'I'm sorry?'

'That day. When we parted. One of the ships was from the north, and they recognized her.'

'Oh. I see.'

'But . . .' and the lad lowered his voice, 'you're not very popular around here.'

He raised his brows. 'I imagine not.'

He sat, and they waited. Dorrin was very quiet for a young lad, and still, and Kyle realized why: it was difficult for him to get around. He reflected on the few amputations he'd seen amid all the fighting he'd known – because the Crimson Guard and the Malazans had had enough trained cadre mages familiar with basic Denul magics. Not so in these wilds, obviously.

It was late and dark when he heard the guards shift to attention outside the door. Moments later, it opened and Lyan entered. She wore her mail armour and her sword at her hip, but now a thick cloak of black and grey wolf fur hung over one shoulder. She carried her helmet in one hand and set it on a table. Her auburn hair was neatly braided and she was far cleaner than the last time he'd seen her.

Her face, he noted, was carefully flat and composed. She nodded to him. 'Kyle . . . good to see you again.'

'Lyan.'

She turned to Dorrin. 'It is late. You should lie down.'

'But . . .'

'Kyle and I have much to discuss.'

The youth picked at the bark of his tree-branch crutch. 'But he just got here.'

'Tomorrow, Dorrin.'

He heaved an aggrieved sigh, thumped the crutch to the dirt and eased himself from the chair. 'Good night, then.'

'Yes, Dorrin,' Kyle said. 'Good night.'

The lad's straw cot was at the very back of the cabin. After the blankets fell between them, Lyan went to the door and opened it a hand's breadth. 'You're dismissed,' she said.

'Not one guard?' enquired Turath from beyond.

'I don't think there will be a sortie this night,' she answered, quite dryly.

'Very good, commander.'

She closed the door, bolted it, went to the table and poured two glasses of wine. She gave one to Kyle and motioned him to remain silent. The cabin possessed one window opening, next to the door, and she peeped out to make certain the guards had gone before closing the wooden shutters and pulling a muslin cloth across. She crossed to him and raised the glass.

He smiled and opened his mouth to speak, but she silenced him with a raised finger. Leaning close, she whispered, 'Are you a fool to have come here!'

'I know . . . I know,' he murmured back, his voice low.

She continued, fierce, hissing, 'There are veterans here from Korel!'

He raised both hands, surrendering. 'Yes. I agree. We'll have to leave tonight.'

'We?'

He was surprised to see her confused, but then she seemed to recover and she set down the wine, her gaze lowered. When she once more met his gaze he understood; she'd taken too long to find her words. 'Kyle . . . there are riches, and more, to be won here – I can't throw all that away . . .'

He set down his glass as well, fought hard to keep all expression from his face. 'You were right.'

'Right?'

'I was a fool.'

Stung, she shook her head. 'No . . . it's not that. Don't you understand?'

'Leave. Now. With me. You and Dorrin. That I understand.'

But she took up her glass and walked away. 'Now you *are* being a fool. A romantic fool.'

He picked up his wine as well, threw it back hard and swallowed. He regarded her across the beaten earth floor. In his anger it occurred to him: was this why she still wore her armour? Hadn't even unbuckled her sword? He murmured, 'You're the fool, Lyan.'

Her face stiffened, and she inclined her head as if in farewell. 'Thank you for saying hello to Dorrin. You mean a lot to him. For his sake, please do not get yourself killed.'

'For his sake?'

He watched her closely, saw the muscles of her jaw tighten against an answer she might have given, watched her resolutely refuse to speak.

He crossed to the door, unbolted it and glanced out. The muddy mass of tracks and wagon-ruts that was one main way of Mantle town lay mostly empty. He turned back to give her one last look. 'Give my apologies to Dorrin.' And he slipped out.

He might have imagined it, but it appeared as if she lurched towards him as he left, but it was too little and too late. So much, he decided, for what might have been between them. He now wondered whether he'd imagined it all – as a romantic fool might.

He yanked his hood low and pulled his cloak tightly about himself, tucking his hand within his shirt to grip the white blade. He meant to head out north immediately, get out of the encampment as swiftly as possible. His route took him past a few timber houses of the old Mantle town. As he crossed in front of one entrance it burst open and out spilled a crowd of rowdy drunken outlanders in a glare of yellow lantern-light. They stumbled into him and he righted one with a quick, 'Careful, there.'

It was a woman, and she blinked at him, frowning, even as she clenched a fistful of his cloak. He answered the frown, puzzled. She shoved her other hand into his face, showing him the bandaged stump where a thumb would jut.

'It's that damned Whiteblade!' she yelled.

In answer, Kyle yanked free the blade and swept it across her neck in one swift motion. The crowd of outlanders shouted and gagged their horror as her head fell in a gout of jetting blood. He attempted to yank free but her fist still held him tight by the cloak. He chopped off that hand at the wrist.

Other hands grabbed at him and these he severed as well. The crowd – those not clenching stumps of wrists and forearms – now scrambled to give him room. He fled north.

But yells and alarm preceded him. Armed soldiers exited a large tent right in front of him. A few quick cuts crippled these and he pushed inside. He sliced the main centre pole, and as the heavy sail-cloth tent billowed down around him he cut his way out at the rear. Now he ran.

Calls for archers sounded all about. He tried to keep to the darker patches of the tent encampment, but more and more torches were being lit as troops crowded the ways. Ahead, across trampled fields and a creek, lay woods. He pounded for the creek. Troops from tents nearby attempted to slow him by blocking his way. The white blade severed shields, vambraces, spear hafts, and two crossbows before their handlers had finished cocking them.

Several arrows hissed past him. One plucked his cloak, then he was tumbling down a muddy slope into a shockingly chill rushing creek. He slogged on. A tossed burning torch crashed into his back, sending him off his feet into the creek. Arrows nipped the waves about him.

'Get him!' someone yelled from the shore.

A new voice bellowed, commandingly, 'Stay out of his reach! Archers, form up!'

Kyle lurched to his feet and stumbled on. He was surprised, then, to see a thick night fog now rolling out of the forest. He couldn't understand it, but it was a blessing and he made for it.

'Damned northern giants!' someone yelled.

'Fire now!' the commander ordered.

Kyle dived under the swift waist-high waters. The current buffeted him and the water seemed to suck all warmth from his body. He simply attempted to stay under for as long as he could. He gripped at boulders his questing hands found in the bed, tried to bring his legs down.

Holding his breath, he reflected that never in all his years did he imagine how much he would owe old one-handed Stoop of the Crimson Guard for all those enforced near-drownings in swimming lessons. Finally, his lungs burning, he had to come up and he pushed his face to the surface to suck in a fresh breath of air. He blinked, finding that he'd entered a world of dense swirling banners of fog. Voices shouted, sounding very far off for some reason, as if the fog muted or distorted them. He slogged onward. Gaining the far shore, he heaved his frozen stiff body up the mud and bracken to lie panting, thankful just to be out of that numbing water.

A wide hand gathered up the cloth at his back and yanked him to his feet. 'What are you doing here?' a deep voice demanded. Kyle wiped water from his face and peered up at a bearded giant of a fellow in cured leather armour, a spear in his other hand.

'I'm looking for the Losts.'

The hand released him and urged him along with a push at the back. He nearly fell as his legs wobbled, numb and tingling. 'They're coming. We must move.' Through the curling vapours behind, Kyle glimpsed blurred orange flames bobbing. 'The fog and creek should delay them, but we'd best give them some room.'

On a hunch, Kyle guessed through numb lips: 'Are you Baran? Baran Heel?'

'Yes. And you are the one my mother escorted off our Holding.' At Kyle's start, the fellow chuckled. 'I saw you in the distance.'

'What are you doing here?'

'Hunting.'

Baran pushed him on. In the fog it was hard to tell their direction, but Kyle thought it north. The haze thinned as they jogged through the forest. As the night sky cleared and the land rose, he knew they were indeed headed north.

'This is Bain Holding, isn't it?'

'Bain Holding is no more. It has gone the way of my mother's, and so many others before it.'

'Oh – I'm sorry.'

'What is it to you? An outlander.'

He'd never considered himself proud of where he'd come from – quite the opposite, in fact – but the accusation irritated him deeply. 'I'm no outlander. I'm from the southern plains.'

Baran peered back, grunted. 'Ah. That explains much, then.'

Kyle waited, but the fellow offered no further explanation. Much later in the night, when they reached the wooded crest of the valley, Baran turned and peered back once more. He grunted again, sounding impressed, or mystified. 'What did you do to rile them up so?'

Kyle struggled up the crest and squinted down and behind. Far off, torches bobbed and wove through the woods. 'Killed a few,' he said.

'Hunh. Well, they've never shown much offence at murder before.' He motioned to one side. 'This way.'

As they jogged, Kyle remembered Yullveig's words. 'Is your sister here?' he asked. 'Erta?'

'She has returned north. I believe she came to see more sense in my father's words.'

'But you do not.'

Baran's large teeth flashed bright in the dark. 'I prefer to fight to the end. I do not care if there is no grace in my leave-taking.'

'Your father refuses to sink to their level. I respect him for that.'

'Yet all your respect will not save his life.'

Kyle bit his lip. That barb struck hard and true. Also, it was this man's people and way of life being swept from the face of the earth – best not to argue the finer points of it with him.

Baran was now leading him due east across a wide shallow valley. With dawn, he halted, pointed onward. 'Lost Holding beyond.'

Kyle had to wait to catch his breath before he could answer. Keeping up with Baran had taken all he had. 'My thanks. Won't you reconsider? Come with me? We should all gather together, present a united front.'

The Heel flashed another grin behind his russet beard. 'Form our own army, you mean? Speaking of sinking to their level.' He shook his head. The wind blew his loose mane about. 'No. That is not us. Not how we do things.'

Kyle nodded his understanding. 'Then, this is farewell. Thank you, Baran, for saving my life.'

The Iceblood inclined his head in salute. 'It was nothing.'

'Good hunting.'

Baran hiked up his spear and grinned again. 'Indeed. Let us hope they've followed far further than they ought.' He jogged off.

Kyle watched him go until he disappeared into the woods, then turned to the east and Lost Holding hidden somewhere among the morning mists flowing down the shoulders of the Salt range.

*   *   *

She awaited them on the crest of a low hill: a single dark figure in ragged untreated hides standing slim against the purpling north sky. Tall spring grasses and blue wild flowers blew about her knees. Her black hair whipped in the contrary winds.

Silverfox eased up from driving her lathered mount and the beast immediately halted. Foam dripped from its lips with each laboured breath. Steeling herself, she wrenched one numb leg to raise it up over the pommel of her saddle. The scraping of her raw thighs was an agony to her. She almost fell when her feet hit the ground, only managing to remain upright by grasping at the saddle's girth-strap.

Old, she reflected grimly. I am already old. Yet I see myself as a young woman. Perhaps everyone comes to do so, and I have simply reached the self-revelation prematurely. An achievement for a girl not yet into her twenties. But not surprising, considering I carry millennia-old awarenesses within.

Rubbing her thighs to ease feeling back into them, she hobbled up the rise to join Kilava.

'Summoner,' the ancient Bonecaster greeted her.

Silverfox flinched – the woman always managed to infuse such disapproval into each use. 'Kilava.'

Behind the woman, down a series of gently descending grassy hillsides, lay the glittering surface of a broad bay, and the body of a wider lake, or sea, beyond. Ships lay at anchor in the bay, and a camp of sorts was spread out along the shore. Smoke from fires rose into the air. Already, mounted scouts were cantering out to investigate their presence.

'What is this?' she asked Kilava.

'The locals name it the Sea of Dread.'

Studying the waters, she could well imagine why they would do so; the rigid grip of the Jaghut magics of Omtose Phellack yet lay hard upon it, though it was rotting and slipping away even as she watched. Like ice beneath the heat of a summer sun, she reflected. In this case, the end of its time here upon the land.

'It is all that remains of a great ice-field that once covered all this region,' Kilava explained. 'One of the last remaining glacial lakes.'

Silverfox motioned to the north, where mountains remained visible in the dusk – the unmistakable gleam of ice shone about their peaks. 'Yet some remains.'

Kilava did not turn to look. 'Yes,' she allowed. 'High in the mountains.'

She did not need to add . . . *our destination*.

Silverfox sensed the presence of Pran and Tolb as they came walking up. Her Imass followers arrived to stand ranged along the crest of the hill. They were motionless but for their tattered leathers and hanging fur wraps and cloaks flapping in the wind. She watched the closing mounted scouts suddenly wheel, wrenching away, to turn and gallop back to their camp. One even fell from his mount and ran now, arms waving, after his horse.

'Where are they?' she asked Kilava.

'Close now. Very close.'

'You have not spoken to them?'

The Bonecaster shook her head, brushed her hair from her face. 'No. They know my choice. They would attack. I might not be able to extricate myself.'

That casual admission brought home the slenderness of their chances to Silverfox. We are too far outnumbered. She wondered, then, whether she was in truth driving them before her. Or were they merely pursuing their goal while she chased after? One and the same, perhaps. In any case, the restrictions imposed upon Tellann in this region inhibited them all.

We walk as in the old days. Tirelessly, yes. But just the same.

Chaos had broken out within the camp. Figures ran to the boats drawn up upon the gravel beaches, pushed them out.

'And who are these?'

Again, Kilava did not turn away to glance. 'Outlanders. Strangers. Not a scent of the Jaghut about them.'

Silverfox nodded her agreement. She, too, saw none of the other race in them. 'We follow the coast north, then?'

Kilava lowered her chin in assent.

Silverfox drew breath to speak again, paused, then continued regardless. 'And . . . did you warn many off?'

'All those I could reach.'

'Thank you.'

Irritation wrinkled the Bonecaster's features. 'As I said – I did not do so to soothe your conscience.'

Silverfox fought to subdue her own annoyance. 'None the less . . . thank you.'

Something heavy fell to the ground behind and Silverfox turned; her mount had collapsed. Its side shuddered for a time, drawing in and out like a bellows. Then this too stilled.

Two Imass broke ranks to jog onward down the hillside. Silverfox turned an eye on Pran Chole. 'What is this?'

The mummified mask that was the Bonecaster's face remained immobile as ever. He extended a stick-thin arm of bone and hanging ligaments towards camp. 'You have need of a horse.'

Silverfox thought about that, then tilted her head. Yes, she supposed she did.

CHAPTER XI

THE PRAIRIE WAS ONE OF TALL GRASSES WHIPPED BY A CHILL WIND. Tall menhirs leaned drunkenly like a giant's set of toys tossed and forgotten across the landscape. Why Shimmer found herself here, she had no idea. The sky was clear, a hard frosty blue, with the moon low in the south. Strangely, the moon looked different: larger, and far less mottled. Another bright object also blazed in the day's sky, something that trailed a long train of fire behind, just as the Visitor had. To the north – if indeed that direction was the north – lay a horizon-to-horizon wall of snow and deeper azure blue glowing ghostly in the moonlight.

She wondered if this was Hood's demesne, his Paths, where the dead wander eternally, forever wringing their hands as they bemoan past choices, mistakes and lost opportunities.

As if on cue, a figure rounded one of the nearby markers and approached. He was grey-haired and bearded, in long tattered brown robes that bore scorch marks and a scattering of burn holes across the weave. She recognized Smoky. One of the Crimson Guard dead. What they called their Brethren.

It occurred to her at that moment that in fact the Brethren constituted by far the majority of the Crimson Guard. The chained spirits of their dead, held to the mortal realm by the power of the Vow they swore to K'azz. The Guard, then, could in truth more accurately be regarded as an army of the dead.

Smoky gave her a nod in greeting. 'Shimmer.'

'Where are we?'

The mage scratched his chin beneath his scraggly beard. 'We don't rightly know. Most of us think it's the spot we swore the Vow – only how it looked long ago.' He shrugged. 'No one knows for certain.'

'You're remarkably unconcerned about it all.'

'I'm dead, ain't I?'

'Why am I here?'

He regarded her more closely. 'Looks to me like you're making up your mind.'

'Making up my mind? About what?'

'About where you belong.'

'Making up my mind? You mean, about whether I'm dead or not?'

'Something like that.'

She snorted her impatience. 'Well . . . I want to return, of course.'

He shrugged his bony shoulders once more. 'Yeah. Figured as much. Off you go then.'

'What? Just like that?'

The old fellow looked annoyed. 'What do you want? A band to play?'

'But isn't this . . . Hood's realm?'

He shook his head. 'No. These are not Hood's Paths.'

'So what do I do?'

He waved her off. 'Just – decide.'

'Right.' She decided, then, that she did not belong here. At that moment another figure rounded the rock to regard her from a distance. She immediately recognized his rotund form. His sodden robes. He raised an arm in sad farewell.

She lurched forward, *'Petal!* No . . .'

But the ground slipped from beneath her feet, her vision dimmed, and she found herself spinning in a way she had no words for. She was suddenly certain she was going to be sick.

She coughed, nearly vomiting, and sucked in a great chestful of cold crisp air.

A man yelped in surprise directly above her and she snapped her eyes open. She was lying on some sort of cot, naked, her arms tied above her head, while a man, similarly naked, sat between her spread legs.

'Hey, Rosell,' the fellow called. 'She ain't dead after all. Like you said.'

'Told ya,' a voice answered from outside her vision.

This fellow leaned over her and slapped her cheek – none too gently. 'Just warming you up, sweetheart. You're so cold in there you near shrank my cock.' He grinned down at her with broken grey teeth. 'Welcome to Destruction Bay.'

Her answer was to hitch up her legs round his neck, twist her hips, and spin him over the side of the cot to slam his head into the dirt floor with a satisfying snap of his neck. She then brought her legs up over her head and pushed against the wood headboard she was tied to. The board burst. She rose from the frame in time to block a knife-thrust from Rosell, wrap the cord strung between her wrists around his throat, and set her knee against the back of his neck. She pushed there until she began to see black spots in her vision, then she let him fall, limp, and stumbled to her own knees, utterly spent.

After catching her breath, she used the knife to cut the cord. She scavenged trousers, a shirt, and oversized leather shoes from what she could find among the meagre possessions scattered about. She then staggered from the hut's entrance, a mere hanging rotten blanket, and stepped out with the knife tucked up her sleeve.

She was on a broad mud flat, perhaps a raised floodplain. A clutch of dilapidated huts and shacks lay about. White smoke rose from a few smoke-holes. Great chunks of flat ice dotted a shore of black gravel. She lurched down to the shore. To the south rose the tall ice cliffs of the channel they had just navigated – or failed to navigate. She studied it and was dismayed to see that she was on the south shore. The wrong shore.

For some obscure reason this one further development was too much for her. She felt an uncontrollable urge to howl. She splashed out up to her knees in the frigid waters then collapsed, her face in her hands, and shuddered in spasms of weeping. She felt disgust and revulsion at everything: the cold, the touch of the grimy clothing, her sweaty clinging hair. She splashed the clean frigid water over her face and squatted there until she was utterly numb.

The coarse physicality of it all nauseated her beyond explanation. Gods! She'd come back to *this*?

Footsteps crunched in the gravel of the strand. She closed a fist on the grip of the dagger and raised her eyes a touch to peer over one forearm. It was Bars in his leathers, a mail coat over one shoulder. He extended a hand. 'Knew you were about.'

She felt as if a death sentence had been reprieved. She clasped his hand, rising. The mail coat was hers and he handed it over. 'Thank you,' she told him. She was surprised by how much his massive presence reassured her. 'Any others?'

'Gwynn's here. Lean and Keel.'

She stared, horrified. 'That is all?'

'No. Gwynn says K'azz is on the north shore with others.'

She nodded at his words. 'Then we must rendezvous.' Bars did not answer and she turned from peering across the channel. He was watching her with a strange expression in his dark sad eyes, something like worry. 'Yes? What?'

'We must go on?'

'Yes. We must. We have come too far. Paid too high a price for anything else.'

'Do you really think there are answers to be found here, Shimmer?'

'K'azz does. He knows the truth – and I swear I will get it from him.'

The big man heaved a troubled sigh, eyed the north shore. 'Well, then . . . we'd best be going.'

She peered about: rowboats and launches lay pulled up on the strand. 'Gather the others. I'll secure a boat.'

Bars offered a mock salute and crunched off across the gravel. Shimmer headed to one of the larger launches.

She had their boat-master guide the vessel close along the north shore of the Sea of Gold. They had agreed upon a price for the crossing, but it was no doubt dawning upon the man that any said pay might be long in coming, if it came at all. With nightfall, she had him put in and they built a fire and lay down round it, save for Bars and Keel, who took turns guarding and sleeping in the boat. When morning came, Shimmer was surprised that the man was still with them. But then, the boat was his livelihood, no matter where he might find himself.

Bars made tea that morning. And with that familiar ritual, she felt that some sort of normality had returned.

They were packing up when footsteps sounded among the surrounding rocks and K'azz appeared in his hunting leathers, hopping from boulder to boulder. With him came Cowl, Black the Lesser, Turgal, and Blues.

Shimmer clasped each in a great hug. 'Good to see you,' she kept saying. 'Good to see you.'

Blues accepted her greeting with an embarrassed flinch. 'I'm sorry . . .' he began.

'There was nothing you could've done.'

He wiped his eyes. 'Still . . . it galls.'

'Yes. I'm sorry.' She turned last to K'azz. The man appeared unchanged; same painfully thin features, same skull-like mien with pale sky-blue eyes that sometimes seemed completely colourless. His leathers, however, looked far worse for wear. 'The ice fell on us,' she told him.

'Yes. Bad luck.'

She shook her head in slow negation. 'Not good enough. It targeted us.'

He pursed his thin cracked lips. 'The Vow, then. No doubt.' He made a move to enter the boat but she blocked his path.

'Not good enough any more, K'azz. What about the Vow?'

The commander glanced about and she followed his gaze. Bars was standing very close with his thick arms crossed; Gwynn stroked the snow-white beard he was growing; Lean stood nearby, truly lean now, having lost so much of her plumpness; and Blues was frowning as if troubled by his own suspicions.

K'azz did not look to Cowl, who stood behind, hugging himself, rocking back and forth on his heels, grinning crazily as usual. The mage even offered Shimmer a wink. Completely dismissive of him now, she merely pulled her gaze away.

K'azz would not look up. He drew a hard breath. 'It concerns the Vow, Shimmer. We aren't welcome here.'

She nodded at that. 'Very well . . . that's a beginning. What else?'

K'azz raised his eyes and she was shocked to see actual pleading in them. 'Isn't that enough, Shimmer? Isn't it clear we must not continue?'

'No.' The denial was blunt and harsh. 'I see that you still refuse to speak and so we must continue onward – to get the truth of this. We owe it to all who have fallen.' She thrust an arm to the south. 'They paid with their lives! And I will collect on it.' She brushed past him. 'Either speak up or stand aside.'

He was left standing alone on the shore. For a moment, she saw him as nothing more than a thin ragged figure, haunted and torn, then she hardened her heart and turned to Bars. 'Push off.' K'azz stepped on board at the last instant. She faced the boat's master, who held the side-mounted tiller. 'What lies up the coast?'

'Scattered camps, ma'am. One big one the gold-hunters established over an old town up there. They call it Wrongway. Past that they say is a fortress named Mantle.'

She eyed K'azz where he sat alone in the bow. 'Are you going to help?'

'The path is due north. Follow the coast for a short time then strike upland.'

'Thank you.' She nodded to the boat's master. 'You have your orders.'

'Yes, ma'am.' He eased back, resigned to his situation, and spat over the side. 'If you lot would step the mast that would be a big help.'

The figures came shuffling out of the deeper gloom in the middle of the broad subterranean chamber that was the no-man's-land separating the feuding Sharr and Sheer families of Exile Keep. Othan Sharr, now the Sharr of Sharr with the death of his elder brother, paused in his gnawing of a roasted rat carcass and narrowed his own rather beady, rat-like eyes upon the strangers.

'What Sheer trickery is this?' he growled to his cousin-wife, Amina Sharr, on his right.

She pushed back her nest of frizzy hair, narrowed her eyes, then hissed a grating breath and gripped the battered table with both sinewy hands. 'Didn't I say with Geth and Lurnan gone they'd try something?'

The rest of the Sharrs lined up along the table facing the no-man's-land slowly set down their cups and crusts of bread.

'What foolishness is this?' Sharr of Sharr called out to the now motionless figures. 'There can be no parley or truce between us – you know that!' The slim shadowy shapes remained silent. The Sharr of Sharr squinted his tiny eyes even further. 'What are they doing? I can't quite see. Are those . . . costumes?'

Across the empty chamber, along the far wall, sitting at the table of the Sheer family, Gurat Sheer, the ancient Sheer of Sheers, similarly squinted into the gloom. 'What are those asinine Sharrs up to now?' He fumbled at the littered tabletop before him, found a stick, and hit the elderly man next to him. 'What is this, Jatar?'

Jatar, Gurat's eldest nephew, wiped the spilled wine from the front of his shirt and glared at his uncle before glancing out across the dusty flagstones of the chamber. His greying brows rose. 'Looks like a full frontal assault.'

The Sheer of Sheers banged his stick against the table for attention. 'Haven't had one of them in generations.' He pointed across the chamber, shouted, 'So desperate now are you, Othan, you dried up rat?'

The figures paced closer. Jatar pushed himself back from the table, frowning. Gurat snorted his contempt. 'What foolish trick is this?'

Amina Sharr raised her unruly nest of hair even further from her face to better see. The figures – they looked very thin.

'Such costumes of bone and rags will not terrorize us!' the Sharr of Sharr laughed.

Amina touched her cousin-husband's arm. 'I do not believe those are costumes, husband dear.'

The Sharr of Sharrs lost his smirk. His beady eyes narrowed to slits as he studied the bizarre skeletal apparitions. 'Oh dear. They resemble descriptions of the dread army of bone and dust.'

As one, the skeletal figures drew long blades of stone from ragged belts and sashes of rotting uncured pelts. Shrieking her rage, Amina Sharr surged to her feet, thrust with her hands, and actinic power lit the low-roofed chamber like a blast of lightning.

Along the other wall, the Sheers kicked back their chairs, some leaping over the table. The Sheer of Sheers slammed his stick to the table, breaking it. 'Send them back to their nether-realm, boys and girls!'

The no-man's-land of shattered furniture and dust erupted into a firestorm of unleashed power where flurries of lancing iron shards peppered stone, the air itself solidified into sheets of rock-hard ice, the flagstones parted revealing black gulfs, and raw unleashed chaos itself roiled through the air in clouds consuming all it touched.

Through this blistering conflagration of energies the figures of bone and rag hides advanced. They threw milky brown flint knives that sliced Sharr and Sheer mages, or rebounded from defensive glyphs. A heaved stone broadsword, a full arm's length of razor-sharp black chalcedony, arced through the air to take the head from young Manadara Sheer. Her arms fell and the channelled raw chaos she had been summoning gushed on to the table, consuming it and the flagstones beneath. The nearby Sheers scrambled in either direction.

The foremost warrior of bone and dust pushed through curtains of ice shards so impossibly keen and hard that they penetrated even its fossilized bones to stand like daggers. It reached the Sharrs' table. A single blow from its grey flint longsword parted the timbers in an eruption of dust and slivers.

Amina Sharr confronted it. 'To annihilation!' she howled, and, leaping, she locked her legs about the creature's torso and released all hold upon the arcing energies sizzling her flesh. The two burst into a cloud of ash and soot that dispersed about the coursing, contrary winds of the chamber.

The Sharr of Sharrs, coughing, waving the ash of his cousin-wife from his eyes, slid along a wall. He tried to right himself but found that for some reason he couldn't. He peered blearily at his arm where it ended at the elbow. He remembered, vaguely, a sword flashing before him, raising an arm . . . Shaking his head, he continued sliding along the wall. Perhaps if he made it to the entrance to the lower regions . . .

His path brought him to a shadowed figure awaiting him. He pulled up short, raised his gaze.

The skeletal figure punched its stone longsword through his chest. Coughing anew, the Sharr of Sharrs smiled and dragged himself even closer. He cupped his hand against the discoloured naked bone of the skull as if caressing it and peered into the darkness of the empty sockets. 'We will take you with us, you know,' he promised. 'We neither can outlive the other.'

'Just so long as you go,' the creature's answer came, breathless and faint.

Hand and skull exploded into shards of bone. Both bodies fell.

*

Lanas Tog and Ut'el Anag silently watched the thick sooty smoke gush from the shattered entrance of the stone structure. Through the pall emerged the remnants of the warband they had sent within. They waited until no more appeared, then Lanas Tog said, 'This deviation has cost us dear.'

'The nest had to be extirpated.'

'We cannot delay.'

Ut'el swung his nearly fleshless face to the south. 'True. They are close.' The head tilted, as if in thought. 'Yet numbers are still with us. Perhaps we should turn upon them. This structure could provide a trap . . .'

Lanas Tog reached out as if she would grasp the Bonecaster's shoulder but pulled her hand of sinew and bare bone back at the last moment. 'Remember our task. Once it is completed, there will be no more argument between us. All shall be moot.'

The battered skull turned to her. 'True. Why blunt our weapons upon each other when our quarry lies so near . . .' He motioned the gathered T'lan onward, stepped close upon Lanas. 'However, remember that I will allow nothing to come between me and the completion of our sworn task. I have waited far too long for this.'

'We, you mean,' Lanas observed, her voice even fainter than usual. 'We have all waited far too long.' In answer, Ut'el merely held his carious face close for a time as he stepped around her, then walked off.

After a lingering glance to the south, Lanas followed.

Reuth was not impressed by what he saw of the gold-seekers' tent town of Wrongway. It stank, and appeared disorganized even to his inexperienced eye. Tents and huts lay all about with no clear avenues or paths, as if everyone had simply set up camp wherever they wished. And with a heavy spring rain last night, it was now a cesspool of mud tracks and overflowing latrines.

Storval went ashore, accompanied by Riggin, the nominal leader of the ten Stormguard. The rest of the Stormguard, plus the new captain's closest supporters among the hireswords, were under orders to remain on board. It did not take him long to realize that this was so the rest of the Mare crew did not simply slip the mooring ropes and sail off.

With the evening coming, he decided that this was to be his chance. At the stern, he'd hidden a bundle of what few spare clothes he possessed. He collected a meal of old bread and dried fish and sat there close to the stern-plate to wait long into the night.

Yet he was not alone. Two of Storval's closest supporters hung about as the hours slipped by and the twilight deepened. Then he realized Storval had set a watch upon him. He, their prisoner pilot, a valuable asset, would not be allowed to slip away.

He wanted to cry then, and he damned his lack of worldly experience. He'd never fought or trained for such things. He was a scholar! When other children were scuffling and drubbing one another he was kept indoors and forced to learn his letters.

Wiping his sleeve across his face, he leaned against the ship's side, set his chin on his arm and watched the shore. Fires were rising all about the sprawling camp. He could hear loud voices, snatches of laughter and songs from the many informal tent-taverns.

He wondered what Whiteblade would do in this situation. The answer was clear enough – he'd swim to shore. Only, like most, Reuth couldn't swim. It was a rare talent indeed. Yet, thinking of it, there were other ways. Wood floated, and sailors' lives had been saved by grasping hold of such things as oars and timbers. He dropped his gaze to the mooring pole lying at his feet. That would do.

He would have to be quick. Toss it over then jump after.

But what if he missed? When then? Like any sailor, he had a terror of drowning.

Yet who said this would be easy? Of course he'd have to take a risk. No gain without it.

Very well. This would be it.

He lifted his bundle of clothes from where he'd stuffed it from sight and set it next to his feet. Then, fighting to steady his breathing, he reached down and lifted the pole from its housing and threw it overboard.

'Hey? What's that?' his minder demanded across the stern deck.

Taking a deep breath, Reuth grabbed hold of his sack and vaulted over the side. The water was shockingly cold and his head sank beneath the surface. He immediately abandoned his bundle to flail blindly for the pole. His searching, grasping hands found nothing. In his panic, he inhaled a mouthful of water and then complete frenzied terror took over. He lashed the water, opened his mouth to scream, but only more water rushed in. He inhaled further, sucking the fluid deeper into his lungs.

Something jabbed his side and scraped a flaming tear across his ribs.

Sudden noise, shouts, splashing, even laughter. He was hanging gaffed: a boathook had him by his clothes. He was yanked up the side of the hull, gagging, vomiting, to thump down on the deck like some sort of hooked fish. Someone kicked him in the side. He pushed his hair back and peered blearily up at Jands, the new first mate.

'That'll teach ya,' the mate said. 'Storval won't like to hear of this!'

The gathered hireswords had a good laugh then wandered off, leaving him under guard. He let his head thump to the timbers of the decking and pressed a hand to his side. He'd failed. Made a mess of it. Unlike Whiteblade, who'd made them all look like utter fools.

Seemed there was more to it than just the need and the desire. There had to be some sort of accompanying experience and skill. Well, how could you gather the required experience unless you tried? At least he'd tried. Couldn't take that from him. He curled up to try to conserve his warmth, and wept fiercely into his fists. At some point in the night one of the Mare sailors dropped a blanket over him.

The next morning, Storval came aboard and announced that they were sailing for Mantle to pledge their swords to the leader of the invader army there, some sort of veteran Letherii commander named Teal. His next act was to manacle Reuth to the stern, next to the rudder.

Reuth wouldn't have minded the position had Gren still been the steersman. However, the big friendly Jasston native hadn't recovered from the arrow wound in his leg and had died of infection. Reuth suspected neglect was closer to the cause, as the man had been no friend of Storval or his hiresword lackeys. The new steersman was one of Storval's hangers-on – he certainly didn't owe his position to any skill with the rudder.

So it was that the next few days passed in a series of cuffs, sour glances and curses sent Reuth's way. It was as if this fellow Brener, a dense Katakan native, somehow resented Reuth personally for some slight or wrong the lad couldn't even remember.

At last, they anchored close to the shore just short of the cliffs and the guarded harbour of Mantle. Storval and the Stormguards had all the crew go ashore. All but two – two guards set to watch the *Lady's Luck*, and no doubt Reuth as well.

As the evening darkened, Reuth sat hunched with a few feet of chain manacling him to the timbers of the stern deck. He decided right then that this truly must be his night, and that was all there was to it. No more half measures. No more running. He'd come to realize that there were no easy escapes for him. He considered his freedom incalculably important – valuable enough to be bought with blood. Others', and probably some of his.

What set his plan in motion was the sight of Gren's pair of big fighting dirks tucked between the boards just behind the gear next to the stern-plate. Big enough to hack away the meat of the timber round the pin securing his chains. Big enough to take a man's life, if necessary. Though he still hoped he could avoid that.

So he waited, behaving himself, while the coast came to life in campfires, and voices called to one another, and he overheard snatches of distorted shouting and laughter. To the east, cliffs rose straight from the shore and now they stood black as night. Night birds emerged and fish splashed snapping up insects in the calm waters of the bay. Across the clear night sky the Goddess's Wall, as the Korelri had it, emerged to shine as a horizon-to-horizon barrier, where, they said, she kept watch against all manner of uncanny demons.

At least that was what they said now that she had been banished from the physical realm.

He waited long into the night, and would have waited even longer but for the fear that Storval, or others, would return or be sent back to the vessel. He took up one of Gren's fighting dirks and reversed it to hold it tight to his stomach.

'Emmel,' he called, 'the anchor's come loose and we're sliding in towards shore.'

'The Lady's Ire we are,' Emmel growled and, coming up to him,

394

dutifully leaned out to test the chain. Reuth saw his chance and lunged, hammering the man high in the back and sending him tumbling over the side.

Things all rushed together then. Jands called, sharpish, 'What was that?'

Emmel managed one gurgled call before going under. Emmel, it appeared, belonged to that majority of sailors who did not know how to swim. Reuth yelled: 'Gods below! Emmel's fallen overboard!'

'*What?*' Jands appeared in a rush.

'He was testing the anchor chain . . .'

Jands, too, leaned out. But something tipped him, perhaps the strangeness of the situation, or Reuth acted too quickly. In any case, his push, intended to send him after Emmel, merely had the first mate tumbling to the deck.

'Lying little sneak!' the man growled, and came at him obviously intending to beat him to a pulp. The point of no return had been reached for Reuth. He swiped the blade out across his front as the man lunged. He hadn't wanted to, and he closed his eyes and flinched backwards as he did so.

Jands let go a fierce yelp of surprise combined with a disbelieving snarl of pain and rage. Reuth forced himself to open his eyes to see the man staggering back, a hand clenched to his forearm where a long deep gash welled blood that dripped from his fingertips to hit the deck in big wet droplets.

'Bastard sneaky snotty upstart,' Jands was cursing under his breath as he made his way to the mid-decks. Reuth knew what the man was going for and turned to the pin that secured the chain of his manacles. Using the heavy knife like an axe, he hacked at the wood on either side of the pin. Chips of fresh bright yellow wood jumped to the deck.

Jands yelled from somewhere out of sight: 'Shoulda killed you right away! There's those of us who argued so. But no, Storval had to save your skin till we reached the goldfields. Well, you brat . . .' he appeared, a rag tied around one arm and a shortsword in his other hand, 'we're here now, aren't we.'

Reuth hacked at the timber in near-blind panicked desperation. The man closed and swung. Reuth parried the awkward blow and realized that the man was swinging with his off-hand. Thank the gods for that. Snarling, Jands swung again, and Reuth, completely unfamiliar with knife-fighting, or any other sort of fighting for that matter, barely managed to deflect the blow, which struck him high in the head and sent a white-hot spike of pain across his mind.

Through a pink haze he saw Jands pulling the weapon back for a straight killing thrust. He remembered then, almost giddy, that Gren always carried two dirks. No sooner had he thought that, or imagined it, than he threw with all his might, falling forward to the wet decking as he loosed the blade.

Some time later, perhaps a mere heartbeat or two, he blinked to wakefulness. He could only see out of one eye. Something slick and hot coated the other. Jands lay a short distance off, awkwardly, one leg twisted back beneath him. He was holding the grip of the dirk where it protruded from his lower stomach, just above his crotch. He was groaning and babbling.

Blinking, shaking with shock and pent-up panicked energy, Reuth used the ship's side to lever himself to his feet. He pulled the second dirk free and set to hacking at the timber once more.

Jands turned his head to him. 'You've done for me, you damned piece of worthless shit.'

Reuth kept hacking. Every blow sent shockwaves of agony through his head. Black spots danced across his vision – including his gummed-shut eye. A loud roaring came and went in his hearing, as if the vessel were approaching an immense waterfall, or raging surf.

'Me! Poor Jands, who never hurt no one!'

Reuth kept swinging. Gods! Would he have to cut the ship in half?

'You're a useless sneaking backstabbing snivelling spoiled rat! That's what you are.' Jands panted to gather breath for another rant. 'I can't believe you've done for me!'

Leaning forward – which took some doing without blacking out – Reuth took hold of the iron pin and tried to yank it back and forth. It gave . . . a little. He returned to bashing at the wood.

Jands was crying now. 'It's just not fair! That's what it is. How could you have killed me? It just ain't fair!'

Reuth had to pause to gather his own breath. He reached down for the pin – and couldn't find it. In a sudden horror he fell to his knees, pawing at the cleft where it had been. Where was it? How could he have lost it? What a fool!

Then he spotted it on the deck where it lay amid the curled chips, still driven through its link of chain. Relief surged through him. Thank Ruse! He thought he'd lost it. He picked it up, or tried to, as when he raised the thing it was yanked from his hand.

Reuth stood blinking at the loose end of chain for some time. Then he realized – oh yes.

He went to the anchor stanchion, dragging the chain behind,

found the storm release, and pulled it free. The length of anchor chain went rattling and slithering free like a hound released from its leash.

The next thing would require him to make it to the bows. And that would mean . . . Jands lay in his way. He edged as close as he dared. The man was still alive. He was panting as if running, his lower torso, crotch and thighs a wet mess of blood. His eyes were open and glaring murder and hatred upon Reuth's head.

Reuth gingerly raised his leg and stepped over the man.

A wet slick hand snapped up to grip his sailcloth trousers. Reuth almost screamed his horror. 'Save poor Jands,' the man begged. 'Please . . . be a good lad and bring help for your old friend . . . poor Jands.'

Smothering his terror, Reuth reached down and brushed the hand from its clutching grip the way one might remove a clinging piece of dirt or mud.

The hand fell to the deck timbers with a heavy thud. 'Heartless murdering piece of shit!'

Reuth then did the hardest thing. He walked away from a man who would soon be dead. A man he had killed. The first – well, the second – man he had killed. He felt diminished as a person as he limped away. But he also felt a childish sort of surge of triumph and energy.

What followed was so much easier. The plain setting of the small foresail, the return to tie off the rudder. Only then did he dare allow himself to relax. He sat on a small stool the steersman was sometimes allowed to pull out, and leaned upon the arm.

The night seemed somehow darker. He blinked, jerked his head up. Then he slid from the stool and banged his head on the deck. He couldn't stop the spinning after that and he was unable to get up.

A voice roused him to wakefulness. Someone spoke, 'Hasn't pulled free. Been a fight.' A heavy step sounded close by. 'Look at this.'

Another voice: 'Mutineer?'

Chain rattled. Someone yanked his leg. 'An escaped prisoner. Or a slave.'

Reuth forced open his eyes, or tried to. One was glued shut. He saw a giant towering over him. A bearded soldier in a long mail coat that hung to his knees. Over his armour the man wore a pale cloth surcoat.

'You are safe now, lad,' he said. 'We offer you sanctuary. And we among the Blue Shields take such offers very seriously.'

Reuth let his head fall back to the decking. Sanctuary? The word troubled him; sounded too much like the pious mouthings of the Stormguard. Was he no better off? After all that . . . The idea was just too much for him and he had to choose between weeping or slipping away into darkness.

He chose the easier of the two.

*　　*　　*

Orman and the Reddin brothers returned to the Sayer Greathall as swiftly as they could. They jog-trotted up the forested valleys, splashed through streams of run-off, and laboured their way up steep bare rocky ridge-slopes. When at last Orman broke through the forest surrounding the cleared fields he was relieved, and also vaguely uneasy, to see the hall still standing, but quietly so, as if abandoned. No one walked the fields or patrolled the yards, though a thin white plume was climbing from the longhouse's smoke-hole.

Was it truly abandoned? Would they enter to find slain corpses? But of course not – the Greathall would certainly be aflame if that were so.

He shook off his dread and continued on. The Reddin brothers, as was their wont, said nothing of their thoughts.

No one challenged them as they leapt up the wooden stairs to the wide open entrance. Just within the darkness of the long hall, Heavyhand awaited them. He was armoured for war in a long mail coat over leathers manufactured in the old-fashioned manner, with the rings as large as coins and riveted to the leather hauberk. His wild mane of greying hair was pulled back and braided, his beard tied off with strips of leather. The spear he held carried a blade as large as an axe.

He allowed them to pass, but offered no greeting, and his gaze was reserved. Beyond, Jaochim and Yrain waited in their raised wooden chairs, one to either side of the central empty one. Orman crossed to stand directly before them and inclined his head.

'I am sorry,' he began. 'But . . .' He found he could not speak the news he'd run all this way to give. His throat constricted as if in rebellion. The words for what he had to say remained burning in his chest.

Jaochim raised a hand in acknowledgement. 'The Eithjar have informed us, Orman. They say also that you slew Lotji with Svalthbrul.'

'Yes.'

398

'That is good. They are gone then. More blood has been spilled, but the feud between us is done.'

Orman could not prevent himself from frowning his amazement and disapproval. This was their main concern? Not the loss of Vala and Jass? He glanced between the two. 'Good? What of the invading army? They will return. The Bain Greathall is only the first . . .'

He broke off because Yrain surged to her feet. 'Do not presume to lecture us, hearthguard. The Bain Holding is merely the most recent of some twenty others. All gone. Every disappearance witnessed by us. Do not think us unmoved by this creeping valley-by-valley pogrom we have been forced to endure. You presume to judge us by your standards. Please do not do so. It is misguided – and in error.'

Her gaze was so severe Orman almost thought himself personally responsible for the centuries of murders and purgings her story implied.

She lowered her gaze then, releasing him, and sat once more. 'We are the last. We few remaining Holdings. It is up to us how to greet this final nightfall of our kind. We choose to meet it at our hearth's side, face on. Without running. Without flight. For truly . . . there remains nowhere to run.'

Still panting, Orman wiped the sweat from his eyes and turned to the Reddin brothers. They shared a silent glance and nodded. Deep down, Orman wanted to run. He desperately wanted to live. But he could not shame himself in front of the brothers, or Jaochim, nor, of course, the memory of Jass. So he swallowed his fears, his yammering need to flee, and nodded as well.

Jaochim and Yrain smiled as if this was to be expected, then stood. 'Very good,' Jaochim announced. 'We were right in offering you the roof of our hall and the food of our table, and the rings from our own hands. Sayer Greathall shall not fall so easily.' He raised his gaze to Bernal. 'Heavyhand, what say you?'

Bernal crossed his thick arms, hugging the haft of his pole-arm to his chest. 'The outbuildings should all be burned. All the stored grain and foodstuffs should be moved inside. The animals should be scattered.'

Jaochim nodded his agreement. He motioned them out. 'See to it.'

The Reddin brothers turned and went. Orman was slow to follow; he still had so many questions. But the two Icebloods descended to the rear of the raised wood platform. He reluctantly followed the brothers out.

In the muddy open ground before the Greathall he hurried to match strides with Bernal. 'They really do not expect to withstand a siege, do they?' he demanded. 'We cannot defend against fifty, or a hundred. They'll just burn the place down around us.'

The veteran huffed into his thick russet beard. 'Do not dismiss Iceblood magics, lad. They're still powerful up here in the highlands.'

'But Vala . . .'

Bernal pulled a hand through his beard. 'What I heard suggests she chose her end, lad. She chose to pass beyond with Jass.'

Orman felt tears welling up once more. He wiped his sleeve across his eyes. Yes. She did that, didn't she.

'Now, as for us,' Bernal began, 'you lot can start bundling all the useful supplies into the Greathall.'

Rather than answering, the Reddin brothers inclined their heads and jogged off. Orman coughed to try to clear the burning heat from his throat, and followed.

*　　*　　*

It began before Jute noticed it. He and Ieleen had been surprised, and pleased, to see a longboat come their way from Tyvar's vessel, the *Resolute*. In it came a contingent of Blue Shields together with its commander himself. One trooper carried what appeared to be a wounded sailor up the rope ladder and brought him immediately to Jute. It was a young man, and he was unconscious.

'An escapee from the besiegers,' Tyvar announced. 'Perhaps a slave or a prisoner.'

Jute called to his wife: 'Ieleen, a patient for you.'

She stood. 'Bring him to the crew's quarters – and someone must guide me.'

Jute signed to his crewmen to obey. Tyvar motioned to his troopers to follow the sailors' lead.

Once the wounded fellow and Ieleen were below, Jute turned to the commander. 'Why all the fuss? There must be many such deserters and escapees.'

'His hands,' Tyvar replied, rather enigmatically.

Jute frowned. 'I'm sorry?'

'Soft, pale, unscarred, and stained black under the nails. No oarsman or servant, that one. Literate. And the ship we pulled him from was a Mare war galley.'

Jute's brows rose. A Mare vessel? Quite the prize.

Tyvar reached into his belt and pulled forth an instrument Jute instantly recognized: an alidade. 'And he carried this.'

Jute reached out and Tyvar set it in his hands. It was a beautiful piece of cast and polished bronze. Crude by Falaran standards, of course, what with their tradition of open-water exploration. But more important, he could see this one had been designed to personal order. He shook his head, amazed. What an accomplishment for someone coming from a region of shallow-water navigation!

He blew out a breath. 'I see . . . Well, won't you stay for a drink, commander?'

Tyvar pulled a hand down his beard and offered Jute a wink. 'I do believe I shall.'

In his cabin, Jute poured two tiny thimbles of Falaran distilled spirit made from the seeds of a low bush that grew on the islands of their archipelago. They called it Peuch. When he turned from the cupboards, however, he found that they were not two, but three. He was annoyed, and rather alarmed, to find that Khall-head hanger-on from the Wrongway camp sitting at the table.

'What in the name of damned Mael are you doing here?' He pointed to the door. 'Get the Abyss out.'

Tyvar raised a hand to beg permission to intercede. 'If I may, captain?' Jute subsided, grumbling beneath his breath. The Blue Shield commander then surprised Jute immensely by saying slowly, and gently, as if addressing an infant: 'You really should ask permission before entering the captain's quarters.'

The Khall-head raised his brows in slow-motion surprise. His yellowed eyes roamed the chamber as if only now fully aware of his surroundings – which Jute did not doubt.

Tyvar continued, 'So wait outside, won't you?'

The fellow smiled then – his eerie empty raising of the lips – and bestirred himself. Despite his antagonism, the state of his limbs raised a wince of empathy from Jute. The man was emaciated, scabbed by sores and the old weeping cuts of an unhealthy body hardly functioning, let alone healing.

He shambled from the cabin. Jute eyed the huge commander. 'Who is he to you?'

Tyvar cleared his throat, tossed back his thimble of spirit and sucked his teeth. 'Cartheron told me his tale. A man worthy of our pity. A sad tale that . . .' His voice tailed off and his gaze swung across the cabin to the door.

'What is it?'

'It's begun,' Tyvar announced.

'What? What's begun?'

'An attack on Mantle.' Two broad steps took the man to the door

401

and out. Jute hurriedly knocked back his shot of Peuch, coughed, and followed.

He found Lieutenant Jalaz also on deck. She wore only a plain padded undershirt that hung to her knees. She was gazing up at the cliff top.

'What—' Jute began, but Tyvar lifted his hand. Jute strained to listen, but all he could hear was a strange sort of murmuring from above, as of many voices and sharp sounds commingled.

'They've rushed the walls,' Tyvar announced.

'Really? How can you . . .'

'By the time we climb those stairs it'll be over,' Giana grumbled.

Tyvar nodded his grim assent. 'Still, the effort must be made. Prepare yourself, lieutenant. You and I must climb to see who now holds Mantle.'

'I will come too,' Jute added, rather surprising himself.

Instead of scoffing, as he feared, the two warriors merely shared a knowing, amused smile. Tyvar pulled a hand down his beard, trying to hide his grin. 'Your wife,' the Blue Shield commander said. 'She has complained of your penchant for rushing in where you shouldn't. She made us swear not to . . . ah, encourage it.'

Something in him felt very annoyed by Ieleen going behind his back like that. 'I've come damned far and I swore I'd see this through!'

Tyvar raised a hand in surrender. 'I cannot argue with that, captain. And you may of course travel where you would. However, we ask one thing . . .'

'Yes?'

Tyvar shared a wink with Giana. 'That *you* face her when we return.'

'Leave her to me.'

Giana burst out with a laugh and headed off to get ready, saying, 'I'd rather face these invaders, myself.'

Tyvar held out a hand and his sword, sheathed and wrapped in its belt, was pressed into his grip by one of his troopers. He fastened it round the long quilted aketon that he wore as part of his armour's underpadding, and gestured an invitation to Jute. 'Shall we?'

Giana rushed up to join them as they left the ship. She wore leathers and carried a Malazan-issue shortsword at her side. 'Cartheron?' she asked.

Tyvar shook his head. 'He made it plain he would not be travelling up and down those stairs. "Like a weasel popping out of its hole" I believe were his exact words.'

Jute smiled at that, but was saddened as well. The man clearly hadn't recovered from his gut wound – and probably never would, as he was so very old.

The Genabackan reiver Enguf met them on the dock. His cheery greeting was, to Jute's ears, rather forced. 'Going topside, are we?' The man laughed. 'Good, good. You'll enquire as to the plans, yes? Perhaps I and my crew should be sent for help? Yes? Gather reinforcements?' The crewmen on the dock behind him all nodded their heads enthusiastically.

'I'll . . . suggest it,' Tyvar promised.

'Good, good!' The reiver waved farewell as they passed.

Starting up the stairs, Giana muttered, 'Fifty Malazan orbs says they won't be here when we return.'

'They will be,' Tyvar answered, sounding amused.

'Why's that?'

'Because they know they can't get past my men without my approval. They are, effectively, trapped.'

Jute climbed unhappily, already resenting the effort. Above, the shouts and clash of battle rose and fell like a surf washing a distant shore. The Blue Shield commander's pace was steady and a touch faster than his; he hurried to keep up. His thoughts turned to the man's predicament. He had said that the Genabackan pirate was trapped – what then of Tyvar himself? Was he? Jute cleared his throat. 'Commander?'

'Just Tyvar to you, captain.'

'Thank you, sir. If I may . . . with all due respect. Are you not disheartened?'

The wooden slats of the stairs creaked ominously as the man paused to glance back over his shoulder, a brow raised. 'Disheartened?'

Jute decided that perhaps that was too strong a word. 'Ah, concerned?'

Tyvar resumed climbing. 'Concerned?'

'To have come all this way – followed the commandment of your god – only to find yourself held aside. Hindered.'

The Blue Shield commander nodded profoundly as he continued up the twisting scaffolding. 'I understand. In answer to your question . . . No. We do not. We have faith in Togg, my friend, absent though he may be. All shall be as he foretold. Never fear. Our fate has not come yet . . . but it shall.'

They took another turn in the scaffolding. Giana was gamely

following along behind Jute, grinding her teeth in her frustration, either at the delay, or the rickety construction. After mulling over the Genabackan's words, Jute called up, 'But as you say, many of the gods are gone from this world. Our offerings no longer reach them directly. How . . . isn't it too late?'

Tyvar nodded once more, clasped his hands behind his back – a dangerous move considering their wobbling footholds. 'Haagen and I have spoken much on this. It used to be that guardianship of the spirits of our brothers and sisters resided with us, the Shield Anvil and the Sword. Now, however, with Hood's grip upon all of us released, things have changed.' He spared Jute one quick glance, as if checking to make certain he was keeping up. 'Are you familiar with the old belief that no one truly dies?'

Jute paused in his climbing to blink his confusion. 'I'm sorry . . . ?'

Tyvar paused as well, turned back to face him. 'Oh yes. Reincarnation they call it. We – that is, our spirits, our souls, are reborn from life to life. No one truly ever goes away. It is a very old idea, in point of fact. Ancient.'

For some reason such an assertion profoundly offended Jute. He started climbing once more. 'But . . . what would be the point of that? Is there no purpose to life, then?'

Resuming his climb, his back to Jute, Tyvar raised a finger. 'A-ha. You have grasped the crux of it. What is the point? Or is there any at all? That is the dread. Perhaps one answer is that each life is an opportunity.'

'An opportunity?'

'Yes. For improvement. Or perfection.'

Jute felt quite bewildered by the idea. 'Do you believe this?'

Tyvar glanced back once more. 'Myself? No. It is too far from my previous beliefs. However, Haagen and I agree that we are mortal, yet there resides within us some portion that is non-corporeal, imperishable. Just as some element of Togg and all the various gods remains imperishable. And that now, it is to this that we join or are enfolded after death. And whatever that is could be named the Divine. To *that* will we dedicate our prayers and the care of our spirit.'

More than the vertigo of the ramshackle scaffolding and the blowing wind now tugged at Jute. He felt quite dizzy, and he made an effort to pull his thoughts back to himself. He pressed a hand to his aching brow. 'I really wouldn't know anything about such matters. I am just a modest sailor.'

They had reached the top landing. Tyvar turned to him. 'Perhaps that is what is needed in these uncertain times, my friend. A sailor

– someone used to finding his way upon unfamiliar waters. Who knows?' His brows crimped then, in confusion, and he faced the walls. As did Jute.

All was now quiet, though the northern defenders still guarded the broad semicircle that was the outer walls. They leaned upon their spears and craned their necks to the main gate area. Giana came up beside Jute and frowned her uncertainty. 'A parley?' she ventured.

'Very possibly,' Tyvar answered and strode off across the bailey yard. Jute hurried after him.

They were stopped and surrounded long before they reached the front gate. From the yard, Jute glimpsed so-called King Ronal the Bastard up atop the wall, wrapped in a great bear-hide cloak, crowded round by his bodyguard, apparently involved in a meeting with someone beyond.

Tyvar motioned that he wished to witness. The northern warriors eyed one another, unsure. Taking advantage of their indecision, he simply barged up the nearest dirt ramp. Jute pressed in to follow in his considerable wake. Giana pushed forward as well.

Along the way they passed tents and awnings raised over ranks of wounded being treated. The ramp itself was blood-spattered and littered with the fallen broken accoutrements of war – shattered spear-hafts, battered shields, a hide shoe, slit and soaked in its owner's blood.

When Jute made the wall, he was treated to the breathtaking view of a mass of foreign besiegers, though a rather ragged and poorly armed mass. Dotted among these ranks of men – and Jute felt reluctant to name such shabby specimens soldiers – stood fully armed and armoured obvious professionals. And these all bore the same heraldry upon their shields and banded-iron hauberks – the sigil of a tower.

Jute didn't know the symbol. 'What soldiers are those?' he asked Tyvar.

The commander was obviously wondering the same thing himself as he scratched his beard musingly. After a time, he came to a conclusion and nodded to himself. 'Letherii,' he murmured. 'Some noble or trading house of the Lether Empire.'

Lether? Jute was surprised; the Letherii were not seafarers. But then, there was gold to be had, so he really ought not to be shocked that the Letherii were involved. Jute put their numbers in the hundreds. The contingent also appeared to have two commanders, as they were the only individuals mounted. One of these raised a hand, as if for silence, though no one was talking, and announced, 'Very good, King Ronal. Your silence is answer enough. Remain cornered here in Mantle. You can watch while we take control of all the north.'

The speaker was a younger man in what was obviously an extremely expensive set of banded armour, inlaid and etched with intricate curling designs. His fellow commander sat tall upon his mount, boarding-pole slim, grey-haired, in much-worn leathers.

'Your realm, King Ronal,' the younger fellow continued, 'has dwindled to a stone's throw across. I understand that the custom here is that when the grip of the old ruler weakens, a new one arises to assert control. Who am I to argue with tradition? Sieges, by the way, are all about time. Time and suffering. We go now to take control of the goldfields – first things first, after all. Once that is done, we will return to relieve you of your suffering. Until then.' He offered a mocking bow in farewell.

Wrapped in his bear cloak, King Ronal the Bastard cackled a grating laugh and waved him off. 'Go on! The Icebloods will have your heads!'

The Lether noble was not concerned. 'I think not. I wonder, in fact, whether there are any of them left.' He turned his mount and cantered off, followed by his companion officer. King Ronal stormed from the wall. His bodyguard and crowd of court followers nearly tripped and fell over one another to keep from underfoot.

Tyvar pushed towards the man's path. King Ronal caught sight of him. Indeed, it was hard to miss him as he was as broad as a haystack. The king pointed, shouting, 'What in the name of the ancients do you want?'

Tyvar bowed his head. 'Once more, King Ronal, I humbly offer my—'

The Bastard threw his spindly arms into the air. 'Another damned foreigner making demands upon me! To the Hooded Taker's grip with all of you!' and he barged onward without another glance. His entourage hurried after him.

Jute and Giana moved close to Tyvar, who had remained quite still, his features controlled, but impassively so. Jute could not help but let out a growl. 'I cannot believe such treatment. Tyvar, sir, you show astounding patience . . .'

The Blue Shield commander gave a wave as if to brush that aside. 'If dedication to something infinitely greater than oneself should teach anything, it is humility.'

Jute remained unconvinced. 'Well . . . I'm dumbfounded. Especially given the fame of your brother order the Grey Swords, and what they managed against the Pannions. This is plain stupidity!'

Tyvar shook his head. 'No. It is pride. We outlanders have taken his kingdom from him. Brushed his people aside. Why should he be favourably inclined towards us?'

'Pride . . .' Giana ground out. Something in her tone made Jute glance at her. She was scowling ferociously. 'Just another word for stupidity . . .' She was staring off towards the wall as she spoke and Jute followed her gaze to find the old Malazan woman, the emissary of that empire, staring back. Her hands were busy adjusting the folds of her black layered blouse and skirts, brushing her face, primping her tightly pulled-back hair. He realized that she and Giana were somehow communicating, and that Giana was not happy. He returned his gaze to the ex-lieutenant to find her glaring straight at him. He hurriedly looked away.

Tyvar let out a breath, loosened his shoulders. 'It would appear that we must yet wait a while longer.' He invited them to follow him back to the stairs. 'Perhaps when they get hungrier they will be more amenable to negotiation.'

*   *   *

The grit of pulverized rock crackled beneath Silverfox's sandalled feet as she walked the subterranean chamber. With her toes she edged aside shattered wood from a chair to approach a sprawled corpse. A woman. Sliced through by the clean unmistakable cut of an Imass stone weapon. Nothing sharper, she thought, feeling very distant from it all. Even in this day and age, after all these centuries.

Her minders, Pran and Tolb, hovered nearby, she was certain, though she couldn't see them at the moment. Prudent, that, given what she felt rising up within her.

She thought she'd managed to contain it all. Tamp it down, choke it off. She'd told herself she could live with all this killing. This murder. Now her numbness scared her. A new worry clawed at her stomach – was she becoming what she despised?

Oblivion would be preferable.

Yet . . . the dread within her whispered: *what if not even oblivion is for you?*

She raised her gaze to the stone ceiling where colossal wild magics had gouged and scarred the root rock. She blinked to clear her vision. The stink of rotting flesh assaulted her nostrils and raised acid in her throat.

I deserve this reek. I should live with it always. A reminder—

No. I should not need reminding. That I would ever need reminding is . . . unforgivable.

Grit crackled again as she made her way to the next corpse – an elderly man thrust through numerous times. Strong in his Jaghut blood, this one – he appeared to have ignored several mortal wounds to continue fighting – yet without the obvious strong markers of his heritage, the pronounced jaws and tusk-like teeth, the height. Without those. So did communities change over time. Look at the diversity of the peoples she knew – all from a common ancestor.

Ancestors she walked with now, who yet appeared far from her blood with their thick robust bones, their squat build and wide jaws.

Flies swarmed the dark holes that once held this one's eyes. She was grateful that she did not have to meet his gaze, even a fixed death stare. She suspected it would be too much. She felt she was on a knife's edge of . . . shattering. The faintest, most innocuous sound might send her tumbling over that edge to where she could never find herself again.

She'd driven her flesh beyond exhaustion, beyond what it should be expected to endure. Yet that was as nothing to the agony her soul had inflicted upon itself. Could a person choke on self-loathing? She felt she was as much a walking corpse as her companions.

Quick light steps across the littered floor swung her about: she caught a glimpse of a slip of a girl, her glaring eyes bright and wild in the gloom, her shirt and long skirting tattered and scorched, before the child launched herself upon her. Instinctively, Silverfox caught her arms and they rocked there, straining, limbs outstretched.

No reason remained in the hatred and rage pouring from the wide eyes. The broken nails of the clawed fingers stretched for her. *Protect yourself!* the voice of Tattersail shouted within. *Destroy her!* the Thelomen bellowed.

Yet Silverfox did not raise the powers of the magery at her command. Instead, she fought to catch those rolling eyes and said, her voice cracking, 'Why?'

Perhaps it was the strangeness of being addressed – or the strangeness of the question itself – but she felt the girl's arms ease. The mouth, working and twisted, fell into a frown of disbelief.

'Why . . . ?' the girl repeated as if testing the word. '*Why?*' She pulled away, clasped her hands behind her back as if to restrain them there. 'You dare ask *why*? You, who slew my family?'

What could she say? The time for 'Sorry' was long past. Ten thousand years past. No, the gulf was too profoundly deep to be bridged by any such gesture. 'What I mean,' she said, 'is why must we kill each other?'

The girl fairly quivered in the grip of emotions no doubt as profound as those afflicting Silverfox herself. Blood-smeared and ragged, she looked like a lost waif. Silverfox had to resist the urge to reach out in an effort to soothe her.

'*You* attacked us!' the girl accused.

'And who are we?'

'You are the enemy we thought would never come. A legend. Stories to scare children. The Army of Dust and Bone.'

So that may be the legacy of the Imass, Silverfox mused. A legend. A frightening threat from the dark night of the past. Even that, she decided, would be eminently preferable. She cleared her throat to speak as she could hardly force out the words. 'Well . . . it is over. No one will threaten you now. You are in no danger.'

The girl's frown eased, though she remained wary, her brows clenched in worry. Then she seemed to come to a decision and her mouth twitched upwards in something like a strained mask-like smile. 'In that case—' she began, then jerked, her eyes bulging.

The point of a brown flint sword punched through the front of her chest. Yet her eyes held Silverfox's. As they dimmed, it seemed to the Summoner that they poured forth a child's hurt at a profound betrayal, and this grief broke Silverfox's heart. The girl slid off the blade revealing Pran Chole behind. Silverfox stared her horror at the Imass. She whispered, 'What have you done?'

'Summoner . . . she was—'

Silverfox threw up a hand to command his silence. The presence of Tattersail, the old Malazan mage, was now choking her in its outrage. '*Answer this crime!*' the ghost-presence of the woman demanded.

But no. No more retaliation. She was done with it. Done with them all. The raised hand now waved dismissal, but it was she who staggered off, lurching, almost blind. She wondered why tears would not come. Am I that hardened now? Instead, anger possessed her: a heated sizzling rage. To think they once held her pity! Chained to a ritual sworn ages ago! Unbending. Immovable. Intractable! They will not change.

Suddenly, it was clear what she had to do. If they were incapable of change, then it was up to her to force it upon them. She was, after all, the Summoner.

The entrance was a half-choked glare of light. She kicked her way through the rubble towards it. Her hand was still extended out behind her, daring anyone to follow.

In the darkness behind, broken rock crackled once more as Tolb Bell'al joined Pran Chole. The latter extended his withered foot in its tattered leather remnants to press open the hands of the dead girl. A thin knife blade clattered to the stones, its edge dark with venom.

The two exchanged a silent glance.

'Shall we ever convince her of it?' Tolb asked.

Pran shook his head, the leather of his neck creaking. 'Best not to bring it up again, I think.'

Tolb nodded his agreement. 'Perhaps so.'

Silverfox exited the stone portal like a swimmer broaching the surface after a too-long dive. She gasped for breath, lurching, grasping at the wall for support. The waiting ranks of Ifayle and Kron flinched from her as they sensed her rage. She stormed off, up a grass-thatched dune, to a single figure standing alone, her long black hair whipping in the wind.

'I am done with them,' Silverfox announced, coming abreast of Kilava.

The ancient Bonecaster crossed her arms. 'Strange how all those who meet the T'lan Imass eventually come to that conclusion. Those who survive, in any case.'

But Silverfox could not share the woman's detachment. 'Tell them to keep their distance. I will go on alone in this. Meet Lanas on my own.' She paused. 'That is, unless you wish to witness?'

Kilava pushed her hair from her wide face, the broad cheekbones and thick, almost brutal brow ridge. 'I would witness.'

CHAPTER XII

KYLE AWOKE TO THE HISS OF RAIN AND UNCONTROLLABLE shudders. He was sitting upright against the trunk of a tall spruce amid needles and twisted roots. Yet even here the night's constant misting rain had found him as it came running down the trunk. He didn't know the north of these lands, of course, but this was the wettest and most icy spring he could remember. Straightening, he muffled a groan and stretched, then pulled his sodden leathers from his legs and back. He needed a fire to warm up, but there appeared little chance of getting one going. He settled instead for that other way to warm oneself, and set off at a jog in an easterly direction.

Ground-hugging fogs snaked through the woods he threaded. Sodden leaf mulch and moss were silent beneath his soft-soled moccasins. Drops of the icy vapour fell from his hair to his shoulders and ran down the back of his neck. The day was dark, hardly warmer than the night. Banks of cloud obscured the heights where breaks in the tree cover allowed a view. He heard the strong pounding of run-off driving through deep ravines and chasms in the distant slopes, but could see only courses of haze that ran down from the heights like rivers themselves.

Strange spring weather. Felt more like autumn.

He crossed over to an easterly valley and started north. The bruises and stings from the clashes the night before – he'd jogged an entire day and night since – slowed him with cramps and a tightness round his chest. Pausing, his breath sending up great plumes of steam, he damned Lyan for a fool. She didn't really think she'd come out on top, did she? Still, she was an experienced war commander – and how many of these Icebloods could there be left anyway? Perhaps it *was* worth the gamble.

411

Yet what of Stalker and Badlands and Coots, should he actually find them? A possibility that appeared to be diminishing by the day. What if she and he were to meet on opposite sides? He snorted as he pushed his way through a prickly, dense patch of brush. Let's not get ahead of ourselves, y'damned idiot. Looks like you're not going to even *find* any of the Losts.

And if they had any sense, they'd all have packed up long ago, anyway.

The next day he reached a broad, flat stream bed of washed gravel where the water chained and sheeted in a thin but icy flow, and he followed the course for the morning. His feet became numb blocks of ice themselves, as did his hands, despite his effort to keep them tucked under his armpits as much as he could.

He was hungry, but not unbearably so; he'd endured far worse. Mushrooms, nuts and berries filled the void for the time being. He'd snared a rabbit the night before and kept an eye out for a dry spot, with tinder enough, to build a fire to cook it. So far he'd found nothing.

Towards mid-day, a discolouring wash came streaming down with the waters. The stain was so washed out it took him some time to identify it as thinned blood. He crouched low and continued on, splashing from the cover of one patch of tall grass to another. Slowly, bit by bit, he came across sodden tatters of torn cloth, scraps of leather. Then the heavier litter of a boot, the broken wooden handle of a shovel or a spade.

Shattered equipment lay ahead. He recognized gold-sluices and hand-held sifting frames. Amid the wreckage lay the bodies of its owners. Hands tucked in his shirt, Kyle carefully studied the remains. Unarmoured, in tattered old jerkins and trousers. A pretty ragged lot. Most were poorly armed as well, as nothing larger than broad heavy knives lay in the water.

He felt sickened. A slaughter. A damned slaughter. These prospectors didn't stand a chance. It was obvious this lot had nothing to do with burning Greathalls, or warring against the Icebloods. Killing them solved nothing. If anything, it invited retaliation.

Stupid. Damned stupid. Such bloodletting only made things worse. Again, the senselessness of vendetta and blood-feud reprisals and vengeance killings impressed itself upon him. Joining the Guard had opened his eyes to how self-defeating and petty these endless cycles of family or clan retribution were.

Something shifted nearby and he straightened, damning himself. Speaking of stupid . . .

He turned. A man had emerged from the tall green grasses. He was burly, in a torn hide shirt, wide leather wrist-guards, moccasins, and leather leggings up over buckskin trousers. 'Should've run when you saw the bodies, lowlander,' the fellow growled.

Kyle stared. That voice. The wild mane of kinky black hair – the hair all over, actually.

The man charged, long-knives flashing. Kyle rapidly backed off while trying to get the name out. He swung and Kyle fell into the water to avoid the blade.

'*Badlands!*' he managed, half stuttering in his amazement.

But the Lost brother splashed after him as if in a bloodlust fury – this was not the laughing, easy-going Badlands he knew! He lunged in, thrusting. Kyle drew to cut across his front, hacking off Badlands' blade in a loud screech of tempered iron.

Badlands flinched away, blinking his disbelief. Kyle rose to a crouch, the frigid water dripping from him. 'It's me, Kyle,' he said.

Badlands retreated another step. He frowned as if half-comprehending. 'Kyle, lad?'

'Yes, it's me. I've come to find you and Coots and Stalker!'

Now real confusion wrinkled his hairy brow and he waved the shorn weapon in his hand. 'But you was in Korel!'

Kyle sheathed the white sword back under his arm, eased out a long breath. 'I was. Greymane died.'

Badlands dropped his gaze. 'Yeah. I heard the stories.' He let out a hiss, dropped the ruined weapon and squeezed his thumb. 'You cut off the end of my blasted thumb, dammit!'

'Sorry.' Kyle fumbled to find a rag or a piece of cloth to tear.

'Never mind!' The Lost brother surged forward and clasped Kyle's shoulders. 'Look at you now! All growed up. No more the scrawny steppe wolf-pup old Stoop bought from the slave-pen! You look like a damned brigand! Didn't even recognize you with the moustache 'n' all.'

He squeezed Badlands' forearm. 'Glad to have found you. How's Coots and Stalker?'

The Lost brother dropped his grin. He half turned away. 'Coots didn't make it.'

Coots? How could Coots not make it? He'd always seemed so . . . indestructible. All Kyle could manage was an unbelieving,

'I'm sorry.' Badlands gave a shake of his shoulders as if to brush the topic aside. 'And Stalker?'

'Stalk's his same grim old self. Only more so.'

Kyle didn't comment that Badlands struck him as very different from his old self. The old Badlands he knew would never have murdered a gang of dirt-poor barely armed prospectors. But then, his brother was dead. His land was being stolen from him. And his culture – his people – were being swept from the face of the world. Understandable, one might say.

The Lost's thoughts must have run along lines similar to Kyle's as he clapped him on the shoulder and urged him along. 'Still – great to see you, lad. Just like old times, hey?' And he laughed, but rather crazily – or so it sounded to Kyle. 'Remember ol' Greymane's face when we showed up after that big Malazan fracas? He sure wasn't expecting us.'

Kyle laughed as well, though not nearly so wildly. 'Yes. He probably thought we were Claws come for him at last.'

Badlands led him north. He sucked on his wounded thumb and glanced back, looking him up and down. An amused, speculative light came into his eyes. 'So,' he announced. 'You *are* the White-blade, then.'

Kyle dropped his gaze, shrugging. 'Yeah.'

'Well, well. Ain't that somethin'?' He chuckled. 'We can probably hold off all these damned invaders now.'

The remark annoyed Kyle, as if Badlands had somehow enlisted him into something he might not agree with. 'What do you mean?'

'I mean not only are you Whiteblade, but we all was Crimson Guard together. And damn the old Oddsmaker if that ain't the oddest thing . . .'

Now Kyle was thoroughly perplexed. In fact, he wondered about the man's state of mind. 'Just what are you getting at?'

'I mean remember that talk we heard of the missing Fourth Company?'

Kyle remembered hearing how the Guard, after barely repulsing a Malazan expeditionary army sent to Stratem to destroy them, had divided itself into four companies to pursue contracts around the world. Eventually, those contracts brought the First Company, under Shimmer, to southern Assail where he, along with the Lost cousins, had joined. Long before then, though, the Guard had lost contact with the Fourth and none knew of its whereabouts, or fate. 'What of it?' he asked.

Badlands laughed. His mirth did not reassure Kyle. Before, the man's laughter had been of the most innocent, teasing sort. Now, it sounded as dark as a hangman's welcome. 'Well . . . who do you think Stalk found camped on the mountainside, every sword against them? None other than Cal-Brinn and his Fourth!'

Kyle was amazed. The Fourth found? Here of all places? Yet why not? The First, under Shimmer, was in the south. Plenty of warfare and potential patrons up here. 'How many?'

Badlands nodded at the question. 'Ah! Just the sole survivors of years of fighting. Sixteen of their Avowed.'

Sixteen Avowed! No wonder the Lost Greathall still stood! Then the thought came, what of the rest in Stratem? 'We should get word of this to K'azz.'

Badlands continued nodding as he climbed the slope ahead. 'Yeah. We talked about that. Cal says they'll come. He says, eventually, they'll have to come.' He gave an eloquent shrug. 'What he means by that I have no idea. Anyway, the Eithjar sure don't like them hanging around. They hate them. Told Stalk to get rid of them! Funny that. Competition, maybe, hey?' and he laughed again, darkly, without humour.

Kyle offered a weak answering laugh then was quiet. He now almost regretted finding his old friend. Compared to the old Badlands, this new one only made him sad.

Two days of climbing through intermittent rains, fording swollen run-off streams, and crossing high mountain vales brought them to a temperate mist-forest in a narrow valley. Kyle reflected that they must now be at enough of an elevation to have entered the clouds that hugged the highest slopes of the Salt range. That, or the weather was one of persistent low cloud cover. He'd heard of wet springs, of course, but this felt extreme.

They exited the tall mature forest of ash and hemlock to enter a series of what appeared to be overgrown fields. Younger deciduous trees dominated here, birch and poplar, and the ground cover was thicker, high brush and bramble. Kyle judged these particular fields uncultivated for decades. Past these once-cleared tracts they came to a tall grass pasture where a number of cattle grazed, apparently unsupervised. Beyond, up the gentle rise of the vale, rose the grass-covered pitched roof of the Lost Greathall. Badlands led the way.

Fog and a light misty rain that draped down like folds of cloth hugged the colossal structure. Broad, rough-hewn log steps led up to the main entrance, which gaped wide. Kyle noted how wet green moss grew like a carpet over the steps.

Rainwater pattered down across the doorway. Just within stood two guards, bearded, in much-battered layered leather armour that appeared to have once been stained a deep red. Two Avowed, Kyle assumed. They greeted Badlands. Kyle gave them a nodded hello and almost told them he was of the Guard as well, but he stopped himself as he considered how asinine that would sound coming from someone who obviously was *not* currently of the Guard. Badlands pushed on, the rain pattering from his shoulders.

Within, it was dark, and Kyle paused to allow his vision to adjust. The hall was huge, cavernous, almost all one long main room. Light streamed down from a smoke-hole near the middle of its length over a broad hearth ringed in stones, dark now, hardly smoking at all. Badlands trudged in past long tables cluttered with a litter of old hides and cloaks, bowls and knives. Spears stood leaning against the tables. Kyle noted the dust coating their broad iron heads. From the darkness beyond the reach of the light streaming down from the smoke-hole came the murmur of music – the slow strumming of some sort of stringed instrument.

At the far end, a man sat at a long table covered in bowls and platters. He glanced up, revealing long straight sandy hair, a drooping blond moustache, and bright hazel eyes – Stalker Lost.

'Another guest,' Badlands called out.

Stalker growled, 'Another? We're gettin' overrun here.' Then he frowned beneath his moustache and half rose. 'You look familiar.'

Kyle nodded, grinning. 'Yes.'

'Kyle, lad? That you?'

'Yes, Stalker.'

The head of the Lost clan came round the table. 'By all the false gods! It is you! Look at you!' He set his hands on Kyle's shoulders. 'You've filled out.'

The strumming stopped. A figure emerged from the dark, tall and lean with long straight dark hair. He moved with the grace of a courtier and carried what looked like a wooden box set with strings across its face. Stalker motioned to him. 'Fisher. Fisher Kel Tath.'

'Fisher? The bard?'

The man bowed. 'Indeed. And you are Kyle . . . not the Kyle once of the Crimson Guard, companion to Greymane, the Stonewielder?'

Kyle was embarrassed, but nodded. 'Yes.'

The bard's brows rose high. 'I have sung songs of you. There is a name for you now, you know.'

Kyle glanced away, unable to disguise his discomfort. 'Yes.'

Another figure emerged from the dark, and despite himself Kyle stared. A Tiste Andii with skin like midnight and black sable hair that bore streaks of white. Tall and muscular. Not at all lean. The bard's gaze, Kyle noted, was moving swiftly between them, back and forth, as if expecting something.

'This is . . . Jethiss,' the bard said, introducing his companion. 'Kyle.'

Jethiss nodded a greeting which Kyle answered. For some obscure reason the bard appeared disappointed and he stroked his chin thoughtfully.

Stalker motioned to the table. 'Have a seat, lad! What in the Seven Mysteries brings you here?'

Kyle laughed. 'I gather it's not the best of timing, but I came to look up old friends.'

Stalker shared the laugh then looked up, surprised, as Badlands appeared from the depths of the hall carrying two tall earthenware tankards. One he set down in front of Kyle and the other before the bard, then he disappeared once more. Stalker glowered at the empty table before him.

The drink was a homebrew, warm and weak, but Kyle thought it delicious, as it had been a long time since he'd had anything resembling beer. Badlands returned with two tankards. One he set before Jethiss and the other he kept as he sat.

Stalker gestured to the table. 'What about me?'

'Get your own.'

The elder Lost cousin rolled his eyes, but rose and stomped off.

'You are making quite a name for yourself,' Fisher told Kyle.

Again, Kyle felt acutely uncomfortable; here was the composer and singer of so many epic lays about ancient heroes telling him *he* was making a name? Was he making fun of him? He didn't know what to say and so he merely shrugged and muttered, 'Just trying to stay alive.'

Again the bard glanced between him and the Andii. 'You never met Anomandaris, did you?'

Kyle did not hide his perplexity at the question. 'No, never. Why?'

The bard was nodding to himself, his hand still at his chin. 'Just wondering. As a poet, the parallels interest me.'

'Parallels?'

Stalker re-joined them, sitting at Badlands' bench.

'Did you know that Anomandaris carried another title beyond Son of Darkness?'

Kyle had no idea what the man was getting at. He shook his head.

The bard's gaze flicked to the Andii, Jethiss, who sat solemn and quiet, as if carved of jet. 'Another name the man carried was Black-sword.'

Some sort of alarm now widened Jethiss's dark eyes, and the line of his sharp chin writhed as he ground his jaws.

Kyle tilted his head, recalling. 'I remember hearing that once or twice.'

Fisher nodded. 'Now he is gone from us. The black sword is broken. And almost immediately what should arise but another blade . . . a white blade.'

Kyle wanted to leap from the table. How could he put these two things together? It wasn't comparable at all! 'Now wait a minute . . . what are you suggesting?'

The bard leaned back, raising his open hands. 'I'm not suggesting anything. I am merely observing. These facts couldn't escape the notice of any singer.'

Kyle scowled, irritated by the observation. Gods! As if he didn't have enough troubles already! 'Well . . . I'd really rather not hear any such speculations.'

'As you will.'

The Andii, Kyle noted, drew breath to speak then, but checked himself and turned his attention to Badlands instead. The Iceblood – for that was what Kyle now knew all these northerners for – had been giving the discussion hardly any attention at all as he sat forward on his elbows, staring down at his tankard. The Andii cleared his throat. 'Badlands,' he began, 'tell me – what lies to the far north of here?'

Fisher actually winced at the question. 'Nothing that concerns us,' he put in quickly.

The Lost brother slowly raised his head and Kyle flinched inwardly upon seeing his face, for it hardly resembled at all the laughing and joking Badlands he had known before. The mouth was a grim line etched in granite, the eyes hollow and flat and empty. How hard it must be for the man to sit here surrounded at every turn by reminders of what was gone from him. He must feel severed in half.

One corner of those humourless lips edged up. 'The far north? You mean the heights? The peaks of the Salt range?'

Jethiss nodded.

'Those are just legends,' Fisher cut in, giving Badlands a warning glare.

But the Lost brother answered with his own scornful look. 'Right, *bard*. Just stories and fanciful songs.' He turned his attention to Jethiss. 'Up above the Holdings are the ice-fields of the Salt range. Snake-like rivers of ice that descend from a broad plateau of blue-black ice some thousand feet thick. We rarely venture up there as there's little hunting to be had. The only one who haunts those heights is old Buri. The Sayers claim him as an ancestor, but really he's a forefather of us all seein' as he's older even than some clans.' Badlands took a sip from his tankard. 'Beyond the ice-fields are the peaks – wind-blasted bare rock faces where nothing ever grows. No plants at all. No moss or weed. Just dry, cold and barren.'

'There's an old story, though,' Stalker began, easing into his cousin's tale. 'Our uncle, Baynar Lost, travelled to those heights. He told of seeing bizarre things, hallucinations, maybe. He claimed he saw something that resembled a tower of rock. Stones heaped up tall into something like a dwelling.' Stalker turned his bright golden eyes on Fisher. 'How's that tale go, Fish? Our origins?'

Jethiss turned his expectant gaze upon the bard. Fisher let out a long hard breath, shot Stalker an annoyed glance. 'Our legends say that's where we were born. We Icebloods. That our ancestor guards the heights. Mother of us all.'

The title *ancestor* startled Kyle. He remembered the words of the Silent People's champions and their shamans: 'Go to the great mountains to stand before our ancestors . . .' He'd thought it referred to these people, these so-called Icebloods. But perhaps it had a more literal meaning. A real ancestor to stand before – the one and only true ancestor.

Jethiss, he noted, appeared troubled now, even disappointed. He frowned as if puzzled. 'And that is all?' he asked, his gaze searching.

'Regarding the heights?' Badlands answered. He shook his head. 'No . . . there's one more legend about the peaks.' He looked to Fisher. 'Ain't you going to tell it?'

But the bard would not raise his eyes. 'It's just a child's night-story,' he murmured reluctantly. 'Silly nonsense.'

Badlands snorted. 'Well, you've sung of it often enough in the past.' He turned to Jethiss, sipped his beer. 'The legend claims there's a reason the old name for this whole region is *Assail*.' He raised a hand and pointed to the sky. 'That they're there sleeping hidden in caves at the peaks. The Forkrul Assail.'

Stalker grunted his agreement. 'And it's said they'll grant the wish of anyone foolish enough to treat with them.'

'This is all just fireside entertainment,' Fisher interrupted. 'Pure fiction.'

The Losts appeared bemused by the bard's vehemence. 'You've sung of it yourself,' Badlands observed.

419

Jethiss leaned forward. 'Why do you say foolish – foolish to treat with these Forkrul?'

Stalker answered, 'Why, everyone knows about their ways. "Forkrulan justice" is a saying for any harsh, but just, judgement.'

'I am unaware,' Jethiss said, 'as I have lost many of my memories.'

Badlands' tangled brows rose in understanding. 'Ah! Well . . . there's one old story from another land far to the south and west. Its name's forgotten, but the story goes of two champion swordsmen from that land who had met and fought numerous times, to the satisfaction of neither. Finally, to settle the matter of who was the greater swordsman, they decided to request that the Forkrul adjudicate.'

The Losts shared savage grins. 'And they did,' they announced together. 'They killed both of them!' And the cousins roared with laughter and raised their tankards.

Kyle watched the bard shoot his companion, Jethiss, a sideways glance. The Andii appeared to be holding his features carefully neutral.

'Then neither of them must have been any good,' a new voice said from the dark and Kyle half jumped from his seat. But the Losts were not startled. They waved the newcomer forward.

It was an old man – no, a middle-aged man who had endured a very hard life, Kyle thought. He was startlingly dark, of Quon Tali Dal Hon descent. His close-cut kinked hair was shot with grey. His features were drawn and thin, a rough landscape of wrinkles and scars. A man who had endured a harrowing time. He wore a suit of light leather armour that from its much-worn appearance probably served as under-padding for a heavier banded or mail coat.

Stalker made introductions. 'Kyle, this is Cal-Brinn, Captain of the Crimson Guard Fourth Company. Cal-Brinn, Kyle, once one of the Guard with me 'n' Badlands.'

Kyle stood and extended his arm. The captain took his forearm in a firm grip. His smile was small and tight, but appeared genuinely warm. 'Welcome. So, you were in the Guard with the Losts here?'

'Yes.'

'And you helped rescue K'azz?'

'Yes.'

'Then I am in your debt.'

'Not at all! I just wanted to do the right thing.'

'I believe that you did.'

'What news, Cal?' Stalker asked, easing back on to his bench.

'I have a Blade watching the Bain border. They report activity. It looks like they are scouting routes east.'

Stalker nodded grimly. 'Then they're coming.'

'You routed them once,' Badlands observed.

Kyle spoke up. 'I don't think you will this time.'

All eyes turned to him. 'Oh?' Cal-Brinn enquired.

He eased back on the bench. 'I was in Mantle not five days ago. They're besieging it, and they're no longer a ragtag mob of fortune-hunters, marauders and thieves. The core of an army has arrived and they're knocking them into shape.'

'Soldiery?' Stalker asked. 'From where?'

'Lether, I believe.'

Cal-Brinn grunted. 'Never faced them. What numbers?'

'Of regulars? A few hundred, I'd estimate.'

Stalker frowned down into his beer. 'So they have a spine now. That's bad for us.'

Fisher faced Stalker directly. 'Now you must see the foolishness of remaining here in the Greathall. They'll just surround you, cut you off, and burn you down.'

Stalker's long face hardened. 'Been away too long already.' His tone brooked no objection.

Fisher sent a despairing glance Cal-Brinn's way.

The battered Dal Hon mercenary pursed his lips. 'There's always the chance of a small desperate group breaking free of any encirclement.'

Badlands had been drinking from his tankard and he slammed it down and wiped his mouth. 'That's us I'd say. Small and desperate.'

*

The hall possessed no outer defences so they started digging a ditch and piling up the earth in a ring all along the inner slope. It wasn't particularly deep, but it was something to stand behind. They set sharpened sticks, pointing outwards, along its top.

Stalker also set them to filling every vessel and container the hall possessed and scattering these about the inner walls. Of what animals the Losts had collected – a few cattle, sheep, and chickens – they drove off the cattle and slaughtered the rest. No one said it aloud, but the possibility of a lengthy siege wasn't even considered.

At the end of the second day, Cal-Brinn's pickets sent word that a large force had crossed the border, marching in column and heading straight for the Lost Greathall. They would arrive on the morrow.

That night they gorged themselves on a full sheep carcass Stalker had roasted over the hearth. The weather had remained cold and rainy through the days and Kyle sat close to the fire, attempting to dry himself. He imagined he must have looked as dispirited as a wet dog, for Badlands cuffed his shoulder and said, laughingly, 'Don't worry yourself! You'll probably kill so many of them they'll run away!' Then he called loudly, 'Hey! Songster! Let's have us a tune!'

Fisher, off in the darkness, stirred at that, nodding. 'An appropriate request.' He lifted up his box-like instrument and strummed, adjusting it and humming to himself. And then he sang as he gently drew his fingertips across the strings:

> 'And when our blood mixes and drains in the grey earth
> When the faces blur before our eyes in these last of last days
> We shall turn about to see the path of years we have made
> And wail at the absence of answers and the things left unseen
> For this is life's legion of truth so strange so unknown
> So unredeemed and we cannot know what we will live
> Until the journey is done
> My beautiful legion, leave me to rest on the wayside
> As onward you march to the circling sun
> Where spin shadows tracing the eternal day
> Raise stones to signal my passing
> Unmarked and mysterious
> Saying nothing of me
> Saying nothing at all
> The legion is faceless and must ever remain so
> As faceless as the sky'

A long silence followed the last muted tones from the instrument as they faded into the emptiness of the hall. The song was far too grim for Kyle – though certainly appropriate. He noted, blinking as he came out of its spell, that Fisher's gaze, glittering in the flames, had held the face of Jethiss throughout, while the Andii had kept his night-black features as immobile as stone.

At length, Badlands stirred, clearing his throat. 'Can't you play any happy songs on that old kantele, bard?' he complained. 'There's that one about the innkeeper's wife and the dwarf . . .'

Fisher lovingly ran a hand across the face of the oddly angled box. 'A magnificent instrument. My compliments to your ancestor.' He set it aside. 'Not tonight. Tomorrow night, perhaps.'

Meaning, Kyle translated, most likely never.

'That's enough anyway,' Stalker announced from where he lay near the hearth. 'Get some sleep. You'll need it for tomorrow.'

Kyle agreed most earnestly with that. He found a clear spot within reach of the hearth's warmth and tossed down a sheep's hide to lie upon. Badlands grumbled nearby about how unreasonable it was that they didn't get thoroughly soused this, their last night on earth. Kyle tucked his arm under his head and stared up at the soot-darkened log rafters far above. The question nagged him how he could calmly lie here in this hall while an army marched upon it. The answer was obvious and easy: because his friends defended it. And if Greymane were here, he'd do just the same.

That settled, he curled up and tried to get some sleep.

*

He awoke to a frosty unseasonable cold. His breath steamed in the hall's still air. Hoar frost covered the sheepskin where it lay across his face. He straightened, groaning and shivering. Stalker was up feeding the fire, blowing and stirring the embers. 'It's damned cold,' Kyle complained.

The Iceblood offered a savage grin. 'Is it now? Must be our cousins preparing a reception committee for our invaders. Perhaps the Sayers, or the Heels.' He poured a steaming cup of tea and offered it. Kyle took the stoneware cup, wrapped himself in the sheepskin, and shuffled to the entrance.

Thick turgid fogs obscured the valley and the distant woods. They coursed and twined like rivers of frozen breath. All the wood gleamed with ice crystals. The surrounding fields of tall grasses stood stiff and frozen, as white as sword-blades. In the outhouse, Kyle eased his bladder as quickly as he could then shuffled back inside.

Fisher was up, and Kyle asked, 'What is this weather?'

The bard nodded. 'Omtose Phellack awoken. We are far north. It clings here still.'

Yet the man did not seem pleased about it; in fact, he appeared deeply troubled. Enough so for Kyle to press, 'Shouldn't you . . . that is, we . . . welcome this?'

Fisher looked to the south and shook his head. 'These invaders – people from distant lands – none of them should trouble Omtose. Only – well . . .' The man regarded Kyle in silence for a time, as if studying him. Then he laughed and cuffed him on the shoulder. 'Pay no attention to an old worrier. We have more than enough to handle this day, yes?' He drew on thick leather gloves backed with interlocking iron rings, raised them admiringly. 'Look at these. Another gift of Stalker's ancestors. Have a look around – need a spear?'

Jethiss joined them; the Andii had found a set of thick leather armour consisting of overlapping layers set with studs and bronze rings. Fisher nodded approvingly. The man rested his hands on the long handle of a twin-headed broad-axe. Badlands passed them on his way out, caught sight of the axe, and swore. 'Gods, man, that monstrosity has rested on the wall since I was a babe! No one wields those clumsy things any more.'

Jethiss shrugged modestly. 'I'll do my best. The haft is a hard wood, is it not?'

'Aye. Ash. Why?'

'I had simply hoped so.'

Shaking his head, the Lost brother walked off.

Three figures obscured the light from the entrance then marched within. Cal-Brinn led, followed by a man and a woman, nearly identical in battered coats of mail that carried the remnants of once having been enamelled or lacquered a deep dark red. Cal-Brinn saluted Stalker. 'Our scouts report the enemy entering the valley. Their own scouts are already watching the hall from the woods.'

Stalker nodded. 'Very well. Everyone – take a skin of water and extra weapons and spread out.'

Kyle had pulled on a hauberk of boiled leather, its leather sleeves sheathed in mail, and belted on a set of heavy fighting knives. Into the belt he now gingerly tucked the sheathed Whiteblade.

When he looked up he saw everyone eyeing him, and he glanced down to see that the grip and pommel, carved from whatever unknown material, glowed now like ivory in the darkness of the hall. Feeling acutely ill at ease, he snatched up a spear and headed out, saying, 'Yes . . . let's go.'

When they had been readying the defences, Stalker had explained how he wanted everyone to spread out around the circumference of the building. They would hold the earthworks for as long as possible before falling back to the hall. The invaders would no doubt set it alight. Once that happened, they were to make a break to the north out of the rear.

That at least was the plan. It appeared more and more flimsy as Kyle gripped the cold wood of the spear-haft and watched the three columns of the enemy, accompanied by many skirmishers, smoothly spread out to encircle them many layers deep.

The last stamp of marching feet resounded from the forest.

Hundreds of breaths plumed the air. The front rank knelt a good spear-throw's distance from the earthworks. All was silent until a nicker and a ringing of jesses announced a horse being urged forward.

The mounted figure gently eased his way through the ranks until he was directly opposite the entrance. Kyle stood off to the right, just within ear-range, with a Crimson Guard swordsman on either side.

'Let us talk,' the man called.

Stalker set one booted foot up on the earthworks and leaned forward on his sheathed longsword. 'About what? The weather?'

The enemy commander had a narrow, puckered look to him. He rode stiffly, was bean-pole lean and straight, and wore a mail coat that fitted him too loosely about the chest and yet was too short. His breath steamed as one edge of his lips drew up. 'About your future – of which little remains.'

Stalker pulled a set of heavy gloves from his belt and drew them on. 'What is your offer, then?' he asked, as if bored.

'Drop your weapons and move on. Where you go, I care not.'

'And who are you to make such demands?'

'Marshal Teal. In the name of—'

'Remember me, Marshal?' Fisher's voice shouted out, cutting the man off. Startled, Kyle glanced over to see the bard approach, a longsword at his side. The marshal's eyes, already half hidden in their nests of wrinkles, slit even more. '*You?*' he breathed. 'How is it . . . what happened at the bridge?'

'We escaped.'

'Escaped . . .' the marshal breathed, wonderingly. '*We?* Ah – I understand. Well, congratulations. I am pleased you emerged unhurt.'

The bard bowed at the waist. 'And now I would offer you advice, Marshal. Turn away this day if you wish to escape as well.'

The marshal shook his head as if entertaining a fool. 'I am sorry to see you in the enemy camp, Fisher. But do not think that because you are a songster it will save your life when all here are put to the sword.'

'Even though my companion's sacrifice purchased your life at the bridge?'

'He did not save my life – he saved the lives of a third of my party. And it wasn't a sacrifice. It was a request.'

Now Fisher shook his head, but sadly. He crossed his arms. 'That night, Marshal, I saw revealed the man behind the Letherii calculation of exchange and advantage. It is to that man I give warning. Sail away and live. The risks here far outweigh any potential gain.'

Stalker muttered half under his breath, 'You're wasting your time.'

'Is this the extent of your negotiation?' the marshal demanded.

Fisher gave a nod. 'That is so.'

Teal's answering nod was curt. 'Then in the name of King Luthal Canar of Goldland, I—'

Stalker burst out laughing: 'King *who* of *what*?'

The marshal looked to the sky and tapped his fingers against his saddle. 'King Luthal Canar – the new king of these lands. Which he has decided to name Goldland.' He tilted his long thin hound's head. 'You don't like it? We think it should attract settlers.'

Stalker thoughtfully rubbed a finger over his lean jaw as he regarded the mounted marshal. At last he opined, 'I'd name it Pompous Ass Land, myself.'

The mocking smile fell from the marshal's lips as his face paled. He gathered his reins. 'Very well. None of you will see the dusk.' He wheeled his mount about, bellowed, '*Archers!*'

Kyle ducked as a fusillade of arrows came whistling straight over the earthwork mound to slam into the Greathall log walls. Crouching, Stalker laughed. 'That got his shirt in a twist!' Kyle glimpsed Fisher dodging his way back to his place in the ring of defenders.

'Keep your head down!' one of the Avowed shouted.

'Let them fire,' another called. 'We can use the arrows.'

Kyle kept one eye on the front ranks of swordsmen, searching for any motion that might reveal a charge. More arrows slashed the air above him. The banners of mist and vapours thinned as the sun rose, but the sky remained heavily overcast by a blanket of clouds that hung so steady and unmoving as to seem fixed about the mountains. Kyle shifted to lie with one shoulder in the cold damp earth. Even through the leather under-layers, the chain of his sleeve chilled his arm.

The Avowed on his right, he noted, in a long mail coat, gripping two longswords, was a wiry young-looking woman with short dark hair under an iron dome helmet. He shouted, 'What's your name?'

'Leena,' she answered. She did not ask his name. Everyone here called him the name that made him wince each time he heard it.

A loud deep horn sounded and an answering roar arose from the gathered ranks.

'Here they come!' Leena yelled.

Kyle straightened and readied the spear he'd collected for just this moment.

The ground seemed to drum as the solid mass of men came roaring and yelling. Most carried swords and medium-sized shields. Kyle scanned the ranks until he found the one who'd marked him. He bore a scruffy beard and his eyes were wild with rage and terror as he drove himself to the task of risking his life.

Aye, my friend, Kyle answered to himself, *like us all*.

He met him with the spear in his gut as the fellow slashed his way through the maze of pits and sharpened sticks. The man collapsed round the weapon and Kyle cursed. It was caught fast. The fellow's neighbour hacked the haft, snapping it. Kyle thrust it at him as he lunged but the broken end wasn't strong enough to penetrate the man's leather hauberk and merely winded him. Kyle drew the white blade as the man straightened and was pushed forward by those closing behind.

To his right, the Avowed mercenary, Leena, was clearing the mound in businesslike sweeps and thrusts, skilfully entrapping weapons between her crossed blades, counter-striking, and easily deflecting wild swings.

The Letherii soldier before Kyle now held the high ground and he closed, chopping downward from his advantage. Kyle stepped inside the blow to take off the man's hand just above the wrist. The fellow gaped, astonished. Then, enraged, he shield-bashed Kyle, pushing him back even further.

'Hold the wall, damn you!' Leena snarled, sounding more anxious than angry.

The invaders did not press their advantage, however. These Letherii soldiers flinched and winced as forces behind them thrust and shouldered them aside. Kyle was amazed to find himself staring at the band of blue-cloaked Stormguard from the *Lady's Luck*.

Their captain pointed and yelled, triumphant. 'Found you again, Whiteblade! Some day one of us will take you!'

Kyle realized they'd wanted him dead all along. From the very moment they saw him. He now understood his mistake in his use of the weapon in his hand. Ruthlessness. Pure, bloody-minded callousness. He'd been too timid. To the Abyss with the limbs! Cripple and finish them!

He took the man's spearhead off then swung low and severed his leg beneath the knee. He returned the swing to slice through four thrusting hafts, and the second rank fared no better as Kyle now understood that to properly exploit this vicious weapon he had to set aside normal swordplay.

He waded in, shield on his left, hacking through the spears, then forelimbs, taking any portion of anatomy within reach. Thighs, knees, it mattered not; the shock of the deep cuts slowed any opponent for the finishing return blow. He regained the earthworks, now a bloodied steaming heap of half-dismembered corpses.

Still the rear ranks pressed forward. Sick of shearing through thrusting spear hafts, he waded onward down the steep side into the flinching ranks. Shorn lengths of hafts flew until he was met with arms, then shoulders, and the thighs of braced legs.

The screams of the wounded now drowned out the clamour from any surrounding engagements. A hand yanked him backwards by his hauberk and he jumped to one side, swinging. Badlands' raised forearm blocked his own just inside his grip on the white blade. The Lost's eyes held his, close enough for their steaming breath to meld into one. 'That's enough, lad,' he warned, urging him back. 'Leave some for the rest of us.'

Kyle spun to the ranks; only Letherii troopers remained, and these held off behind shields, swords raised. Their eyes, white all around, were filled with something Kyle had never before seen in any opponent: open dread. Badlands slowly walked him backwards.

'*Archers!*' came a familiar bellow.

'Run for it!' Badlands shouted and pelted up the mound.

Kyle had time for three panicked steps in the yielding mounded dirt and a leap before arrows whisked the air over his back and punched the heavy logs of the Greathall.

He lay panting in the muddy ground, his front wet with gore and pooled rainwater.

'Up for another rush!' Leena warned.

Groaning, he staggered to his feet and hefted his shield, which, from the weight of it, seemed to have been transformed into lead. Badlands padded off to continue his watch on the defence. All about the ring of mounded dirt the new ranks of attackers came storming up, shouting and slamming swords into shields. He waited, tensed, the white blade readied, but none appeared at his section of the perimeter. No cursing wild-eyed soldier came charging up the slope.

The Avowed on his left was a broad giant of a fellow who crashed his wide infantryman's shield down on top of the smaller, lighter shields, bearing them low for thrusts over the metal rims or down on to heads and shoulders.

Leena, on his right, had her hands full taking on a mass of pressing infantry. He half lunged, meaning to lend her his aid, only to catch himself, realizing that he dared not leave this section open and undefended. In any case, he couldn't have gotten close enough

– he knew well enough not to crowd a warrior who fought the two-swords style. She swung both full round for smashing, sweeping blows, never quite halting their blades' figure-eight weaving over and under in a mesmerizing dance. Attackers who could have pressed round her flinched away when their paths took them too close to Kyle.

When the wave eased the Letherii infantrymen backed away, dragging their wounded with them. The Avowed swordswoman came to him. She was heaving in great panting breaths, almost dragging her weapons behind her. She thrust one blade into the soft earth to dab at a cut across her mouth, then leaned over to spit out a red bloody stream.

'Looks like we'll have to move you to a new spot,' she croaked, her voice sand-hoarse.

Kyle offered his waterskin, which she took gratefully. 'Where did you learn to fight like that?'

After a long pull at the waterskin, she swallowed and said, 'From my father. He was a veteran of the Iron Legion.'

He'd heard the name once or twice. 'The Iron Legion?'

She looked annoyed. 'You've not heard of it? The elites of the Talian Iron Crown?'

Kyle blew out a breath. 'Well, of course I've heard—'

She waved the matter aside. 'Never mind. Why should you have? The old emperor crushed them long ago.' She pressed a fold of cloth to her cut mouth once more. 'Hard for me to remember it's all ancient history.' She urged him off. 'Find Cal before they come again. Tell him you should move.'

The Avowed's words had startled him for an instant, until he recalled that of course this woman might be older than his grandmother. He dipped his head in assent and jogged off.

He passed the Andii, Jethiss, now gripping two short-hafted hatchets. He supposed the great broad-axe's ash haft hadn't held up after all. The man's scavenged armour was notched and battered, but he appeared otherwise whole. He inclined his head as Kyle passed, his long black hair hanging loose, and greeted him with a murmured, 'Whiteblade.'

Kyle found that to be addressed in such a fashion, by such a man, made his breath catch and he nearly tripped, at an utter loss for words. Finally, he bobbed his head, muttering, 'Jethiss,' and hurried off. He found Cal-Brinn standing on the front entrance's log steps. All about him arrows studded the logs like tossed quills while before him the air wavered and shimmered in ribbons of night. He saluted the Crimson Guard captain. 'Rashan?' he queried. Cal-Brinn nodded. 'I've seen little of the Warrens here in Assail.'

'The Elder Omtose is dominant here. It suppresses any other conjurings.'

The roar of another charge arose from beyond the earthworks and Kyle spun. Arrows nipped the air only to whirr away from the wavering ribbons before Cal-Brinn. The captain motioned to them, murmuring, 'The best I could do.'

Kyle watched while the Avowed within sight, together with Fisher and Stalker, answered the charge. They resembled bobbing corks in a choppy sea, tossed and battered, about to be submerged. 'We cannot hold,' he told Cal-Brinn.

'Perhaps,' he granted. 'Yet in battle every exchange is a potential surprise. No one can say what turn will come. Who knows?' He descended the steps to stand close to him, and, leaning down to bring his face close, he whispered, 'Have you not considered that it is *they* who might lose heart?'

Kyle ducked his head, thoroughly chastened. But the captain softened his comment with a wink, and, bellowing a war-cry, drew his longsword and charged into the line next to Stalker. Kyle felt his blood rise and nearly sing in his ears at such a sight, and he took a fresh grip on the white blade and ran to join the fray.

It was late after the noon when Kyle next roused himself, blinking. He was only standing because he was leaning against the rough logs of the Greathall. His throat gagged him as if scraped raw, while his limbs hung numb yet screaming in the stinging, twitching pins of exhaustion. His shield was a battered wreck on his left forearm. He forced his fingers open upon the leather strap and let it slip to the ground.

Badlands came jogging round the defences and joined him. The Lost brother was a mass of cuts and scrapes, a bloodied cloth was wrapped round his left upper arm and a severe gash across the side of his head had peeled back a portion of his shaggy hair leaving that ear a mass of drying gore.

'Well – we ain't dead yet!' the Lost greeted him with an elated grin.

Kyle roused himself further. He had to wet his throat to answer, 'But it's still a good day.'

Badlands laughed uproariously and clapped him on the shoulder, nearly sending him to the ground. 'Now you're getting into the spirit of it!'

Kyle didn't say that it was the Lost brother who appeared to have reclaimed his old spirit. He spat and croaked, 'How many?'

Grinning, Badlands raised a hand as if to hold him back. 'Enough! Don't you fear – more than enough. They've decided to grind us down.'

The flickering light of flames now sent shadows whipping over them. Tossed torches came arcing out from behind the ranks. Some thumped to the ground in splashes of sparks and ash, but others struck the grassed roof of the Greathall to catch, sputtering and smoking.

'Looks like they've changed tactics,' Badlands observed.

Kyle carefully sheathed the white blade. He studied the steep roof. 'Shouldn't we go up there?'

'You'll be poked full of arrows, lad.'

More torches came flying overhead, together with skins of what must have been some sort of oil. The roof suddenly roared to life in orange flames.

'Have to find Cal,' Badlands said, and jogged off.

'Hold the line!' an Avowed shouted above the crackling of the flames. Kyle staggered to the earthworks and peered over. The Letherii soldiery had assembled a short distance off in double ranks, bows held before them, arrows nocked. The shifting light of the flames danced from their helmets. They were ready to repel any attempt at escape.

The roof was now a deafening inferno. Its heat pummelled Kyle's back. Drifting sparks stung his neck and billowing black smoke choked him. A tap on his shoulder revealed Badlands returned. He yelled into Kyle's ear: 'Time for that desperate break out somebody mentioned a while back.' He motioned for Kyle to follow and led him to the rear of the Greathall.

He found Stalker, Fisher, Jethiss and Cal-Brinn assembled there. All appeared to have taken wounds of greater or lesser severity. Cal-Brinn was crouched, a hand above his head against the heat and drifting embers. 'They are expecting us!' he shouted over the con-flagration battering them with its yammering fury.

'We can't wait!' Stalker answered.

'I know!'

The wool surcoat of one of the Avowed standing guard nearby suddenly burst aflame. The man calmly yanked it over his head and tossed it aside.

'I will try to raise my Warren,' Cal-Brinn called out. 'It may be too much – you might have to carry me!'

'No!' Jethiss pushed forward. 'Allow me. I managed this once before . . .'

Kyle remembered Coots falling and the darkness descending – yes, he'd somehow summoned sorcery before.

The man stood utterly still, concentrating, Kyle imagined. Everyone, meanwhile, danced and batted at embers of burning hay and wood that came drifting down to sting flesh and singe hair. Yet Jethiss did not stir, even when embers touched upon him, sending up wisps of smoke to join the black clouds churning about them.

Kyle came to despair: they'd be consumed before anything manifested! He wiped coals from the mail of his sleeves and his gloves smoked. Perhaps it was his dimming vision then, but the light changed. The blinding incandescence of the inferno seemed to brighten even more as black streams of night snaked away over the bared bloodied ground. He'd banished the darkness?

Barely audible over the thunder just above their heads came shouts of panic from out beyond the earthworks. Jethiss turned to them, gesturing outwards. 'It is done.'

Cal-Brinn raised an arm, signing, and the Avowed converged. Coughing almost uncontrollably, Kyle joined the rush over the mound. He did not know what to expect out beyond the defences but complete chaos and confusion was not it. The Letherii lines had disintegrated. Soldiers ran all about, falling, flailing, batting at twisting ribbons of dark that twined about them like snakes.

Cal-Brinn gestured and the remaining Avowed formed a perimeter round their small party and they quickly pushed through to the forest beyond. Few blows were exchanged, though arrows did fly their way from distant portions of the ranks far from their point of escape. Kyle did a hasty count and came up with twelve of the Guard. They'd lost four in the defence.

They jogged on. No one suggested a halt, despite pronounced limps and ragged breaths. At length, Cal raised his fist and the party staggered to a stop. Kyle leaned over, hands on his knees, gasping. Some collapsed to the ground. Despite his dizzying exhaustion, he turned to study their rear. He found a glow through the trees in the valley below that betrayed the Greathall. He glimpsed no torches in the woods between. Perhaps Marshal Teal was content in having driven them off. Groaning, straightening his back, he crossed to where Stalker and Cal-Brinn spoke in low tones.

'You need not come,' Stalker was saying. 'You've done enough.'

'We would see you safe,' Cal answered, his tone firm.

'We will be safe in the heights.'

'What was that?' Fisher demanded, straightening from examining the wounded side of an Avowed.

Stalker drew his fingers down his moustache, his lips tightening. 'We're heading to the heights. Any survivors from the other Holdings will have made their way there.'

Fisher waved his arm in a broad arc. 'Strike east or west. All directions are open. Head for the coast. Escape this region!'

'But avoid the spine of the Bone range,' Badlands muttered.

Through this Stalker was shaking his head. 'No, Fisher. We can't avoid it any longer. It's our legacy – and yours too, lad,' he added, speaking to Kyle. 'We share the blood.'

'What of it?' Badlands asked.

Stalker began cleaning his blade on a handful of moss. 'I mean it's coming to a head – isn't it, Fish? What do you say?'

The bard drew breath to speak, but checked himself. Kyle almost thought his expression fearful before he suddenly turned away.

'Speak, damn you!' Stalker yelled. 'Or hold your tongue from this point onward!'

The bard suddenly swung round, his lips clenched so tight as to be almost white.

From the edge of his vision, Kyle caught Jethiss stepping out of the dark. The Andii had his hands raised, open. 'We are all of us run ragged. Our blood is high. Perhaps now is not the time . . .'

But Fisher had drawn himself up straight and with both hands pushed back his long, sweaty grey-streaked hair. 'You would have me speak, would you? Very well. All I have are suspicions, hints, lines from old sagas, but what I dread may be very real. I fear both what lies ahead and what lies behind. And for the life of me, I cannot say which is the lesser of the two! Omtose Phellack is stirring. And why? What could raise its ire? Badlands,' he demanded, pointing, 'I spoke of this before and you dismissed it – who is the old enemy?'

The Lost brother's brow wrinkled in confusion at first, but then understanding came and he snorted his scorn. 'You can't be serious, man!'

'I fear it!' Fisher answered, insistent. 'And we are leading them on higher!' He turned to Stalker. 'And what sleeps in the heights?'

Stalker scowled in obvious rejection of the bard's words. He turned away and raised his head to the heights gleaming silvery-blue through breaks in the forest's canopy. He was quiet for a time as he smoothed his long drooping moustache. 'You're letting your imagination get the better of you – jumping at maybes and phantasms.' Yet his tone told Kyle that he was half convinced. 'We'd better talk this over with the others.' As if struck by a thought, he faced Jethiss. 'My thanks for getting us out of there.'

The Andii inclined his head a fraction. 'No – it is I who should thank you.' He glanced to Fisher. 'Calling upon whatever it is in me that allows this manipulation has jogged free more of my memories. I believe I now know why I am here.'

Strangely, instead of being pleased, as Kyle had thought he would be, the bard actually appeared wary. He offered a subdued, 'Oh?'

'Yes.' Jethiss turned to Kyle. 'Our people once had a champion who carried a blade that guarded us. Now we are without such a protector. I believe I have been sent to remedy that lack. I believe I have been sent for a sword.'

Kyle could not help but close his fist on the grip of the white blade. All eyes, he noted, now rested upon him. He felt his breath whisper away in an unmanning clutch of dread.

Jethiss frowned then, studying his face in puzzlement, then his brows rose and for an instant a strange expression crossed his face. What to Kyle appeared a wince of hurt. He waved a hand. 'Do not worry, friend Kyle, I would never – that is, your weapon is safe.'

'Then where,' the bard asked into the lengthening silence, 'do you believe you will find this weapon?'

The Andii's alien night-black eyes released Kyle to shift to Fisher. 'In the north.'

Kyle found himself blinking and weaving slightly as he dropped his sweat-slick hand from the sword. Only now did he note how both Stalker and Badlands flanked him, while Cal-Brinn had eased away, closer to the Avowed now quiet and watchful across the copse of woods.

'A desperate option,' Fisher remarked, rather dryly. 'Do you think it wise?'

'I think it necessary.' And the Andii walked off into the woods, heading upland.

Kyle and the remaining three exchanged silent looks. We are of the blood, he realized. As Stalker said, I, too, have a stake here.

'So what do we do?' Badlands growled, and adjusted the blood-soaked cloth round his upper arm.

'I do not know,' Fisher answered. 'I'm not even sure we could stop him if we wished.'

'Is he – you know . . . *him?*'

The bard shook his head in frustration. 'I do not believe so. He appears so different. But then . . .'

'Yes? What?' Stalker prompted, irritated by the bard's habit of withholding his thoughts.

Fisher raised his shoulders in a helpless shrug. 'He *was* a shapeshifter.'

'Oh, wonderful,' Badlands snarled, and he let out a breath like a fart. 'That's a big help.' He waved Cal-Brinn over, calling, 'Let's put more room between us 'n' them Letherii bastards, shall we?'

*　　*　　*

Reuth started up from his bunk in a panic. It was dark and all he could see were Storval's hands reaching for his throat from the night. He blinked away the ghost-memory from his nightmares. He remembered that he was safe now, on board the *Silver Dawn*, in the care of a blind Falaran pilot and her husband, the ship's captain. He had a sudden sense of the solid presence of his uncle, Tulan, wrapped in his bear-hide cloak, smelling of grease, and tears came to his eyes. He was gone, and the crew that betrayed him was now part of the invader army camped outside the walls of Mantle, high on its cliff-side perch.

Though it was long before dawn he knew he'd never get back to sleep, so he swung his feet over to the cold boards of the cabin and dressed. The air was surprisingly chill and he shivered as he pulled on his woollen outer shirt and vest. Last, he drew on his goatskin shoes, slipped each leather thong over its horn toggle, and stood to stamp his feet on the boards to bring warmth to them. Indeed, so cold was the night air that he drew on the extra cloak he'd been given and clasped it at his shoulder with its round bronze brooch.

Ducking his head, he opened the door and stepped out of what was the cabin of the captain and his wife – the only private cabin on board the vessel. He remembered, vaguely, being moved here. He drew in a long breath of the chill air and nearly coughed, so harsh was it. His lungs felt frozen. To the south, the night sky was dark and clear, the stars glimmering brightly. But thick black clouds choked the sky overhead and further north. They crowded so low as to cut off the heights of the Salt range.

'Felt it too, yes?' murmured the rough voice of his caregiver, the ship's pilot, Ieleen.

He turned to the tiller arm where she sat, long-stemmed pipe in mouth, hands clasping a short walking stick. 'Felt what?'

'The change.' She took hold of the pipe and gestured. 'All these days the wind has been coming out of the south, bringing warmth and the spring.' She pointed the stem north. 'But now the air is coming down from the mountains, bringing an unnatural cold.' Her eyes, milky blind, somehow found his. 'Ever felt the like?'

Being of Mare, Reuth had to admit that he had. So dreadful was the similarity he was reluctant to give it voice. As if saying it would somehow lend it solidity. 'The false winter of the Stormriders,' he finally admitted, hunching and shivering.

'Aye. Your Stormriders. The ignorant speak of the winters of the Stormriders and the Jaghut as if they are the same thing. But that is not so. The Riders are alien. Not of this world. Indeed, some argue that in their original form they were of the frigid black gaps between the worlds – but that cannot be decided. No, this cold is more familiar, is it not? We've faced it before, or at least our ancestors have.' She drew on the pipe in a loud hiss and popping of whatever strange leaf she burned. 'This crew is of Falar, and south of our lands are mountains capped by a great ice-field. The Fenn range, we call it. It, too, is a place where the old races yet hold out. Giants and Jaghut – the Fenn and the Thelomen-kind. We both know this cold, yes? It is the breath of the Jaghut winter blowing down our necks.'

Reuth shivered again. 'But it's spring.'

The old woman's snow-white orbs gleamed in the yellow glow of the pipe-embers. 'It was. I fear spring's been cancelled. As has summer.'

'That's impossible!'

'Not at all. It's happened before. Many times. In many regions.'

'Greetings, *Silver Dawn*!' a gruff voice called from the dock. 'Permission to come aboard?'

Reuth glanced to Ieleen then shook himself, remembering her blindness. 'What should I do?' he whispered.

She waved him onward. 'Give him permission, lad!'

He hurried to the side. It was a barrel-shaped fellow he recognized as a Genabackan. 'Granted,' he answered.

The big fellow came puffing up the gangplank. He was all smiles behind his greying beard. 'Morning! Morning. And a damned frosty one too! Cold enough to freeze the tits from a—' He caught sight of Ieleen and clamped his lips shut. 'Sorry, ma'am.'

But she just smiled indulgently as she drew on the pipe then exhaled a great gout of blue smoke. 'Look at us three,' she murmured, choosing to ignore her own handicap. 'A Falaran pilot, a Genabackan mariner, and a Mare navigator. We three smell it. Us with the knack of sensing the currents of sea and air. Yes, Enguf?'

The Genabackan was nodding as he stroked his beard. 'Aye. The wind's changed. It's strong out of the north now. Not a good sign for us.'

'I agree,' Ieleen said around the stem of the pipe. 'We must be ready. We may have to slip anchor in a rush.'

The Genabackan pirate cocked a brow. 'Think you so? Unsettling news. The lads and lasses won't like that.'

'They sound miserable already.'

Enguf winced and dragged his fingers through his beard. 'Aye. This whole venture's been nothing but one disaster after another. I've had to put down three, ah . . . spirited debates regarding my leadership.'

Ieleen laughed with the pipe stem clamped between her teeth. 'Look at it this way. You might be the only ship to return to the Confederacy. You can tell whatever stories you damned well please, then.'

Enguf laughed uproariously and slapped Reuth's shoulder. The fellow rather reminded him of his uncle. 'And I shall!' he promised. 'You can be damned certain of that!' He straightened. 'I'll keep your words in mind. Always prudent to weigh the words of a Falaran sea-witch. Until later, then.' He clomped off to the gangway.

Reuth's eyes had grown large at the man's words. A sea-witch! Growing up in Mare, he'd heard nothing but ghastly stories of such sorceresses. Human sacrifices, eating babies, drinking blood! Every wicked practice imaginable! Swallowing to wet his throat, he ventured, 'He called you a sea-witch.'

The old woman's blind hoarfrost-white orbs swung to directly meet his own. Her wrinkled lips rose in a slow smile that seemed to promise she knew all he was thinking.

'It's just a term of affection,' she said.

*   *   *

Mist sensed the approach of yet more newcomers. She was pacing before her throne, hands clasped behind her back, wondering on the mystery of this untimely chill flowing down from the north like an unwelcome breath. Had these pathetic invaders caused more trouble than she'd imagined?

Who, she wondered, would dare approach now in the mid-day? None of the horns had sounded announcing landing vessels – and she was certain none of her people would neglect that. Still, in the past, some parties *had* arrived overland, harrowing though the passage might be. She turned to the rear of the great meeting hall, calling, 'Anger! Wrath! Rouse yourselves, you sodden wineskins! We have unannounced guests.' Deep basso grumblings answered her from the dark.

She sat on the throne, arranged the long trailing tag-ends of her gown, and summoned her sorcery. It was a melding she had crafted over the centuries of her innate access to Omtose Phellack and such lesser portals to power as were available in these southern lands.

Shadows moved in the light streaming in through the open way, out beyond the entrance hall. The flickering light pulled her gaze and she paused, bemused by what she sensed there. Something unfamiliar, yet also teasingly recognizable . . . like something she had sensed recently. Something she hadn't liked.

Her magery now swirled about her in gossamer filaments and ribbons, spreading out to enmesh the entire hall in readiness. She turned her attention to the figures now entering the hall and the twitching tag-ends of coalesced fog, together with the scarves of vapour, all flinched as one.

Creatures out of legend. The threat so long predicted she'd long since laughed it away. The unrelenting, undying hunters. The Army of Dust and Bone.

The lead figure wore a cloak of stiff hide on which only a few sad patches of what was once perhaps white fur still remained. The eyeless head of the beast rode atop a mummified mien hardly any better preserved. A forest of bear claws rattled and clattered at his hollow chest. Ragged tattered pelts and skins wrapped a torso of flesh hard to differentiate from the leathers. A blade of pale brown flint, its grip wrapped in a leather strip, rode at a belt of woven leather.

The next one was in even worse shape, could that be possible. She, for Mist intuited that the dried cadaver had been female, had obviously been driven through by many savage blows. The cured leather of her hides hung in shreds. Wide tannin-stained cheekbones seemed to elongate the empty orbits of the eyes. Upper canines glinted copper-sheathed.

Behind these two leaders more of the undying entered, spreading out across the hall. Bony feet slid and clacked on the stone flags of the floor, dry hides brushed and rubbed. Mist imagined she could almost hear their joints creak and grate as the hoary ancients swung their heads to regard her.

She found that a sea of dark empty sockets casts a heavy weight.

She remembered who she was – her lineage – and loosed her grip on the armrests of her throne. She raised her chin, defiant even in the face of these foretold avengers, and worked to force the usual disdain into her voice. 'What is it you wish, accursed ones?'

'You know what we have come for,' the lead undying answered – its voice was as the desiccated brushing of dead twigs across stone.

'Then you have travelled far for nothing, as you shall not leave this hall.'

'We shall see.' He lifted a gnarled mangled hand of sinew and ligament-wound bone to his fellows.

'A moment,' Mist called, 'if you would.'

At a small gesture from the foremost the female undying paused. 'What is it?' she answered, utterly uninflected.

'May I know the names of those who would presume to level their ages-old judgement upon me?'

The lead one fractionally inclined its ravaged head. 'I am Ut'el Anag of the Kerluhm T'lan Imass.' He indicated the one next to him. 'And this is Lanas Tog of my clan.'

Mist bowed her head a touch. 'Greetings, ancients. I am Mist. And, with your permission, won't you allow me to introduce my two sons?' She raised her hand, beckoning, and to her hidden relief, heavy thumping steps sounded from the rear.

Unlike all her previous audiences, however, these visitors did not flinch nor back away as her sons emerged. She spared a glance up-wards and saw that they, too, were not acting as usual. Instead of their confident laughing grins they now wore hardened expressions. Their eyes were slit and lips compressed. Only the tips of their blunt yellowed tusks showed. They held their weapons readied.

'This is Anger,' she indicated, 'and Wrath.'

Ut'el Anag regarded each in turn. 'Such guards will not help you escape us.'

'You misjudge me, Ut'el. I have no intention of escaping.' And she swept her arms forward, unleashing her sorceries.

The closest ancients made straight for her throne. Sweeps from Wrath's man-tall sword and Anger's great broad-axe knocked them all flying backwards to crash into the stone walls in a clatter of bone and fallen stone weapons.

Mist clenched her fists, enmeshing all within the tangling coils of her scarves of fog. Without thinking, she wasted precious seconds squeezing their throats, then remembered just who, and what, these were, and cursed herself.

Her sons waded in, roaring their war-bellows. Great blows from Wrath's sword hacked mummified corpses right and left. Yet those not scattered into tangles of broken bone regained their feet, weapons of flint and obsidian readied.

A quick slice from one of the undying severed the rear of Anger's ankle, bringing him falling to one knee and hand. His bellow of pain shook the stone ceiling and brought dust sifting down. Mist sought to wrap the undying in her coils of vapour, immobilizing them. But their stone weapons cut the ribbons and scarves just as one might rend rotten cloth. They closed upon Anger, severing his hand from its wrist. In powerful two-handed blows they chopped his head from its neck. Hot blood gushed across the flags as the giant's oxen heart laboured yet.

Mist shrieked her horror and gripped the throne's armrests – the mists curled away, dispersing as she gaped at the fallen corpse of her son.

Wrath swept all aside with a great wide swing of his axe. And that would have been the end but for the fact that these were undying, and so those that could stood again, re-gripped weapons, and advanced. A thrown blade of flint took him in the throat and he reared up tall, gurgling, searching for the shard at his neck. The other leader of the band, Lanas Tog, lunged in and severed the back of his knee. He tottered, swung the axe wildly to smash shards and pulverized dust from the wall, and fell. Others closed in, swinging. Before Mist's stunned gaze they dismembered her other son.

The tip of a stone sword raised her chin. She unwillingly pulled her eyes from her fallen sons and lifted her face to the desiccated flat mien of Ut'el Anag.

'You were . . . overconfident,' he said.

Yes. She had been. Yet could she be blamed? She had faced nothing like this. And yes, the myths warned of this Army of Dust and Bone – but those were just stories, after all, weren't they? She nodded, and said, 'No one expects the past to reach out and destroy the present – or the future.'

The ancient's face bore hardly any flesh that could move, yet Mist thought she caught a sort of startled flinch before furious rejection crimped the dried ligaments of the jaws and the arm drew back then thrust forward. Cold stone penetrated her chest. It slid through her heart, and exited into the soft wood of the seat-back behind. She felt her muscles relaxing yet the blade supported her upright, for the moment. Her breath eased from her and in that last moment she felt no panic, no denial. She would go now to that bridge across worlds leading to where, none of her kind knew.

She, at least, had a destination.

Staring hard into the empty orbs of her murderer, she saw that he did not. These undying had abandoned everything – even their hope for a future for themselves. They had sacrificed everything before the implacable pursuit of their goal. In that moment, as her life fled from her, she saw deeper into the essence of these undying and saw that she was mistaken – that there *was* something. A possibility. 'Do not despair,' she spoke with that last breath, 'there is yet hope for you . . .'

Ut'el Anag retreated from the half-breed corpse. He turned to Lanas Tog. His dust-dry words carried wariness, 'What could she mean . . . "there is hope"?'

Lanas Tog's desiccated features, the lips pulled back from her yellowed grinning teeth, the cheeks sunken to the barest strips of leather, remained immobile. The teeth and shell fragments woven into her hanging white hair rattled as she turned away. Her hands creaked clenching into fists of bone. 'She knows nothing of us. Come, we must go. The Summoner is close. I feel her presence.'

'We could yet deal with her.'

Lanas glanced back. 'As I have said – there is no need. Once we have dealt with all these, the argument will have resolved itself.'

Ut'el's voice still held its wariness. 'So you say, Lanas. So you say.'

CHAPTER XIII

ORMAN, THE REDDIN BROTHERS, BERNAL AND THE SAYER HOUSE-hold servants Leal and Ham had three days to prepare be-fore Keth jogged up from the lower valley to report that the outlander army was approaching and would arrive before nightfall.

These last three days it had been alternately raining, sleeting, and snowing. It was as if the weather could not make up its mind. Orman was glad for the damp chill. It would work against the invaders, or so he told himself. He worked piling the last of the equipment and furniture on the barricade of logs and hastily cut down trees they had raised surrounding the Greathall. All bolstered by lashed barrels, heaped sod, and any tangled bric-a-brac they could pull from the outbuildings before they fired them.

And what of his resolve? he wondered as he tied down a great heavy table of solid logs turned on to its side. Had the weather dampened it? He straightened and pressed a hand to the patch over his eye. Hard to know it was still there when he couldn't see it. Was he an utter fool not to have run off one of these past nights? Bernal said to have faith in Jaochim – easy for him, as he'd known the Iceblood for decades.

No, faith in the Icebloods wasn't keeping him here. It was, rather, the faith they had shown in him. They had simply taken his word that he would see this through, and that trust was what kept him steadfast. That, and the answer to the question what would he do if it were Jass who stood now beside him? Could he abandon him?

The absurdity of the idea of his ever deserting Jass made Orman laugh aloud. The carefree barking chuckle startled him and raised Kasson's head from where he worked mounding the earthworks.

'There is something of Old Bear in you, I think,' Jaochim said behind Orman and he turned, feeling a hot embarrassment for his outburst.

'I have been watching you these last few days,' the lean Iceblood said, peering down at him. 'I have seen you struggle with your resolve to remain despite not knowing what was to come.' He gestured for Orman to follow him back to the Greathall. 'Come – I have something for you.'

Within, the Iceblood elder dug about in a remaining large wooden chest and pulled out a cloak of thick black bear fur. 'Here. Wear this. It is going to get cold.' He helped Orman slip it on then pinned it at one shoulder with a wide bronze brooch. He seemed to study Orman for a time, then nodded to himself. 'Good. Now, do not interrupt me as I speak. Yrain and I have no intention of allowing these outlanders to take us and luckily – though . . .' and here he paced, thinking, 'perhaps luck had nothing to do with it . . . In any case, we have had time to fully sense Buri's plan. And we support it. Therefore, when the time comes, you will take everyone and find him once more—' Orman drew breath to object, but Jaochim carried on, 'You will take him this message – that he is to use all that we have given him. Yes? You will do this?'

At first Orman would not answer. He kept his jaws clenched only to mutter, low, 'I will not abandon you.'

'You are not abandoning us. You are fulfilling a last obligation.'

Orman felt hot tears come once more to his eyes, even his ruined one, and this embarrassed him yet again. 'Do not send me away.'

Jaochim nodded his understanding. 'Yrain and I have spoken, and we will not have you fall in our defence. That would be selfish of us. You and the brothers have many years before you. You shall carry our legacy into the future. For that possibility alone, Yrain and I are glad to send you like a spear thrown onward into the years to come.' He clasped Orman's shoulders in both hands. 'Will you do this thing? For our sacrifice? And for Vala and Jass's sacrifice?' Unable to speak, his throat and chest choked with emotion, Orman gave a curt jerked nod. Jaochim squeezed his shoulders. 'My thanks.'

Bernal appeared in the sunlight streaming in the entrance. 'They are here.'

Jaochim released him. He turned to Bernal. 'When the time comes – go with Orman here, yes?'

Bernal bowed from the waist. 'Very well.'

'You will know when,' he told Orman. He gestured to the far end of the Greathall, where the thrones stood on their raised wooden dais. 'Yrain and I will wait here. No others should be present.'

Seeing Orman hesitating, unwilling to go, he gently motioned to the front. 'Bernal – please greet our guests.'

Bernal thumped the butt of his spear to the packed dirt of the hall floor and lowered himself to one knee. 'As you order, m'lord.' Straightening, he urged Orman out. 'Come. There's more than enough for all of us.'

Though it was a grey overcast day, Orman still had to blink as he stepped outside. Once his vision cleared, he saw that Bernal was right. There were a damned lot of them. Far too many, in fact. The ranks were parting as they approached, no doubt meaning to encircle the Greathall. It was not a ragtag mob of marauders and raiding fortune-hunters. This was an army. Someone had come with more in mind than scavenging gold. He quickly descended the steps and jogged to where he'd left Svalthbrul leaning up against the barricade.

The soldiers formed up two ranks deep encircling them. They wore plain leather armour and carried medium-sized triangular shields, with shortswords at their sides. Behind them ranged the skirmishers: remnants of the force they had routed days earlier. These carried a mishmash of weaponry. Some bore no armour at all. It looked as if all those better equipped had been taken up into the ranks.

A man pushed forward and stepped out ahead of the front rank. He was by far the best armoured of the lot, bearing banded iron engraved and inlaid with a silvery spider-tracing that glimmered as he moved. His hair was long and loose, but his beard was short and neatly trimmed. He waved an arm before himself as if in disbelief.

'What is this?' he called. 'I see only three of you.'

Bernal stepped up to the barricade, thumped his spear to the ground. 'There's one more in the back.'

'Is this some sort of insult?'

'Is this what you call parleying?'

The man, whom Orman assumed to be their commander, looked to the sky in what he might have thought was a gesture of self-control, but which was also actually an insult. 'I am not parleying,' he sighed. 'I am in truth attempting to do you a favour.'

'And what favour would this be?' Bernal enquired innocently, leaning on his spear.

'The offer of your lives.' He raised his voice, calling, 'Set down your weapons and walk away and you may live!'

Bernal turned his head round to glance behind to the right and left, then returned his attention to the man. He shrugged.

444

The commander sighed once more, rubbed his brow. 'I see.' He glanced to the men next to him and explained, 'Barbarians. The same everywhere. All façade of nobility and honour. They yearn to demonstrate how brave they are. We of Lether have dealt with this before, have we not? They wish to prove they do not fear death? Very well. We shall oblige them.'

Orman ached to plant Svalthrul in the man's sneering heart, but then the weapon would be beyond the barricade, out of his reach. 'At least give us until nightfall to consider your offer!' he shouted.

The man glanced to Orman then looked up at the dense ashen clouds above and shook his head. 'No. I think not.' He bellowed, 'Torches!'

Orman flinched. This was not what he'd been expecting.

Shortly, a barrage of lit torches came arcing up from behind the ranks to sail over and land on the wooden planks of the Greathall roof. Most rolled back down to fall to the ground. But some remained, sending up gouts of black smoke. Orman tore his gaze from the roof to return to facing the men ranked before him.

More torches flew overhead. Behind him grew the crackling and snapping of burning wood. Was this what Jaochim meant by the right moment? But what were they to do? Charge the ranks? That would also be certain suicide.

Bernal came limping a circuit of the barricade. 'Steady, lad,' he murmured. 'They won't charge us now, will they?'

'What of . . .' He jerked his head to the Greathall.

Bernal rested a hand on his shoulder. 'They've made their choice, they have.'

'But what should we do?'

'We'll see, lad. We'll see.'

The crackling swelled to a constant roar. A growing heat punished his back. Smoke billowed, blinding him and tearing at his throat. A wind rose with the flames. He heard nothing but the ravening fire and the explosive popping of resin.

Dear ancestors, this was it. Oddly enough, he felt utterly resigned. Just as Jass went, so too would he. It was an . . . elemental way to go.

Squinting through the smoke he saw, rather than heard, the ranks retreat a step. To a man they now stared above him, wonder and a touch of dread on their faces. Orman dared a glance behind.

The fire appeared to be diminishing. He might be mistaken, but here and there the blackened beams of the room showed through, smoking, yet free of flames.

And from the Greathall entrance, descending the log steps like a river, came a steady course of dense fog. It curled outwards past Bernal's sandalled feet, spreading as it went.

Something frigid kissed Orman's own feet and he leapt, flinching. More fog now ran out from beneath the hall. It appeared to be spreading to all sides. It coursed through and over the barricade, swelled onward.

Many of the soldiers retreated as it came.

'Stand firm!' the commander bellowed. 'Mere barbarian witchery. I—' He stopped himself, staring upwards in disbelief. Orman followed his gaze and was astonished to see that the roof fire was now completely out. Exposed blackened beams smoked, but no flames could be seen. The commander once more pressed a hand to his brow. He sounded an aggrieved sigh. 'Oh – just kill them.'

Sergeants among the ranks bellowed, 'Charge!'

The front rank surged forward to the barricade. They chopped and yanked at the heaped logs, barrels and equipment. One screamed as Bernal's spear found him. Orman shook off his hesitation and thrust as well, jabbing at every soldier within reach.

He fully expected the soldiers to climb or push their way through the barricade in moments; it was undefended for almost all its length. Yet this did not happen. The men he fended off with thrusts of Svalthbrul retreated, nursing wounds, but so too did nearly all the others. These gasped and flinched, hunching, their breaths steaming. Many fell amid the dense fog. Over these humped shapes he glimpsed a fine glittering armour of hoar frost grow and thicken.

He stood back in wonder. True, it was damned cold; the air biting at him and his own breath plumed, but somehow the frigid streamers were not so deadly to him. He ran to find Bernal.

The disembodied voice of the enemy commander shouted from somewhere behind the wall of churning vapours, 'What are you waiting for? It is just a fog! Advance, damn you!'

Bernal stood on the log stairs together with one of the Reddin brothers, Kasson, Orman was fairly certain. 'Now is the time,' he said as he arrived.

Bernal curtly nodded his agreement. 'You and the brothers must go.'

Orman cast a quick glance into the hall. Mist choked it, but he could see thick layers of ice crystals gleaming across the walls and floor, while at the far end sat two figures, immobile, streaming with vapours – no doubt the very source of them. Iceblood magics, obviously. He turned back to Bernal. 'What? No. All of us. Now.'

446

Bernal smiled behind his beard as he shook his head. 'No. I will stay and hold the door. Now go.'

'Leal and Ham, then.'

The commander's voice sounded again: 'I order you to advance!'

Bernal urged him onward with a push of his shoulder. 'They sit now with the master and mistress. As I shall – so go, quickly. The spell is fading.' He pushed Kasson off also.

Orman edged back down the stairs; he had his one last duty to perform. 'Very well. Kasson, let's find your brother.' Backing away, he saluted Bernal with Svalthbrul. The fellow raised his great spear in answer and waved them off. Orman and Kasson jogged away round the Greathall.

They found Keth at the rear, the bodies of fallen soldiers all about him. 'Jaochim has tasked us to bring word of this to Buri,' Orman said.

Kasson nodded. 'Bernal told me.'

Characteristically, Keth said nothing. He merely started climbing the thin barrier of logs. Orman joined him.

Vapours slid about the fields, sinking now into pools and depressions, like water. They jogged past fallen soldiers who lay shuddering, their arms clenched to their chests as if against a terrifying cold. Orman headed for the nearest patch of woods and they crashed through. The tree limbs and brush snapped like icicles. Orman reflected that he might be inured to the magics because of his shared blood, but the air was so appallingly frigid it still hurt his nose and lungs with every breath.

They jogged onward, heading north and upland. He heard no sounds of pursuit.

*　　*　　*

The night watch woke Jute, reporting of strange sights and sounds to the west. Still groggy, but happy to have his cabin back now that the Mare youth had recovered and moved to sleeping in the hammocks with the crew, he pulled on his boots, wrapped himself in a thick fur cloak, and headed out.

The night air shocked him with its bracing cold. His fingers tingled. This didn't feel like spring at all. Had more of the smell of autumn to it. The sailor motioned to the far shore, where it lay barely discernible in the dark overcast night – only the diffuse glow of the moon and stars behind the clouds allowed any visibility. Torches and lanterns swung and bobbed there, movement. A great number of people on the move in the dead of night.

Jute scratched his chin, wondering. Those would have to be the people from Wrongway up the coast. Given up on the goldfields, perhaps. But what would drive them onward through the night?

'Jute Hernan,' he heard Ieleen call, and he turned. She stood wrapped in a blanket in the doorway, a hand on the jamb.

'Hmm? What is it, love? Sorry if I woke you.'

Her blind gaze was on the west and he was surprised to see her brows crimp in worry. 'Sound the wake up and get dressed. Visitors.'

He stroked his chin. Well, if she insisted . . . it seemed quiet to him, but he'd lived this long by respecting her instincts. He nodded to the crewman. 'Sound the alarm. All hands to readiness.' He returned to their cabin as the hanging bronze alarm was banged, and feet pounded the deck.

When he returned, he found the crew at their posts and the ship's marines at the sides together with the Malazans. Both officers, Letita and Giana, armed and armoured, stood before him. 'Captain,' Letita greeted him. 'Your orders?'

He glanced to Ieleen sitting next to the tiller arm. She held her pipe in her mouth, but it wasn't lit. The Mare lad, Reuth, sat cross-legged on the deck beside her. She withdrew the pipe and motioned to the bows. He followed the motion to see Cartheron leaning up against the side, peering to the west. He nodded to Letita and Giana to excuse him and went to the captain. His voice low, he asked, 'What's going on?'

The old fellow ran a hand over what little of his bristled hair remained. 'Damned if I know . . .'

'Commander Tyvar!' one of the crewmen called out.

Tyvar came pounding up the gangway. Behind him came another person, startling Jute. It was the unmistakable tall figure of the foreign sorceress, Lady Orosenn. He bowed to her and she returned the courtesy.

'Captain,' she said. 'I must apologize. I thought that disguising my presence would buy us more time – but I can see now that I need not have bothered.'

Jute blinked his confusion. 'Your presence?'

Tyvar motioned to the switchback staircase. 'I must get my men up at once.'

'Their King Ronal will treat you as just another invader and attack,' Cartheron warned. 'Malle has made that clear.'

'Malle of Gris?' A new voice spoke up and everyone turned. It was that bedraggled Malazan Khall-head, straightening from where

448

he'd been slouched next to the gangway. Somehow, Jute – everyone – had overlooked him. 'She's up there?' he breathed, and he squinted at the heights.

Cartheron followed the man's gaze. He started for him, 'Don't you dare . . .' But the fellow slipped away down the gangplank with a fluid speed that surprised Jute. Cartheron hurried after him, cursing. He reappeared a moment later, rubbing his chest and wincing, winded. 'He got away, damn his eyes.'

'Never mind him,' Jute said, wondering why it should matter if the fellow ran off.

But Cartheron was staring off at the cliff top. 'The shit will well and truly fly now,' he announced. Then he lowered his gaze, grinning savagely. 'Malle will not like this, but she'll have no choice.'

'I see no one on the stairs,' Tyvar said as he scanned the night.

'He used his Warren,' Lady Orosenn observed.

Jute felt his brows shoot up. Really? That broken-down derelict? He shuddered in memory of the insults he'd sent the fellow's way.

'Our troubles remain,' Tyvar commented impatiently. 'We will climb regardless. Now.'

Cartheron raised a hand for a pause. 'Wait. Give it one glass's time. If I know my man, this shouldn't take long.'

'Who? What?' Jute demanded, frankly rather irritated with the old Malazan commander.

Cartheron leaned back against the gunwale, crossed his arms and nodded as he accepted the reasonableness of Jute's annoyance. 'He is, well, *was*, an imperial Claw. An assassin,' he explained, speaking to Lady Orosenn. 'I recognized him. Seen him around. Rose up through the ranks under, ah, the old emperor's regime.'

Jute snorted at this. 'That wreck?'

Cartheron's lips clenched and he lowered his gaze. 'Something happened to him. Something that shattered him.' And he added, softly, as if speaking only for himself, 'Something that hurt all of us.'

The Blue Shield commander was still scanning the west shore. Jute glanced over. The bobbing torches and lanterns were closer now, waving furiously, as if the people had now broken into a run. Tyvar actually growled as he spun away. 'Lady Orosenn,' he demanded, 'if what you say is true we *must* go now. My people are ready. We will climb ten at a time. We must prepare.'

The foreign sorceress regarded Cartheron silently. Her almond-shaped eyes seemed to glow like those of a bird of prey, probing and gauging. The Malazan returned the stare without flinching. Jute reflected that the man must have faced down some pretty powerful entities in his time. She slowly nodded her inhumanly long head. 'You have your time, Cartheron Crust.'

It was not many minutes after that that a crash sounded on the boards of the dock close to the base of the cliff. As if he'd been expecting exactly that, Cartheron nodded to everyone, turned, and jogged down the gangway. Tyvar, Jute and Giana followed.

It was the fellow himself, lying slashed and bloodied amid the broken timbers of the dock. Cartheron knelt and gently cradled his head on his lap. A smile raised the man's lips as he croaked, 'Didn't get the landing right. Got him, though. Damn if those boys aren't good with their spears.'

'Don't talk,' Cartheron murmured, though it was clear from the many thrusts the man had taken that it would make no difference.

Then tears came to the man's eyes and he clamped a blood-smeared hand on Cartheron's arm. 'I'm sorry!' he gasped, suddenly panicked. 'I'm so sorry she fell. I failed her. Do you forgive me?'

It was fairly clear to Jute that, like so many in dying, the man was now rambling of his past.

'We all failed her,' Cartheron answered, and Jute was surprised by the strength of emotion in his voice. 'Only after she was gone did I see how much we needed her.'

The man clenched savagely at Cartheron's arm as if he would pull himself erect. He left bright bloody smears down the Malazan's sleeve. 'I'm so sorry,' he barely breathed.

Cartheron gently pressed shut his eyes and, with an effort, pushed himself erect. Peering down, he murmured so low Jute hardly heard, 'I can forgive *you* . . .'

'Who was he?' Jute asked. 'What's going on?'

'There's a light flashing from above,' Giana observed, scanning the heights.

'What does it say?' Cartheron asked. He was still regarding the strange fallen fellow, who Jute gathered must have been more than a passing acquaintance. The old captain now suddenly appeared much older, much more beaten down by his years. He raised his gaze to blink at Jute as if only now recognizing his presence. 'As I said. He once was a Claw. Bodyguard to Empress Laseen, in fact. They used to call him Possum.'

Laseen! The slain empress! So . . . this broken man . . . One slip, one mistake, and his entire world ended. How he now regretted his earlier harshness. 'He was a friend, then?'

'No. Couldn't stand him myself.'

Giana came to the commander's side, murmured low and respectfully, 'It says we can come up.'

Cartheron gave a tired nod. 'Very good, lieutenant.' He turned to study Tyvar. 'You have your invitation to the party, Mortal Sword of Togg.'

*

Jute joined the file to climb even though, on the *Dawn*, Ieleen had made clear with her silence that she did not approve of his choice to go. They went in small groups. Tyvar's Genabackans were by far the majority. Cartheron joined the file even though he'd sworn he'd never climb the damned stairs again. With the old commander went Lady Orosenn followed by her servant, Velman or -mar, Jute couldn't remember. Lieutenant Jalaz led the contingent of every Malazan veteran from both ships.

As they gathered awaiting their turn upon the stairs, the Genabackan captain Enguf appeared. He swore the ships would all be safe with him and his crew remaining behind to guard them. He wished them all the best of luck then hurried back to his ship.

Jute found the night climb easier than his first ascent. It was either that he couldn't see his actual height clearly, or he'd done it already and so had lost his fear of it. In either case, it was over far more quickly than the first climb. The structure groaned and shifted alarmingly, but he found he could put that out of mind more easily by concentrating on his handholds on the dried grey slats of the scaffolding.

It was dark at the top, though there was a glow of moving torches and lanterns beyond the outer curtain wall where it arced in a broad semicircle from cliff edge to cliff edge. Tyvar was there, whispering commands to his officers. Cartheron and Lady Orosenn stood aside, scanning the crowded grounds. The old Malazan looked very much worse for having made the climb. He was pale, pressing a hand to his chest, apparently in some measure of pain.

Giana Jalaz gained the top and nodded to Cartheron, awaiting orders. The old captain waved for her to take to the walls. She bowed and jogged off with her command.

A knot of the locals, spears in hand, came marching up. Almost invisible in their midst was the short and wiry shape, all in black, of Malle of Gris.

The company halted before Cartheron and stamped their spearbutts to the ground. Malle stepped forth and indicated one of the party: a youth, and like these locals tall and slim with a great mane of brown curls. He was studying Cartheron and did not appear to be impressed by what he saw.

'This is Voti,' Malle began, 'nephew of King Ronal who now lies upon his bier, cut down by an outlander assassin sent by the besiegers . . .' her voice quite hardened at that last part as she eyed Cartheron. She bowed to the lad, Voti. 'May I present Cartheron Crust – a great veteran commander of the Empire.'

The lad, the king presumptive, Jute assumed, gave the merest nod. 'Malle tells us you know these outlander ways. You may advise during the coming battle.'

Cartheron was experienced enough not even to blink as he inclined his head. 'My thanks.'

The lad next turned to the figure of Lady Orosenn, dressed now in her tanned hunting leathers, a long-knife at her side. Tall she was, even in this company, her auburn hair unbound in a great wild mane. Jute was suddenly struck by the resemblance between her and these people in their features and general build.

He remembered then her saying that she was returning home.

'You look familiar . . .' the lad said, addressing her, frowning as if trying to recall just where he'd seen her.

She inclined her head. 'I do not believe so. My name is Orosenn. I have been a long time away. It is merely the family resemblance.'

The lad grunted at this, satisfied. 'Very well.' Then, as if suddenly remembering his duties, he added, gruffly, 'You are welcome.' He strode off followed by his bodyguard of spearmen.

Malle, however, remained. Her glare, fixed upon Cartheron, could've melted iron. The commander, still pale and haggard from the climb, raised his hands in a gesture of surrender. 'I know, I know.'

'I thought I made it clear,' she hissed, her lips tight, 'the old ways of doing things are over.'

'I'm all tradition, Malle.'

She snorted her agreement, but then a new light came into her eyes – something like grudging admiration. She gestured to the nearest section of wall to invite Cartheron, Jute, and Lady Orosenn forward. 'Well, by now you've guessed the Empire saw its chance for a toehold on this continent and we were sent to establish relations. What I didn't expect was to find myself in the middle of a full-scale invasion.'

'There is far more at stake here than a mere change in rulership,' came the rich tenor of Lady Orosenn.

Malle stopped short and turned to peer up at the woman. She did not flinch, and Jute realized just how apposite Cartheron's warning about not getting in the woman's way had been. She appeared wrought entirely of iron, from her iron-grey hair to her thin arms of twisted iron bar. 'I know your heritage, sorceress. I know the name of the cold winds blowing down from these mountains. I know we sit at the feet of a Jaghut refugium.'

'But do you know that your being here is no accident?' the sorceress countered, her voice hardening as well. 'That we should be here at all is entirely your fault?'

Malle was clearly rocked by the accusation. Her mouth drew down into a sour scowl. 'Explain yourself, sorceress . . .' Even Jute heard the cold menace in the old woman's words.

'You Malazans,' Lady Orosenn continued. 'Your being here is no accident. I knew this the moment I encountered Cartheron here on his way to these lands. And so I enrolled Tyvar and his Blue Shields in helping escort him north.'

Cartheron almost jumped at that. 'What the . . . ?' He coughed, utterly shocked. 'I'm just making a delivery.'

Orosenn nodded. 'Yes, for this woman to use to back up a Malazan client state here in the north – conveniently near a goldfield.'

Now Malle's gaze narrowed. Her hands disappeared among the long black lace trimmings at her wrists. 'You are too well informed, sorceress.'

Cartheron raised a hand in warning. 'Malle . . . don't.'

Jute's hair rose as he realized that this woman fully intended to attack the sorceress. The servant – whatever his name was – tried to push forward but Orosenn held him back.

'Why this delay!' boomed a new voice as Tyvar came jogging up. His armour jangled loudly and he carried his helmet in a fist, his other on the long leather-wrapped grip of his sword. 'Those without the walls are clamouring to be allowed in. Our fair ruler refuses. And,' he added, his tone sharpening, 'm'lady, of the enemy you mentioned, there is yet no sign at all . . .'

Jute felt as if he could suddenly breathe once more. Malle's hands reappeared among the hanging lace at her wrists. She demanded, 'What army? What state's? More Lether reinforcements?'

'We should have until dawn,' Lady Orosenn answered Tyvar. She turned her attention to Malle. 'What army, you ask? One might argue that it is the army of the past that comes now to throttle the future.'

Jute felt his face wrinkle up in confusion. What nonsense was this now?

'The army of the past,' Malle echoed, wonderingly. Her gaze shot to Cartheron. 'It cannot be . . .'

Jute was surprised to see the old general's face harden and lose all hint of his habitual mocking humour. 'You're on dangerous ground hinting at such things, Lady Orosenn.'

'I? I am on dangerous ground? You Malazans have no idea what you've been meddling in. The old war was over until your emperor broke the balance. Now all this blood spilled is your fault and you must make reparation.'

Jute cleared his throat loudly. 'Please, Lady Orosenn – of what do you speak?'

The sorceress turned to him and her features softened. A smile came to her lips, but it was a wistful one. 'Jute of Delanss – I am sorry. You are right. We dance around the subject because it is almost too terrifying to name. I speak of course of the T'lan Imass, reawoken by the old emperor. Their Summoner nears even as we speak.'

Cartheron was shaking his head in hard denial. 'No. You say we're culpable. But we helped bring them this Summoner, Silverfox.'

'Or she emerged in a desperate effort to right the imbalance,' the sorceress countered.

'Word is, Silverfox has nothing against the Jaghut,' Cartheron growled.

'Evidently she does not speak for all clans.'

Malle snapped up a hand. 'Enough. This cannot be settled now. Sorceress – you claim the T'lan Imass are marching here. Yet what is this to us? I gather they seek these Icebloods, who I suspected are Jaghut. They will ignore us and pass on into the heights to track down their old enemies. It is sad and regrettable . . . but we could not interfere even if we wished.' Malle made a show of studying the sorceress up and down. 'Indeed, Lady Orosenn, I understand the fierceness of your advocacy. And considering this, you would be well advised to flee immediately yourself.'

'Tell them what you told me,' Tyvar Gendarian rumbled, his voice deep with suppressed emotion.

The sorceress sighed and there was now compassion in her gaze as she studied Cartheron. 'This is a hard thing to tell you Malazans, but all these locals who live in the north, who occupy this keep, who farmed and lived here . . . they all share some measure of Jaghut blood. The T'lan Imass are marching north and killing all as they come. They will take this keep by storm and slay every living original inhabitant of these lands.'

Jute found that he almost blacked out at the thought of it. His vision darkened and his face and hands became frigid and numb. *All the gods forfend!* How could such things be allowed? Surely the injustice of it must offend all. He'd never considered the idea of evil before, but surely such an act must be condemned as such.

If Jute felt sickened, he could not imagine what Cartheron was feeling now. The man had appeared haggard and tired before, but this news seemed to age him decades as a weight slowly settled upon his shoulders and gouged fresh depth in the already creased and furrowed brackets at his mouth and eyes. He pulled a shaking hand down his face. 'If that's so, then there's nothing we can do.'

'We have a chance,' Lady Orosenn offered. 'Omtose Phellack hampers them. They must march as any other army. They must climb defences. Receive blows. Those that are broken will not arise again. We can defend. Their Bonecasters will attempt to raise Tellann, but I shall work to suppress it. Together, we may have a chance.'

The age-spotted hand that Cartheron had been drawing so hard down his face now brushed the grey bristles of his chin. He turned his head to study Tyvar for a time. 'And what of you, Mortal Sword? I don't believe Togg has done you any favours here.'

The swordsman regained his savage grin. 'I disagree. We have been blessed with the greatest challenge we could hope for. No force has ever repelled the T'lan. The Blue Shields intend to be the first.'

Cartheron gave a curt nod. 'So be it. To tell the truth, I would like to have a word with these Imass.'

Lady Orosenn bowed to Cartheron. 'My thanks, commander. We all have our posts, then. I shall be at the entrance to the inner keep.' Bowing again, she headed off, followed by her servant.

Malle regarded Cartheron with a speculative glint in her dark eyes. 'The right thing, Crust?'

'Right enough,' he answered, roughly.

'And what of your cargo?'

He shook his head. 'Not right for this – unless you want to destroy our own walls.'

She pursed her thin lips. 'A shame. Very well . . .' She inclined her head. 'Commander. I shall be at the wall with my men.'

Jute watched her walk away then turned to Cartheron. 'Excuse me, captain . . . but just who is that woman anyway?'

Cartheron was rubbing a hand over his bristled chin once more. 'Who? Her? Ah – Malle.' An expression came to his face that was similar to the admiring look the woman herself had given him. 'The Empire has one academy where its imperial Claws are trained, Jute.

For thirty years that gal ran it.' He clapped his hands. 'Well, I'm for the walls. Apparently I'm in command of the foreigner contingent here. You can stand with me if you like – as good a view as anywhere of the coming goddamned end of the world, I suppose.' He headed off.

Jute stood unmoving. He knew where his post should be – back at the *Dawn* with Ieleen. She'd be worried, he knew. Yet . . . to walk away from witnessing the T'lan Imass confronted? To describe such an opportunity as once in a lifetime would be a laughable understatement. Once every ten thousand years, more like. He simply could not tear himself away. Besides, the *Dawn* was in the best of hands with her. And the crew was loyal.

He hurried to catch up. Beyond the tall stone walls, the glow of torches still bobbed and swept about. Voices clamoured, and, above the bellowed orders and shouts of plain panic, he heard the crash and groan of equipment being moved and the thump of axes on timber.

Climbing a ramp of beaten earth, Jute found Cartheron with Lieutenant Jalaz at his side. He took the commander's other side. They overlooked Mantle town, or at least its remains. The camp of the besiegers was in turmoil. Glancing far to the east, where the glow of coming dawn painted the sky a brightening purple, he glimpsed a bedraggled line of distant figures in retreat – those who wouldn't stop even for the presumptive safety of the camp and what portion of the invader army remained. From what he'd heard of the wilds of the Bone Peninsula, he imagined such refugees wouldn't long survive.

Those elements that had retained their organization were now feverishly assembling a barricade to the rear. They obviously had completely reversed themselves to face the enemy they believed to be coming for them. Jute groaned his helpless frustration and disbelief, 'But the T'lan don't want them!'

Cartheron sighed. 'Malle's been trying to tell them that.' He lifted his bone-thin shoulders. 'They're terrified. They won't listen.'

'Better if they had all fled,' Jute grumbled.

'Really?' Cartheron shot him a quick glance. 'Bastards might actually get lucky, you know. Take down a few of the Imass.'

The sentiment made Jute shudder. He'd forgotten. Their time together had fooled him into thinking the man at his side was a relatively harmless old codger – but he wasn't. He was a retired commander of Malazan forces, once a High Fist. And to defend his command he was obviously prepared to sacrifice every one of these poor unfortunates arrayed on the field before him.

Jute wrapped his cloak tighter about himself, turned to study the walls. A small complement, a watch, now stood the walls. He spotted the night-black shape of Malle at the wall, flanked by two figures, an old man and a young girl, who he believed had to be imperial cadre mages. Most of the defenders, locals, the Malazans, and Tyvar's Genabackans, were lying down across the grounds. Jute shuddered again as the sight of all the prone figures crowding the broad yard made him think of a field of graves.

Gods! The T'lan Imass. We won't see the noon. Yet all I would have to do is drop my weapon and they would pass me by – would they not? Somehow, when the time came, Jute knew he would not yield. He would do his part. And defending walls is spear-work. Thankfully, there were plenty of racks at hand. He collected a spear and leaned upon it.

Out among the demolished houses and huts of Mantle town, along the line of hastily raised barricades, one figure constantly marched back and forth, cajoling, yelling orders. From the voice, Jute knew this officer was a woman. She wore a long coat of mail and a helmet with a faceplate, raised at the moment.

At one point Tyvar came past on an inspection and he paused at Cartheron's side to motion to the officer. 'See that one?'

Cartheron nodded tiredly. 'Yeah. I see.'

'I'd know that style of armour and helmet anywhere,' Tyvar continued, sounding almost excited. 'That's a Shieldmaiden out of northern Genabackis, I'm sure.'

'They fought us in the north,' Cartheron observed, a touch irritated – he'd been asleep standing up.

Tyvar gave a serious nod. 'Aye – as we would've if you'd reached the south.' And he slapped Cartheron on the back and continued his circuit.

Jute blinked heavily then, leaning on his spear, and the next thing he knew there were screams from below and he blinked anew, clutching his spear haft. It was brighter now, fully dawn, though it was hard to tell because of the dense low bank of clouds that hung like a smothering blanket crowded up against the slopes of the Salt range. Men and women among the defenders and civilians below were now pointing west. More among them broke and ran for the east, abandoning their posts and fleeing. The Shieldmaiden sent curses after them.

Jute squinted into the gloom of the west. Figures were approaching just inland from the coast of the Gold Sea. A wide front of shapes. Not a file, or a column, but rather a broad skirmish-line of walkers. The image came to Jute of a net, a line of beaters, driving their prey before them. The image made him almost faint with dread. T'lan Imass. So terrifyingly ruthless and unrelenting. They won't let anyone escape them.

The Shieldmaiden now shouted encouragement to her troops, who readied their spears. She drew her own sword and climbed the barricade.

'Good for you . . .' Cartheron murmured beneath his breath.

The T'lan came on, scarecrow thin, unhurried, yet somehow inexorable – like the tide, Jute thought. Their skirmish-line passed between the burned and scavenged husks of the few houses of Mantle town. They brushed aside the canvas of tents, kicked through smoking campfires. Closer now, Jute saw how their cloaks hung ragged and full of gaping tears. Some wore animal bones as armour in the shape of wide scapulae lashed across the chest, or skulls of enormous beasts upon their heads. They came with their slim stone blades gripped negligently in their fists. He put their number at over a hundred.

They met the logs and overturned wagons of the barricade and those blades flashed to hack through the thigh-wide trunks as if they were kindling. The defenders thrust with their spears. They rocked backwards a few of the attackers, but these merely shook off the thrusts and returned to the task of chopping the barrier.

Further panicked yells sounded where individual Imass succeeded in pushing their way through. Defenders closed, spears abandoned and swords drawn. Next to Jute, Cartheron ground out a muttered, 'Fools . . .' yet he sounded admiring all the same.

Jute saw the commander of this desperate – yet needless! – defence charge in to join one fray. A great swipe from her heavy blade chopped down through an Imass at juncture of neck and shoulder. That one fell, evidently crippled. A great cheer arose from the defenders, and Jute noted that Tyvar's Blue Shields joined in the huzzah.

More Imass came as they pushed and hacked through the heaped wreckage. Defenders fell. However, to his relief, Jute saw now that the Imass were lashing out with their fists and the sides of their blades as they swung to bash the men and women down. Oddly enough, he almost felt grateful to these elders for their restraint – if that was what one might call it.

The Shieldmaiden fell then, taken by a blow to her helmet that laid her flat. A shudder of pain seemed to run through the line of defenders, and it broke. Jute, who had never seen a land battle before this journey, sensed it even as it happened. It seemed as if all it took was one defender half stepping back, or flinching, and his fellows shied away as well. Instantly, it seemed, like a contagion, this backpedalling spread up and down the ragged line and men and women were outright fleeing, scrambling, all streaming towards the east.

The T'lan halted their advance to watch them go. Their flat ravaged profiles turned to follow the men and women as they fled. Those same cadaver heads then swung up to regard the walls.

Jute felt his mouth turn ash-dry while at the same time his hands were slick upon the spear haft. He wiped them on the thighs of his woollen trousers.

At some silent order, the T'lan resumed their advance. They stepped on dropped shields and abandoned spears as they came.

As they neared the stakes driven into the ground before the ditch beneath the walls, Cartheron leaned forward, cupped his hands to his mouth and shouted down, 'We of Mantle Keep greet you! With what clan do I speak?'

The ranks halted to stand as silent and still as a file of statues. A weak wind brushed at the hanging tattered ends of hides and fur cloaks.

Jute saw the local young king presumptive, Voti, followed by Malle, arrive next to Cartheron. The lad stood with his arms crossed, the haft of his spear hugged to his chest. Jute heard a steady murmuring among the local defenders gathered at the walls. Their accent was difficult for him, but eventually he made out the repeated litany of wonder: '. . . bone and dust . . .'

He turned to the nearest of the locals, a woman, perhaps a mother standing the wall to defend her children within. 'What does this mean,' he asked, '"bone and dust"?'

'An old legend among us,' she replied, sounding oddly resigned. 'An old story that our world will end with an invasion of the dead.'

Jute could only shake his head in wonder. Ye gods! Was this prescience? Or merely chance? But, he thought, the war between Imass and Jaghut was incalculably ancient. Perhaps this legend was a memory of an earlier clash. One that might even have occurred upon another continent halfway round the world.

Closing now, up the silent unmoving ranks, came two figures. Both were of course of Imass stock, yet they differed strikingly. One was lean while the other markedly squat. The lean one wore the mangy and raggedy hide of what appeared to have once been a white bear. The beast's head rode his own, the upper fangs hanging down before his mummified face. Necklaces of yellowed bear claws rode his chest, and the clacking and clattering of these were the only sounds Jute could hear.

The other Imass was among the most damaged of those present. She – Jute intuited somehow that it was female – appeared to have been thrust through multiple times. She bore a primitive face with a broad shelf of a brow and wide jaws. Her canines jutted quite prominently and they glinted copper in the early morning light. Shells laced about her ragged leathers swung and clattered.

The Imass in the bear hide stepped forward. His voice, though as wispy as brushing leaves, somehow reached Jute: 'Greetings. I am Ut'el Anag, Bonecaster to the Kerluhm T'lan Imass. Who addresses us?'

'I am Cartheron Crust of the Malazans. We greet you as allies and friends.'

Ut'el shifted his skull-like face to his companion Imass. 'I understand that alliance no longer holds. You and all those not native to these lands are trespassers here. Stand aside and you will not be harmed. Our quarrel is not with you.'

'This is the will of Silverfox?' Cartheron called, much louder.

The Bonecaster paused only very slightly. 'It is our way.'

'But not hers, I gather. She is coming, is she not? Perhaps we would prefer to wait to hear her counsel on this matter.'

The bear head dipped as the Kerluhm Bonecaster nodded. 'You may wait. Meanwhile, Omtose Phellack is rotting. I sense a powerful elder Jaghut within, but even she, being flesh and blood, will tire. Soon we shall be free to move as we wish.'

Jute turned to mutter to Cartheron, 'He is right in that. What shall we do?'

The old commander answered beneath his breath, 'Don't worry yourself. They may be ancient, but they're still awful at cards. They can't bluff worth a damn.'

Smiling broadly, the ex-High Fist answered with a welcoming sweep of his arm. 'Then sit yourself down and let me tell you all about my childhood on Nap. Do you know Nap? It's an island south of Quon Tali. 'Course in your time it was probably a mountain top. In any case, I was born on Fanderay's High Holy day – not that that's done me any good – though my mam claims it shaped my character just as my brother Urko was born in a quarry—'

Ut'el raised a withered hand for silence. 'So be it. You should not

460

invite our attack. Do not think we will spare you as we did these other outsiders.'

'I did not imagine so.' Cartheron turned to the new king and Malle. 'Find your place at the wall, ah, sire.'

The lad nodded and sauntered off, determined to show how unimpressed he was. 'They were going to attack anyway,' Malle said.

Cartheron waved her onward. 'I figured as much.'

Jute took a renewed grip on his spear haft, found he had to wipe his hands once again.

The attack came as before, without warning or shouted orders. As one, the Imass simply advanced, spread along the arc of the wall. They clambered down the slope of the moat, pushed through the mud, then started climbing the wall using handholds in the rough stone slabs.

The defenders, local northerners, Malazans, and Blue Shields, thrust with spears to dislodge or stave off the wave. The Imass ignored these stabs as they climbed. Many defenders soon understood that thrusting weapons were ineffective against this ancient army, and so the spears, billhooks and pikes were thrown down and swords and axes readied.

Jute abandoned his own spear standing from the shoulder of an Imass. The creature calmly took hold of the haft, yanked it free, and returned to its slow deliberate ascent. Jute drew the weapon at his side and was appalled to remember as he saw it that it was a shortsword. He cursed Mael and himself. How could he have not foreseen . . . He madly searched about for a larger weapon.

Long-hafted axes lay gathered at the inside base of the wall. Jute scrambled down the ramp to collect one. He lifted one and was about to return to the wall when he heard a strange sound coming from the rear – from the cliff side. It was the methodical thump of wood being chopped.

He could hear this because the battle was eerily silent. The T'lan, of course, made no noise at all. The defenders merely grunted, swore and exhaled noisily in their efforts, while wood and iron clattered from stone.

He wondered what could possibly . . . Then he knew and his hair stirred to stand on end. He ran for the cliff top. A crowd of the locals had gathered here, peering down and pointing. Jute pushed through to the fore. Down below, four Imass had climbed out along the cliff to reach the stairway and were in the process of demolishing it. Even as he watched, sections of the stairs tore free of the rocks to tumble in awful slowness.

The *Dawn* was below! He looked to the vessels, and realized the crews had seen this coming and had already slipped moorings and were in the process of pulling away: the *Dawn*, the *Ragstopper*, and the Genabackan pirate's. Even the *Resolute*, though Jute had no idea who might be crewing it.

The wreckage of timber crashed and burst upon the rocks. Entire lengths of the stairs had been cut from the cliff face. Jute watched the vessels raising sails and he silently bid Ieleen farewell. He knew now he would die here. His need to be part of negotiations, to witness events – to poke his nose in where it didn't belong, as Ieleen had it – would finally finish him. As she had so long predicted.

Everyone at the cliff top now saw the four T'lan Imass climbing the rocks headed straight for them.

As the battle raged on behind them, these locals, most of them non-combatant women and old men, began heaving rocks down upon the Imass. They took axes to the uppermost section of the stairs, Jute included, and managed to send it tumbling down as well. One of the Imass fell a short distance, but caught himself, possibly breaking the bones of his arm.

The lead three reached the top where soil and sod curled over the lip. As they dragged themselves over, people crowded in to hack at them. It was frantic and panicked – ugly to any soldier, no doubt, as utter disorder reigned. People got in each other's way, even injured one another with their wild swings. Jute caught himself sobbing and cursing as he tried to get a blow in.

One Imass lost an arm and slipped back over the lip, presumably to fall. The two others righted themselves beneath a flurry of blows and drew their stone blades. A lucky swing took one's hand off where it gripped the blade and this Imass lashed out to clutch its adversary's neck. Trachea and vertebrae popped and crunched audibly, then it tossed the limp corpse over the edge behind it. Spears thudded into its torso to stand like decorations. It knelt to retrieve its blade odd-handed. The other Imass slashed down a woman. Two men threw themselves on to it, wrapped their arms around it, and the three tottered backwards to slip off the edge and disappear in complete deathly silence.

The remaining Imass slashed about itself. Men and women fell clutching at deep eviscerating cuts that spilt blood and bile over the grass. The Imass waded into the crowd, which exploded in wild panic. Jute knew that he could not let this attacker come at the wall from the rear, so he backed off to allow it to pass and then slowly, deliberately, began to stalk it.

Perhaps it was simply too intent upon slaughter to notice his approach, Jute did not know, but he raised his long-hafted axe up over his head for a great swing, charged the last two steps, and brought the iron wedge-shaped blade down upon the mangy, desiccated half-bare skull, and split it nearly in two.

The blade wedged at the base of the neck. As the creature swung round it tore the haft from Jute's grip. Jute backed away, appalled. *Ye gods! What does it take . . .*

The creature slashed, catching Jute's upper arm. He gasped at the sizzling pain of the cut and kept retreating back towards the cliff edge. The Imass kept after, incensed perhaps by this fellow who dared split its head with an axe. His right arm hung blood-soaked and numb. He knelt one-handed for an abandoned spear and gripped it hard, tucking the haft under his armpit for further stability.

The T'lan Imass came on. When Jute's very heels were at the cliff's lip, he lunged, striking the spear home in the Imass's chest. It raised its blade to hack at the haft. Still gripping the weapon, Jute danced a half-circle and pushed with all his might. The Imass sliced through the haft, but not before it staggered backwards and overbalanced, to slip suddenly from view.

Jute lurched back towards the tower and the wall beyond. He gripped his arm where the blood still welled. His vision seemed to darken and there was a roaring in his ears – he suspected it was his laboured pulse. Coming round the base of the tower, he found the ground before the entrance blackened and smoking. Three corpses, no more than white bones and charcoal, lay upon the scorched earth. Two were Imass, the other Jute assumed to be the sorceress's servant, since she herself sat up against one wall of the entrance, her chest heaving, her leg and a hand bloodied.

He tottered to her. 'Can you stand?'

She nodded tiredly. 'Barely.'

He helped her up then surveyed the corpses. 'Your servant saved your life.'

'He did.'

'I can't remember his name.'

'It was Velmar.'

'Ah.' He scanned the walls, blinking to clear his vision. Perhaps he was seeing things, but it seemed that half of those who'd stood defending the walls were gone. Bodies lay thick upon the catwalk. The local northerners were still fighting side by side with the Blue Shields, all struggling to push back the T'lan Imass. Malle and the

Malazan veterans held the east arc of the wall. Jute watched amazed while the young cadre mage's roaring streams of flame cleared a swathe across the top and the lean older mage thrust with his staff, somehow driving individual Imass off as if punched. Yet more took the wall than were repelled. The young cadre mage jerked, the flames snapping away. She toppled backwards impaled upon a slim cream-hued blade. Sections of the top were being yielded to the Imass. A hoarse bellow of alarm from the old Malazan mage marked his rush to an exposed Malle. He charged, knocking Imass from the wall, clearing a section, only to totter, slashed through to hanging ribbons of cloth and red gashes, and fall forward from sight.

The defenders retreated down the ramps in a solid wedge. The Blue Shields held the rear, fending off the T'lan in their slow advance.

'We will not last,' Jute murmured, now certain of it.

'No. They will win through.'

'Well, I will guard you now.'

She turned the same affectionate look upon him that he had often noticed. 'You are gallant, Jute of Delanss. But Ieleen would have you back. Even now she fights to protect you.'

He blinked again, bewildered. 'Oh? How so?'

'She is helping to pull the wind out of the heights.'

'A wind?' He had noticed how cold the air was and how the banners snapped and whipped.

'Yes.' The sorceress's eyes slipped closed and she stumbled back against the stone wall. She clasped a deep cut in one thigh that poured blood and fought to open her eyes once more. 'It brings news from the ice-fields. I only hope their Bonecaster will notice.'

She would have fallen but for Jute catching her, one-armed, and lowering her to sit up against the jamb. They found him like that, kneeling before her, rubbing her hand and whispering that she come back to them.

She smiled then, her eyes shut, and murmured, 'Ieleen is a lucky woman, Jute of Delanss.'

It was Cartheron who gently urged him aside. He felt for her pulse, then pressed a hand to her chest.

'Will she . . .' Jute began.

'She'll live. That we could even dare face them is thanks to her.'

Jute peered about. He was astonished and alarmed to see Tyvar here. The man's chest was heaving, his mail hacked through across his torso and arms, helm gone, his cheek and scalp slashed – the blood from these head wounds was soaking his neck and shoulder. Yet his eyes were shining with joy.

'What happened?' Jute demanded.

'They'd reached the bailey in places,' Tyvar explained, each word a laboured breath, 'and so we pulled the locals back even as they refused to retreat. Then, all at once, the T'lan drew off.' He appeared as bewildered as Jute.

'I saw it,' Cartheron said. 'Their Bonecaster, Ut'el. All of a sudden his head snapped round to the north and he took off without hesitating. The rest followed him.'

'They are hurrying to the heights to stop it,' said Orosenn, her voice dreamy with fatigue.

'Stop what?' Cartheron asked.

She raised an arm and Jute took it to help her up. She leaned back against the wall, drew a ragged breath. 'The Imass have their ritual of Tellann, you know. They used it to create the T'lan. We have our ritual as well. The Raising of Phellack. Someone in the heights has invoked it. What powers I possess are as a raindrop in the ocean compared to the might I sense being marshalled there. And when it comes . . .' She shook her head, almost falling once more. 'All of you must flee – now.'

'What is it? What comes?' Jute asked, almost unable to believe that anything worse could possibly happen.

She smiled again, but sadly this time. 'The true end of the world, Jute of Delanss.'

*   *   *

They walked in silence, for there was nothing more to say. None called for a halt for a meal. No one stopped when the sun set, nor when the sun rose. It seemed unnecessary, even tedious to Shimmer to consider halting so close to their goal.

K'azz led through the woods and high ridges. He pushed through frigid streams and up steep valley slopes. Shimmer followed next in line. Bars came after, then Lean, Keel, Black the Lesser, Turgal, Gwynn, and Blues in the rear. Where Cowl had gone, or even whether he still followed, she did not care.

They were high in these northern mountains now, the Salt range. They parted thick hanging cloud banks as if walking through an underworld of mists. Banners of the opaque fogs wove about them like the sinuous bodies of dragons. For brief moments she would note how loose her mail coat hung from her; how her hair lay tangled about her face and shoulders; how ragged her leather boots had become, yet she walked on, uncaring. K'azz promised their fate lay ahead. The secret of the Vow – which was clearly now a curse.

They came to a high meadow, a clearing that had once been a series of cultivated fields, now long abandoned, and they spread out. K'azz, on her right, was a vague silhouette in the low churning clouds, as was Bars on her left. A burned empty husk of a Greathall emerged from the mists ahead. Whatever tragedy had happened here had been wrought long ago. Saplings grew within the tumbled logs.

Past the overgrown remains of the burned hall stood a modest log cabin, sod-roofed. Here two figures rose from the tall grasses to confront them. They reared, enormous to Shimmer's eyes, both far taller than any normal man or woman, yet both obviously young in years. The lad wore supple tanned leathers and possessed a thick curled mane of russet hair and a beard to match. The girl was equally sturdy, in hunting leathers, her long blazingly red hair plaited.

The lad drew two hatchets to stand protectively before the girl. 'You'll not take us easily, damn you.'

K'azz raised his open hands. 'We intend no harm. We seek the heights and those who live there.'

'You intend no harm?' the lad repeated, incredulous. 'You who have slain all our kin?'

'We have slain no one. We are mercenaries out of lands far to the west.'

The lad frowned his disbelief then rubbed his eyes and examined them more closely. He jerked a nod. 'I am sorry. For a moment there I mistook you for . . . for someone . . . else.'

'What has happened here?' Shimmer asked.

The lad slipped his hatchets into his belt then gestured to the cabin. 'Our parents lie within, side by side.'

'And these others you speak of,' K'azz said, 'they did this?'

The girl shook her head. 'Nay,' she said. Her voice was flat, yet full of wonder. 'They simply chose to go. They bade us seek our elders in the heights then lay down together side by side.'

'I am sorry,' Shimmer offered.

The lad shook his head. His great mane of wild hair blew in the strong winds out of the north. 'No. We do not weep. It is good to see them here together, holding hands. So loving, yet so different. Yullveig the Fierce they called her, and Cull the Kind. Apart too much in life – together now in death.'

Shimmer regarded the modest cabin. The lad's words pulled at her distantly. There was something here, an ache that fought to squeeze her chest, yet she felt lost in a fog, or dullness, that held her numb to feelings.

'We travel to the heights,' K'azz said. 'We may travel together?'

The two nodded a sort of bruised agreement.

'Do we leave them in this manner?' Blues asked the girl.

'Yes. No flame will burn there now. We will leave them. None shall disturb them.' She inclined her head to Shimmer. 'I am Erta and this is Baran.'

Shimmer, K'azz and the rest introduced themselves. The two gathered up small rolls of gear and they headed upland once more.

The higher they climbed the thicker the fogs became and the more intense the cold. It was as if they had entered a realm of frigid winds and coiling mists as dense as streams. Ice now sheathed the trees and blades of tall grasses and they clattered and rattled as Shimmer pushed through. The light was diffuse, yet held a silvery shading, like pewter. It was almost impossible to tell whether they travelled in night or day. The slopes steepened, became half barren ridges of grey and black rock, the only colour a mute orange and yellow of lichen.

K'azz and Baran, at the fore, halted here, as did the rest of the file in turn. The clattering of rocks no longer echoed about the shrouded steep valley they currently walked. Shimmer moved up to join K'azz. He and Baran stood peering ahead into the blowing, churning clouds where a figure was approaching. It was a girl. Yet she stood man-high, slim, in trousers of wool and a leather shirt that hung to her knees, decorated in bright red and blue beadwork. Her hair blew about her, long and in tangles. Streams of tears darkened the ash and dirt that smeared her face.

'Greetings,' Baran called gently. 'I am Baran of the Heels.'

'Siguna of the Myrni,' she stammered, her voice soft and wary.

Erta knelt before her. 'What happened, child?'

Her wide eyes darted about as if expecting attack at any moment. 'They came out of the river gravel,' she said, awed. 'I saw them myself. They came out of the ground. I ran home. There was a fire. Uncle sent me away.'

'Who came?' Shimmer asked.

The girl's terrified gaze flicked to her. 'Demons. The Army of Dust and Bone.'

Siguna travelled with Erta in the middle of the file. K'azz and Baran led. The closer they were to their destination the more their old general seemed to have shaken off his reluctance and self-imposed isolation. Shimmer for her part was content to leave him to command; she'd begun to suspect that something was wrong with her. When she looked at the young Myrni child alone in the world she knew that something ought to move within her, yet all she felt was a remote poignancy as of an old loss, now a distant memory. She searched her feelings only to find a landscape as desolate and lifeless as these barren rocky slopes.

She was terrified of what was happening to her.

Some time later in the climb, the loose rocks shook beneath her feet. Everyone paused, peering about in alarm. Rocks and boulders came tumbling down out of the ground-hugging fogs. Everyone moved to a nearby ridge and gathered together. Blues came to stand next to her, his arms crossed. She noted how ragged and torn his leather jerkin had become, his scruffy beard and hollowed dark cheeks. Far above, beyond the immediate shoulders and slopes between them and the uppermost peaks, the clouds churned as if being drawn into a funnel. A glow suffused the region – a dazzling azure brilliance muted only by the cloud cover.

The ground shook again and Shimmer was alarmed to sense that the entire ridge of rock had actually moved. Baran and Erta shared a shocked glance.

'What is it?' Shimmer demanded. 'An earthquake?'

'This is no earthquake,' Blues growled, his eyes fixed upon the heights.

'We must reach the ice-fields,' Baran called over the crash and hissing of tumbling stones. 'Quickly.' And he set off, leaping from boulder to boulder. K'azz followed while Shimmer and Erta brought along Siguna. Bars and Turgal helped any of the rest who struggled to keep up.

A howling, biting wind punished them as it came driving down into their faces. Shimmer scrambled her way up the slope of loose rock. She had the strange sensation of actually travelling backwards as she advanced. The shifting talus and gravel seemed to heap even higher before them. She came across the trunks of fallen trees, shorn of branches, slowly edging their way down towards them like battering rams.

She clambered over the trunks only to hear a despairing call behind. She urged Siguna onward and stopped to peer back into the moiling fog. Others, she knew not who, passed as blurred shapes in the mist. Something closed upon her foot and ankle between the logs and she was yanked to her knees. A churning mix of gravel and soil had her. It was burying her as it came shifting down the slope. It rolled over her side and up her chest as it advanced. She drew breath to scream but took in a mouthful of dirt. Beneath the soil larger rocks squeezed her legs until she knew her bones would be shattered to splinters.

Then a tight grip at the mail over her chest, an agonizing yank, and she was free on the surface, gagging and coughing, lying on her side. Someone stood over her, his gaze watchful – Cowl.

He helped her clamber to her feet. She stood swaying, unsteady, as the ground felt like the deck of a ship. 'Thank you,' she managed, spitting out dirt.

'You will not thank me. *You*, above all, I want to make it. I want you there to see what he has done to us. I want you to see it.'

'Who has done what?'

The mage retreated down the slope. 'I know already. It is for you to discover. *Then* I want you to face him! Now go.'

'*Cowl!*' she yelled after him, but he was gone.

The very ground groaned and vibrated beneath her feet. She dashed up the rocks, pushing against the loose debris as it came sloughing down the entire valley slope to either side.

She made the crest of fresh steaming earth, and stopped, utterly amazed. A dry frigid wind battered her as she stared at a wide wall of dirty glacial ice that stretched from side to side across the entire high mountain vale before her. Far ahead, tiny figures, the rest of the party, struggled up the first of the leading lobes of dirty ice. Nearer, Blues and Bars ran towards her, stopping now and waving.

She waved back. And she might have been imagining it, but it seemed to her that the entire gargantuan frozen river itself, a very mountain of ice, was moving.

CHAPTER XIV

THEY KEPT TO THE FOREST AS THEY FLED UPLAND, THOUGH as they climbed higher the woods thinned. Spruce now predominated, and those thin and scraggly. Fisher and Jethiss stayed with Kyle, while the remaining Crimson Guard spread out about them. No one had formally set out the marching order. Kyle wondered whether it was to protect him – he who least needed protection. Stalker and Badlands ranged widely, sometimes scouting ahead, other times keeping an eye on the rear.

At least they travelled through the constant cover of the dense clouds that hugged these high slopes of the Salt range. Eventually, during the morning – if he judged aright the diffuse yellow glow of the sky – Cal-Brinn called a halt and they collapsed where they stopped to lie panting, sucking in great shuddering breaths of the frigid air. Water skins made the rounds.

The Crimson Guard captain came to where Kyle, Fisher and Jethiss sat leaning against the backrest of a toppled fir. 'Sleep,' he told them. 'We will keep watch.' He moved on. Kyle did not argue, and neither did his companions. They rolled themselves into whatever cloaks or blankets they had managed to salvage or pack. In Kyle's case, it was an untanned bear hide he'd rolled and roped over his back before the fight. He lay down and his thoughts went to the lowlands, to the shores of the Sea of Gold. What was happening there? Were Lyan and Dorinn safe? Of course she might not even *be* there – she might have accompanied the army north. But somehow he did not think so. These Lether officers and soldiers were claiming the north for themselves. To them, she and her Genabackans were outsiders. Perhaps even a threat.

Some time later he was woken by the poke of a spear-butt and he sat up, shivering, bleary and coughing. The sun was a smoky, silvery orb among the clouds. Tendrils of steam rose in wisps all about, and a clawing cold wind slithered down across them from the heights.

'The weather is strange,' he commented to Fisher.

The bard did not appear pleased. In fact, he had been in an uncharacteristically grim mood since they fled the Greathall. 'It is no weather,' he replied.

By now Kyle was accustomed to having to draw information from this man the way one must shake coins from a miser. A strange manner for a bard. 'Then what is it?'

Fisher drew a hard breath as if he would rather not say, but then he allowed, 'It is power coiling and tensing. Preparing itself for an unleashing. An invocation of Omtose.'

Kyle noted Jethiss paying close attention. 'What will come?' the Andii asked.

'I do not know for certain what form it will take,' Fisher admitted. 'But I fear the worst it might.'

Stalker and Badlands emerged from the dense fogs. 'They are with us still,' Badlands announced.

When he was younger, Kyle might have expressed his confusion. They'd pushed them out – the Holding was theirs. Why pursue? But he was older now, hard truths of the world had been beaten into him, so he merely shook his head at the inevitability of it. Of course they were coming. What else would they do? To ensure their grip on the land these new rulers had to eliminate all last vestiges of any prior claim. Any survivors would be a potential menace as they might raid, or form alliances and return some day to try to reclaim their ancestral holdings. In this Marshal Teal had no choice. Usurpers – claim-jumpers – had to be thorough.

Stalker stopped before Kyle. 'Far enough north for you?' he asked.

Kyle laughed. 'Aye. Perhaps for them as well.'

The Iceblood's hazel eyes held amusement. 'Well, I've never been up much higher. No call for it. From here, though, we can descend into the Sayer or Heel Holding if we would. I only wish I knew the best route.'

'Our line is good for now,' said Fisher. He shook out his cloak. 'Straight on.'

Everyone eyed the bard as he clipped the cloak tightly about his shoulders. Stalker studied the man as he drew his thumb and forefinger down his long moustache, smoothing it. Fisher, for his part, said no more.

It seemed to Kyle that the man had left the role of bard behind. He was something else now and Kyle wasn't certain just what that might be. Then, unexpectedly, he remembered the instrument the man had been strumming . . . the way he had held it. Like a treasure. 'It's not your fault,' he said.

The bard turned a puzzled frown upon him. 'I'm sorry?'

'That old stringed instrument at the Greathall. We had to flee. There was nothing you could have done.'

Understanding blossomed in rising brows and a broad smile broke through the man's dark mood. He squeezed Kyle's shoulder. 'Thank you for your thoughts, Whiteblade. But not to worry.' He raised the shoulder bag at his side. 'Such a rare thing should not be left to destruction.'

'So there is hope yet, then,' Kyle said.

The bard appeared startled. His gaze went to the shrouded heights. 'You are right, of course. The skein of our fates is unknown. Or at least is not for me to say.'

Badlands slumped on the fallen trunk. 'Now that that's settled – did anyone think to bring any food?'

It turned out that Cal-Brinn and the Guard always carried pouches with a few days' worth of dried rations pressed into bricks. It was hardly edible, but Kyle found that if one kept a knot of it tucked into the cheek, it slowly softened into something resembling food.

Cal-Brinn signed that they should get going, so they packed up their gear and set off jogging upland once more. They trotted through the rest of the day, as the light through the black clouds deepened to a silvery pewter. Kyle knew he would be freezing if it weren't for the heat of his exertions. His breath steamed and plumes of mist rose through his armour from his sweat-soaked tunic beneath.

Stalker ran with him and Fisher and Jethiss for a time. He gestured ahead, where the valley slope rose in a steep ridge of naked rock. 'We are nearing the top of the Lost Holding. Beyond that ridge lies a wide run-off stream, the Stonewash. Past that are the ice-rivers that descend out of the frozen wastes above.'

'Will they follow us?' Kyle asked.

He gave a non-committal shrug. 'They may send a party to dog us.' He eyed Jethiss. 'You are intent upon continuing?'

'I am.'

'There may be no one there.'

'In which case we are all free to choose whichever direction we wish.'

Stalker drew off his conical iron helmet and rubbed a hand

472

through his matted hair. 'Well, I have to admit to being rather curi-ous myself.'

'Not a good enough reason,' Fisher muttered.

'And you a bard,' Stalker remarked. He pulled the helmet on once again and turned his attention to Kyle. 'You still wear it, I see,' he said.

Kyle's brows drew down. 'I'm sorry?'

'The stone you're always fingering.'

He realized he was rubbing the amber pendant at his neck, as he often did. He dropped the hand. 'Yes.'

Stalker nodded solemn agreement. 'He was a good friend, Ereko. We miss him too.'

Kyle cleared his throat. It still pained him to hear the Thelomen-kind, Thel-Akai as he had it, mentioned. He'd forgotten that during their earlier travels Stalker had spent as much time with the giant as he. He answered the Lost's nod. 'Yes.'

'I know that name,' Fisher said, his eyes narrowing in thought. 'He was said to have been one of the oldest of those raised up by the earth.' He studied Kyle anew. 'You travelled with him?'

'Yes.'

'I would have that tale.'

Stalker flashed his teeth in a smile. '*Now* you're sounding like a bard.' He jogged ahead to start climbing the slope.

From the knife's edge of the ridge-top they could see nothing. The mists enveloped them. Stunted long-needle pine and juniper clung to the rocks here, damp with fog. Stalker and Badlands started down into the vale, which promised to lead higher up this shoulder of the Salt range.

Close to the floor of the narrow valley, the Lost cousins raised their hands for a halt. Dense banners of fog obscured all ahead. A fiercely cold wind buffeted them. 'What is it?' Fisher asked.

'Listen,' Stalker said.

Kyle focused on what sounds he could make out. Other than the moaning, gusting wind, all he could hear was a distant cracking and booming, accompanied by the occasional crash as of rocks falling.

'Those are the sounds of the great ice-tongues,' Fisher said. 'Some name them frost-serpents.'

Stalker tilted his head in agreement. 'Yeah. That's right. But what's strange is that we shouldn't be able to hear that above the roar of the stream that comes down here.'

'I hear no stream,' Kyle said.

Stalker's moustache drew down. 'Yeah. Something's odd. Wait

here.' He gestured Badlands to the right and he took the left. They disappeared into the roiling sheets of mist. Cal-Brinn signed for the Avowed to form a defensive perimeter. Kyle nodded a greeting to Leena, who winked back.

After a brief time, the two figures came jogging back through the fog. Their boots crunched on the stones and gravel as they closed. Stalker stood breathing heavily, his breath steaming. He smoothed his moustache while he shook his head in wonder. 'It's gone,' he told Fisher. 'The run-off stream is dry – well, muddy, but free of any flow. Can't figure it.'

'I can,' Fisher answered, grimly.

'And?' Badlands prompted.

The bard scowled as if he regretted saying anything. Finally, he offered, 'The ice has awakened. There'll be no spring or summer.'

Badlands barked a laugh. 'Ha! You've sung too many old sagas, Fisher. Such things no longer happen.'

Fisher gave Kyle a long-suffering why-do-I-even-try look. Kyle hid a smile and thought that perhaps he now understood something of the bard's reticence.

'We'll cross then climb the ice-serpent, though it will be treacherous with crevasses,' said Stalker, and he gestured to invite them onward.

They followed what was essentially a shallow empty riverbed of green-grey silt flats and broad gravel patches, all punctuated by boulders that emerged from the mists like sentinels. The way led them upslope. The wind was punishing now – a blasting current of cold that was oddly dry and desiccating. It carried the cracking and popping of the massive hidden field of ice. The eruptions burst as loud as the explosive munitions of the Moranth.

Stalker raised a hand to call for another halt. He came crunching across the gravel to Fisher, motioning for Cal-Brinn to join them. 'You lot can carry on until you reach the foot of the ice. Badlands and I will check on our friends. We'll re-join you upslope.'

Fisher and Cal-Brinn curtly nodded their agreement. Stalker waved for Badlands to accompany him and they set off jogging down the gravel bars and silts of the riverbed. In places they hopped from rock to rock as they descended.

Cal-Brinn and the Guard turned to walk on, as did Kyle, but at the last instant something urged him to turn back. Some sensation that brushed at the nape of his neck and made the small hairs on his arms stand on end. He suddenly knew they were no longer alone. He glanced about, alarmed, but saw that, of the party, Fisher alone had turned back as well. He met Fisher's troubled gaze, and realized, *we two are of the blood . . .*

Rocks clattered below, gravel shifted. Movement among the silts caught Kyle's eye. Shapes were rising from the riverbed. Down below, Stalker and Badlands had halted and turned back as well.

Ragged skeletal shapes straightened. Clots of clay and silt fell to the ground. They wore rotting lengths of coarse hides and furs. Some carried the remains of a sort of crude armour of stitched straw. Stained brown skulls, some hairless, turned to him and Fisher. The faces were as he expected – dried and mummified with empty sockets and fleshless grins. T'lan Imass. The enemy of the Jaghut.

And, he realized with a terrified sickening jolt, *his* enemy.

'*Over here!*' he heard Stalker bellow from below. There was a clash of weaponry and several of the carious heads turned that way – Badlands had charged the nearest. 'C'mon, you bastards!' Stalker yelled.

Kyle started forward. Hands grasped him from behind. 'We must flee,' said Cal-Brinn, now next to him.

Badlands was backing away down the slope, drawing the nightmare shapes after him. '*Go*, damn you!' he yelled to Kyle.

'Protect him!' Stalker called, then he was off, running down the slope. This quick movement somehow settled the matter as the Imass started after him. Kyle counted some seventeen. He ought to follow – they would need the white blade!

'We're going to say goodbye to Coots!' Badlands called, laughing, as he jumped from stone to stone. Their outlines disappeared into the mists.

More arms and heads were emerging from the gravel beds even as Kyle stood there, frozen, horrified.

Fisher appeared before him. He set his hands on his shoulders. 'We must go. *Now.*'

Kyle blinked, remembered to breathe. He met the bard's gaze, pleading. 'We must help . . .'

'They will outrun them. Do not worry.'

'But . . .'

'They will be safe. Perhaps they mean to lead them into the Lether troops! Imagine that, hey?' Hands tugged at him. He stumbled backwards. The bard's voice hardened, 'Do not ruin their gambit! More are coming!'

This shocked him and he took a sharp breath of the frigid air. He jerked a nod. 'Yes. All right. Yes.' He turned and started up the gravel. Fisher's tight grip on his upper arm urged him onward.

Higher up the slope, a wide expanse of dirty white emerged from the clouds. The serpent of ice. Far closer, however, down the wash towards them clattered stick-thin figures in rags and beast armour. Kyle snapped a glance behind to see their pursuers closing.

'Circle up!' Cal-Brinn ordered, and the Crimson Guard closed into a tight circle that pushed Kyle, Fisher and Jethiss inside.

Kyle fought to join the line. 'You will need my blade!' he shouted to Cal-Brinn.

'You may yet have the chance,' the Dal Honese answered grimly.

Their pursuers, further T'lan Imass that had risen behind, reached their circle first. Flint blades swung, meeting Crimson Guard shields in a clash of stone on bronze and iron. Kyle was startled to see the Imass using the flat of their blades upon the guardsmen and women. One of the women fell to a blow from an Imass fist.

Then he realized: they do not want these people . . . They are after us alone. His back shivered in a sensation that only hunted prey could know. He hefted the white blade, waiting for one to break through.

Next to him, Jethiss, his two hatchets readied, saw his chance and bounded out to join the defence. A blow of one hatchet split the skull of an Imass and shattered the haft of that weapon. He flung it aside. Another thrust for him but Jethiss swung, severing the arm at the shoulder.

Kyle watched this, amazed. *Who could do such things to the T'lan Imass?*

Then the newcomers from above closed upon them then, washing round the mêlée, and Kyle was further stunned as these Imass assaulted their attackers. Imass fought Imass in a ruthless terrifying whirl of flint swords and hard dry limbs, and then it was done, seemingly in an instant.

Eight standing T'lan Imass stood motionless, regarding them with their eerie empty sockets. One raised an arm of bone and hanging dry flesh to point upslope. 'Run, now,' it breathed in a voice like falling sand.

'Who are you?' Kyle called, even as Leena tugged at him.

'We are of the Ifayle. I am Issen Li'gar. I came seeking my sister Shalt Li'gar, gone so very long ago. Now, run. We shall guard.'

Leena pulled Kyle backwards. He wanted to ask so much more of this Ifayle, but of course they could not delay. He turned and kicked up the loose gravel as he went.

They pushed their way across a muddy flat of thick grey-green silt. It clung to his leather shoes and smeared all the way up to his knees. He'd served for a time in the Guard, and had heard the stories that the Imass had never attacked them. At the time he'd dismissed such tales as rather too self-promoting. 'They wouldn't kill you,' he panted to Leena, still amazed.

'They never have.'

'Why?'

'I believe they respect us,' she answered, short of breath as they tramped through the thick mud. 'Everyone calls us mercenaries, but the truth is we do not fight for money. We have honour, and this is their way of respecting that.'

Kyle thought of the Crimson Guard swordswoman they had picked up from the mud, groggy, spitting blood from the blow across her jaw. The Imass had an odd way of showing their high regard. As daughter of an Iron Legionnaire, Leena might think it was honour. The Legion had probably been esteemed for its noble values, and she had absorbed that. But he did not think such things would impress the Imass. No. There must be some other reason.

Ahead, across the broad gravel wash, now empty of run-off, the valley-wide dirty expanse of the ice-serpent rose ahead. They picked up their pace. A short hurried dash later and they reached the cliff-like leading edge of the nearest lobe, or tongue, of the ice-river. Great caves of aqua-blue gaped at its base, where, Kyle imagined, rivers of water once flowed.

Something had halted that natural melting process. A few of the Guard, and Jethiss, clambered on to the dirty-grey leading edge and crunched their way up. They beckoned everyone to follow. A glance back revealed what Kyle thought might be stick-like motionless shapes through the tatters of scudding clouds. He climbed up on to the ice.

*　　*　　*

Orman walked blind through the heaviest snowstorm he had ever known. He, Keth and Kasson had strung themselves together with belts. They took turns leading the way. Whoever was at the fore thrust at the ice with Svalthbrul, searching for crevasses hidden beneath the fresh snow cover.

This snowfall was so thick it came up to their knees. A brutal wind lashed them, numbing Orman's face and finding any gap in his leathers. He reflected sourly how unfair it was that even though he shared Iceblood, he should still feel the damned cold. He supposed that he simply wasn't *immune* to it. Occasional quakes, or massive cracking, shook the broad plain of ice beneath them and they rocked, arms out, steadying themselves.

They were making for a strange azure light that glimmered and sizzled far up upon the ice-field. The black clouds seemed to congregate there, licked by sheet lightning. It appeared to be the focus of this massive storm that smothered the entire north. Through passing gaps in the churning overcast layer he caught brief glimpses of the barren rocky peaks of the Salt range above, grey and forbidding.

They pushed against the wind, fighting their way across the ice-plain. Even as they walked, Orman had the definite sensation that it was moving beneath them – crackling and rumbling profoundly as it shifted downslope.

He was walking onward, pushing at the snow ahead, when the deafening howl of the wind faded away and he found himself standing in relative calm, the dense fat snowflakes drifting down nearly straight. He looked to the brothers in wonder. Here all was quiet, though the massive cloud front churned above as it blazed with lightning and flickering mage-fire. Ahead, a figure sat waist-deep in the snow; pillows of it covered his shoulders. Buri. They approached. The snow crunched beneath their feet. Their breath steamed in the chill air.

'Buri?' Orman called, hesitantly.

The figure stirred. The head with its great mane and beard of hair as white as the snow lifted. The long almond-shaped eyes flickered open. He smiled and inhaled a long steady breath. 'Ah, Orman. You have brought Svalthbrul. Good. It will help immensely.'

'Is it . . . yours, then?' he asked.

The smile became wistful, like Vala's just before she walked into the flames. 'No. Not mine. It is a weapon taken from the T'lan Imass long ago – your Army of Bone and Dust.'

Orman and the brothers studied its faceted leaf-shaped stone head of deep brown flint, the colour of earth. 'The enemy? Then . . . how can it help?'

The smile turned rather savage. 'You have heard of those who drink the blood of their enemies? Who hope to claim their strength? Well, there is magic there, Orman. Power the one who first laid this ice barrier used. A kind of magic I too shall exploit.'

'What must I do?'

The Elder now looked upon him with compassion. 'Must you ask? Sacrifice must be made – has been made. The old enemy must be forestalled.'

He felt his heart racing in awful panic; he could not breathe. Sacrifice? Jaochim and Yrain? Vala? Who knows how many others? Perhaps even . . . *Jass*? He flinched from the man – the Iceblood – sickened. 'No . . . never.'

Buri would not release him from his steady gaze.

Orman tried to shift his hands on the cursed weapon but found that they were frozen to the wood haft. 'I am sorry, Buri. I . . . cannot. I dare not.'

'You must. To complete the invocation.'

'I'll not kill you the way Lotji slew Jass.'

The Elder blinked heavily, swaying, utterly spent from his efforts. 'Ah – I see. No, Orman. That had nothing to do with this. If Jass were here now, I would demand the same of him. But it was fated that he should not be. It is up to you to act that another should not have the blood upon his hands.' He gestured, weakly, to Keth and Kasson. 'Would you leave the task to one of your friends?'

'Of course not!'

'Then you must do what must be done and take it upon yourself.'

Orman closed his eyes against this Elder's relentless logic. He loathed having to do anything so terrible, so dire. Yet it would be shameful to hand the responsibility, and the consequences, to another. He gave a weak nod of submission.

'Very good. Through the back, if you would.'

The Reddin brothers moved to stand off at a distance. Orman slowly made his way around behind the cross-legged Elder. 'I'm sorry . . .' he began, but Buri interrupted him.

'Nay. Do not be sorry. Be glad. I have prepared for this for a long time. You will complete it and for that I am thankful.' He rested his hands on his knees and straightened his slim bare back.

Orman raised his arms high, Svalthbrul angled downwards. He pressed the tip of the stone blade against the Elder's back high and to the right of the spine. He intended to thrust downward at an angle through the heart.

Buri remained immobile throughout. He appeared to be gathering himself, and after a time he let out a long breath. He was waiting. Still Orman could not bring himself to thrust. Perhaps the Elder understood this and knew what he needed, because he murmured, softly, 'Now.'

Orman thrust. The spear slid in smoothly to pass through the man's chest and on to sink into the ice before him. Orman hadn't intended to strike so deeply but something seemed to yank upon Svalthbrul and demand that the stone blade pierce the ice as well.

Buri remained sitting upright, impaled and affixed to the ice. His head was tilted forward, his long snow-white hair hanging.

Orman wept. Hot wetness stung both cheeks as tears also fell from his ruined eye. He could not be certain but it seemed as if a profound vibration emanated from where Buri sat, expanding in all directions, like an immense stone tossed into a lake. He gritted his teeth and worked to remove his hands from the Imass weapon. Skin tore off in strips as he yanked each free. The blood that came froze swiftly; only a few drops stained the snow at his feet.

He turned to the Reddin brothers. The wetness at his cheeks was now frozen ice as well. He felt oddly numb. All sounds seemed muted. He examined his hands – bloodied. I have blood upon my hands. I am kinslayer now in truth. Uncles from both sides of my line have I slain.

He did not know how much of these thoughts showed upon his face, but the brothers knelt on one knee before him, bowing their heads, just as a hearthguard may to his lord.

If anyone is to be damned, it will be me. I have spared them that. He turned to the south.

Now let us see what we Icebloods have wrought upon the land.

*   *   *

Bodies, old and new, dotted the mud flats along the shores of the Sea of Gold. They lay amid the remains of broken rickety docks. Silverfox numbly observed to herself, these nuggets are hardly gold. This sea should change its name to something more . . . appropriate.

She stood on the grassed lip of the shore cliff, peering south to the slate-hued water beneath the overcast sky. She wondered whether she faced this way because she dared not glance east.

What she might see there would make all this appear pleasant.

She felt, rather than heard, Pran Chole take his place at her side. 'Almost all human, Summoner. I sense no recent fallen who carry the Jaghut taint.'

'This is supposed to cheer me?'

'There are . . . many,' the Imass allowed. 'These invaders do not appear to be handling themselves well.'

She stole a glance at the ancient being. She had ordered him to remain behind but he had simply refused to obey. The nearest thing she might claim as a father, and he millennia old. We are a strange family, she mused. He, I, and – she cast a quick look about for

Kilava, found her standing far off staring north – and the disappointed aunt.

'So they fled,' she sighed, more relieved than she dared contemplate. Yet her aged and crooked hands still shook and even she sensed it, fragility. That she was composed of four souls, four awarenesses, made her particularly susceptible to . . . shattering.

'They are close. A few days' journey. Gathered together.'

'Yes, I sense them. A last stand, perhaps.'

Pran Chole added nothing to this, as there was no more to say. The mummified sinew of his joints clung to his bones as if he were strapped together, all animated by the eldritch ritual of Tellann. Most of the dried leather flesh of his face remained, though patches of it had fallen or been worn away. Mostly along the ridges of bone: the sharp edges of the cheekbones, the upper orbits of his empty sockets, or where the flesh had been thinnest, such as across his forehead where the skull peeked through, smooth and polished like old seasoned wood. The skullcap of the ancient deer he wore as a helmet had fared far worse. Grey with age it was, and utterly dried. It would probably weigh next to nothing in her hands. Its muzzle where it rode high above Pran's head was longish and narrow.

She knew she was drifting . . . delaying.

'Summoner,' Pran began, and he always used this form of address when he wished to be stern with her. She could almost hear him clearing his throat, had he breath to do so. 'We cannot delay any longer. We must confront them.'

No. *We* mustn't. She had made her decision. 'This time you must remain behind.'

If a desiccated mien of bared grinning teeth could express surprise and dismay, Pran's features came closest. 'Summoner . . .' his breathless voice whispered. 'Do not cast us off.'

'I alone must speak to them. You have brought me this far and for that I thank you. Now you must remain. I won't—' She stopped herself. 'That is, I cannot risk losing any of you.'

'And what of you?'

'You know I will be safe. Fetch my horse.'

He inclined his head until the empty sockets of the beast skull seemed to stare at her in direct remonstration. 'As you order, Summoner,' he murmured in his sad dry voice.

He shuffled off and she went to talk to Kilava. A cold wind buffeted them all, slicing down out of the mountain heights. The beaded laces of her shirt rattled and her long tangled grey hair tossed about her face. She drew it aside. She sensed something, far in the heights behind the dense cloud cover. But just what it was she couldn't be certain. Oddly enough, she had no interest in the Jaghut themselves, or their sorcery. Her purpose was not to prosecute the Jaghut; her purpose was to bring an end to the ritual of Tellann. No doubt, however, it was this stirring that had so distracted Kilava these last two days.

She stopped next to the squat muscular woman whose midnight black hair, being even longer than hers, lashed violently in the gusting wind as if reflecting her angry thoughts. She stared north for a time, trying to see what this elder Imass Bonecaster might be seeing.

'You have not seen a Jaghut refugium before, have you?' Kilava asked.

She shook her head. 'I am a child of the warm prairie.' She might not have seen one, but in response to the Bonecaster's question there came a cascade of images provided by the three awarenesses that shared her being: Nightchill, crossing one such windswept waste beneath hanging curtains of flickering lights tinged pink at their frills; Tattersail, sailing past gleaming night-blue cliffs of ice far taller than those they glimpsed just to the south; even Bellurdan, sharing a fire with a Jaghut elder within one of these remaining enclaves.

'I see them through other eyes,' she said.

Kilava nodded her understanding. 'What *I* see troubles me. It has been a long time . . .' she glanced to her, 'an unimaginably long time – but what I sense hidden there reminds me . . .' She frowned then, losing whatever memory it was she hunted. 'Well, perhaps we will have to chase the Kerluhm even there.'

'I hope it will not come to that.'

The Bonecaster turned to Pran, Tolb, and the waiting T'lan. Silverfox looked as well. How painfully few this remaining handful, some thirty only. Yet incalculably precious to her.

'You have hurt Pran's feelings,' Kilava observed.

'They have no feelings.'

Kilava raised one silken black brow. 'You know that is not so.'

'Yes,' she sighed, exhausted. She was just so tired of their company. Their rigidity. Their silence. Their unrelenting . . . alienness. 'Yes,' she sighed again. 'They feel twice with their spirits what they can no longer feel with their flesh. I know this.'

'Do not forget it. It is too easy to forget.'

Pran arrived, leading the watered and rested mount. Tolb followed, his withered hands clasped at his ragged belt. 'We are to remain behind,' Pran told Kilava.

The Bonecaster eyed him. 'I see. Yet why should the Kerluhm listen to her now?'

Silverfox stroked the bay's neck, avoiding her gaze. 'I'm not going to ask this time.'

'Then perhaps I should follow at a distance,' Kilava offered.

Silverfox felt her brows rising. This was a day of days. The legendary Kilava being obliging. 'There is no need.' She added, mounting, 'You would be too far away to intercede in any case.'

But the three Bonecasters were paying her no attention. All three had turned to the north, as had the faces of the rest of the Imass. She glanced that way, shading her eyes. What was it? She sensed there, behind the bunched soot-black clouds, the stirring of Omtose – was that it?

Then she saw it. Through her own Bonecaster's vision she glimpsed a kind of wave descending the upper slopes. Invisible, yet visible by the disturbance it evoked as it came, like a wave through water. It came on, descending the slopes at astounding speed.

Kilava spun to her. 'Protect yourself!' she ordered.

She could only gape. What was this thing?

Then a hammer struck her across the head and she tumbled sideways off the horse to land numb with the shock of it. Pink coloured the swirling visions that assaulted her. She sensed her awarenesses, like survivors lashed to a raft, battling to remain afloat. The most potent of them, Nightchill, appeared to swim before her. *Not in ten thousand years have they dared!* she snarled, in stunned amazement. Bizarrely, behind the cracks widening between her shared essences, came the bellowed joy of Bellurdan as the giant gloried in the unleashed puissance washing over them. Darkness took her then.

*

A jolt awoke her to the utter blackness of a deeply overcast night. Except in one direction where bright mage-fire flickered far off in banners of pink and emerald. She was being carried over steep ground while lying flat in some sort of litter. Distant thunder rumbled and murmured and she thought it odd that a storm should be rising – perhaps it was all these clouds. She closed her eyes.

When she woke again it was day, or a fog-choked attempt at one in any case. Branches of conifers passed overhead. The ground was rough. Four T'lan Imass carried her. Again distant rumblings and eruptions rolled over them in sharp distinct blasts. Were they moving into a thunderstorm?

483

'What happened?' she asked, rather groggily.

Kilava's head appeared in her vision. Black flakes of dried blood marked where her nose and eyes bled. 'You are with us still – good. They were of course quite worried.'

'Worried that I had fallen apart?'

The Bonecaster nodded her agreement. 'Something like that.'

She rubbed her forehead where it seemed as if a spike had been driven between her eyes. 'What happened?'

'We are privileged,' the Bonecaster remarked with something like very dry humour.

She blinked, not certain she understood. 'Privileged?'

'To witness something thought long gone from the world. The birth . . . well, the rebirth of a Jaghut ice barrier. The T'lan are understandably rather . . . angered.'

She'd like to see that – an angry T'lan Imass. How would one know?

'What of the Kerluhm?'

'They travel north as well. The, ah, disagreement has been set aside until we have dealt with this new threat.'

Silverfox allowed her throbbing head to fall back to rest upon the cloth of the litter. 'Good.'

Kilava, however, appeared not to share her relief. She walked along, one hand on one of the wooden poles of the litter, and brushed aside branches that rained cold droplets. Nearby, rocks clattered and crashed in a slide. 'Do not be glad, child, nor think those survivors safe. The rejuvenated ice barrier will grind them to splinters of bone if they do not flee.'

'They will retreat.'

'Let us hope so.'

She rubbed her head, astonished to find no wound upon it. The impact must have been sorcerous alone. A wave of Omtose Phellack colliding with Tellann. Fraying it with its intensity. She and Kilava, both alive, both Bonecasters, felt the punishment of this dismembering. The T'lan, being undying, remained immune. Thus the ritual of Tellann.

'So we travel to it, then,' she murmured, and winced as the litter jerked in the hands of its bearers.

Kilava's darkly tanned features took on an odd look, almost pained. 'Well . . . the truth is, it is coming to us.'

The constant low rumblings took on an awful new meaning in Silverfox's awareness. She raised her head to try to see, but all she could make out was an army of mist-shrouded trees on a steep rocky slope. Somewhere, though, stones shifted and hissed, punctuated by the crash of a tree falling. Like an enormous beast arising from the black depths, the awareness of what was coming clarified in her thoughts and she eased her head down in wonder. *Gods. They really went and did it. And we drove them to it. I hope the damned Kerluhm are happy now!* And perhaps they are. Perhaps this was what they wanted all along: proof of the Jaghut's threat. *And now it's a threat that would swallow us all.*

*   *   *

K'azz, Shimmer and Blues led the way up the wide course of the ice-tongue. To either side naked ridges of rock rose like knife-edged barriers. It was snowing now, and above, through brief gaps in the massed storm clouds, the white expanse of the ice-field glittered in a hard cerulean light. They prodded the ice ahead with trimmed branches they had collected, searching for hidden crevasses in the creaking and groaning surface beneath their feet. Indeed, this course of ice, this frost-serpent, struck her as nearly a river in truth as she imagined it bucking and writhing under her boots. She had the unnerving sensation that they were actually moving backwards and making no progress at all.

Yet they struggled on. All without a spoken word. More than ever now was she determined to see this thing to its utter end. They had come too far. Too many had fallen. She could never face the Brethren if the day came and she had no answer for them. So she planted one tattered leather boot before the other and leaned upon the long branch, prodding and probing as she went.

Something, however, seemed to be resisting her. Some force pressed down upon her, dimming her awareness. Each footfall felt like an eternity. At times she had trouble lifting her boots as the ice seemed to grip and pull at them. Once or twice she found herself on her knees; these spells she shook off and lurched to her feet once more.

A hand tugged at her mail armour and she turned, blinking. It was the Myrni girl, Siguna. 'I have been calling,' she shouted, looking oddly panicked.

Shimmer frowned. Calling? Whatever could she mean?

'Your friends! They have fallen behind! One won't rise. Another is missing!'

Shimmer had to force herself to concentrate upon the words and their meaning. *Missing? Fallen?* Understanding finally reached her

485

and she nodded her thanks. She pointed to where she'd last seen Blues through the swirling fat flakes of snow. 'Get Blues.'

The girl gave a quick nod and ran off.

For a moment Shimmer watched her go, wondering at her energy and lightness of foot over the snow. Whatever was weighing upon her didn't seem to be affecting the girl at all. Then she shook her head and began tramping back to find the rest of the column.

A knot of figures, no more than dark outlines amid the brushing curtains of blowing snow, waited below. She found Gwynn, Bars, Black the Lesser and Turgal with the two Heels, Baran and Erta. They stood around a figure kneeling in snow up to her waist. Lean.

Gwynn greeted her, gestured to Lean. 'She will not get up.'

Shimmer knelt before her friend, gripped her chin and lifted it to study her. The woman's face was slack, her eyes unfocused. 'Come to me, Lean,' she called.

Lean blinked. The eyes searched, found Shimmer's face. 'Let me sleep,' she mumbled through lips nearly frozen shut.

'No. Time to move out. We're waiting.'

'I'm too Togg-blasted tired.'

Blues joined them, followed by K'azz. Shimmer looked up. 'What should we do?'

'Where is Keel?'

Bars' hollow gaze was haunted and desolate. He gestured down behind them. 'I'm sorry . . . I should've noticed.'

'None of us did,' Gwynn said.

K'azz raised a hand to end the matter. 'You four will go back. Take Lean with you. Find Keel. Cross to a rock ridge. Get off the ice. Wait there.'

Bars' face revealed his shocked disbelief. 'You can't send us back!'

K'azz's voice softened. 'Not back, Bars. Off the ice. It is dangerous for you.'

'But not for you, or Shimmer, or Blues?'

'We . . . seem able to fight its effects better. Now, pick her up and go.' He gestured Gwynn to him, 'Make sure they all make it off.'

Gwynn, his long staff in his hands, nodded grimly. 'Yes, K'azz. We will await you.'

'Thank you.' He turned to go but Blues and Shimmer planted themselves directly in his path. 'And what of us?' Blues said.

Their commander offered a lift of his bird-like bony shoulders beneath his torn leather jerkin. 'You wished to find your answers . . . they await above.'

486

'And Cal-Brinn?' Shimmer demanded. 'Aren't we here for him as well?'

K'azz nodded. 'He is near. The same . . . difficulty . . . is affecting him. If we do not find him above, then we shall search for him.'

Shimmer stood aside. 'Very well. But we had better find him.'

K'azz closed his eyes in tired agreement. 'We will, Shimmer. I swear.'

The man appeared exhausted, his eyes sunken, his cheeks hollow. And clearly the strange spell of general lassitude pulled upon him as well, but she thought there was something more weighing him down, he was sad. So very regretful. What was it that affected him so? Whatever the answers were, they seemed to be breaking his heart.

At that moment she was almost ready to agree that they ought simply to find Cal-Brinn and go. If whatever lay above was so distressing to K'azz, perhaps it was best left alone. Yet to have come so far . . . and they were so near . . . She shook her head. Whatever it was, perhaps it would weigh less heavily upon him if they all shared it. It seemed almost near to breaking him even as she watched.

Yes, that was it. He need not bear this all by himself. She turned to the rest of the Guard gathering to retreat. Bars, she saw, was steadily returning her gaze. It was a good few moments before a voice spoke in her thoughts: *what are you waiting for? You should go to him*. She did so, and a strange relief flickered across his face. She stood close, peering up at him, and raised an arm to slip it behind his neck.

'You have been distant of late,' he said.

'Yes, I have.'

'We must get to the bottom of that.'

'Yes, we will. When I return.'

'Very well. When you return.' He bent to kiss her and jerked away, shock on his face, 'You are so cold!'

'Is that a complaint?'

'I mean it. Here, take this,' and he moved to slip off his woollen cloak.

She closed her hand on his. 'Keep it. I do not feel the cold.' He frowned, troubled. 'Do not worry. I will return.'

Something of his old manner slipped through as he growled, 'See that you do.'

She turned to where K'azz and Blues waited, then gestured, inviting them, Baran, Erta and Siguna onward. She turned for one last wave farewell, wondering again: *what is wrong with me?*

Marshal Teal stood at a brazier in his command tent high in the upper vales of the southern slopes of the Salt range. He warmed his hands over the charcoal and considered his next course of action. Scouting parties would have to be sent, of course, to determine whether the last renegades had chosen to hang about. His orders from Luthal had been explicit; his future position depended upon his thoroughness.

Still, he was confident. This was, after all, a mere mopping up. He was eager to return to clean out Mantle. Once their grip was secure upon this north coast of the Sea of Gold, they could consider their next move. Consolidation of the south coast, most likely. Then onward to the Bone Peninsula.

All funded by their war-chest of gold dust.

Thunder rumbled beyond the hide tent walls. A storm was on its way. Good. Perhaps the renegades would die of exposure and save them any further expenditure. Still, he would like to get his hands on that white blade. It would bring a fortune in Lether, or Darujhistan. He could name his price.

The thunder intensified into a constant deep ongoing roar that Teal thought he could feel through his feet. Then the ground moved. The brazier would have fallen had he not steadied it and singed his fingers. Panicked shouts sounded without. He threw open the tent flap, demanded of a guard, 'What is going on?'

'Earthquake, sir.'

'Yes, I know that!' He waved to indicate the men rushing about bearing torches. 'What is everyone upset about?'

The guard swallowed hard. 'Well, sir. Most of these lads have never experienced one. They say . . . well, talk is, the northern gods are angry at us.'

'What a load of bullshit. You get out there and you calm them down!'

The guard saluted crisply. 'Yes sir!' He ran off, waving for others to accompany him.

Teal drew in a deep breath of the cold clean air. Gods give him patience! What could he possibly be expected to accomplish with these pathetic recruits! Give him drilled and trained regulars over these amateur foreigners any day.

He crossed his arms, hugged himself for warmth against the fiercely cold wind and peered into the low clouds to the north. It looked as if something was moving there behind the swirling banners of mist. He took a few hesitant steps, squinting. It was almost as if the entire slope above them was slowly shifting. Had the earthquake triggered a rockslide?

The ground beneath his feet began to vibrate. Not in the rolling of any earthquake he'd ever experienced, but as a constant low drumming vibration. A distant avalanche, perhaps?

The swirling clouds parted then, as if thrust aside by some broad front of wind. Through the dimness of the overcast night he saw that the slope above was much steeper and closer than he remembered. And it was moving – roiling and churning as it came. Even as he watched, entire swathes of tall spruce and fir fell before its advance, only to be sucked beneath the leading edge of tumbling rock and soil.

True panicked yells sounded now about the camp, all nearly drowned by the roar of the coming cataclysm. Teal stood transfixed. In his experience this was unanswerable. How could anyone respond to such an onslaught? There was simply nothing to be done.

Lieutenants came, shouting to be heard, but he merely waved to them to flee. 'Save yourselves,' he mouthed. And they fled. He chose not to. There was something inexorable, almost magisterial, in what he was witnessing. Running might gain one a few more minutes of life, but why fall in an undignified mad scramble?

He preferred to meet what was coming. And he did – just before the end.

The screen of conifers above the camp was the last layer of trees still standing before the mountain of churned-up soil and rock tumbling its way down upon him. The ground now juddered as if in agony; he could barely keep his feet. The avalanche roar was so loud it deafened him.

And he glimpsed, above the mounded-up tons of loose soil and talus, something glowing with an inner cobalt-blue light. A broad and low wall descending out of the heights, pulverizing rock, and growling an immensely deep basso rumble that was shaking the ground, and his breath left him in awe.

How beautiful, and how terrible . . .

*   *   *

'You must all flee.'

They were in conference within the stone tower at Mantle. Lady Orosenn stood with the aid of Jute's shoulder – he winced whenever her full weight threatened to bow him – and he with one arm bandaged and bound across his chest. They stood together with the new king, Voti, and Malle at his side. Cartheron was there, gritting his bristled jowls, and Tyvar, dabbing a cloth to the cut above his temple that would not stop bleeding.

The young king continued to shake his head. 'This is our home. We will not leave.'

Lady Orosenn shifted her entreating gaze to Malle, whose black skirting was now slashed and spattered with dried blood. Having seen her fighting upon the wall Jute felt even more terrified of the woman: she threw slim knife blades, then hatchets that had snapped back the heads of more than one Imass. Now, though, she merely pursed her thin colourless lips as if to say: *there is nothing I can do* . . .

Orosenn shifted one awkward step backwards, signalling that she would go. 'But reconsider while there is still time.' Jute helped her turn round. Cartheron and Tyvar followed them out. 'Stubborn fools,' she complained as they went.

'We cannot force them to go,' Tyvar observed as he refolded the bloodied cloth.

The Jaghut sorceress, for that was what everyone now knew her to be, studied the Blue Shield commander for a time. 'No. But there *is* something you can do. The task that perhaps you were truly sent here for.' She headed off, limping, for the eastern curtain wall. 'Come with me.'

Jute helped her up the ramp to the catwalk. She gestured over the wall to the ragtag encampment the invaders had set up along the shore east of the fortress. Smoke from countless camp fires hung over it before gusting southward over the sea, driven by the fierce frigid winds blowing down from the heights. Jute put their numbers at close to six thousand.

However, he was far more interested in the five vessels anchored a safe distance off the coast. Though it was foggy, he would recognize the *Dawn* anywhere. With it lay the *Ragstopper*, the *Resolute*, the *Supplicant*, and that Genabackan pirate's galley.

Seeing the direction of his gaze, Tyvar said, 'They are wise to stay off shore.'

Jute nodded. 'Aye. They'd be swamped immediately.'

'You see these people?' Orosenn asked Tyvar, who stroked his beard, a touch mystified. 'In less than two days they will all be dead if they do not move south.'

The mercenary commander narrowed his gaze. 'You are certain?'

The sorceress let out a hard breath. 'I know what is coming.'

490

'What, then, would you have us do?'

'Tyvar Gendarian, you said Togg gave you one last geas – to save innocent lives. Well, there lie thousands. I believe that is truly what our god had in mind. Not battle. *Saving* lives! You are the Blue *Shields*, are you not? Escort them south! Organize the evacuation of the women and children on to the vessels, then guide the rest down the Bone Peninsula. Guard them. Ward them. See them safe. There is a true challenge!'

The commander studied the rambling camp and his brows tightened. 'We are fewer than one hundred now,' he murmured.

'Work with that woman who was organizing their defence – she lives still.' Her eyes rose to the heights, where some sort of lightning storm flickered and glowed behind the dense cloud cover. Jute could hear the rumblings of the thunder even from this distance. She returned her gaze to Tyvar, fierce. 'This is my request of you, Tyvar. See them safe. I'm sure Togg would approve.'

He had been stroking his beard. His eyes now glittered with renewed passion. He bowed his head in assent. 'Saving innocents,' he answered. 'Yes. Togg would approve. Thank you for reminding me of my purpose, my lady. We will go at once.' He jogged down the ramp, shouting for his lieutenants.

'And what of us?' Jute asked. 'Will we be safe here?'

She turned a warm gaze upon him. 'You will return to Ieleen on board the *Dawn* and sail south, Jute of Delanss. You have lingered here too long.'

'But will you be safe?'

'Never mind about us. See the evacuees safe. Enjoy your life. Give your love to Ieleen. She is very worried for you.'

'But what of you?'

'Go. Now. Leave me here at the wall. I wish to . . . study the storm for a time.'

He was unwilling to abandon her, or Cartheron for that matter. She had arguably saved his life twice now. Thinking of the Malazan gave him an idea. He bowed his leave and went to find the old commander.

It took him a long time to track the man down. Eventually he was pointed to the cliff edge and there found the fellow peering down at the sea. He had the look of a man who'd forgotten something he suspected was important. He nodded a distracted greeting to Jute. 'Damned thorough, those Imass,' he muttered. 'Took out our access to the water. Now I know what it's like to be on the other end of their stone swords.'

'Sir,' Jute began, attempting to grab his attention, 'you have to talk sense into Malle. Something tells me she wouldn't ignore a direct command from you.'

The fellow lifted his chin in assent. 'Once, aye. But there's a new regime now, and I'm not welcome. In fact, I'm officially drowned.'

'The sorceress has asked Tyvar to escort all the newcomers south. I believe he'll do it.'

'Sounds like an impossible task. I'm sure he'll relish it.'

'We can get the women and children into the vessels.'

Cartheron nodded approvingly. 'And you go with them, Jute. But not the *Ragstopper*.'

'Why not?'

'She's full of water. Won't sail no more. And I have to admit I'm kinda curious 'bout what's coming. I have my suspicions.'

It took some time for Jute to accept what he was hearing. 'So . . . you're saying you're going to stay?'

'Aye. I believe it could be quite a sight.'

'And the crew?'

He shrugged. 'They can choose, o' course.'

Jute let out a long breath. He didn't know what to say. He discovered himself plucking at the edge of his shirt. 'Well, then,' he sighed. 'I guess I'd best go and help.'

Cartheron gave him the old salute of a hand to the chest, then waved him away. A few paces off, Jute turned back and called, 'What was he like?'

'Who?'

'The old emperor.'

Cartheron pulled a hand down his greying jowls, nodded his understanding of Jute's interest. 'I could never make up my mind if he was the biggest fool I'd ever met, or the most cunning bastard.'

The answer wasn't what Jute had expected, but the commander, once a High Fist, turned away to stare out over the waters of the Sea of Gold, and so he went to find Tyvar.

The vessels, it turned out, were wisely allowing none to approach. Early in the morning, Jute went out alone in the battered old skiff that the invaders' commander, Lyan, had sent out through the night to beg for berths. He arranged for the young and the wounded to be taken out to the *Resolute* and the *Silver Dawn*. Lady Orosenn also offered up the *Supplicant*. Jute was wary, but when he climbed a rope ladder, one-handed, and inspected the vessel, he found it completely empty of any crew. He did not know where the silent figures he'd glimpsed had gone, now that the sorceress had no more use for them. He had his ideas, of course, but these he kept to himself.

The Genabackan pirate, Enguf, offered berths to the highest bidders, and in this manner did well out of the venture after all. He was the first to sail off, if rather sluggishly, with a perilously slim freeboard, as he'd taken on far too many passengers. Greed, Jute reflected, seemed immune to all setbacks.

Next went the *Resolute*. As passenger on board this vessel went a crippled youth who seemed to be family to the Genabackan Shield-maiden officer. The woman, however, remained with the camp. She seemed satisfied with the protection that the Blue Shields offered, sending five of their number with the vessel, together with their pledge to reunite her and the boy in Elingarth.

The *Supplicant* followed slowly, its crew of veteran sailors from among the invaders doing their best with the unfamiliar lines of the strange vessel.

This left the *Ragstopper* and the *Silver Dawn*. Jute clapped his hands on young Reuth's shoulders and looked him up and down. The lad appeared to be prospering; gone were the bruises of his escape – at least those apparent in the flesh. He was eating well and even occasionally smiled. Jute had noticed that he asked almost every new passenger for news of a 'Whiteblade'. An ex-Malazan swordsman.

He waved the lad off and turned to Ieleen, who sat in her usual place next to the tiller arm, hands on her short walking stick, her head tilted to the wind. It seemed to him that she'd been watching him out of the edge of her snow-white orbs. He rubbed a hand over his unshaven cheeks and cleared his throat.

'You're staying, then,' she said, and he jumped, startled.

'How did you know?'

'I know that throat-clearing.'

He continued to brush his fingers over a cheek. 'I have to see this through to the end, love.'

'Why?'

'I don't know.' He gazed about the deck, now crowded with evacuees. 'Curiosity, I guess. I have to see how it ends.'

She banged the stick to the deck. 'It could end in your death!'

'Don't let's fight, dear. Not during my leave-taking.'

'I'm supposed to like it?'

'Don't worry. The *Ragstopper* remains. We can evacuate in that, if we must.'

She shook her head in a knowing negative. 'That hulk sounds as full of water as a bathtub.'

'Well . . . it's still afloat. In any case, we can always run for it.'

She continued shaking her head. Her grey curls blew about in the wind. 'I've always feared your curiosity will be the death of you.'

'I'll be careful, dearest.'

Her silver orbs narrowed, promising her wrath. 'You'd better be.'

'Of course I will. I'll await your return. If not here, then further south down the coast. Yes?'

She tapped the stick to the deck thoughtfully. 'I do not want you to go. But if you must . . .' She shook her head. Sadly, this time.

'Thank you, my chick.' He pecked her on the cheek.

She urged him off with the stick. 'Go on, then.'

He saluted the ship's weapons master, Letita, who appeared miserable herself, her eyes red and her cheeks wet. He recalled that Lieutenant Jalaz was remaining with Cartheron. Then he climbed down one of the rope ladders to a waiting skiff.

The shore was now empty. Where a temporary encampment of thousands had arisen, only smoking fire pits and the trash of torn canvas, abandoned boots, broken tools and mining equipment remained. The unruly mob of civilians had been urged, cajoled, and plain browbeaten by Tyvar and his remaining Blue Shields, plus the Shieldmaiden and her Genabackan veterans, into marching south down the coast.

Walking back up the slope of the rise topped by Mantle, Jute noted the closing storm from the north. The cloud front had rolled down the upper heights of the Salt range and was now obscuring the vales immediately above. The constant roar of thunder shook the ground and strong winds lashed the branches. He spotted elk and deer bounding along the treeline just above the fields. Flights of birds came peeling out of the fog in ragged lines of ravens, gulls, ducks. And, apart from these, soaring higher, the outlines of prey-birds – eagles and falcons.

Something was driving all before it. The thing Lady Orosenn spoke of. All that Jute could imagine was a sort of huge landslide or avalanche, churning its way down the slopes.

He found Cartheron and Lady Orosenn in conversation at the wall, also looking north. Cartheron was gesturing, explaining something. 'Am I interrupting?' he asked, approaching up the earthen ramp.

'Always welcome,' Lady Orosenn greeted him. 'Commander Cartheron was just explaining the geography of this location.'

'*Commander* Cartheron?'

'Considering his experience, King Voti has placed him in charge of Mantle's defences.'

'For what it's worth,' the man grumbled.

'It is worth a great deal,' Lady Orosenn corrected him. 'I myself had hoped to reach the north and there kneel before my mother and beg her forgiveness. But,' she pressed a hand to her wounded thigh, 'it is not to be. Now we must weather the coming storm from here.'

'And this storm,' Jute now dared ask, 'what is it exactly?'

The Jaghut shared a glance with Cartheron. 'You know the great ice cliffs we passed to the south?' Jute nodded, he had seen such along many shores. 'Like that, only moving across the land.' Jute blew out a breath – he couldn't even imagine what that would be like. Nothing, it seemed to him, would be spared such a grinding passage. 'And Commander Cartheron has some ideas on this front.'

The old Napan held his hands out over the wall as if describing an inverted V. 'This is bedrock we're built on. Been here for ages. This is the highest piece of land across the entire north coast. See how we're atop a wedge that slopes down away before us and off to either side?' Jute nodded. 'We can use that natural rock incline.'

'How so?' Jute asked, still mystified.

Lady Orosenn was examining the slope. Free of her headscarf and veil, her features were rather harsh, Jute thought – the jaw too square and heavy, the cheekbones too jutting. But her wide expressive eyes still held their glamour for him. They carried sceptical calculation now. 'Why are we discussing this? You would need some sort of immense push even to get the motion going.'

Cartheron winked. 'Oh, I got me a big motivator.' He looked around, found Lieutenant Jalaz where she waited nearby for orders, and waved her to him. 'Send word to the *Ragstopper*. I want it brought in to shore and Orothos up here.' Jalaz saluted and jogged off. 'Now we wait.' He peered round again and shouted to a nearby local spearman, 'Hey, how about a meal? I'm starving up here.'

A meal eventually appeared, comprising a trencher of bread, cold venison, a block of hard cheese and a leather tankard of beer. With the meal came Malle. She shot Cartheron a knowing glare and raised her chin to the cloud front descending the forested vales amid a now constant reverberating booming. 'What's the plan?' she asked. She had to raise her voice to be heard above the din. 'Do we jump into the sea?'

'Might come to that,' Cartheron agreed. Then, aside, 'Ah! Here we are.'

His first mate, Orothos, came walking up the dirt ramp. His shirt hung in tatters from his emaciated form, as did his trousers of canvas, which were tied up with a worn hemp rope. 'What now?'

the mate grumbled in a manner far from respectful. 'I'm busy bailing.'

Cartheron ignored the tone – or possibly it meant nothing to him. 'I want the springals and scorpions mounted on the wall here. And I want all the consignment brought up for use.'

The first mate blinked his incredulity. 'What? *All* of it?'

'It's of no use to us at the bottom of the Sea of Gold.'

The man gaped at his captain. He spluttered, 'But that's our nest egg. Our retirement fund! What're we gonna do without it?'

'The king here has offered us a place. I understand I'm takin' over as foreign adviser once Malle here leaves.' The wiry old woman tilted her head in agreement.

'If there's anything left!'

Cartheron finally snapped: 'Then let's see to it! Now do as I say!'

The first mate glared his defiance, which Cartheron met with a scowl, and then the man slapped a hand to his forehead, spun on his heels, and slouched his way down the ramp, muttering to himself, '. . . *now* he drops anchor? . . . not Nathilog? . . . damned nowhere . . . not one tavern to be found . . .'

In the silence following the mate's departure, Malle clasped her hands and stepped up to Cartheron. 'I, too, must express my concern. I mean – must you use *all* of it?'

'It's it or us, Malle. And I intend to hit it with all I got.'

A strange smile crept up one edge of her thin lips. 'Well . . . that *is* the old Crust I remember.'

The ex-High Fist snorted, then gestured Lieutenant Jalaz to him. 'Take the lads and lasses and see to the unloading.' She saluted again, and offered a savage grin.

All the Malazans, including Malle's guard, lent a hand. As the light darkened to the honey-yellow of late afternoon, four siege weapons were mounted and test shots were executed with weighted stones to measure distance. A steady train of black wooden chests came up from the *Ragstopper*, each sealed with a silver sigil. Lieutenant Jalaz came to Jute as he studied the chests and she pointed out the seals. 'See the sceptre? Sign of the imperial arsenal at Unta.' She ran a caressing hand across the wet black wood. 'When K'azz's Crimson Guard attacked the capital they blew the main imperial depot. All the Moranth munitions were supposed to have been lost. But look at this. A cache such as no one will ever see again.'

'So this is rare – even for you Malazans.'

The lieutenant choked down a laugh. 'Rare? Captain . . . you could buy a kingdom with this.'

'Perhaps that's what Cartheron aims to do with it.'

To her credit as a one-time servant of the throne, Jalaz flinched from such frank language. 'He sees a chance to defend an ally and he does not shrink from it.'

Jute would not release her from his steady gaze. 'Lieutenant, you are from Genabackis. I am from Falar. Our fathers or grandfathers were conquered by the Malazans, yet here we are. Why?'

Giana Jalaz turned away to stare off at the massed clouds that hung overhead like a fist about to crush them. She hugged herself against the chill wind, tucking her hands under her arms. 'When I was a child,' she said, after a time, 'my world was very small. Just my village and the valley we and the neighbouring villages occupied. To travel beyond it was unthinkable. You would be robbed or enslaved or killed out of hand as a stranger – an interloper. But then the Empire came and my world broadened beyond measure. I could travel from Cat in the north to Pale or even to Darujhistan if I wished . . . all under the aegis of the imperial sceptre. I was treated as equal, able to sign up to serve. I could hold what was mine under the law and the law held. That was what the Malazans brought. Granted, there were abuses, corruption, just as there had been under the old provincial rulers – human nature doesn't change. But the opportunity was there. Hope was there. At least a chance.' She lowered her gaze to him. 'And now the new emperor is from Falar, isn't he?'

Jute pulled away, but not because of the rearing head of imperial politics. 'We don't speak of *him* in Falar.'

'No? Why not?'

Jute straightened from the stacked chests, glanced about. 'You have been frank, and I thank you. That is a rare gift. I am only a ship's captain, a small-time recovering raider. But we of the sea trade in Falar know of the old blood-cult, the Jhistal. Its followers terrorized our islands for generations. He—' Jute broke off as a gang of Malle's guards arrived to carry the chests up to the top of the wall. Once they were gone, he turned back to Giana and lowered his voice: 'You speak of limited horizons. We in Falar had squirmed in the grip of those priests for generations. To speak up was to find one's children selected as the next sacrifices to the sea. The Malazans broke that grip and for that I will be forever grateful, despite the cost. But the new emperor . . . he tries to rewrite the history of it, but there are those who still dare to whisper that he came out of that hierarchy. That he was once a priest of the Jhistal. And so as long as he may rule we will never speak his name.'

The lieutenant blew out a long ragged breath and held out her hand. He took it in a tight grip. 'Honesty is a rare gift among strangers,' she said with feeling.

'An easy gift, since we may not see the morrow.'

She lowered her gaze to the chest at their feet. 'Well then . . . let's get to it.'

They each took a handle, and together they carried it up to the top of the wall.

Lady Orosenn was on the catwalk speaking to Voti and Malle. Beyond, up the valley, the fog appeared to be breaking up. The rumbling was not diminishing, however. Even atop the wall, Jute felt the vibrations hammering through his boots.

'This is your people's last chance,' Lady Orosenn was saying. 'There will be no escape once it is upon us.'

The young king's mouth pulled down, accentuating his long jaw. 'We will not abandon what is ours.'

Lady Orosenn dipped her head in acceptance. 'Very well. I have to confess – I hold little hope.'

Voti bowed. 'Thank you for that frank admission. I will go to tell my council.'

Lady Orosenn answered the bow and he descended the ramp, followed by his bodyguard of ten spears. Malle remained. She leaned against the shaking stone blocks of the wall, peering out.

Cartheron arrived and nodded to Lieutenant Jalaz. 'Time,' he said. She gave a curt bob of her head. 'You'll need eight veterans.'

Malle turned from the wall. 'Riley and his boys are up for it.'

Cartheron gave his assent.

'Time for what?' Jute asked, feeling a strange sort of growing unease.

Lieutenant Jalaz squeezed his shoulder, grinning. 'Wish me luck, Jute of Delanss.' She jogged off down the ramp. Malle leaned out over the catwalk and snapped her fingers. The majority of her remaining guards rose where they'd been squatting below among the chests.

'What is going on?' Jute asked everyone.

Cartheron shouted down, 'Open the gates!'

'Open the gates? What for?'

But Cartheron ignored him, going to the wall to lean out, peering down. Jute went to his side. Below, the gates of bronze-sheathed timber swung open. Lieutenant Jalaz appeared, jog-trotting north at the head of a train of four munition chests, each carried by two men and piled with shovels and picks.

'What is this?' Jute demanded.

Cartheron finally turned to him. He was rubbing a hand over his balding pate. 'A gamble.'

'A gamble? What sort of gamble?'

'Orosenn assures me that all the soil and dirt 'n' such is going to be scraped up, so no point in burying a charge. But there's rock crevices and cracks where the bedrock comes mounding up. They're gonna look for some of those at our maximum range. Push a few munitions down there for a little extra oomph.'

Jute snapped his gaze to where Lieutenant Jalaz and her team were disappearing into the banners of ground fog. 'There's no time for that!'

Cartheron just brushed his fingers down his jaw. 'It's a good throw. Worth four chests.'

Jute could not believe such callousness. 'Four chests! What of nine people?'

That must have stung, as the old commander's gaze flicked to him and he grated, his voice tight, 'Don't lecture me, son. They're good people doing what they do best, so leave them to it.' He walked off, unsteady, looking bowed. Jute moved to follow, but Malle caught his arm.

'Let him go. Do not add to his pain. Nine lives, you say? Well, what of all of us?'

'But—'

The hardened old woman stopped him with a look. 'There will always be buts, captain. The important thing is that choices be made. Now comes the hard part.'

'The hard part?'

'Yes.' Her gaze shifted to the north. 'Now we wait.'

The walls became crowded as the evening passed. Everyone wanted to watch, perhaps out of a kind of perverse fascination to see the end. Conversation was impossible. One had to press one's mouth to anyone's ear to be heard over the groaning earth, the rumbling avalanche, and the growing thunderous grinding of tons upon tons of moiling rock and earth.

To make it worse, it was now blowing snow. The fat flakes came out of the heights, driven by a cutting wind that only grew in intensity. Far to the east and west, all along the uplands as far as Jute could see, the thinning clouds hinted at a wall of white covering the heights – an unbroken sheath of snow that was utterly featureless except where tall ridges of black rock poked through like knife-edges.

He scanned the domed rock before the fortress where it descended to the north. The bedrock carried only low brush and dwarf trees, but it combed downward into a forest of cedar, fir, and birch. Just at the fringe of these woods was where Giana and her team were supposed to be digging. He could see no sign of them, however.

The vibration punishing everyone's feet was becoming almost unbearable. One of the pounded dirt ramps collapsed into a heap of soil, soundlessly it seemed, as the cacophony of the leagues-wide avalanche grinding down upon them drowned everything out.

Squinting into the blowing snow he could make out entire swathes of forest disappearing as if swept down by an invisible hand. The enormous blocks of the wall juddered and bounced as if toys. The last screen of trees between them and the avalanche fell towards them, their crowns swinging down as if bowing in farewell. *Come on!* he urged Giana. *Run!*

Something appeared through the curtain of snow but it was not what Jute expected. To all appearances it looked like a flood of extremely muddy water creeping up the slope of the bedrock. Sticks and detritus roiled amid the froth of the approaching tide. It took him a moment to grasp that the sticks were in fact the stripped trunks of mature trees, and that the coming tide was a churned froth of mud, silts, soil, and sand, all being scooped downslope towards them in front of a solid wall of one of the ice-tongues.

And before this flood emerged six figures, running pell-mell for the high land and the wall.

Jute tottered and stumbled his way down the ramp to the gates, where a team of locals waited to swing closed the twin leaves. The figures, completely mud-covered, ran on while the very earth jumped and shuddered beneath them. Now Jute counted only four.

The quartet came barrelling in, dripping, sheathed in mud and streaks of blood, and fell to the ground, panting and gasping. King Voti's people shut the doors. Jute and a number of Malazans stooped to the four, rubbing away muck, pulling a shattered length of wood the size of a dagger from the arm of one of them. To Jute's immense relief Lieutenant Jalaz emerged, bruised and bloodied, from the layers of clinging muck encasing another of them.

'You fool!' he growled, though of course she could not hear. She understood, however, and shrugged weakly. He waved for her to stay where she was and tottered up the ramp.

What he found above reminded him of what Lady Orosenn had

said about there being no escape. Entire forests of tangled trees were building up amid the coursing wash of suspended soil and earth that was passing to either side of the rise. Orothos, under directions from Cartheron, had his crews blasting these logjams to pieces. Meanwhile, the roiling mass of coming earth just kept mounting higher and higher. Of the township of Mantle there remained no trace. The effect of all this was as of the worst naval engagement Jute had ever endured. He ran to Lady Orosenn, motioned that he wished to speak. She lowered her head. 'What are they doing?' he yelled.

She made a pushing gesture. 'Moving it along.'

'Why?'

'We don't want it to catch and heap up.'

'Why are they firing into the mud?'

'We don't know when the ice will arrive,' she called back. 'I suspect the leading edge to be thin. Under the muck at first.'

After that, Jute was too hoarse to continue yelling so he merely nodded and allowed Lady Orosenn to return to studying the flow. He tried to imagine what it must be like on the shores of the Sea of Gold as all this earth and gravel and loose rock came thrusting out on to the mudflats, perhaps taking them with it. It suddenly occurred to him, horrifyingly – could the entire sea be erased? All that water heaved further south? How far away were the ships? Had they made it through the channel yet? He prayed to the gods that they had. If not, they were in for a memorable ride.

One of the crews on the springals thrust their arms skyward, shouting soundlessly, and Jute scanned the base of the rise. Pulverized white flakes came floating down from an eruption. They momentarily painted white the foaming, shifting flow, only to be sucked beneath. Cartheron was gesturing, signing to the crews, who shifted their aim. He raised an open hand and the crews waited, hands at the releases.

Why was he waiting, Jute wondered. Shouldn't he be punishing the ice now that it had arrived? Perhaps he was waiting for the flow to thicken – no point in blasting the thinnest leading finger. Perhaps. Then he noticed that the commander's gaze was fixed upon Lady Orosenn, who had a hand outstretched as if reaching for him.

The walls rocked then, as in a true earthquake. Or perhaps a collision. Jute turned his head to the north, terrified of what he might see. There, what he'd taken earlier for a thick wall of falling snow revealed itself to be a steep upward-sweeping wing-like slope that went on and on, perhaps for leagues, up the entire lowest shoulder of the mountains: an ungraspable immensity of ice and weight and might all bearing down upon them like a war dromond striking a water beetle. He knew it to be a plain physical manifestation of ice and rock, but he couldn't help also feeling a palpable sense of deliberate menace and ruthless will pointed directly at him – and he the size of a flea beneath it.

Lady Orosenn snapped her hand down and Cartheron made a fist.

All four siege weapons fired.

The four cussors arced upwards, disappearing into the driving snow. Almost immediately spouts of smashed ice shot upwards, without any accompanying sound. Jute was appalled. The best they had. Like a child throwing a rock at a landslide. Cartheron signed to fire again. The four now simply kept firing and reloading, pounding that one same spot. Jute imagined that that must be where the cussors had been jammed down into cracks and crevices in the bedrock – if they hadn't yet been plucked out.

The eruptions came almost continuously now, in a constant shooting spray of pulverized ice that arced high into the blowing snow. Jute thought the pushing lip of the ice-tongue was climbing the hump of bedrock. Soon, he imagined, it would sweep them off like dust from a tabletop.

All four crews kept pounding, and it did seem to Jute that larger chunks of broken ice now flew with each eruption. He gripped the topmost stone of the wall before him, itself many hundreds of pounds of rock, and felt the immense power of the grinding advance transmitted to his bones through the juddering of the stone. *Break, damn you!* he exhorted the ice. *Break!*

He'd seen towers brought down by one or two well-placed cussors. Entire harbour defences reduced to rubble with just a few casts. And now this man, Cartheron Crust, was pouring half the imperial arsenal of Moranth munitions into this unstoppable mountain of ice in a colossal contest of wills that would grind all else into dust.

The blocks of the wall jerked towards him then, knocking his hand aside as if it were alive and flinching. Ahead, through the curls and scarves of snow, a great fountain of white was burgeoning upwards like a dome swelling over a surfacing swimmer. Enormous shards of emerald and white ice now arced skywards. They blossomed outwards in all directions. A roar washed over Mantle that overcame even the valley-wide growling of the ice.

Smaller chunks fell all about him. They burst to shards against the wall. Some punched through the timbers of the catwalk. Nearby, a man fell as if mattocked, his head a shattered ruin. Jute ducked, arms over his head, and staggered down the ramp to take cover under the catwalk. Here, beneath his hand and his rump, the bedrock shook as if drummed. A deep wounded-animal sort of groan mounted into a high-pitched cracking. In his mind's eye, he imagined the stupendous weight of the ice pulling it downslope to the east and to the west, naturally tugging in opposite directions. And so it would split – not of intent, but because the great ice-river merely wished to find the lowest level. He rose and clambered out to look. The ramp had been shaken to nothing more than a heap of dirt, and this he climbed to pull himself one-handed up on to the catwalk. The huge blocks of the wall were now misaligned and uneven in their course, and it seemed wondrous to Jute that the snow still fell as if nothing had happened. To the right and left coursed the dirty snow-blown river of ice, down to where the two arms came together again before sweeping out over the obliterated shore of the Sea of Gold.

They sat atop a scoured-clean island of naked rock.

He went to find Cartheron and spotted him collapsed against the wall, watched over by two of his crew. He was pale, squeezing his chest, his face clenched against pain. Jute knelt next to him. The roar of the creaking and groaning ice was still like a thunderstorm, and he had to yell to make himself heard. 'Are you all right?'

The old man laughed weakly. 'When Lady Orosenn sewed me up she told me to avoid any stress.'

'Good thing you're taking it easy, then.'

There was a tremor in the Malazan's hands that he didn't seem to notice. 'Yeah,' he said, 'it's the retired life for me.'

Jute stood. 'I'll get Orosenn.'

The old commander was too exhausted even to respond. Jute ran, searching for the sorceress. He found her at the extreme southern end of the catwalk close to the wall's edge overlooking the cliff. She was watching the great tongue of ice where it crept out over the Sea of Gold.

Gaining her attention, he put a hand to his mouth to shout, 'Cartheron is in a bad way.'

She nodded. 'I've done what I can for him. It's a miracle he's still alive.'

He gestured out towards the sea. 'What can we do?'

'We wait.'

'Will it be like this for ever?'

She bestowed the familiar affectionate smile upon him once more. 'No, Jute of Delanss. This was a ferociously rapid invocation. It will fade faster than most. Perhaps a mere hundred years.'

Oh. A *mere* hundred years. 'So it is over,' he breathed, immensely relieved.

But the sorceress shook her head, her long black hair blowing like a banner and her wide mouth hardening. 'No. This was only the opening salvo. The true confrontation is taking place high above. I wish I could be there to add my voice.'

'Add your voice?'

'Against the rekindling of an ancient war. And I do not mean the animosity of the T'lan Imass for the Jaghut. There have been far older wars, Jute of Delanss. And there are some who never forget, nor forgive.'

He did not know what the sorceress meant. He did not have her deeper vision of events. He only knew that a friend was in pain, so he gestured once more that they should help Cartheron, and Orosenn nodded, squeezing his arm.

CHAPTER XV

THEY WERE ONLY A SHORT DISTANCE UP THE WIDE SINUOUS SERPENT of ice when Kyle halted. Blustering snow obscured the distance. He could just make out tall spine-like ridges of iron-grey rock that rose as barriers far to the east and west.

Fisher came to his side. 'What is it?'

'I can't walk away.'

'I told you – they're safe. The farther from here the better.'

But Kyle couldn't shake the feeling that he was betraying the Losts. It felt wrong, just turning his back. Even if they didn't want him to follow. 'No. I have to go back.'

Cal-Brinn joined them. 'They're closing. We must keep moving.'

Kyle shook his refusal. 'We should go back.'

Cal-Brinn's already wrinkled and burnished features creased further in a frown of consideration. After a moment, he dipped his head in assent. 'It is early yet, but I was going to have to tell you that we of the Guard cannot continue in any case. There is something pushing against us. So I must send my people back to find Stalker and Badlands while I remain. Will you accept this?'

Kyle clasped the amber stone at his neck. It was warm in his chilled hand. 'I should go. They are my friends.'

'Your loyalty is to be commended. But it is you our pursuers want, not us. And the Losts are our friends as well.'

He released the stone – the numbness from the bitter cold had gone from his hand. 'Very well. I just feel . . . that I have let them down.'

Cal-Brinn inclined his head once more. 'They would be angry if you showed up. Now go.' He motioned for Fisher to hurry him along, then turned to his company. 'Jup, Leena, attend me!'

The bard took Kyle's arm and urged him onward. 'You and I must speak for the Myrni and the Losts above,' he said, his breath steaming.

Kyle tried to bring his brows down to show his confusion, but his face was too numb. 'What do you mean?'

'I mean that any survivors will have been driven to the highlands, just like us. There will be a meeting of the families such as has never taken place.' He waved to Jethiss, who waited ahead.

Kyle glanced back, still reluctant to go. Cal-Brinn now walked with them, his hands clasped behind his back. His long coat of armour kicked up snow as he pushed through the drifts. 'A meeting? What for?'

'To decide what to do.'

They caught up with Jethiss, who was carefully prodding the hidden ice with a broken branch he'd picked up when they had run across the dry stream bed. Kyle was grateful for this, as the great serpent of jagged ice heaved and groaned as if in constant pain. Explosions of cracking ice would shudder beneath them, sounding up and down its length. The snowstorm and dark clouds obscured the way ahead, but it appeared to be steepening.

Night gathered as they walked, yet shifting curtains of lights provided some illumination. They seemed to wreathe the heights, and they reminded Kyle of similar veils he'd seen in Korel, above the Stormriders. He thought they were some sort of manifestation of the manipulations of energy, whatever the source. They tramped on. Jethiss showed no need or inclination to pause. Kyle glanced back often down the sweep of the great serpent behind. Once or twice, through the gusting snows, he thought he glimpsed slim dark figures arrayed across the ice, tatters of cloth whipping from their shoulders.

They reached a plain of ice that lay like a plateau beneath a low bank of black clouds. Through gaps in the clouds he glimpsed a series of slim pinnacles, all bare ash-grey sheet-like rock. The peaks of this easterly range of the Salt Mountains. Then Fisher gestured ahead to where a group of dark dots marred the pristine silver expanse of blowing snow.

As they neared, the group resolved into four individuals, one sitting cross-legged in the snow, the other three lined up before him. They were a martial group, tall, in leather armour. Closer now, Kyle noted how young the three were, and that the sitting one, an older fellow, was impaled upon a wicked-looking spear.

Jethiss halted and Fisher stepped up to the fore. He raised his hand, calling: 'Greetings! My name is Fisher and I speak for the Myrni. This is Jethiss, of the Tiste Andii. Kyle, who speaks for the Losts. And Cal-Brinn, of the mercenary company the Crimson Guard.'

The middle lad raised his hand. Kyle saw fresh scarring where a thrust had taken his right eye. A thick bearskin cloak clasped by a large bronze brooch humped his shoulders. 'Welcome. I am Orman. This is Keth and Kasson. We speak for the Sayers.' The lad half turned to the silver-haired elder. 'This is . . . was . . . Buri.'

Fisher's gaze, snapping to Kyle, was wide with wonder. 'Buri in truth?' he breathed, awed.

'Indeed. It was he who summoned the ice-barrier anew.'

'And who did this to him?'

The lad's jaws writhed with suppressed emotions. 'I did,' he finally ground out, his voice ragged.

'And why?' Fisher asked very softly, and gently.

'Because he asked that I do so – to seal the invocation.'

Fisher was nodding. 'I see. That must have been a . . . difficult . . . thing to do.'

With his one good eye, Orman was studying Fisher. 'You give the name Fisher – not *the* Fisher, the bard?'

'Yes.'

The Sayer was obviously quite impressed. He took a deep breath to steady himself. 'My father spoke of you. We are honoured.'

Fisher inclined his head in recognition of the compliment. 'Any others? The Heels? No Bains survived?'

Orman shook his head, saying in a bitter tone, 'The Bains are gone.'

'Then we must decide upon our course of action.'

The Sayer glanced back to exchange a look with his two fellows. 'How so? It is over. We can reclaim our Holdings.'

'The Holdings are beneath rods of ice. But more to the point, we are pursued.'

'Pursued? The outlanders?'

'That would be a simple matter. No, I speak of another enemy.'

The lad started in recognition. He exhaled a steaming breath in wonder. 'The old enemy?'

Fisher nodded. 'Aye. Our Army of Dust and Bone – the T'lan Imass.'

'I know them only as the Undying Army.'

'Close enough.'

'But,' Orman gestured back to the corpse of Buri, 'the invocation was completed – this was his purpose . . .'

Fisher pressed a hand to the lad's shoulder. 'I know. And it has been successful. But some it seems are resisting enough to advance. Or a Bonecaster, one of their shamans, has come. In any case, we must flee.'

The Sayer lad appeared almost shattered by the suspicion that he had done what he did for nothing. Kyle could not help but step up as well, saying, 'It is working – few are coming. We will escape, I'm sure.'

'Someone is coming now,' Jethiss announced, staring south. Kyle spun, his hand going to the grip of the white blade tucked in his belt.

Two tall figures emerged from the blowing snow, a young man and woman. Everyone readied their weapons. Kyle took a few hesitant steps as he realized he knew the one with the great bunch of wild curly hair. He raised his hand. 'It is the Heels.' He ran down to meet them. 'Baran, welcome!' He took his hand. The lad smiled behind the rime hardened round his beard. 'Cull or Yullveig?'

The smile faded and Baran shook his head. He turned, pointing, 'We aren't alone.'

Kyle squinted into the gusts. Thin figures approached. Their tattered leathers and cloaks snapped and lashed in the wind and he shivered – for a moment he thought them Imass. They closed, and to his astonishment he recognized them . . . Shimmer, Blues and K'azz of the Crimson Guard. And with them a fourth person, a young girl, of obvious Iceblood heritage.

K'azz came forward. He walked bowed, as if struggling beneath a great weight. Kyle was shocked by his condition. The man appeared even more emaciated and haggard, his cheeks hollow as if clawed. He was hardly more than skin and bone. Yet fire flashed in his eyes and he offered up a warm smile. 'Kyle of Bael lands,' he said. 'It is good to see you.'

Kyle took his hands, found them frozen into rigid claws. 'What by all the gods . . .' he wondered aloud. 'Why are you here?'

Shimmer approached and he embraced her, flinching when he found her skin as cold as the snow. It even held the same silvery paleness. 'Kyle,' she said. 'We hear great stories of the white blade.' He could only laugh as he gripped Blues' hand.

Then he remembered, and invited them on. 'Come. There is someone you must meet.'

He watched while they wearily trudged towards the rest of the gathering. The girl crossed to stop at Erta's side. He watched as Cal-Brinn took a few faltering steps towards them, then ran, kicking up snow, and they embraced, the four, all together.

He went to join Fisher and Jethiss while the group spoke in low tones. To his eyes it was an oddly subdued reunion. Then he noticed the tears running down Fisher's cheeks, his lips clamped as against a moan. In a moment the man lurched away, hugging himself.

'What is it?' Kyle whispered. 'Are you sick?'

Fisher jerked his head savagely, his eyes clamped closed. Then he seemed to master himself and raised his head to the ash-grey clouds above, the falling snow, blinking back tears. He offered Kyle a wounded smile. 'Only now do I see it. Only now.' He glanced back to the four Crimson Guard. 'It was before me all this time, yet I failed to see.' He raised his face to the dark sky once more, drew a rasping breath. He clenched the bag holding the instrument at his side and raised it to press it to his brow as if he would break it. 'There are no words,' he groaned. 'No words for this song.' He staggered away into the gusting snow and playing lights of the shifting banners above. Kyle moved to follow, but Jethiss caught his arm.

'Leave him. All he needs is time.'

'Do you know what he speaks of?'

The Andii shook his head, his narrowed gaze upon the mercenaries. 'No. But I am beginning to see more and more the higher we venture.' He raised his chin to the heights above. 'I see that we are not alone.'

Kyle squinted to where the dark peaks reared naked and jagged high above. Movement pulled his eyes down. A single large figure was closing upon them; it looked to possess the height and narrow build of a full-blooded Jaghut. It wore tanned old leathers, trousers and a long jerkin. As it closed, the Sayer lad, Orman, let out a gasp of recognition. The newcomer was a Jaghut woman who limped with one stiff leg. Laces of stones shone at her neck and hung woven in her wide mane of hair.

'You!' the Sayer lad exclaimed.

This newcomer offered him a small puzzled smile, then nodded. 'Ah, you met one of my daughters. Yes. Greetings, Orman Bregin's son, of the Sayer.'

And the lad actually knelt on one knee before her, saying: 'Great Mother.'

Mother? Kyle wondered. Then, in turn, the Heels knelt, and then the Myrni girl. If Fisher were here Kyle imagined that he might actually kneel too. Then it struck him – he ought to as well. This creature's blood flowed through his veins.

'So few,' she whispered, an edge of anger hardening her voice.

She crossed to Buri's corpse, still upright, impaled, covered now in a fine layer of snow. She rested a hand upon his bowed head, then walked round to take hold of the spear that pinned him to the ice. She yanked, and the weapon slid free. The slick, wet haft steamed in the chill air. She raised the weapon, studying its length. 'It has been a long time,' she murmured.

For a time no one spoke, until Jethiss broke the silence, saying, 'It is not safe here.'

The Jaghut elder tilted her head as she looked him up and down. 'You, I did not see.' She glanced to K'azz. 'Nor you.' She limped to Orman and extended the weapon. The lad's face actually wrinkled in loathing, but none the less he took it from her hands. 'But you are right,' she said. 'We must go higher.'

Kyle squinted to the south. He could just make out small dark shapes pushing through the field of white. A line that seemed to extend all the way across the ice-plain. He began backing up. 'They are coming,' he said, though he was sure they all knew.

'This way,' the elder said, and she started up the slight incline that led to the peaks.

The three Sayers followed with the Heels and the Myrni girl. Kyle and Jethiss came after, followed by the four Crimson Guard, who spread out as a laughably slim rear guard. They climbed the shallow rise. The snowfall thinned, as did the ground-hugging clouds. Looking back, Kyle was amazed to catch glimpses of the level tops of the packed cloud cover below looking like the calm surface of the ocean itself, extending off as far as he could see.

The wide face of the nearest peak closed before them, dominating the north. It appeared to consist of nothing more than jagged rock cliffs and heaps of broken talus. Their boots crunched upon loose stones as they climbed. His chest burned now. He felt as if he could never catch enough breath.

Past the snowfall, higher on the rock slope they climbed. Ahead, Fisher straightened from among the boulders to await them. As the woman limped onward, swinging her leg awkwardly as she came, he called down, 'Come no higher.'

She paused, glanced back briefly and answered, 'They will not relent.'

The lines of the bard's mouth appeared graven in stone. His grey-streaked long hair whipped in the strong winds and his gloved hand was upon the grip of his Darujhistani longsword. 'Go east or west. Hide anywhere but here.'

The elder continued to close. 'You would draw a weapon upon me?'

'If I must. You mustn't disturb what lies above.'

'What lies above is our only chance of escape.'

The bard's features appeared ready to crack. He gasped as if pleading, 'There are other ways.'

Kyle's own hand went to the blade at his belt as he saw how the Sayer lad's fists tightened upon the spear, and the two with him prepared to draw their longswords.

The elder shook her head as she advanced into sword-range. 'Will you draw upon me?'

Some terrible emotion shuddered through the bard and his face broke as he groaned, defeated. His hand fell from the sword grip and he slumped to the rocks to sit hunched, his head in his hands.

The elder passed him. She rested a hand upon his head for a time, as in blessing, then walked on. When Kyle reached him he extended a hand. At first the bard refused to raise his head. But then he held up a hand, which Kyle took to pull him upright.

'There is no dishonour here,' he told him.

Fisher shook his head, fierce. 'She is a fool if she thinks she can control them. Or dictate terms. No one can.'

'We shall see,' Jethiss said. His gaze was on the heights, where a blasting wind punished the bare rock above.

'The same goes for you,' Fisher told him.

A peculiar smile came to the Andii's lips. 'I merely have one simple wish.' And he passed them, climbing once more.

The Crimson Guard reached them. Kyle noted how the bard regarded them now with a bruised look in his eyes of which the mercenaries seemed oblivious. Blues carried his sticks in his hands and he gestured back with them. 'They're gaining and there're too many of them.'

'Our guide believes she has a secret weapon,' Fisher spat, hugging himself.

'Well, we'd better find it damned soon,' Blues grumbled. He urged them on.

Kyle almost groaned himself as he forced his legs to move. Dizzy spells came and went and he had to rest, sitting a few times, until one of the Guard appeared to chivvy him along. He had no idea how long they'd been climbing, though the sky was clear now and he could see that it was late in the afternoon. He felt as if he'd been wandering across the entire mountain range for an eternity.

*

Shimmer found that she climbed in a fog, even though they had left the mists and snow of the cloud cover far behind. Above, the Jaghut elder, the obvious matriarch of all these northern clans, led the way. Her distant descendants followed. The ex-Guardsman Kyle came after them, filled out now to a rangy, fierce-looking plainsman and fitting bearer of a storied blade. He kept fitting company as well – this strange Andii, and the legendary bard.

K'azz had them spread out to serve as a rear guard. She could not stop peering over to Cal – just to make certain he really was still with them. What a shock it had been, finding him. The man hadn't appeared much different, only more careworn than before. Yet she must have changed. She saw the distress of it in his eyes when they embraced. And his shock upon seeing K'azz's condition couldn't be hidden from any of them.

'The others?' K'azz had asked, and he had replied, 'Waiting be-low,' and that had been the extent of the conversation. Then they fell in together and it was as if nothing had intervened and no time had passed at all – though in truth, nearly two decades had come and gone.

She climbed. Rocks clattered and shifted beneath the ratty broken leather that was the remains of her shoes, and she wondered how it could be that so much time could have disappeared without her no-ticing it. Perhaps, she reflected, that was how lives went by. Long or short, they ran out like sand through your fingers before you could even think of closing your fist. And by then it was too late, and the sands were gone.

A shout snapped her head up. A warning from Blues. She turned, drawing her whipsword all in one motion.

They faced a closing skirmish line of T'lan Imass. Some twenty in all. Cal-Brinn had his longsword out, Blues his sticks. K'azz stood with arms crossed.

Two Imass approached from the line. One wore the rotted hide of a northern white bear. Necklaces of bear claws rattled about his withered neck. The other was squat and bore a trim of white hair about its skull, tied with what looked like stones or shells.

'Stand aside,' the white bear one whispered, his voice carrying as if he yelled.

'Remember your manners!' K'azz answered, startling Shimmer with the sudden new anger in his voice. 'I would know who speaks!'

The lead one's features, dried and withered, almost conveyed surprise. He inclined his head in assent. 'I am Ut'el, of the Kerluhm T'lan Imass. Who is it that knows the old formulas?'

'Well met, Ut'el. I am K'azz, of the Crimson Guard. Know that we will not allow you to pass.'

'You will be brushed aside,' stated the Imass next to Ut'el.

'You may try,' K'azz invited.

One of the line advanced, whispering, 'Enough talk.' It swung its long chalcedony blade at K'azz, who stepped inside to block the arm, twisting. Bones snapped like dry branches and K'azz took the weapon while kicking down the Imass.

The entire gathering of T'lan Imass became utterly still, as did Shimmer, watching but not believing. How could that have happened? How did K'azz do such a thing?

After remaining frozen for a time, Ut'el tilted his ravaged head and whispered in a voice like the wind scouring the rocks, 'Who *are* you?'

'Greetings, old enemy!' came a bellow that made Shimmer jump. It was the Jaghut, coming down the slope, awkwardly, one leg stiff, stepping sideways. Her descendants were arrayed before her, spears lowered and swords readied.

Fisher and Jethiss accompanied her.

Ut'el straightened in obvious recognition. 'I did not think to see you again,' he answered. He pointed a withered finger to the lad, Orman. 'That is my spear you hold.'

'You deserve it,' Orman grated. He raised it to throw.

The Jaghut reached out and lowered the spear-point with her hand. 'There will be no hostilities. We are in the shadow of the Forkrul.'

Ut'el turned his flat dried mien to right and left. 'I see them not. They sleep – as is their nature.'

'Dare you risk that?'

He waved to encompass everyone with her. 'Dare you?'

She crossed her arms. 'We are at stalemate, then.'

The Imass edged his head beneath its bear skull in the faintest of negatives. 'I think not. You yet have everything to lose. While we . . . possess nothing.'

'I believe you will find that you are wrong in that, Ut'el,' K'azz said, loudly and suddenly. He lowered his head a touch to indicate the lower slope. Ut'el and the one with him turned. An instant later, all the Imass spun as well.

Shimmer peered past them to what looked to be four more T'lan Imass approaching. She could see nothing in this. Four more meant nothing as there were already too many to withstand. Yet what of K'azz and his defeat of one? There was something in that – some hint of an idea that, for some reason, she could not bring into focus. Something that made her look away from her commander.

The four proved to be two obvious T'lan and two living women – one old, the other of middle-age. From the manner in which the two T'lan followed the older woman, Shimmer thought her the leader, though the other woman, dark and wind-tanned, stood apart.

To Shimmer's astonishment, the gathered T'lan Imass knelt to one knee before the old woman in her worn tanned leathers and neck-laces of turquoise and green jade. Ut'el, the leader, knelt as well, murmuring, 'Summoner. You honour us.'

'You are?' she demanded.

'Ut'el, Bonecaster to the Kerluhm.'

The woman turned from him to rest her attention upon the other Imass. This one stood firm and impassive beneath her hard gaze. 'Lanas,' the woman said at last, and there was no welcome in her voice.

The Imass dipped her head, the teeth and stones woven into her remaining white hair clattering in the chill air. 'Summoner.'

From what she'd heard of events in south Genabackis, Shimmer now understood this Summoner to be Silverfox, a living Imass Bonecaster – the first in millennia. And born, it was said, to fulfil their Vow. This must be so, she decided, as she noted how Silverfox ignored the Jaghut matriarch. Yet the surviving Iceblood, the Heels and the Sayers, were lined up before their ancestor, ready to defend her. Standing apart was the small grouping of Kyle, Fisher and the Tiste Andii. It occurred to her that, being from this region, Kyle might also be a target of the Imass. She signed to K'azz: *Shall we defend?*

He answered: *Wait and see.*

After studying this second Imass, and perhaps communicating some soundless message, the Summoner dismissed her. In passing, her gaze fell upon K'azz, and Shimmer saw how it fixed there. The woman started, almost stunned, it seemed, by what she saw. An entire gamut of emotions crossed her wrinkled, sun-burnished features in surprise, disbelief and amazement, followed by near horror and stricken grief.

K'azz, for his part, simply lowered his head as if in shame.

Recovering her bearing, the woman tore her gaze from K'azz to face the Bonecaster. 'You have done well, Ut'el, to sustain so many against the pull of Omtose Phellack. For that I salute you. But I must ask, what is it you believe you will accomplish here?'

'I merely serve the demands of the ritual, Summoner.'

514

Silverfox answered, her voice hard: 'I decide what does, or does not, serve the ritual, Bonecaster.'

Ut'el bowed his head, acknowledging her authority. 'Forgive me, but all was set out ages ago. It is our legacy. It is all we Imass have left to us.'

'All you have . . .' Silverfox echoed, wonder in her voice. She turned on the one named Lanas. 'I see . . . My apologies, Ut'el, I had thought you Kerluhm deliberately blind. But I see that I was mistaken.' She closed to stand directly before the female Imass with her copper-capped incisors and ravaged torso of countless sword thrusts. 'You, Lanas Tog, have withheld the gift of the Redeemer.'

'Time for that afterwards, Summoner,' Lanas answered, her voice faint and dry as falling leaves. 'There will always be time . . . afterwards.'

'What does the Summoner speak of, Lanas?' Ut'el demanded.

'You will not show them?'

The Imass remained immobile in her defiance.

Silverfox turned to Ut'el. 'I speak of a gift that is not mine to give.' She invited one of the Imass with her to stand forward.

Ut'el nodded his welcome, murmuring, 'Greetings, Pran Chole of the Kron.'

Pran answered, 'We honour the Kerluhm.' He held out empty open hands that were no more than bundles of sinew-wrapped bone. 'Tellann is suppressed here, Ut'el. May I offer a gift that was given us, unbidden and unlooked for, in lands beyond these?'

The bear-head hood covering Ut'el's head dipped as he gave his assent. Pran advanced to press his hand to the Bonecaster's forehead. It seemed an instant later that the Kerluhm Bonecaster snapped backwards as if having received a blow from a hammer. He raised his hands to his face and studied them. His sockets were empty pits, but it seemed to Shimmer that open wonder and amazement filled his features. He murmured in awed tones, 'Who gave the T'lan Imass this gift of hope of a realm for our spirits?'

'We name him the Redeemer.'

At that, the Kerluhm Bonecaster appeared to flinch, stricken by pain. He bowed to Silverfox. 'I can do naught but strive to honour it,' he whispered, his voice even more faint and breathless. He turned to the one named Lanas, who waited, immobile, her incisors bright in the hard light of the heights. 'You knew of a realm where we might find peace after the ritual . . . yet you withheld it?'

'We each sought to serve the ritual in our own way.'

The Bonecaster shook his lean desiccated head beneath its hood of curving bear fangs. 'I thought such hope long gone from us, Lanas. Yet it lives again and I repent of my despair. Think on this during your ages-long dismissal.' He swept his hand and the Imass dissolved into a scarf of dust that the wind immediately scattered across the snows.

Ut'el turned to Silverfox. He knelt on one knee. 'We of the Kerluhm offer ourselves to your judgement, Summoner.'

Silverfox laid a hand upon his bear headdress. 'There can be no punishment worse than that which the T'lan have already endured tenfold, Ut'el. Stand with me. The Kron and the Ifayle welcome the Kerluhm.'

Ut'el stood and he and the two other Bonecasters grasped one another's forearms: Pran Chole, and the other Shimmer now recognized as Tolb Bell'al, whom they had met on an ice-floe during their journey to Jacuruku. The Summoner, she noted, looked to the other woman, the short powerful one with hair like a long black mane that whipped in the wind. This one stood immobile, her arms wrapped tightly about herself, her cheeks wet. For an instant she appeared familiar to Shimmer. A ghost memory of having seen her before drifted across her awareness, only to waver away. Somewhere – she'd seen her before – she was certain.

As if summoned, this woman now strode towards her. An unreasoning urge to flee grasped Shimmer's throat. She couldn't breathe and she felt the hair rising upon her arms and neck in terror. *Something awful is coming*, she realized. Yet her feet in their frayed boots remained frozen to the ice, her lips numb with cold, and her arms heavy – so very heavy.

The woman faced Shimmer and K'azz and Blues and Cal-Brinn, lined up as they were to challenge the Kerluhm should they attack. Yet there was no hint of challenge in her wind-darkened features. No, what horrified Shimmer was the pain there, the open compassion in her dark eyes.

The woman called to Silverfox, over her shoulder, 'One more task awaits you before we may go, Summoner. One I do not envy you.'

Silverfox drew a heavy shuddering breath. Her hands closed to pale fists at her sides. 'This is not my burden, Kilava,' she answered, resolute.

The woman, Kilava, closed her eyes for an instant, let her arms fall. 'But it is.' She added, 'I'm sorry.' Yet to whom she was apologizing was unclear to Shimmer.

Swallowing through her dread, Shimmer addressed K'azz, 'What is this?'

The man was holding himself rigid. His bruised sunken eyes made him look so very ill. Was this what they were speaking of? That he is near to death? 'I'm so very sorry, Shimmer,' he answered, his voice choked and ragged. 'This wasn't what I wanted – please believe me.'

'What is it, please?' she begged.

Silverfox seemed to drag herself to stand before them, flanked by Tolb Bell'al and Pran Chole. She studied them each in turn and the anguish in her eyes terrified Shimmer. 'The Crimson Guard,' she murmured, nodding to herself. 'If only we had met earlier in Genabackis. I would have recognized it immediately, K'azz.'

'You are the Summoner,' he said, his voice hardly more than a groan.

'Yes. So the task must fall to me though I wish it otherwise.'

Something in what they were saying made Shimmer dizzy. The *thing* lurking behind their words threatened her so much she thought she would lose her reason. She raised a hand, pointing to Kilava. 'I have seen you before . . .'

The woman nodded. 'Yes. Once. The day of your Vow – Shimmer, is it? That day your Vow touched upon Tellann and so I came to witness.'

Touched upon Tellann . . . the words spun like a destroying whirlwind in Shimmer's thoughts. Echoes of their Vow washed over her. *Eternal opposition* . . .

Kilava addressed K'azz, 'What do you think lent power to you Avowed? Sustained you all this time?'

K'azz nodded, his eyes downcast. 'I knew. For some time, I have known.'

Silverfox gently raised a hand and pressed it to K'azz's forehead. 'Though it brings me terrible pain to do so, I welcome you, K'azz D'Avore, Commander of the Crimson Guard.'

Tolb Bell'al inclined his ravaged skull. 'We of the Ifayle are also saddened, yet we welcome you gladly. Long has it been since we have welcomed a new clan among the T'lan Imass. We offer our greetings to the D'Avore T'lan Imass. The Red Clan.'

'Gods above and below,' Shimmer heard Blues moan.

'We thank you,' K'azz answered, the words jagged with suppressed pain. Then he turned to Shimmer, took her hand – his fingers so cold. 'I'm sorry, Shimmer . . . please . . .'

But she hardly heard him. The *thing* in her mind was close now. The truth she did not want. It all made sense now. Now she knew why she'd run from this knowledge. Avoided it at all costs. Why she'd refused to see it. She understood, and could see the truth of it. Her hand rose to press against her chest where, weeks ago, a blade from the Sharr attack had struck, and she knew. She finally accepted that for some time now – she'd been dead.

With that giving up to the fact, that yielding, came darkness and nothing more.

*

When Shimmer collapsed into her commander's arms the man gently lowered her to the ground and the others, Blues and Cal-Brinn, knelt with him next to her. Kyle could only wonder on the shock of such an unveiling. The Crimson Guard Vow – a curse in truth, just like that of the T'lan. He shook his head at the horrifying injustice of it. Then jerked, startled, as the Jaghut elder raised her arms, calling, 'Summoner! We have delayed here too long.'

Silverfox spun from the kneeling figures, sudden panicked awareness in her face. 'T'lan, guard us!' she ordered.

The ranks of the Kerluhm came clattering forward across the rocks to form a broad defensive circle around the Crimson Guard and the Jaghut elder and her descendants.

Fisher, Jethiss and Kyle pushed forward into the circle. Moments later the Icebloods, the three of the Sayer, and the son of the Heels, joined them.

Beyond the nearest boulders and debris of this high shoulder, there rose all about them ash-grey shapes from among the broken rocks. Kyle had never seen them before, but he immediately knew them for what they were. Their slate-hued, thin and elongated shapes revealed them as the Forkrul Assail. He also knew at that moment that it was unlikely that they would get off the mountain alive.

The alien figures remained immobile, as if carved of stone themselves. The Imass waited, obsidian and flint swords readied. Kyle drew the white blade and to his astonishment – and extreme discomfort – saw the attention of the Forkrul shift to him as their slit eyes all moved at once.

Jethiss moved to confront them but Fisher snapped up a hand to grasp his arm, pulling him back. 'Not yet,' he murmured, 'if you must at all.'

The Andii eased backwards, acquiescing to the bard's urgings – at least for now.

The Forkrul then raised arms to point up the slope to a higher ridge of stone. Kyle glanced up to see two there waiting. Stones crunched as the Jaghut elder passed through the circled Imass. She paused then, looking back to them. 'One from each of us gathered here must come,' she said. The words troubled Kyle in that he sensed something deeper behind them. Something profound and ritualized.

Further steps sounded over the stones as Silverfox stepped forth. With her came Kilava and Pran Chole. The Sayer youth, Orman, joined the Jaghut elder. He cradled the wicked-looking spear in his arms. The Matriarch gestured, inviting up Jethiss. He turned to Fisher, who nodded, and in turn reached out to pull on Kyle's arm. Kyle resisted. 'There are enough,' he said.

'No. The white blade must come. I understand this now. This is no accident, Kyle. This is why we are here.' Fisher peered about, his eyes widening. 'Great Abyss,' he murmured, 'Four. We are four again.' He pressed his sleeve to his face, daubing away a sheen of sweat. 'Gods guide us!'

Not understanding the bard's words, but granting the man's urgency, he relented, and followed up the slope.

Here, two Forkrul, no different from the others as far as Kyle could discern, awaited them. They stood tall, equal even unto the Jaghut, on gangly strangely jointed legs that looked able to bend backwards, with frail-looking thin arms, and long pinched heads. Oddly, each face bore a vertical scar, or suture, that ran from chin up to sloped skull. Kyle was not fooled by their frail appearance. He knew that they faced a great danger here, and not only they. All in this region faced destruction should these Forkrul bestir themselves.

One tilted its head, studying the Jaghut. 'You trouble us again,' it said.

'Through no choice of mine,' she answered.

'False,' broke in the other Forkrul, its voice as harsh as cracking stone. 'You chose.'

'Do you dispute this judgement?' the first one asked.

The Jaghut sighed her assent, then, raising her chin to regard them more closely, asked, 'What do we call you?'

The first inclined its head as if to grant the appropriateness of the question. 'That you ask reveals you are aware that names are irrelevant among any community of unadulterated Assail. All are equal. However, when communicating with you lesser kinds we adopt titles as we understand you require such props. Therefore, you may name me Arbiter, and this one Penance.'

'Very well,' the Matriarch answered.

'So,' Arbiter spoke again. 'You trouble us though you know we could cleanse this landmass as we have others before. Do you dispute this?'

She clenched her lips in distaste, but nodded her curt agreement.

'Cleansing would avert further irritation,' put in Penance.

'You Forkrul,' Silverfox suddenly announced. 'Your conceit is matched only by your arrogance.'

Arbiter fixed its slit eyes upon her. 'Of all parties present, you Imass bear the greatest weight of guilt.'

'Do you dispute this guilt?' Penance demanded.

Silverfox's aged features paled. She exchanged a look with Pran Chole, then cleared her throat warily. 'If you mean the Vow, then, no. I do not dispute this.'

'The hostilities between you and the Jaghut is what we reference,' Penance clarified.

Silverfox pointed to the elder, outraged. 'They started the war!'

'Provocation matters not,' said Arbiter. 'What matters is you Imass broke the ancient founding of the peace.'

Kyle tensed as Fisher stepped up. The bard raised his hands, saying, 'And we are four now, gathered here once more.'

Arbiter tilted its head once again. 'Four?' Its gaze fell upon Jethiss and it let out a long hissing breath. 'Ah. I see. The K'Chain Che'Malle are for the most part gone from the lands. Yet a new race now stands among us. Dare you pledge to a new founding of the peace?'

Jethiss turned to study Fisher for a time. Kyle was oddly reassured to see the man's hands shake slightly as he rubbed them down his thighs. He took a deep breath. 'Yet there are other races . . .'

'True,' Arbiter acknowledged. 'But they have not moved together in all-out hostilities against other kind. As all of us gathered here have.'

'We never did,' the Jaghut elder corrected.

'So you insist,' Penance answered brusquely. 'Yet here you are.'

Arbiter raised a hand for silence. 'I sense that while the others may not be here . . . they may have cast a vote.' To Kyle's horror the Forkrul pointed a crooked finger directly at him. 'You – child of the Imass and Jaghut both. You bear a potent token. Would you bring it forth?'

Kyle shot an uncertain glance to Fisher, who nodded his encouragement and gestured him forward. Stepping up, Kyle drew the white blade. He offered it grip first.

To his astonishment, the Forkrul shied away from the weapon and waved it aside with a disdainful flick of its fingers. 'Not that thing of chaos. We speak of the token at your neck.'

Now Kyle flinched back, confused and shocked. *Not the stone –*

anything but that. He clenched his free hand to the amber at his neck, sheathed the white blade. He shook his head. 'I'll not give this up.'

'It speaks well that you will not. May we examine it?'

Kyle glanced again to Fisher. 'On the understanding that he does not relinquish it,' the bard said.

'Of course,' Arbiter answered, sounding almost irritated. 'It would be of no value otherwise.' It held out a long-fingered hand.

Kyle snapped the leather thong and handed over the modest token of polished amber – the one thing he had left of his time with the giant Ereko. The Forkrul held it in its palm, closed its eyes for an instant, then peered up with a strange new expression in its alien face. 'We were almost as brothers, you know,' it said. 'We regard ourselves as children of the earth. It is . . . surprising . . . that you should carry such a gift from the Thel Akai.'

'Speaking for the T'lan,' Silverfox announced, 'we pledge to a peace between us.'

A long silence followed this as even the Forkrul seemed at a startled loss. 'You so swear?' murmured Penance, a dangerous note in its voice.

Pran Chole bowed his head to Silverfox and she nodded her grave agreement. 'We so pledge.'

The Forkrul extended its hand and Kyle took the necklace. 'What of the Jaghut?' it asked.

The woman motioned the Sayer youth, Orman, forward. The young man adjusted the patch on his eye and stepped up with his spear held straight. He thumped its butt to the stones, saying, 'We so pledge.'

'And the Tiste Andii?'

Jethiss nodded solemnly. 'I believe I have been sent here to make this pledge. And to ask of you a boon . . .'

The two Forkrul exchanged a glance. 'We will adjudicate that in time,' answered Penance.

'As to this new founding of the peace,' intoned Arbiter, 'we Forkrul pledge our honouring.' It gestured curtly and the many Assail scattered among the rocks clambered quickly up the slope. All in eerie silence.

Kyle examined the modest lump of amber in his palm. Did you know, Ereko? Was this why you left this behind? Yet how could you know? Perhaps it was a hope only. A seed cast into the future with the hope that it would find the right conditions, the right soil, to germinate. He retied the lace about his neck.

'Well done,' Fisher murmured low to him. The bard sounded

infinitely relieved. 'The giving of that stone is a tale I would have you tell.'

'It is a sad one.'

'Of course. All the important ones are.' Then he turned away, his breath catching, and Kyle glanced over. Jethiss now faced the Forkrul. Fisher was at his side in an instant, taking his arm. 'You need not pursue this,' he hissed.

'I wish to,' the Andii answered, quite calm.

'It is perilous beyond your grasp.'

'My memories are slowly returning, Fisher. I believe that this will complete them.' The Andii offered a crooked smile. 'Finding out who you are in truth is always a perilous undertaking.' He faced the Forkrul. 'I ask a boon.'

Arbiter nodded. 'Speak.'

'Once, we Andii were blessed by the protection of a powerful champion and weapon. A storied blade. Now he and it are gone. I ask of you Forkrul a weapon worthy of us Andii. Worthy to protect us. Will you grant me this boon?'

The Forkrul glanced to one another once again and Kyle intuited a great deal of communication was exchanged in each of these moments. They broke off the gaze and Arbiter turned to Jethiss. 'We shall fashion for you a blade worthy of you,' it answered.

'I accept,' Jethiss said even as Fisher drew breath to cut in with a shout.

'No!' the bard yelled. 'That wording. I fear that wording. There is something there. Some hidden danger.'

The Andii merely let out a long exhausted breath, his shoulders easing. 'It is too late. What is done is done. Now we shall see what the Forkrul can provide.'

In answer, Arbiter curled its thin fingers, inviting Jethiss onward. 'Come.' The Andii followed the two up the slope. Eventually he disappeared from sight behind a boulder.

Fisher sat heavily among the rocks. He hid his face in his hands. 'I fear we shall never see him again.'

Kyle eased himself down next to him, sighed his utter weariness. 'We shall see.'

Footsteps sounded and a shadow loomed over them. Kyle squinted up at the Jaghut Matriach and Orman with her. 'You will await your friend?' she asked.

'Yes.'

'He is a fool to ask anything of the Forkrul. They are vicious, cruel, and amoral.'

'Then it is best we do not disturb them,' Fisher observed, sharply.

The Jaghut woman tipped her head to him. 'I have a modest abode nearby. I will bring you some food and blankets.' She limped off. The stones rattled and crunched beneath her sandals.

Kyle studied the young man, Orman. 'You will return to your people?'

He leaned upon the tall spear, touched self-consciously the patch over his eye. 'Yes. When the ice melts – and Mother assures me it shall eventually – it is my wish that we should build a new Greathall where we shall all reside. All we Icebloods. The blood-feuds and vendettas between us, I hope, will be things of the past.'

'A worthy goal,' Fisher said.

'You will always be welcome in our hall.'

'I shall look forward to such a visit in the future.'

'And you too, Kyle, friend of the Children of the Earth, and wielder of the white blade.'

'I thank you.'

'Until then,' and Orman bowed and headed down the slope, thumping the butt of the spear loudly to the stones as he went.

Fisher let out a heartfelt breath. 'That spear makes me as uncomfortable as your sword.'

'There is something primal about it. And it is an Imass weapon, after all.'

Silverfox approached with Pran Chole and the woman Kilava. Kyle and Fisher scrambled to their feet to bow to her. 'Summoner,' Fisher welcomed.

She waved off their formality, addressed Kyle. 'Thank you, White-blade. I do not know what it is you carry, but somehow it tipped the scales in our favour. I am not naïve enough to believe that the Forkrul have hearts, but perhaps it touched something within them. A sense of nostalgia, maybe.' She shrugged. 'In any case, you have my gratitude.'

'I think of what I carry as friendship,' Kyle said.

'Friendship?' She brushed back her wind-tossed hair. Kyle was struck by the unexpectedly girlish gesture from such an apparently aged woman. 'Would that they could understand such a thing,' she murmured.

'You are off?' Fisher asked.

'Yes. We head south. I would gather up as many of the T'lan as I can, then we shall continue our search.'

'Your search?' Kyle asked.

'Yes. I will find them all, friend Kyle. And when I have found

523

them they will know the gift of the Redeemer and I shall release them. None shall be left behind.'

Fisher bowed once more. 'I wish you success.'

Pran Chole gave them a nod, dipping his deer headdress. 'Farewell. Or not. Perhaps we shall meet again.'

'Perhaps,' Kyle acknowledged.

Last came Kilava. The short powerful woman now carried a half-smile on her lips. 'That went far better than I had hoped or expected. Well done, Whiteblade.' She faced Fisher. 'Bard. Good to see you again.'

'And you, Kilava.'

She leaned forward and planted a light brush of a kiss on Fisher's cheek, then walked off. Kyle watched her go, astonished, then returned his wondering gaze to the bard.

'You were once . . .'

Fisher sat once more, sighing, his hands hanging loose over his knees. 'Another time, Kyle.'

They were alone now with the moaning, gusting wind. The thick deck of clouds churned below, effectively cutting off the world beneath. It seemed to Kyle that here among the frigid peaks they were in the realm of the gods. The day was cooling. The sun had descended behind the cloud cover to the west.

He blew upon his hands to warm them and knew that without his Iceblood, his Jaghut heritage, he would be frozen stiff.

Fisher opened the satchel at his side and withdrew the stringed box, the kantele of the Losts. He examined it to make certain it hadn't been harmed.

'Will you play?' Kyle asked.

He shook his head. 'No. Too cold.' He wrapped the instrument and gently returned it to its case.

'What tale will you tell of what has occurred here?' Kyle asked.

The bard nodded profoundly. 'Ah yes. That is the question.' He extended his legs straight out before himself and crossed them at the ankle, meshed his fingers over his chest. 'One mustn't feel constrained by the facts.' He shot Kyle a sideways glance. 'Poetic truth is a higher truth, you know. Names and events must be changed to disguise the mundane – and invariably disappointing – truth behind.'

Kyle smoothed his now long and drooping moustache, smiling. 'Of course. In other words, you'll make up what you want and claim that's what happened.'

'Of course. Now, tell me the tale of your finding of this stone.'

Kyle eased back among the rocks as best he could. He shot a glance high above, searching for any sign of Jethiss, then pulled his cloak tighter against the wind. 'Well . . . I didn't *find* it. It was given to me. Left behind by a friend.'

EPILOGUE

SHIMMER OPENED HER EYES TO FIND HERSELF ONCE MORE STANDING among the grassy hills and broad ring of canted stone menhirs mottled orange and olive-green by lichens. It was chill, the day was bright, the sky blue and dotted with wispy clouds, yet she could not see the sun. Now she understood why she was here, and she sighed, hugged herself, and started walking a circuit of the stones.

Soon she discovered she was not alone. Smoky, the dead mage – who was not dead in truth – walked with her. His sandalled feet kicked the frayed and scorched edges of his brown woollen robes. He walked with his hands clasped behind his back, resolutely not looking to her . . . waiting.

After a time, she asked, 'How long have you known?'

'We didn't really *know*,' he answered while he scratched at his patchy beard. 'We suspected.'

'Yet you said nothing.'

'We would not burden the living.'

'Among which I no longer number,' she observed, and was surprised by the lack of bitterness in her voice.

'Yet you could return, as before. The option remains for you.'

She halted. 'Why just me? Why not any of you?'

He stopped with her, rubbed his chin ferociously, his gaze lowered. 'Not just you, Shimmer. K'azz was the first to discover this.'

Though she understood that she was not breathing in this place, Shimmer felt her breath catch and her chest tighten in dread – old habits. 'What do you mean?' she asked, slowly.

Still unable to match her gaze, he said, 'He died long ago, Shimmer. When Skinner and Cowl buried him alive – he died. Yet he did not die. He discovered the truth of the Vow then. Eventually, he clawed his way free.'

He drew a heavy breath – perhaps merely in a gesture to put her at ease. 'I'm sorry. Anyway,' and he shrugged, 'had to happen some time. And we are coming back. Slowly. Eventually, we will return.'

She nodded her understanding. 'I see. Like the T'lan Imass.'

He answered her nod, his hand at his beard. 'Yes. Somehow, our Vow echoed theirs. Perhaps it was the location – the physical source of this spirit realm. Or K'azz's words. Or the spirit of our intent and conviction.' He lifted his bony shoulders once more. 'Who knows?'

'But we can never . . . leave.'

'Yes.'

She faced him. 'So . . . everyone is here? All the fallen? Petal? Sept? Cole? Even . . . Skinner?'

'Yes. All the Brethren.'

She peered round, seeing no one. 'Well? Where are they?'

'We've found it best not to overwhelm. First things first.'

She studied him, her gaze narrowing. 'Such as?'

'As before. Do you wish to return?'

'Return? You mean . . . I may? I can?'

'Yes.'

For some reason she felt terribly unworthy of this gift. Unwilling to pursue it, as if it would be an insult to all the Brethren who had come here before her. 'Why me? Why not the others?'

He raised a hand as if to calm her. 'I understand, Shimmer. Do not worry yourself. Some choose not to. Some do. In time, they will.'

She took another steadying breath, though she knew it for a deceit. 'Very well. Then yes, I choose to return.'

He nodded at this and smiled crookedly. 'We all knew you would.' He held out his hand. 'Farewell . . . for now.'

She reached for his hand but somehow her fingers passed through his and she blinked, the world growing dim, then she blinked again to glowing brightness that made her flinch and cover her eyes. Someone held her hand and she saw that it was K'azz.

'Welcome back, Shimmer.'

'I wasn't really gone, was I?' she said in wonder.

'No. Not really.' He and Blues helped her up and steadied her. They still stood upon the ice-field.

'Did you know?' she asked of Blues.

He scowled his dismay and amazement. 'I knew something wasn't adding up, but . . .' he took a shuddering breath, 'I still can't believe it.'

Cal-Brinn offered his hand and she took it, squeezing.

'You knew, yes?'

The old mage nodded. 'I suspected. Omens and hints from Rashan told me to wait. That answers would come here. And so I waited.'

'I see. What now, then?'

'Now we wait a little more,' and he gestured to the gathered Icebloods. They were peering up towards the cloud-obscured heights. Even the Imass faced the north. The wind sighed and hummed as it whipped between their bones.

'And what of us?' she asked K'azz.

'We return to Stratem – all of us.'

She nodded her heartfelt agreement. 'Yes. All of us.'

They waited in silence then. Shimmer now understood their long shared silences. They were Avowed. They could wait. A thought struck her, and she asked, 'And what of Cowl?'

K'azz had been gazing off down the mountain slope and the immense vista beyond of snow and twisting spine-like ridges of black stone. He lowered that gaze to his feet, his brow clouding. 'Yes. Cowl. He blames me still. He would destroy me if he could, I think.'

'I see that now. He thought I would share his rage.'

He shot her a brief, wary glance. 'And . . . do you?'

She shook her head, sighed, and crossed her arms. 'No. It was not deliberate. We all chose to swear. No. I am not angry.'

She felt the tension fading within him, saw the easing of the coiled dread and hurt about his eyes. He murmured, his voice thick, 'Thank you, Shimmer.'

The afternoon lengthened. The light beneath the clouds darkened to a silvery pewter where shadow and light seemed to melt together. Movement drew her eye where a lone figure descended the rocky slope. A thick bear cloak draped his shoulders and a patch covered one eye. He walked thumping his long dark-wood spear to the stones as he came and Shimmer felt an atavistic shiver upon seeing him.

'Success, it would seem,' K'azz remarked.

The Sayer, Orman, went to his brothers and sisters among the Icebloods and clasped arms. Next came Silverfox and the Bonecaster, Pran Chole, followed by Kilava. These went to the Imass and the other Bonecasters, Ut'el and Tolb Bell'al. Their sharing was in silence.

First to come to them was Silverfox. She walked alone to stand before K'azz. Her face it seemed could not help but carry sadness and hurt when she looked upon him and the rest of them. 'I'm sorry,' she began again, but K'azz raised a hand to silence her.

'There is nothing for you to apologize for. What happened above? Are the others coming? Kyle?'

She drew a weary breath – one touched by a measure of disbelief. 'We struck an accord. I have formally sworn off all hostilities towards the Jaghut. For reasons of their own, the Forkrul decided not to intervene.'

'Well done.'

'Do not thank me. Your friend, the Whiteblade, was instrumental.'

'And where is he?'

'He waits above with the bard for their companion, the Andii, who has entered into an exchange with the Forkrul . . .' The shake of her head told what she thought of that decision, and of his chances.

'I see. Well, I congratulate you, Silverfox. I have heard the tale of your coming into your birthright in south Genabackis. The Pannion wars. I believe that all those who had a hand in your raising would feel vindicated and immensely proud right now.'

Shimmer saw that these words struck the woman deeply. She blinked back tears, nodding. 'Thank you, K'azz. You are generous even when . . .' she could not continue, and had to break off to master herself. 'Even as the curse of the T'lan Imass has fallen upon you and yours.'

He held out his open hands. 'We came to this of our own accord. It probably would not have emerged, otherwise.'

She tilted her head, agreeing, and pushed back her greying curls behind an ear. 'You understand that I am not the Summoner for you?'

His answering smile was gentle. 'Yes. We understand. We must await ours.'

She tilted her head again and offered Shimmer a shy smile of farewell that was so incongruous on the face of an elder that she had to answer with her own. 'Good luck,' Shimmer offered.

After she left, Kilava joined them. She regarded K'azz with a critical eye – perhaps her normal expression. 'So, K'azz of the Red Clan. Full circle.'

He nodded his grave agreement. 'Indeed.'

'This was never our intent. The opposite, in fact.'

'I know. What of you, then?'

She frowned her uncertainty. 'I believe I will walk for a time with the Summoner – at least until we cannot bear each other's company. We shall see.'

K'azz offered his hand, which she took. She took Blues' and Cal-Brinn's hands as well, but when Shimmer offered hers, the woman pulled her close and hugged her with alarming strength. 'I'm glad to see you are back with us,' she whispered, and released her. Shimmer stood rather shocked, unable to frame a reply. 'Farewell, Red Clan,' she said. 'We will see one another again.'

The T'lan Imass set off across the ice-field. To her eyes they appeared so lonely, so frail, yet she knew this was not the truth at all. She felt that she was watching something timeless, yet something that would perhaps never be seen again.

The Iceblood Orman came to them next. He was flanked by his twin guards, both quiet and watchful. He leaned upon his tall spear and regarded them with his one good eye. He still loomed taller than they.

He nodded to Cal-Brinn. 'My thanks, Crimson Guard, for your defence of the Losts. I am grateful. What now for you? Will you await your friends above?'

K'azz shook his head. 'They will know where to find us, if they wish. We are for our homeland, Stratem. Best of fortunes to you, Orman of the Sayer. I hope you can carve out a homeland as well.'

The lad's eye glittered with a new confidence. 'Oh, I believe we shall.'

'Farewell, then.' And K'azz bowed his head, as did Shimmer, Blues and Cal-Brinn. They headed off, following in the tracks of the T'lan Imass.

Cal-Brinn, however, turned back as if struck by a thought. 'Orman,' he called.

The lad looked up, 'Yes?'

'The Losts. Stalker and Badlands. They may still be alive. It's just that . . . they're lost again.'

Orman ruefully shook his head. 'I see. Thank you,' and he waved a farewell.

They returned to tramping through the snow. 'Let us collect our scattered people,' K'azz said as they pushed onward through the drifts. He offered Blues a joking smile. 'Shall we split up to do so?'

Blues waved his arms in alarm. 'Gods no! No more goddamned splitting up!'

Shimmer's quiet smile was so fierce it almost hurt her lips. It was good to have K'azz back with them.

She thought of the meeting ahead and the man waiting for their, and her, return below.

Oh, Bars! What could she possibly say? The man has endured so much already! *Do not let it be me who finally breaks your heart!* And as for her own – well, it was too late for her, was it not? She had waited too long, delayed and put off reaching out until there could be no hope of it now.

And yet, was it not true that they now faced an untold stretch of time ahead together? Time enough, perhaps, for them to finally come to understand one another.

*

Orman watched the foreign mercenaries, this Crimson Guard, wading their way through the snow down the ice-field. Beyond them, far down the serpentine slope, the Imass, the Army of Dust and Bone, had already disappeared. How odd it seemed to him now that he should pity them, his former enemy, labouring as they did beneath an endless curse. Yet endless no longer. Their Summoner had come. Perhaps, then, they would find deliverance.

They might no longer be enemies – at least for the time being – but he hoped never to see them again.

He turned back to his people. What he now saw as his extended family. Keth and Kasson followed, walking just behind at each shoulder. He planted Svalthbrul and examined these three – all survivors like himself. All knowing the true perils and secrets of these heights.

He nodded to them. 'It seems these upper slopes are ours once more. I doubt we shall ever see the Army of Dust and Bone again. If their queen has her way they shall remain of the dust and the earth. So, my offer stands. Shall we rebuild a Greathall and hold it together?' He looked to Baran and Erta of the Heels.

The brother and sister exchanged bruised and exhausted glances. Baran pulled on his tangled beard. 'The question is where? These valleys are all scraped clean of trees and soil.'

'If I may,' the Myrni girl, Siguna, began timidly, 'there are woods on the slopes farther to the west.'

'What of the heights?' Baran asked.

'We must guard them still,' Orman answered. He understood now what Jaochim and all the other elders had been doing all this time. Guarding the Holdings, yes, but more importantly barring the way to these heights and the secrets they contained. The hidden places that mustn't be opened. He would honour that heavy purpose and guard these secrets. Perhaps, in time, he would come to be feared or cursed by the lowland newcomers as a hoarder of mysteries. But better that than the end of the world come again – perhaps in truth.

'And the Matriarch?' Erta asked.

'She will remain. She will call us if she needs us.' He studied the Myrni girl, turning his head slightly to see her better. 'You will guide us west, then, Siguna?'

She bowed. 'Yes, Orman.'

One last thought struck him and he turned to Baran. 'Oh – I have heard that the Losts were last seen alive to the east. Will you hunt them out?'

Baran bowed also, smiling behind his beard. 'With pleasure.'

Orman leaned more of his weight upon the thick haft of Svalthbrul. He nodded to Siguna. 'Find us a favourable high vale that we may call our home.'

*

Jute haunted the cliff tops of Mantle Keep. They overlooked the one narrow clear channel that allowed access to the Sea of Gold through the ice cliffs. Great chunks of carved ice floated there, bumping and clashing on their way out to wander the sea. More fell daily, calving in massive eruptions of splitting ice.

Sometimes the Jaghut sorceress joined him to exercise her leg. Yet her gaze was drawn not out to sea, but to the north, and he knew she was considering leaving soon to make the journey up the great serpentine ice-floe where she claimed her mother abided.

Sometimes Cartheron walked with him, though any extended period of exertion tired the old campaigner and he would sit instead, grumbling about the food, the cold chambers, or the lack of circulation in his feet.

Other times the former lieutenant Giana Jalaz joined him. She, too, was quite eager for word from the outside world. King Voti of Mantle, it turned out, had been generous in rewarding the defence of his keep. His people had been residing here for a very long time on the shores of the Sea of Gold and had had ample opportunity to amass a considerable hoard of its namesake. All hidden below in chambers carved from the rock – all of which could have been swept away by the ice-serpent had not Cartheron intervened.

In any case, Giana was eager to transport her newfound riches home, where a certain plot of land awaited repurchase from the rapacious moneylenders of Mott. Jute knew also that a rather large chest sat in Malle's chambers with his name upon it. None of that interested him, however, more than the sight of a certain vessel returning from its southern journey.

This day Cartheron sat in the sun while Jute paced back and forth, casting the occasional glance to the channel. Nearby, carpenters hammered and sawed a new stairway from the surplus of fallen logs surrounding them.

'She made it, I'm certain,' Cartheron assured him for the hundredth time as his pacing brought him past. 'Question is, how far south did she go? Did she drop them off on the Bone Peninsula? Plenty of towns and cities down there, I understand.'

Jute nodded. Yes, he'd been through all that countless times in his mind. Always, he asked himself, what would I have done? How far would I have taken them? All the way to Genabackis? Gods, please, no!

He kneaded the still raw slash across his arm, shuddered in the chill air wafting off the ice. 'We could build a new vessel before she returned,' he complained.

Cartheron laughed. 'Usually it's the womenfolk home fretting for years – how does it feel to be on the other end?'

'Ieleen and I always travelled together.'

The ex-High Fist straightened in his chair. 'Ho? What's this?'

Jute squinted out to the very mouth of the channel. Something dark was moving there amid the drifting chunks of frosty-blue ice.

'Looks like a visitor,' Cartheron observed.

It was still too far away for Jute to identify, but its general size and cut appeared encouraging.

'Looks two-masted,' Cartheron affirmed.

Crew were poling aside the ice as the vessel came on. Recognition came to Jute as the lines of its hull and the arrangement of its sails resolved into familiar lines. It was the *Silver Dawn*.

He waved frantically from the cliff's edge. They drew nearer, sails were reefed and sweeps emerged. The *Dawn* advanced warily up the centre of the channel. It neared the wreckage of the docks and fallen lumber of the stairway in the waters at the base of the cliff.

Jute continued waving, one-handed, as his off-arm was still too stiff to raise.

And from the stern, next to the long tiller arm, though he knew she did not possess normal vision to see him as others did, a figure there returned his wave. His beloved Falaran sea-witch.

*

In the end, the ferocious relentless wind drove them to seek shelter at the Jaghut matriarch's dwelling amid the bare rock of the peaks. It was no more than a heap of stones, a tomb rather than a home. He and Fisher took turns fetching wood for the meagre fire they kept.

Of the Matriarch they saw little. She invited them in yet quit the dwelling herself. Kyle felt uncomfortable for having driven her from her own home, yet he was also thankful for her absence, as the slim cave was hardly large enough for him and Fisher.

The bard passed the time composing on the kantele. Kyle listened with one ear while he scanned the lifeless windswept rocky slopes, his legs out, half asleep. One morning he overheard the bard singing faintly to himself as he strummed.

'In these rows there are tales
For every line, every broken smile
Draw close then
And dry these tears
For I have a story to tell'

He also heard lines concerning ancient races of giants, hidden valleys, maidens of war, and powerful weapons whose curses doom their bearers. These last phrasings made him eye the bard sidelong.

By the fourth night he'd started wondering how to broach the subject of moving on when a huge dark shape emerged from the gloom. The Matriarch announced, 'Someone is coming.'

Fisher eased the instrument back into its satchel and Kyle tightened his bear-hide cloak about his shoulders. They set out, leaning away from the slicing winds.

The bare broken rocks clattered and grated beneath their boots as they slowly ascended. They sought the place the Matriarch had told them was beneath where the Forkrul came and went. It was a hike of a few leagues from her dwelling.

Below, the clouds had not entirely dispersed. Broad sweeping vistas of woods and glittering lakes spread out for as far as the eye could discern. Except for one entire face of the range. Here, a broad river of ice descended from the wider field below. It gleamed sapphire and white, looking much like a serpent of frost.

The desiccating winds had long cracked Kyle's lips and clawed his throat raw. He and Fisher had also taken turns fetching snow and ice to melt for drinking water. But it was never enough, and this was their greatest want.

They tramped on. Kyle focused upon raising one foot after the other. These extreme heights, Fisher had explained, can poison the lungs and bring delusions and mirages to those who would trespass. All Kyle knew was that no matter how deeply he inhaled, he seemed to never have enough breath. And breathing too hard made him dizzy.

The light deepened to a murky purple, tinged by blood red in the west. Fisher raised a hand for a halt. Kyle came abreast of him. The bard was squinting up where the slope steepened. Movement. A dark figure descending.

He and Fisher waited. Whoever it was, he appeared wounded or exhausted. He would stagger then pause, righting himself, only to lurch onward once more. Kyle cast an uncertain glance to Fisher, who motioned that they should wait.

It was Jethiss. He still wore the old armoured hauberk he'd salvaged. Yet something was odd about his outline. As he neared, his steps now audible over the rocks, Kyle's breath truly caught as he saw that the man's left sleeve of leather and mail hung loose. It swung empty in the winds.

Somehow, in some manner, the man had lost an arm.

Only now did the Andii appear to become aware of them. He halted, taken aback, then changed direction to approach. Though the air was bitingly frigid and the winds punishing, a sheen of sweat covered his face and ran dripping from his chin. The Andii possessed near black-hued skin, yet Kyle would have said that the man was pale – perhaps from shock, or loss of blood.

He halted, weaving slightly, before them, his chest heaving, and nodded his greeting.

Kyle's gaze fell to fix upon the strange new weapon now sheathed at his side. The pommel was an oddly contoured knob. It and the grip appeared to be constructed of the same material: pale, like ivory, but not glowing like his white blade. Portions of the pommel and grip were smooth while others possessed a rough and porous look. Slowly, the realization came of just what he was looking at – what the sword had been moulded from – and he raised his appalled gaze to where the man's sleeve hung empty.

Not even the cruellest gods would dare . . .

Jethiss nodded to them again, affirming their guess. He raised his arm to wipe the sweat from his face, swallowed hard. 'The justice of the Forkrul,' he whispered hoarsely, 'is harsh indeed.'

'A sword worthy of you . . .' Fisher breathed in wonder, his face sickly.

The Andii was breathing heavily. The trial he'd endured must have been ghastly. He nodded his agreement at Fisher's words. 'Yes.'

'And your memories?'

'With me once more.'

'Then,' Fisher asked, 'would you give us your name?'

'Mother Dark offered a title.'

Fisher's breath caught. He spoke low, as if not daring to say the words aloud: 'Son of Darkness . . .'

Jethiss gestured, inviting them to descend with him. 'Now more of an honorific, in truth.'

The Andii's tone was light, but Kyle saw with what trouble he walked, the rigid control he was forcing upon himself to remain erect. He wanted to reach out to help steady the man, but his instincts told him that he mustn't.

'There was a terrible battle,' Jethiss murmured aloud as they descended. 'At the feet of a gate. I wandered lost for an unknown time. A woman's voice spoke to me from the Eternal Night. She told me I was needed to stand as I had before. But that the cost would be great. That I would have to lose myself to find myself anew.' He paused to press a hand to Fisher's shoulder. 'And so I have. My old name no longer fits. I am Jethiss. As for the title . . . we shall see if I prove worthy.'

'Where will you go?' Kyle asked, careful to give the man room as he walked at his left side.

'I would travel to Coral,' Jethiss answered. 'There is a modest barrow there I would pay my respects to. A good friend. Many evenings we spent together playing Kef Tanar.' He offered them a smile. 'I would be honoured if you would accompany me.'

'The honour is mine,' Fisher answered.

'And mine,' Kyle added, feeling eminently comfortable with the idea of travelling with the Andii. It seemed to him altogether fitting and strangely proper that the White Blade should be found walking alongside what he imagined, one day, might come to be known as the Blade of Bone.

GLOSSARY

Elder Races
Tiste Andii: Children of Darkness
Tiste Edur: Children of Shadow
Tiste Liosan: Children of Light
K'Chain Che'Malle: one of the Four Founding Races, presumed
    extinct
Imass: an ancient race of which only the undead army, the T'lan
    Imass, remain
T'lan Imass (the Armies of the Diaspora)
    Logros, Guardians of the First Throne
    Kron, First to the Gathering
    Betrule (lost)
    Ifayle (lost)
    Orshayn (lost)
    Kerluhm (lost)
Trell: an ancient race of nomadic pastoralists
Jaghut: an ancient race of recluses
Thelomen/Toblakai: an ancient race, pre-agriculturalists

The Warrens
Kurald Galain: The Elder Warren of Darkness, Elder Night
Kurald Emurlahn: The Elder Warren of Shadow, Elder Shadow
Kurald Thryllan: The Elder Warren of Shadow, Elder Light, also
    known as Liosan
Omtose Phellack: The Elder Jaghut Warren of Ice
Tellann: The Elder Imass Warren of Fire
Starvald Demelain: The Eleint (dragon) Warren
Thyr: The Path of Light
Denul: The Path of Healing

Hood's Paths: The Paths of Death
Serc: The Path of Sky
Meanas: The Path of Shadow and Illusion
D'riss: The Path of the Earth
Ruse: The Path of the Sea
Rashan: The Path of Darkness
Mockra: The Path of the Mind
Telas: The Path of Fire

ABOUT THE AUTHOR

IAN CAMERON ESSLEMONT has worked as an archaeologist and has taught and travelled in South East Asia. He now lives in Fairbanks, Alaska, with his wife and children. His previous novels, *Night of Knives, Return of the Crimson Guard, Stonewielder, Orb Sceptre Throne* and *Blood and Bone*, are each set in the fantasy world he co-created with Steven Erikson.

To find out more about the world of Malaz,
visit www.malazanempire.com